Myths
of
Religion

ANDREW M. GREELEY is a distinguished sociologist, journalist, and priest—and one of America's most prolific writers. His bestselling novels include *The Cardinal Sins, Thy Brother's Wife, Ascent Into Hell, Lord of the Dance, Virgin and Martyr, Angels of September, Patience of a Saint,* and *God Game,* as well as his Blackie Ryan mystery series and his second science fiction novel, *Final Planet.* In addition to his novels, he is the author of over one hundred scholarly works and more than fifty nonfiction books, including his highly acclaimed *The Making of the Popes 1978.* Andrew Greeley divides his time between Chicago, where he works as a research associate at the National Opinion Research Center at the University of Chicago, and Tucson, where he holds the post of professor of sociology at the University of Arizona.

ALSO BY ANDREW M. GREELEY

FICTION

Death in April   *The Cardinal Sins*

THE PASSOVER TRILOGY

Thy Brother's Wife   *Lord of the Dance*
Ascent Into Hell

TIME BETWEEN THE STARS

Virgin and Martyr   *Patience of a Saint*
Angels of September   *Rite of Spring*

MYSTERY AND FANTASY

The Magic Cup
The Final Planet
God Game
Happy Are the Meek
Happy Are the Clean of Heart
Happy Are Those Who Thirst for Justice

NONFICTION

The Irish Americans: The Rise to Money and Power
Sexual Intimacy: Love and Play

ANDREW M. GREELEY

Myths of Religion

WARNER BOOKS

A Warner Communications Company

Biblical quotations in *The Sinai Myth* under the chapter headings, as well as those within the text, are from THE TORAH: THE FIVE BOOKS OF MOSES published by The Jewish Publication Society of America, Philadelphia, 1962. Reprinted by permission.

Unless otherwise indicated in *The Sinai Myth,* all other biblical excerpts are from *The Jerusalem Bible,* copyright © 1966 by Darton, Longman & Todd, Ltd. and Doubleday & Company, Inc. Used by permission of the publisher.

A Warner Edition

This Warner Books edition is published by arrangement with the author.

Warner Books, Inc., 666 Fifth Avenue, New York, NY 10103

W A Warner Communications Company

Printed in the United States of America

First Warner Books Printing: March 1989

10 9 8 7 6 5 4 3 2 1

Designed by Giorgetta Bell McRee

Library of Congress Cataloging-in-Publication Data

Greeley, Andrew M., 1928–
    Myths of religion / Andrew M. Greeley.
        p. 576
    Bibliography: p.
    Contents: The Jesus myth—The Sinai myth—The Mary myth.
    ISBN 0-446-38818-1 (pbk.) (U.S.A.)
    ISBN 0-446-38819-X (pbk.) (Can.)
    1. Theology, Doctrinal—Popular works.   2. Jesus Christ—Person and offices.
3. Ten commandments—Criticism, interpretation, etc.   4. Revelation on Sinai.
5. Mary, Blessed Virgin, Saint—Theology.   6. Femininity of God.   7. Myth.
8. Catholic Church—Doctrines.   9. Christian ethics—Catholic authors.   I. Title.
BT77.G838   1989   88-33683
232—dc19   CIP

Contents

Myths
of
Religion

Introduction

I wrote these three books, now combined for the first time in one volume, in the late sixties and the first half of the seventies, as I worked out in my own head the relationship between religion and sociology. Without realizing it at the time I was also doing the groundwork of a theory of the nature of religion that would later lead me to write novels.

The key tool in this work is the notion of "myth." I mean by it not fairy tale or legend, not make-believe or fiction, but rather a story that points beyond itself and gives meaning, purpose, and direction to life. Thus this book is about three stories—the story of Jesus, the story of the Jewish people formed in the experience at Sinai, and the story of Mary the Mother of Jesus who represents the mother love of God.

I agree with my teacher Mircea Eliade and my colleague Wendy O'Flaherty that the important thing about myths is their content—what the stories say—and not their structure. Thus I disagree with Joseph Campbell that all myths are basically the same because they have the same structure. As Professor O'Flaherty puts it, all skeletons look pretty much alike and are similarly uninteresting.

Each of the stories is true—the disparate and ragtag Hebrew tribes did feel themselves constituted a people by God's intervention in the desert near Sinai. Jesus did live and die and was experienced as risen again by his followers. And he did have a mother who has fascinated his followers ever since. When I call these stories "myths" I mean that in addition to their historical truth, they carry a deeper and broader meaning, an explanation of what human life means and how one ought to live that life.

In the first two books I was engaged in updating my own understanding of the Bible in light of the brilliant work of the professional scripture scholars who emerged from under a cloud of suspicion during the Vatican Council. I found that far from undermining the Christian faith, the insights of these scholars made my comprehension of the Bible richer and deeper.

My account of the story of Mary the Mother of Jesus is a more complicated effort. In the middle seventies I was powerfully influenced by the "narrative theology" of my friends John Shea and David Tracy. In the book I was trying to integrate this approach to religion with that religious symbol that Henry Adams had said was the most important symbol in fifteen hundred years of the history of Western Culture, a story that was uniquely Catholic and at the same time despised and rejected (foolishly I believed and still believe) by many of the post-conciliar enthusiasts within the Church.

If narrative theology could reinterpret the Mary story successfully, I felt, then it could be applied to any component of my own religious heritage.

Two years later when I would begin to write my first novel, *The Magic Cup*, a story heavily influenced by my research on the Mary Myth, I paid tribute to Mary the Mother of Jesus by giving her a "walk-on" role (albeit one of critical importance) in the plot. Later when Father Edward McKenna wrote an opera based on the novel, the Mother of Jesus was given two beautiful arias, one filled with themes from Gregorian Chant hymns to Mary.

Subsequent sociological research on the religious imagination revealed that the Mary symbol was still the most powerful religious symbol for young Catholics and an appealing symbol for young Protestants. In both cases it was the men especially who benefited religiously and personally from an image of God as mother.

Autobiographically, then, these books are the story of a parish priest and sociologist on his way to becoming a novelist. Intellectually they are the story of how I came to believe that poetry and fiction and metaphor were superior not inferior to propositional prose, and that image and experience and story came before intellectual religion and not after it.

Obviously I still believe in the importance of reflective religion and discursive writing or I would not be composing this introduction. I am rather suggesting that imagination is not a poor relative to reason in the human personality but an equal partner, a spouse who provides both the origins and the raw power for religion.

—ANDREW M. GREELEY
Grand Beach
Lady Day in Harvest
1988

PART ONE

The Jesus Myth

*To two men who in very different ways
made this book possible—*

Clifford Geertz *and* **J. Michael Hartnett**

l'amour de Dieu, c'est folie . . .

—from the French Easter liturgy

Note

The word "myth" is used in the title of this volume in a specific and definite sense. A myth is a symbolic story which demonstrates, in Alan Watts's words, "the inner meaning of the universe and of human life." To say that Jesus is a myth is not to say that he is a legend but that his life and message are an attempt to demonstrate "the inner meaning of the universe and of human life." As Charles Long puts it, a myth points to the definite manner in which the world is available for man: "The word and content of myth are revelations of power." Or as A. K. Coomaraswamy observes, "Myth embodies the nearest approach to absolute truth that can be stated in words."

Many Christians have objected to my use of this word even when I clearly define it specifically. They are terrified by a word which may have even a slight suggestion of fantasy. However, my usage is the one that is common among historians of religion, literary critics, and social scientists. It is a valuable and helpful usage; there is no other word which conveys what these scholarly traditions mean when they refer to myth. The Christian would be well advised to get over his fear of the word and appreciate how important a tool it can be for understanding the content of his faith.

Chapter 1

The Founder of the Firm

This is a book about the Founder of our firm, one Jesus of Nazareth. It is not a scientific biography, since we do not have the materials for such a biography. It is not an original theological work, since I am not a theologian. Even though it is based on the most recent research on the New Testament, it is not an exercise in New Testament studies, since I am not a Scripture scholar, either. All the book can claim to be is a series of reflections from the religious symbolism of Jesus.

To say that Jesus is a religious myth or symbol, albeit the most important religious symbol in the Western world, is not to deny him reality. There is nothing more real than men's symbols and myths. To say that Jesus is a symbol does not say that his life and message are legend. Quite the contrary, it is the very core of the myth of Jesus that his life and message were real historical phenomena; phenomena which, even though we perceive them through the theological understanding of the primitive church, still have powerful historical value in the strict sense of the word.

There was a time, not so long ago, when many scholars were persuaded that the story contained in the gospels was mostly a fabric of legends derived from the Hellenistic world to which Christianity had moved after the fall of Jerusalem. In particular, it was argued that much of the symbolism of Christianity was derived from the mystery cults which were contemporaneous with it in the fading world of Greece and Rome.

We now understand, however, that the symbolism of primitive Christianity is mostly Jewish, that the Christian "mysteries" owe very little, if anything, to the mystery cults of Hellenism, and that even the logos theme of St. John is more Jewish than Greek. Furthermore, we have also discovered that, while there may be an occasional similarity in language or theme between the Christian symbols and the symbols of pagan legends, the really striking thing is not the similarity between Christianity and the Orphic or Dionysian mysteries, but rather the immense difference. In dealing with the symbolism of Jesus of Nazareth we have to contend with a symbol that is drastically different from the other religious symbols of his own time or indeed of any time.

One hears it said frequently today that Jesus and his message are "irrelevant" to the problems of the modern world. The irrelevance of Jesus is not however a new discovery. He was irrelevant to his own world, too; so irrelevant that it was necessary for him to be murdered. The symbolism of his life and message was no more adjusted to the fashionable religious currents of his day than it is adjusted to the fashionable ideological currents of our day. Much has been made recently of the similarity between the message of Jesus as contained in the New Testament and the beliefs of the monastic Jewish sect which lived in the hills overlooking the northern end of the Dead Sea. Surely the Dead Sea community tells us much about the religious atmosphere of Palestine when Jesus appeared on the scene, but, as we shall note in a later chapter, the striking thing about the relationship between Jesus and the Dead Sea community is not the similarity but the great diversity. Some of the categories of expression, some of the religious tools were the same, but the content of the message was profoundly different.

The symbolism of Jesus, then, was as much out of harmony with his own time as it apparently is with ours. One reflects at length and in depth on the symbolism because despite its apparent continuous irrelevancy it has still managed to survive and, indeed, become the dominant religious symbolism for a substantial segment of the human population. One hears that today the influence of the Jesus symbolism has finally run its course. But even announcement of the decline of the influence of Jesus of Nazareth has been made repeatedly since the soldiers rolled the stone across the door of the tomb. Nonetheless, somehow or other, the symbolism has managed to survive. One is therefore rather well advised to be skeptical about the demise of Christianity. It becomes, therefore, appropriate to try to probe the meaning of the symbolism of Jesus if only to learn whether despite its obvious irrelevancy it might still say something important about the human condition.

The religious reflections on the symbolism of Jesus contained in the present volume result from the fact that some time ago I became "hooked" on New Testament studies. In my work in the sociology of religion I have been more and more influenced by the writing of Professor Clifford Geertz, who thinks of religion as a set of symbols which provide man a "meaning system" that can answer his fundamental problems about the interpretability of the universe. The "templates" which guide the behavior of animals are for the most part provided by innate instincts, but man has rather few instincts and is capable of surviving in the world not because he is endowed with an elaborate system of instincts but because he is able to evolve culture; that is to say, a series of meaning systems with which he can interpret and organize his life. Man's religion is the most fundamental of his meaning systems because it is one which provides an answer to the most puzzling and basic questions about the meaning of existence itself. In Geertz's words, "Without religion; that is to say, without a basic meaning system, it is not merely that man cannot interpret the meaning of problems like death and suffering and unexpected events, but he finds himself threatened with an uninterpretable universe. Without religion, interpretability collapses and man is immersed in chaos."[1]

Geertz's point is not that every man believes in God or that every man requires the sacred or even that every man agonizes frequently during his life over problems of ultimate interpretation and interpretability. His point is rather that most of us need, at least implicitly, some sort of rough and ready answers to questions of whether life has meaning,[2] of whether good triumphs over evil; or evil, good; of how the good man lives; of whether the really real is malign or gracious; and of whether man is capable of establishing relationships with the real. Our

---

[1]Clifford Geertz, "Religion as a Cultural System" in *The Religious Situation*, Donald Cutler (ed.). Boston: Beacon Press, 1968, p. 668.
[2]Is Macbeth right when he says that life is a tale told by an idiot, full of sound and fury, signifying nothing; or is Teilhard de Chardin right when he says something is afoot in the universe?

religious symbols contain, frequently in highly poetic form, the ultimate meaning system or interpretive scheme which we use to cope with these questions.

My interest in the writings of Geertz began with a conviction that those who, like Dietrich Bonhoeffer or the younger Harvey Cox, argued that secular man no longer needed a religion, completely misunderstood the nature of the human condition. An anthropologist, Geertz discovered in his work in Java and Morocco that modernization and "secularization" of these societies, far from eliminating religion, made religious needs more acute, precisely because the meaning questions now became very explicit and conscious. Bonhoeffer is quoted less frequently, and Harvey Cox has gone far beyond the walls of the secular city, and I found myself increasingly faced with the question of what it meant to say that Christianity was a symbol system or an interpretive scheme. What were the "privileged" Christian symbols and what sorts of answers do they provide to the fundamental questions of interpretation and interpretability of the universe? Was it possible that both Christian theology and Christian controversy had become so involved in peripheral issues that the role of Christianity's principal symbols as providing interpretation of the universe had been overlooked?

There isn't much doubt that Jesus of Nazareth is the central symbol of Christianity. His life and message as contained in the gospels either would contain the main themes of the Christian interpretive scheme or these themes would not be found anywhere. But at this point I found myself in a rather surprising position. Even though I thought I knew what the Christian answer would be to the basic questions about the meaning of the universe in Geertz's sense, I was hard put to link those answers with the person and life of Jesus. In my mind, and I suspect in the minds of most of my contemporaries, the symbol of Jesus has become so encrusted with piety, theological controversy, and ecclesiastical triumphalism that it means very little. Piety is clearly outmoded. Controversy seems to pertain to issues no longer of much moment and which were, perhaps, never anything but peripheral, and triumphalism seems designed almost deliberately to obscure Jesus behind Byzantine robes and ritualism.

It must be understood that a Catholic clergyman of my generation learned practically nothing about New Testament studies in the seminary— or Old Testament studies either for that matter. We were led to believe, though perhaps not deliberately or explicitly, that most New Testament scholars were agnostics or skeptics or "liberals" who were basically concerned with denying the uniqueness or the authenticity of Jesus and quite possibly both.[3] While my generation of Catholic clergy has been able to assimilate the impact of Old Testament literary criticism, we have not turned our attention to New Testament criticism. Indeed, the little we heard about it (usually from some of the younger clergy who had read a book or two or heard a lecture about Rudolf Bultmann) persuaded us that when the New Testament critical scholars were finished there was nothing much left of Jesus and not much in the way of historical basis for our faith.

I must make it plain that I was not especially concerned that my faith would be in danger if I wrestled with the writings of the New Testament scholars. Faith is not rooted in scholarship, and anyone who adjusts his fundamental orientation toward the universe so that it fits what university faculty members are currently writing simply has no notion of either the mutability of academic thought or its extreme limitations as a means of coping with reality.

However, I had heard enough about the conclusions of those scholars who had ruled out the possibility of a realistic search for the "historical Jesus" to conclude, quite wrongly as it turned out, that there was not much to be learned from them about the content of the Jesus symbol. I would later discover to my dismay that those friends of mine who had read a book or two and announced that we could know nothing about the historical Jesus were twenty years out of date and that the post-Bultmannians had a great deal to say about the historical Jesus.

But I was ready to accept Bultmann's unhappy compromise. It seemed to me to be sensible to settle for the symbolism which the early Church in its New Testament writings perceived in the Jesus phenomenon if one could not break through to the phenomenon itself. With this in mind, I turned somewhat skeptically to the New Testament literature and began to plow through the writings of men like C. H. Dodd, J. Jeremias, Rudolf Bultmann, R. H. Fuller, E. Kasemann, N. Perrin, W. Marxsen, A. J. B. Higgins, T. W. Manson, G. Bornkamm, with increasing fascination and enthusiasm.

---

[3]Unquestionably, at one point in the development of New Testament studies such a charge had some validity.

I am not engaged in a sociological analysis of Jesus of Nazareth, but I did begin with the perspective of the sociology of religion. Nor did I begin seeking confirmation for a faith about which I had doubts, much less seeking arguments to convert others to my faith (I have a hunch that usually these last two enterprises are the same). On the contrary, I approached the work of New Testament scholarship with respect for the abilities of the men who engaged in it, with increasing fascination for their brilliance and skill, and in search of deeper understanding of the faith to which I was firmly committed. I now propose to share my reflections on this literature with the readers of this book, because it seems to me that the fears and misunderstandings which most educated Catholics have toward New Testament studies deprive them of insights which could be of extraordinary importance for their religious life. As Professor Hams Küng has put it:

> The background to the gospels, and in particular the first three synoptic gospels, is not legend and speculation, but living experiences and impressions, reports handed down about the living Jesus of Nazareth. If not directly, at least through the evangelists' testimonies of faith we can hear Jesus himself speaking. Anyone who comes to these documents with essential rather than peripheral questions and puts them seriously rather than casually, will receive answers which are remarkably clear, consistent and original; answers which are obviously not just the product of a chance coincidence of various theological versions of the truth, but which—however much occasional details may seem historically dubious—speak to us with the original words of Jesus.[4]

The myth about New Testament studies that is widespread among the Catholic clergy and educated laity—and not merely among those of us over thirty-five—has not progressed much beyond the understandings of A. Harnack or A. Schweitzer. We are more or less convinced that what the critical studies have concluded is that Jesus was an itinerant ethical preacher making no special claims to being a messiah, much less God's son, warning of the imminent end of the world, and paying with his life for the revolutionary implications of his ethical preaching. He had no intention of founding a church. The

[4]Hans Küng, *The Church*, trans. by Ray and Rosaleen Ockenden. New York: Sheed and Ward, 1967, p. 44.

signs that he was supposed to have worked were made up by his followers. The prophecies he made were derived after their fulfillment instead of before. The resurrection was an extremely dubious event. The Gospel of St. John was produced under powerful Gnostic influence. The concept of mysteries in the writings of St. Paul shows the influence of the Greco-Roman mystery cults. The virgin birth was a Hellenistic idea absorbed rather late in the day from pagan religions, and most of the words and deeds reported in the New Testament were piously fictional creations composed by the early Church.

This summary of New Testament research, which I believe many Catholics accept as accurate, corresponds to what some writers were saying at one period in the development of the New Testament studies. They began with an assumption of a closed universe in which only those things that could be verified by empirical science could be considered as legitimate objects of human knowledge. The rationalists, the skeptics, the empiricists had their day in New Testament studies just as they did (and do) in most other scientific disciplines.

I am asserting that the thrust of the New Testament studies in the last two decades has gone far beyond the debunking skepticism practiced by some authors in days gone by. Most of the elements of the caricature described above were simply inaccurate. Jesus was not basically an ethics teacher at all. He apparently resolutely refused to set a time limit for the complete fulfillment of the Kingdom. He did not found the Church in the sense of setting up a formal organizational model, but he left no doubt as to how the community of his followers were to behave. Even though he may have been executed because he was suspected of being a political revolutionary, he was not especially interested in the political issues of his time. At least some of his prophecies were clearly made before the events occurred. The tradition of Jesus as a man who performed marvels is so primitive and so powerful that some writers say the only historical explanation possible is that marvels did occur. St. John's gospel was not Gnostic; it was written before Gnosticism began and was basically Jewish in its orientation. And St. Paul's concept of history owed practically nothing to the pagan mystery religions. Finally, we can be historically certain that the early Christians had a profound experience of Jesus as still alive sometime shortly after his death. Historical science cannot say what the exact nature of these visions of Jesus was, and only faith can say what they mean; however, the fact of the experience cannot be questioned.

But I was to discover something much more important. When the "post-Bultmannians," by their rigorous and very skeptical methods of form criticism, finally got that body of material which they think can be attributed to the historical Jesus, we do not find obscurity and uncertainty but rather a basic teaching and a fundamental self-understanding of incredible clarity and power. While the theological reflections of the early Church on the person and teaching of Jesus are of immense importance to us, it is still useful to follow the post-Bultmannians on their project of stripping them away and getting back to that which can beyond reasonable doubt be attributed to Jesus himself. For when the symbolism of Jesus stands forth, unadorned by the reflections of the early Church, he is even more challenging than when he is obscured by the theological problems and concerns of primitive Christianity. Jesus was not an ethical teacher or an apocalyptic prophet. He did not think of himself in such a way and did not behave as either rabbis or prophets behaved. His self-understanding and his message were unique, original, and startling. It is small wonder that he shocked and frightened his contemporaries and that they would not accept what he said. It is also small wonder that we have done our best to obscure the shocking nature of the symbolism of Jesus ever since.

It is not my intention in the present book to summarize the work of the New Testament scholars. Rather, I propose to offer religious reflections based on my reading of their works. Anyone who wishes to pursue their work in the original can certainly do so on their own. (He would be well advised to begin with Gunther Bornkamm's *Jesus of Nazareth*.) I will occasionally attempt to summarize some of their conclusions as a basis for my own reflections, but these summaries will necessarily be brief and lacking in the complexity of much of the work of these scholars. I will limit myself for the most part to reflections on material which many of the post-Bultmannians confidently think comes from the historical Jesus. I do this not because I doubt the merits of the theological reflections of the early Church as contained in the books of the New Testament, but because I think it is a useful religious experience to reflect on the very core of the symbolism of Jesus. It is worth noting that the methodology of New Testament criticism is to include in the corpus of "historical" material only those passages which can be established as certainly historical beyond any reasonable doubt. It does not follow that a historically doubtful passage is certainly unhistorical; it simply is that its historicity has not been proven. Thus, most of St. John is not included in the certainly historical category because methods have not yet been discovered by which the scholars can confidently separate the various layers of tradition to be found in that highly complex gospel.

One should not assume that the New Testament scholars are in complete agreement among themselves as to what material can confidently be said to be historical. There are lengthy and complicated debates, for example, over whether Jesus actually referred to himself as the Son of Man, and there are also debates over the extent to which Jesus explicitly applied to himself the suffering servant themes from Deutero-Isaiah. I am not qualified to make any judgments on these controversies. Jesus certainly seemed to have been reluctant to apply *any* titles to himself. However, there does seem to be general agreement that his attitude, his behavior, and his preaching were such that the use by the early Church of religious categories such as the Suffering Servant and the Son of Man to describe him was certainly valid. It ought to be noted that the thrust of these controversies tends to swing back and forth. What one generation of scholars assumes to be true beyond all doubt another generation calls into serious question. Such is the nature of the academic enterprise in every discipline. This is not to say that nothing is certain in New Testament study, but one must be wary of staking his religious commitments and convictions on the scholarly opinions currently in fashion. I know of one priest who left the Church because (so he claimed) his analysis of St. Mark convinced him it was impossible to believe in the myth of the empty tomb since it was so clearly a legend created by the Hellenistic Jewish community out of which Mark's gospel came. I was not competent then and I am even less competent now to follow the logic of his argument; however, the most recent scholars are now currently convinced that Mark was Palestinian rather than Hellenistic in its origins. I suspect that the priest in question will not return to the Church despite the fact that the scholarly opinion he used to justify his departure has been discredited. It is worth keeping in mind that positions on specific controversies are quite likely to change in any academic discipline from year to year, and that these controversies exist in a different order of knowledge and meaning than does one's ultimate interpretation of the universe, or at least they should exist in different orders of meaning.

A number of other observations about New Testament studies from the point of view of an outsider may be pertinent:

1. The intellectual capabilities of many of these men engaging in this field of scholarship are immense, even awesome. The skills, for example, that have gone into the recreation of the original Aramaic text of the "Our Father" are very impressive indeed.

2. Unlike most other practitioners of the social and historical disciplines, the Scripture scholars seem to have what Thomas Kuhn calls "paradigms" in his book *Structure of Scientific Revolutions*. Paradigms for Kuhn are statements of the nature of the problem which define clearly the context within which scholars can work. Once a discipline constructs a paradigm, immense and rapid progress can be made in puzzle solving. Form criticism and the quest for the historical Jesus seem to have provided precisely such a paradigm for New Testament study. However, as Kuhn notes, paradigms bring problems, and one of them is that those working within the paradigm are so caught up with the fascination of puzzle solving that they are quite unaware of issues which may not be stated in the paradigm. I find myself, for example, just a little bit surprised that most of the extraordinarily brilliant New Testament scholars seem unaware of the profound religious implications for our own time of the work in which they are engaged. (Joachim Jeremias is one outstanding exception to this stricture.) The concluding paragraphs of their books will occasionally provide a note of faith and piety, but beyond this they do not seem inclined to go.

3. For the English-speaking reader the work of New Testament scholars is made more difficult to understand because so much of it is done in Germany, and the German professorial style of discourse is obscure at best (even in good translations). It becomes even more opaque when it is mixed, as in many of the post-Bultmannians, with doses of Heideggerian existentialism. However, despite the complexity and the obscurity and passion for minute technical detail, as well as the occasional arrogance of their work, anyone seriously interested in deepening his understanding of Christianity can ill afford to ignore the work of the New Testament scholars.

Let me make it clear for whom I am writing this book. First, I suppose I am writing primarily for myself, to clarify and deepen my own understanding of the meaning of the life and teaching of the Founder of our firm. Second, I am writing for all those like me who are trying to deepen their understanding of the faith to which they are committed in this disturbing era of change and confusion. I will not "defend" Christianity from the attacks of skeptical critics, nor do I propose (as a reviewer of one of my other books suggests) to reassure any "troubled" middle-aged Christians. (That reviewer, I am afraid, would have deemed anything other than a complete rejection of Christianity to be directed at those unfortunates in the middle years.) I certainly do not propose to try to explain Christianity to the agnostic secularist who has been labeled "modern man." It is not my intention to persuade the "young" that Christian symbols are "relevant."[5] Nor, finally, do I wish to argue with those members of the clergy for whom radical skepticism has become a personal stance excusing them from thought, inquiry, personal maturation, and religious commitment. I surely do not wish to deny the importance of any of these groups in modern society, but I assert that the position all of them take, each in its own way, rules out on a priori ground the necessity and even the possibility of trying to determine what Jesus means.

If this volume is any use at all, it will be limited to two groups of people: (1) Those Christians who wish to understand the core of their faith more deeply and to think about the implications of that faith for our particular segment of time and space. (2) Those non-Christians who are curious as to how the core of the Christian message is understood by one Christian social scientist living and working in the secular academic world.

Will we be able to conclude that Jesus is relevant? I think if we put quotes around that much abused word "relevant" and restate the question to say, Does the message of Jesus respond to contemporary intellectual and social fad? Then we will assert that Jesus is certainly

[5]Professor Mary Daly tells us that many of the young do not find New Testament symbols relevant. I rather doubt the representativeness of Miss Daly's sample, but if some members of the younger generation are so shallow and superficial as to dismiss symbols that have shaped human thought for two millennia without investigating deeply the meaning of such symbols, that is their problem and not mine.

not "relevant" today, no more than he was in his own time. If, on the other hand, the question is stated, Does Jesus throw down a challenge which has profound implications for men of every era? The answer is that Jesus is most certainly relevant and will be until the human race grows tired of pondering the meaning of life.

Chapter 2
Jesus and His Times

Perhaps one of the reasons for the many controversies that have raged over Jesus of Nazareth is the difficulty in classifying him. For some, he seems a simple ethical preacher; to others, a mystical prophet; to others, an eschatological visionary; to yet others, a political revolutionary; and to still others, the founder of a church. It is not merely the different presuppositions that we bring to our study of Jesus that create the confusion. He is a hard man to categorize. He does not seem to fit into any of our neat labels, and this problem of figuring out where exactly Jesus stands is not a new one. Even in his own time he puzzled most of his contemporaries. In the concluding pages of his *Sayings of Jesus,* T. W. Manson summarizes Jesus' paradoxical behavior.

His hearers were amazed by the authority with which He spoke. He dominated the crowds, and He was, without ever striving for mastery, easily the Master of His band of disciples. Yet He constantly insisted that He was the servant of all, and as constantly demonstrated the genuineness of that strange claim. . . .

The religious authorities were horrified by the freedom with which He criticized doctrines and practices hallowed by centuries of pious observance. Yet He was wont to go to the Synagogue on the Sabbath; and He enjoined the healed leper to do what Moses commanded in the matter of his healing. . . .

Respectable people were scandalized by the freedom and familiarity of His intercourse with the disreputable. He was nicknamed "Friend of publicans and sinners." Yet the quality of the friendship was determined by Him, not by the publicans and sinners. . . .

The rank and file of the Jewish nation were estranged in the end by His lack of patriotism. Yet He wept over the impending fate of Jerusalem; and He was executed as a political agitator along with two rebels against Rome. . . . [1]

In other words, Jesus went about providing answers to questions that no one was asking and refusing to answer the questions everyone thought important. He resolutely refused to permit himself to be part of any of the principal religious or political currents of the environment in which he lived. One can imagine that a frequent question people asked about him was, "But where does he really stand?"

Palestine was in chaos when Jesus arrived. The Herods presided over what was little more than a Roman puppet regime. The Temple priesthood, somewhat influenced by Hellenistic thought, cooperated with the occupying power to preserve a little bit of their own autonomy. Political revolutionaries were engaged in never-ending plots often exploding into rebellions before, during, and after Jesus' life until the final destruction of the Temple of the Jewish nation. The Pharisees, an unofficial group of zealous laymen, were popular religious innovators who attempted to regulate all human conduct by appeal to the Torah. The Essenes and similar groups (including the community on the banks of the Dead Sea) shared with the Pharisees a zeal for the law, but, unlike them, emphasized the priestly element in the Jewish religion and, also unlike the Pharisees, felt it necessary to withdraw from the mainstream of Jewish life. The scribes were scholars of the law and obsessed with trivial debate over the interpretation of the letter of the law. The principal popular religious themes were either messianic or apocalyptic. To fulfill messianic hopes, a royal offspring of the house of David was expected to drive out the Romans and restore the political kingdom of Israel. In the apocalyptic strain an eschatological son of man was awaited who would introduce the kingdom of peace and plenty and prosperity for all. The messiahs, it was thought, would triumph with miraculous political and military

[1] T. W. Manson, *The Sayings of Jesus*. London: SCM Press, Ltd., 1964, pp. 344–45.

victories; the Son of Man would arrive in the midst of cosmological marvels. For almost all the inhabitants of Palestine, the political and religious situation was intolerable. The past was superior to the present, and a much better future was eagerly anticipated. Pharisees, Essenes, Zealots eagerly awaited a better world, whether it be messianic or apocalyptic; and Jesus satisfied none of them.

The Pharisees were appalled at his casual disregard of the law and his vigorous condemnation of their moral self-righteousness. The Zealots could find in his preaching no promise of success in political revolutions. The Essenes were undoubtedly horrified by his proclamation of a kingdom for all men. Those who expected a political messiah were disillusioned when Jesus refused the claim that he was such a messiah and would have no part of the schemes to make him king. And finally, those who expected an eschatological apocalypse were told that they would see no signs from heaven and that they would hear from Jesus no guess as to when the last days would be fulfilled. In other words, Jesus rejected the titles, the categories, the theories, and the aspirations of all religious movements of his time. He did preach a kingdom, but it was a kingdom not of this world; he did announce an eschaton, but it was one quite free from cosmological signs and wonders. Instead of insisting on the old law, he proclaimed a new one. Instead of extolling the uniqueness of the Jews, he preached Good News for all men. Small wonder that when the chips were down he found himself quite without friends or allies.

Without stretching the comparison too far, we can see that many of the religious ideas and movements in Jesus' time have their counterpart in our own day. The Sadducees, the corrupt, politically minded heirs of the ancient church, were an Establishment. The Pharisees were liberal reformers filled with self-righteousness and zeal. The Essenes were perfectionists, who had withdrawn from a corrupt society to build the new and more perfect world of their own. The Zealots were revolutionaries who believed that drastic political action would provide salvation from the injustices they saw all around. Those who expected a messianic kingdom are not unlike contemporary Marxists who think that new forms of political and social organizations will make the world a better place in which to live. And, finally, those affected by the apocalyptic spirituality were not too dissimilar from our own revolutionary utopians such as Professor Charles A. Reich and the other admirers of Consciousness III.

I am not, however, trying to argue that our time is more like the time of Jesus than other epochs in human history. My point is, rather, that the religious and political currents in Palestine in the time of Jesus represent certain fundamental themes that are reasonably typical of the human condition. The names may be different, but the Pharisees and the Sadducees and the Zealots and the Essenes are always with us and so are those forms of popular piety which sees salvation in political revolutions or the dawning of new paradisal ages. Reformers and revolutionaries, puritans and perfectionists, dreamers and defenders of the old order have always sought to find support for their positions in the teachings of Jesus, but he eludes their grasp just as effectively as he eluded the grasp of the movements in the currents of his own time.

To the Pharisees and the Sadducees, to the Essenes and the Zealots, Jesus responded in effect by saying that they were asking the wrong questions and using the wrong categories. It was necessary, of course, as they all said, that God's will be done, but the will of God meant something rather different to him than it did to those who questioned it. As Manson puts it:

> For Pharisaic Judaism it was holiness and righteousness as revealed in the Law. For those Jews who nourished their souls on the Apocalyptic literature, there was added an intenser assurance of a Divine power that would destroy evil and vindicate righteousness, and that right early. For many the Kingdom of God meant the downfall of Rome and the exaltation of Israel to world-dominion. For Jesus the will of God is primarily the forgiving, reconciling, redeeming love of God. And being what it is, it must express itself in a Divine act for men rather than in a Divine demand upon men; though this demand follows inevitably upon the act.[2]

The answer was not a satisfactory one, not to the Essenes, the Pharisees, the Sadducees, the Zealots. It said nothing about purity or zeal for the law, or the upholding of the priestly tradition, or the restoration of the kingdom of Israel, or the beginning of the messianic or apocalyptic age. It said in effect that none of these questions mattered very much and what counted rather was God's forgiving love, but to that his hearers shook their heads in dismay. You couldn't restore a kingdom with God's redeeming love, nor could you protect

[2]*Ibid.*, p. 345.

the law from those who violated it, or maintain the dignity of the priestly tradition. It was no help in getting rid of the Romans, and it certainly didn't seem likely to lead to any reform of Jewish religious life. As a matter of fact, there wasn't much you could do with the message of Jesus at all.

Except believe it, and that was too easy and too difficult. It was too easy because it didn't involve fulfilling minute regulations or taking the field in combat against the Roman barbarians. It was too difficult because it meant depending on God rather than on oneself, and nobody was about to do that.

Neither then nor now.

Much has been made, particularly in the totally irresponsible articles by Edmund Wilson in the *New Yorker* magazine, on the similarity between Jesus and the separatist Jewish community of Wadi Qumran on the shores of the Dead Sea (a group which may or may not have been the same as the Essenes which the Jewish historian Josephus mentioned). That there are some similarities in vocabulary and category is not to be denied. The discoveries at the Wadi Qumran have made an immense contribution to our understanding of the religious atmosphere at the time of Jesus, but few responsible scholars today would argue that Jesus was part of the community whose members spent so much time bathing themselves in the sun-drenched rocks overlooking the Dead Sea. In his pamphlet, "Jesus and the Wilderness Community at Qumran," Ethelbert Stauffer notes nine differences between Jesus and Qumran. These differences nicely illustrate just how much at odds with his own day Jesus really was.

1. The Qumran community was heavily clerical; priests played a larger role there than in any other Jewish community of that time. But in the life and ministry of Jesus there is no reference to the priestly tradition.

2. The wilderness community was almost compulsively committed to ritualism. Jesus, on the contrary, argued that purity was internal rather than external.

3. The monks in the wilderness community were required "to love all the sons of Light and hate all the sons of Darkness," but Jesus insisted that we must love all men.

4. The Qumran sect was deeply involved in revolutionary militarism. Jesus argued that all that take the sword shall perish by the sword.

5. The Qumran community was obsessed with the minor details of the Jewish calendar. Jesus completely ignored the calendar controversies.

6. The wilderness community was committed to secret teachings and traditions. Jesus, on the contrary, insisted that he had spoken publicly for months and years and had said nothing in secret.

7. The Qumran community expected two messiahs: the kingly one from the house of David; the priestly one from the house of Aaron. Jesus, on the contrary, is completely unconcerned about genealogies and not very much occupied with messianic questions.

8. The Qumran sect was intentionally critical of Jerusalem priesthood and the Temple cult, claiming that it was illegitimate, deviant from the proper hereditary line of the priesthood. Jesus, on the contrary, took part in the Temple celebration and, while he was critical of the abuses, made no comment at all on the question of priestly genealogy.

9. Stauffer summarizes the differences between Jesus and the wilderness community with the rather startling assertion that they would have murdered Jesus as readily as the Pharisees and the Sadducees.

> In addition to the manifest differences and certain readily admitted points of contact between Jesus and the spirit of Qumran, are there also antitheses? Is there anywhere a genuine "either/or" which is a life-and-death matter? I answer that there exists at least one major antithesis between Jesus and the spirit of the Qumran sect . . . the attitude toward the Torah. By the Torah I mean the Mosaic law, as recorded in the five books of Moses and as found in its central formulation, the Ten Commandments. I contend: had Jesus fallen into the hands of the Wilderness sectarians, they would have murdered him as ruthlessly as did the Pharisees. For in the climactic period of his ministry, Jesus opposed the spirit of the Wilderness sectarians just as relentlessly as he did the spirit of the Pharisees.[3]

The wilderness community was even more rigid in its insistence on the law than Jerusalem either in its Phariseeic or Sadduceeic manifestations. The Torah was the measure of all things, and a man who breaks the Torah cannot be a man from God. And as good a measure

---

[3]Ethelbert Stauffer, *"Jesus and the Wilderness Community at Qumran,"* trans. by Hans Spalteholz, Facet Books Biblical Series—10. Philadelphia: Fortress Press, 1964, pp. 20–21.

of the importance of the law are the regulations of the Sabbath. In Stauffer's words:

> The Sabbath laws were considerably more rigorous in Qumran than in Jerusalem. However, not only did Jesus altogether reject this heightening of the law; what is more, he fundamentally repudiated the Mosaic Sabbath law itself. For this reason there could be no fellowship between Jesus and Qumran, no understanding, no tolerance. There was simply no place for Jesus in the world of the Wilderness sect. Had he sought such a place, had he fallen into the hands of the Wilderness sectarians, according to their logic and exegesis of the Torah, they would have condemned to death the rebel against the Sabbath in Qumran; they would have had to condemn him—just as it actually was done in Jerusalem.[4]

The early Church chose to use many of the categories of Jewish thought—Son of Man, Messiah, Suffering Servant—to describe the ministry of Jesus, but what is striking about the way these categories are used is that if we compare the Christian use of them with the pre-Christian use, whether it be among the sectarians at Wadi Qumran or in popular Jewish piety, the content of the category undergoes drastic change. The early Church claimed that Jesus was the Messiah, Son of Man, the Servant, but the words now meant something rather different, and necessarily so, because if Jesus was a messiah he was unlike any messiah that had previously been expected, and if he was an apocalyptic son of man, the signs and wonders and the eschatological age introduced by them were drastically different, and if he was the servant of God, the *ebed* Yahweh, he infused service with a meaning that was certainly not understood by those who had pondered over the implications of the later chapters of Isaiah.

It would appear that Jesus deliberately avoided titles because the titles that were popular in the religious atmosphere of his time could only lead to a distortion and misunderstanding of his message. When the early Church fell back upon these titles because it needed some kind of category, because it had to have some kind of theological concept to explain its experience of Jesus, it was forced to modify drastically the content of the titles so that they meant something quite

[4]*Ibid.*, pp. 33–34.

different from what they did to the compulsive hand-washers of the Wadi Qumran and the zealous puritans of Jerusalem.

The point of all this is that Jesus was appallingly unique. He was a man of his time—born in Judea, raised in Galilee, speaking Aramaic, understanding Hebrew, honoring the central tenets of the Jewish law, and dying under the unjust administration of Roman justice. But his style, his message, and his challenge ignored rather completely the critical religious and social controversies of the day and, indeed, quite explicitly aimed to transcend such controversies. The symbolism which Jesus' life and message represent is profoundly original and quite unlinked to the social and cultural epoch in which he lived or, indeed, to any social or cultural epoch.

Jesus came to preach a simple, profound, but quite straightforward message, one that jarred his audiences and led them to conclude, first of all, that he was irrelevant and, second, that he might very well be dangerous. His message was rejected by all the leading groups of his society, and because he persisted in it, it was necessary to get rid of him.

And if he was irrelevant to his own society, he was far more irrelevant to the deterioration of Greek culture and Roman government that constituted the frightful hodgepodge of the Hellenistic world with its cults, its sects, its mysteries, its obscure philosophies, and its endless political intrigue. Perhaps the principal difference between the reception Jesus would have received in Rome as compared to the one he received in Jerusalem is that in Rome it would have taken much longer to decide that he was an enemy of the people.

It is my contention that nothing much has changed. The revolution-aries, the establishmentarians, the liberal reformers, the utopians, the philosophers, the cultists, the mystics, and the schemers of our era are no more impressed by Jesus of Nazareth than were their counterparts in his own time. He was irrelevant then; he is irrelevant now. He was dangerous then; if people really began to take him seriously today, he would be perceived as dangerous now. Stauffer says he would have been condemned to death at Qumran as much as at Jerusalem. In our more humane era we might dispose of him by trying to turn him into a television personality rather than by executing him. But if we would not slay Jesus, we would at least imitate our predecessors and try to ignore him.

Some of the more enthusiastic Catholic political revolutionaries would have us believe that the gospel of Jesus legitimates their cause (I shall say more about this in a later chapter). They are quite wrong, of course. Jesus did not advocate political revolution; neither did he condemn it. But he argued that human happiness and human salvation would be achieved, if they were achieved at all, by other means. However, in a sense deeper than politics, Jesus was indeed a revolutionary. Indeed, even more radical than the revolutionaries. His message was distorted; he himself was disposed of because he was a threat to everyone in sight, left and right alike, and he would continue to be misunderstood, misinterpreted, and distorted down through the ages for precisely the same reason.

The rather simple, straightforward, and shocking message which Jesus came to bring was an attempt to redirect the course of human history, to change the style of human behavior and transform the nature of human relationships, and to reorder human life. It was an attempt which was not notably successful in his own time and has not achieved very much success since then.

It may not be legitimate for Jesus of Nazareth to ask that we accept his message, that we believe his Good News, but surely he has a right to insist that we listen to what he really says and that we respond to what in fact he is telling us and not to the misrepresentation and distortions that our own concerns bring into his message. As I say, he has a right to ask this, but, on the basis of performance, past and present, his expectations that his rights will be honored cannot be very great.

In the last paragraph of his book *The Sayings of Jesus*, Professor Manson summarizes the Good News.

> The essence of the Gospel is that Jesus—His life and death and victory over death, His ministry, His teaching—Jesus is the divine act, the fulfillment of God's redemptive purpose, the incarnation of the Kingdom of God. The ministry of Jesus is no mere prelude to the coming of the Kingdom, nor even a preparation for it: it *is* the Kingdom at work in the world. His ethic is no mere "interim ethic" to bridge the gap between the present and the future: it is the will of God which, whenever and wherever the Kingdom comes, is done on earth as it is in heaven. God was in Christ reconciling the world unto Himself. It is probable that the key to the teaching and the ministry of Jesus, and indeed to the whole New Testament, lies in a single phrase, which expresses, as perfectly as words can, the supreme

interest of our Lord, that for which He lived and died, for which He
endured hardship, loneliness, and obloquy, that to which He gave
His whole undivided devotion—not "the Law and the Prophets,"
not "the Kingdom of our father David," but "the Kingdom of my
Father."[5]

So the question we must face then is, What is the kingdom of his
father that Jesus preaches?

---

[5]Manson, *op. cit.*, p. 345.

Chapter 3
The Kingdom Is at Hand

The phrase "the kingdom of my Father," with which we ended the last chapter, has been heard so many times down through the course of nineteen hundred years that we have lost any sense of what a bombshell it was when Jesus first uttered it. All three words are important: "kingdom," "my," and "father." In this chapter we will reflect mainly on the first word, and we shall use the word "kingdom" because it is the one most familiar to us from the Scriptures. However, we must note that the word meant something rather different to those who first heard it than it does today. Not only were they steeped in the eschatological writings of the Scriptures but they also had some sense of the power and the majesty of the king, a sense which is lost today when most of our kings have little power and most of our men of great power do not choose to call themselves kings. The word "kingdom" might be more appropriately translated as "reign" (as C. H. Dodd translates it) or "power," or perhaps the same idea might be conveyed if we mentally note that whenever Jesus says, "The kingdom of God is at hand," it can be understood as meaning, "The promise of God is about to be fulfilled." It was the notion of fulfillment of an age-old promise which most excited the crowds when Jesus emerged for his brief ministry of preaching. Something staggering, immense, overwhelming was about to happen, for God's age-old promise of redemption was now being fulfilled.

We can summarize the core of Jesus' message around five propositions:

1. One must change one's life, for the kingdom of God is at hand.

2. The day of salvation has dawned.

3. The principal sign of the kingdom and its salvation is God's loving mercy.

4. No matter how the kingdom is opposed, and no matter what happens to it, the kingdom will triumph.

5. Since now we have heard the Good News of salvation of the triumph of the kingdom, we must rejoice.

The message is very simple and, through repetition down through the centuries, has become trite. But its simplicity and its triteness should not obscure for us the fact that the message responds to the most basic and agonizing question that faces all who are part of the human condition: Is everything going to be all right in the end? Jesus' response was quite literally to say, "You bet your life it is." Or, to put the matter only slightly differently, to the question of whether life was ultimately a tragedy or a comedy, Jesus replied with the absolute assurance that it was comedy.

1. The theme of Jesus' preaching was indicated in the first chapter of St. Mark, fourteenth verse, and in the fourth chapter of Matthew, seventeenth verse. Gunther Bornkamm quotes the two texts and observes:

> "Now after John was arrested, Jesus came into Galilee, preaching the gospel of God, and saying: 'The time is fulfilled, and the kingdom of God is at hand; repent and believe in the gospel' " [Mk. i. 14ff.]. "From that time Jesus began to preach saying, 'Repent, for the kingdom of heaven is at hand' " (Mt. iv. 17). With these words the first two evangelists sum up the whole message of Jesus. Each does so in his own language: Mark clearly in the language of the first Christian mission, Matthew in the language of the first Jewish-Christian community, which shuns the name of God, saying "kingdom of heaven" instead of "kingdom of God." There is no difference in substance: God's kingdom is near! That is the core of Jesus' message.[1]

The word in Greek for repent is *metanoia*. It means more than giving up sinful habits. It means, rather, the transformation of the basic structures of one's life. The intervention of God in history which

[1] Gunther Bornkamm, *Jesus of Nazareth*, trans. by Irene and Fraser McLuskey with James M. Robinson. New York: Harper & Row, 1956, p. 64.

had been expected for ages was now about to occur; indeed, was in the process of occurring. Old styles of life, old forms of religious behavior, old attitudes and dispositions must be cast aside because they are no longer pertinent. We simply cannot continue as we have in the past. The whole situation has changed. Jesus' hearers were in no doubt as to what he meant. They knew the passages from the Psalms about the kingdom of God.

> "All thy words shall give thanks to thee, O Lord; and all thy saints shall bless thee!
> They shall speak of the glory of thy kingdom, and tell of thy power,
> to make known to the sons of men thy mighty deeds, and the glorious splendour of thy kingdom.
> Thy kingdom is an everlasting kingdom, and thy dominion endures throughout all generations" [Ps. 145: 10–13].
> "The Lord has established his throne, in the heavens; and his kingdom rules over all" [Ps. 103: 19].[2]

And if they were in any doubt, Jesus quickly clarified the issue for them. In the scene in the synagogue of Nazareth, which St. Luke uses as the introductory theme to his theological reflections on the message of Jesus, one sees Jesus standing in the synagogue reading an eschatological passage from Isaiah:

> The spirit of the Lord has been given to me,
> for he has anointed me.
> He has sent me to bring the good news to the poor,
> to proclaim liberty to captives
> and to blind new sight,
> to set the downtrodden free,
> to proclaim the Lord's year of favour.

Jesus then quite calmly rolled up the scroll, gave it back to the attendant, and sat down (as was appropriate when one was preaching in the synagogue), and, with all eyes fixed upon him, serenely announced, "Today this scripture passage is fulfilled in your hearing." Foolish arguments would rage down through the ages about whether Jesus thought he was the messiah or not. What he thought of himself

---

[2]Quoted in Bornkamm, *Ibid.*, p. 64.

(which we will turn to in a later chapter) is less important than what he thought was happening. He clearly thought that the messianic age, the reign of God's kingdom, the eschatological banquet, call it what we will, had begun, and it had begun in and through him.

2. "Now is the day of salvation." In responding to inquiries from the disciples of John the Baptist, Jesus (Luke 7:22, Matthew 11:3) once again, somewhat freely, quoted Isaiah. The blind see; lame walk; lepers are cleansed; deaf hear; poor have the gospel preached to them. Jesus is not necessarily claiming that all these events have occurred, but that once again the "Day of the Lord," the day of salvation, has begun. The old age is finished; the turning point in human history has arrived; a new era has begun. The dream of Isaiah has become a reality. In Professor Joachim Jeremias' words, "Salvation is here; the curse is gone; paradise has come again." It is time not to repair old garments with new cloth but to put on new robes. It is time when new wine must be poured into new wineskins. It is a time of a new harvest and a new vintage, and the intoxicating wine of salvation is now available for all men. (Noah planted a vine after the Deluge, Israelite spies brought a bunch of grapes from the Promised Land, and Jesus creates a superabundance of wine in Cana in Galilee, each act indicating a new age is beginning.) As Professor Jeremias summarizes it: "The old garment and the new wine tell us that the old is passed, and the New Age has been ushered in."[3]

This turning point in history is described in a number of different poetic images. A new shepherd is sent for the lost sheep. He gathers his little flock around him. A physician has come to the sick. A messenger comes with a summons to a wedding feast. A head of the family gathers the family around him and invites guests to the table. An architect builds a new temple. A king makes a triumphal entry. These images indicate the same theme: a decisive turning point has occurred. And Jesus has come to announce it.

3. The intervention of God in history is not one of punishment and judgment but rather of mercy and love. This is what is especially good about the Good News. Salvation is sent to the poor and Jesus has come as a savior for sinners. Four of the parables of Jesus emphasize this theme: the parable of the Prodigal Son (or, as Professor Jeremias calls it, the parable of the Father's Love), the parables of the Lost

---

[3]Joachim Jeremias, *The Parables of Jesus*, trans. by S. H. Hooke. Charles Scribner's Sons, 1963, p. 118.

Sheep and the Lost Drachma, and the parable of the Good Employer.
In the parable of the Prodigal Son, the emphasis is not on either the
sinfulness of the son or the jealousy of his brother but on the love of
the father. In the parables of the drachma and the sheep that are lost,
the emphasis is on the utter foolishness of hunting down one lost sheep
or spending so much time on one mislaid coin. Only a crazy shepherd
or a foolish housewife would act so absurdly, just as only a slightly
demented father would shower honor on him who was a wastrel.
Finally, only an employer whose generosity had caused him to take
leave of his senses would pay to those who had worked only one hour
a whole day's wage.

Men have always suspected or at least hoped that God might be
good, might even love us. The message of Jesus was not new simply
because it vigorously confirmed that suspicion. The novel element in
his Good News was that God's love was so powerful that it pushed
Him to the point of insanity. God's passion for his people is so great
that he dispenses with the normal canons of discretion and good taste
in dealing with us. The Loving Father does not even give the prodigal
son time to finish his nicely rehearsed statement of sorrow. The son
has barely begun before he is embraced, clothed in a new robe and
propelled into a festive banquet. The woman taken in sin is not
required to express her sorrow or promise amendment. Before she can
say anything Jesus sends her away with forgiveness. *L'amour de Dieu
est folie* as the French Easter liturgy puts it.

We are scandalized by such behavior on the part of God. Why does
he not behave with more dignity and respectability? If we were in his
position we would have heard out the prodigal son and then told him
to come back in a few weeks when we had made our decision. And we
would have taken every precaution to make sure the adultress really
was not planning on dashing back to the arms of her lover. Nor is our
sense of scandal new. Apparently the story of the sinful woman was
left out of the early versions of the gospels because, even though it
was part of a very ancient tradition, it described a standard of leniency
that was shocking to the strict moralists of primitive Christianity. They
had already begun to try to remake God into the stern judge that they
thought he ought to be. The stern judge might be foreboding, but at
least he isn't embarrassing. The trouble with the God that Jesus
claimed to represent is that he loves too much.

The parable of the Good Employer is especially interesting when one ponders the fact that there was a rabbinical story with which Jesus' audience was certainly familiar that was quite similar to it. But the point of the rabbinical story was that the workers who came at the last hour worked so hard they accomplished more than those who had come at the first hour and actually deserved to be paid the whole day's wage. But in Jesus' version of the story, the emphasis is not on the hard work of those who came at the end but rather on the generosity of the employer. As Professor Jeremias observes, "Thus in this apparently trivial detail lies the difference between two worlds: the world of merit, and the world of grace; the law contrasted with the gospel.[4]

Jeremias notes that the parables of Jesus were generally tools of controversy used to defend his Good News against the attacks of those who would not accept it.

> It was not to sinners that he addressed the Gospel parables, but to his critics: to those who rejected him because he gathered the despised around him. . . . Again and again they ask: "Why do you associate with this riffraff, shunned by all respectable people?" And he replies: "Because they are sick and need me, because they are truly repentant, and because they feel the gratitude of children forgiven by God. Because, on the other hand, you, with your loveless, self-righteous, disobedient hearts, have rejected the gospel. But, above all, because I know what God is like, so good to the poor, so glad when the lost are found, so overflowing with a father's love for the returning child, so merciful to the despairing, the helpless, and the needy. That is why!"[5]

We must not pass over these parables quickly because we have heard them all before. We may not understand fully the dizzy incredibility of their meaning. Jesus is saying in fact that God's love and mercy are so generous that similar generosity in humans would be deemed madness. God's generosity in human affairs would be a sign that a man had become irrevocably demented. It is not merely that he has set up an accounting system in which a considerable amount of credit is deposited on our side of the ledger; it is also that he has in a moment of insane generosity thrown away the account book entirely and provided us with a checkbook full of signed blank checks.

4. The kingdom of God will certainly triumph. Professor Jeremias

---

[4]*Ibid.*, p. 139.
[5]*Ibid.*, pp. 145–46.

describes four "contrast-parables" (contrasting the beginning with the end) as expressing Jesus' confidence concerning his mission. The parables of the Mustard Seed, the Leaven, the Sower, and the Patient Farmer are all part of "the great assurance." The emphasis in all four is one of the inevitability of process. The mustard seed is planted and the processes of nature are such that it becomes a tree no matter how small the seed. Similarly, the tiny bit of leaven initiates a process of fermentation which will certainly transform all the dough. The sower casts his seeds on the ground and, despite the perils to which they are exposed, they nonetheless bear fruit. The farmer plants his crop and waits patiently, knowing that there is nothing more for him to do until the inevitable natural process produces the harvest. Not only is the Good News being announced, but the certain triumph of the Good News is being guaranteed absolutely. It is as certain as yeast transforms dough; as the seed grows into a tree; and as the crop comes to harvest. Nor does the certainty, in the final analysis, depend on the strength of human opposition or the weakness of human faith. God has intervened to begin the New Age, and no matter what we do it will continue. We can no more stop it than we can stop the sun rising in the morning.

5. It is therefore necessary for us to rejoice. The kingdom is like a treasure that someone finds in the field. He is so delighted with it that he sells all he has to buy the whole field. All the way to the real estate office and all the way back, the man bubbles with joy because he knows what a splendid find he has come upon. Similar is the man who finds a pearl in the marketplace. It's a terribly expensive pearl, and he realizes upon examination that it is a priceless find, worth far more than is being asked for it. Even if he has to sell all he possesses to buy it, it is still easily worth the cost. The pearl is far more valuable than everything he possesses and more. Norman Perrin summarizes the joy and surprise theme of these two parables:

> The original form of these parables, then, has a double element: surprise and joy. They both speak of a man going about his ordinary business who is surprised by the discovery of a great treasure, and, in this respect, they reflect the sympathetic observation of the men of first-century Palestine that we claim is so strong a feature of Jesus' parables. In a land as frequently fought over as ancient Palestine the chance discovery of valuables hidden for safe keeping in some past emergency was by no means unusual, and every peasant ploughing

his field must have had some such secret dream. Similarly, pearls could be of fabled worth, and every merchant whose business took him to far places must have speculated upon the chance of stumbling across one such pearl. So we have the secret dream suddenly and surprisingly fulfilled, and the overwhelming joy that then seizes the man and determines and dominates his future activity. The analogy is clear: so it is with the Kingdom of God. A man can suddenly be confronted by the experience of God and find the subsequent joy overwhelming and all determinative.[6]

One must of course realize the extent of the treasure; one must grasp what the pearl is really worth. And when one has gained insight into the immense value of that chance finding, then no cost is too great, no inconvenience too serious to prevent obtaining the treasure. Indeed, the cost and the inconvenience are minor because in any rational calculation the treasure is worth far more. The man who sells all his goods to obtain the treasure does not think he's making any sacrifice. Quite the contrary, he knows he has stumbled on an extraordinarily profitable transaction; hence, he rejoices at the thought of the payoff.

Again we are forced to note the extreme simplicity of the message of Jesus. An old era is done. God is intervening to begin a new age. It is an era of incredible generosity. One must change one's life in order to benefit from the generosity, but so great is the payoff in accepting the abundance of the new age that our *metanoia* ought to be one not of sorrow and sacrifice but of wonder and rejoicing.

This message speaks to the most fundamental questions a man can ask: Is reality malign or gracious? Jesus replies that it is gracious to the point of insane generosity. Is life absurd or does it have purpose? The reply of Jesus is that not only does it have purpose but that God has directly intervened in human events to make it perfectly clear what the purpose is. What is the nature of the Really Real? Jesus' response is that the Really Real is generous, forgiving, saving love. How does a good man behave? The good man is a person who is captivated by the joy and wonder of God's promise. In the end, will life triumph over death or death over life? Jesus is perfectly confident: The kingdom of his Father cannot be vanquished, not even by death.

Jesus is saying that in the end it will be all right, that nothing can

[6]Norman Perrin, *Rediscovering the Teaching of Jesus*. New York: Harper & Row, 1967, p. 89.

harm us permanently, that no suffering is irrevocable, that no loss is lasting, that no defeat is more than transitory, that no disappointment is conclusive. Jesus did not, as we shall see in a later chapter, deny the reality of suffering, discouragement, disappointment, frustration, and death, but he simply asserted that the kingdom of his Father would conquer all of these horrors, and that God's generosity was so great that no evil could possibly resist it.

The message of Jesus, the Good News of the kingdom of his Father, deserves to be accepted or rejected for what it is: an answer to *the* most fundamental questions a man could ask. If we are to reject it, then let us reject it because we believe that evil triumphs over good, that life is absurd and is a tale told by an idiot, that the Really Real is malign, and that only a blind fool would believe that things will be all right in the end. For it is on this ground that we must accept or reject Jesus, not on matters of papal infallibility or the virgin birth, or the stupidity of ecclesiastical leaders, or the existence of angels, or whether the Church has anything relevant to say about social reform.

But the contemporaries of Jesus did their best, nonetheless, to avoid the issue. Jesus confidently announced that in the end all would be well, that a new age had dawned, that God was intervening in human history, and that the only appropriate response for us was to be delirious with joy. His audience did not say, "Yes, we believe you," or, "No, we think you're a fool." They rather said, "What about the cotton-pickin' Romans?" or "When are you going to produce the apocalyptic sign?" or "Why aren't you and your disciples within the Jewish law?" or "Which side do you take in the various legal controversies?" Jesus replied by saying that the Romans were not the issue, that the law was not the issue, and that cosmic miracles were not the issue. God's insanely generous love for us was the issue, and, in the face of that fact, the Roman and the Torah became peripheral. But his listeners stubbornly refused to concede that the Torah could possibly be peripheral or that the Roman domination of Palestine could possibly be a marginal question. The Torah and Rome—these were the relevant problems—and what did Jesus have to say about them? But, once again, Jesus responded that he had not come to discuss the law, nor had he come to challenge the Roman Empire. He had come to bring Good News that the Really Real was love, and to demand from men joy and response to that love. Sober, hardheaded, realistic people in his audience simply shook their heads. Why did he not address himself to the really critical questions?

But it was not merely those in his audience who ignored the point. Since Jesus first appeared on the scene to announce that the day of salvation was at hand, we have elaborated vast theological systems, we have organized a worldwide church, we have filled libraries with brilliant scholarship, we have engaged in earth-shaking controversies; we have done battle with all kinds of political tyranny; we have engaged in crusades, inquisitions, renewals and reforms; and yet there are still precious few of us who go about with the same kind of joy as does the man who has found buried treasure or who responds to the baffled happiness of the prodigal son showered with gifts by a father who has every reason to ignore him.

One can imagine what the dismay of Jesus was like. He came to bring the best news that man had ever heard, and, no matter how many different ways he stated it, nobody seemed to hear him. They were so concerned with their own petty fears, ambitions, and causes they simply did not seem to be able to grasp the plain and obvious content of what he said. But perhaps after a time it became clear to Jesus that in one level of their personalities they most certainly understood what he said; they pretended not to understand precisely because they realized the full implication of his Good News and understood the staggering *metanoia* that would have to occur in their lives if they should take him seriously. For if everything was going to be all right in the end, then there was nothing left to worry about. One of course had responsibilities and obligations. One could not ignore the political, economic, social, or cultural world, but all of these terribly seductive human activities would be seen in a very different light. In fact, they might even be understood as games, games which the players knew they would certainly win. Jesus was asked about the Romans and about the law and about the cosmic signs because his audience did not want to face what life would be like if Jesus was right. They refused to listen to what he was saying not because it was burdensome, not because it was threatening, not because it was a vision of gloom and doom punishment, but because it was too spectacularly good, much too good, in fact, to be true. Jesus was rejected and ultimately executed not because of greed or ambition or fear, but, rather, because of cynicism. If there is any prophet more obnoxious than a prophet of doom, it is a prophet of joy.

It was cynicism, pessimism, and despair which defeated Jesus and continues to defeat him. So precious few of even those who claim to be his followers live lives that would lead one to suspect that they had indeed discovered a treasure in the field or had spotted a pearl of great price in the marketplace or, to use a somewhat more modern simile, a long-lost Rembrandt painting. Not very many Christians live lives of men who have been intoxicated by the eschatological wince of a new age. Quite the contrary, the average Christian is every bit as gloomy and sober as his non-Christian neighbors. Not many Christians go about with the bright eyes and the singing heart that were characteristic of the prodigal son. The typical Christian's eyes are downcast and his heart is heavy and dull. Only a few Christians live with the serene confidence that the triumph of goodness is as certain as the fermentation of dough by yeast. The typical Christian is at least as anxious as his non-Christian neighbor.

Many young Catholics think it is the height of fashion to say that Christianity isn't any different from good humanism, and even such a distinguished scholar as Father Gregory Baum seems astonished to discover that there are many good, generous, and helpful people in the world who are not Christians. Sometimes I suspect that both the young people and even Father Baum are not fully aware of how much modern secular humanism is merely Christianity in another guise. However, the important point that I think they miss is that Jesus made no claim to preach a gospel that was "different." His message was not a new attempt to define the good or the true or the beautiful. It was not a revelation of some deep substantive truth that men had not understood before. He was not a Gnostic providing a secret way to wisdom. The gospel is not to be compared to the Koran or the Book of Mormon. There is but one secret that Jesus wished to reveal, and it was what man had always rather hoped was true: Reality is gracious. Jesus merely went one step further and said: "Reality is love. The kingdom of my Father is the kingdom of love, and all you have to do is accept that kingdom and joyously receive His love."

If the Christian is to be different from other men, it is not because he believes certain creedal propositions, or because he follows certain norms, or because he engages in certain ritual activities, or because he takes certain stands on social action issues. What marks the Christian off against everyone else is that the Christian is, in Brian Wicker's words, "The humanist who is sure of the ground on which he stands."

The Christian knows that God is Love, that the Really Real is insanely generous in his affection toward us, that it will be all right in the end. The Christian may, of course, express his insight in certain propositions. He may believe that certain moral behavior is appropriate to him. He may engage in certain ritual acts. But the really important thing about him is that his confidence and joy transfuse everything he does.

But to the enthusiastic young Catholic who has suddenly discovered that there are people in the world who are not Catholic and wants to know how Catholics are different, one can only point out that by no means everyone in the world is willing to say, in Teilhard de Chardin's words, "Something is afoot in the universe." Not everyone in the world is willing to give himself over to ecstatic joy because he believes he has found the pearl of great price. Not everyone is willing to live life as though he has discovered a treasure whose richness will never diminish. Indeed, the irony is that not even most Christians are willing to live in such a way.

He who accepts the gospel of Jesus rejects nothing that is good in the world, turns his back on no human endeavor, runs away from no human problem, but he asserts by word and deed that there is nothing to fear, nothing to worry about, nothing over which to be dismayed. What he does is much less likely to distinguish him from others as the way he does it. The way he does what he does is the way of the man who has found the buried treasure.

So the modern searchers-after-relevance say to Jesus of Nazareth, "But what do you have to say about peace?" And Jesus replies to them, "My Father loves you." They say to him, "What is your position on the race question?" And he responds, "You ought to rejoice over my Father's love." And they say to him, "What do you think about the ecological crisis?" And he answers, "Nothing can stand in the way of my Father's love." And the young apostles of relevance shake their heads in dismay. Clearly this strange Jewish preacher is completely out of it. He doesn't understand the issues at all. What in the world does God's generous love have to do with peace or ecology or race?

When I try to summarize Christianity, as I have in the previous paragraphs, some people have said to me that I am merely promising to those who suffer, "pie in the sky when you die." But such an answer shows little insight into what Jesus was talking about. He was not simply preaching the existence of heaven or an afterlife in which the good would be rewarded or the evil punished; he was rather saying something more basic and fundamental. There was not the slightest taint of cheap consolation in Jesus' message. He did not deny the reality of suffering or death; he simply asserted that God was Love and that love triumphed in the end. He did not say that injustice was to be quietly accepted. He did not say that suffering was to be overlooked or that pain was to be denied. He did not say that death was not a terrifying reality. Rather, he addressed himself to something much more elemental and asserted that, despite suffering, despite injustice, despite misery, and despite death, everything would still be all right in the end. Because his Father was love.

We have said repeatedly in this volume that the message of Jesus was irrelevant in the sense that it did not address itself to the problems that his contemporaries thought pressing—and no more does it address itself to the problems deemed relevant today. And yet in a deeper sense the answers of Jesus were shatteringly relevant in his time and our own. For despite all the social progress we have made since A.D. 30, distrust, suspicion, hatred, injustice, misery, fear are as pervasive in the world today as they were in Jesus' own time. It has not dawned on us that a man's fundamental view of the nature of reality can have a profound effect on his ability to cope with social and human problems. Jesus did not deny the existence of injustice, much less did he excuse his followers from concern about the problems of the human condition. He simply insisted that they seek first the kingdom of his Father with the confidence that all other things will be added to it. What would have happened if the crowd believed Jesus? What would happen if we believed him? What if cynicism and distrust, suspicion, fear, and hatred began to melt away? What if a rapidly increasing proportion of the human race did believe in the fundamental reality of his love? Probably the only answer to this question is that we don't know because it hasn't been tried. But one can say with a great deal of confidence that it certainly would not hinder the solution of social problems, and at this stage in history it ought to be clear to us that every enthusiastic social movement the world has known has broken up on the rocky shores of human apathy, cynicism, and fear. The naïve conviction of some of the youthful radicals that they are the first ones to be concerned about injustice merely demonstrates how little history they know. And their disillusionment when their bright visions are frustrated—as every bright vision before them—ought to be an indication to them and to their middle-aged admirers that crusades based on self-righteousness, scapegoating, and compulsory virtue (imposed on others) never work. Something new and far more profound is needed in the way of transformation. Yet man stubbornly refuses to recognize that his enthusiasm, his passion, his vision, is no more adequate to cope with the problems of his condition now than it was two thousand years ago. The message of Jesus is relevant precisely because it provides the underpinnings of conviction about the basic nature of reality without which we will never be able to change the world. The world is still pretty much the place it was when Jesus came; the reason why is that so few people have thought to take Jesus seriously.

But why is one's fundamental world view so important? Why does it really matter what one thinks about the nature and destiny of the universe? Isn't it enough that we agree with other people on proximate ends without having to share ultimate values with them? These questions, frequently and mindlessly asked, miss the point entirely. Of course we can work with those who share proximate ends with us. The relevant question is not who we can work with but rather what contribution our world view has to make.

There is no room for discouragement. We have the Great Assurance that love will triumph, that it will be all right in the end. Such a conviction does not make things easier. Our bright hopes are frustrated; our dreams blighted. Faith is not an inexpensive tranquilizer that eliminates the need for suffering. All it does—and this of course is critical—is enable us to keep going.

As I write these words the college campuses of the country are quiet. The students with whom I have talked assure me that they and their contemporaries have given up on political action. As one young man expressed it, ''We got all excited last spring and didn't accomplish anything, so now we've decided there's not much point in trying.'' Oh, man of little faith. One effort, without careful analysis or hard work, leading to an emotional outburst, and it becomes permissible to be disillusioned. The young people did not take to the streets to support peace candidates in the 1970 election, and Ralph Nader says they have copped out on the ecology-pollution issue. The present generation of enthusiasts has set an all-time record for shortness of commitment.

Their discouragement has only just begun, as anyone who has tried ever so slightly to modify the human condition can tell them. Frustration, discouragement, defeat, and disappointment are constant. If one does not have some fundamental conviction, he will either give up in cynicism or become authoritarian, determined to force men to be virtuous whether they want virtue or not.

Furthermore, in the agonizing complexities and uncertainties of personal relationships, the temptation to quit is overwhelming. Unless one believes that somehow it will be all right, that no matter how much pain and suffering there is in developing an intimate relationship, the struggle is not without purpose.

Discouragement and disappointments, both in social action and human relationships, become even worse as the years advance and one's health and vigor begin to fail. One hoped for so much and so little seems to have occurred. One worked so hard; the payoff was so small. One dreamed such dreams and the reality is so shabby. Maybe Macbeth was right after all; the idiot's tale means nothing. Whether it be the young enthusiast, frustrated because Congress did not change its policy once he has explained his conviction, or the aging reformer who has discovered that even the success of all his plans does not really seem to alter the human condition, discouragement is the ultimate foe; a foe which can be overcome only if one's notion of the fundamental nature of the universe forbids surrender to it.

In G. K. Chesterton's "Ballad of the White Horse," Alfred the Saxon sits disconsolately on an island in the Thames River lamenting the defeat of his armies by the invading Danes. The Mother of God appears to him standing above the reef of the river. He asks her for a sign that his struggle is not in vain. She tells him that a sign he will not get, for while the men in the East may read signs in the stars that give them courage to go on:

> But the men who are signed with the cross of Christ
> Go gaily in the dark.

> I tell you not for your comfort,
> Yea, not for your desire
> Save that the sky grows darker yet
> And the sea rises higher.

> Night shall be thrice upon you
> And heaven an iron cope
> Do you have joy without a cause
> Or faith without a hope.

"But the men who are signed with the cross of Christ go gaily in the dark": as good a two-line summary of the message of Jesus as one could find. And Alfred the Saxon stands up, buckles on his sword, and goes forth to do battle in the White Horse Vale: as good a Christian response to the message as one could ask for. For Jesus does not say that discouragement will go away; he merely asserts that discouragement is not ultimate. The dark is not any less dark; the gaiety of the Christian is not based on any sign that penetrates that dark, but rather it is a conviction that somewhere ahead there is light which the dark will never extinguish.

A man signed with the cross of Christ can go gaily in the dark precisely because he has the Great Assurance. If one objects that there has been precious little gaiety in the two thousand years of Christian history, the only possible response is that there has been precious little confidence in the Great Assurance. But if gaiety is relevant to the human condition—and I suspect that nothing is more relevant—then the Great Assurance and the Good News of the kingdom are too, so frighteningly relevant in fact that most men will do their best to pretend that neither exists.

He who believes in the kingdom has no choice but to respect and reverence fellow citizens of the kingdom. No cause, however important, justifies his turning his fellow citizens into objects. If God is generous in forgiving, so, certainly, must be His followers. White racists, ethnic hard hats, reactionaries, or, on the other hand, radicals, Communists, and hippies must all be treated with sympathy and respect. No cause, however sacred or just, can legitimate hatred; and no oppressed people, no matter how virtuous, have any right to denounce other people as a class. The long years of discrimination and bigotry, of white against black, do not legitimate black hatred or stereotyping of white. Hatred, stereotyping, bigotry, prejudice of whatever sort have place only in a cynical universe; they are irrelevant in a world in which madly generous Love is defined as the core of reality.

One must be stubborn about the point: the message of Jesus of Nazareth is absolutely meaningless unless it produces men and women who can go gaily in the dark without the need for enemies to scapegoat. There is no way to prove as yet that gaiety and generosity can indeed reform the world, but it's worth noting that their opposites, cynicism and scapegoating, have not succeeded.

The late George Orwell once remarked that all revolutions fail. But not all the failures are the same. Some revolutions, one presumes, fail because they are beaten and others fail because they succeed. The message of Jesus of Nazareth suggests that attempts to change the world fail because, in the final analysis, men lose their nerve and their confidence. They lose their nerve and their confidence because they do not believe in the kingdom of his Father, a kingdom of love and generosity. Christianity denies no human aspiration; it rather asserts confidently that these aspirations are valid. But its very confidence modifies the style of our pursuit of our aspirations in such a way that now, for the first time, achieving them ought to become possible. To believe it of course takes a tremendous amount of trust in the fundamental goodness of Reality and a good deal of faith in the message which asserts such goodness. If the kingdom of God is at hand and it is moving toward victory with the inevitability of the seed growing into the tree, then we need never lose our cool. For in the long run nothing, not even death, can hurt us. But the people who have kept their cool in the last two thousand years have been few and far between. It is, after all, hard to be cool when one's principal concern is those cotton-pickin' Romans.

By no means does self-definition as Christian guarantee that a person really believes in the kingdom, really accepts the Great Assurance, or really is capable of going gaily in the dark. At some point in the distant past, a decision was made that in the absence of internal acceptance of the Good News, external conformity to it would suffice. It was much easier, of course, to arrange for external conformity because it is much easier to pretend to be a Christian than really to be one. One's attempts at gaiety may be halfhearted, one's celebrations may be lackadaisical, one's confidence in the Great Assurance may be cautiously guarded, but one can still go through the motions. The training in Catholic schools, seminaries, and novitiates was carefully arranged so that going through the external motions could almost be guaranteed. One's commitment might be rather weak, but the external supports propping up the commitment were quite powerful.

But since the Vatican Council, this strategy has collapsed. We find considerable numbers of priests, religious, and laity who have discovered that their commitment to the kingdom is weak, if it exists at all. One, for example, hears women religious in their middle thirties say that they're not sure their religious order will survive, they're not sure that there will be anyone to take care of them in their old age, that therefore it is necessary for them to leave the community and find an occupation and, eventually, a husband in order that they might have some security. Go gaily in the dark, indeed! Similarly, we hear from priests that they're not sure what the priesthood means anymore, and they do not know whether the Church has a future. But this is simply another way of saying that they never did know what the priesthood meant and they never did know what the Church meant, and they never did commit themselves to the good news of the kingdom. Their lives are not lives of joy and wonder and surprise now because they never were, but in the absence of external support, the weakness of their faith and commitment becomes all too obvious. And Catholic laity are profoundly shocked either by the dramatic changes in the Church or, alternately, with the failure of the Church to change enough. But if their commitment to the kingdom, their belief in the Great Assurance, if their gaiety in the dark depends upon the structures of the organized Church, then it never was much in the way of faith to begin with. It is not that any of these three groups have suddenly lost their cool; rather, they never had the cool in the first place and the collapse of the structures of external conformity simply makes the deficiency obvious. They may try to persuade us that they don't know whether they believe anymore, but the point is that they never really believed at all. But then, very few of us have.

The message of the kingdom is an absurd one. Prudent, careful, cautious, and cynical men will never accept it. They will ask irrelevant questions or pretend to believe the message and then live without confidence and gaiety. I suppose that Jesus was not surprised. He surely understood that the last thing in the world men wanted to hear was good news.

Chapter 4
The Call for a Decision

In the last century repeated efforts have been made to characterize Jesus as an "ethical teacher." For some men, like A. Loisy and A. Schweitzer, the ethics were essentially gentle and peaceful. More recently some theologians have tried to characterize Jesus' ethical system as revolutionary; many see it as ethics of *political* revolution. But these attempts to find behavioral formulas to specify a response to Jesus are not new. In the very early Church there was a dispute as to whether response to Jesus required obedience to the Mosaic law. In later years those who were most enthusiastic in their response were expected to demonstrate that enthusiasm by venturing forth into the desert or hieing themselves to monasteries where rigidly prescribed rules of conduct were thought to represent the best way of achieving perfection in one's response to Jesus. The religious life as it came into the twentieth century was firmly committed to the notion that, if one followed certain prescriptions and, of course, in every respect the will of one's superior, then one could be confident of the worth of one's response to Jesus. Most recently, some of those on the margins of Christian existentialism see response to Jesus in "personality fulfillment," and in some cases even as "fulfillment" is achieved in sensitivity and encounter groups.

There is a good deal to be said for the religious life and for personality fulfillment, though endorsing both does not endorse the bizarre aberrations of "pop psychology" or some of the monastic practices such as the penitential disciplines of sixth-century Ireland. In those cases one can be sure that some kind of mental disturbance, sometimes of an extreme variety, has intervened between the message of Jesus and response to it.

But neither can the genius of the religious life nor the quest for personal fulfillment be reduced to formulas; and, a fortiori, the response to Jesus is not subject to description in terms of ethical formula. Indeed, it does prescribe an ethic, not as a way to enter the kingdom, but as a result of an acceptance of the kingdom. One did not earn admission to the kingdom by being virtuous; the kingdom was a pure gift. Once one had accepted the gift, then there are certain inevitable consequences for an ethical life. Norman Perrin summarizes this insight very nicely:

> In speaking in the way of recognition and response, we are intending to cover ground that might be considered under such a rubric as "ethics." But "ethics" is a misleading word, because it carries with it the assumption that there is a Christian ethic as there is a Socratic or humanistic ethic. So far as the teaching of Jesus is concerned, this latter is simply not true. There is nothing in that teaching about standards of conduct or moral judgements, there is only the urgent call to recognize the challenge of the proclamation and to respond to it. To talk about the "ethical teaching of Jesus" is to talk about something that can only be found by a process of abstraction and deduction from the teaching as a whole. While we may sometimes wish to carry out such a process, let us recognize that it is always a process which does violence, to a greater or lesser degree, to the intent of the historical Jesus.[1]

Jesus came to preach good news: the kingdom of his Father was at hand. The fundamental ethical challenge was to accept the kingdom, to choose decisively in favor of it, to become a part of it *now* before it is too late. The splendid, glorious opportunity is at hand, and Jesus pleads with us not to miss it.

The parable of the Ten Virgins has this theme precisely. A great feast is being prepared; the Lord, our God, has come to begin his reign, and the banquet will celebrate that feast. We have a choice of entering into this splendid, joyous celebration or standing aside from

[1]Norman Perrin, *Rediscovering the Teaching of Jesus*. New York: Harper & Row, 1967, p. 109.

it. We are urged to decide which we will do, and we are warned of the fate of those who, like the foolish virgins, procrastinate. If we put off choosing for the kingdom of Jesus' Father, we may find that the opportunity has passed us by.

The same theme is to be found in the parable of the Last Supper, where, according to the Scripture scholars, in Jesus' original version the emphasis was not so much on those who were called from the highways and the byways but on those foolish people who refused the invitation to the brilliant and exciting festival. In Jeremias' words:

> This parable, too, is not fully understood until attention is paid to the note of joy which rings through the summons: "everything is ready" (v. 17). "Behold, now is the accepted time; behold, now is the day of salvation" [II Cor. 6:2]. God fulfills his promises and comes forward out of his hiddenness. But if the "children of the kingdom," the theologians and the pious circles, pay no heed to his call, the despised and ungodly will take their place; the others will receive nothing but a "Too late" from behind the closed doors of the banquet hall.[2]

Jesus pleaded repeatedly with his audiences to respond; indeed, many scholars regard the parables of Jesus as essentially a weapon he used in controversy to demand a response from the listening crowds.

The story of the Unjust Steward (Luke 16:1–9), which has scandalized so many pious Christians, has but one single point—we must act decisively while there is still time. Norman Perrin translates the parable into a modern idiom.

> There was a certain labor racketeer who had grown rich on sweetheart contracts and illegal use of the union pension fund. One day he found that the FBI was tailing him and he began to suspect that there was no escape for him. So what did he do? Carefully, he put a large sum of money away where no one could touch it and then faced trial. He was duly convicted and after he had exhausted all his rights to appeal, he finally served a sentence in the Atlanta Federal penitentiary. Having served his time, he took his money and moved to Miami Beach, where he lived happily ever after.[3]

[2]Joachim Jeremias, *The Parables of Jesus,* Revised Edition. New York: Charles Scribner's Sons, 1963, p. 180.
[3]Perrin, *op cit.,* p. 115.

The steward (labor racketeer) was scarcely an admirable person, but at least he was capable of decision. When he was in a difficult situation, with time running out, he acted decisively. He saw a crisis which threatened him with ruin and disaster, and he did not let things overwhelm him; he acted. And while he acted dishonestly, he did act. So, we too are faced with disaster if we pass up the invitation to become part of the kingdom. Like the unjust steward we must act boldly, resolutely, and courageously, for if we do not, we will have suffered a tragic loss.

Similarly, Jesus urges us to keep our hand on the plow and not look back. His audiences of course knew what he meant; the Palestinian plow was a light wooden implement, and if someone looked away from the furrow he was digging, it could easily swerve to one side and the furrow would become crooked. There is not time for us to look back; we must move ahead decisively. If we hesitate and look back, the furrows of our lives will become crooked and we may steer ourselves outside the kingdom.

Jesus' famous saying about the need to hate one's family if one wishes to be worthy of him (a saying of such scandalous vigor that the critics are agreed that it must have come from him) is another way of trying to create a sense of urgency in his audience. The matter at hand is of such grave consequence that even one's family must not be permitted to interfere with his making the decisive choice in favor of the kingdom of the Father.

The ethics of the kingdom, then, are a consequence of the choice that one makes. Perrin points out to us that even the parable of the Good Samaritan, which is surely an ethical parable par excellence, is a parable rooted in Jesus' eschatological message of the kingdom of the Father.

> Because one knows God as responding to human needs in terms of
> the eschatological forgiveness of sins, one must respond to the needs
> of a neighbor in terms of whatever may be appropriate to the
> immediate situation.[4]

The Jew and the Samaritan were bitter enemies, but because God had expended loving forgiveness to the Samaritan, he in turn extends love to the Jew he finds in need. As Perrin puts it, "In the context of

[4]Perrin, *op. cit.*, p. 124.

God's forgiveness men learn to forgive, and in the exercise of forgiveness toward their fellow man they enter ever more deeply into an experience of the divine forgiveness.[5] Or, in other words, as men experience God's love for them, they respond to other human beings with love and, in that response, come to understand God's love better.

The behavior of the Christian, then, is indeed the behavior of a man transformed, a man who has undergone a *metanoia*. But repentance is not accomplished the way one acquires skills at waterskiing, knitting, or writing books. It is rather a transformation of one's life that is accomplished in a basic existential leap in which we decisively choose for the kingdom of God, decisively commit ourselves to the notion that the Really Real is in fact insanely generous love. The ethical behavior of the Christian is a consequence of that leap, not an automatic consequence, indeed, because the leap is never perfect or complete; not a consequence which requires little effort, but a consequence that follows inevitably just the same. For if we permit ourselves to experience God's love, then that love is so powerful that it bursts forth from our personality and spreads to all around us. The light breaks forth in the darkness, and the darkness cannot put it out.

So much of the approach to Christian ethics in ages past has been the other way around. Whatever the theological differences have been, and whatever the theoretical debates, in fact most of us have preferred to believe that our ethics earn us admission to the kingdom. During the Reformation, for example, both the reformers and the fathers of the Council of Trent agreed that one could not merit on one's own the initial admission to the kingdom. But in fact, Protestants and Catholics alike since the sixteenth century have lived their lives as though Christianity was an exercise of certain carefully detailed specific responsibilities. The New Testament provides no grounds for such an assumption; on the contrary, Jesus makes it clear that the essential challenge is to accept the kingdom. That is the major ethical act. When that is accomplished all else follows "naturally," even if not without pain and difficulty. Jesus resisted attempts to categorize the behavior of those who accepted the Father's kingdom in terms of specific regulations. The parable of the Good Samaritan was the response to just such a question which sought for a neat juridical definition of what a neighbor is. Rather, the emphasis in Jesus' teaching

[5]*Ibid.*, p. 152.

was on concrete situations and concrete responses to the situations. Norman Perrin, in discussing the concept of faith as described in the miracle stories (and he does not doubt, by the way, that there is a hard core of authenticity in the miracle stories), writes:

> Today, the pupils of the original form critics are prepared to accept elements of the tradition their teachers rejected. We cannot, of course, diagnose the diseases and their cures over the gulf of two thousand years and radically different Weltanschauungen. Nor can we accept the necessary authenticity of any single story as it stands at present in the synoptic tradition; the "legendary overlay" (Kasemann) and the influence of parallel stories from Hellenism and Judaism on the tradition are too strong for that. But we can say that behind that tradition there must lie a hard core of authenticity. . . . [6]

Faith in a concrete situation, faith in Jesus' demands of his followers, is not acceptance of some abstract, theoretical proposition, but rather the commitment of the total person, the concrete situation presented by God's intervention in history in the form of the kingdom proclaimed by Jesus.

I am not suggesting, of course, that there is no room for theory in Christianity, no room for abstract propositions, no room for philosophical systems. Man must reflect and he must especially reflect on those central symbols around which he organizes the whole meaning system of his life. But the symbols precede analysis; they do not follow it. The full understanding of the implications of our decision to accept the kingdom of Jesus' Father goes not before we have committed ourselves to the kingdom but after.

The whole history of Christianity is the history of people claiming to have responded to Jesus' urgent demand for decision, while in fact they have not responded to it, of people proclaiming that they believe all the truths of the faith but of hesitating to commit the whole reality of what they are to the fundamental truths of the insanely generous love of God for us.

Jesus made the issue very simple and pleaded with us to make up our minds, and we have responded by making the issue very complex. We pretend that we have made up our minds and try to live in the world between commitment and noncommitment, between apathy and

[6]*Ibid.*, p. 136.

joy, between going to the wedding banquet and staying away, between seizing the opportunity of the moment and decisively rejecting that opportunity. Like the ten foolish virgins, we sit at the door of the feast and proclaim that in just a minute we are going to go in, but never quite get around to walking over the threshold.

If one views the story of Christianity as a long chronicle of how people have evaded the decision that Jesus expects of them, a lot of puzzles are solved, but one still must ask, why? Why are we so afraid to respond to Jesus' urgent demand for an answer?

I once had an opportunity to work with a small group of people who in their history together seem to have recapitulated the whole story of Christianity. They discovered almost by chance that there was a possibility of leading a different kind of life, a life of hope and love and joy, of giving themselves over to commitment to the kingdom which Jesus had come to preach. But, then, suddenly they realized the immense demands that the commitment would make on them for the rest of their lives, how much they would have to give up, how many of their foolish fears and defenses they would have to put away, how open their lives would be to ridicule and laughter, the many risks they would have to take. It was not at all clear that the joy and love were worth the price that had to be paid. Rather than take the chance, the group, both as individuals and as a collectivity, fell back on the defensive patterns of their childhood. Some became silent, some became aggressive, some became manipulative, some became disruptive. It was decided that they were not a religious group but merely a friendship community. God, Jesus, Christianity, the kingdom were mentioned only at the risk of exposing oneself to sarcastic laughter. It was argued that all of us must accept everyone the way they were, that no demands, no challenges, no insistence on *metanoia* were acceptable. Ours was a friendship community and friendship meant "total acceptance." Those who tried to preach and practice something else were driven forth, and though the original group soon lost all vitality and direction, and indeed practically all trust and affection, it still persists, if only so as to assure the remnants of its membership not merely that no negative decision was made, but also that no response had ever been required.

The most appalling part of the story is not the rejection of the kingdom which was inherent in this group's history—and I am completely persuaded that the group did indeed reject Jesus and his message—but the dishonesty of the refusal even to acknowledge that Jesus was rejected. One can imagine the Lord saying, "Why won't you at least say no to me, if you will not say yes? Why do you persist either in pretending that there is no need to say yes or no, or in pretending that you have already said yes when, in fact, you live as though you had said no?"

But this little band of people was no different from those who listened to Jesus in Palestine two thousand years ago, and most of those who have claimed to follow him ever since. People do not want to let go. If Jesus will let them reduce his message to certain formulary that can be scrupulously carried out, fine. If one can obey canon law or be "totally open and honest" in an encounter group, if one honors all the precise regulations of the constitutions in one's community, if one zealously pursues the radical party line on every moral issue that occurs, then one is only too willing to be a follower of Jesus, because in all these responses one is still in control. One's own selfhood is still nicely contained. The force of God's love is carefully limited. The stirrings of the spirit are neatly arranged. The precise timetable has been prepared for the coming of the kingdom. But the response that Jesus demands, the existential leap of being in the world, this we would rather not do because we would not be able to control ourselves or contain the power of the spirit or the fierceness of God's love.

The only difference between the little community of which I have spoken and its predecessors in the long and sorry history of Christian refusal to respond to Jesus is that this community was sophisticated in matters psychological. It not only used childish defense mechanisms to keep God and one another at bay, but it became quite self-conscious about these mechanisms and tried to persuade itself that its real problem was not the absence of religious commitment but rather the presence of interpersonal difficulties. That psychological stresses and strains were there was surely true—they are present in every human relationship. What was also true was that these strains were jealously guarded and eagerly promoted because as long as one could concentrate on interpersonal hangups there was no need to address oneself to the ever-present but conveniently obscured challenge of Jesus.

In the forties and fifties (and for centuries before, for that matter) there was little awareness of the connection between religious commitment and personality growth; in the last decade, the pendulum has swung in the opposite direction and the two have been equated. Psychological categories are extremely helpful in helping us to understand the nature of man's religious problem, but it is of utmost importance that one think clearly about the relationship between faith and personality.

In their very root, one supposes they are the same, for acceptance of the kingdom and acceptance of life in all its fullness are virtually the same act. Anyone who responds positively to the invitation to the wedding feast has opened himself up to the world and to his fellow man in hope, love, and joy and is on his way to human wholeness. The reason for this is that the Good News asserts that man's hunger for the absolute and the ultimate, for life and love, is a valid hunger and one to which Life and Love will respond. The message of the kingdom asserts that the fundamental thrust of the human personality is in fact a response to the Really Real.

Thus, religious growth and personality development go hand in hand. The fundamental difference that the Christian message makes is simply that it provides greater assurance and deeper confidence that the thrust is not a vain one. One can develop and enrich one's personality without accepting explicitly and consciously the Christian message. In every thrust of the human person to transcend the limitations of his being, there is certainly an implicit, at least at the time of commitment, notion that reality is good. What Christianity adds is a great deal more confidence and assurance that the struggle for wholeness is worth the price and that it will ultimately end in triumph. The difference between the Christian seeking to become fully himself and the non-Christian may simply be the difference between explicit and confident acceptance of the Good News and an implicit and tentative acceptance of it. But that is the whole purpose of Jesus' coming with his message: to make explicit and conscious that which had previously been implicit and very tentative.

The consequence of this line of reasoning is that when someone is explicitly faced with the message of Jesus and understands what that message is, a response which says, "I will proceed to develop my personality" is something less than an adequate response, because Jesus' challenge, at least to those who hear and understand, is a challenge for explicit, conscious, confident and permanent response. He who understands this challenge and tries to limit his response to an implicit affirmation is caught in a difficult if not impossible psychological bind. He says in effect, "I am not ready to commit myself totally to the proposition that the Really Real is insanely generous Love, but I am going to try to become a fuller human being, although I hesitate to make such a commitment and may refuse to do so." This is, of course, a response which declares that life is indeed a tale told by an idiot. He is really saying, "I will live my life in such a way that, if nothingness is my reward, it will be an unjust treatment of me and my life."

In any case, it must clearly be established that Jesus demanded far more in the way of response than that of the atheist or agnostic existentialist who says, "I will become more fully human despite the fact that I think life is absurd," or of the modern Christian who says, "I will become more fully human without addressing myself positively or negatively to the invitation of Jesus." For that invitation is a highly concrete invitation with a highly concrete promise. Jesus demands that we accept his Good News that reality is love and that we open ourselves up so that love flows into us and out of us to all around. The enthusiastic acceptance of the invitation to the wedding feast involved in this challenge may not be the only way to become more fully human, but one is forced to assert that it is the best way that man has yet devised.

Almost at once the question arises, "Why are there so few Christians who are the kind of loving, living, rejoicing human beings that response to the message of Jesus seems to imply?" The answer to that question is that when a Christian is defined as one who explicitly and consciously says yes to the invitation of Jesus, there are not very many Christians and never have been.

Personal transformation, then, of the gospel message comes about not from engaging in certain ethical acts but from a total transformation of one's life from unbelief to belief. Try as we might to cloud the issue, Jesus will have none of our evasions. He who is not with me is against me. He who does not gather with me scatters. Either the absurd message of joy that Jesus brings ought to be rejected out of hand as blithering idiocy or it must be accepted and lived by. The solution most of us Christians arrive at is to accept it and live by it just enough to get by, just enough to be able to say to Jesus, "At least we are not against you. We can't be with you enough to really enjoy the wedding feast, to become fully and richly ourselves at the feast, and we probably won't be gay and joyful enough to attract others in, but here we are anyway." In other words, we say to Jesus, "Okay, we'll go up on the mountaintop and light a candle—I hope nobody gets a good look at our light."

Let there be no mistake about it: indecisiveness is ultimately a rejection of the message of Jesus, and there is much in the history of the Church that represents rejection. Triumphalism, which puts confidence in the power and the splendor of the Church rather than in the power and love of God, is a rejection. Parochialism, which is too willing to prevent the Father from working outside the Church or the Spirit from inspiring those who are not Catholic, is a rejection. Dishonesty, which tries to obscure the all too obvious human failings in the Church organization, is a rejection of the message of Jesus. The validity of that message does not depend on the virtue of those who preside over that community which is attempting to respond to it. One of the worst of all forms of rejection is authoritarianism, which attempts to compel people to be virtuous. Jesus made it very clear that we had to choose and that the choice must be a completely free one. He compelled no one to follow him, and when the Church uses coercion to win followers for Jesus, it utterly perverts his style and message. Stereotyping and scapegoating, which blame other people for what is wrong in the world, is an utter perversion of the message. When old blames young and young blames old, when white blames black and black blames white, when Catholic blames Protestant and Protestant blames Catholic, each refuses to look into his own heart to see how he has failed to respond. But then it's always so much easier to analyze somebody else's failures instead of our own.

But if the Church frequently fails as a collectivity to decide for or against Jesus, so too do individuals. Pietism is a failure because it confuses commitment with performing certain virtuous acts or developing certain virtuous styles. Zealotry is a failure because it makes us think we can demonstrate our commitment by forcing a commitment on others. Rationalism is a failure because it ultimately refuses to admit the possibility of a special intervention of the Real in the person of Jesus. And faddism is a failure because it confuses being up to date and being "with it" with penetrating the root questions which all men must ask and for which Jesus claimed to have a spectacular answer.

Is there then a crisis of faith in our times? Perhaps there is, but then there always has been a crisis in faith. The difference in our time is merely that many people who have thought that one or more of the evasions mentioned above were in fact faith have now suddenly discovered that these evasions are not indeed adequate answers to the challenge of Jesus, and that he is still insistently urging us to make up our minds whether we want to come to the wedding feast or not. Some of us who always thought that we had accepted the invitation are now discovering that in fact we had not. The masks and props which have supported us have been taken away and we find ourselves faced with the necessity of deciding whether there is indeed a wedding feast and whether we want to go to it. We hesitate at the doorway. There is music and love and laughter within but maybe it's all a trick. Besides, how many of our problems can be blamed on the people who have organized the feast, and what is the position of those inside on race or on peace or on pollution? They keep saying that if we come into the feast everything will be all right in the end, that black and white will come to love one another, that men can live in peace with each other, and that the world, groaning for redemption, will be redeemed. That's all well and good, we say in response, but would they please give us some sign, and in the meantime, what are they going to do about the Establishment or the military-industrial complex, or about the war? and they answer, "Seek first the wedding feast and all else will be taken care of." Still we hesitate. At one time we thought we were at the feast, but we discover that the banquet that we were attending was only a pale imitation—a counterfeit. Maybe this new wedding feast will be a fake too. We are angry at what happened before. Why should we choose again? After all, what do we owe those people in there at the banquet? What do we owe the one who has convened it? While we hesitate in the doorway, a man comes to the entrance, looks us directly in the eye, and says, "You'd better come in before it's too late. My Father isn't going to keep the door open forever." We know who this man is. He has been preaching this message of urgency for a long time, so we don't feel obliged to take him too seriously. In fact, nobody has ever taken him very seriously.

Chapter 5

"Who Did He Think He Was?"

In the Irish community I know best the question, "Who does he think he is?" (or if directed to the person, "Who do you think you are?") is the most devastating and sarcastic of conversational ploys. It may be a relic of the poverty of the old country in which virtually all Irishmen shared. When anyone dared to raise himself up as being just a little bit better off than his neighbor, it was felt that he really had no right to do so; that by becoming a little bit affluent he betrayed the cause of Ireland by selling out to the Anglo-Irish Establishment. "Who do you think you are?" is not just a challenge to an upstart but a charge of treason. It was in something of the same sense, one suspects, that Jesus was challenged to explain who he was. Not merely was he a relatively uneducated Galilean peasant, he was also preaching a doctrine which could easily affect the future of the battered Jewish nation. He had better explain himself and explain himself clearly. Who, after all, did he think he was?

Jesus gave a very clear answer, so clear that there ought not to have been any doubt, and yet down through the centuries people have come up with interpretations which would explain away the answer. They are still busy doing so.

One troubled priest observed to me, "But what if Jesus really didn't claim to be the Messiah after all?" I must say that whenever I hear a question like that I find it hard to suppress my amusement. It is as though we are imposing on Jesus the requirement that he speak in exactly those categories that would enable him to fit smoothly and painlessly into the categories of Apologetics 101. In other words, why wasn't Jesus considerate enough to provide ready-made answers for the questions which we happen to think are pertinent today? Why did he not give us nice neat discourses on the Trinity, the Incarnation, infallibility of the pope, collegiality of the bishops, and all the other important theological questions? It would make things a lot easier for all of us, or so we like to think.

But did Jesus really think he was the Messiah? The first thing that must be said is that he apparently was extremely reluctant to apply titles to himself, in part because titles represented religious themes that he could not accept. Thus, the Messiah was thought of as a Davidic political king, and Jesus did not only not claim political kingship but explicitly rejected it. Whether he described himself as "the servant of the Lord" or "son of man" is debated by the contemporary scholars. To put the matter more precisely, by the strict canons of their science Scripture scholars cannot exclude the possibility that those two titles were not attached to Jesus by the early Church, so they cannot say that the use of them was a part of the message of the historical Jesus.

Most writers would agree that the combination of the son of man and the suffering servant in St. Mark's gospel and their application to him by the early Church were perfectly legitimate conclusions from what we know to be Jesus' authentic message, whether he used them himself or not. It must be kept in mind that Jesus was not preaching himself. He was proclaiming the Good News of his Father's kingdom. Nor was he (despite many decades of writing in this century to the contrary) primarily concerned with some future event. He was proclaiming the kingdom of God as present *now* and demanding a response to that kingdom—even though he knew that the kingdom was not yet fully present.

However, after Easter, there was an inevitable shift in emphasis and Jesus the Proclaimer became also the one who was proclaimed. While Jesus was still among them his followers were constrained to concentrate on the message that he preached. But when he had departed and they had their overwhelming experience of him as alive after his death and burial, they had to explain not only the proclamation but the one who proclaimed it. They fell back on the categories they had at hand, the Christ, Son of Man, Servant of God, the Prophet, though obviously they used these categories in a somewhat different fashion than they were used in other contemporary religious thinking. What the early Christians did was what any man must do: they took the symbols available to them and tried to use them to convey the reality of their experience.

At one stage in New Testament criticism, it was at least implied that this early Christian theological thinking about Jesus was consciously or unconsciously a plot in which the basic message of the person of Jesus was distorted. More recent scholarship, however, emphasizes that the experience of Jesus was too powerful for anyone to dare to try to change it. The tradition recounting his life was too sacred to be treated with anything but the utmost respect. What the early Christians, preachers and then writers, attempted was to use symbols to convey and in part to explain their experience of Jesus. The symbols they used were the best ones they could find to relate honestly what they had seen and heard and felt. Furthermore, contemporary writers like Reginald H. Fuller[1] emphasize that according to what we now know about the historical message of Jesus, the symbols the early Christians chose to use were quite appropriate. What the scholars still disagree on is whether the servant and the son of man symbols were also used in some fashion by Jesus himself. Nevertheless, the use of them by his followers was true to the reality he represented.

Fuller goes even further. He demonstrates at great length and in considerable subtle detail how the theology of the Church as contained even in the first Council is consistent with the intuition of those who wrote the New Testament as well as with the experience of those who knew Jesus. In Fuller's words, "... in Jesus Christ an event occurred which transcended all human possibilities. The transcendent salvation became completely immanent in him."[2] He goes on to say:

And we shall, it is to be hoped, continually return to the ontic mythology when we sing in our Christmas carols:

> Sacred infant, all divine,
> What a tender love was thine,
> Thus to come from highest bliss,
> Down to such a world as this.

---

[1] Reginald H. Fuller, *The Foundations of New Testament Christology.* New York: Charles Scribner's Sons, 1965.
[2] *Ibid.*, p. 256.

> And we shall continue to mark with reverence the words of the
> Nicene Creed, "And was incarnate by the Holy Ghost of the Virgin
> Mary, and was made man." For although both carol and creed are
> couched in mythological language, they are the very life-blood of
> Christian faith and truth, which asserts that Jesus Christ is the saving
> act of God.[3]

Fuller's account of the development from the experience Jesus'
followers had of him through the first primitive theology of the
categories used in the New Testament to the far more elaborate
theologizing necessitated by contact with the Greek world and culminating in the work of the early councils may be profoundly shocking to
those Christians who think that it is necessary for Jesus to have
thought of himself in exactly those categories used by the Councils of
Ephesus and Chalcedon. But if we reflect for just a moment we will
see how absurd such an assumption is. From the point of view of the
social scientist, I must say that Fuller's account makes a great deal of
sense. First of all, man experiences God profoundly, powerfully, as
being present in a very special way. In trying to describe this
experience to others, he uses, modifies, and adjusts the religious
symbols available to him. Then as he moves into other cultures, he
tries to integrate into his presentation philosophical symbols. Finally,
when the community of those committed to that experience becomes
organized, he strives to elaborate a precise theological synthesis,
hoping, of course, that the clarity and precision of the synthesis does
no serious harm to the vitality and energy of the original insight and
experience. It does seem to me that anyone who is committed to the
notion of Chalcedon, that Jesus was truly man, will not be shocked
that his followers understood him and expressed that understanding in
a truly human way.

So whether Jesus called himself the Christ or not (and he probably did
not) is a rather irrelevant question. What is relevant is whether the early
Christian use of this word regarding him was true to his message. And
whether he called himself or thought of himself as the Son of Man or the
Suffering Servant (and he may have) is of less importance than whether
the use of these symbols does convey to us something very important
about who Jesus was and what his message was. The work of men like

---

[3]*Ibid.*, p. 256.

Fuller and A. J. B. Higgins[4] makes, it seems to me, an entirely persuasive case that the use of these symbols was perfectly valid.

But then how did Jesus think of himself? To answer this question, we must turn more to his words and deeds than to any titles that he appropriated for himself. Jesus claimed that in his words the kingdom of God is really present. In the solemn introduction, "Truly, I say to you," by this " 'Amen,' Jesus pledges," Fuller says, "his whole person behind the truth of his proclamation."[5] In the message of Jesus, in other words, one is confronted with the actual presence of the kingdom of God not only in his words but in his deeds also.

Jesus claims that God is present by acting through him. As Fuller puts it, "It is demonstrated by logia which pass all the criteria of authenticity."[6] Jesus addresses people with the phrase, "Truly I say to you." He is not interpreting or reporting a tradition like the rabbis do. Nor is he relating a message received from a distant God like the Old Testament prophets did. God is not distant at all; he is near enough to be called by the intimate title, "Abba." In Fuller's words:

> The nearness of God is *now* a reality precisely in his drawing near in Jesus' eschatological ministry, which is therefore implicitly christo-logical. Jesus can call God "Abba" because he has known him as the one who has drawn nigh in his own word and deed . . . [7]

All of Jesus' behavior—his announcing of the kingdom, his call for decision, his demand for a response, his teaching about the nearness of God, his urging others to follow him, his eating with publicans and sinners—"forces upon us the conclusion that underlying his word and work is an implicit Christology. In Jesus as he understood himself, there is an immediate confrontation with 'God's presence and his very self' offering judgment and salvation."[8]

Fuller concludes his argument by asserting:

> . . . he was certainly conscious of a unique Sonship to which he was privileged to admit others through his eschatological ministry. For,

[4]A. J. B. Higgins, *Jesus and the Son of Man*. Philadelphia: Fortress Press, 1964.
[5]Fuller, *op. cit.*, p. 104.
[6]*Ibid.*, p. 105.
[7]*Ibid.*, p. 106.
[8]*Ibid.*, p. 106.

although there is no indubitably authentic legion in which Jesus calls himself the "Son," he certainly called God his Father in a unique sense.[9]

In other words, Jesus thought of himself, preached, and behaved as though he was the Son of God in a special and unique sense. This was how his followers perceived him, this was the message they conveyed in the New Testament, and this is the experience and the message which the formularies of Chalcedon and Ephesus tried to reduce to theological precision.

In a way, that's all that really matters. Jesus is the Son of God, God is uniquely present in him, both in his words and his deeds; and when we experience Jesus we experience contact with the Father who is present in him. What he chose to call himself on different occasions is quite irrelevant compared to the overwhelming import of his words and deeds.

But one would have thought that it was obvious. A. J. B. Higgins, speaking of both the Son of God and the Son of Man and their Christologies, observes: "The genesis of both Christologies, however, is undoubtedly to be found in the thought of Jesus, only the result is further from that thought in the case of the latter than in that of the former, for Jesus certainly believed God to be his Father in a unique and special sense."[10] He concludes his book with the observation:

> Jesus' fundamental understanding of his mission thus went far beyond . . . the thought of the humiliation and exaltation of the righteous in contemporary Judaism. It was conditioned by a much more profound consideration—the consciousness of his sonship to the Father, Abba.[11]

Fuller and Higgins both state it nicely. (British Scripture scholars writing in the Anglican tradition have a much more graceful way of expressing themselves than those who write in the German Lutheran tradition.) But how could there have been any doubt? If one reads the New Testament to find an absolutely precise justification of the formulations of Ephesus and Chalcedon, he will be disappointed. If

[9]*Ibid.*, p. 115.
[10]Higgins, *op. cit.*, p. 202.
[11]*Ibid.*, p. 208.

one reads to discover how Jesus thought of himself, the evidence is overwhelming that he thought of himself as the Son of God in a special and unique way. He believed that the Father was closely and intimately present in him, and that those who followed him followed the Father also. Jesus was not the pious, ethical teacher; nor was he the prophet come to announce an immediate apocalypse. As we shall see in a later chapter, Jesus was not especially interested in the end of things. He was concerned about the present challenge. The notion that Jesus was an ethical teacher and apocalyptic prophet is one of the most extraordinarily clever and systematic conspiracies that man has ever developed. The New Testament presents Jesus as claiming something entirely different. He asserted that in him and through him God was intimately present in human events, an idea completely foreign if not repugnant to all the religious currents of his time (or any other time, for that matter). He was either what he said or a madman, and the attempt to write him off as something else is false both to the New Testament as we have it now and to his own message revealed by the Scripture scholars as they probe beyond the words of the New Testament to find the historical Jesus himself.

The German scholar Joachim Jeremias in his pamphlet, *The Lord's Prayer*,[12] and his book, *The Central Message of the New Testament*,[13] makes much of the word *abba*. Indeed, Jeremias argues that if we only had the two authentic words of Jesus, *amen* and *abba* (and both are indisputably authentic), we would have enough to be able to understand his message. For the word *amen* indicates he was one who preached on his own authority, and the word *abba* indicates that he was one who claimed the most intimate of possible connections with God, his Father. Jeremias does not feel that he exaggerates a bit when he says that all we know of both the person and the message of Jesus can be summarized in those two words.

Jeremias attaches enormous importance to Jesus' use of the word *abba*: "To date nobody has produced one single instance in Palestinian Judaism where God is addressed as 'my Father' by an individual person."[14] Furthermore, nowhere in the immense literature of ancient

[12]Joachim Jeremias, *The Lord's Prayer*, trans. by John Reumann, Facet Books Biblical Series—8. Philadelphia: Fortress Press, 1964.
[13]Joachim Jeremias, *The Central Message of the New Testament*. New York: Charles Scribner's Sons, 1965.
[14]*Ibid., Message*, p. 16.

Judaism is there a single instance of the invocation of God as *Abba*. It is a word of utmost intimacy and familiarity. It was the babbling sound that a Jewish infant used toward his father, the equivalent of "dada." But it was more than that. Grown-up sons and daughters called their fathers *Abba* as well, but only in the context of the greatest tenderness and familiarity. It is never used in Jewish prayers because "to a Jewish mind," Jeremias says, "it would have been irreverent and therefore unthinkable to call God by this familiar word."[15] For Jesus to dare to use this word, to speak with God as a child speaks with his father, intimately, simply, and securely, is for Jeremias, "something new, something unique, and something unheard of . . ."[16]

Beyond all doubt, *abba* is a word that Jesus did use, and when we have established that he used it:

> We are confronted with something new and unheard of which breaks through the limits of Judaism. Here we see who the historical Jesus was: the man who had the power to address God as *Abba* and who included the sinners and the publicans in the kingdom by authorizing them to repeat this one word, "*Abba*, dear Father."[17]

For Jeremias, then, the "Our Father" is a prayer of utmost importance. His booklet is extremely interesting reading because it shows the fantastic scholarly care and cleverness by which the Scripture researcher recreates the original Aramaic text of the Lord's Prayer. As Jeremias notes:

> . . . in the Lord's Prayer Jesus authorizes his disciples to repeat the word *abba* after him. He gives them a share in his sonship and empowers them, as his disciples, to speak with the heavenly Father in just such a familiar, trusting way as a child would with his father. Yes, he goes so far as to say that it is this new childlike relationship which first opens the doors to God's reign: "Truly, I say to you, unless you become like children again, you will not find entrance into the kingdom of God" [Matt. 18:3]. Children can say "*abba*"! Only he who, through Jesus, lets himself be given the childlike trust which resides in the word *abba* finds his way into the kingdom of God. This the apostle Paul also understood; he says twice that there is no surer sign or guarantee of the possession of the Holy Spirit and

[15]*Ibid., Message*, p. 21.
[16]*Ibid., Message*, p. 21.
[17]*Ibid., Message*, p. 30.

of the gift of sonship than this, that a man makes bold to repeat this one word, "*Abba*, dear Father" [Rom. 8:15; Gal. 4:6]. Perhaps at this point we get some inkling why the use of the Lord's Prayer was not commonplace in the early church and why it was spoken with such reverence and awe: "Make us worthy, O Lord, that we joyously and without presumption may make bold to invoke Thee, the heavenly God, as Father, and to say, Our Father."[18]

The phrase "we presume to say" or "we dare to say" is very ancient. It goes back into the first century. I suppose that most of us who repeated the words every day at Mass "*audemus dicure*" thought of it as a quaint Latin phrase. We did not realize how bold and daring, how outrageous, how almost blasphemous it was to use such a word of God. Indeed, some of the untrained liturgical enthusiasts quickly dropped the phrase when liturgical reform began. Once again we missed the point completely. Jesus was not merely the one so intimate with the Father that he would dare to address Him in a familiar tone; he was also the one to make it possible for the rest of us to speak to God, the Really Real, the Ground of Being, the Absolute, the Ultimate, the Infinite, in terms of affectionate familiarity. When Jesus called God *Abba* he urged us to do so too; and that is the core of the message he proclaimed. We have called God *Abba* down through the centuries, but whether we have actually lived as though we were on such intimate terms with the Really Real is another matter entirely.

Louis Evely, the resigned French priest, has recently launched a fierce attack on the "Our Father," suggesting that it inculcates fear, insecurity, dependency, and anxiety. Nowhere in his attack, which in my judgment borders on the blasphemous, is there any awareness of what men like Fuller and Jeremias have come to understand is the implication of the use of the word *abba*. Evely is obviously very angry at what the Church has done to him—so angry that he would sooner attack the "Our Father" than address himself to the challenge and demand for a response that the word *abba* clearly conveys. Evely is not the first man to miss the point; nor is he the last. It is so very easy to be angry at the mistakes of our teachers and leaders. It is so difficult to penetrate beyond our anger to face the horrendous existential challenge implicit in the life of a man who thought himself to be God's son, called God, "Daddy dear," and instructed us to do so too.

[18]Jeremias, *"The Lord's Prayer," op. cit.*, pp. 20–21.

In another book, *The Gospels Without Myth*, Evely urges that we strip myth away from the gospel, arguing a popularized and bowdlerized version of R. K. Bultmann. But religious thought without symbols is impossible, and Evely only substitutes his symbols of psychological self-fulfillment for those of ancient Jewish thought, which were, after all, the only ones available to the writers of the New Testament. It would have been much more helpful and more scholarly, too, if Evely had suggested that we strive to understand the fundamental religious experience the New Testament authors were trying to convey through their use of the terms Messiah, Son of Man, and Suffering Servant. That perhaps they struggled to communicate their encounter with the man Jesus, who claimed that the distant God was near—indeed, present—in his word and deed; and that God was not only available to him on terms of affectionate familiarity but also available to us in the same terms so long as we followed him.

One must imagine how profoundly disconcerting Jesus' words and deeds were to his contemporaries. Not only did he refuse to answer what they thought were relevant questions, he refused to put a label on himself that would enable them to pigeonhole him in categories of their own religious thought. More than that, he introduced a completely new set of categories—startling, shocking, blasphemous categories. The way Jesus spoke and acted was unsettling, jarring, troubling. Any man who dared to use such language was bound to cause trouble. The language was so new and startling that it was difficult to say even what the nature of his trouble would be. Finally, the authorities settled on the kind of trouble they thought would be most appealing to the Roman government. The Romans could only have thought anyone using "Daddy dear" to address God was a harmless madman; they had to consider him a potential rebel. So, although Jesus denied that he was a political messiah, he was still executed on that charge. But deep down inside, the real problem was that he made himself like God; he even went so far as to suggest that in his name we could too.

We have incarcerated this claim of Jesus into harmless, trite formulations which, though frequently repeated, have no concrete impact on our lives. Theological arguments by angry men like Louis Evely are most welcome because they provide us with an escape from having to face and deal with the apparent blasphemy of Jesus' behavior. It is better to denounce mythology, or to argue about *homoousios* or *homoiousios*; better to repeat mechanically the Our Father a hundred times a day than to permit ourselves to face the historic and terrible reality of Jesus' claim.

Would it not have been wiser for Jesus to compromise just a bit? Even if he did think of himself as being able to say *amen* and *abba*, would it not have been more discreet and prudent to avoid such language? Could he not have conveyed the Good News of God's loving eschatological intervention in history without adding the bizarre claim that that intervention was somehow personified in himself? The message was hard enough to accept. Why create additional scandal by identifying himself with that message? Those who came after him would have to cope with not just the message, not just the absurdity that God is a lover, passionate to the point of insanity, but also with the blasphemy that God becomes intimately available to us in the person of Jesus. Would it not have been more difficult for us to evade the message of Jesus if he had not also included himself as someone, in a way, even more terrifying than the message? Why was he not content with the perfectly exciting Good News that God did love us and was intervening in a merciful and saving way? Why did he have to embellish the Good News with the even more incredible announce-ment that through him we could address the Ground of Being as Daddy. As we noted in a previous chapter, men don't particularly like those who bring good news, especially when that news is so good as to seem ridiculously absurd. Why did Jesus have to make the Good News so fantastically good? Why did he have to suggest that he was intimately part of the Good News? Could he not have soft-pedaled somewhat the whole *abba* and *amen* business?

All of which is, of course, another way of wondering if Jesus couldn't have pulled his punches just a bit. We are no longer asking, Who did he think he was? We are now asking, Why did he have to burden us with the knowledge of who he thought he was?

But there is no sign of his willingness to compromise; no indication of his willingness to make concessions to our disinclination to take the risk of believing him. He was a man with serene confidence in the nature of his mission and absolute uncompromising integrity in its execution. He was sorry when people would not believe him, sorry to the point of weeping over the city of Jerusalem, but he neither pleaded nor threatened, neither argued nor cajoled. He was not defensive and did not apologize. He was authentic but not with the phony authentici-ty that is so popular today—that kind of authenticity that attempts to overwhelm others. He was patient in the face of those who deliberately missed the point. He explained, but it usually made matters worse instead of better. He clarified, but it seemed to confuse his audience even more. They tried to provide him with ways out, but he resolutely refused to take them; on the contrary, he put himself into even deeper trouble with them—and with us.

If only he had backed down just a bit. It would have been much easier for his contemporaries and for us. But then of course, how can you back down when you are convinced that you can call God *Abba*? At times Jesus indicated that he would rather have liked the burden of his mission to pass from him; nonetheless he persisted. Great events were occurring, a sense of urgency was absolutely essential. He was conscious not merely of God's presence in loving intervention but he was conscious that God was present in *him*. It was not the urgency of threatened punishment; it was that of a splendid opportunity not to be missed. Why, oh why, did we not see how marvelous it was and how happy we would be if, like him, we dared to call the Father *Abba*? Even if we were prepared to accept the urgency of his message, we seize upon passages in the New Testament which have some kind of an apocalyptic element in them to emphasize the urgency of escaping judgment instead of the urgency of accepting love. Jesus did not rule out judgment and punishment, nor did he deny apocalypse. (Much of the apocalypse in the New Testament apparently represents attempts by his followers to convey the eschatological, that is to say, the saving intervention, nature of Jesus' message.) But he was not primarily concerned with judgment or punishment and much less with the awful events of the Last Day. Indeed, he persistently refused to pay much attention to questions about when the End would come. He even made the scandalous statement that he did not know (a statement which scholars argue must be authentic because the New Testament writers would certainly not have permitted Jesus to utter something so scandalous unless he had beyond doubt said it). No, what Jesus was concerned with was the offer of love and the demand that we accept that offer.

But why can we not accept love? Perhaps because its demands never end. If this God of ours is so insanely generous, so passionately concerned with us, it is obvious that He never means to let us go. He will never leave us alone. We will never be able to do enough for Him. His affection for us will never stop. This Jesus whom He has sent is also a man who obviously makes immense demands. He constantly calls forth the very totality of our persons. And if we give ourselves over to these demands, what will we have left for ourselves? If we respond to a loving God and his challenging emissary, what will be left of us? They will consume us in their passion and their affection. They will never leave us alone, ever again. Isn't it enough that they created us, put us on this earth? Why can't they provide us with some sort of privacy, some opportunity to escape their insatiable demands for our affection? Why do they want us to be intimate with them? Why do they demand that we address them with the incredible term *Abba*? Wouldn't it be much better for all concerned if God and man were a little bit more formal, more restrained, more judicious, more stoical, or more platonic? If God were going to intervene in history, why didn't he choose the Greeks or Romans? They were rational people. But the Jews were crazy madmen, already engaged in a strange love affair with their rather odd God, Yahweh. They were perhaps the only race that could produce a bizarre notion of a God so intimately and familiarly available to all of us. As Hilaire Belloc put it, "How odd of God to choose the Jews."

Why was Jesus killed? In the final analysis, it was for the same reason that all great men are killed: they bother us. Jesus bothered us immensely. He bothered his contemporaries and he bothers us now. His contemporaries killed him, but he didn't even have the good taste to stay dead. He continues to bother us. We evade him, distort him, attempt to turn him into a preacher or a prophet, a political radical or a serene moralizer. But his authenticity and his integrity are too strong for our attempts to categorize him. He keeps breaking those bonds even as he broke out of the tomb. There he is again, still confronting us with the demand that we should believe in the kingdom of his Father; that we should address the Father, presumed head of the kingdom, with the same familiarity and affection, almost contempt, that he used.

Oh yes, indeed, it would be much better for all concerned if Jesus, the self-proclaimed Son of God, would go away. But he hasn't, and he won't, and he never will.

Chapter 6

Jesus the Man of Hope

The image of Jesus that many of us acquired in our early training frequently seems to reduce him to being a puppet. There was a scenario that the heavenly Father had designed. The role of Jesus had been written for him. He went onto the stage, played his part knowing exactly how it would all end, and departed to permit the rest of the drama to continue. In such a view of things there was little room in the life of Jesus for hope. He knew what was going to happen to him, he knew how the act would end, and how the drama would continue. Hope was no more pertinent an orientation for him than uncertainty of outcome would be for an actor in a play.

But such an image of Jesus has precious little to do with the reality of the New Testament. It is only by completely evading the evidence and distorting the language that we can conclude that Jesus was not hopeful.

But what is hope? It is the conviction, a modest conviction, that God is not mad—or, if one happens to be Christian, that God's insanity is benign. It is the belief, as Father Gregory Baum has expressed it, "that tomorrow will be different," or, as a young friend of mine has put it, "it is the assumption that the universe is out to do you good, and therefore it's all right to do good for yourself."

Ours is an age deeply concerned with hope. Because more than in any previous age we have a sense of history and of man's evolution, we are more concerned (pathologically so, perhaps) with the future than with the past. We are frequently aghast at the horrors and ugliness of the present in which man's capacity to do evil seems to have been multiplied one hundredfold by his new technological cleverness. Despite the ugliness of the present, we strive desperately to believe that the future will be better. The cult of science fiction among the young, the popularity of Father Teilhard among Catholics, the astrological conviction that the Age of Aquarius is dawning, Charles Reich's announcement of the advent of Consciousness III, the writings of the Marxist philosopher Bloch—all strive to obtain the conviction that despite all our trials and tribulations the human race is moving forward.

The trouble with many of these cosmic visions of hope is that there doesn't seem to be much room for the individual. The race will get better, the species will get better, the lot of the working class will improve, the third world will find abundance, America will eventually be green: these are exciting and challenging visions, particularly when one is young and expecting to see some of these visions come to fruition. But when one is older, he is not readily persuaded that these Splendid Days will dawn for him and that hope for the species which does not necessarily involve hope for himself seems rather empty and foul.

Jesus' message of hope is somewhat different in that it is much less future-oriented. The kingdom of God is yet to come in all its fullness. There will be an ultimate day of vindication. But the full message of Jesus is based on not so much the expectation of something that is yet to come as on the announcement and celebration of something already present.

As Christian Duquoc points out in a 1970 issue of *Concilium*, Jesus' hope will exist with the utter weakness of his personal situation. He refuses to display any sort of messianic strength. He does not work apocalyptic signs, he does not win great victories, he does not wield political power.

> The source of the revolution or the transformation of society would have been supernatural. It would not because of this cease to be earthly. For the sign of his messianism would have been power, and to understand power does not demand a "conversion" of the heart. Jesus is dedicated to the very feeblest of means. To "convince" he has only his attitude and his word. This extreme weakness, this renouncement of all the apparatus of power even to allowing himself

to be accused of imposture, are the sign of the greatest hope in
God . . . [1]

Duquoc adds, "Jesus, Prophet and Revealer, assumes the risk of
proclaiming the coming of the Kingdom in the feebleness of the Word.
The risk was not imaginary: it was verified by his condemnation to
death."[2]

Do not misunderstand this weakness of Jesus. This absolute and
resolute refusal of his to yield to the messianic temptation is not naïve.
He knows what is in man; he knows the scribes, the Pharisees, the
Sadducees, the chief priests; he knows the fates of all the prophets; he
knows what is going to happen to him.

> He pursues his path with no less audacity. Serene audacity, it is true.
> Patient audacity. He knows the stakes of his preaching. . . .
>   To found the Kingdom by power would have been to hide the face
> of God and to contradict the very meaning of Revelation. To found it
> in weakness and freedom was to take the risk of not seeing it come
> into being. Jesus enters actively into this risk. One person to sow
> and another to reap. God is faithful and it is in the "now" of this
> fidelity that the promised Kingdom is coming.[3]

One sees immediately the differences between this hope and the hope
we have discussed in previous paragraphs. Jesus indeed believes that
the universe is out to do us good, but he feels no need to put
constraints on the Really Real—constraints that the exercise of power
and the working of signs would involve. He is so confident in God
that he can afford to be feeble and thereby give the Really Real
complete freedom to manifest his love for us. Hope is based not on the
evolution of the species or on any action of man; neither is it to be
found in some strange mysticism inherent in the universe (either the
Age of Aquarius or Consciousness III). Hope and the dawning age are
the free and gratuitous loving intervention of the Really Real. So
powerful is this intervention that he who manifests it can afford to
appear weak and feeble. Jesus' hope, as Duquoc tells us, is not based

[1]Christian Duquoc, "The Hope of Jesus," *Concilium: Dimensions of Spirituality*, ed. by
Christian Duquoc. New York: Herder and Herder, 1970, p. 26.
[2]*Ibid.*, p. 26.
[3]*Ibid.*, p. 27.

on blind optimism. It is rooted in the experience of God present in him, loving and transforming the world.

Jesus is therefore willing to wait. Instant victory is not required. It is not necessary to force the hand of God or to hasten the time of fulfillment of the kingdom. It is not necessary to have a detailed timetable for the realization of the kingdom. One does not have to supply answers to questions of when and where and how. One does not expect to know exactly how the individual is to survive in the kingdom that is simultaneously present and coming. It is sufficient merely to know that God loves. Man must have absolute trust in the power and goodness of this love.

As Duquoc puts it:

> If Jesus' hope had been founded on an estimation of the evolution of societies, on an improvement in human relationships, it would only be optimism needing verification. It was never that and that is why he was able to risk everything so that eternal communion with God could be shared by men.[4]

Jesus was not a utopian or a dreamer. He did not deceive himself about the failure of his own preaching. He was angry at the stupidity of his audiences. He was pained by the pettiness of his disciples. Jesus was a deeply disappointed man, but none of his disappointment, none of his failure caused him to lose hope because, as Duquoc puts it, "the Kingdom is where there exists neither self-assessment nor demonstrations of power but communion with God."[5]

Note the great difference between Christian hope as manifested by Jesus and other forms of hope. The Marxist, for example, says that, even though the present state of society is unsatisfactory, the process is known by which society will evolve into a more perfect state, and his personal frustrations and disappointments will contribute to that evolutionary process. The apostle of Consciousness III declares that political action is not necessary, that all our discouragements need not be taken seriously because the messianic community—the youth culture— is already alive and ready to transform the world. In other words, one's hopes, disappointments, and discouragements are not seen in

4*Ibid.*, p. 30.
5*Ibid.*, p. 30.

these visions of hope as real. They are, rather, a part of the inevitable historical process tending toward victory.

But for Jesus and the Christian, defeats, failures, disappointments are very real indeed. One puts hope not in the collection of defeats culminating in victory but in the promise of the Father that victory is already present and will eventually manifest itself completely. Christian hope is frequently accused of promoting and fostering illusion, but the Christian is at least enough of a realist to recognize defeat and failure for what they are and not insist that they are part of some inevitable process toward victory. The Christian is also enough of a realist to be able to say that man left by himself has not been able to make the world a much better place. If love is to triumph eventually, some external force is going to have to intervene. Non-Christian hope still persistently believes, despite all evidence to the contrary, that we can do it alone.

Curiously enough, it is the Christian, precisely because he does not believe that a utopia will come by evolutionary process, who is more likely to sustain his commitment to the human condition. As Juan Alfaro says, "Man lives in so far as he has aspirations and plans, that is to say, in so far as he hopes."[6] But even if the non-Christian can deceive himself into believing that somehow the frustrations and uglinesses which he endures will contribute directly to some ultimate victory, he must still face the fact that he will not be around to enjoy the victory; for he must die. The awareness of death, that horrendous contradiction, demands consciousness of his own being. As Alfaro puts it:

> In its very proximity to nothingness death is, thus, a frontier of the transcendent, a radical call to take the decision of hope. Being totally unable to render his existence secure, man can only hope for the gift of a new existence. Death presents man with the option between an autonomous existence, limited to its possibilities in this world (a choice which is fundamental, whether it takes the form of heroic or fatalistic despair, of nausea at living, or an alienated existence ignoring death), and a brave open existence trusting in hope of a transcendent future. Death, then, is a frontier for man's freedom in the option it places before him between hoping and not hoping beyond the scope of this world. And because death is

[6]Juan Alfaro, "Christian Hope and the Hopes of Mankind," *Concilium: Dimensions of Spirituality, op. cit.,* p. 59.

permanently present in human existence, the whole of life is a frontier of hope. In the response he makes to "transcendental hope" each individual interprets his own existence (every interpretation of one's own existence involves a choice) and decides its definitive meaning.[7]

In other words, when he is faced with the possibility of death, man has no choice but to face the fact that he is as weak and as feeble as Jesus was when he faced the envy of the Jewish leadership and the awesome power of Rome. Jesus refused to work signs and wonders; he refused to stop the sun or to call down the twelve legions of angels to protect him in his weak and feeble condition. We might very much like to do that when we are faced with death, but we are unable to do so. We are therefore forced to either give up hope or to accept the promise of a new existence as pure gift. The Christian by the very fact that he can transcend death with his expectation of such a pure gift is more likely to hope, more likely to have aspirations and plans, and more likely to be committed to life. Christian hope, Alfaro tells us, is an "exodus," that is, "a going out of oneself, renouncing any guarantee of salvation provided by human reckoning, in order to trust solely in the divine promise: a breaking of the moorings of all assurance in oneself and in the world, and a tossing of the anchor into the bottomless depths of the mystery of God in Christ."[8] Yes, man hopes, and in the act of hoping he experiences love by God. With that love he is possessed by the certainty of the promise.

The Christian hope is not so much in an afterlife and existence after existence; it is, rather, a hope in existence itself: in the goodness and permanence of one's own being rooted in God's promise. Even though Christians have frequently misunderstood this and acted as though they could ignore their present existence in favor of some better existence to come, the fact is that Christian hope necessarily commits the Christian to the fullness of his present in the knowledge that God will transform it into a new existence. In Alfaro's brilliant concluding paragraph, he says:

> Far from alienating man from his mission of transforming the world, Christian hope stimulates him to carry out his intramundane task and integrates his commitment to the world in his responsibility

[7]*Ibid.*, pp. 62–63.
[8]*Ibid.*, p. 67.

before God and before men, who are his brothers in the firstborn among men, Christ. The Christian lives according to the hope (founded in faith) that man's action in the world will neither end in failure nor lose itself in an endless search for a fulfillment which will never come; his hope in a definitive fulfillment sustains him in his worldly activity. Moreover, the grace of the Absolute Future does not remove but on the contrary radicalizes his responsibility as an actor with a part in history (just as the gift of justification does not suppress but is on the contrary fulfilled in the free response of faith); the salvation of man and of the world come about in the dialogue between the Absolute Freedom of God in his self-communication to man and man's responsible freedom before the call of the God-Love. Charity, the fullness of hope, demands from the Christian a radical involvement in the tasks of the world for the good of mankind. Precisely in the fulfillment of his responsibility to mankind, the world and history, Christian hope anticipates the coming of the Kingdom of God in Christ.[9]

The Christian, then, believes in failure just as Jesus believed in failure, but he knows that failure is not the end. He believes in fulfillment though he knows that he cannot achieve it himself. He knows that he is weak and will be defeated; but he knows that with God's help he can transcend that defeat to achieve victory. It is therefore impossible for him to quit; he cannot give up. When all around him have given up hope, the Christian, conscious of his feebleness and fragility, his weakness and his impotence, is still absolutely committed with the fullest confidence to the strength and love of God. When the charity of others runs out because of age, infirmity, discouragement or frustration, the Christian knows that this is not an option available to him. His hope demands that he continue working no matter how hopeless the situation.

There is a very fine line between the Christian's conviction that he must continue to work to humanize the world and the belief that his work will by itself accomplish that humanization. Hard work does not create the kingdom: it comes of itself through God's power in His own good time. Even the resurrection of Jesus could not cause the coming of the kingdom; it merely manifested it. We do not fully understand the complexity of things. We know that the kingdom is a gift, and we know that we must work toward it. We even understand that in some

[9]*Ibid.*, p. 69.

sense the kingdom is dependent upon our work and our response, though work and response will not cause it. So our effort matters. We commit ourselves to the works of justice and charity not just because we know that love will ultimately triumph because of God's power but also because we understand that the triumph of love works somehow or other through us even though we are not its principal cause. The Christian cannot afford the luxury of relaxing and waiting for God to do everything. Jesus *cared*. He cared deeply and profoundly despite the fact that he knew the kingdom was to come inevitably. In the final analysis, to reconcile our care and commitment, on the one hand, with the inevitability of the coming of the kingdom, on the other, is beyond our human powers of comprehension. We do at least understand this: it is practically impossible to sustain care and commitment in the face of discouragement and the prospect of death unless one is able to believe in the coming of something which transcends us and our efforts.

The tension between the free coming of the kingdom and our own effort is a hard one to balance. I remember giving a lecture at a meeting of college chaplains in which I suggested that the campus ministry could expect to have little direct impact on the life of the university and that therefore what the campus clergy and their flocks should strive to do is to create a model of human relationships of love and trust which would be a light on the mountain to which the rest of the campus could look if they wished. One of the Protestant clergymen present was highly irate. I was preaching a form of Pietism, I was arguing for irrelevance and justifying a cop-out from the demands for involvement. He was astonished that a social scientist could possibly think that faith and love were enough to change American higher education.

I responded that, as a sociologist, I was astonished that he thought anything else would change American education. Furthermore, my social scientific analysis of the role of the church on campus led me to believe that in terms of any direct action toward reform the campus chaplain and his flock could count on nothing more than marginal effectiveness.

His reply was that at least at his university this was not true. He had attended faculty meetings and marched on picket lines; he served on committees promoting educational reform. He was making the Christian voice heard in these situations. Alas, anyone who knows higher education knows that nothing ever happens in committees or at faculty meetings, and that picket lines generally affect only symptoms and not causes. My Protestant minister friend was totally irrelevant to the life of the campus. His frantic efforts to attain relevance by compulsive activity were bound to end in frustration and defeat.

We must, of course, work for higher educational reform. We must, I suppose, go to meetings and even occasionally march on picket lines. But we deceive ourselves if we think these activities are nearly as effective as the witness of a life of commitment, confidence, trust, and love. I hope higher education can be reformed eventually. (Although I don't really see how. I think it may take some special interventions from the heavenly Father to really stir this most recalcitrant of institutions.) I know that if it is ever to be reformed by men, they must be men whose confidence and hope are rooted in something much deeper than attending faculty meetings, marching in picket lines, or participating in the latest campus crisis. Nothing is more hilarious six months after the Kent State–Cambodia demonstrations than to read the apocalyptic articles in the divinity school journals. Such great hope was placed in the fervor of the May moment, and but a half year later, that ferment has been poured down the sink like stale beer. The good divines on these faculties would have been better advised to root their hope in something more permanent, to work with the serence confidence of men who need not see results to have their hope confirmed, who need not exercise power to be confident of the coming and presence of the kingdom, who need not feel strength to know that they labor not in vain, who can experience frustration and discouragements as painful but not ultimate conditions.

On another occasion I was asked to give a speech about the future of religion in the contemporary world. I suggested that its future was probably as secure as its past, because men were not likely to stop asking those questions about meaning they had asked since thought began. Indeed, it seemed to me that the crises of the present days were, if anything, driving men to ask more explicitly and more vigorously the questions of meaning which are at the core of any human value system. After my talk the Methodist cleric who had convened the conference (to force the churches to "take a stand on social issues," as it turned out) announced that we heard too much about faith and not enough about action, and that it was time for the churches to go on record as favoring action.

I certainly would not want to oppose the churches' going on record in favor of action, but what happens after they are on the record and the pace of social change does not accelerate? I wonder if my Methodist friend would then begin to consider the possibility that resolutions at the end of meetings are relatively meaningless, and that social action commitments without a profound transformation of one's world view are likely to turn sour. That social change in the long run is likely to be accomplished not so much by men who insist on immediate action but by men who are deeply committed to faith and see the pertinence of that faith to the agonies of the human condition. To repeat a theme I mentioned in the previous chapter, the commitment of the Christian is such that he realizes that discouragement is simply a luxury he cannot afford, at least not for very long. Quitting is a self-indulgence that he cannot permit himself. Even if he knows he is going to lose now, he knows that in the long run he will win. Jesus knew he would lose; he did not stop trying or caring. He was able to sustain his effort only because he also knew that through the power of his heavenly Father he would eventually win.

The commitment to the notion that the world is out to do us good and in the long run we will win is also absolutely essential if one is not to turn away in terror from the paralyzing fear of giving oneself to others. Josef Goldbrunner says:

> To surrender myself, to put myself defenseless into someone else's hands in total trust, to do this at the risk of being exploited and misused, all this grows into a true experience of dying as we grow older. The sudden changeover to a life with a new quality, the personal quality, is only possible by dying to the protective armor-plated world we have built around ourselves. A person who does not give his self away cannot break through his isolation, nor escape from the prison of meaninglessness, cannot open up, trust, ask, forgive, love.

> Change, metamorphosis, renewal, resurrection—all these words picture what happens when an event bursts upon us and calls us forth, and the answer is not given by reason or some emotion, but by the personal self. This center of my self is called upon, and then actuated and shaped by the response to this call. "Above" and "below" find themselves united again in me in a new way.[10]

[10]Josef Goldbrunner, "What is Despair?" *Concilium, op. cit.,* pp. 74–75.

In despair, one faces the certainty of failure in one's efforts to change the world and the experience of terror at being cut off from others. To maintain commitment in the face of frustration, to take risks in the face of terror, requires a profound conviction that the world is indeed out to do you good. Personal existence, whether manifested in personal responsibility for the world or in discovering the lost dimension of ourselves and radiating it to others, requires the absolute confidence that defeat or rejection is not ultimate and that though our plans fail and our friends spurn and reject us, tomorrow we will be different. I am not suggesting that Christians have a monopoly on this conviction. Men sustain effort and faith in the face of discouragement and continue to break through the armor plate of their defensiveness without the benefit of the full and explicit Christian message. I am asserting that he who does possess that message is better equipped to sustain hope because he has complete confidence in final victory and final resurrection. But one must say more than that. It is not merely that hope ought to be more possible for a Christian; it is also more necessary for him. The existential commitment that he makes demands that he be hopeful. In Alfaro's epigram " 'Justification by faith' means 'salvation in hope.' "[11] The Christian who is not a man of hope stands revealed as not being a man of faith. Hope is a necessary though always difficult and painful consequence of the commitment of faith. Hope is not only a possibility for us; it is in the final analysis an obligation.

One of my agnostic colleagues summarized his theology this way: "God created man and grew very dissatisfied with man's evil. Therefore, He condemned man to hell, which is the situation in which we presently live. Then God took pity upon us and permitted us to escape this hell—by death."

I am not sure that my friend fully believes this theology. He does not, it seems to me, live by it, but, in any event, a man who truly accepts that view of the universe is surely not hypocritical when he gives up his efforts to reform the world or when he quits trying to break through the barriers of fear and suspicion that separate him from other human beings. Indeed, quitting, giving up, waiting for the liberation of death, is perfectly consistent with his position. But the opposite position, which I take to be that of the Christian, is the one

[11]Alfaro, *op. cit.*, p. 67.

manifested by Jesus of Nazareth. Because we believe in the presence of the kingdom, because we believe that we do have the privilege and the obligation to call God *Abba*, because we are fully conscious of our own weakness, we continue to plug away. Indeed, one might even say, plug *merrily* away, because we know the future to be ours.

It has often seemed to me that if the Really Real did want to communicate with us, He selected in the symbol of Jesus an extraordinarily effective means. Sometimes we would think that the Real would have been better advised to produce active signs and wonders, but, as Father Duquoc mentioned in his aforementioned article, that would have been to compromise the fundamental nature of the message that he apparently wished to communicate to us.

Given the constraints under which, for reasons of His own, the Real chose to operate, He did come up with a marvelously effective symbol. But the symbol hasn't worked for most of us, or at least it has worked poorly. In some sense the Real must be criticized for this—not so much for putting together a bad symbol but for choosing to create and to bother with such a stubborn and thickheaded creature which has developed such incredible skill at ignoring, evading, misunderstanding, and misinterpreting perfectly good religious symbols.

The Bethlehem symbol, to which we turn each year at Christmas, is one whose persistence and power man could never have expected. Granted, of course, that the Bethlehem scene cannot be reduced to scientific history like some of the other sections of the gospel. Nonetheless, according to the most recent scholars, it is part of a very ancient tradition which goes back to Palestine in the decade immediately after the death and resurrection of Jesus. The secret of the power of the Bethlehem symbol is the extraordinarily ingenious combination of power and weakness, or, to use Cardinal Newman's words, "omnipotence in bonds." And yet, on a priori grounds, who would have thought that the image of a man, a woman, and a child in a cave with animals and shepherds hovering in the background could possibly have any religious significance? Many hundreds of thousands of times the scene must have been reenacted in the course of human history. People could pass by and not even notice save for a brief moment of compassion for a mother and child in such uncomfortable circumstances. Yet the scene has exercised a magnetic attraction for almost two millennia, and it has survived all the vulgar commercialism of our own time as well as the phony joy of so many Christmas celebrations.

It has survived precisely because its very commonness, its very ordinariness, its very universality, make it such a powerful and appealing message of hope. The Bethlehem scene is nothing more than that fundamental message of Jesus reduced to a setting we can all understand and with which we can all identify. Bethlehem stands for hope because it conveys the message that God loves us so much that we can find Him manifested in the mystery of human life in the most ordinary and commonplace circumstances. Jesus was a man of hope because he was completely committed to the message he preached—a message symbolized for us by the Bethlehem scene. Those of us who claim to be followers of Jesus have no choice but to live in the same hope. And for us, alas, the Christmas symbol is more than just a charming sign of God's love, more than just evidence of the power of the Real to inspire us to heights of poetic imagery. It is a demand that if we take the symbol seriously, we can never permit ourselves the delightful melancholy cynicism of despair.

Chapter 7
That His Will Might Be Done

In the Lord's Prayer, the kingdom of the Father and His will are different aspects of the same reality. The kingdom is God's loving intervention in human history. His will is that man responds to that invitation. He must respond first by accepting the gift and then by giving a life which will manifest the kingdom of God with a light shining on the mountaintop.

We noted previously that Jesus did not come specifically to preach a new ethic; he came to proclaim a kingdom. He also made it clear that we would know the members of the kingdom by the way they lived. Jesus' attitude toward ethics and morality is nicely illustrated by his reaction to the Jewish law. His condemnation is not so much the essence of the law itself, particularly as it is manifested in the Decalogue, but rather the juridic, legalistic interpretations which had been fastened on it like a straitjacket.

Those who have made the existential leap of commitment in accepting the kingdom of the Father are not held to the narrow legalistic interpretation of the law; they are held to something far more difficult: the spirit of the law. They cannot manifest the kingdom by simply asserting that they have fulfilled a certain number of highly specific, neatly codified, and exhaustively listed regulations. It is not enough that they avoid murder, which is relatively easy; they must respect one another, which is very difficult. It is not enough to avoid adultery, which is moderately difficult; they must preserve in marriage a reverence and respect for one's spouse, which is extremely difficult.

It is not enough to guarantee one's truthfulness by swearing an oath; one must also guarantee it by being so transparent that an oath becomes unnecessary. It is not only enough to love one's friends, one must also love one's enemies.

But it is also not enough to reduce chastity and charity and honesty and patience and respect to juridic categories—as we Christians have all too frequently done. Gunther Bornkamm points out that obedience to the law as Jesus enunciated it is not something measurable, something that can be demonstrated, something that can be subject to reckoning, and counterreckoning, to merit and debt, to the economics of double-entry bookkeeping.[1] The will of God is not that we pile up merit for ourselves or that we honor specific, neatly delineated rules which apply to all circumstances. What is necessary, rather, is that we live the kinds of lives of openness and love which will demonstrate that we have indeed responded positively to the challenge of the kingdom which Jesus proclaimed.

Jesus wants no part of legalism. He rejected the legalism of the Pharisees, and there is no reason to think that he expected his followers to engage in newer and higher levels of Pharisaism. Bornkamm notes:

> . . . the words of Jesus in their concreteness have nothing to do with the casuistry of Jewish legalism. Characteristic of this legalism is its endeavor to enmesh man's whole life ever more tightly. With each new mesh, however, it forms a new hole, and in its zeal to become really specific it in reality fails to capture the human heart. This "heartlessness" is characteristic for all casuistry. The concrete directions of Jesus, however, reach through the gaps and holes for the heart of man and hit their mark where his existence in relation to his neighbor and to his God is really at issue.[2]

Yet, Christianity has not been free, to put the matter mildly, of those who have instituted a "higher grade of Pharisaism, more rigorous and more painstaking even than that of Jesus' adversaries."[3]

In *The Sermon on the Mount*, Joachim Jeremias notes that there have been two misunderstandings of the "ethics" enunciated in the

[1]Gunther Bornkamm, *Jesus of Nazareth*, translated by Irene and Fraser McLuskey with James M. Robinson. New York: Harper & Row, 1960.
[2]*Ibid.*, pp. 105–6.
[3]*Ibid.*, p. 107.

Sermon.[4] I will call one misunderstanding "Catholic" and the other "Protestant." The Catholic misunderstanding is to see the ethical ideal laid down by the Sermon as a counsel of moral perfection rather than a strict moral imperative. Those who wish to or are able to are strongly encouraged to live by the Sermon on the Mount, but it is not expected of all men.

According to the "Protestant" aberration, the Sermon is indeed a description of a strict moral imperative, but one which man cannot possibly respond to. Therefore, when faced with both the imperative and his own weakness, man has no choice but to throw himself to the mercy of God and plead for forgiveness for his inadequacy.

Both interpretations assume that Jesus is in fact laying down an ethical code, more noble indeed than that of the Pharisees, but fundamentally a code demanding maximum effort to see that each of its regulations is honored. But, as Jeremias observes, if we look at the life described in the Sermon on the Mount in its proper context, it does not represent an ethical code at all. It is a description of an eschatological reality.[5] The "hunger" and "thirst" are not physical; they are a yearning for God's kingdom. The "mourning" is not for earthly suffering but for the fact that the kingdom has not yet been fulfilled completely. So the Sermon on the Mount is a description of how those who respond positively to the invitation of the kingdom will be able to live. They will be the "light of the world" and "the salt of the earth" precisely because their happiness, their love, their freedom, and their joy will make them new kinds of men—men of truthfulness, generosity, patience, chastity, and goodness.

The Sermon on the Mount does not present a moral or ethical code that must be adopted to earn entrance into the kingdom. It is rather the way those who have decisively chosen for the kingdom will in fact behave—not always, of course, and not perfectly, surely, but at least consistently enough so that the whole quality and tenor of their lives will be demonstrably different from that of those who have not yet committed themselves to the kingdom. Bornkamm describes this "new righteousness" as a qualitatively new and different attitude.

---

[4]Joachim Jeremias, *The Sermon on the Mount*, translated by Norman Perrin, Facet Books, Biblical Series—2. Philadelphia: Fortress Press, 1963.

[5]Indeed, Luke's version of the Beatitudes with which the Sermon begins is clearly an eschatological variant of St. Matthew's more catechetical version. Most authors think Luke's Sermon on the Plain is an earlier form of the Sermon on the Mount.

The truth is that the new righteousness is qualitatively a new and different attitude. In accordance with the biblical idiom elsewhere, neither the concept "righteousness" nor that of "perfection" could be exceeded. "You, therefore, must be perfect, as your heavenly Father is perfect" (Mr. v. 48). This is not an ideal which may be achieved step by step, but means "wholeness" in comparison with all dividedness and brokenness; a state of being, a stance whose reality is in God. In the demand which he makes upon them, Jesus points the disciples, with the greatest emphasis, to God—the God who will come and is already present and active. To live on the basis of God's presence and in expectation of his future, this is what Jesus aims at his commandment: "That you may be the children of your Father who is in Heaven!"[6]

In a strange paradox, those who have committed themselves to doing God's will are both liberated from the world, since they no longer feel tied to onerous and legalistic regulations, and at the same time put back into the world in the sense that their lives now make them "a light on the mountaintop" and the "salt of the earth." The Sermon on the Mount is not a program for legislative and social reform. It is a description of a lifestyle by which we will know those who have accepted God's kingdom; a lifestyle which flows, albeit not easily, from the joy and happiness and love which one experiences when one has decisively responded to the invitation to the wedding feast. The Sermon on the Mount, then, describes a mode of conduct for the eschatological banquet. It portrays the way guests will act at the splendid party to which God has invited them. Why must one love other men, even those who are enemies, even those who are Samaritans? The reason is quite simple. As Bornkamm notes: "The ground of his command of love is simply because it is what God wills and what God does."[7] The fact that love has no limits does not mean that all the boundaries among men are eliminated. The frontiers between friend and foe, Jew and Samaritan, neighbor and stranger, Pharisee and tax collector still exist, but God's love is not limited by those boundaries, and neither must ours. God is so insanely generous as to permit His rain to fall gently on the crops of both the good and the wicked. He refuses to distinguish between His friends and enemies; and we have no right to make such distinctions in our love either.

[6]Bornkamm, *op. cit.*, p. 108.
[7]*Ibid.*, p. 114.

The Sermon on the Mount, as we have said before, does not provide a blueprint for remaking the world. It does describe a lifestyle, a mode of relating to our fellow men without which the world will never be remade. The world has not yet been remade, not because the Sermon on the Mount is inadequate or too lofty as an ideal but because the commitment to faith which it presupposes has not been made completely and totally enough by very many people. As G. K. Chesterton put it, "It is not that it has been tried and found wanting, it has been found hard and not tried."

And if we do not see many Christians whose relationships with their fellows do act like the "light on the mountaintop" described in the Sermon, if there are not many Christians whose behavior is like that of the good Samaritan, then the reason is not that Christianity has failed or that the ethical ideal of love laid down in the Sermon on the Mount and the parable of the Good Samaritan is inadequate. The reason is simply that there haven't been very many Christians.

Juridicism, whether it be of the "Catholic" or "Protestant" variety, is a manifestation of the same pervasive human temptation to which the Pharisees succumbed: the temptation to insist on the letter as a substitute for the spirit, to feel that morality can be reduced to doing certain things instead of a way to do all things. We have vigorously and more or less successfully ignored Jesus' teaching in this respect, and in many cases succeeded in out-Phariseeing the Pharisees in evolving a vast complex of moral obligation, some binding under "mortal sin," some under "venial sin," and some simply binding under the pain of being guilty of "imperfection." This approach to morality is perhaps being left behind; yet one wonders how in view of the Sermon on the Mount it could ever have been taken seriously. I am not at all persuaded that a new "liberal" or "existential" or "psychological" juridicism will not replace the old moral theology juridicism. There are certain kinds of behavior, for example, which are as rigidly prescribed by sensitivity and encounter groups as were other norms of behavior prescribed in days gone past by novice masters and mistresses. The Pharisees we always have with us, even if now some of them appear in the guise of T-group leaders.

I am not arguing for the abolition of moral systems. Jesus didn't argue that either. As he pointed out, he came not to abolish the law but to fulfill it. Man cannot do without moral systems, without ethical codes, for *ethos*, as Clifford Geertz tells us, is but the other side of the coin of *mythos*. Man's conception of how the good man behaves is but a reflection of his concept of what Reality really is. Even the "situationists" or the "contextualists" end up almost necessarily with some new form of systematic morality, though usually one which takes a more benign view of sexual aberrations than the older systems—a view which is in its turn often rooted in a simpleminded misunderstanding of psychoanalysis.

For some strange, perverse reason there has always been a tendency to believe that liberation from moral juridicism means that man has greater freedom to engage in illicit behavior; that he is no longer constrained to be good. But Jesus insisted on liberating his followers from the legalism of the Torah not so that they were now free of sin but so they were free to be good. Moral systems are not thereby abolished. They are seen as being quite incapable of providing "righteousness." They may be necessary, useful, helpful guides, but by themselves they do not provide the good life, and honoring them to the letter is not a sign that one has acted decisively in favor of the kingdom. The liberation implicit in the Sermon on the Mount is less a liberation from an obligation to honor minutiae as it is a liberation for practicing love even in situations where a moral code provides no strict and explicit regulations. To do God's will means to love our neighbor in the concrete circumstances in which we find him. A moral system can be an extremely helpful guideline as to what we ought to do in those concrete circumstances, but those who are part of the kingdom will not point with pride to their implementation of the strict literal norms of the moral system as evidence that they are indeed acting like "lights on the mountaintop."

From one point of view we can say that Jesus' whole ministry was an effort to persuade men that they could find security nowhere else save in God. The difficulty with the rich young man was not so much that his riches were evil, but that he sought his own personal security from them. But if there are dangers from riches, there is certainly no automatic justification from poverty. The poor man was more likely to hunger and thirst after God's kingdom because he was not able to afford the luxury of the rich man's thinking he could find security in his wealth. But neither can security be found in poverty, which no more justifies a man than riches console him. We can only find salvation by accepting God's love and responding to it. Honoring the explicit, specific regulations of a moral law does not justify us;

poverty does not justify us; giving alms to the poor does not justify us; striving to become virtuous by our own unaided efforts does not justify us: only by God's love are we justified. Only when we decisively accept that love and respond to it with the same almost mad generosity that characterizes His love for us can we feel secure. Indeed, the love of God and love of neighbor cannot be separated. As Jesus insists in the twenty-fifth chapter of St. Matthew, "What we do to others, we do to God." We cannot respond positively to God's love for us unless we manifest that love to the least of our brothers. It is not an indirect love achieved by a detour through our love of God; it is, quite the contrary, an overflowing of God's love accepted by us and radiating out from us to all with whom we come into contact. Once we permit God's love to operate in us, our own love floods out and engulfs others.

There is something of a mutual causality at work here. We cannot love others, at least not in the way described by Jesus as the will of his heavenly Father, unless we first accept God's love for us; and in the very act of loving others we experience that love yet more deeply. The very difficulty we experience in loving the very least of our brothers forces us back upon the love of God. And in that deepening understanding of His love, we turn with love toward our brothers once again.

All of this has precious little to do with the juridicism of the Pharisees and the novice masters, of moral theology books, and of catechisms. But neither has it much to do with the sloppy sentimentality of those contextualists who are bent on justifying premarital sex at any cost. The will of the heavenly Father as described in the Sermon on the Mount, the parable of the Good Samaritan, and in Matthew 25 is not terribly concerned with what we can't do or what we can do. Virtue is not achieved in that fashion. The will of the heavenly Father is rather that we love even as we are loved; that we be as generous to others as God is to us. Such a position is neither juridic nor sentimental; it demands the courage, persistence, tenacity, and generosity that can only be sustained by a man filled with hope and quite conscious of being passionately loved.

Another of Jesus' sayings, that about paying tribute to Caesar, bears directly on this point. Jesus was asked a political question; he gave an eschatological answer. The point was not (at least not principally) that it was moral to pay taxes to political authority. The emphasis is not on rendering to Caesar those things that are Caesar's but rather on rendering to God those things that are God's. Once again, Jesus refused to be trapped by the perspectives of his questioners. It was not so much that the political issue was unimportant as it was that it was rather less important than the message he had come to preach. If men paid taxes to political regimes, however grudgingly, how much more they were held to the requirements of God. Caesar wanted taxes, so give him taxes. God wants love, your love; therefore, render to him that love he has the right to require. Caesar is satisfied with the payment of coin. It is not that simple with God. He does not want specific actions from you. He wants *you*.

There have been a few people in the course of history who have ridiculed the Sermon on the Mount, seeing in it a surrender of the dignity and integrity of the individual, the destruction of man's will to live by a God who wishes to reduce man to a state of total dependency. Such a view may have given nineteenth-century German philosophers a chance to work out some of their personality problems, but it is obvious, I trust, that it is based on a fundamental misunderstanding of the will of God as described in the New Testament. We are not called to surrender our vigor or our strength. We are urged, rather, to exercise them in making a decisive commitment and then in living the life that commitment makes possible for us. Almost two millennia of sermons may have made the vision of the Sermon on the Mount seem weak and effeminate. Being a "light on the mountaintop" is no great challenge to us when it seems vague, shallow, "pious," and unhuman. Just as we convert Jesus into a nice, simple, moral teacher to avoid having to face what he really was, so we turn his moral code either into an impossible ideal or a manifestation of a passive, dependent personality. Then we can easily dismiss it; we will not have to face Jesus' insistent demand that we love even as we are loved.

I trust that the reader will excuse me for quoting one more question after a lecture. (Lecture questions seem to embody in the purest form possible the evasions we have developed for ourselves.) Speaking to a group of educators, I once noted that it seemed to me that the educational experience was most effective when the process was marked by love between teacher and student and among students. After the talk, one black educator rose demanding to know whether I was saying that black students should love white teachers and white administrators after the centuries of tyranny, oppression, and suffering they had endured from the white man. I could have said that black students today have not endured centuries of suffering and oppression since they haven't lived that long, or I could have asked whether he thought those of Irish background should hate professors of English background, especially since the Irish died during the potato famine in far greater numbers than the blacks did at any time of their white domination. But these would have been *ad hominem* arguments which only indicate the foolishness of hatred.

I replied by saying that the only answer I knew was that of a Christian. If hatred could be justified, a convincing case could be made for blacks hating their white oppressors. But, as a Christian, I did not believe that hate could ever be justified. Many of the blacks in the audience and some of the liberals violently disagreed. Only by hating, they argued, could the black man be free. Only, in other words, by reacting to white men as white men had reacted to them could the black man escape the results of the white man's hatred. Those senseless and foolish humanists! Hatred merely breeds further hatred, and no one in human history has ever become free by hating. Does it impose a heavy burden on black men to ask that they love white men? Of course it does. But the demand to love is a great imposition on anyone. And Jesus leaves no doubt that responding to the love of his heavenly Father necessarily impels us to love others. The Samaritan should have hated the Jew, but that wouldn't have made him any more free of the Jew, it wouldn't have made him any more proud to be a Samaritan. He would not have been able to go back to Samaria proclaiming that "Samaritan is beautiful." His hatred would have made him no better a human being than he was before encountering the Jew and no better than the Jew who hated him. The Christian may well be able to understand why men hate, but, given his commitment, it is something he cannot accept for himself or approve as a political or social strategy.

In the dark, passionate, romantic period in which we presently find ourselves, hatred is fashionable again. Anti-Semitism has reared its ugly head under the guise of anti-Zionism. The counterculture urges the young to hate the old and their Establishment. Black extremists urge their compatriots to hate whitey, and white militants pursue their own policies of vengeful hatred. Young radicals are urged to hate and, if necessary, to destroy their enemy. International congresses of Catholic theologians adopt resolutions endorsing the actions of revolutionaries who want to deprive other men of their freedom and their lives.

Women's liberation in some of its forms actively urges women to hate men, and the white liberals encourage, and even on occasion demand, that young blacks manifest hatred for whites.

All of this hatred is justified in terms of being necessary that men might be free. It seems incredible that after all the years of bitter experience the race has not yet learned that hatred never frees anyone. Presumably, our present romantic era will end, and we will recognize once again that hatred is no solution. So it will be put aside or repressed into our unconscious, and we will pretend again to love. But it will be a careful, antiseptic love, even among most of us Christians. We are, of course, prepared to love our fellows, but to love with the same generosity that God gave to us through Jesus is simply not possible.

That is correct. It is not possible—not unless we have already made the decisive commitment to accept with joy and celebration God's love for us.

Chapter 8
The Disciples

Jesus came to invite all men to the wedding feast. The Good News was for everyone. Those who accepted his invitation would live lives of love which would make them the salt of the earth and the light of the world. All those who responded to his invitation would be his followers.

But also within the band of followers there was a special group: his immediate followers, his disciples. It is clear from the New Testament that Jesus did have such a select group of intimate followers; but it is difficult for us to sort out which of his instructions were specifically for them and which were aimed at all his followers. There are two reasons for this difficulty. The first is that Jesus himself apparently drew no firm line of distinction between the two groups. Furthermore, the early Church, in recounting Jesus' words and deeds, frequently made use of the stories to reinforce and emphasize certain points of Christian beliefs that were pertinent to the situation for which the writers of the New Testament were directing their books. Jesus' chiding the disciples for their lack of faith, for example, must be understood as a story told not so much to recount Jesus' actual words to his disciples but to use Jesus' words to chide some segments of the early Christian community for their lack of faith.

Nevertheless, it is clear that there were some men who were assigned special roles. They did not choose their roles, they were chosen by Jesus. They were called to come after him with a special call not received by others. They had to be prepared to leave behind their ordinary lives. They were expected to be as mobile as Jesus without necessarily finding a place on which to lay their heads. They had no reason to think that their faith would be any different from the faith of Jesus or that they would receive any more acceptance than he did. They were advised to reckon costs carefully in responding to the special invitation. It was not wise for them to be rash. If they were to build towers, they should have enough money to finish them lest they be mocked by their friends. If they were going to war, they would be sure to have an army strong enough to win; therefore, if they were going to follow Jesus, they must be sure that they knew what they were getting into and that they were willing to pay the price.

But the demands being made on the special disciples were not a new moral code designed for a handpicked elite. It was not an ascetic ideal which Jesus demanded from a precious few. They were called not to be ascetics, not simply to be holy men; they were called upon to help Jesus to proclaim the kingdom of God. And it is the kingdom, this eschaton, this special intervention of God in history, that is the only foundation of the call. In Bornkamm's words:

> The special demand made upon the disciples must, therefore, not be understood at all as a moral code for an elite, as a proclamation of an ascetic ideal which Jesus exacts only from the few, little as he elsewhere rejects earthly things as such: vocation and property, sex, marriage, and family. The kingdom of God is the sole foundation of Jesus' call to follow him. It imposes upon the disciples a special task, a special destiny, but also grants them a special promise.[1]

The task of the apostles' was to be fishers of men. But they are fishers not by trapping or cajoling, much less by tyrannizing them. Rather, they proclaim the victory of the kingdom; they are called to share the healing power, the authority, and the triumph of Jesus, but they must be prepared to share his suffering and his death.

As Father Raymond Brown points out in his splendid little book on the priesthood, *Priest and Bishop*, we cannot make an automatic transition from the apostles and the Old Testament to the bishops and priests of today. The evolution of the Christian ministry to its present

---

[1]Bornkamm, *op. cit.*, p. 148.

form was more complicated even in the first century. Nevertheless, the priest today in the present state of the Church is expected to play a role roughly equivalent to that of the disciple as described in the New Testament. (Though the priest may not be the only one called upon to play such a role.)

A Catholic theologian writing in the magazine *Commonweal* suggested that, since the sacred was no longer a useful category in the human experience, there was obviously no meaningful distinction between priests and lay persons in the Church and that therefore the title "priest" ought to be abolished. The death of the sacred, it turns out, was premature, as *Commonweal* itself announced about a year after. But the title "priest" is not at all indispensable. Father Brown suggests that in New Testament days the one who presided over the Eucharist was not necessarily the one who was the *presbyter-episcopos*. Neither of these two roles was the same as the role of the apostles. One could, perhaps, separate the roles again. But the important point is not what we call him or what his task is. The point is that one can scarcely think of a community of Jesus' followers without thinking of some people exercising the role of disciple, that is to say, of the immediate follower who has a special challenge and commission to proclaim the kingdom—a challenge and commission which he has not chosen, but for which he has been chosen.

As we will note in a later chapter, Jesus did not devote himself to the founding of the Church in the sense that he laid out a neat organizational plan or, much less, that he had tucked away in the back of his head the schema of the code of canon law. Jesus came to proclaim the kingdom and to summon men to follow after him in that kingdom. He was well aware that those who believed his message would form a community. He did found a church in the sense that his message and his instructions provided a mandate for that community.

Jesus would certainly not have approved of hard and fast caste distinctions between those who would play the role roughly equivalent to the fishers of men and others in the community, for all were to be lights on the mountaintop and salt of the earth. But it is hard to read the New Testament and escape the conclusion that there were some men in his community who would be chosen by him for a special mission. The significant thing about the disciple was not his special position and surely not his assumption of moral excellence. The important thing was the proclamation of the kingdom: to proclaim the insane generosity of God and the fabulous marriage feast to which all had been invited. The disciples were marked as men not merely by the quality of their lives but also by active and presumably full-time preaching of the Good News.

That priests—of whom it can be said they are officially commissioned to the role of discipleship—and laity might be restless and dissatisfied with the way this special mandate had been institutionalized in the pre-Vatican Church is surely understandable. In the layman's point of view, priests were a separate caste having all the power and the privilege in the Church. From the priest's point of view, he was cut off not only from his people but also from the human condition. But railing against transitory institutional structures ought not to lead us to overlook the fact that the notion of a special call to some men to devote their lives to the proclamation of the kingdom is unquestionably rooted in the New Testament. As Father Brown vigorously notes, "Can we overlook the fact that the New Testament leaves no doubt at all that these special followers of Jesus are called to a life of extreme dedication and sacrifice?" The dedication is of course not tied to any specific norms. As we know by now, Jesus wanted no part of juridic categories. It is not legitimate, for example, to say that one man is a good disciple because he owns a Volkswagen and another man a bad disciple because he owns a Pontiac, and yet another man is the best of the lot because he only owns a Schwinn bicycle. Such moralistic categorizing, so immensely popular for two millennia of Christian history, is completely foreign to the message of Jesus. Forms of dedication to the proclamation of the kingdom, to the heralding of the wedding feast, will change in time and place. Celibacy, for example, may be an extremely helpful asset to the disciple. Father Brown goes so far as to suggest that one could make a strong case from the New Testament that the Church has the right to require this of those who play the disciple role. But while the Church may decide to require it at certain times and certain places, and may even legitimately do so, it does not follow that Jesus has specified it as essential for his closest followers. They must simply be ready to follow him wherever he calls, indeed, follow him enthusiastically. What this means concretely in given situations is something that Jesus leaves to those who came after him; he refuses to legislate himself.

A lay reader of this chapter might well wonder why there is such confusion and uncertainty in the clergy about the role of the priest. The New Testament makes it clear that the disciple is one who is to dedicate his life to the explicit proclamation of the kingdom. Why isn't it clear to many troubled clergymen that that indeed is their role, even if they have other roles in addition, such as administering the Church's communal affairs and presiding over the Eucharist? (One can view the presidency of the Eucharist, of course, as at the very core of the proclamation mission.) If the disciple is really to do the same thing Jesus did, then why doesn't the priest understand that his task is to announce to all that there is a wedding feast being convened, a banquet being assembled, a splendid party just getting under way, and that everyone should come to the party before it is too late?

St. John's narrative of the life of Jesus begins, we are told, with an account of the marriage feast at Cana because John wants to emphasize the festive nature of the proclamation of Jesus. Why don't priests understand, then? They are indeed celebrants, men whose role it is to announce and preside over a festive celebration.

One of the reasons, I suspect, is that the role model of the priesthood that was provided for us in our training said very little about festivity and celebration and practically nothing about zeal for proclaiming the kingdom. In all my years at the seminary I heard countless talks on the necessity for obedience to the will of God (always interpreted for us by the pastor). I cannot recall a single talk about zeal. I was warned repeatedly about the loneliness and difficulty of the priestly life (though I don't know that I have ever felt particularly lonely, save for a couple of days when I found myself marooned in Istanbul), but no one ever suggested to me that I was supposed to announce and preside over a splendid celebration.

What happened, of course, was that because the Church could not really be sure of the internal convictions of its clergy, it decided to settle for external conformity. If we were not really to be men obsessed by the Good News of the kingdom and by a passionate desire to share that News with others, then at least we would be men who lived the model of the clerical life as set down by the Council of Trent and by the various congregations of the Roman Curia. Just as for the laity it was not necessary so much to accept decisively and totally the Good News of the kingdom as it was to keep the commandments, so for us it was more necessary to say the breviary and avoid contact with women than to give ourselves over with delirious enthusiasm to proclaiming the presence of the kingdom and the dawning of the messianic age.

I am not angry, either at the institutional Church or at my seminary teachers. The style of evasion we practiced was centuries old; it may even contain somewhere deep within it some authentic insight. I am conscious that even now I am repeatedly trying to evade the challenge of the kingdom and the challenge of discipleship, so I cannot blame my predecessors for having developed a whole system of institutionalized evasions. We have not been much of a church down through the centuries. The point is that we are the only one there is, and even though we have fogged the message of Jesus and obscured the Good News of the kingdom, we are still the only community that exists for the purpose of proclaiming the kingdom and spreading the message. Anger at our failures is considerably less appropriate than understanding the reasons for the failures and resolving to do better.

But in the rigid structures of clerical culture, faith in the kingdom was not nearly so important as careful external conformity. It was not necessary that we be celebrants so long as we were obedient. We were not called upon to invite people to the wedding feast so much as we were expected to be on time for confessions on Saturday afternoons and evenings. As long as those structures were firmly maintained, we were not even aware of how shallow our convictions and how bland our enthusiasms really were. Nor did we understand that a life of celibacy can be painfully lonely if it is not somehow or other rooted in an experience of the fantastic Good News of that insanely generous and passionately loving God. It was not so much that we were not lonely but rather that our lives were so organized and routinized that we really did not have an opportunity to become aware of the fact of our loneliness.

The present crisis in the priesthood is, I think, based on the fact that the routines, the organizations, the structures, the props, and the masks have all been swept away, and we are being challenged to face our questions of conviction and commitment and to recognize our loneliness—a loneliness which for some personalities must be intolerable and which for many others can become meaningful and constructive and healthy only when the leap of existential commitment to the

Good News has been made. I would not suggest that the problem for many priests (and for other, perhaps less official, disciples) is that they have "lost their faith" so much as it is that they have discovered their faith to be very inadequate and incomplete; that now for the first time in their lives they are being forced to face the challenge of the kingdom for what it really is. We know from historical precedent that men will try to evade the challenge of the proclamation of Jesus if they possibly can. It seems to me that the priesthood today, at least in the United States, is going through a difficult and painful period of recognizing Jesus' urgent call for decisive choice and trying to evade the stark fact that Jesus is demanding a response.

Some lay people have observed to me that from priests today one hears just about everything but proclamation of the Good News of the kingdom. One hears about race, about pollution, about war; one encounters priests who are counselors, community organizers, recreational supervisors, candidates for political office, T-group leaders, interior decorators, and even, on occasion (heaven protect us), sociologists. None of these roles prevent proclamation of the kingdom; all of them can be successfully integrated with the proclamation, but not a single one of them is an adequate substitute for issuing invitations to the wedding banquet. Many priests seem hesitant to commit themselves to the role of an eschatological herald because they are no longer sure that they believe in that role—another way of saying that they never really did believe in it. They do not think that such a role can be "relevant" in our "secularized" world, and they are not sure that people would take an eschatological herald seriously. The point is that to be really a disciple of Jesus one must be as committed to the message of the kingdom as he was, and to preach it whether or not the audience chooses to take it seriously or deem it relevant.

This book is not the appropriate place to discuss the "secularization" myth, but such an easily refuted sociological theory is embraced by many priests. The reason, it seems to me, is that it has proved a useful means of evading the challenge inherent in the New Testament. If Jesus is to believed, if his message is to be taken seriously, if God indeed has intervened with loving and saving mercy, then the message is supremely relevant and the issuance of invitations to the wedding banquet is supremely important. But the fundamental issue is not whether men happen in the present time to deem the message relevant;

it is whether it is a true message. This can be decided only by a leap of commitment. One cannot be a disciple without being committed, and if there are many hesitant disciples today, the reason is that they have not yet made an active commitment, perhaps even not yet had a full-fledged opportunity to choose for or against Jesus.

And make no mistake; that's what the issue is. The young cleric or nun who tells me that Jesus was a political revolutionary is not speaking either of the Jesus of the New Testament or of the Jesus of history as the New Testament scholars have discovered him. What they are speaking of is a Jesus created out of their own fantasy to help them evade the challenge of the New Testament. And when the young cleric or nun argues that he or she is not sure whether the New Testament is relevant anymore, they are evading the real issue, which is whether the message of Jesus is *true*. For if an eschatological age has dawned, if God really was present in Jesus in a unique way, if we are really privileged to be in intimate contact with the Real on a basis of affectionate familiarity, then this Good News is overwhelmingly relevant.

I do not reject the social concerns of the younger clergy and the religious, though sometimes I wish they were rooted in better informed and more sophisticated social analysis, but I am saying that if these social concerns are not integrated with the self-definition as herald of an eschatological banquet, as proclaimer of Good News, then the priest or nun is simply not living the life of a disciple as Jesus described it. They may be admirable and virtuous human beings. They are not disciples of Jesus. As I have said in previous chapters, for a Christian, personality growth and social reform are a consequence of the fundamental commitment to the Good News of the kingdom, to good news of God's fabulously generous love for us. Similarly, for one who is a special herald of the kingdom, concern about social injustice and human relationships is admirable, praiseworthy, even necessary; but as a consequence of one's proclamation of the marriage feast and not as a substitute for it.

If some of the clergy and religious do not want to proclaim the marriage feast, that is, of course, their privilege. Vast numbers of people down through the ages haven't proclaimed it. But if they will not proclaim it, they will do themselves and us a great favor if they do not claim to be disciples of Jesus and do not try to serve up to us a

Jesus that has nothing to do with the man we discover in the New Testament.

Sometimes I allow myself to think that we may have reached a turning point in the development of Christianity in the Church and of the role of disciple of Jesus. We know so much more now about the real meaning of the New Testament. We also have far greater understanding of the workings of human societies and the development of human personalities. This new knowledge will make evasion much more difficult. The decision for or against the kingdom, a choice of either attending the marriage feast or not, will be much more difficult to evade in the years ahead.

But perhaps this hope of mine is foolish. We have shown remarkable ingenuity down through the centuries in coming up with new evasions when the old ones are stripped away. It may well be that extrinsic faith as a substitute for existential commitment is finished, but we may find ourselves a new substitute in the form of either radical social action or interpersonal aggressiveness masquerading as honesty. I am not so sure that I would like to choose between these two evasions; they are both singularly unattractive.

Most of those who are ex officio disciples have not lost the faith in the sense that they no longer believe at all in Jesus and his message, but many of them do not yet have the faith in the sense that faith means a definitive and total commitment to the Good News of the kingdom. The future of the Church in the United States, perhaps for centuries, depends on how many people in this present time of crisis are able to make such a leap. Or, to put it even more bluntly, how many will see that radical social action, be it of the romantic or intelligent variety, and interpersonal openness, be it of the sick or healthy variety, are not adequate substitutes for the proclamation of the Good News?

I have not watched the TV program "Laugh-In" for almost a year, but when I did, there was an ongoing party inhabited by those bizarre "Laugh-In" characters. It never ended. Whenever the camera shifted, the party was rolling along with its characteristic frantic excitement. I often thought the "Laugh-In" party could easily be viewed as a secular symbol of the kingdom. For the wedding banquet to which we are invited is a party which never ends. Those of us who have decisively chosen for the Good News of Jesus are permanent participants of the banquet, and those who are called to be disciples of Jesus not only participate in the banquet but like Jesus venture forth to insist that those who have not responded to the invitation don't know what they are missing. But one can hardly renew an invitation to the banquet if one has never been inside.

Chapter 9

The Game Plan

The prophet Isaiah was popular with the early Christian writers. Believing as they did that with the preaching of Jesus an eschatological age had begun, the Christian writers found a wealth of ideas and imagery in the writing of Isaiah. This was extremely helpful to them in recounting their experience of Jesus. Especially popular was the *Servant of Yahweh* poem in the fifty-third chapter of Isaiah. As C. H. Dodd points out in his pamphlet, *The Old Testament and the New*,[1] only one of the twelve verses of the poem is not quoted in whole or in part somewhere in the New Testament. Indeed, one sentence or other from the chapter is quoted, or at least alluded to, in all four gospels, in Acts, Romans, Philippians, Hebrews, and I Peter. Dodd notes that even if the original text of Isaiah had been lost, it would still have been possible to reconstruct the servant song from allusions to it in the New Testament. In Chapters 8, 9, 10, Mark prepares the reader for the death of Jesus and clearly emphasizes that the sign to which Jesus would look would not be the sign of an apocalypse or a messianic military victory; it would be the sign of the Suffering Servant. Indeed, it is precisely the combination in these chapters of Mark of the apocalyptic Son of Man notion from Daniel with the Suffering Servant notion from Isaiah which many writers take to be the core of the Christian insight. The

[1]C. H. Dodd, *The Old Testament and the New,* Facet Books, Biblical Series—3. Philadelphia: Fortress Press, 1963.

eschatological age is not begun with marvels and wonders, much less
with messianic victories. The Son of Man triumphs, rather, by becoming a Servant.

St. Luke begins his account of the public life of Jesus by relating
the incident in the synagogue at Nazareth where Jesus applied to
himself the passage from Isaiah 61:

> He came to Nazara, where he had been brought up, and went into
> the synagogue on the sabbath day as he usually did. He stood up to
> read, and they handed him the scroll of the prophet Isaiah. Unrolling
> the scroll he found the place where it is written:
>
>> *The spirit of the Lord has been given to me,*
>> *for he has anointed me.*
>> *He has sent me to bring the good news to the poor,*
>> *to proclaim liberty to captives*
>> *and to the blind new sight,*
>> *to set the downtrodden free,*
>> *to proclaim the Lord's year of favor.*
>
> He then rolled up the scroll, gave it back to the assistant and sat
> down. And all eyes in the synagogue were fixed on him. Then he
> began to speak to them, "This text is being fulfilled today even as
> you listen."[2]

John begins his gospel with a description of a wedding feast, an
indication to most commentators that John is referring to the frequent
Isaiahian theme of the new age, the messianic era, being a banquet. In
other words, Jesus is the Suffering Servant of Isaiah who begins the
era of the messianic banquet and who by his suffering brings glad
tidings to the poor, liberty to captives, sight to the blind, and the
release of prisoners—all as a sign of favor from Yahweh.

There is no doubt, then, that the New Testament writers thought of
Jesus as beginning the messianic age as described by Isaiah, and
interpreted Jesus' life and especially his death in terms of the Servant
song from Isaiah. But an important question we must ask is whether
Jesus used the Isaiahian imagery, particularly the Servant song, of
himself. If he did, we have not only a perfectly valid interpretation of
his life devised by the early Christians but also the interpretation Jesus
chose for himself.

---

[2]Luke 4:16–22, *The Jerusalem Bible*. New York: Doubleday & Co., 1966.

Here is the Servant song in its entirety:

"Who could believe what we have heard,
and to whom has the power of Yahweh been revealed?"
Like a sapling he grew up in front of us,
like a root in arid ground.
Without beauty, without majesty (we saw him),
no looks to attract our eyes;
a thing despised and rejected by men,
a man of sorrows and familiar with suffering,
a man to make people screen their faces;
he was despised and we took no account of him.

And yet ours were the sufferings he bore,
ours the sorrows he carried.
But we, we thought of him as someone punished,
struck by God, and brought low.
Yet he was pierced through for our faults,
crushed for our sins.
On him lies a punishment that brings us peace,
and through his wounds we are healed.

We had all gone astray like sheep,
each taking his own way,
and Yahweh burdened him
with the sins of all of us.
Harshly dealt with, he bore it humbly,
he never opened his mouth,
like a lamb that is led to the slaughterhouse,
like a sheep that is dumb before its shearers
never opening its mouth.

By force and by law he was taken;
would anyone plead his cause?
Yes, he was torn away from the land of the living;
for our faults struck down in death.
They gave him a grave with the wicked,
a tomb with the rich,
though he had done no wrong
and there had been no perjury in his mouth.

Yahweh has been pleased to crush him with suffering.
If he offers his life in atonement,
he shall see his heirs, he shall have a long life
and through him what Yahweh wishes will be done.

His soul's anguish over
he shall see the light and be content.
By his sufferings shall my servant justify many,
taking their faults on himself.

Hence I will grant whole hordes for his tribute,
he shall divide the spoil with the mighty,
for surrendering himself to death
and letting himself be taken for a sinner,
while he was bearing the faults of many
and praying all the time for sinners.[3]

Joachim Jeremias in his book, *The Central Message of the New Testament*, devotes ten pages to discussing the question of Jesus' interpretation of his own death. By careful textual analysis he first demonstrates that Jesus did indeed anticipate his death before it occurred. He also assures us (p. 45) that anyone who knows anything of the importance of the idea of the atoning power of suffering and death in late Judaism will admit that it is "completely inconceivable that Jesus would have expected to suffer and die without having reflected on the meaning of these events."

Jeremias next carefully analyzes the five passages in the New Testament where Jesus applies the Servant song to himself. It is not our purpose here to engage in complicated exegetical debates, which are the proper field of the Scripture scholars, but let us quote one paragraph from Jeremias on what he considers to be the most important of the allusions to the Servant song, that found in the words of the institution of the Eucharist.

Among the texts in question, first of all attention must be drawn to the Eucharistic Words. What matters here are the words "for many." I will restrict myself to two remarks. In the first place, these words are preserved in all versions of the Words of Institution which the New Testament hands down to us, although with some variations as to position, and phrasing. Mark 14.24 says "for many," Matt. 26.28 "on behalf of many," I Cor. 11.24 and Luke 22.19, 20 have "for you," and finally John 6.51 writes "for the life of the world." Of the different versions of this expression, Mark's "for many," being a Semitism, is older than Paul's and Luke's "for you." Since Paul is likely to have received his formulation of the Eucharistic

[3]Isaiah 53, *The Jerusalem Bible, op. cit.*

Words in the beginning of the forties in Antioch, Mark's "for many" leads us back into the first decade after Jesus' death. Whoever wishes to drop those two words as a secondary comment ought to realize that he is abandoning a very ancient piece of tradition and that there are no linguistic grounds on which he can stand. In the second place, the words "for many" are a reference to Isa. 53, as Mark 10.45 confirms. The idea of substitution as well as the word "many" alludes to just this passage, for "many" without the article, in the inclusive sense of "the many," "the great number," "all," abounds in Isa. 53 and constitutes something like the keyword of this chapter. Thus, the phrase "for many" in the Eucharistic Words shows that Jesus found the key to the meaning of his passion and death in Isa. 53.[4]

At the end of his analysis of the five passages, Jeremias concludes that the primitive Christian interpretation of the death of Jesus as a fulfillment of Isaiah 53, that is to say, a suffering and death of service for many, can be traced back to Jesus himself *with great probability.* He adds that absolute certainty is not to be expected. One can be absolutely certain that the Servant song interpretation and the related allusions to other passages in Isaiah date back to the first few years, certainly well within the first decade, after Jesus' death. In all likelihood, the Isaiah interpretation goes back to Jesus himself.

It is, I think, legitimate for us to consider the Servant theme to be at the very core of the message of Jesus. If he did not use the words of Isaiah 53 himself, he acted in such a way that almost immediately after his death his followers virtually unanimously concluded that the Servant song imagery was the best possible symbol they had to describe what Jesus stood for.

But then what does it mean to say that Jesus was the *ebed-Yahweh?*[5] The Servant is, first of all, the Servant of Yahweh. He comes to do the will of his Father, even if it means his suffering and death for "many."[6] He came then, to serve Yahweh and to do His bidding.

[4]Joachim Jeremias, *The Central Message of the New Testament.* New York: Charles Scribner's Sons, 1965, pp. 45–46.

[5]That word *ebed*, used in the Servant songs of Isaiah, is also used in the synoptic gospels to describe the religious experience of Jesus after his baptism. The voice of heaven is depicted as saying, "This is my 'servant' [*ebed*] in whom I am well pleased."

[6]It is well to note that in his original preaching Jesus did not expound a complex theology of atonement such as is to be found in the later books of the New Testament or in theological writing after the New Testament era.

However He bade Jesus also to serve others, to free them from captivity, to help them to see, to walk, to hear, and to leap with joy. The primary service was to preach the Good News, to challenge the people to faith and then to encourage them to make the decisive act of responding to the challenge. It would be to read back into the first century our own more modern notions to think that "service" as it is used in the gospel means the kind of social action commitments which many Christians today try to justify as part of the *diakonia* of the Church. But the primary service of the *ebed-Yahweh* is service of Yahweh Himself. The secondary service is that of preaching the Good News of Yahweh's love.

However, the extension of this service to include a vast multitude of service activities to one's fellow man is certainly not invalid. The parable of the Good Samaritan, Jesus' compassion toward the poor, the sick, and the hungry, the warning that what is done to the least of the brothers is done to them, the insistence that the apostles serve one another as he had served them, all indicate that service is to be understood by the followers of Jesus as characteristic of all their relationships. But they must not forget that the primary service is owed to the heavenly Father. Other services are a consequence of that commitment. The heavenly Father has sent Jesus with the Good News for "the many." Jesus serves Him by preaching the Good News even to his death for "the many." The followers of Jesus are also to preach the Good News and thereby join in the service of Yahweh. But their commitment to the Good News and to its proclamation involves them necessarily and inevitably in lives of open, generous, serving love.

In effect Jesus said to his audiences, "A sign indeed you shall have, but it will not be the sign of the Romans being driven into the sea, nor a sign of the sun darkening; it will be a sign of the Servant of Yahweh, to be manifested first in my life and then in my death and also in the lives of my followers. Their joyous commitment to the Good News of my heavenly Father's kingdom will be so powerful that they will live lives of dedication and service that will permit no doubt about the validity of my message. The ultimate credentials I offer as spokesman for my Father in heaven will be the kind of lives I and my followers after me lived."

A perfectly splendid game plan I think we will all admit. For if the followers of Jesus did indeed live the kind of life he described, their witness would be irresistible. One servant of Yahweh could easily be put down by the human race (though as it turned out not permanently), but hundreds, thousands, millions of such servants would overwhelm the world. Human beings of the integrity, the authenticity, the commitment, the generosity of Jesus, even human beings who are pale imitations of Jesus, would have been the most spectacular sign in the history of the human race. A great game plan indeed, but as the pro football writers say, "It's a shame they didn't have the personnel to execute it." For never in the long history has there been more service than talk of it. By no means have all those who claimed to be followers of Jesus been servants in fact. They did not serve the little children as Mark (9:30–37) interprets the story of the little children. Nor do they imitate the meekness and humility of a child in the sense of Matthew and Luke. Far too many popes, bishops, priests, and laymen in the history of Christianity have become arrogant, domineering tyrants more concerned with their own powers, privileges, and prerogatives than with serving the people of God. Only he who is blind and thinks the effectiveness of the Christian message depends on the perfection of churchmen will deny this fact. Some of us have not been servants because we have been proud and even ambitious men, but others of us, alas, have refused to be servants from motives which have appeared to be virtuous.

If we are to be servants, we must leave others free to make their own religious decisions. We do not, however, wish to trust others with their freedom. We are afraid that, if they are free, they would make the wrong decisions, so we decide to reject the role of servant to assume the role of lord and ruler, not from ambition but from the desire that men and women be virtuous. We force them to do right *for their own good*. How much tyranny and oppression, how much lack of respect for the dignity and integrity of the individual person has masqueraded under those words?

But this is not the way of Jesus. He forces no one, he does not try to decide what people should do for their own good. He demands service and acts as a servant himself.

There is much contemporary criticism of ecclesiastical authorities for the pomp of their vestments and ceremonies, the ridiculously elevated titles with which they are addressed, and the isolated lives they live. I don't worry very much about any of these things. What a man is called or how he dresses or even where he lives are important only if he permits himself to think that titles and clothes and mansions make him somehow a superior man. I'm afraid the problem runs in the other direction. Ecclesiastical leadership has retreated behind titles, robes, and mansions because it was afraid of service. Elaborate paraphernalia are an effect and not a cause; remove the cause and the effect is of peripheral importance. The cause, I suspect, is less that some ecclesiastical authorities are ambitious, though many of them truly are, but rather that many more of them are not really ready to trust their followers to make the right religious decisions. The servant role for such leadership is transformed into one of the imposition of virtue. It is an arduous and difficult role with few rewards and consolations. It may even be thought of as a form of service. But it is not the service of the New Testament; not the service of the invitation.

But why blame ecclesiastical leaders for a trait characteristic of all of us? Are parents really ready to be servants to their children, facilitating their offspring's growth in the freedom to make their own decisions and to live their own lives? If parents are followers of Jesus of Nazareth, they must serve God by serving their children in the way Jesus served us. A parent not ready to respect his child's freedom of choice (appropriate, of course, to the age of the child) is scarcely in any position to be critical of ecclesiastical leadership which substitutes repression for invitation.

Service also ought to be characteristic of the relationship between husband and wife. The passage in Mark 10:2–16 about divorce is set in the context of Mark's development of the theme of the "cost of discipleship." Jesus is teaching that all who imitate his role as servant must approach even the marriage relationship with an attitude of service. Divorce is an easy escape from service to one's spouse, and it is rejected by Christians.

This passage from Mark has been so battered and beaten in attempts to use it to support now one side and now the other side of the debate on divorce that its whole striking emphasis is lost. It is worthwhile for us to consider it at some length, if only to get an idea about what Jesus meant by service.

It is necessary to remember that for the Jews adultery meant intercourse between a married woman and a man other than her husband. A woman could commit adultery against her husband and a man could commit adultery against another man, but a man could not commit adultery against his wife; that is to say, infidelity on the part of a male was not considered adultery in Jewish law. Thus, the teaching of Jesus in Verse 11 was strikingly novel, for it put husband and wife on a plane of complete equality. A man may no more put aside his wife than she can put him aside. It is this revolutionary attitude toward marriage that struck the apostles as being very harsh and making a fierce demand on their masculinity.

The prohibition of divorce in Mark 10:11 is absolute and is apparently both older and more authentic than the passage in Matthew which, at least in one text, seems to admit of an exception (Matthew 19:9). However, responsible Catholic scholars such as Alexander Jones are careful to point out that, while there is no doubt that Jesus is clearly laying down the ideal of Christian life, he is not specifying the exact marital legislation which would be appropriate for his followers in attempting to carry that ideal out in practice. It is extremely difficult to justify divorce in the face of its explicit proscription, but as Jones says, the passage must be interpreted "in the spirit," just as must all passages in the gospel. Thus, because Jesus leaves no question as to what the *ideal* of Christian marriage ought to be, this does not exclude the possibility of problems for those who through no fault of their own are not able to honor the ideal.

Jesus, however, was not attempting to provide information and quotations for the debate between Protestants and Catholics on divorce. He was, rather, speaking in the context of debates of his own time over the interpretation of Deuteronomy 24:1. The followers of Rabbi Shammai (who lived sometime before Jesus) were willing to permit divorce only on grounds of unchastity, whereas the disciples of Rabbi Hillel would permit divorce on much slighter grounds such as ugliness or even bad cooking. Jesus' statement of the ideal relationship between a man and a woman rejects the grounds of the debate.

Some Pharisees approached him and asked, "Is it against the law for a man to divorce his wife?" They were testing him. He answered them, "What did Moses command you?" "Moses allowed us" they said "to draw up a writ of dismissal and so to divorce." Then Jesus said to them, "It was because you were so unteachable that he wrote this commandment for you. But from the beginning of creation *God made them male and female. This is why a man must leave father and mother, and the two become one body.* They are no longer two, therefore, but one body. So then, what God has united, man must not divide." Back in the house the disciples questioned him again about this, and he said to them, "The man who divorces his wife and marries another is guilty of adultery against her. And if a woman divorces her husband and marries another she is guilty of adultery too."

People were bringing little children to him, for him to touch them. The disciples turned them away, but when Jesus saw this he was indignant and said to them, "Let the little children come to me, do not stop them; for it is to such as these that the kingdom of God belongs. I tell you solemnly, anyone who does not welcome the kingdom of God like a little child will never enter it." Then he put his arms round them, laid his hands on them and gave them his blessing.[7]

Jesus shows here that the love between a husband and wife ought to be so strong and vigorous that there would be no thought of divorce between the two of them, that, indeed, the husband and the wife are equals. There is no more double standard by which a woman is held to moral requirements of which a man is free. In the next passage of Chapter 10 in Mark, Jesus shows that the openness and trust of little children, their docility, and their willingness to grow and to learn are to be other characteristics of his followers. It is not foreign to the context of these passages to link the two: only when husband and wife are willing to take on the style of little children in their relationship with one another, being as open and honest and trustful as children are, can the ideal of Christian marriage be achieved.

Fear and suspicion are the two principal reasons for the decline of married love. We are afraid that if we permit our mate to know us as we really are, we will be ridiculed or taken advantage of. We are afraid that, if we open up to the other, we will lose our rights and be trampled upon. If we "give in" at all, we will never again be able to draw a line beyond which the other cannot come. We are suspicious of the other. He is a stranger, no matter how long we have lived together. We do not trust each other. We are not sure that he will be faithful and not desert us. We suspect that he will use our weakness and openness as an opportunity for cunning and selfishness, to cheat and make a fool of us. These emotions which cause us to harden our hearts in self-defense are part of the human condition. We use them to keep strangers, even friends, at bay. And in the most intimate relationship,

---

[7]Mark 10:2–16, *The Jerusalem Bible, op. cit.*

that between a husband and wife, it is "natural" that we fall back on these defenses. But if it is natural, it is also disastrous, because these sorts of defenses make marital happiness impossible. It is precisely those defenses of fear and suspicion that Jesus asks us to give up if we are to be his followers.

The beginning of marriage is at its best a commitment to try to develop friendship—a commitment to begin a relationship of being servants to one another. But just as the whole Christian life is an experience of constantly growing in the skills of service, so must Christian marriage be an experience that never stops growing. Christian marriage is not a life that can be lived apart from the rest of the Christian mission. Only he who is willing to be a servant in marriage can be a servant beyond it, and only he who sees the servant theme as part of all of his life will have the courage, the bravery, the openness and trust to be a servant in marriage too.

We can get some idea how the early Church used the implications in the Suffering Servant theme if we continue to analyze Mark's gospel.

James and John, the sons of Zebedee, approached him. "Master," they said to him, "we want you to do us a favor." He said to them, "What is it you want me to do for you?" They said to him, "Allow us to sit one at your right hand and the other at your left in your glory." "You do not know what you are asking," Jesus said to them. "Can you drink the cup that I must drink, or be baptised with the baptism with which I must be baptised?" They replied, "We can." Jesus said to them, "The cup that I must drink you shall drink, and with the baptism with which I must be baptised you shall be baptised, but as for seats at my right hand or my left, these are not mine to grant; they belong to those to whom they have been allotted."

When the other ten heard this they began to feel indignant with James and John, so Jesus called them to him and said to them, "You know that among the pagans their so-called rulers lord it over them, and their great men make their authority felt. This is not to happen among you. No, anyone who wants to become great among you must be your servant, and anyone who wants to be first among you must be slave to all. For the Son of Man himself did not come to be served but to serve, and to give his life as a ransom for many." (Mark 10:35–45)

In the passage preceding those quoted above, Jesus makes his third and final prediction of the Passion. He is explicit: he is going up to Jerusalem, he will be delivered to the Gentiles, executed and on the third day he will rise. Mark makes the point that Jesus deliberately set his face toward Jerusalem, the known source of all his enemies, and thereby consciously and freely accepts his messianic destiny.

Mark does not report the immediate reaction of the apostles to the prediction (as he does in Chapters 8:32 and 9:32 with the first two Passion presentiments). Instead, he relates the selfish request of James and John and the equally selfish response of the other disciples, which in the original tradition are probably unconnected. Thus Mark indicates that, once again, the disciples completely misunderstood Jesus' principal theme.

In his direct response to the sons of Zebedee Jesus makes two points: that positions of honor in God's kingdom are awarded in accordance with the decisions of a righteous God who could not be moved like some petty Oriental despot, and that in the days of his flesh their request lies completely outside Jesus' competence to fulfill.

He also points out that if there is to be any special place it will be for those who have rendered special service to others even to the extent of giving their lives through martyrdom.

The last paragraph of the above-quoted passages appear in completely different contexts in both Luke and Matthew, indicating that they were part of collections of the sayings of Jesus which circulated without any particular context. Mark inserts them here because he finds them appropriate to his theme of Jesus as Suffering Servant and that the followers of Jesus be men committed to a life of service.

Mark ironically contrasts in these chapters Jesus' conception of his own role as Suffering and Ransoming Servant with the apostles' conception of his role as a political messiah. No matter how frequently he predicts his death, no matter how insistently he describes himself as a Suffering Servant, they simply will not understand. And in the midst of all his predictions, two of his followers manage to be so completely out of it that they are still worried about their own positions in the kingdom. Even as Jesus is on his way to Jerusalem to fulfill the will of the Father, his followers are engaging in trivial squabbles about their own prestige and status. It is easy for us to ridicule them for missing the point. However, haven't we missed the point too?

Jesus is asserting in this passage that his death is not an accident or a tragedy but an offering which is made freely and eagerly. He would give himself, and from this gift something of immense value would come. Every follower of Jesus must think of himself as freely, generously offering his life in the service of others. Our deaths ought not to be accidents or tragedies (though of course they will have an element of tragedy and perhaps accident, too). They should rather represent merely the conclusion of a life which has been from the beginning to end an exercise in gift-giving. But the question those who follow Jesus must ask themselves is, are we really giving life? Does our living bring ransom to any captives? Do our efforts bring release to any prisoners? Are we bringing hope and faith and love to very many people in the world around us, indeed, to anyone? We are called to give life; to give life to others by giving our own lives to them; to bring others hope and joy because of our hope and joy; to offer them faith because of the strength of our faith; to teach them how to love by the power of our love. If we live in such a way, then our death is as much an enthusiastic, conscious acceptance of God's will as the death of Christ. As we live, so we will die.

Mark concludes his tenth chapter with a final story to complete this extraordinarily brilliant theological reflection on the servant theme.

> They reached Jericho; and as he left Jericho with his disciples and a large crowd, Bartimaeus (that is, the son of Timaeus), a blind begger, was sitting at the side of the road. When he heard that it was Jesus of Nazareth, he began to shout and to say, "Son of David, Jesus, have pity on me!" And many of them scolded him and told him to keep quiet, but he only shouted all the louder, "Son of David, have pity on me." Jesus stopped and said, "Call him here." So they called the blind man. "Courage," they said, "get up; he is calling you." So throwing off his cloak, he jumped up and went to Jesus. Then Jesus spoke, "What do you want me to do for you?" "Rabbuni," the blind man said to him, "Master, let me see again." Jesus said to him, "Go; your faith has saved you." And immediately his sight returned and he followed him along the road. (Mark 10:46–52)

This passage acts as a transition between Jesus' Galilean ministry and his ministry in Jerusalem, and it concludes Mark's lengthy commentary on the need for followers of Jesus to imitate him as Suffering Servant, an imitation which Mark is urging on the early Christian converts.

The location of the miracle is important. Jesus is now drawing near to Jerusalem, Jericho being only fifteen miles away. It is his closeness to Jerusalem that justifies the end of Mark's "messianic secret." The fact that Jesus is the Messiah is no longer to be hidden for fear it will be misunderstood. All too soon he will demonstrate the precise nature of his messiahship—that of triumph through suffering and death rather than dazzling military victories. Jesus quite explicitly does not reprimand the blind man for proclaiming his faith in Jesus' messiahship. The passage is Mark's way of saying that now the lid is off.

Most authorities agree that the vivid details of the story indicate that it is being recounted by an eyewitness, though certainly its precise place in Mark's gospel is hardly accidental. The story contributes to the development of Mark's narrative and probably was part of the very early Christian catechesis even before the gospel was written, since it illustrates so precisely one of the important dimensions of discipleship— the need for enthusiastic faith.

Mark apparently intends us to contrast the enthusiasm and the faith of the blind man with the dullness of the apostles. The blind man does not have eyes and yet he really sees. The detail of Bartimaeus' throwing off his cloak indicates eagerness and enthusiasm, the promptness and spontaneity which are required of the man of faith. By leaping to his feet and dashing to Jesus he shows the enthusiasm that the apostles, who see but do not see, who follow but slowly and reluctantly, so sorely lack.

We of course wish to put ourselves on the side of Bartimaeus. We much prefer the blind man who saw and eagerly sought to follow Jesus. But in fact we probably have far more in common with the apostles. Bartimaeus knew what his problem was. How could one escape the obvious fact of physical blindness? He knew how utterly helpless he was unless the Messiah took pity on him. He knew that he could not exercise tight, unyielding control of his own life. He had to throw himself on the mercy of the Son of David. Our situation is as helpless as his. We, too, are utterly dependent on God's mercy, but we don't realize our dependence. We like to think that we are still in control of things. We like to think that we can impose our own carefully devised schedule on God's operations. Bartimaeus was blind and he knew it, so he could really see. Like the apostles, we are blind and do not know it, so we really cannot see. Jesus tries to open our eyes just as he tried to open the eyes of his apostles, but we obstinately refuse to open them because we are convinced that we already do see.

We also find ourselves embarrassed by Bartimaeus' headlong response. He dashes to Jesus, throwing off his mantle as he runs to him, and breathlessly pleads for his sight. He is a violently active man. He does not carefully fold his robe, neatly place it on the ground, and say to someone, "Look after this until I come back." He leaped and didn't look. We are cautious before jumping to our feet, and we are very careful about committing ourselves fully. Indeed, after carefully and cautiously evaluating the situation, we frequently do not leap at all. Jesus wants us to be headlong enthusiasts in our exercise of discipleship. When someone says to us about Jesus, "He is calling you," Jesus expects us to leap up and dash to him filled with throbbing, panting enthusiasm. It has been a very long time, I fear, since there was much throbbing, panting enthusiasm in most Christians.

Notice how the crowds try to throw a wet blanket on Bartimaeus' enthusiasm. They tell him to be quiet, not to bother Jesus with his request. They advise him that his enthusiastic faith and his eager commitment to the possibility that Jesus can cure him are foolishly optimistic. Who does he think he is that Jesus could possibly be concerned about him? Why should the Son of David, assuming that he is indeed the Son of David, possibly be concerned about a poor, ignorant blind begger? Forget your enthusiasm, Bartimaeus, he does not care about you. Shut up. Be quiet. Do not disturb the crowds. Do not upset the solemn occasion of the Master's trip to Jerusalem. Restrain your crude, foolish enthusiasm. That's what the wise men of the world tell the simple man of faith. But Bartimaeus is a tough customer. He does not quiet down. He does not take the advice of the wise men. He believes that the Son of David really can and does care about him, and so he keeps shouting. And what is the response to his enthusiasm? What is the response to his almost blasphemous belief that Jesus would care about him? The response is quick and simple: "Be on your way, your faith has saved you." And then what did Bartimaeus do after he received his sight? He began to follow Jesus on the road to Jerusalem. Maybe that's why we don't want to be enthusiastic about the possibility that Jesus really loves us; then we, too, would have to follow him on the road to Jerusalem.

We have quoted the tenth chapter of Mark and commented on it at considerable length because it is a splendid illustration of how even that first and most primitive of the Christian gospels is in fact a brilliant, complex theological reflection, complete at the very end with a story of a blind man seeing just as the eschatological vision of Isaiah predicted that the blind would see in the messianic age. Bartimaeus' blindness is used as a symbol of the spiritual sight he already had but we lack. Jesus came that we might see, and the really important seeing is that by which we become conscious of the signs of the new eschatological age which has begun. Mark has used the tradition handed down to him as a means of instructing the early Christians on how they ought to live in response to the invitation of Jesus.

The question of how much of the tenth chapter is a literal repetition of the words and deeds in the life of Jesus is academic. Mark was not trying to fool us, not trying to hide Jesus from us, not trying to distort his message. He was trying to explain to us, or rather to his immediate readers and through them to us, how he and the other early Christians experienced and understood the words and deeds of Jesus. And they experienced them as a profound call to service—a call which could be beautifully and brilliantly symbolized by allusions to the servant song of Isaiah. Jesus in fact was a Suffering Servant of Yahweh, even if he did not choose to call himself the Suffering Servant. Those who follow Jesus are also to serve Yahweh and, once committed to Him, are to lead lives of service to one another.

Chapter 10
More About Basic Themes

There are three other basic themes in the message of Jesus about which I think it is appropriate to comment: (1) universalism, (2) anger, and (3) hunger.

One of the most painful problems for modern Scripture scholars, as they try to penetrate beyond the layers of tradition to the original message of Jesus, is that the writers of the New Testament documents were dealing with very specific problems of their own. Mark, for example, was trying to explain to his readers why suffering was still necessary, why it was necessary for even Jesus to suffer when the messianic age had already begun. Luke was trying to explain why Jesus did not return though Jerusalem had fallen. Both writers also faced the need to exhort the early Christians who were often persecuted and discouraged. The rigorous canons which the Scripture scholars follow compel them to refuse the label "authentic" to any passage which cannot be clearly excluded from the literary concerns of the writers. Thus, if in a gospel we read of an incident in which Jesus apparently indicates that the Parousia will not occur in the near future, the scholars would say that it might very well be a literary device of the gospel author to cope with the problem of the delayed return of Jesus. Such a decision is, of course, not final, because other canons of criticism might restore the passage to the authentic category. Thus, if in the same incident Jesus is depicted as saying something unthinkable for the early Church to say, then the passage is more likely to be authenticated. So, when Jesus himself says that even he does not know when the Parousia will occur, the probability of that passage being authentic is enhanced. It must be remembered of course that "authentic" has for the critics a rather narrow meaning. It indicates that a given passage can be considered certainly, or at least with a high degree of probability, to be something that Jesus actually did or said and not a theological interpretation, reflection, or explanation of the early Church. If a passage is labeled "unauthentic" it does not indicate that the words or events did not happen; it means only that we cannot have a high level of confidence in it.

The problem of separating the theological and pedagogical concerns of the early Church from the actual events is especially difficult when one attempts to cope with the universalism of Jesus' message. By the time the gospels were written, the decisive choice had been made by the early Church to go beyond the synagogue into the Gentile world. Many of the Jewish Christians found themselves profoundly shocked by this decision, and, hence, all the gospel writers found themselves under severe constraints to justify what had been done. This does not mean that they distorted the tradition they received. But they eagerly searched for everything in the tradition which would have some bearing on the question of the universalism of the Good News.

Some scholars observe that the astonishing restraint of the gospel writers in the way they treated the traditional material they received is evidenced by their rigorous refusal to fabricate incidents in which Jesus visited Gentile countries or conversed with Gentile men and women. It would marvelously have suited their purposes to have provided a considerable number of stories of such events. Yet they recount only a few conversations and a couple of visits to Decapolis and to Phoenicia, which indicates that, however strong their controversial needs were, they simply did not feel at liberty to "doctor" the tradition. We can therefore assume that Jesus' healing of the daughter of the Syro-Phoenician woman does contain within it the core of a historically authentic trip. If one such story was made up, there was no reason why many more could not have been made up.

As we read through the gospels, we encounter many incidents in which the mission to the Gentiles is prefigured. For example, in the fourth chapter of St. Luke, Jesus is pictured as engaging in a rather bitter dialogue with his fellow citizens at Nazareth. He comments that a prophet should not expect honor in his own place. "Indeed, let me remind you there were many widows in Israel in the days of Elijah, when the heavens remained closed for over three years and a great famine spread over the land. It was to none of these that Elijah was sent, but to a widow of Zarephath near Sidon. Recall, too, the many lepers in Israel in the time of Elisha, yet none was cured except Naaman the Syrian." For such a sarcastic comment, Jesus was promptly thrown out of the synagogue.

The Scripture critics are at a loss when faced with a passage like that. How much of it actually represents a historical incident, and how much is Luke's theological reflection? The biting irony of Jesus' words gives at least some plausibility to the notion that they are too strong for his devoted followers to dare to put into his mouth.

But if it is difficult for us to say exactly how many of the references to the Gentiles found in the New Testament are considered to be historically authentic, it is not at all difficult to say that the message of Jesus was universalistic in its orientation. He may have spoken with few Gentiles and only occasionally traveled into Gentile land. He may not even have made many references in his preaching to them. The important point is that he preached the love of his heavenly Father—a love which transcended all boundaries, Pharisee and publican, Jew and Samaritan, rich and poor, young and old. What is important in the Good News of Jesus is not who one is or where one comes from, but whether one responds to the invitation. Even if the Good News was announced in but one country originally and only to the members of one tribal group, it completely transcends the boundaries—political, religious, intellectual, and geographic—of that group. There were hints in Isaiah, of course, that the eschatological age would be for all men, and the Gentiles would beat a path to Zion. Apparently by the time of Jesus, Zion was thought to be some sort of political capital to which other tribes would come in respectful tribute. Just as the message of Jesus rejected completely the notion of a political messiah, so it also rejected the idea of an Israelite empire. The kingdom to be centered in Zion would be a kingdom of those who responded to the invitation of the heavenly Father to call him "Father dear" and to enter into his splendid wedding festival. The resistance of many of the Jewish Christians to following the implications of that message to its logical conclusion is understandable, as was, indeed, the resistance of the citizens of Nazareth. It was bad enough that God loved them, it was even worse that God loved all men. We are not at all sure that we want to accept the Good News, but it is even worse if we are faced with the annoying fact that we must share it with others. In fact, if part of the Good News is that God loves everyone, we begin to rather doubt that it is *Good* News. We don't want to believe in God's love when it is directed just at us, but when it is directed at everyone else it seems much better not to believe in that love at all.

When we describe the response to Jesus in such a fashion, the absurdity of the reaction seems obvious. Yet the citizens of Nazareth had no monopoly on it. It is as difficult for us today to accept the universality of God's love as it was for them. If Jesus came into our town and announced that God loved the Chinese, the North Vietnamese, and the Russians every bit as much as he loved us, he would run a serious risk of being pushed over a cliff once again.

And if he should attend a meeting of the most radical or liberal Catholic enthusiasts and tell them that his heavenly Father loved the white ethnic racists and the polluters of the environment and even the fat cats of the Establishment, he would be very lucky to get out of that meeting without having obscenities hurled at him.

We have, of course, made some progress since the time of Jesus. We now love some others not part of our own racial, religious, or ethnic group. It is now fashionable in certain circles to love blacks, particularly when they are of the militant or violent variety, young people, particularly if they are drug addicts, and poor people, especially if they march on picket lines. But it is hardly expected of us to love hardhats, or middle-class Americans, or suburban executives, or Republicans, or squares. Fashions change of course. The ethnic hardhats thirty years ago were the "working masses." Professor Michael Lerner tells us of his colleague at Yale who when he heard that Italian candidates were daring to challenge Mayor Lindsay for that unenviable role commented, "If there is one inferior people in the country, I am convinced it must be the Italians."

The reader may suspect by now that I am more than a little fed up with the snobbery, the faddism, and the selective compassion of academia. Not all academics behave that way, of course. The point is, however, that even in the most enlightened and sophisticated segments of what is supposedly a progressive and intelligent society bigotry is still very much with us. It did not go out of fashion when Jesus passed through the crowd at Nazareth and shook the dust of that obscure little hamlet from his feet. Selective compassion, the lionizing of one group (so long as it acts according to our prescribed expectations), has absolutely nothing to do with the message of Jesus of Nazareth. Jesus tells the university professor that he must love the Polish hardhat and even try to see the world from his perspective in order to understand sympathetically the other's position. He tells the white racist that he must strive to understand the reasons that lie behind the black man's militancy, and he tells the black militant that he must make every effort to understand and even sympathize with the fear of the racist. He tells the old that they must not write off even the most repulsive inhabitants of the youth culture, and he warns the youth culture that the generation gap is not a virtue but a barrier. Scapegoating, no matter how popular and pervasive a human activity, is not permitted to the follower of Jesus. The only men legitimately villains are ourselves, and the only villainy is that of refusing to accept the invitation to the kingdom.

This is a hard saying. Hatred is so marvelously useful to mobilize human emotions, to give movements their energy and drive, to force causes toward fulfillment and victory. We do not want our movements and our causes to be fundamentally rooted in hatred, but we do use "just a little bit" to be sure that the energies and enthusiasms of our colleagues do not lag. Only there is no such thing as "a little bit of hatred," and any cause which allows itself to be infiltrated by it will ultimately be destroyed by it.

And yet we profoundly suspect those who are different from us. The Hindus fight the Moslems in India; the Malays and the Chinese struggle in Singapore; the East Indians and the natives eye one another with suspicion in the Fiji Islands; black and white war with each other in South Africa, and black and brown in the Caribbean islands; English and Welsh and Scots revive old animosities in Great Britain; and the last battles of ecumenism will surely be waged in the streets of Belfast and the plains of Derry. The Ibos fight the Hausas to the death in Nigeria; the Chinese and Russians spar with one another along the two-thousand-mile border; in Canada the conflict between British and French grows more serious; and across the English Channel, even after the departure of Le Général, one frequently doubts that the Hundred Years' War ever ended. As Jesus of Nazareth contemplates this fantastic array of hatred, he must say to himself, "I don't think they yet understand what I was talking about."

There is an incredible amount of diversity in the world. Some of us are tall, some short; some fat, some thin; some of us have straight hair, some of us have kinky hair; some have thin noses, some wide;

some brown skin, others white, yellow, and everything in between; some of us enjoy sexual attractiveness to a voluptuous extreme and others display a more austere, restrained sexuality (not necessarily less powerful). Such diversity is one of God's jokes, it seems to me. He could have made the human race in a much more standardized form. But as in so many other things, he outdid Himself. He produced a staggering amount of diversity, which probably vastly amuses Him. He undoubtedly wonders and is disappointed that we do not get the joke. For instead of enjoying the diversity of the race, we have used it as an occasion for conflict and hatred. Wars have been fought over skin color, hair length, eating habits, languages, and almost every other conceivable difference. Amazingly enough, sometimes these differences are not distinguishable to those not party to the conflict. Most Americans, I dare say, would be hard put to distinguish between a Biafran and a Nigerian. And most Nigerians would not think an English Canadian was at all different from a French Canadian. Even the faintest of differences can mean not just that we notice the difference but that we feel the other is inferior and may be plotting against us; therefore we must destroy him before he destroys us.

No, the citizens of Nazareth were not the last ethnocentrics.

And the point of Jesus' message is as pertinent today as it ever was: unless we believe in the heavenly Father (or a Really Real), who does in fact love all of us to a point of insane generosity, we human beings are simply incapable of being generous in our love of others. We may honor such universality of love and compassion in theory, but in practice we end up with our scapegoats and our villains, with our "good guys" and our "bad guys," with those whom we feel constrained to love and those whom we feel perfectly free to hate. What a pathetic character man is. He has an immense capacity for love, but a great fear of what it will do to him; so he defends himself against its demands by retreating behind the barriers of hatred. Jesus of Nazareth says, "If you believe that my heavenly Father loves you, if you believe that the universe is out to do you good, then you know you have nothing to fear; you do not run so very great a risk by putting aside the defenses of hatred and permitting yourself to make that terrifying leap of faith which is called love."

Who knows, you may even be able to love the Samaritans.

One of the more astonishing aspects of the person of Jesus, at least to me, is his capacity for anger. The meek and mild Jesus of the nineteenth- and early twentieth-century biographies is simply not to be found in the New Testament. He is a man who speaks his mind, even at the risk of offending others. He vigorously denounces hypocrisy and injustice, and angrily excoriates those who impose foolish religious burdens. And while he is patient with the weakness and frailties of his disciples, he never permits them to deceive themselves as to what he thinks of their foolishness. His "Get thee behind me, Satan" statement to Peter (most likely an authentic logion, because the early Church would scarcely present Peter in such an unfavorable light) comes from a man not at all hesitant to give vent to the emotion of anger.

The humanist psychologists, such as Abraham Maslow, insist that the capacity to love and the capacity to be angry are closely related; that we can only be free to love when we can be free to be angry. The man who tries to love while restraining his anger is apt to become a passive-aggressive personality. He uses his love as a means of controlling and manipulating others as he is unable to experience anger in his relationships with them.

For some strange historical quirk, which I do not fully understand, popular piety has insisted on portraying Jesus as a passive-aggressive person, one who meekly and patiently loved and only rarely expressed the opposite side of passion, anger. And the model of the Christian life urged on so many of us in seminary and novitiate days was the model of the passive-aggressive person or "the nice guy." Not only were we not permitted to express our anger, we were urged to pretend we didn't have it. We were told that the meek would possess the earth. They never told us that the word "meek" in the Beatitudes actually means "one who is humble and open-minded to the inspiration of God's spirit." The only sort of anger we thought could exist was that of blind fury, and of course that was generally the kind of anger we experienced; it devastated others like a hurricane.

When I speak of anger, however, what I really mean is the capacity to assert our own dignity and our own integrity and our own reality in our relationships. It is the ability to be ourselves even when that offers a challenging demand to our role opposite in a relationship. The angry man understands that an expression of his own selfhood in a relationship may cause some suffering, but he realizes that less suffering is involved in the long run than if he were to restrain his anger, hide his selfhood, and pretend to a peace and tranquillity that do not in fact exist. One presumes that Jesus knew he would hurt Peter when he called him Satan and told him to get behind him. He certainly understood that it might hurt his mother when he indicated to her that her time would come only after his death, and surely he realized that James and John would be offended when he abruptly rejected their claim for priority in the kingdom. But he did not compromise, he did not equivocate, he did not evade; he bluntly and firmly asserted his own selfhood.

I suppose I am particularly impressed by this phenomenon because one of the major defects of my own personality is my inability to express anger. I can do it (perhaps all too well) in the written word, but in face-to-face relationships, I find myself almost compelled to shy away from the possibility of causing pain to someone else. It would be easy to scapegoat my seminary training (blaming the seminary is one of the great indoor sports of the clergy today), but I am aware that this problem goes far back beyond seminary days. I am getting somewhat better at it, at least in certain relationships, and I am not "a nice guy" who attempts to manipulate others by serving them. On the contrary, I am more inclined to express my anger by assuming the martyr's role in my relationships with others. However, the step from a long-suffering, patient, sainted martyr to a raving, ranting man possessed by a towering rage is all too short.

And it is a step that is frequently taken at the wrong time. Any unfortunate who happens to cross my path at the wrong moment is likely to be the victim of a rage long building up.

I remember one particularly disgraceful incident when I was presiding over what was, alas, the largest teen club on the South Side of Chicago. It had been a bad night. I was being harassed by a pastor, a mother superior, a janitor, a parents' committee, an irresponsible hi-club president, a dizzy female vice-president, a couple of thieves, beer drinkers, an incredibly incompetent policeman, and a number of ingenious characters who thought that the great challenge of the evening was to find a way to avoid paying the twenty-five-cent admission fee. About ten-thirty, two young men who were among my closest friends and coworkers in the parish arrived on the scene two hours later than they should have. One of them jokingly remarked, "You really don't expect us to pay our twenty-five cents, now, do you?" After the first three seconds of my tirade, they fled in terror.

Half an hour later I found them to apologize. But I think to this day they don't quite understand what happened.

I become autobiographical at this point because I suspect that in this matter I am typical of countless Catholics. We hold our anger back, being afraid of vigorously and forcefully asserting ourselves in human relationships for both personality and religious reasons. If the result is not an occasional towering rage, then it is something worse, a subtle but pervasive punishment of others under the guise of love. Of the two, I think the towering rage is preferable.

But whichever choice we make, it ought to be perfectly clear that it cannot be justified in the person or the word or the deed of Jesus of Nazareth. He allowed himself to be led to the cross, indeed, like a lamb to the slaughter; he almost exulted in his own weakness and frailty. But at no point did he stop being himself. We need to read only the account of his trial to realize that this was not a passive-aggressive man. He was not afraid to be angry, but neither did he need to be angry. It is almost as though the presence or absence of anger was no great problem for him. He was conscious of his mission: he had come to proclaim the kingdom of his Father and to invite everyone to share in the festivities of that kingdom. He would tolerate no perversions of the message of the kingdom, and when anyone attempted to pervert it, his reaction was quick and powerful. Even his closest and most adoring follower heard the terrible words, "Get thee behind me, Satan."

Finally, when one reads the New Testament, one cannot escape the impression that there is an immense amount of talk about food. There are wedding banquets, miraculous meals in the desert, descriptions of people hungering and thirsting after righteousness, the assertion by Jesus that he is the Bread of Life, the Last Supper with the apostles. The emphasis shifts back and forth from the real to the symbolical. Jesus' compassion for the crowd because they were hungry is both a sympathy for their physical hunger in the desert and, perhaps more, a sympathy that they do not even realize how hungry they are for the Bread of Life. And in the sixth chapter of St. John, the alternating emphasis on Jesus as Wisdom and Jesus as Eucharist reduces such a skillful, clear writer as Father Raymond Brown to using diagrams. But the important hunger is, of course, the eschatological hunger, the hunger for the fullness of God's kingdom, the hunger for the completion of the love which Jesus has come to announce.

And yet the meals described in the New Testament are by no means simply symbols. The wedding feast at Cana and the Last Supper, for example, are real assemblies of real people with real hopes and real fears. Some Scripture authorities even suspect that the Last Supper was not by any means the first supper, and that the meals that Jesus had with his disciples throughout his public ministry were not just functional events but at least some of them took on the significance of a religious banquet, a simultaneous and foreshadowing of the banquet in the kingdom of the heavenly Father. The Last Supper and the Eucharistic celebrations after the resurrection were a continuation of a religious custom already being celebrated during the active ministry of Jesus.

Eating is such a basic and primal human activity that, like that other basic and primal activity, sexuality, it almost inevitably takes on religious symbolism. It represents man's basic union with the physical forces of the universe and also his communion with others with whom he shares this vital human activity. We are hungry for the banquet in the kingdom of God not merely as individuals but as members of a community. The fact that eating is a communal activity almost demands that those who share in the meal which foreshadows the fullness of the messianic banquet be themselves a community. Even if we had no other evidence that the message of Jesus necessarily led to the emergence of a community of Christians, the symbolism of the messianic banquet and the fact of the communal meal of Jesus and his followers would certainly indicate that even during the public life of Jesus a church was slowly coming into being.

Hunger, in the final analysis, stands for human loneliness, the desperate longing of man for union. When we eat we take the physical world into our bodies in order to assuage our physical hunger. But man also has a capacity for the infinite, a hunger for everything, a longing for the absolute. When Jesus proclaimed himself the Bread of Life, that he came to offer man food after which they would never hunger and drink after which they would never thirst, he was asserting that the Good News of his heavenly Father's kingdom was a response to man's yearning for the Infinite, his hunger for the Absolute. It was just one more part of the Good News that was too good to be true.

Chapter 11
He Lives

After a fairly long period when Catholic theology paid little attention to it, the resurrection is once again on center stage among Catholic concerns, and that is, of course, where it ought to be, because it is impossible even to imagine the existence of Christianity in the absence of the Easter phenomenon.

My own personal hunch is that the resurrection issue will become more and more important as the years go on. The human race has discovered that man is never too old to grow and that personality growth and development come through a process of death and resurrection; the experience of putting off the fears and protections of one's defensive armor plate in opening oneself to a new life. St. Paul's description of putting off the old man and putting on the new turns out to have been rooted in a very sound psychological insight. Experiencing resurrection is a constant dimension of life, a resurrection preceded by and made possible through a death. Modern man will, I think, shortly have to ask himself which of these two intimately related realities is the ultimate one.

But if the resurrection is center stage in Catholic thought, it does not follow that the discussion of it is always helpful. There are in Catholic circles, it seems to me, four "fallacies" which seem to focus on the Easter phenomenon:

1. Emphasis on the resurrection which ignores the cross.

2. Emphasis on the individual resurrection which ignores the communal nature of New Life.

3. Emphasis on the facts of the resurrection narratives without much attention paid to the meaning of the Easter event.

4. Emphasis to a point almost of compulsiveness on future personal resurrection while isolating this from the rest of the message of the kingdom.

In his book, *Jesus Means Freedom*, Ernst Käsemann devotes a brilliant chapter to the discussion of Paul's dealing with the resurrection issue in his epistle to the Corinthians. Käsemann shows how the disorder and enthusiasm of the Corinthians was founded on the misunderstanding of the nature of the resurrection. The Corinthians thought that the battle was all over, that the resurrection had already occurred, and that all they had to do was enjoy its fruits.

> Anyone who feels himself to be a citizen of heaven and permeated with heavenly strength no longer needs to take the earth seriously. He has all the less need to do so if he has already been drawn into the largely orgiastic doings of the mystery religions, and is accustomed in his proletarian existence to accident and uncertainty, so that one must not assume that his old Adam is strictly regulated. Exuberant religious vitality breaks through every dike and stops for no bourgeois taboo.[1]

In such a view of the resurrection, then, the cross was completely forgotten. Oh, it may have been an action which preceded the resurrection, but it had no particular meaning for the present situation in which men found themselves. The lid was off; the sky was the limit.

> Why should the woman keep silence when the Spirit has come upon her? Why should the slave consent to be dependent on a Christian master? Why should not prophets and those who speak in tongues speak as often as they wish, if they are inspired? Why should one not on the one hand practice asceticism to show that his state is like that of the angels, and on the other hand cohabit with his stepmother to show that Christ has freed us from the moral prejudices of a bourgeois world? Freedom has become the real and the sole mark of the Christian and the church. Do we not renounce all the bliss that has been bestowed on us, if we do not turn it to account incessantly and in relation to everyone?[2]

[1]Käsemann, Ernst, *Jesus Means Freedom*. Philadelphia: Fortress Press, 1968, p. 64.
[2]*Ibid.*, p. 64.

It is perhaps no accident that similar enthusiasms can be found today in certain Catholic quarters. The emphasis on resurrection in the theology from the last decade has removed the cross from many people's minds and produced displays of emotional orgies not unlike that on which Paul had to depend at Corinth. My colleague, Father Raymond Brown, at the International Conference in Brussels in 1970 insisted that the two events could not be separated (much to the offense of some of the amateur theologians in the crowd). Käsemann makes exactly the same point:

> . . . for Paul he remains the Crucified One. That is not meant historically, so that the cross is the way to exaltation, although that naturally was the case. It is meant, rather, that Christ, exalted above the cross in his sublimity, is misunderstood if one separates the exaltation from the cross, and so reduces their relationship to that of two merely consecutive events. The Risen and Exalted One remains the Crucified One; and his sovereignty is not understood and acknowledged if the cross is merely made the last station on his earthly way. . . . [3]

For the battle is not yet over. The sovereignty of Christ is still being disputed by the power of death. The kingdom is not yet fully come. The message of the Good News has not yet been accepted. Even the vindication of Jesus in the resurrection event has not enticed everyone to the wedding feast and therefore the service of the Suffering Servant of Yahweh must continue at least in his church. The resurrection for us is still a promise of the future. As Käsemann notes, ''What ultimately matters is not that we genuinely believe and defend this preaching, but that we accept it as a call to walk as Jesus' disciples and to share his death.''[4]

Käsemann adds later:

> A man counts as a lover of the cross only in so far as it enables him to come to terms rather with himself and others and with the powers and enticements of the world. Under the cross man attains manhood, because that is where God reveals himself as what he really is—our Creator. . . . [p. 76]

[3]*Ibid.*, p. 67.
[4]*Ibid.*, p. 75.

Christ's victory begins in our hearts. That does not eliminate the evil forces that surround us; but if the spell is broken in our heart the good effects spread indefinitely. The church that is worthy of the name is a band of people in which the love of God has broken the spell of demons and strange gods and is now pushing its way into the world.[5]

The resurrection, then, began with Jesus, but with us it is yet to come. Our lives are still lives of suffering service. We still walk the way of the cross.

Anyone knowing merely the risen Lord who has left his cross behind is no longer speaking of Jesus of Nazareth, and so his theology of resurrection can leave us cold. For no theory of the resurrection that does not become a theology of the cross is bound to lead, as the Corinthian example shows, to a wrong-headed enthusiasm . . . there is no sharing in the glory of the risen Lord except in the discipleship of the cross.[6]

One wonders even that it is necessary to say this. Even if the New Testament was not clear on this, we need merely to look at our own lives and recognize how painful the experience of service is to understand that the kingdom is not yet completely come, that the wedding feast has only begun, and that the resurrection exists rather in down payment than in reality. Joy we may have, but surely not yet the fullness of joy. Nevertheless, the intimate relationship between cross and resurrection seems to have been repeatedly misunderstood down through the history of Christianity. The enthusiasts of Corinth were not the last of their breed.

Exultation came to Jesus through service—painful, difficult service— and there is no other option available to us. The enthusiasts who attempt to eliminate the cross from Christianity or attempt to short-circuit the process or to simplify it to an "encounter" session use a massive denial mechanism, a mechanism which at root confuses the euphoria of hope and enthusiasm with faith—and, incidentally, also frequently confuses aggressiveness and hard sell with charity. Suffering service described in the tenth chapter of St. Mark is still the game plan. It is service, of course, mixed with joy. We already are at a

[5]*Ibid.*, p. 76–77.
[6]*Ibid.*, p. 82.

wedding banquet, but it is only beginning. The main course has not yet been served.

If "resurrection without the cross" is a theory that has once again emerged in the Catholic community, the idea of a purely individual resurrection has been with us for a long time. In a rather pedantic article in the Scripture issue of *Concilium*, 1971, Joseph Blenkinsopp ridiculed the idea of the immortality of the individual soul and the resurrection of the individual body separate from a renewed life for the whole of creation. There isn't much doubt that the separated soul is a concept quite foreign to the New Testament. Furthermore, there is also evidence that Jesus came to preach a whole new creation in which life was promised not merely to individuals but to the whole race and, indeed, to the whole material world, which as St. Paul observes is groaning for redemption. Blenkinsopp is perhaps too harsh on the popular piety, because, while its symbols (like all symbols) are inadequate, they did represent a conviction about life which was basically sound. We cannot separate our own destinies from the destiny of the race, and we cannot separate mankind's destiny from that of the universe. The individual of course does live, but he does not live alone. He will find everlasting life only as a part of the human community, only as an element in the whole of creation. The heavenly Father's love, which Jesus announces, is a love for the whole of creation manifested in and through man and permeating to the very outer limits of the universe. *Everything* is to be restored in Christ, and the religious inner-directed man working out his own personal salvation and resurrection by himself has missed an extremely important point in the teaching of Jesus.

But it seems to me that the most serious misplaced emphasis, one that has been with us persistently almost from the beginning of Christianity, is that which argues interminably over the details of the resurrection and ignores its meaning. I once sat in on a conversation of very learned theologians in which an argument raged over whether a TV camera at the entrance of the tomb on Easter morning would have recorded anything at all. I must confess that my sense of the absurd got the better of me, for I imagined not just the TV camera but Walter Cronkite or perhaps Howard Cosell and Dandy Meredith commenting on the event. (Indeed, I even thought of Dandy saying, "It sure is good to have ole Jesus back with us again!") I should have thought that the important point is that Jesus lives; that the way the heavenly Father vindicated him in the face of his enemies was considerably less important than the *fact* that the vindication did occur.

I would be quite content to leave the methods by which the Father accomplished the vindication to His own choosing. Incidentally, one must say from purely objective grounds that the vindication has been successful. Those who accused and then executed Jesus thought they would get rid of him, that he would be removed from the public scene and no one would ever hear of him again. They were quite confident that Jesus' days of troublemaking were over. The historical record shows how wrong they were, and even if one rejects completely any new life for Jesus after his death, he still must admit that he won and his enemies lost. They are forgotten, but Jesus and his troublemaking go merrily on.

Gunther Bornkamm makes an extremely useful distinction between the message of the resurrection and the historical problems of the narrative. The message is totally single in its content and import, but the narratives are filled with ambiguities.

> The event of Christ's resurrection from the dead, his life and his eternal reign, are things removed from historical scholarship. History cannot ascertain and establish conclusively the facts about them as it can with other events of the past. The last historical fact available to them is the Easter faith of the first disciples. What the message and the experience on which it was founded mean is not hidden by the New Testament. This belief is not the particular experience of a few enthusiasts or a particular theological opinion of a few apostles, which in the course of time was fortunate enough to establish itself and make a big success. No; wherever there were early Christian witnesses and communities, and however varied their message and theology were, they are all united in believing and acknowledging the risen Lord. . . .
>
> At the same time, just as certainly as—even in a completely historical sense—there would be no gospel, not one account, no letter in the New Testament, no faith, no Church, no worship, no prayer in Christendom to this day without the message of the resurrection of Christ, even so difficult and indeed impossible is it to gain a satisfactory idea of how the Easter events took place. There is an undeniable tension between the singleness of the Easter *message*

and the ambiguity and historical problems of the Easter *narratives*. We cannot deal with this in all its detail here.[7]

So what we do, of course, is concentrate on the ambiguity of the narratives and ignore the message. It is really much easier to do this, because if we can lose ourselves in the conflicting details of the narratives, we do not have to face the facts of the message—that is to say, the fact that the Father vindicated Jesus even as Jesus promised that He would. It is so very easy both for theology and apologetics to simply become highly sophisticated forms of evasion.

The Dutch Catholic Scripture scholar, Bas van Iersel, in an article in the 1971 Scripture issue of *Concilium*, asks whether the resurrection narratives in the New Testament are intended to be information or interpretation. Are they primarily historical accounts purporting to describe exactly how things happened, or are they interpretation, that is to say, do they attempt to assign a meaning to the resurrection phenomena without informing us specifically about events. Van Iersel concludes that only Luke 24:36–43 can be identified as traditional with "sufficient probability."

> This particular traditional matter here seems to show a risen person, tangible, observable, not only with flesh and bones but actually eating in view of all present, and so identifying himself as Jesus. This observation of Jesus does not seem to presuppose faith. On the contrary, the whole passage gives the impression that perplexity, bewilderment, fear, doubt and even disbelief can be overcome by sensual seeing and touching. It seems wholly justified to bring up this tradition as an argument against the assertion that the risen Lord holds himself aloof from observation and any perception which occurs outside the faith. In any case this text should serve as a warning to us not to sever the risen Christ from the tangible Jesus.[8]

Yet van Iersel says that even this passage is more interpretation than information, that it is "polemical and directed against the docetic opinion which began to emerge"; that is to say, it was an argument

[7]Bornkamm, *op. cit.*, pp. 180–81.
[8]Bas van Iersel, "The Resurrection of Jesus—Information or Interpretation," trans. by Theo Westow, *The New Concilium: Immortality and Resurrection*. New York: Herder and Herder, pp. 65–66.

against those who deny that Jesus was a real man rather than a strictly historical narrative.

But if van Iersel thinks that the resurrection narratives are more likely interpretations than information, it is "a way of interpreting handed over to the original community" and, indeed, handed over to it quite independently of the general Jewish expectation of the resurrection of the dead. Van Iersel concludes: "I would therefore say that this way of interpreting is also derived from the facts. But about the nature of these facts and their verifiability we are wholly in the dark."[9]

Bornkamm observes that we must view the Easter stories as evidence of faith and not as records of chronicles, and we must seek the *message* of Easter when we read the stories and not a literal description of Easter.

Comments like these cause profound scandal to some Christians as though somehow or other their faith in the resurrection is based on the New Testament's providing a videotape replay of the event. In that case we have a historically validated fact and we do not need faith. That George Washington defeated the Hessians at Trenton is not an object of faith at all. It is something we can confirm by historical scholarship. But the fact of the resurrection can never be confirmed by historical fact. Even if the narratives we have were literal descriptions of certain events, it would still require a leap of faith to interpret these events as actually meaning that a man had risen from the dead; and much more—that all of us were to rise from the dead. The question is not, do we have an accurate picture of the facts of Easter, but do we believe in Easter? All the facts in the world do not make that leap of faith one bit easier. The message is far more important than facts (though of course the message presupposes some facts). The critical question for us is the message.

We can be quite certain of some facts. The early Christians had a profound experience of Jesus immediately after his death. In Bornkamm's words, "What became clear and grew to a certainty for the Church was this, that God himself intervened with his almighty hand in the wicked and rebellious life of the world, and had wrestled this Jesus of Nazareth from the power of sin and death which had risen against him, and set him up as Lord of the world."[10] This was the way people felt

---

[9]*Ibid.*, p. 66.
[10]Bornkamm, *op. cit.*, p. 83.

shortly after Jesus' death. They experienced Jesus as vindicated even as he foretold he would be. The experience for them was one of faith, as it is for us today, but that the experience occurred is a historical fact. It cannot be written off as a plot, a conspiracy, or a slowly developing evolutionary process. Immediately after his death there was a fantastic experience of him as alive. Jesus' own message of the coming of the kingdom was preached once again, but now he himself, together with his death and resurrection, in Bornkamm's words, "has entered into this message and become the core of it."[11]

How we choose to cope with this experience, whether we accept the interpretation put on it by the early Christians and embodied in the resurrection narratives we have, is ultimately dependent on our faith. But the experience itself is indisputable. Was it a monstrous delusion or is it true that God has acknowledged Jesus, whom the world refused to acknowledge? Was there really an event that took place in this time and in this world even though it puts an end and limit to this time and to this world? That is the issue that must be faced and it will never be faced as long as we quibble about the details of the resurrection narrative.

Bornkamm insists that if we are to face the issue we must look squarely at the contrast between what men did and do and what God has done and accomplished in and through Jesus as this contrast is manifested in the New Testament interpretations of the resurrection. Bornkamm then demonstrates with considerable skill how these two narratives interpret God's vindication of Jesus and the resurrection event.

> The men and women who encounter the risen Christ in the Easter stories, have come to an end of their wisdom. They are alarmed and disturbed by his death, mourners wandering about the grave of their Lord in their helpless love, and trying like the women at the grave with pitiable means to stay the process and odor of corruption, disciples huddled fearfully together like animals in a thunderstorm (Jn. xx. 19ff.). So it is, too, with the two disciples on the way to Emmaus on the evening of Easter day; their last hopes, too, are destroyed. One would have to turn all the Easter stories upside down, if one wanted to present them in the words of Faust: "They are celebrating the resurrection of the Lord, for they themselves are resurrected." No, they are not themselves resurrected. What they

[11]*Ibid.*, p. 184.

experience is fear and doubt, and what only gradually awakens joy and jubilation in their hearts is just this: They, the disciples, on this Easter day, are the ones marked out by death, but the crucified and buried one is alive. Those who have survived him are the dead, and the dead one is the living.

Hence the miracle of the resurrection does not have a satisfactory explanation in the inner nature of the disciples, nor—and this is a quite unbiblical idea—does it have an analogy in the eternal dying and rebirth in nature. . . . It is the resurrected Christ, therefore, who first reveals the mystery of his history and his person, and above all the meaning of his suffering and death. This is movingly told in the story of the disciples of Emmaus (Lk. xxiv. 13ff.), who were joined on their way by the risen Christ, but did not know him. They tell the stranger at their side the terrible tale of their Master, which has disappointed all their hopes; indeed they can even tell the events of Easter morning, but only as a hopeless story, known to everyone except, apparently, this stranger, until he opens his mouth and reveals to them the deep redeeming meaning of the whole story: "O foolish men, and slow of heart to believe all that the prophets have spoken. Was it not necessary that the Christ should suffer these things and enter into his glory?" (xxiv. 25f.). And so he fans the dying flame in their hearts anew, and they are aware of his presence at the evening meal. Truly, even the disciples at Emmaus cannot hold him as they might an earthly travel companion. The risen Christ is not like one of them. He vanishes from them again. But in the words that he speaks to them and in the supper he eats with them, they have the pledges of his resurrection and presence. Thus they return to the circle of their brethren as witnesses, and are met with the joyful confession from their midst: "The Lord has risen indeed, and has appeared to Simon." (xxiv. 34)[12]

It is extremely difficult for us to give up our obsession with facts. The apologetical method with which we learned our catechism, the passion for precise historical detail which is characteristic of an empiricist age, and also the extreme utility of concern about facts as a pretext for evading issues, all combine to make us want to know exactly how things occurred on Easter morning. One can see the TV cameras rolling up with Cosell and Meredith anxiously pacing the ground outside the tomb. But facts don't produce faith. In the very nature of things, they cannot. The issue is presented to us not by a TV

[12]*Ibid.*, pp. 184–85.

documentary, but by a fundamental challenge: are we prepared to believe that God intervened in history in the person of Jesus? Are we prepared to believe that the kingdom was vindicated in the face of its enemies? That really is the issue, and if we are not prepared to make that leap of faith, then a TV cassette recording showing the door rolling back and Jesus bounding forth would not make us one bit more likely to believe.

The real issue is the kingdom and not the resurrection. The resurrection is the supreme vindication of the kingdom and the promise that the kingdom will be fulfilled for all of us. Well, when someone says to me, "I'm not sure that I can accept the evidence for the physical resurrection of Jesus," I am afraid that they rather miss the whole point. One is either prepared to accept the Good News of the kingdom or not accept it; one either believes that God has entered into history in the form of loving service and vindicated the strength of his love or one is not going to believe it. It seems to me that that is where the decision ought to be made. Quibbling about the evidence of the resurrection is quite beside the point.

The resurrection, then, is a symbol; to use a word that offends many Catholics, a myth. By myth I do not mean a fable or a fairy story or a legend; I mean an event that represents a greater event. The Easter phenomenon, the early Christians' experience of Jesus as dead and yet once again alive, is a vindication of the kingdom and a symbol of the kingdom's triumph, a symbol that nothing can stop total fulfillment of the kingdom. To get bogged down in one reality and not to face the greater and more ultimate reality which it represents is to miss the point totally.

And yet, the confused traditional Catholic stubbornly argues, "But will I personally rise from the dead?" For this seems to him to be the most critical issue. What is going to happen to him *personally*? There are two different kinds of answers to the question, both of them, one supposes, valid. One is to say that personal concern is completely understandable, that of course we will live again. The other is to say that we know very, very little about the nature and modality of the new life and that we do not put our faith so much in expectation of a literal physical resurrection as we do in God's love, for, after all, it is God's love that is the cause and the new life which is the effect. He has revealed to us His love and promised to us a new life. We believe the love and accept the gift of new life. We commit ourselves to the reality that God did vindicate Jesus against the powers of sin and death and that that vindication was a promise and pledge of our own life. God lives and loves; Jesus lives; and we, too, will live. That is the proper object of our faith. How the Father proposes to go about arranging these things is a matter which we would be much better advised to leave to him instead of agonizing and quibbling over the details.

"My own personal resurrection is at the center of my faith," said one Catholic to me. One supposes that this is one valid way of putting it. The resurrection is certainly the central part of our faith, but I think it must be emphasized that it is only a part, a part of a larger and more comprehensive message, the message of the Good News of God's love. The resurrection is merely the event that vindicates the message of love. Our proper focus ought to be on the whole message and not just on the vindicating event.

The message is, in the final analysis, that we shall live. One either accepts or rejects that message, and all the factual details in the world cannot command either acceptance or rejection of it. The man stands at the door of the banquet and says to us, "I was dead and yet I lived; my Father has raised me from the dead in order to vindicate the invitation that you all should come into the banquet and live." The critical issue for us, as always, is whether we want to take the risk of going into the banquet to find out what it's really like. There's a strange paradox in this invitation, for it implies that man can decide for himself if he is to conquer death. If we accept the kingdom, we are told, then we will live; if we are ready to believe the triumph of life over death, then in fact we will triumph over death.

In one of the best of the recent theological articles on death, the Jesuit theologian Ladislaus Boros notes that death is the "location" of integral decision. Boros' article should be carefully read by everyone concerned with the existentialist theological approach to death and resurrection. Death is a "yes saying," the final, definitive acceptance of the Good News of the kingdom. In that acceptance of the Good News, man begins to live. Two paragraphs of the Boros article are worth quoting:

> *Death is the "location" of integral decision.* The absolute is "reached" in death. For a person, for a "being" which has wholly "come to be itself," this "reaching" always means meeting—an

encounter. A meeting can take place only between two persons who can express the "I-thou" relationship in freedom. In consequence, man as a person is not dissolved in death, but on the contrary becomes a "full person" for the first time. Therefore, the absolute encounter must be a personal relationship; hence the Absolute itself is a person. The event proper to death is coexistence with or rejection of the Absolute Person by a finite person which has wholly come to be itself. In consequence, death is a wholly personal and total decision in regard to a personal God. Hence,

In death man secures (first of all) eternity for himself. The total realization of the inward man in death is (if it occurs as affirmation) a wholly personal coexistence of a finite with the infinite being, a full participation in God. This participation in love is, however, twofold: On the one hand, it means that the being of the Other becomes our own being; on the other hand, it means that we come to be "ourselves" even more fully. The infinite fullness of the Absolute cannot be fully assumed or exhausted by any finite being. This means that the eternity that comes about in death can be comprehended only as a limitless process of growth into an ever richer completion. In heaven, everything static and quantitative is transformed into an unlimited dynamic process advancing into infinity. The world occurs in its proper form only if and when man, through his freely given Yes to God, enters heaven.[13]

It is a long, long way from the unshakable conviction of the apostles that they had experienced Jesus alive once again to Boros' existentialist terminology, but both the narration stories in the New Testament and Boros' theorizing are an attempt to capture in words an incredible experience and a conviction about the meaning of that experience. The Really Real is Love; so powerful, generous, and determined a Love that nothing can contain it, not even sin and death; and so resourceful a Love that we, too, will live.

The message is the same as it always was, no more easy to believe now than it was when Jesus appeared on the scene and confidently asserted that both he and the kingdom he was preaching would be vindicated. The early Church does not portray its leaders as brave, heroic men, gratefully accepting a vindication about which they were

[13]Ladislaus Boros, "Has Life A Meaning?" *Concilium: Immortality and Resurrection, op. cit.*, p. 17.

confident. Quite the contrary, it portrays them as not wanting to believe, not wanting to accept the possibility of vindication, but being so overwhelmed by the experience of vindication, they believed in spite of themselves. If we are to believe, we too will believe in spite of ourselves.

Chapter 12
The Future and the Church

More ink has been spilled on the subject of "eschatology" in the last seventy years than on any other subject in Christian theology. Jesus preached an eschaton, that is to say, the beginning of a new age marked by a special intervention of God. But, to oversimplify the matter somewhat, the critical question is, when does the eschaton begin? Albert Schweitzer, one of the giants of the early phases of Scripture scholarship in this century, was convinced that Jesus expected the eschaton in the very near future. He was essentially a prophet of the coming of the Last Days and therefore had no thought of a long interval between his death and the beginning of the Last Days or of founding a permanent community.

Schweitzer's influence has been pervasive, and I suppose is still very much a part of the pop theology. But in the 1930s, the brilliant British scholar C. H. Dodd reanalyzed the question of the eschaton and the Last Days and concluded that instead of Schweitzer's "consequent eschatology" Jesus was really preaching "realized eschatology"; that is to say, an eschaton that had already come and was already manifested in his own words and deeds. Even though Dodd's position does not receive the wide popular acceptance of Schweitzer's, the British scholar has by far the better argument, since recent criticism has demonstrated pretty conclusively that most of the passages on which Schweitzer bases his arguments for consequent eschatology are in fact "not authentic"; that is, they are certainly the work of the writers of the New Testament and not of Jesus himself.

The most recent scholarship tends to emphasize an opinion which is a combination of Schweitzer and Dodd, observing that sometimes Jesus spoke of the eschaton as though it had already arrived and at other times as though it were still in the future—an eschatology that is both realized and consequent, that is here present and yet to come. This position, summarized in A. L. Moore's book, *The Coming of the Kingdom*, represents a curious swing of the circle because it brings us back by an immense amount of exegetical and religious sophistication to a position which was prominent enough before Schweitzer. Moore summarizes the position of Jesus' understanding of the future by saying that it is based on twin themes—eschatology and grace. Jesus is sure that the End, being the revelation of his person at work and the end of all ambiguity and contradiction, is near. "On the other hand, he is also convinced that God will allow men time for the event of life and the grace and comfort of His Holy Spirit. Time, that is, to enter into the significance of Christ's work, to exercise faith, hope, and love."[1]

There is not much doubt that many in the early Church expected an early fulfillment of the kingdom. By the time St. Luke wrote his gospel, the "official position" was shifting against such an expectation, but the careful studies of scholars like Moore and Norman Perrin provide no evidence that Jesus himself either encouraged or expected an imminent vindication. Jesus was more concerned about the urgency of the present situation than he was about the future. That concern came not so much from his expectation that time would run out, though he insisted that it would, but rather from the immensity of the opportunity and challenge that it offered. Perrin remarks, ". . . almost all the elements in the tradition which give definite *form* to the future expectation in the teaching of Jesus fail the test of authenticity."[2] Perrin notes that the apocalyptic expectation in Mark 13 is certainly a work of the early Christians, and yet the expectation of the Parousia in Matthew is a development of the Son of Man tradition, and that in turn is an early Christian interpretation of the resurrection. Equally spectacular, notes Perrin, is the way in which sayings that express its imminent expectation fail to stand up to serious investigation. The only elements that can be traced back to Jesus with any degree of

[1]A. L. Moore, *The Coming of the Kingdom*. Leiden: E. J. Brill, 1966, p. 206.
[2]Norman Perrin, *Rediscovering the Teaching of Jesus*. New York: Harper & Row, 1967, p. 203.

certainty are the most general expectations of vindication and judgment. "These express confidence in *a* vindication, but they tell us nothing about its form. The difference between this and the general expectations of the first century, both Jewish and Christian, is spectacular."[3]

Many writers are inclined to attribute authenticity to Jesus' denial that he knew the date of the Final End. Although such an assertion would have fit in very well with the shifting position of the official church after the fall of Jerusalem, these scholars are still skeptical that any early Christian writer would dare to put such an expression in the mouth of Jesus. So scandalous a saying would not have been tolerated if the tradition did not very strongly assert that Jesus very clearly said something along those lines.

This whole examination of the eschatology question leans far more toward the position of C. H. Dodd than that of Schweitzer. The kingdom of God is present, not completely perhaps, but it is present. The present time is filled with the reality of God. Nothing more is to be expected than a complete fulfillment of that experience in the future. The reality is now known incompletely, ambiguously, immersed in conflict and temptation. Clarity and victory are yet to come. The apostle lives in the era of Now but also of the Not Yet. The table fellowship they share is of the kingdom, but it is also an anticipation of a superior fellowship which is yet to come. The future is already present but not completely so.

Perhaps part of our difficulty in understanding this mystery of the eschaton Present and Yet to Come is that we are dealing with a mode of viewing time which is very foreign to our present Western time sense. It also is very likely foreign to the time sense of the early Christians who could not conceive of a vindication in which the resurrection and the final consummation of things would be long separated. Exactly how long Jesus personally estimated the "time of grace" would be is not known, because he apparently avoided making any comment on that subject. His sense of urgency, let it be repeated, is not rooted in the expectation that the end will come next week but rather in the importance of his message. The message is so important, the opportunity is so great, that it almost does not matter when the end will in fact come. One can be quite certain that if Jesus were told that

[3]*Ibid.,* p. 203.

it would be thousands of years and hence that his invitation was not quite as urgent as he made it, he would have been quite surprised, for the urgency of the announcement of the kingdom and the invitation to the banquet were quite independent of how long it would be before the doors of the banquet hall were closed.

But even the early Christians could not separate their sense of urgency from the consideration of measured time. Their solution was to conclude that the time obviously had to be very brief. Our conclusion is that it will be a long time and, hence, there is nothing to get excited about. Jesus' point was that time was irrelevant and that there was plenty to be excited about because the kingdom of his Father was near, indeed, even among us. But, like every other element of his challenging message, the near presence of the kingdom can easily be evaded. We who are his followers will announce that we are about to change our lives, that we are about to begin our *metanoia*, about to respond to his expectations, but then we adjust the pace of our change and the speed of our *metanoia* so that we are guaranteed that even if Jesus should not reappear on the scene for half a million years we still would be too late. Our *metanoia* is under way, but at a rate which makes it absolutely certain that we will never finish. When the End does come, whenever that is, we will have the perfect excuse: "If only you gave us a little bit more time."

The phony urgency of the early Christians—phony because it had to rely on the false expectation of imminent end—is surely more attractive than our apathetic indifference. They at least had a sense of urgency and one sees very little of that among contemporary Christians. Why hurry, there still is plenty of time, we tell each other, and when the man at the door of the wedding banquet says, "Make haste, the kingdom of my Father is at hand," we say, "But you've been telling us that for a couple of millennia; what's all the rush?"

One imagines that the picture must be seen from his viewpoint to understand what all the rush is. There is of course a rather finite amount of time in the lives of each one of us, but, even more important, the point of Jesus' message is that the magnificent opportunity of the kingdom is present for us, at least inchoately, here and now. We are absolute fools to overlook that opportunity. We are cheating ourselves; we are being blind, deaf, stupid, and insensitive. And we cheerfully acknowledge all these accusations and say, "Not just now, Lord; I still have to go out and try my new yoke of oxen. You wait here at the door and tomorrow or the next day at the latest I'll be back, and then I'll come in and see what this party of yours is all about.''

The time between the Now and the Not Yet is the time of the Church. The Church is a community of those who are standing ready for the coming of the Lord who continue to proclaim the message of the Good News, however inadequately and halfheartedly. It is an assembly of those who take the message of Jesus of Nazareth seriously and have confidence in the vindication of that message in the resurrection of Jesus. With characteristic grace, Gunther Bornkamm describes its urgency:

> But this very community who await the coming Lord and, in the spirit, are already certain of his presence, bind themselves consciously, at the same time, to the way and the message of the earthly Jesus, and take his orders and promise as a guide for their own earthly way; not in spite of their hopes which are fixed on the future, but precisely because of them. Their expectation of the coming of the Lord gains its power and its reason for existence in their knowledge of past and present. From now on the great theme of the early Christian mission is the proclamation and delivery of the message of the redemption, which happened through the cross and the resurrection, and the kingship of Jesus Christ over the world.[4]

As I remarked in an earlier chapter, it may not be much of a Church, but it is the only one we have. It has made a rather serious mess of its mission of continuing the proclamation of the Good News. Not very many of its members are lights on the mountaintop or salt of the earth or leaven amid the dough, and not many of its leaders correspond to the ideal model of discipleship as presented in the gospel. But for all its faults, the Church is the only institution in the world that even claims to be continuing the proclamation of the Good News and to be anticipating the fulfillment of the wedding banquet. I suppose, without wishing to get involved in the whole vast theological debate, that, in the final analysis, this is what the infallibility of the Church means. Despite all the frailty of its leadership, all the evasions of its membership, all the incredible mistakes it has made, the Church still continues, however obscurely and inadequately, to preach the Good News and will, if Jesus' confidence of vindication is to be

[4]Bornkamm, *op. cit.*, p. 188.

justified, continue to preach the kingdom until the fullness of the kingdom is achieved.

Railings against the failure of the Church ought to be seen from the perspective we have taken in this book as an utter waste of time. To be angry at the inadequacy of the Church or the pettiness and the occasional corruption of Church leaders may be a superb way of working out the emotional conflicts of our childhood, but it has nothing to do with responding to the message of the kingdom, with attending the wedding banquet, or with living the lives of festive joy to which we are called. Nor has anger anything to do with the proclamation of the Good News of the kingdom. Some anger is perhaps justified, and certainly efforts at improving the human organization of the Church are most praiseworthy, but anger has to be transcended, and organizational renewal, however necessary, does not by itself guarantee the more effective proclamation of the kingdom or more enthusiastic acceptance of it.

Yet contemporary Catholics are obsessed by institutional forms and class-conflict themes in the life of the Church. There are some laymen, for example, whose major religious activity seems to be focused on the insistence that ecclesiastical financial records be made public. I would be inclined to think that the records ought to be public, too, though whether they are or not is rather unimportant compared with the message of the kingdom. Some priests will speak of little more than the need for collegiality or coresponsibility among the priests of the diocese and for the election of bishops by priests, and perhaps people, too. Now I myself am a convinced democrat. I do not believe that we are likely to have reform in the Church or decent leadership until we return to the traditional means of selecting our bishops—that is to say, election. But yet from many of these democratic enthusiasts I hear very little about the Good News and practically nothing about the wedding banquet that's going on. The plea for democracy has replaced the proclamation and this I think is a grave misfortune, because even when we become democratically organized—as we most certainly will—we will not necessarily be any more likely to proclaim the kingdom then than we are now, not unless we go through a *metanoia* by which we understand that democratization is a means and not an end. A democratic Church would be less inadequate as a herald of the Good News than a corrupt and authoritarian one, but democracy is by itself no guarantee that we will become excited once again about the nearness of the kingdom of God.

One way Jesus could have guaranteed that his community of followers would have been adequate to his task would be to exclude all human beings from its membership. A group of specially trained, highly disciplined archangels could have pulled it off brilliantly—at least, for all we know about archangels they could have pulled it off. It may well be that they are as inept as we are.

But once he committed himself to operating with human beings, Jesus was bound to get in trouble. Presumably he knew this, and if he didn't he discovered it very early in his dealings with his disciples. Yet, as we noted earlier in the chapter on hope, Jesus seemed to exult in the weakness and frailty of his methods. He would not underwrite the kingdom by producing at the appropriate moment twelve legions of angels, for that would be to rely on power, earthly power, even though supernatural in its origins. And if we would not ultimately make the guarantee of his kingdom by the appearance of the angelic shock troops, neither would he have it rest ultimately on the most brilliant and charismatic of leaders. For the power of charismatic leaders is also finally an earthly power, and to rely on such power for vindication would be to prove false Jesus' basic theme that the power of the kingdom came not from earth but from God.

Jesus certainly does not reject charismatic leaders and, on the whole, the Church has some reason to be proud of the great men it has produced. But its ultimate vindication will take place quite independently of our charisma, although, in some way we do not fully understand, our charisma is also necessary to prepare the groundwork. Those who persist in judging the message of Jesus by the membership and leadership of his Church are setting up criteria which he explicitly rejected beforehand and whose validity collapses in the face of Jesus' decision to call fragile human beings to be his followers and also to exult in their fragility.

The Church is primarily a local community, or, as the current theologians say, the whole Church is manifested in the local community but not completely contained within it. In another book[5] I will

[5]Andrew M. Greeley, *What a Modern Catholic Believes About the Church*. Chicago: Thomas More Press, 1972.

discuss this paradox at some length. It is sufficient here to observe that the table fellowship, which is at the core of the Christian's anticipatory experience of the heavenly banquet, is necessarily something that is celebrated locally and with a small group of people. The kingdom of God is present in the world most specifically and most specially when a small group of the followers of Jesus band together to share the fellowship of the Eucharistic banquet. But the banquet is a worldwide phenomenon even though it is celebrated only in specific loci. Our little band of brothers, eating on our "location," are nonetheless a part of the worldwide banquet, and we are held together with one another by the common banquet, the common faith, the common expectation of the ultimate vindication of Jesus and the kingdom, and our common commitment to proclaiming both by our life and by our words the Good News of the message of Jesus. Just as the early community had a leadership, we have leadership whose principal job is to devote all their energies to the explicit proclamation of the kingdom, and by so doing to prevent the rest of us from taking our eyes off that goal and to begin to live in such a way that we become like the light of the world and the salt of the earth.

These are the essential things about the Church. Most of the rest is historical development which is important, valuable, and worthy of our reverence and respect. The forms evolved through the centuries are not to be lightly cast aside, especially not because immature and uneducated enthusiasts think they are irrelevant. But neither are these forms to be confused with the essentials. Yet, despite the overwhelming evidence in the New Testament about what is essential and what is not, we still manage to make the essential accidental and the accidental essential. The reason is, I suspect, that we want to, that such confusion simplifies our lives immensely because it evades the challenge.

The Roman Congregation of the Clergy, for example, may be as important as some of its supporters and administrators think it is, or it may be as inept and misguided as many of its critics think it is, but in the strict sense of the word it is irrelevant in terms of the ultimate message. The Congregation of the Clergy cannot guarantee the effective proclamation of the kingdom, much less can it guarantee men's response to the kingdom, but neither can it prevent us from preaching the kingdom. Its mistakes and ineptitudes are no excuse for our not responding to the invitation of the kingdom. The best it can do is to facilitate somewhat the preaching of the kingdom, but it is, from the point of view of the proclamation of the kingdom, a trivial institution—however immensely dignified its membership may be. Because the Congregation is trivial does not mean that it should not exist, just that neither its supporters nor its critics should permit themselves to be obsessed by it.

And yet it is so splendid to concentrate on means and ignore ends; indeed, after a while we get really skillful at it. Our whole lives become a concern over means. That is, of course, the way to build a fully human, open, authentic, honest style of life, a life which is so concerned about means that even to the last it refuses a final, determinative decision about the End.

Jesus had some rather nasty words to say about that kind of life, words that spoke of exterior darkness and weeping and gnashing of teeth.

Chapter 13

Jesus and Political Action

The reader is probably conscious that I have engaged in dialogue in two directions in this book. On the one hand, I am speaking to those who confuse the part for the whole, who turn away from the very fundamental simple message of Good News that Jesus proclaimed to concern themselves with theological details, organizational structures, or historical verifications. On the other hand, I am engaged with, or perhaps against, those who attempt to reduce the gospel to a program for radical political action. Neither of these responses to Jesus' message is so very new. The former is the course of the Pharisees, the latter is the course of the Zealots. In more recent years the Zealot temptation has reappeared with a good deal of seductiveness. The temptation is all the more attractive because the charge for which Jesus was executed was pretty clearly one of Zealotry; he did have some criticism of the existing world in common with them. But Zealotry as a temptation is not to be more radical than Jesus, but to be less radical.

Let me make it clear that my abhorrence of the Zealot temptation, particularly as it is manifested in much of the current "theology of revolution," has nothing to do with the conviction that Christians should stay out of political and social action. As long as I can remember I have been a political and social activist and still am even though I do not burn draft records or march on picket lines. I do not engage in these activities because I am opposed to counterproductive methods of social action. I was an activist long before many of our contemporary fashionable activists, and I suspect I will continue to be one long after they have given up on it and marched off into the desert to await the inevitable eschatological greening of America.

I object to the theology of revolution on two counts: (1) as a social scientist and (2) as a Christian. The latter objection is perhaps more pertinent to this book, but let me take up the social science objection first so as to clear it away.

The call for revolution is usually based on the assumption that the present disorder is the result of malice, selfishness, the concentration of power, and the maldistribution of wealth. The malicious and selfish men are to be swept out of power. If power and wealth are redistributed, then injustice will substantially be reduced if not eliminated and the world will be a better place. The oppressed and the suffering of the earth, in other words, are to be delivered from their oppression and suffering by seizing power and redistributing the goods of the world.

Such an analysis has the appeal of simplicity and clarity. One knows both what must be done and what the effects will be. What the appeal lacks is any understanding of history or of economics or of human society.

If one looks at the so-called underdeveloped nations with any kind of economic sophistication, one has to say that the redistribution of power or wealth is not likely to have much impact on the society in those countries. New models of social organization, acquiring of industrial skills, and drastic economic changes are the only things that will improve the lot of the people in these countries. The passion for political revolution is a marvelous outlet for anger, but it does not necessarily solve the problems of economic and social structure.

We are also told that it is intolerable that a small proportion of the world's population controls most of its wealth and a large proportion lives in poverty. I am willing to agree that it is intolerable, but I do not agree that the poverty can be eliminated by taking goods away from the wealthy of the world and giving them to the poor. Problems of international production and distribution are, alas, far more complicated. The harsh truth is that we do not know yet how to solve most of these problems, but redistribution of goods, however much it appeals to the simpleminded enthusiast, would only have marginal impact on eliminating poverty from the earth.

Quite apart from the fact that enthusiasts for revolution are quite innocent of any social and economic and technological sophistication, there also is the overwhelming evidence that revolutions do not work. As George Orwell said in a quote we noted earlier, all revolutions fail, but not all the failures are the same. Those American liberals, Christian and non-Christian who are enthusiastic apostles of revolution, have for the last half century waxed optimistic about first the Russian, then the Chinese, and now the Cuban revolutions. Evidence is overwhelming that in each instance economic progress was slowed down rather than accelerated by the revolution. The American radicals, somehow or other, have their moral aestheticism more satisfied by the drab gray dullness of Castro's Cuba than by the corruption of Batista's Cuba. Recently, even they have begun to admit that, despite the vast amount of Russian money that has been poured in, the Cuban economy is not much better than it was fifteen years ago.

And one need only note the unending series of revolutions in Latin America to realize that, while the elite holding power may change, the elites still govern pretty much on their own authority without widespread social assent for their own benefit and profit. There is still the pious myth that a Marxist elite will somehow or other promote social and economic progress. But even a small amount of information about the economic and social problems of the underdeveloped countries indicates that what is needed is not a new power elite but rather new methods of and attitudes toward production and distribution of goods and, in many instances, more effective means of population control.

I am not saying that some governments are not oppressive; clearly they are, and perhaps the only justification for revolution is the removal of oppressive and unrepresentative governments. If the revolutionary goals are limited to that, the revolution is likely to be moderately successful (as in America). But if it attempts to remake the social structure and to eliminate suffering and misery by redistributing power, there is no reason in the world to expect success and every reason—historically, economically, and sociologically—to expect failure. It may be much more romantic and dramatic to advocate revolution than to promote economic development; just the same, if one is really interested in improving the human condition, economic development is far more important.

When I try to explain this position to some of the Catholic revolutionaries, their response is, "You may be right but the people won't wait." One is not sure whom they mean by "the people." When some intellectuals in underdeveloped countries, a handful of students, and a handful of nonrepresentative members of minority groups in the United States cry out, "All power to the people," they are hilarious. If the people really had power unrestrained by the government and the judicial system, they would promptly clap the revolutionaries into jail.

In a world where the problems are as complex and intricate as our own, about all that revolution can accomplish is political liberation. Many of those who are most enthusiastic about a theology of revolution seem to be responding to what they consider to be the scandalous identification of the Church with the Establishment. That certain ecclesiastical leaders have become too closely involved with those who possess political power I have no doubt. I am skeptical as to whether replacing one set of political leaders with another really does much to change the structure of society, and while I can understand anger and impatience with those ecclesiastics and self-announced Christians who stand in the way of social progress and change, I do not think the solution lies in blasting them out of their positions of power, satisfying as such an exercise might be. I do not think that anger at reactionaries and "fat cats" represents the specifically Christian response to human social problems.

Jesus was a radical, make no mistake about that. As Oscar Cullmann points out in his book, *Jesus and the Revolutionaries,* he was an eschatological radical. He criticized the existing order but he rejected political movements as the important means of transforming the world order, because political movements ". . . divert one's attention from the kingdom of God . . . and violate by their use of violence the command to absolute justice and absolute love."[1]

Cullmann summarizes his careful examination of Jesus' relationship with the Zealots in the following fashion:

> The eschatological radicalism of Jesus, as we have seen, underlies his absolute obedience to the will of God and the resulting condemnation of legalism, hypocrisy, and injustice. The Zealots also proceed from an eschatological radicalism; but Jesus is much more radical not only with respect to his concept of the kingdom of God, but also with respect to his application of norms. His goal and norms are "not of this world," as is the case of the Zealots. For this reason

[1] Oscar Cullmann, *Jesus and the Revolutionaries.* New York: Harper & Row, 1970, pp. 51–52.

he directs his criticism not only against the defenders of the existing order, but also against the Zealots. That does not infer that it is Jesus' intention that we should in general eliminate our ethical judgment by indiscriminately including all in the same criticism. I have vigorously stressed that Jesus found himself in a certain sense close to the Zealots—as also to the Pharisees. There was for him a Zealotist temptation. But exactly for that reason he warned those to whom he found himself close of the terrible consequences of their fundamental position, which made all their efforts so questionable and ultimately caused them to be transformed from nonconformists into conformists. Their resistance became indeed finally so popular in Palestine that it required courage to criticize them for not taking their norms from the kingdom which is not of this world.[2]

There are then two points in Jesus' program for remaking the world: (1) Man must first accept the kingdom, and (2) man must act according to the norms of justice and love. This is not an escape from political activism, though in Jesus' time the implications of justice and love and for the reorganization of society were not nearly as clear or well developed as they are today. Indeed, one might even say more. Under the impulse of the ethic of justice and love which Jesus preached we have become far more conscious of what the good society ought to be like. What Jesus is saying, rather, is that unless men are prepared to commit themselves to the vision of God's love for us that he has come to preach then they will not be able to love one another. One generation's revolutionaries can turn into the next generation's oppressors. Anyone who knows much history can have no doubt about that, but the argument still remains: Will the plan of Jesus work? Will the conversion to the kingdom of God and the consequent willingness to live by justice and love really transform, or at least notably improve the human condition, even before the complete fulfillment of the kingdom?

I suppose the only answer to that question is that empirically we do not know because the program of Jesus has never been tried.

Revolutions, even violent revolutions, may occasionally be necessary, but they are, at best, risky affairs, and if there is not something more involved than just the redistribution of power and attempted redistribution of wealth, the historical record is clear: the revolution

[2]*Ibid.*, pp. 57–58.

will fail, and may even make things worse instead of better. Jesus did not so much call for the end of revolutions as he called on men to understand that the revolution was a pathetically inadequate means of transforming the human condition and that that condition would be transformed only when men had enough confidence in God's love for them to be willing to take the great risk of loving one another.

It can be objected that in my view of things social change will necessarily be a slow and gradual process and that "the people won't wait." But of course the people will wait and are going to have to wait. If my method is somewhat slower, it is also more likely to be effective. I suspect sometimes that the Christian radicals want success because they realize in their heart of hearts that if they don't have dramatic and rapid success they will lose their enthusiasm. The point is, however, that the Christian by definition is not supposed to lose. His faith in the coming of the kingdom does not excuse him from commitment to the world. On the contrary, it holds him both more firmly and more confidently in his commitment to the world, more firmly because he knows that he has no choice but to love, and more confidently because he knows that in the end love will be vindicated.

I cannot insist too strongly at this point that the Christian is not running away from social problems. He is not waiting for an eschatological kingdom where all will be well. He rather believes that his commitment to the eschatological kingdom tells him to practice love in all his relationships. He has always believed this, but the modern Christian, in addition, perceives the vast social implications of love. He also understands that in some way or other his exercise of love in the social order both proclaims the kingdom and also prepares for—though it does not cause—its fulfillment. He does not, he cannot give up and retreat to some rural commune, but neither can he attempt to short-circuit the process by falling back on hatred and violence. He does not abhor political action. He does not despise politics. He is not even afraid of amassing political power, though he knows that the most that power can do is modify structures to an extent that love becomes feasible; it does not create love, and in the absence of love social reforms have minimum effectiveness.

The eschatological vision does not mean that the Christian is opposed to school desegregation, for example. Quite the contrary, he enthusiastically supports it. He realizes that in the final analysis tension between black and white will be resolved only when there is more love between the two. Equalized power can prevent injustice and may give people opportunity to become fully human. It can even create a situation where love can be possible.

The Christian realizes that he must commit himself to both equalized power and love without ever having the slightest thought of withdrawing that commitment. He cannot therefore engage in demonstrations or revolutionary acts or liturgical gestures and then withdraw from the field with the rather soreheaded complaint that it didn't do any good. Neither can he succumb to the temptation of thinking that he can force men to be virtuous. He may be able to prevent them from abusing others by power and law, but the Christian realizes that you teach men to love only by loving yourself.

There isn't much doubt, after one has read a book like Cullmann's, that this is where "Jesus was at." The Zealots dismissed him as a pious dreamer, the Pharisees dismissed him as a violator of the law, the Establishment viewed him as a dangerous radical, and so the Romans disposed of him—or at least tried to. One has the appalling feeling that his political and social message would receive the same response today. The realists would think it naïve; the defenders of the status quo would think it revolutionary. And yet Jesus was neither a naïve person nor a revolutionary, at least as the word is normally understood; so once again, he was misunderstood and once again, one suspects, deliberately. It is too bad because his plan at least deserves a try, and save on a small scale with tiny groups of human beings, it never really has been tried. It is a revolution that is ultimately not of this world at all, yet one that claims to transform this world too. It is a revolution which begins, curiously enough, with an invitation to a banquet, and if we ever go through the portals of the banquet hall we will find the revolutionary leader beginning the conversation with, "I suppose you wonder why I've called you all together."

Chapter 14

Conclusion

In one of the more splendid "Star Trek" episodes the *Enterprise* and her crew come to a planet which combines first-century Rome and twentieth-century America in its culture. Caesar's proconsul presses Kirk, McCoy, and the pointy-eared Spock into service as gladiators. After the usual number of close calls the officers of the *Enterprise* are saved (at the cost of his life) by a huge gentle gladiator named Flavius. He preaches universal brotherhood and seems to worship the sun. When they have "beamed" back to their starship, the three heroes muse over Flavius, puzzled by his worship of the sun. Uhura, the lovely black communications officer, tells them they have misunderstood Flavius: it is not the "sun" he worshiped but the "Son."

"Interesting, even fascinating," says Spock. "Christ and Caesar—they have them both here even as earth did."

"And Christ is triumphing over Caesar just as he did on earth," murmurs Kirk. "It's happening once more. Wouldn't it be marvelous to be able to watch it again?"

Mr. Chekov is instructed to take the *Enterprise* out of orbit, and at warp factor 2 it proceeds on its pilgrimage through space.

"Star Trek"—and may the Lord forgive the networks for killing it—was the closest thing to an explicit morality play that the idiot tube has ever produced. But this particular episode was one that ought to have stopped every Christian short. We might be tempted to ask, in the words of Alice Meynell's great poem, "... in what guise He trod the Pleiades..."?

> But in the eternities
> Doubtless we shall compare together, hear
> A million alien Gospels, in what guise
> He trod the Pleiades, the Lyre, the Bear.[1]

Whether he trod the Pleiades or not we do not know. We have at least left behind the ethnocentrism (or perhaps one should say cosmocentrism) of those theologians who argued that it was impossible for the Incarnation to occur on any other planet. It is entirely possible that some future counterpart of the *Enterprise* will encounter somewhere in the universe other life forms to whom the Father has manifested His love. We could no more legitimately object to that than the citizens of Nazareth could object to the Father manifesting His love to the Samaritans. From what Jesus has told us of his Father, we would find it difficult to see how He could avoid getting involved with whatever other stray life forms are to be found out there among the galaxies. If He managed to fall in love with us, if He could be insanely generous with such rather low-level life forms as we, how could He not love whatever life should appear in the universe?

It would be interesting to know what He thinks of the Vulcans.

But the important point is not whether Jesus walks in the Pleiades; it is that he walked here on earth. Captain Kirk and the crew of the *Enterprise* might well envy Flavius and his friends for the chance to be part of it all again. But we are part of it now—or we can be if we want to. Our pilgrimage does not take us through physical space like the *Enterprise*, but it is a pilgrimage just the same—a pilgrimage of the human spirit in its restless quest for the Absolute. Jesus is not merely a manifestation of the Absolute; he is simultaneously the assurance that the Absolute loves us and is a guide on the pilgrimage.

The issue is the same for us as it has been for all our predecessors: Do we want to go on the pilgrimage? Do we wish to trust the Absolute? Do we believe the claim of Jesus to be a guide for the pilgrimage? The *Enterprise* moving at warp factor 2, the Israelites following Moses out into the desert, our accepting the invitation to the

[1]Alice Meynell, "Christ in the Universe," *The Golden Book of Catholic Poetry*, edited by Alfred Noyes. Philadelphia and New York: J. B. Lippincott Company, 1964, p. 234.

wedding feast—all manifest a fundamental trust in the graciousness of being, without which pilgrimage becomes impossible. The challenge of Jesus may not be "relevant," but demanding its acceptance has always been and always will be.

In his discussion of religious symbols Paul Ricoeur speaks of the "first" and "second naivete." In the "first naivete" man accepts his religious symbols in a simple, unself-conscious way. He does not need to reflect, to analyze, to explain, to interpret—at least he does not need much of these activities. Such a "naive faith" has been characteristic of most believers in most periods of human history; the Breton fisherman or the Irish washerwoman of pious legend had this sort of faith. So perhaps did our parents and our grandparents, maybe even some of our teachers. It is fashionable in some circles to ridicule "naive faith"; but such ridicule is merely a display of shallow pseudosophistication.

But however admirable the "first naivete" may be, it is not possible for an increasing number of us. We do not simply repeat sacred poetry, we must analyze it, take it apart, interpret it, uncover the various levels of narration and meaning. We are products of an analytic, scientific age, and our myths and poems must be analyzed. We must know what the symbol means.

There is nothing wrong with that. The ability to analyze is one of man's most impressive accomplishments. But can we go beyond analysis? Or do we become like the English professor who is so sophisticated in taking apart the poetry of the Bard that he no longer can enjoy Shakespeare's vision? He can tell us what every word in a line means, but he can no longer thrill at the thought of Juliet as the sun. He has learned prose so well that he can no longer speak or listen to poetry.

I can almost hear some readers say, "But is Jesus real, or is he just poetry?" The only answer is that poetry is more real than prose. Jesus is real precisely because he is poetry, precisely because his life and message are symbols—symbols of God's love for us.

In the second naivete, having achieved a more sensitive and profound understanding of the meaning of the symbol, we give ourselves over to it once again and now the symbol has even more power for us than it did before. The poetry expert who has gone beyond analysis can take even more delight in Juliet as the sun because he has explored all the implications of the image.

A man still hung up on prose says skeptically, "But of course Juliet really isn't the sun, is she?" How badly he misses the point. The whole message of the image is not that she is something less than the real sun, but rather for one who loves her she is something much more. The poetic image is never an exaggeration of reality, it is an understatement of it.

We live in an age of prose. As a race we have left behind the first naivete and have not yet quite made it to the second. We tear our symbols apart and then sorrowfully view the pieces, lamenting that we have wrecked our myths. For prosaic Christians, this age of analysis is one more marvelous excuse. Obviously, we don't have to wonder about whether we ought to accept the invitation to the wedding banquet. After all, the wedding feast is "only a symbol."

This has been largely a book of prose; a book of pilgrimage, perhaps, between the first and the second naivetes. I have "taken apart" the person and the message of Jesus, analyzed, interpreted, and explained. Such an effort is not a foolish one. It is absolutely necessary for men of our time to engage in such a prosaic task. But the critical question for me and for the reader is: Now that we have "explained" Jesus, what do we do about him?

Are we or are we not going to that wedding feast?

PART TWO

The Sinai Myth

Introduction

The God of the Fruitful Mountain: The Sinai Myth

From the mists of prehistory between the thirteenth and eighth centuries B.C. there emerged in Palestine a people with a strikingly different religious tradition. A nomadic and illiterate people, they did not write their experience of God on paper for hundreds of years. When the oral tradition finally did become literary, it was composed of complex tribal laws; ancient poems, chants, and oracles; fables, parables, and legends from a distant past.

This collection of different source materials creates a great problem for our own very literal-minded age. Our understanding of the sources must begin with the realization that the documents which we have are an attempt to record an oral tradition, which in its turn was an attempt to record an extraordinary religious experience. No description of a religious experience is adequate even if it is an individual experience at one particular time and place. The Israelite traditions were an endeavor to record the religious experience of a whole people over a considerable period of time. We may not find their experiences particularly attractive or helpful or we may find them deeply moving. In either case we cannot begin to do justice to the Israelites or their traditions until we realize that we are dealing with something more than a bizarre collection of texts, some of which are confusing, some obscure, and some downright unedifying. In the documents we are confronting an experience of God, and before we do justice to the Israelites we must strive to understand as best we can the nature of that experience. Who was the God that the Israelites encountered in their going out of Egypt? At the foot of Sinai? Upon entering the Promised Land? What did this central religious symbol of the Jewish religion have to say about the nature and purpose of human life?

It is only when we attempt to answer these questions that we encounter the Israelite heritage. Agonizing over where the "Red" or the "Reed" Sea was or what the nature of the disaster that befell the army of the Pharaoh was or where Mount Sinai was or what sort of natural explanation there can be for the manna in the desert is quite beside the point. One can find natural explanations for the manna and the parting of the waters or one can dismiss them as fables. One can assume that the voice of Yahweh really was heard from the top of Sinai (wherever it might have been) or one can say that the Israelites witnessed a volcanic eruption. Finally, one can conclude that the whole Sinai story is a legend made up by clever priests in the eighth century B.C. (None of these explanations seem to be satisfactory to me, incidentally.) But having made these judgments about the description of the Sinai event, we have only begun our work. The critical question is not how did Sinai occur but what does it mean? We cannot understand the Israelites and their tradition unless we first of all understand the meaning of Sinai.

Going out of Egypt, encountering Yahweh in the desert, and entering Palestine were the experiences which gave the Israelites their God and made them a people. Those three experiences constitute the core of the Israelite tradition, and whatever may be said about the historical nature of those events as they come down to us in the Israelite documents, it must be admitted that the nineteenth and twentieth chapters of the book of Exodus record the center of that tradition.

The experience of God on Sinai became the decisive symbol in Israelite religion and theology. If we wish to understand Israel we must understand Sinai. Judaism as we know it today began with the experience recorded in those two chapters of Exodus, and Christianity can claim to be nothing else but a continuation of the Sinai experience. If someone from the outside wishes to understand either Judaism or Christianity he must first comprehend Sinai; and if the Jew or the Christian wishes to understand who and what he is, he, too, must comprehend Sinai. For on that mountain, El Shaddai, the God of the

Fruitful Mountain, became Yahweh, the One Who Causes Things to Be, and the history of the human race was changed decisively.[1]

This book, then, is an attempt to understand the Sinai event as recorded in the nineteenth and twentieth chapters of the book of Exodus.

Let me conclude this introduction with a word about the kind of book this is. It is certainly not an exercise in academic theology because I am not a theologian. Nor is it the work of a professional exegete, because while I have immense respect for their skills, I do not possess them. I have consulted the exegetes, both their books and their persons. It is possible that I have misunderstood them in some respects, but I do not think it likely that I have misunderstood the basic religious symbolism of chapters 19 and 20 of the book of Exodus. My reflections on those symbols are my own. They are submitted to the reader not as an apodictic interpretation of the symbols but for whatever use they may be to the reader's own reflections.

If anything, the book is an exercise in sociology, although scarcely of the sort one would submit to *The American Sociological Review*. It is a search for meaning, an attempt to determine what a given set of religious symbols means, what basis these symbols provide for "a pact against chaos and death," as Peter Berger has put it. Paradoxically enough, the sociologist approaches religion with the same question that the deeply religious man asks: What do these sets of religious symbols really mean? I will scarcely claim that this book is an exercise in scholarly sociology, but I will assert that if I were not a sociologist and had not had the experience of more than a decade of sociological research, I do not think I would have come to ask the question that I am trying to ask in this volume.

Is the book an exercise in "popularization"? I am not sure what that word really means, though it has a certain pejorative sense (particularly when used by book reviewers) that I would not accept. If

[1]There are various translations given for "El Shaddai": the God of the Mountain, the God of the Fruitful Mountain, or even the God of the Breast. I might have chosen the third translation as the title for this book. It emphasizes the fertility cult aspect of pre-Sinai religion and would not be inappropriate given the passionate nature of the relationship between Yahweh and his people. I think, however, that it might not be acceptable in contemporary religious book publishing. I shall explore this aspect of Yahweh in a later chapter.

"popularization" means only the absence of basic research, then I suppose that it is clear that this book is "popularized." "Popularization" may also imply that a work is unserious and watered down, something light and frothy that an author serves up to people who are not as intelligent as he and surely not as intelligent as his academic colleagues. If this is what is meant by "popularization"—and I think such a connotation is usually intended—then this book is not "popular."

This volume is a deadly serious attempt to cope with some of the most fundamental religious questions human beings can ask. Whether the book is profound is not for me to say; I do not equate seriousness or profundity with either obscurity or the scholarly apparatus. I refuse to accept the right of academics and their fellow travelers to define what is important and serious and at the same time to insist that the only worthwhile things are written principally for scholars.

It is important to make this point, I think, at the beginning of any attempt at religious interpretation. We cannot approach serious religious interpretation without the assistance of archaeologists, historians, linguists, exegetes, theologians. But if we cannot understand religious symbols without the assistance of such scholars, we should not equate their brilliant and skillful scholarly work with religion or faith and our efforts to implement religious symbols in our lives. Yahweh did not write a Ph.D. dissertation on Sinai, and Moses never produced an article for a learned journal. Religion, today at least, presupposes solid scholarship, but it does not and cannot stop there.

Chapter 1
Sinai as Turning Point

One of my friends was horrified when he heard I was doing a book "about the Ten Commandments." "No one," he protested, "is interested in them anymore."

What can one say in response to such a comment? It is certainly true that our catechisms and our moral theology books turned the Ten Commandments into a rigid ethical code from which we were supposed to deduce detailed norms for all our decisions about behavior. Such inflexible codes of behavior became first oppressive and then irrelevant. If it be true that no one is interested in the Ten Commandments, the reason may well be that the Decalogue was converted into a harsh, legalistic code despite Yahweh and Jesus. The problem still remains: Why did something, now judged to be so inhuman, have such tremendous importance to so many people for so long?

The Sinai experience was not fundamentally an ethical vision at all. It was a religious event, an encounter of man with God. The ethical code which emerged from that encounter was simple, not especially original, and rather of secondary importance. In our catechism classes and in our moral theology courses we skipped over the first three or four commandments rapidly. Graven images were no problem, taking God's name in vain was only a venial sin, not very many people used Ouija boards or went to fortunetellers, and servile work on Sunday was so difficult to define that nobody paid much attention to it. The really important commandments, the ones on which we spent most of our time, were the seventh, eighth, and ninth. Theft, injustice, and adultery—those were the things worth worrying about!

But in fact the context of the Sinai covenant shows that it is the first three commandments that really count. If one wishes to understand the religious experience of Sinai, one must understand them.

If I am told that no one is interested in the Decalogue as a symbol of a profound religious experience whose impact is still very much with us, I am astonished. There are, of course, people who believe that there is nothing to be learned from the past. They can take Margaret Mead seriously when she asserts that the "now" generation has its roots in the future, not the past; and they can take Alvin Toffler seriously when he argues that "future shock" has eliminated almost all stability and continuity from human society. It would seem to me, however, that anyone with a moderate amount of education or intelligence must be aware that we are all creatures of our past heritages. Indeed, even the rejection of our heritage is normally done in the categories the heritage provides for us. If one turns away, for example, from the Jewish or the Christian religious traditions, one generally does so in terms of a messianic vision of the future of the human race—quite unaware that if it were not for the Jewish and Christian heritages, the human race would be totally lacking messianic concepts. Western man thinks about the future only because somewhere in his past there was a convenant that was a promise. We have the vocabulary and the thought patterns to discuss "future shock" only because more than three millennia ago some of our spiritual ancestors encountered a God who, unlike the other gods around him, seemed more concerned with the future than he was with the past.

But this book is not written to argue with those who say that the past is unimportant. It is for those who wish to respond to the present religious situation in which they find themselves and who wonder whether the symbols available to them from their heritage can have meaning for them now. The Sinai experience and the Decalogue which records it are unquestionably critical religious symbols that are part of our heritage. Before we reject them we should at least know what they mean.

The accounts that we have available to us in the book of Exodus are obviously highly stylized traditions passed on first by word of mouth and then by a number of different written traditions. They are filled with both theological reflection and religious exhortation. It is extremely difficult to get beyond these documents to an understanding of the actual historical events. However, modern scholars are inclined to agree that the stylized accounts of the book of Exodus are not mere fables; that they describe people who actually existed and events which really occurred, although they describe them in a very different way from what we would expect historical narrative to be today.

It would appear that following the defeat of the Hyksos invaders (about 1560 B.C.), the Egyptian Pharaohs began to reestablish their empire. In the process they did battle with some of the "foreigners," the Apiru, who had settled in Egypt and just outside its borders. Some of these Apiru or Hebrews did apparently leave Egypt during the thirteenth century B.C., probably escaping from an Egyptian military detachment that was thrown into disarray by a natural disturbance in the marshlands between Egypt and the Sinai peninsula. At some later point in history, this tribe (or perhaps a collection of tribal elements) combined with other tribes that lived in the desert beyond the borders of Palestine and invaded that land. Some of those who left Egypt, or perhaps some of the other tribal components whom they later encountered, had a traumatic religious experience near a sacred mountain, which may have been in any of a number of places in the Sinai peninsula. (If you require a volcanic mountain, then it has to be on the eastern side of Sinai near the Gulf of Aqabah; if you trust early Christian or even late pre-Christian tradition, then it was the mountain called the Mountain of Moses in the southwestern part of Sinai. Even the Old Testament sources seem uncertain as to where the mountain really was.)

It is entirely possible that the going out of Egypt was experienced by one tribe and Sinai was experienced by another, while the occupation of Palestine was experienced by considerable numbers of people who were part of neither the Exodus nor the Sinai encounter. These questions are fascinating historical and archaeological issues, but they are rather less important in terms of religious symbolism. By the time we meet the twelve tribes of Israel, they are a religious confederation, an amphictyony. Whatever the historical events were that gave rise to the sense of a common religious experience, this sense was well established in the twelve tribes by the time we are able to deal with them on the basis of historical records. It was also that sense which fundamentally constituted them as people.

It is a mistake, then, to think of the Israelite religious experience as one that occurred only in a given place and to a specific number of people. It happened over time, several centuries perhaps, and in varying ways to a whole population. Exodus and Sinai were decisive components of this religious experience in both constituting it and symbolizing it, but they do not represent the totality of the experience as it historically occurred.

How many people were at the foot of Sinai? Were they the same people who went out of Egypt? Was Moses really there? Was there a volcanic eruption or was there a thunderstorm? Did the people imagine that they heard the voice of Yahweh? Or were the sounds of natural phenomena "interpreted" for them by their leaders? Obviously, certain answers to these questions are not possible now. In all likelihood they will never be possible, and while these questions are legitimate historically, they are not especially important from the religious viewpoint. More important than how Israel came to believe that Yahweh was its God is the question of what kind of God he is. The children of Israel experienced over a period of time a number of dramatic events which forced them to interpret the nature of their relationship to the Really Real. The Sinai symbol and the convenant theology which flows from it were the way Israel tied together its striking experiences, interpreted them, and used them as a basis for creating a religious and national unity. Rather than to inquire what really happened at Sinai, the important question to ask is what does Sinai really mean?

However obscure the historical events may be, there can be no doubt that the religious experience which occurred at Sinai and which is embodied in the traditional interpretation of the events is absolutely unique. Let us quickly admit that the Israelite religion did not spring into being completely free from the influence of the culture of which it was a part. Its poetry and its creation myths owe something in language if not in content to the Semite and Babylonian myths which pervaded the ancient Near East. The etymological roots of the name "Yahweh" are obscure but must be located in the cultural heritage of the Israelites or in those cultures that influenced them. It is possible that Israelite monotheism was influenced by the Egyptian monotheism of the heretic Pharaoh Ikhnaton (Amenophis IV), who lived probably a century before Moses. It is also highly probable that in its beginnings the religion of Yahweh did not deny the existence of other gods. The Yahweh who was encountered in the desert was not the only god or even necessarily the chief of the gods. What he was—and this is the decisive part—was a god totally different from any other.

Furthermore, let us be prepared to admit that Yahweh owed something to the mountain gods of the wandering Semitic tribesmen and to the personal gods of family and clan. Indeed, it is quite obvious that the collectors of the Old Testament documents equate Yahweh with the personal and family gods of the patriarchs who went before them.

But having made all these admissions of limitation, it must still be asserted that the encounter of Israel with Yahweh was an absolutely unique religious experience. It was unlike anything else in the ancient world. It took a long time for Israel to understand the meaning of its encounter with Yahweh. (And those of us who are still Israelites, real or spiritual, have yet to exhaust the full meaning of that encounter.) But the uniqueness of Israel's experience is as clear in the first written records of it as in the later sophistication, interpretation, and elaboration of it.

This book assumes that most of the old battles are over, that we no longer have to argue about whether Genesis (which is a book of secondary importance compared to Exodus) is scientific history, about whether Moses really lived, and about whether the book of Numbers was really jotted down in the shadow of Sinai. I take it that having put aside such relatively trivial questions, we can address ourselves to the fundamental question that the Sinai symbol raises for us: What is the nature of the relationship it describes between man and God?

Religious symbols must be explored and interpreted to see what they tell us about God, about the fundamental nature of the universe, and about the purpose of human life. Every religious symbol attempts to offer an interpretation of the human condition, and the fundamental question we must ask about a religious symbol is not whether it teaches us truth but whether it provides useful insights into the nature of the Real. All human religious symbols are valid in the sense that they all shed some light on the human condition. The theologian Schubert Ogden offers us the following principle of the verifiability of religious symbols: "Mythical assertions are true insofar as they so explicate our unforfeitable assurance that life is worthwhile, that the understanding of faith they represent cannot be falsified by the essential conditions of life itself."[1] Ogden goes on to say:

[1]Schubert Ogden, *The Reality of God and Other Essays*. New York: Harper & Row, 1966, p. 116.

> The reality with which mythical assertions must come to terms is not the everchanging world disclosed by our senses, but our own existence as selves, as those who, whatever their external perceptions, always experience themselves and the world as finite-free parts of an infinite whole. It is for this reason that mythical assertions, when true, express an understanding of faith which not only *is* not falsified by our experience, but also *can* not be so falsified.[2]

Following Ogden's norm, what we must ask of the Sinai experience is to what extent it confirms our own basic conviction about the worth and purpose and dignity of humankind. If the Sinai myth does indeed powerfully "re-present" (to use Ogden's word) this primordial religious conviction for us, then it has validity not only for people who first experience it but for those of us who approach it today once again. What we must do is to ask first of all, what does Sinai really mean? And, second, what does Sinai mean for *us*? To anticipate somewhat the conclusion of this book, it means infinitely more than a series of negative prohibitions. It is, rather, a revelation of God's love for man.

I am not suggesting that we come to the foot of Sinai to ask Yahweh for specific answers on issues like birth control, war, racial justice, and pollution. If the pertinence and utility of a religious symbol depends on the capacity of that symbol to provide simple, clear, and direct answers for specific social and ethical problems, then forget about the God of the Fruitful Mountain, because he doesn't have them—but then neither does any other god, or at least no other god who respects the intelligence and freedom of his followers.

Nor should we ask if Yahweh is a revolutionary. In some sense he is; certainly human religion has never quite been the same since the Sinai encounter. But if it is required for Yahweh to be "relevant," that he lay down a concrete program for overthrowing the Establishment (whatever that may be), then Yahweh is no revolutionary. He did not like idolatry and he still doesn't. Any attempt to reduce him to a specific program or a specific set of answers is idolatry, precisely because it absolutizes the relative; it turns that which is contingent and problematic into something that is eternal and unquestionable. Of this sort of thing Yahweh will have no part.

[2]*Ibid.*, p. 117.

If we are to make a pilgrimage to the foot of Sinai at all, our purpose must be to find out what Yahweh says about the meaning and purpose of human existence; then we must determine what the insights we obtain from listening to Yahweh mean for our own lives.

If we wish to approach with reverence, respect, and intelligence the religious symbols which are part of our heritage, we must avoid two extremes. First of all, we must not become so bogged down in the cultural particularities of the situation in which the symbol was first used that we lose sight of its possible pertinence for our own lives. On the other hand, we must not twist that symbol so out of its own proper context as to force it to provide detailed and literal instructions for our own behavior. The first approach is that of the history of religions, which brilliantly and with fantastic displays of erudition describes the religious symbol in its proper context and asks no questions about what challenge the symbol may pose for the life of the analyst. The second approach is that of fundamentalism, which thinks, for example, that Yahweh's dealing with the Amorites is appropriate guidance for our dealing with Communists. In the historical approach, the symbol is left safely in its context; fundamentalism pulls it completely out of context.

Interpretation asks what the symbol tells us about man, God, reality, purpose, meaning, and community. The interpretive art is a difficult one, though I think not necessarily more difficult today than it has ever been. Any of those of us who engage in interpretation—and I suppose all religious people do—should be aware of the tentative and transitory nature of our interpretations. The best we can do is to say that the religious symbol as we understand it seems to mean certain things for us now. Beyond that we must be very wary of imposing our interpretations either on future generations or demanding them of prior ones.[3]

This book is an exercise in interpretation from the perspective of a schismatic Yahwistic sect founded by one Jesus of Nazareth, who claimed to have a unique relationship with Yahweh. The Israelite experience with Yahweh was an ongoing one. In their encounters with

[3]I should like to make it clear that I do not think our own interpretations can ignore those of the past. If every generation must return to the primal religious symbols, it can do so with intelligence, I think, only if it has respect and reverence for how previous generations have dealt with the symbols. It is the most stupid sort of temporal ethnocentrism to refuse to learn from the wisdom of the past. It is also the most stupid sort of religious timidity to refuse to attempt to go beyond the interpretations of the past in our search for meaning.

him in Exodus and on Sinai they discovered that Yahweh was a God of history, a God who acts. So, necessarily, he was to be encountered again and again. It was the claim of the Christians to have had a new experience of Yahweh as he manifested himself in Jesus. Surely, it was not an experience that negated the Sinai encounter but one that continued to develop and enrich it. Christianity—whether some Christians like it or not—is a Yahwistic religion. It may very well represent a notable leap beyond the Sinai symbol, but it was a leap that could only occur in the religious tradition of which Sinai was the central event. From one point of view, the quantum leap of human understanding in which El Shaddai became Yahweh was an even greater one than that represented by the Easter experience of the early Christians. To put the issue in a schematic and oversimplified form: On Sinai we learned that God loves us; in the cross and resurrection we learned how much he loves us.

I have repeatedly used the words "experience" and "encounter." Let me make it clear that I am not speaking about religious "feeling" or religious sentiment. I am talking about a profound human insight that pervades the whole person, intellect, and feeling. The "experience" I have in mind is a revelatory one, or, perhaps more precisely, a response to a revelation that one perceives as having occurred. It is not merely the subjective experience of the modernist but rather a response to objective reality.

But the question may be pressed: Do I really believe that it is God that is doing, God that is acting? Or is the revelatory experience of which I speak something simply that men do by themselves and then postulate the acting God as an explanation? It seems to me that this is an inappropriate way to pose the question. Of course I believe that God acted on Sinai and in the history of Israel and at Calvary and Easter. I believe that God acts in all human events and that he acted in a unique way in the dramatic religious encounters. Do I believe that God really spoke? If one means by this do I believe that he spoke the way he was depicted as doing in the movie *The Ten Commandments,* the answer is, obviously, no. If I am asked if there was really a voice speaking on the mountain that people could hear, I would say maybe. I wasn't there and I don't know. If there was a voice, it was not the voice of God. God does not have a voice. It must have been a modification of the air waves that God produced for the purpose of communicating with people. Such an event would be marvelous indeed, and since I believe in an open universe I would not want to exclude the possibility of such an event; but I will assert that under normal circumstances that is not the way God works. Indeed, which is more marvelous—a God who works through creating modifications in the air waves or a God who works through the growth of human insight and understanding?

In other words, I cannot accept a divorce between God's working and the growth of human insight and understanding. What occurred in the experience that Sinai symbolizes was a fantastic leap forward in human insight, and I think that such a leap is infinitely more impressive and dramatic than voices coming from a cloud on a mountaintop.

In any event, on Sinai, God worked and man worked. They worked together, and the result was an extraordinary religious event. Attempts to explain how the event occurred are much less important than the recognition that it did indeed occur.

Chapter 2
The Religious Background

There are two problems that must be faced if we are to come to grips with the religious challenge presented in the nineteenth and twentieth chapters of the book of Exodus. First of all, we must rid ourselves completely of the notion that the Israelite religion emerged in an instant, fully developed and distinct from the religious and cultural currents which swirled around the ancient Middle East. The cult of Yahweh is unique. Nothing even remotely like it is found anywhere else in ancient times; but the uniqueness comes not from the development of totally new religious material but rather from the organization of existing religious material around a decisively new insight. There were unquestionably certain specific events which had a major impact on the development of the insight (Sinai was certainly one of those events), but the full development of new insight and the rearrangement of existing religious material was the work of years, probably centuries, and with periodic backslidings.

Furthermore, while some individuals, such as the historic Moses, unquestionably played a critical role in the development of the religious insight (how much of a role is difficult to tell from our vantage point), the evolution of the Israelite religion involved a fundamental shift in world view among a whole community of people, especially among its principal religious leaders. The Israelite insight, then, was both individual and collective, the work in part of extraordinarily gifted religious leaders and in part of an anonymous but vigorous community.

Not so long ago, comparisons between the Old Testament documents and other ancient Middle Eastern religious documents were viewed by both believers and nonbelievers as a threat to the uniqueness of the revelation reported in the Old Testament. Even today, many Catholics, both priests and laity, are profoundly uneasy when they hear comparisons between the Genesis creation myth and the Babylonian creation myth. But in the world of serious biblical scholarship the terms of the issue have been changed, for it is clear that however much the Israelites may have borrowed material from the religious environment in which they lived, they transformed it to suit their own particular understanding of how the world began, an understanding whose uniqueness becomes even more apparent when compared with others who used similar mythological symbols.

If one assumes that the Israelite religious insight emerged over time, not merely as the result of individual effort but as the result of the growth of collective belief, then the tools of comparative religion are no longer a threat to our understanding of the uniqueness of the faith of Israel. They become a positive help. Indeed, it is only when we come to grips with the basic questions which the religious insight of Israel purports to answer that we can understand how unique the Israelites' response was.

The other problem, in some ways exactly the opposite of the first one, is the difficulty we have in trying to respect the mythopoetic approach to religion. In our very rational and cognitive age we tend to distinguish between history and legend; the former we take to be true and the latter to be false. Myths are not history, therefore they are legend, and therefore they are false. Of course our own age is not without its legends and its myths, but most of us refuse to face the fact that mythmaking is part of the human condition, as much now as it was in the Middle East of the thirteenth century B.C.

The Israelites broke decisively with the nature myths that pervaded the world in which they lived and replaced them with the Sinai myth. It was an enormous leap forward in human religious understanding, but it neither abolished the mythopoetic approach to religion nor dispensed completely with the symbolic components of natural mythology.

Ancient man was aware that he lived in a world in which there were great "powers." He was aware of the cycle of life and death, of fertility and reproduction, of planting, growth, and harvest. He knew that the sun and the moon and the stars changed their position in the heavens. He realized the immense constraints that family, clan, and tribe imposed on his behavior. If he was Egyptian, he was awed by the rise and fall of the mighty Nile, which dominated every aspect of his life. He knew that sexuality was a force within him that was terribly difficult to restrain. He knew that there was thunder, lightning, storms, and drought; volcanoes, earthquakes, and eclipses. Most fundamental of all, he perceived around him a struggle between order and chaos. He understood the routine systems of both nature and human society, but he also perceived that these could be disrupted: in nature by the tremendous force of natural phenomena gone wild, in society by internal conflict or external invasion. There were, unquestionably, orderly routines in the world, but there was also constant disruption. There were powers of order and powers of chaos. Ancient man wondered (at least some of them) how it came to be that the world was.

We may have grown more skillful at formulating these questions in abstract and theoretical ways, but we deceive ourselves if we think the questions are any less important to us than they were to our ancient ancestors or that our answers produce any more certainty than those of three and four millennia ago. The basic differences between us and our ancestors is that we use a different language to describe our experience of the "powers" which impose themselves on our lives. In the words of Jay G. Williams:

> The polytheistic mythologizer, then, simply sought to describe the variety of powers which affect man. He was not just a superstitious man purveying silly stories about imagined deities. Rather he was seeking to describe as concretely and as carefully as possible the powers which actually exerted influence over the lives of human beings.[1]

Williams continued to describe the mythologizer:

> He does not try to speculate about what the world is like apart from man. He develops no abstract notions about being and becoming or

[1]Jay G. Williams, *Ten Words of Freedom: An Introduction to the Faith of Israel.* Philadelphia: Fortress Press, 1971, p. 32.

about atoms and the void, but instead, through the medium of poetry, tries to express the impact which the various powers of the universe make upon man, how they confront man, and how they are related one to another. The scientist may examine the meteorological causes of the sudden storm. The philosopher may search for principles for understanding change. But the mythologizer simply describes how the storm confronts man concretely and directly.[2]

In other words, myth is truth told not abstractly but concretely. The mythmaker may be a poet but he is not a superstitious fool; he has chosen to grapple with reality with a story rather than a schematic proposition. Ancient man's way of telling the truth was to become emotionally and poetically involved in it.

Man the mythmaker is trying to come to terms with the problem that man the scientist tries—perhaps unsuccessfully—to declare insoluble, for ancient man was puzzled by the greatest mystery of all: the problem of human existence. In Paul Ricoeur's words:

> . . . Still more fundamentally, the myth tries to get at the enigma of human existence, namely, the discordance between fundamental reality—state of innocence, status of a creature, essential being—and the actual modality of man, as defiled, sinful, guilty. The myth accounts for this transition by means of a narration. But it is a narration precisely because there is no deduction, no logical transition, between the fundamental reality of man and his present existence, between his ontological status as a being created good and destined for happiness and his existential or historical status, experienced under the sign of alienation. Thus the myth has an ontological bearing: it points to the relation—that is to say, both the leap and the passage, the cut and the suture—between the essential being of man and his historical existence.[3]

The myth, then, is a comprehensive view of reality. It explains it, interprets it, provides the ritual by which man may maintain his contact with it, and even conveys certain very concrete notions about how reality is to be used to facilitate mankind's life and comfort. The

[2]*Ibid.*, p. 33.
[3]Paul Ricoeur, *The Symbolism of Evil*, translated by Emerson Buchanan. Boston: Beacon Press, 1967, p. 163, paperback.

men who created the myths and lived by them were not superstitious, foolish savages. They were not our predecessors in the evolutionary process. Intellectually, their style was different from ours—at least when we engage in abstract, objective science. But even science as practiced by men like Claude Lévi-Strauss and his colleagues seems to be in the process of discovering that mythopoesis as thought and expression may be indispensable in any comprehensive and adequate system of human knowledge.

The most obvious place to look for influences on the formation of the Israelite mythology is Egypt, whence escaped some of the Hebrew tribes who later settled in Palestine and integrated both the Exodus and the Sinai experience into their religious symbol system. The most powerful factor in the life of the Egyptians was the Nile River. The regular rise and fall of the Nile flood made possible the development of the longest single culture in the history of the human race. R. A. F. MacKenzie summarizes the fundamentally optimistic religion of the Egyptians:

> Life in the Nile Valley was a good life, and any change must be for the worse. History had no real meaning for them; existence was fixed in an unchanging rhythm of natural forces, to which they were well adjusted and which seemed incapable of improvement. There is a Christian formula which, applied strictly to the welfare of man and his harmony with the cosmos, rather neatly expresses the Egyptian outlook and hope: "As it was in the beginning, is now, and ever shall be, world without end." That was the business of the gods. Let them see to it that the Nile flowed regularly through the land, that it punctually and adequately rose in flood each summer, that the crops were abundant, that the north wind continued to blow, that the sun-god in particular made his daily majestic progress from east to west across the sky. Then the Egyptian knew that the gods were in their heaven, all was right with the world.[4]

Egyptian religion, then, was essentially a fertility cult; and the gods, whose names changed at different times in Egypt's history, basically guaranteed the annual flow of the Nile and the annual fruit of the field. In the century before the Hebrews fled from Egypt, there was an attempt

---

[4]R. A. F. MacKenzie, S.J., *Faith and History in the Old Testament*. Minneapolis: University of Minnesota Press, 1963, p. 11.

on the part of the heretic king, Ikhnaton,[5] to establish a kind of monotheistic worship of the solar disk, Aten. There was much that was beautiful in the solar cult, as the following stanza from an Egyptian hymn makes clear:

> O creator of what the earth brings forth, Khnum and Amun of mankind! . . .
> Excellent mother of gods and man, good creator who takes the greatest pains with his innumerable creatures. . . .
> He who reaches the ends of the lands every day and beholds those who walk there. . . .
> Every land adores him at his rising every day, in order to praise him.[6]

But the cult of Aten did not last very long. Apparently it was a rather precious intellectual development presided over by a royal family whose sexual ethics were dubious. (Nefretete was apparently Ikhnaton's half sister. His nephew and successor, Tut-ankh-amun, married his own youngest daughter. However, since he suffered from the same physical deformities as his predecessor, he was probably impotent, so his daughters' paternity is in some doubt.) Certainly, the new cult never penetrated to the masses or even to the priests and scribes. It deteriorated rapidly and was thrust aside with the accession of Rameses I and a new dynasty.

Some of the Israelite tribes were undoubtedly in Egypt at the time of the rise and fall of the Aten heresy. If we assume that there is some historical truth in the legends of Moses' early life, he certainly would have had some access to the theories of Egyptian solar monotheism. Even apart from this, it is unlikely that the Israelites could have lived in Egypt without knowing the official religion of the land despite its limited acceptance. If one wishes to find origins of monotheism in the religious environment of the Israelites, one can also discover such beginnings in their own Semitic tradition.

It may be difficult to document the extent of Egyptian influence on

---

[5]W. F. Albright makes it clear that the king himself was probably incapable of effecting the artistic and religious innovations attributed to him. Anatomical studies of his mummy show that he was physically deformed and underdeveloped in such a way that his emotional and intellectual growth was very likely stunted. Perhaps his mother, Queen Teye, his wife, Nefretete (whose lovely face still haunts us), or some other favorite was the guiding force during his reign. (See William Foxwell Albright, *From the Stone Age to Christianity*. Baltimore: Johns Hopkins Press, 1940, pp. 164–65.)
[6]Albright, *op. cit.*, p. 166.

the Israelite religion, but there is no difficulty in tracing Babylonian imagery. In the famous story of Enuma Elish we have the Babylonian myth that explains the struggle between order and chaos in the universe. Marduk, the great Babylonian hero god, destroys the female sea monster, Tiamet, or "chaos." Out of the darkness of the monster he produces the orderly world. In the cosmogony of Mesopotamia, a god fights a battle over the powers of chaos and conquers them.

There can be no question that traces of this cosmogony can be found in the Old Testament. For example, in Psalm 89:8–11:

> Yahweh of hosts, who is like you?
>   Your power and your faithfulness are your attendants.
> You who rule over the raging of the sea,
>   when its waves rise you subdue them;
> you who crushed Rahab like a corpse,
>   with your strong arm scattered your enemies;
> to you belong both sky and earth;
>   the world and its contents, you have established them.

And in Isaiah 51:9–10, Yahweh is pictured as destroying the monster and providing order in the world just as Marduk did:

> Awake, awake, put on strength,
>   arm of Yahweh!
> Awake, as in the days of old,
>   the generations of ancient time.
> Was it not you that mangled Rahab,
>   that pierced the sea monster?
> Was it not you that dried up the sea,
>   the waters of the great Deep;
> that made the depths of the sea a pathway
>   for the redeemed to cross by?

Since this book is not primarily concerned with the Israelite creation story, there is no need to emphasize the obvious differences between Marduk's fighting the battle against chaos and ordering a preexistent reality and Yahweh calmly and effortlessly by a mere word bringing the whole of reality into being. Father R. A. F. MacKenzie summarizes the very considerable literature which has emphasized the different substance of the Babylonian myth and the Israelite myth.

The language, the conventions, the symbols belong to a fixed and familiar genre, which owes most to the myths of Babylonia. In no other terms could a cosmogony or anthropogony be acceptable or comprehensible to the mentality of early Israel. It had to tell a story; it had to embody its teaching in such images as a wonderful garden, a talking snake, a magic tree.

Secondly, no ancient literature offers any parallel to the profundity, the penetration, with which psychological and theological truths are here so plastically expressed. They all depend on the central figure of the story, who is neither the Man nor the Woman, still less the Snake, but the Creator-God himself. No explanation is attempted of his origin; he is there, given existence; the question is only to explain the origin of his creatures. He does not need them; but he creates them and then lavishes on them his benefactions. The only return he expects from them, and the only one they can give him, is their personal loyalty, their acknowledgment of the truth that they are his. When they deplorably fail in this acknowledgment, and attempt to dispense with him—when they break the covenant of loyalty and gratitude—their punishment is less than they deserve, is tempered with indulgent mercy, and does not completely separate them from him.[7]

The authors of the two versions of the creation with which the book of Genesis begins use some of the imagery of the ancient Middle Eastern environment in which they found themselves, but they put the imagery to entirely different purposes. The Yahweh the Israelites knew in the Sinai experience did not have to fight any battles with monsters. He created the universe; it was all his; and he ordered it to suit his own good pleasure. Marduk is more than a power, perhaps; he had something of a personality, though Father MacKenzie says that it was feebly developed. In MacKenzie's words, "He never issued forth as a complete personality, never stepped out of his function as patron and personification of the city, never really became more than a heavenly symbol of the earthly primacy of Babylon."[8] Yahweh has a personality that is all his own.

If one turns from the Babylonian to the Canaanite predecessors of the Israelites, one finds four different manifestations of divinity that

[7]MacKenzie, *op. cit.*, p. 55.
[8]*Ibid.*, p. 17.

are worth considering in our search to understand whence came Yahweh. First, there was in all likelihood some sort of vague "high god" lurking behind the pantheon of lesser deities. In Egypt, Babylonia, Greece, and virtually all of the other ancient kingdoms there loomed a high god in the background, but he was not important. Among the ancient Semite tribes, they were apparently ignored, probably because like the Greek Kronos they had become irrelevant. There is no record of any cult of the high god. One supposes that in any religion where there is some kind of tradition of a high god, there is the potential for monotheism, but if that god exercises no direct power in the world, the potential rarely becomes realized. There is, after all, no reason for dealing with a god who does not exercise power on earth and is incapable of responding to worship. Yahweh is a high god in the sense that he reigns over all the other gods, but he did not remain aloof. Quite the contrary, there were times when Israel found him altogether too much involved.

The ancestors of the Hebrews were devoted to fertility cults. The reproduction of their animals and, in a later age, the harvest of their fields were what kept them alive. William Foxwell Albright describes for us the fierceness of the Canaanite fertility worship:

> Goddesses of fertility play a much greater role among the Canaanites than they do among any other ancient people. The two dominant figures are Astarte and Anath, who are called in an Egyptian text of the New Empire "the great goddesses who conceive but do not bear," i.e., who are always virginal but who are none the less fruitful. . . . Another dominant characteristic of the Canaanite goddesses in question was their savagery. In Egyptian sources Astarte and Anath are preeminently goddesses of war; a favorite type of representation shows the naked goddess astride a galloping horse and brandishing a weapon in her right hand. In a fragment of the Baal epic . . . , Anath appears as incredibly sanguinary. For a reason not yet known she massacres mankind, young and old, from the seacoast to the rising of the sun, causing heads and hands to fly in all directions. Then she ties heads to her back, hands to her girdle, and wades up to her knees—yes, up to her throat—in human gore. The favorite animals of the Canaanite goddess were the lion, because of its ferocity, and the serpent and dove, because of their reputed fecundity.[9]

[9]Albright, *op. cit.*, pp. 177–78.

There are obvious traces of the fertility cult in the Israelite religion. As we shall see later on, sexuality is at the very core of the Israelite religion. The Feast of the Paschal Lamb, originally in a pastoral context, and the Feast of the Unleavened Bread, originally agricultural (both combined later to become the Passover), were in ancient times fertility rites marking the coming of spring. It was no accident that the two feasts were converted into a celebration of the covenant Yahweh made with his people, a covenant which was viewed as a symbolic marriage from which all life was to come. The power of fertility, then, was seen to be Yahweh's power and a manifestation of Yahweh's love.

Walter Harrelson describes how the Israelite religion took the themes and the symbols of fertility worship and transformed them completely to be utilized by the Israelites' new religious insight.

> Since Yahweh ruled alone as God, there was no place for a goddess as his consort. The motif of fertility, prominent as it is in the Old Testament, seems to have been rigorously curtailed in the official cult of Israel. But the sacred marriage of god and goddess, symbolically represented through acts of sacred prostitution at the shrines and vividly portrayed in the ritual accompanying the New Year's Day acts outside Israel, was one of the most significant cultic acts of the festival. The power of man and beast to produce progeny was renewed and restored through such ritual acts. In no other respect is the Israelite cultus more sharply to be distinguished from the cultus of her neighbors than in the way in which fertility is dealt with. While we have evidence in the Song of Songs and in a few other biblical references for sacred prostitution and for fertility rites at the various shrines, such evidence can best be accounted for by the assumption that various groups at different times brought into Israelite worship this prominent element in the worship of Israel's neighbors. The official Yahwistic cult probably did not allow for such practices.
>
> The theologians of ancient Israel came to understand Yahweh to be the creator of all fertility, providing within the natural order for a continuing appearance of life. It was Yahweh who at the time of creation had provided plants that produced their own seed, and animals and men who could procreate. The mystery of fertility was not eliminated, but the ritual acts and mythological explanations of those acts were slowly demythologized and fertility was drained of much of its numinous power in this way. God's good earth teemed with the power to produce living plants. On this good earth, means

were provided for the birth and sustenance of animals and men.

Fertility was related to the history of Yahweh's salvation also. The prophet Hosea depicted Israel as the bride of Yahweh, but this bridal imagery was connected with the covenant made between God and people (Hosea 2), a covenant once made in the wilderness and thenceforth binding upon all the people. The Deuteronomistic historian was bitter in his opposition to the practices associated with fertility (Deuteronomy 23:17–18). But this historian and tradition out of which he came saw in Yahweh's promise of a good land, flowing with milk and honey, rich in all the goods that made life full and complete, clear indication of Yahweh's control over the powers of fertility. This historian too, in his way, demythologized the mystery of fertility, relating it directly to the promise of Yahweh made to the forefathers, a promise in process of fulfillment, awaiting the End appointed by Yahweh when the entire earth would be transformed into a veritable paradise.[10]

Another Semite manifestation of the divinity was the tribal god, the deity whose particular responsibility and concern was with a given tribe. For the Semitic tribes this god (who frequently doubled as the male fertility principle) was thought of as living on a high mountain. The patriarchs of Israel knew this god as El Shaddai, the God of the Mountain or, as we suggested earlier in this book, the God of the Fruitful Mountain. This mountain deity is also a storm god, vaguely related to the Accadian Amurru, that is, the Western One, the god who is responsible for the storms in the west. The God of the Mountain, then, was responsible for fertility, the weather, and for protecting the tribe.

But the most important of all the Semite deities was the personal god of a man and his family. In Albright's words: "... the Hebrews, like their nomadic Semitic forefathers, possessed a very keen sense of the relationship between a patriarchal group (clan or family) and deity, who was therefore an actual member of the clan and could be addressed by a mortal kinsman as 'father, brother,' and even as 'kindred.' "[11]

One did not get involved in such intimate relationships with Aten or Amon-Re or Marduk or Astarte or even with El Shaddai. The personal

---

[10]Walter Harrelson, *From Fertility Cult to Worship*. Garden City, New York: Doubleday Anchor Books, 1970, pp. 54–55.

[11]Albright, *op. cit.*, pp. 186–87.

god of the family was different; he was someone you could talk to and understand. In the Genesis records we have indications of the various family gods: the Shield of Abraham, the Fear of Isaac (or maybe the word means the Kinsman of Isaac), and the Mighty One of Jacob. These were deities that were in some sense distinct from El Shaddai and were combined in later Israelite tradition to become the "God of the fathers." Since they didn't have a place of their own, the Semitic tribes were perhaps more inclined to develop a cult of the family god. After all, El Shaddai was on his mountaintop (wherever that was) and when you were a long way from the mountain, he might be interested no longer. The only god available, then, to fall back on was the one who was already a member of the family. Albright describes the two religious conceptions of the early Hebrews (both of which were characteristic of their environment) as follows:

> **1.** a dynamistic belief in an undefined but real blood relationship between a family or clan and its god(s);
> **2.** a recognition of the right of an independent man or founder of a clan to choose his own personal god, with whom he is expected to enter into a kind of contractual relationship. In combination, these ideas must have led to a form of tribal religion where both the collective and personal aspects of deity were present, the former in tribal acts of religious nature and the latter in individual worship.[12]

What the Sinai insight involved was the recognition that El Shaddai and the God of the fathers were really the same God, the ruler of fertility and natural powers but also a close personal friend. Yahweh is, of course, more than just a combination of El Shaddai and the God of the fathers. But it seems reasonable to guess that the insight which combined these two manifestations of the deity was the first movement in the religious quantum leap that produced the notion of Yahweh, which we shall explore in the rest of this book.

Two other elements of the pre-Sinai tradition deserve mention. The first is the religious idea of "promise," which the interpreters of the Sinai experience would develop into a theology of "covenant." It is generally agreed that the verses in Deuteronomy 26:5–9 represent one of the most ancient texts of the Israelite tradition (notice, for example, that there is no reference to Sinai in the brief kerygma):

[12]*Ibid.*, p. 189.

Then, in the sight of Yahweh your God, you must make this
pronouncement:

"My father was a wandering Aramaean. He went down into
Egypt to find refuge there, few in numbers; but there he became a
nation, great, mighty, and strong. The Egyptians ill-treated us, they
gave us no peace and inflicted harsh slavery on us. But we called on
Yahweh the God of our fathers. Yahweh heard our voice and saw our
misery, our toil and our oppression; and Yahweh brought us out of
Egypt with mighty hand and outstretched arm, with great terror, and
with signs and wonders. He brought us here and gave us this land, a
land where milk and honey flow.[13]

There is in this text only a dim implication of a promise from
Yahweh; that notion will be developed and become central in the
Hebrew people's reflection on their own experiences. In Gerhard von
Rad's description of the developments:

> . . . the era of the patriarchs as a whole is understood as the time of
> the promise, as an elaborate preparatory arrangement for the creat˙on
> of the people of God and for its life. What is new in this view is not
> the use of the idea of the promise in itself— . . . the promise of a
> land and of children already formed a part of the oldest traditions
> deriving from the patriarchal age. What is new is rather the theologi-
> cal employment of this twofold promise as a word of God which set
> in motion the whole of the saving history down to the conquest
> under Joshua. Behind this conception lies a prolonged and insistent
> reflection upon herself on Israel's part. The Israel which had become
> conscious of her peculiarity now felt the need to visualize how she
> came into being. Thus, there lies behind the patriarchal history in the
> Hexateuch a mighty amazement at the far-reaching preparations
> which Jahweh had made to summon Israel into being.[14]

Finally, the contemporary Israeli scholar Yehezkel Kaufmann points
out that Moses may very well have been a *kāhin,* an Arab pagan
prophet, frequently part of a family of seers. Moses, Aaron, and
Miriam were all spokesmen of God. Kaufmann illustrates the *kāhin*ic
nature of Moses by noting the similarity between the roles played by
him and Mohammed among their respective peoples:

[13]Deuteronomy 26:5–9, *The Jerusalem Bible.* Garden City, New York: Doubleday, 1966.
[14]Gerhard von Rad, *Old Testament Theology,* Vol. I. New York: Harper & Brothers,
1962, p. 170.

Like the *kāhin,* Moses is not connected with an established temple or cult. Whether Moses was ever himself a *kāhin* or not, he seems to have grown up among a family of such seers, and this surely affected him. The ancient Hebrew *kāhin*-clairvoyant was the social type that served as the vehicle of his appearance as prophet and leader. The case of Mohammed in later times is an instructive parallel. Mohammed was not an actual *kāhin,* but his visions and poetic expression grew out of the soil of *kāhin* prophecy. At first Mohammed feared that he was nothing but a possessed *kāhin,* until he became convinced that an angel was speaking with him. If the content of his prophecy was not *kāhin*ic, its form was, and his influence and acceptance among his contemporaries were founded on the current belief in *kāhin* prophecy. Similarly, the new message of Moses clothed itself in a form familiar to the people of those times. That a divine spirit revealed itself to a lonely seer was not an incredible thing; that this man should become a leader of his people was also not unheard of. And, since the ancient Hebrew seer was not bound by a specific cult or temple, Moses enjoyed the freedom necessary for the expression of a new idea. To this seer, however, there appeared not a familiar spirit but a supernal, omnipotent God. Moses returned to his people not a clairvoyant, but a messenger of God.[15]

Moses' experience of God in the burning bush and the various ecstatic or quasi-ecstatic experiences of the journey through the desert can be seen as having some correspondence to the experiences of the ecstatic prophets of the ancient Semitic tribes. Moses was both the last and the first: He was the last Hebrew *kāhin* or seer and the first messenger of God. It was Moses who told the disparate Israelite tribes the name Yahweh, and it was he who united them under that name with Yahweh's promise of redemption.

It is easy for us to feel greatly superior to all the ancient threads of cult and paganism that may be traced in early descriptions of Yahweh. We do not need a god to explain fertility or the weather, or to protect us against the vagaries of wandering in the desert; our family lives are quite secure without postulating a deity lurking on the hearth or in the attic. The powers of the universe no longer threaten us; on the contrary, we control many of them and are hopeful that someday we will control everything. We don't need El Shaddai or Marduk or Amon-Re or Aten or any other of those weird and rather frightening

[15]Yehezkel Kaufmann, *The Religion of Israel,* translated and abridged by Moshe Greenberg. Chicago: The University of Chicago Press, 1960, pp. 227–28.

characters. And while there is a certain charm in the Shield of Abraham or the Kinsman of Isaac, we don't see them as being much more relevant than patron saints or guardian angels. God may or may not be dead, but the gods long ago ceased to have any meaning for human life. Man, as Dietrich Bonhoeffer told us, has come of age, and gods are not only no longer required, they must be dismissed as a threat to man's freedom and his full humanity.

Well, maybe. But for all our wisdom, it could be questioned whether we have any more satisfactory ultimate answers to the mystery of human life and death than our nomadic predecessors did. Nor can we explain human sinfulness, the struggle between order and chaos, the tragedy and comedy, the glory and the disappointment of human existence any better than they could. And it turns out that our immense powers over the physical world frequently serve to pollute and destroy that world, and thus, eventually, to destroy us. Human existence may be a bit longer and somewhat less uncertain than it was in the thirteenth century before Christ, but it is still a chancy, problematic affair. If we no longer explain thunderstorms by such mythological creatures as giant vultures, we still are content to create mythological monsters like the "Establishment" to provide simple and comprehensible explanations for the problems that beset us. We desperately look for some functional equivalent of Marduk (preferably possessing Consciousness III) to slay the great monster Establishment, establish order, and make America green again.

Our sophisticated explanations of the weather, the fertility cycle, and the progression of the stars across the heavens do not provide either answers for the most fundamental questions man can ask or ethical norms which enable us to live with each other in peace and harmony and constructive respect for our physical world. That we are religiously superior to the Babylonians or the Egyptians or the Canaanites or the pre-Sinai Semites is not immediately obvious. We may know more than those ancient peoples about many things and we may have a higher degree of ethical sensitivity, but those problems which baffled them also baffle us, and man's tragic inability to live in peace with his fellows was surely no more destructive in their time than it is in ours.

Perhaps, after all, we ought to journey to the foot of Sinai to see what is going on there and to learn what this Yahweh god has to offer.

Chapter 3
Covenant

The covenant symbol contains the basic theme of the Sinai revelation and of the Jewish religion. By the covenant symbol Israel claimed a unique relation with the deity. In other ancient religions God was identified either with nature or with the society that worshiped him, but for Israel the relationship with God was the result of a positive action on the part of Yahweh himself. It was an action that demanded a positive response from Israel. It was not part of the necessary conditions of human existence, either natural or social, but was rather a relationship that was free on both sides.

The emergence of the covenant symbol may well be the most dramatic change in the whole history of human religions. Even the later cross and resurrection symbolism of Christianity are, in the final analysis, merely a further development of the covenant symbolism. Most of us, unfortunately, are so familiar with the idea of covenant (in the bad translation of the word into English as "testament") that we take the symbol for granted. It is part of religious environment, and we rarely pause to realize how striking and dramatic it is. God has made a covenant with us? Well, of course, so what else is new?

Undoubtedly, the idea of a covenant between God and his people had its origins in the pre-Sinai tradition of a "promise" made by the God of the fathers. The covenant symbol could be used to reorder and reinterpret the pre-Sinai traditions. But a covenant, as we shall shortly see, is far more than a promise, and Yahweh on Sinai is far more than a Kinsman of Isaac. A covenant (the Hebrew word is *berith*) was very

201

much part of the social life of the ancient desert countries. It was a treaty, a pact, an agreement that established a permanent relationship between those who entered the agreement. The parties to the relationship could be two individuals, two families, or two peoples. Covenants between kings, acting either as individuals or for their collective units, were especially frequent. The result of a covenant was an extremely close bond, indeed, one equivalent to the closest natural bond. Those who entered the covenant bound themselves under penalty of curse and destruction to fidelity and to assistance. There was a special word to describe responsibilities resulting from a covenant relationship; the word in Hebrew is *hesed*. We shall see more of this word in a later chapter. Father R. A. F. MacKenzie's comments on it are appropriate at this point: "Though impossible to translate adequately, since it combines the ideas of love, loyalty, and ready action . . . it may be rendered 'loving kindness,' or perhaps better 'covenant love.' "[1] God and Israel had made a pact freely entered into on both sides, which bound God and the people to one another in a most intimate sort of relationship, one in which he committed himself to act toward his people with loving kindness.

There are other symbols in the Old Testament which attempt to cope with Israel's experience of Yahweh. It is described as a father-son relationship, as a shepherd-flock relationship, as a king-subject relationship, a relationship among kin, and, especially, as a marriage relationship. However, it is generally agreed now that a covenant symbol is the basic one and the key to all the others, though as we shall see in a subsequent chapter, the very language used to describe the covenant makes the marriage symbol almost immediately obvious.

The last four books of the Pentateuch are, in effect, simply variations on the theme of the covenant between Yahweh and his people. There is some question as to exactly when the theme became central in Israelite religion. Men had a religious experience and then attempted to describe that experience to themselves and others through the use of whatever symbols were available to them, however inadequate those symbols might be. The apostles, for example, had a profound religious experience of Jesus both before and especially after Easter. Jesus himself was apparently rather reluctant to use any titles or labels. It was sufficient for him that he announced the kingdom of God, the

---

[1]MacKenzie, *Faith and History in the Old Testament, op. cit.,* p. 38.

kingdom of *his* Father. But the apostles had to describe and explain the experience, and so they fell back necessarily on the vocabulary of their time and spoke of "Messiah," "Son of Man," "Prophet," and "King." Similarly, the Israelites had an experience of Yahweh and found in the covenant customs of their time a symbol which told them and then others what the experience had meant. It is not easy for us to reconstruct the nature of that experience, but it had something to do with the collection of disparate and wandering tribes suddenly becoming conscious that they were a people, that God had made them a people, hence, inevitably, *his* people. They were a disorganized assemblage of nomadic tribes and suddenly they were one, not under any earthly ruler, only under Yahweh. Yahweh had intervened and made them a people; this intervention seemed to correspond to other agreements that kings made with their peoples, and so, for them, it was a covenant.

We wonder, of course, how long it took for this sense of union as a people to become translated into the covenant symbolism. Most scholars at this time are ready to concede that the covenant symbolism probably emerged in the desert even before the invasion and occupation of Palestine. Hence, the symbol probably came into being rather quickly after the event. The tradition with which we are especially concerned as recorded in the nineteenth and twentieth chapters of Exodus probably dates, though hardly in its present form, to the desert experience. The account of the covenant in the twenty-fourth chapter of the book of Joshua is more likely to be a version with its origin to be found in Palestine after the occupation.

The covenant, according to George E. Mendenhall, is a "suzerainty treaty by which a great king bound his vassals to faithfulness and obedience to himself."[2] Mendenhall traces evidence of the existence of covenants to Babylonia, Assyria, the Hittite Empire, and Egypt. There are generally six components in the Hittite covenant treaties that are available to us (Hittite covenant treaties are the only ones available of those ancient cultures):[3]

1. The preamble, which names the king and gives his background.
2. The historical prologue, which sets forth the previous relation-

---

[2]George E. Mendenhall, "Law and Covenant in Israel and the Ancient Near East," reprint from *The Biblical Archaeologist*, Vol. XVII, No. 2 (May 1954). Pittsburgh, Pennsylvania: The Biblical Colloquium, 1955, p. 26.
[3]Cf. *Ibid.*, pp. 32–34.

ship between the parties—generally in an "I-Thou" form of address.

3. The conditions imposed upon those with whom the covenant is made. For example, the prohibition of other foreign relations, the maintenance of peace, military assistance, and confidence in the king.

4. The requirement that the treaty be deposited in the temple and that it be read to the people periodically.

5. A list of the gods who witness the treaty.

6. Curses and blessings for violation and fulfillment of the treaty.

In addition there are other factors involved which generally did not appear in the written form of the treaty: the formal oath of obedience, a solemn ceremony which accompanied the oath and its renewal, and, finally, a procedure for taking action against a rebellious or unfaithful partner of the covenant.

The various descriptions contained in the books of Exodus, Deuteronomy, and Joshua of the covenant between Yahweh and his people parallel rather closely the Hittite treaty forms. There is a preamble ("I am the Lord, thy God"), a historical prologue ("who brought you out of the land of Egypt"), a set of stipulations (Exodus 20, the Ten Commandments), and a ceremony of oath and commitment of the sort described in Exodus 24:4–8. There is no explicit statement of curses and blessings, though surely the first commandment of the Decalogue implies that it would be just as well not to anger the "impassioned" Yahweh. Nor is there a list of gods as witnesses, but of course Yahweh doesn't need any other gods to witness the covenant which he enters. Finally, while there is no description of a requirement for periodic reading or deposit in the temple, we do know that every seven years in Palestine there was a great ceremony at Shechem renewing the covenant; there is every reason to assume that the present text of chapters 19 and 20 of Exodus were part of that liturgy of covenant renewal.

The account, then, of the beginning of Israel's relationship with Yahweh was designed, in all likelihood explicitly and consciously, to parallel the treaties by which individuals and tribes constituted themselves a people together with their king.

But it would be a mistake for us to think that the covenant with Yahweh was like any other covenant that existed in the ancient Middle East. For if it were simply a treaty binding together a number of tribes under a new leader, the covenant would have been with Moses; he was the leader of the tribes. But Moses did not present himself as the overlord with whom the covenant was made. On the contrary, he was the go-between—humble, frightened, and not always reliable. It was no earthly leader Israel dealt with, and it was no brilliant monarch who forged them as a people. It was Yahweh, the Lord of Creation. The stipulations he makes are totally different from those of other suzerains. He is not concerned about military might and pledges of assistance in time of war. He does not need these things; he demands the fidelity of his people, a fidelity evidenced by their loyalty to him. Nor are the stipulations he imposes on his people complicated or rigorous, not, at least, in their most primitive form. Other than fidelity to him, he demands nothing in the way of specific action; he only forbids behavior which is inappropriate for a people who are his followers: They shall not lie or steal or commit adultery. The way they choose to respond to his love is left to their own free determination. In later years, these stipulations would be expanded into a complex legal system, imposing a vast number of obligations, which purported to measure the amount of response to Yahweh's commitment. There was considerable resistance to this development. Deuteronomy may well have been the last effort to resist the rigid formulation of obligations. As von Rad says, "Indeed, in reducing all the profusion of the commandments to the one fundamental commandment, to love God (Deut. 6:5) and in concerning itself so earnestly with the inner, the spiritual, meaning of the commandments, Deuteronomy rather looks like a last stand against the beginning of a legalization."[4]

Even though Deuteronomy was a relatively late book in the Israelite religious tradition, there seems to be little doubt that the command "Hear us, O Israel, the Lord is our God, the Lord alone. You must love the Lord, your God, with all your heart and with all your soul and with all your mind" represents all the basic insight of the ancient Sinai covenant far more adequately than all the detailed legislation that later became part of "the Law." On Sinai Yahweh stipulated that his people love him in response to his love for them, and that was about all that he demanded. The legalism that emerged in later centuries was a manifestation of the apparently incurable human tendency to deal with God by keeping rules rather than by responding with love.

What the covenant symbol says, then, is that the God of Moses is not a mountain spirit but a free agent and Lord of the Universe. He

---

[4]Von Rad, *Old Testament Theology,* Vol. I, *op. cit.,* p. 201.

can convert an outlawed shepherd like Moses into a prophet; he can turn an unorganized group of slaves into a closely knit people. What is more, he can make this people his people, whose mission it was to bring his word to the noncovenant peoples. The whole nation was a priestly nation because the whole nation was called to bear witness to Yahweh's love. Israel was the light, the priest, and the sacrificial victim offered for the sins of all the people.

But the covenant was more than just a mystical event. It was a structured relationship between God and man; it was a record of the experience of a disorganized, disparate welter of tribes who were suddenly a people, and who could think of no other explanation for the emergence of their federation than the intervention of a proximate and passionate God, deeply, one might say, desperately involved in human affairs. He would use this people of his for worldwide, cosmic purposes.

Just as their social and political bond had nothing to do with royal families, religious hierarchies, and military confederations, so the mission of the people had nothing to do with flood control, defense, or the establishment of empires. The mission of Israel was to reveal Yahweh's love.

In form, then, the covenant was like other covenants, but in purpose, in content, and, above all, in origin it was completely different. Gerhard von Rad summarizes this use of the covenant theme to explain Israel and its history:

> Thus, in the final state of the Hexateuch, the following division of the traditional materials into periods emerges. God created the world and man. After the destruction of the corrupt human race by the Flood, God gave to a new human race laws for its self-preservation, and, in the covenant with Noah, guaranteed to it the outward continuance of the world and its orders. He then called Abraham, and in a covenant which he made with him, promised him a great posterity, a special relationship to God, and the land of Canaan. The first promise was fulfilled in Egypt, when the patriarchs grew into a people; the second was fulfilled at Sinai, when with a fresh covenant Israel received the regulations for her community life and her intercourse with God; and the third was fulfilled when under Joshua Israel took possession of the land of Canaan. Thus, by means of the covenant theology, the entire mass of the Hexateuchal traditions was set beneath a threefold arch of prophecy and fulfillment. Initially,

there were only the patriarchs: they are not yet a people, they have not entered into the promised special relationship with God, nor do they possess a land. Then, from the patriarchs a people comes into being; but it is without the special relationship with the land. And finally, in what is perhaps really the most exciting period, Israel, which is entirely ordered in one direction only, that is towards Jahweh, towards the last promise, the land of Canaan.[5]

The covenant, both the reality and the symbol, would suffer many vicissitudes in the history of Israel; for Israel would not always remain loyal to Yahweh. Furthermore, at a later time in its history, the covenant was thought to exist not so much between Yahweh and the whole people as between Yahweh and the Davidic monarchy. In most classical prophets, there is no reference to covenant—even though the idea of Yahweh's love for his people was still of the highest importance to the prophets. But in Jeremiah and Ezekiel the idea of covenant returns, and now it is suffused with that which was only implicit in the book of Exodus—the symbolism of marriage.

Furthermore, the covenant was presumed to be between Yahweh and the whole people; salvation was a collective, not an individual matter. Only very slowly and gradually did the idea emerge that Yahweh also had a relationship with individuals. Nevertheless, despite failures in the practice and understanding of the covenant, it remained, at least implicitly, the central theme of Israelite religion. It is also, though in a different fashion, the central theme of the Christian religion.

What are we to make of this whole affair? A group of Semitic slaves escapes from Egypt. Some of their neighbors have a peculiar experience near a sacred mountain in the desert. They come together with other tribes around a desert oasis. There is no political unity and no one strong enough to become king. Out of the sheer necessity of maintaining some sort of peace with one another an amphictyony emerges, that is, a tribal confederation based on a common religious belief. The tribes discover that this religious belief, centered on one God, isolates them from neighboring cultures and forges them into one people. They occupy Palestine, and to maintain their unity in new circumstances, they periodically recommit themselves to the covenant. Later, their religious thinkers begin to use the covenant theme to interpret past traditions and to explicate a universal mission for this

[5]*Ibid.*, p. 135.

rather grab-bag collection of tribes now transformed into a self-conscious nation.

A collection of remarkable events, perhaps, certainly unique in the ancient world. One could understand why the experience of becoming a nation would be so astonishing to the disparate tribal collectivity, particularly when it was simply a belief in one common God which merged them. Obviously, it had to be a powerful God to accomplish such a feat. The experience of becoming a people through common worship forced the Israelite tribes to postulate a rather extraordinary God, who intervened in their affairs to accomplish a unity they were unable to accomplish themselves.

The random probability of political, social, economic, geographic, and cultural forces in the desert south of Palestine had produced a situation in which the development of new religious symbols was both necessary and inevitable. The event was remarkable, nonetheless; and some of the men in it must have been religious and political geniuses.

And so, having analyzed the emergence of Yahwism and having provided reasonable and plausible explanations for it, we sophisticated modern men think that we understand what happened, and we turn our faces from Sinai with the firm conviction that we need not take Yahweh very seriously.

It never occurs to us that the emergence of a brilliant and dramatic new religious insight out of a historical, social, and cultural experience might be more marvelous than Yahweh's personally engraving letters on stone tablets ever could be. Nor does it occur to us that Yahweh's promise to the patriarchs and to the Israelites that they would reveal his name to all nations has turned out to be a remarkably accurate one. Finally, we see no reason at all why, after we have explained the social and cultural factors that produced Yahwism, it should also be necessary for us to ask the most fundamental religious question: Does the symbol of a God entering a treaty with his people tell us something about the nature of the Really Real that must be listened to and either accepted or rejected quite independently of our explanations of how this symbol came into being?

As we shall see in the subsequent chapters of this book, the Yahweh who appears on Sinai is far more than is required merely to hold a tribal confederation together. We learned moderns may persuade ourselves that we understand his origins and thereby we limit him by our categories, but unless we are the kind of men and women who believe that all reality can be contained in books in the library, we must still ask ourselves the question, what if Yahweh is real? What if the universe really is what the covenant symbolism tells us that it is? What if the Ground of Being, the fundamental creative principle, really does intervene in human events? What if he is a proximate and passionate God? What then?

To have explained more or less effectively the social and cultural origins of Yahwism does not provide answers to those questions. We may reject Yahweh because he is absurd and because the vision of reality which he symbolizes is much too good to be true. We may also dismiss him because a God who meddles in human affairs and converts a wandering collection of tribes into a people is an unworthy God. No God with any self-respect would bother with such affairs. (Hilaire Belloc says in his famous poem, "How odd/of God/to choose/the Jews." Such an oddity surely can't be a real God.)

Or we may choose to accept him. We may, to paraphrase slightly Schubert Ogden's comment about Jesus, say that any God who does not correspond to the covenant-making Yahweh is not a God worth believing in. But any response of acceptance requires an act of faith and commitment. Social and historical explanations, no matter how great the erudition in which they are rooted, will not provide sufficient grounds for a commitment of faith. The important question for faith is not how the Israelites came up with the notion that the deity is deeply involved in a love relationship with us; the important question is are we willing to commit our lives to the notion that basic Reality is loving? Anybody who thinks he can answer that question with historical or archaeological or cultural or scientific data simply doesn't know what he is talking about.

The fundamental insight of Israel is that God is *involved*. He is committed; he *cares* for his people. As we shall see later, he cares passionately for them. This insight so transcends the culture of the ancient Middle East, indeed, even the culture of our own time, that it still is literally incredible, literally too good to be true. It is rejected today or believed only weakly by those who profess it because its absurdity is too great for our cynical human intelligence.

There is, I think, more than just the notion that Yahweh is a God who *cares*. The Sinai symbolism tells us that he is a God who cannot help caring. He is involved because he has no choice but to be involved. I am certainly not denying the obvious fact that Yahweh is depicted as freely entering the covenant. Yet, once he has entered into it, he is portrayed as someone who is deeply concerned about its continuation. He does not need anything his people have to offer, but at the same time he desperately wants *them*. Francis Thompson's famous poem about God pursuing man like a hunting dog is grounded ultimately in the covenant symbolism. Yahweh *wants* his people. He is satisfied with nothing short of their whole devotion and their whole love. He demands their complete trust in him and will accept nothing less than that. Yahweh is not merely a God, not merely a Jewish God; he is a pushy Jewish God who refuses to leave his people alone. The idea seems ridiculous if not blasphemous. Why should God push his way into our lives? Why should he elbow himself into our condition? Why can't he leave us alone? Why does he bother with our silly problems? Why should he have bothered with the problems of those illiterate and unattractive desert tribes of the thirteenth century B.C.?

An aloof desert god on the mountain, a warm and cozy family god to whom you could talk, a fertility goddess who guaranteed the continuation of the food production cycles—all of these are reasonable gods. So, too, is Marduk, who keeps chaos at bay, and the storm gods, who must be propitiated by magic. They behave the way gods ought to behave. They are independent, stern, aloof, cold. While sometimes they have all too human frailties, their emotions are not really anthropomorphic. They may, as in Greece, get involved with attractive individuals of the opposite sex, but they don't really care much about the human race. Such gods are easy to believe in and easy to reject. When many moderns reject Yahweh, they think it is that kind of god they are rejecting. We who are supposed to depend on the Yahwistic tradition have been so inept in proclaiming it that men can reject him, thinking that they are, after all, rejecting someone rather like Marduk or Amon-Re or Zeus or even El Shaddai. To accept or reject such a god is relatively simple, particularly since neither decision will have any impact on our lives. But to reject Yahweh means to turn one's back on the idea that love beats at the core of the universe. It means to reject the best news the human race has ever heard. On the other hand, to accept Yahweh—well, that means a radical and profound transformation of everything we do, because it means we can lead lives of trust and confidence. It is much better to explain how the Israelite tribes came up with the idea of Yahweh or to argue interminably about whether he really exists or not; for if we can occupy ourselves with these questions, we do not have to take seriously the challenge of a deity who says to us, "I am the Lord, your God, who have brought you out of the land of Egypt . . . an impassioned God, showing kindness to the thousands of generations of those who love me."

As far as we are concerned, it would be much better if that sort of God had remained on Sinai and kept his strange, pushy ideas to himself.

Chapter 4

Preparation

On the third new moon after the Israelites had gone forth from the land of Egypt, on that very day, they entered the wilderness of Sinai. Having journeyed from Rephidim, they entered the wilderness of Sinai and encamped in the wilderness. Israel encamped there in front of the mountain, and Moses went up to God. The LORD called to him from the mountain, saying, "Thus shall you say to the house of Jacob and declare to the children of Israel: 'You have seen what I did to the Egyptians, how I bore you on eagles' wings and brought you to Me. Now then, if you will obey Me faithfully and keep My covenant, you shall be My treasured possession among all the peoples. Indeed, all the earth is Mine, but you shall be to Me a kingdom of priests and a holy nation.' These are the words that you shall speak to the children of Israel."

Moses came and summoned the elders of the people and put before them all the words that the LORD had commanded him. All the people answered as one, saying, "All that the LORD has spoken we will do!" And Moses brought back the people's words to the LORD. And the LORD said to Moses, "I will come to you in a thick cloud, in order that the people may hear when I speak with you and so trust you thereafter." Then Moses reported the people's words to the LORD, and the LORD said to Moses, "Go to the people and warn them to stay pure today and tomorrow. Let them wash their clothes. Let them be ready for the third day; for on the third day the LORD will come down, in the sight of all the people, on Mount Sinai. You shall set bounds for the people round about, saying, 'Beware of going up the mountain or touching the border of it. Whoever touches the mountain shall be put to death: no hand shall touch him, but he shall be either stoned or pierced through; beast or man, he shall not live.' When the ram's horn sounds a long blast, they shall come up unto the mountain.''

Moses came down from the mountain to the people and warned the people to stay pure, and they washed their clothes. And he said to the people, ''Be ready for the third day: do not go near a woman.''

On the third day, as morning dawned, there was thunder, and lightning, and a dense cloud upon the mountain, and a very loud blast of the horn; and all the people who were in the camp trembled. Moses led the people out of the camp toward God, and they took their places at the foot of the mountain.

Now Mount Sinai was all in smoke, for the LORD had come down upon it in fire; the smoke rose like the smoke of a kiln, and the whole mountain trembled violently. The blare of the horn grew louder and louder. As Moses spoke, God answered him in thunder. The LORD came down upon Mount Sinai, on the top of the mountain, and the LORD called Moses to the top of the mountain and Moses went up. The LORD said to Moses, ''Go down, warn the people not to break through to the LORD to gaze, lest many of them perish. The priests also, who come near the LORD, must purify themselves, lest the LORD break out against them.'' But Moses said to the LORD, ''The people cannot come up to Mount Sinai, for You warned us saying, 'Set bounds about the mountain and sanctify it.' '' So the LORD said to him, ''Go down, and come back together with Aaron; but let not the priests or the people break through to come up to the LORD, lest He break out against them.'' And Moses went down to the people and spoke to them. (The Torah, Exodus 19)

I suppose that most people who attended Catholic grammar school, high school, and college probably heard about the Ten Commandments at least once a year throughout the years of their education. It would be a safe wager that for practically all of us at no time in those sixteen years did we ever hear anything about Chapter 19 of the book of Exodus as a preparation for Chapter 20. Here were the ten rules God had laid down: no adultery, no bad thoughts, no lying, no stealing, no coveting (whatever in the world that was), go to Mass on Sunday (never mind that Sunday wasn't the sabbath), do what your parents, teachers, and pastor tell you to do, and, oh yes, don't use God's name irreverently, and don't fool around with spiritualistic séances under pain of excommunication.

If one assumes that the Decalogue is essentially an ethical code containing at least in embryonic form all the appropriate proscriptions of human behavior, then such an approach is perfectly valid. The rather bizarre events in Chapter 19 of Exodus—indeed, throughout the whole book—have nothing to do really with moral proscriptions. They are interesting accounts, filled with rather odd imagery; but since they don't tell us when "bad thoughts" turn from venial sins into mortal ones or how much work on Sunday violates the sabbath or how late you can come into Mass without having to hear it all over again, then there is nothing to be learned from Exodus about the meaning of the Ten Commandments.

In fact, however, the Ten Commandments are not basically an ethical code at all. In Gerhard von Rad's precise words, ". . . Israel certainly did not understand the Decalogue as an absolute moral law prescribing ethics: she rather recognized it as a revelation vouchsafed to her at a particular moment in her history, through which she was offered the saving gift of life."[1]

For many Catholics and, indeed, for many non-Catholic Christians, this notion is terribly difficult to accept. It involves a wrenching away from past preconceptions. All our lives we have believed that the Decalogue is the basic outline of a detailed code of moral behavior by which we earn life from God. Now we are told that that is not the way ancient Israel viewed it at all. It was rather an element in a saving gift that God offered to his people. The Decalogue is not an isolated moral code; it is part of a religious revelation. Our proper response to it is not so much to worry about keeping ethical rules as it is to believe in the gift of life that has been offered.

I am not suggesting that there is not an ethical component in the Sinai revelation, for there certainly is, though it is a very generalized one. The important point is that the component is a consequence of the covenant that Yahweh made with us; it is not the essence of that revelation. Yahweh did not appear on Sinai and say, "These are the rules of the game. You must keep them." He said rather, "I am the Lord your God. I love you and you will be my people. Since you are my people and since you have responded to my love with faith, these are some of the things that you will not do." Thus, honoring one's parents and not killing, stealing, or committing adultery are conse-

[1]Von Rad, *Old Testament Theology*, Vol. I. *op. cit.*, pp. 194–95.

quences and evidences of the acceptance of Yahweh's love. They are not a set of conditions imposed on us for earning that love. We keep the Commandments not because Yahweh has told us we must but because he loves us. Insofar as the Decalogue has an ethical component, it is an ethic that follows from God's love for his people. If our abstinence from murder, theft, adultery, and covetousness is not permeated by our faith in that love, then it has nothing to do with the Yahweh who spoke to us from Sinai.

I argued in my book *The Jesus Myth* that contemporary scripture scholarship, far from weakening religious faith, makes the dimensions of that faith much clearer. The interpretation that critical scholarship puts on chapters 19 and 20 of Exodus is a classic example of this point. It was easy enough for us to pull the Ten Commandments out of the religious context in which they are set and convert them into a detached ethical system when we didn't understand what the context was. But now the scripture scholars are quite certain that we have in chapters 19 and 20 (and at least segments of the subsequent chapters) a liturgical text, part of a worship service. Taking the Decalogue out of that text and trying to develop from it a philosophy of human life makes no more sense than to remove the Gloria from the Eucharistic liturgy and deducing from it the essence of Christianity.

It is now generally agreed that in Israel during the time of the judges, and indeed probably even after that time, the Decalogue was read as the midpoint of the solemn renewal of the covenant, a festival which occurred every seven years at Shechem. As Gerhard von Rad says:

> If Israel at regular intervals celebrated the revelation at Sinai in the cult in such a way, we can in turn deduce from this how ardently she looked on this divine revelation as momentous. With this proclamation of the divine law something came about for her, and that not only in the so-called "spiritual sphere"; rather did this conveyance to Jahweh have its consequences principally on the plane of concrete historical events. For in the cultic celebration Israel gave expression to the fact that the event which took place at Sinai had an undiminished importance for each age: it was renewed upon each succeeding generation: it was for all of them "contemporary."[2]

[2]*Ibid.*, p. 193.

The text that we have, then, in Exodus 19 and 20 is part of a celebration of a momentous experience of God, a celebration designed to recreate, so far as was possible, the awe and wonder of that primal experience. It is an experience of a righteous God, but his righteousness consists not so much in the punishment of sin as in the revelation of his loyalty and his community relationship with Israel. In the renewal of the covenant Yahweh is presented as asserting once more his *hesed*, his loving care of his people. As von Rad puts it, "There is no terror here, and no sighing, as if they were a burden, but only thankfulness and praise."[3] The purpose, then, of the festival of the covenant renewal was to put to the children of Israel once more the challenge of the past. Israel encounters Yahweh once again, and once again, it is forced to a decision about life and death. As von Rad says, "When Israel heard this utterance, she was put in a position from which there was no more going back."[4] Thus, the texts of Exodus 19 and 20, as we have them, are not so much a demand for moral integrity as they are a demand for faith. The renewal at Shechem was not an exercise in memory or an examination of conscience about moral failings; it was rather a renewed challenge to faith. The ceremony of which our text was a part did not ask Israel in effect, Do you commit sins? but, Do you still believe in Yahweh's love?

In this perspective the Commandments are but an outline, a Decalogue that, as von Rad says, "confines itself to a few basic negations; that is, it is content with, as it were, signposts on the margins of a wide sphere of life to which he who belongs to Jahweh has to give heed."[5] Von Rad continues:

> Within the sphere of life thus circumscribed by the commandments there lies a wide field of moral action which remains completely unregulated (after all, idolatry, murder, and adultery were not constant occurrences in Israel's everyday life). If then these commandments do not subject life in any way to a comprehensive normative law, it is more appropriate for us to say that in certain marginal situations they demand avowal of Jahweh, and this avowal consists precisely in abstaining from doing certain things displeasing to him.[6]

---

[3]*Ibid.*, p. 196. Von Rad adds, "Israel only encountered the law in its function as judge and destroyer at the time of the preaching of the prophets" (p. 196).
[4]*Ibid.*, p. 196.
[5]*Ibid.*, p. 194.
[6]*Ibid.*, p. 195.

Von Rad adds that at least ancient Israel, before ossification set in, understood what the Commandments meant.

> Israel regarded the will of Jahweh as extremely flexible, ever and again adapting itself to each situation where there had been religious, political, or economic change.... Jahweh's will for justice positively never stood absolutely above time for Israel, for every generation was summoned anew to hearken to it as valid for itself and to make it out for itself. This once again makes clear that the commandments were not a law, but an event, with which Jahweh specifically confronted every generation in its own *hic et nunc,* and to which it had to take up its position.[7]

What was said on Sinai in effect was that "there are moral implications of accepting Yahweh's love, and these negative commandments I give you specify some of the things that simply will not appear in the lives of those who love me. But how you respond positively to my love is something you yourself will know in different times and places if you really believe in me and my love."

The distinguishing characteristic of the followers of Yahweh is not so much that there are certain kinds of things they do not do as that they believe in his love and respond to it. Their response will have a profound effect on their behavior, but Yahweh is not attempting to describe that behavior in any detailed, legal code. That in later times Israel attempted to create a moral and legal system and identify it with the response to Yahweh's love only serves to measure how poorly that nation understood what transpired on Sinai. However, those ancient Israelites who gathered at the festival at Shechem realized that what happened on Sinai was only in a very minor sense concerned with morality and ethics. It was a reenactment of an experience of encounter with a powerful, passionate, and loving God.

There will continue to be, no doubt, vigorous resistance to the idea that Israel and Christianity are not basically ethical systems at all. Every religious symbol system has an ethical counterpart. As Clifford Geertz has observed, "Ethos is the reverse side of the coin of mythos." A myth tells you what is the nature of the Real and also inevitably implies how man behaves in response to the Real. The Sinai covenant symbol of a God who pushes himself into human events with

[7]*Ibid.,* p. 199.

a passionate love obviously prescribes an ethic by which men love one another. The way this love can or should be exercised is left largely to man's own freely determined, love-motivated decisions in time and place. Certain broad guidelines are set down. That is all Yahweh is going to do. Neither the religion of Sinai nor its offspring, the religion of Easter, contains anything in its basic symbol system which authorizes the elaboration of detailed, legalistic ethical codes, which can lay claim to specify the requirements of the Jewish or the Christian life. Yahweh wants faith and love. He has no need for legalistic codes.[8]

A friend of mine suggested that instead of a book about the Ten Commandments, it might be more appropriate to write one about the New Sins. (Ronald Knox once wrote a hilarious essay on the subject.)

It may be necessary for the Roman Catholic Church to have a code of canon law with more than two thousand rules (though that issue may be debatable), but it should be clear that the code of canon law is a set of bylaws of a particular time-space development of an institutional structure. Such a code has nothing to do with being a Christian and responding to God's love. Indeed, one could keep every single one of the canons (some are rather difficult to violate) and still not be a Christian at all. We modern men think we are categorically different from our predecessors. Everything we do has little continuity with the past, so obviously there have to be new sins, sins that only sophisticated, secular men who have "come of age" can commit. I would suggest that a development of a list of new sins would be simply one more exercise in legalism. For the Israelite and the Christian there is but one sin: not to love the Lord our God with our whole heart, our whole mind, and our whole soul. All other sins are merely the result of that basic infidelity. Refusing to respond to Yahweh's love is nothing new in the human condition. As Exodus tells us somewhat ruefully, even in the desert around Sinai, there were many gods to worship, indeed, to whore with. If good old Yahweh expected people to remain faithful for very long, the book of Exodus seems to say, he was disabused of that idea in short order.

---

[8] I abstain in this book from commenting on the elaborate requirements of Jewish law. Like the code of canon law, these can be justified, I suppose, by particular circumstances of time and space. I presume that no devout Jew, however, would equate the precise fulfillment of the law with the obligation to "love the Lord your God with your whole heart and your whole mind and your whole soul." In any case, a Catholic writer has more than enough to do to cope with the legalisms of his own religious community without offering unsolicited and uninformed advice to others.

Yahwistic religion, then, doesn't ask much from us in the way of detailed behavior. On the contrary, it asks merely one thing; but if we give Yahweh that one thing, we have given him everything. For if we really believe in his passionate *hesed,* then our whole lives will be transformed.

It is much easier to elaborate lengthy, detailed ethical and legal requirements than to turn ourselves over to Yahweh's *hesed.* The advantage of a legal code is that it can be fulfilled. It may require a great effort, tremendous sacrifice, vast amounts of pain and suffering, but at some point we will have kept all the requirements and honored all the rules and then we can sit back and relax and say, "See, Yahweh. We have done just what we were supposed to and now we are your true followers."

Yahweh will say, "Not yet." He will explain that holiness does not come from making and keeping rules. Whatever holiness we have comes from the fact that a God who loves us has chosen us for his people and we are by definition holy. We do not become holy through effort; we rather accept the holiness the Yahweh has tendered us. The trouble with Yahweh's gifts is that there are strings attached; once we have accepted them, we realize that what he wants from us is not specific legal and ritual behavior but our total lives, our complete response with enthusiastic trust, confidence, and love. There is no limit to the demands of Yahweh's love. He is not about to let us sit back and say we have done everything we had to. Like any passionate lover, Yahweh refuses to be content with the ritualization of a relationship. He will not accept from us what so many husbands and wives accept from each other—a "settling down" of a marriage relationship in which everything has become routine with no excitement or adventure. Yahweh wants a romance that never ends. He will be content with nothing less. That is the reason why the stipulations he sets down in his covenant are broad and general and deal only with the outermost limits of human morality. The Sinai covenant does not deny that ethical and moral systems are important for human life; it simply asserts that in the final analysis these systems have little to do with Yahwistic religion.

So, lists of sins, new or old, may well be useful and appropriate as guidelines to assist men in the difficult ethical judgments they must make in their lives. The follower of Yahweh is different in his approach to these ethical problems not because he has a different set of ethical principles but because his personality and his being is pervaded with a faith in God's love and a trusting confidence in his response to the fundamental graciousness of Reality. He does his best to make the proper ethical decisions according to the wisdom of ethical systems, but he makes them from the perspective of one who has been on Sinai and knows that Yahweh loves him. However, he understands that his moral decisions, while they may be influenced by his faith in God's love and are in their shape and style a consequence of that love, are not to be confused with the love of Yahweh, much less to be thought of as a means of earning that love. Yahweh once complained to Israel that he was appalled by the stench of their sacrifices. I should think he would equally be appalled by the stench of our ongoing efforts to convert the revelation of his love into a rigid moral code.

It is now possible to understand the importance of a rather strange event described in Chapter 19 of Exodus. God calls Moses to Sinai; he points out that he brought Israel out of Egypt as on eagle's wings; he informs him that they are a treasured possession among all the peoples, a kingdom of priests and a holy nation. Then the Lord informs Moses that he will come in a thick cloud and the people will hear his voice. Moses tells the people that they must purify and discipline themselves in preparation for the holy event that is to occur. Finally, after three days of waiting, there is thunder and lightning and clouds; the mountain trembles and there is fire and a blaring horn. The people are warned not to draw close to the mountain. It is a marvelous and awful event; great things are afoot: The Lord is about to utter his covenant!

One can well imagine that the participants of the Shechem festival thrilled at the retelling of the story. The drama of the imagery must have stirred their hearts and made their blood beat faster. A great religious event was about to occur once again.

The nineteenth chapter of Exodus makes it as clear as possible to us that we are dealing with a mighty and profound religious experience. If after all the thunder and lightning, the trembling of the earth, and the sound of the horn, the best Yahweh was able to do was to tell people not to commit adultery, bear false witness, kill, and steal, then he would have produced one of the great anticlimaxes in all history. What was revealed in the twentieth chapter of Exodus was the revelation of God's loving care for his people, a *hesed*. God made a covenant, a *berith*, and the world was changed.

Chapter 19, then, tells us what is happening. It is both an anticipation of and a commentary on Chapter 20. It makes clear for anybody who has eyes to read that the principal event in Chapter 20 is a revelation of a commitment of Yahweh to his people. Anything else that occurs there can only be understood as part of that commitment. It is simply impossible in the light of the anticipation and commentary contained in Chapter 19 to view Chapter 20 or any part of it as being fundamentally the establishment of an ethical system or a moral law. God revealed not the law but himself.

Before we turn to the actual content of that revelation there are two problems that must be noted. First, relatively little has been said thus far about the "monotheism" of Hebrew religion, mostly because it appears now that monotheism is less an important part of the Israelite religion than we had once thought. In the early years, there was no explicit denial of the existence of other gods besides Yahweh. Israel was to stay away from those "strange gods," who were obviously inferior to Yahweh, and Israel's principal concern was to be the existence of Yahweh, not the nonexistence of other gods. The important thing in the Sinai revelation was not the proclamation of one god, but rather the proclamation of the kind of God the God of Israel really was. In later years, the Israelites would deduce that if Yahweh is that kind of God, the other gods or "powers" are of trivial importance and cannot be said to exist in the same way Yahweh exists. Was Moses a monotheist? In some sense, of course, he was, but the important thing is not whether or not he was a monotheist, but what kind of monotheist he was. William Foxwell Albright answers the question:

> If by "monotheist" is meant a thinker with views specifically like those of Philo Judaeus or Rabbi Aquiba, of St. Paul or St. Augustine, of Mohammed or Maimonides, of St. Thomas or Calvin, of Mordecai Kaplan or H. N. Wieman, Moses was not one. If, on the other hand, the term "monotheist" means one who teaches the existence of only one God, the creator of everything, the source of justice, who is equally powerful in Egypt, in the desert, and in Palestine, who has no sexuality and no mythology, who is human in form but cannot be seen by human eye and cannot be represented in any form—then the founder of Yahwism was certainly a monotheist.[9]

[9]Albright, *From the Stone Age to Christianity, op. cit.,* p. 207.

The important thing about Yahweh, then, is not that he was the only God but rather that he was a God who made a covenant with his people.

The other question is whether Israel's God is anthropomorphic. Many moderns are deeply offended by the attribution of human characteristics to gods. They are willing to believe in God, perhaps, but certainly not in a "personal" God. Some social researchers delight in pointing out the decline in our belief in a personal God. (Researchers always seem to assume, incidentally, that there was once a time of greater belief in a personal God than there is now.) The trouble with the use of the word "personal" as an adjective modifying the word "God" is that the meaning is not at all clear. For many of us, perhaps most of us, "personal" means "human." No one, not even the wildest Israelite anthropomorphist, believed God was human in the sense we are human. The issue is not whether God is "like us" but whether the Ultimate Reality is capable of entering into a love relationship with those of us who are less than Ultimate.

There is a certain kind of pseudo-sophisticated agnosticism that is willing to concede some sort of divine principle yet denies that that "divine principle" could possibly be concerned with us. This position obviously goes back before Sinai and turns God either into the indifferent Kronos or high god or into some mountain cousin of El Shaddai, who loses track of his people when they get too far away from his own mountain. If one is willing to postulate some fundamental principle in the universe, it escapes me why that fundamental principle is to be denied the capacity for love. I suppose that it is a great leap of faith to admit that there is a Real. I should think it would be a relatively less important leap to concede that the Real is capable of love.

My problem is trying to figure out how anything can exist. By rights, it seems to me, there should be nothing. Once something is, especially such a creature as man, capable of knowledge and love, then I see no great intellectual problem in accepting the notion that love is at the core of Reality. How come man? Once there is man, then God is rather less of a problem. But that is an intellectual and philosophical statement of the issue. The profound difficulty with a God who loves is not intellectual at all but religious. One can readily concede the plausibility of his existence and still be offended and frightened by the necessity of responding to him.

Bishop Robinson in his *Honest to God* (misunderstanding Paul Tillich, I think) takes serious offense at anthropomorphic notions of God. I fail to understand how a man can cope with God in any other than human terms. If we are to speak of him at all, we must speak of him with human words. (And presumably we can dismiss as religiously irrelevant those logicians who wish to refuse us permission to speak of God. The human race will simply not take such prohibition seriously.) When man postulates that God is Thou, he does so because there is no other way to speak of him. He understands that God is a Thou in a different way than his human friends are thou, yet he is asserting his conviction that God loves. How can anything that is Thou not love?

My friend Gregory Baum, in his extraordinarily insightful and helpful book *Man Becoming,* suggests that thinking of and speaking to God as a Thou is not appropriate because it imprisons God in our own conceptions. I do not see how else one can be faithful to the Jewish and Christian traditions of a loving God unless one thinks of him, analogously at least, as a Thou. If Father Baum can produce a set of categories and symbols by which we can think of ourselves as dealing with a loving Reality which need not be called Thou, I will happily accept them. Until such symbols are produced, then I am afraid that most of us have no other choice than to conceptualize, however inadequately, the ultimate loving Reality as a Thou.

One theologian put it to me this way: "It would not be appropriate to deny to the deity perfection of those human characteristics that we speak of as knowledge and love." I suppose that this is a precise and legitimate theological way of putting it, though as poetry and symbol, the theologian's words are worthless; but once he is prepared to concede that it would be improper to deny to God the perfections of those things in man that we call knowledge and love, the theologian is really no different from the ancient Israelite arguing with Yahweh. The latter's sense of poetry and imagery may be far more exuberant, but it does not follow that the former really knows anything more about God.

It would be arrogant of us to assume that the simple anthropomorphisms of the ancient Israelite tribesman were either naïve or ignorant. He was no more unaware, I daresay, than is the modern theologian that we can only speak analogously of God. The cultural context in which he found himself made it less necessary, perhaps, than today constantly to remind all present that the vocabulary was analogous. On the other hand, neither was he quite as likely as some modern theologians to get so hung up on the use of words as to become incapable of saying anything about God.

I am certainly not denying that there are dangers in anthropomorphic categories. They have led to abuses in the past and they will probably lead to more in the future; but because some people misunderstand poetry and insist on taking it literally, it does not follow that poetry should be abolished or that we should conclude that poetic imagery tells us nothing about Reality.

William Foxwell Albright has some appropriate comments to make on this subject, too:

> ... it cannot be emphasized too strongly that the anthropomorphic conception of Yahweh was absolutely necessary if the God of Israel was to remain a God of the individual Israelite as well as of the people as a whole. For the limited few who are natural mystics or have learned to employ certain methods to attain ecstatic state, the theological concepts attached to deity matter relatively little; there is a striking parallelism between the psychology of mysticism in Judaism, Islam, Buddhism, and Christianity. For the average worshiper, however, it is very essential that his god be a divinity who can sympathize with his human feelings and emotions, a being whom he can love and fear alternately, and to whom he can transfer the holiest emotions connected with memories of father and mother and friend. In other words, it was precisely the anthropomorphism of Yahweh which was essential to the initial success of Israel's religion. Like man at his noblest the God of Israel might be in form and affective reactions, but there was in Him none of the human frailties that make the Olympian deities of Greece such charming poetic figures and such unedifying examples. All the human characteristics of Israel's deity were exalted; they were projected against a cosmic screen and they served to interpret the cosmic process as the expression of God's creative word and eternally active will.[10]

Since I am committed to the notion that symbols and poetry are not merely effective means of describing Reality but are in fact the only effective means of describing the Ultimate Reality, I shall not hesitate to use anthropomorphic terminology throughout this book. I would

[10]Albright, *op. cit.*, p. 202.

remind all nit-picking theologians that I am well aware that I am using my language analogously.

But I am further aware that no matter what one's language, the fundamental theme of the Sinaitic revelation is that God is a loving God. The trouble with our anthropomorphic imagery is not that it leads us to believe in a love that is not there, but rather that no matter how brilliant or daring it may be, it is much less than adequate as a description of the length and breadth, the height and the depth of Yahweh's love for his people.

Chapter 5
I and Thou

"I am Yahweh your God who brought you out of the land of Egypt, the house of bondage. You shall have no other gods besides me."

Verses 2 and 3 of Chapter 20 of the book of Exodus are the preamble and the historical prelude characteristic of the covenant form. Yahweh identifies himself and he describes his vast relationship with his people. Both the identification and description are starkly simple, bald statements of fact. So simple are they that we may miss the point that they contain the core of both the Jewish and the Christian religious traditions. Indeed, the whole of Yahwism is summed up in the first phrase, "I am Yahweh your God." It affirms that there is an I-Thou relationship between God and his people, a relationship of personal intimacy in which the people belong to Yahweh, but Yahweh also belongs to the people. This is the whole story of both Judaism and Christianity. All else is commentary and explication.

How many times as children did we recite the Ten Commandments, mindlessly repeating the sentence "I am the Lord thy God; thou shalt not have strange gods before me." It was an easy commandment to remember because it had a certain rhythm to it, and we could confidently begin our recitation because we knew we wouldn't stumble over the first component of the Decalogue. We didn't know exactly what it meant, of course. We were told that we shouldn't build idols, an explanation which didn't quite make sense considering all the statues in our churches. No one taught us that it was the central expression of our faith—mostly, I suppose, because none of our teachers knew it was the central statement of our faith. Nor did it seem to occur to anybody why God could possibly care whether we took strange gods seriously. Why should he be offended if we went to an occasional fortuneteller or had someone read our tea leaves?

As we shall see in more detail in the next chapter, we are not to seek after other gods precisely because such idolatry violates the intimate love of the covenant relationship. Yahweh has pledged himself to be our God and that relationship of intimate love is violated if we have other gods instead of him. The "command" part of the first commandment flows from the nature of an intimate relationship, and the important part of these verses of Exodus is not the command but the description of the relationship from which the command flows.

Professor J. G. Williams beautifully describes what Yahweh's commitment in verse 2 means:

> It means that the Power which governs the planets in their courses, causes water to evaporate, the vegetation to blossom, makes the human heart beat and the human mind think is a power who can and does identify himself with the word "I." This "I" does not simply stand over against us; this "I" surrounds us, envelops us, constitutes us. This is the "I" which cannot help but disturb, indeed overwhelm us if it is heard at all.[1]

This "I" who envelops and surrounds us and proclaims himself our God tells us his name is Yahweh. There has been endless scholarly debate about the meaning of the name. Today, there seems to be some broad agreement that it is a fragment of a longer name, Yahweh-Aser-Yiweh, in Albright's translation, "He who brings into being whatever comes into being." Therefore, in its root meaning, the name proclaims Yahweh as the all-powerful creator. However, we should remember that the Israelites were not a metaphysical people. They certainly could not understand the idea "the essence of God is his existence." Nor were they sophisticated in etymology; they may have had only vague notions of all the implications of the name by which they called upon God. We must be content with the conclusion that the name "Yahweh" indicated to them that their God was a powerful God;

[1] J. G. Williams, *Ten Words of Freedom: An Introduction to the Faith of Israel.* Philadelphia: Fortress Press, 1971, p. 70.

indeed, more powerful than all the other gods—so powerful in fact that he could legitimately demand that all other inferior gods be ignored. A speculative philosophy of creation was as unlikely in the desert as was a speculative theory of monotheism. It was sufficient for the Israelites to know that Yahweh dominated *everything*. Their later adaptation of the Babylonian cosmological materials indicated how decisively superior they believed Yahweh's power was to all the other powers in the universe. Yahweh was the all-powerful creative force. If we asked the desert tribes whether he created *ex nihilo* they would not have known what we were talking about, and they wouldn't have much cared.

We do not fully appreciate the heroism in the covenant religious conception. It meant that the people who were committed to the pact with Yahweh would abandon forever dealing with the "powers" now that they belonged to The Power. They could no longer bargain with the rain gods or the fertility gods or the tribal gods. Now they must commit themselves to trusting totally the Power on which all other powers in the universe depend, realizing that they are depending totally on the gracious love which he has promised them. Walter Harrelson describes Yahweh's followers:

> If God will tolerate no rivals, how can a people take account in their worship of the presence of the dark powers that threaten to destroy them? What is to be done with the indubitable power of evil, of malevolence, of rottenness in this world? Must God be blamed for it all? Or must man bear all the blame if God is freed of responsibility? Worship clearly represents a response to the Holy that is designed, among other things, to ward off the powers of chaos and destruction. How is one to turn the power of evil into power for man's good, if in principle demonic forces and other gods are denied existence? Israel's theological answer—clearly not accepted by all members of the community at all times—is that Yahweh brings evil upon his people for their faithlessness to his will, and the same faithlessness affects the natural order. Worship of God, then, offers a means for evoking God's power to forgive, to restore, to heal a broken humanity and a wounded earth. And fidelity to God's will in daily life offers the means for the earth's continuing fruitfulness and for God's continuing blessings upon his people.[2]

²Walter Harrelson, *From Fertility Cult to Worship, op, cit.,* p. 13.

In the desert, Israel encountered the Holy, the Totally Other, the Reality simultaneously fascinating and terrifying. All religious experiences are an encounter of some sort with the Holy, but the Holy as perceived by Israel was both more powerful and more benign than that encountered in any religious experience before or since. (I here presume that the Easter experience of the apostles is fundamentally a continuation of Sinai.) The Holy was not passive, was not withdrawn; rather, it was creative, active, demanding, involved. It was an incredibly dynamic power, but a power that was essentially loving. The depths and the power of this holiness are, as Gerhard von Rad tells us, essentially manifested in the first commandment in "Jahweh's curt claim . . . to be the only God worshiped."[3] Von Rad continues:

> This intolerant claim to exclusive worship is something unique in the history of religion, for in antiquity the cults were on easy terms with one another and left devotees a free hand to ensure a blessing for themselves from other gods as well.[4]

Israel's choice of the covenant symbolism to convey its experience of the Holy made it inevitable that the exclusivity of worship became a central theme of Israelite religion. Note well what happens. Israel had an experience of the Holy, an experience of Reality that was almost unbearably powerful. So powerful—and so good—is this Holy perceived to be that the human response to it is to say, "There can be no other Holiness besides this Holiness." God did not create the covenant symbolism, Israel did. The covenant idea described the nature of Israel's relationship with the Holiness in terms of a demand for exclusive love. The covenant was the tool Israel chose to describe primarily for itself but also for others the nature of the Holy it encountered. Speculative monotheism and the doctrine of creation *ex nihilo* would come later, much later. Even the beautiful marriage symbolism would come somewhat later. In its rawest and most primitive form, Israel experienced Power—Power that was both overwhelming and gracious, Power demanding response. In the time and place in which Israel found itself, an exclusive I-Thou relationship, precluding any dealing with lesser gods, was the best symbolism

[3]Von Rad, *Old Testament Theology,* Vol. I, *op. cit.,* p. 207.
[4]*Ibid.,* p. 208.

available for describing what had happened. More than that must be said, however. For all our progress, we may not have come up today with a better symbolism of man's relationship to God than that contained in the insight that God is an "I" who wishes to relate to us as "Thou."

If we understand that the whole history of Israelite thought is an attempt to clarify the experience of the powerful but benign Yahweh, we can then begin to make some sense out of the Old Testament religious poetry, which frequently seems so peculiar to us. Thus, Yahweh continues to dominate creation:

> Lift your eyes and look.
> Who made these stars
> if not he who drills them like an army,
> calling each one by name?
> So mighty is his power, so great his strength,
> that not one fails to answer. (Isaiah 40:26)

> I it was who made the earth,
> and created man who is on it.
> I it was who spread out the heavens with my hands
> and now give orders to their whole array. (Isaiah 45:12)

He makes both the dawn and the darkness:

> For he it was who formed the mountains, created the wind,
> reveals his mind to man,
> makes both dawn and dark,
> and walks on the top of the heights of the world;
> Yahweh, God of Sabaoth, is his name. (Amos 4:13)

> It is he who made the Pleiades and Orion,
> who turns the dusk to dawn
> and day to darkest night.
> He summons the waters of the sea
> and pours them over the land.
> Yahweh is his name. (Amos 5:8)

He measures the water in the hollow of his hand:

> Who was it measured the water of the sea in the hollow of
>   his hand

and calculated the dimensions of the heavens,
gauged the whole earth to the bushel,
weighed the mountains in scales,
the hills in a balance? (Isaiah 40:12)

He gives breath and spirit to those who walk the earth:

Thus says God, Yahweh,
he who created the heavens and spread them out,
who gave shape to the earth and what comes from it,
who gave breath to its people
and life to the creatures that move in it: (Isaiah 42:5)

If Yahweh is superior to the gods of fertility, it still must not be
thought that he is not involved in fertility. On the contrary, fertility is
Yahweh's gift to men. It is not Baal but Yahweh who bestows the
fruits of the soil:

She would not acknowledge, not she,
that I was the one who was giving her
the corn, the wine, the oil,
and who freely gave her that silver and gold
of which they have made Baals.

That is why, when the time comes, I mean to withdraw my
    corn,
and my wine, when the season for it comes.
I will retrieve my wool, my flax,
that were intended to cover her nakedness;
so will I display her shame before her lovers' eyes
and no one shall rescue her from my power.
I will lay her vines and fig trees waste,
those of which she used to say,
"These are the pay my lovers gave me";
I am going to make them into thickets
for the wild beasts to ravage.
I will put an end to all her rejoicing,
her feasts, her New Moons, her sabbaths
and all her solemn festivals.
I mean to make her pay for all the days
when she burnt offerings to the Baals
and decked herself with rings and necklaces

to court her lovers,
forgetting me.
It is Yahweh, who is speaking. (Hosea 2:10–15)

He, further, is the one who is responsible for the progeny of men and beasts and fruit of the field:

He will love you and bless you and increase your numbers;
he will bless the fruit of your body and the produce of
your soil, your corn, your wine, your oil, the issue of your
cattle, the young of your flock, in the land he swore to
your fathers he would give you. (Deuteronomy 7:13)

They will come and shout for joy on the heights of Zion,
they will throng towards the good things of Yahweh:
corn and oil and wine,
sheep and oxen;
their soul will be like a watered garden,
they will sorrow no more. (Jeremiah 31:12)

He gives and withholds rain:

He will send rain for the seed you sow in the ground,
and the bread that the ground provides will be rich
and nourishing. Your cattle will graze, that day, in
wide pastures. (Isaiah 30:23)

And it is most sure that if you faithfully obey the
commandments I enjoin on you today, loving Yahweh your
God and serving him with all your heart and all your
soul, I will give your land rain in season, autumn rain
and spring, so that you may harvest your corn, your wine,
your oil; (Deuteronomy 11:13–14)

Come, we must fear Yahweh our God
who gives the rain, the early rain
and the later, at the right time of year,
who assures us
of weeks appointed for harvest. (Jeremiah 5:24)

But while Yahweh is responsible for the blessings of fertility, he is himself superior to the process. Yahweh dominates fertility; he is not a fertility god.

It is no longer thought that Yahweh was originally a storm god, though surely there were storm gods in the Israelite religious background. Nevertheless, the Israelites thought of the power of Yahweh when they experienced the tremendous natural forces of storm, earthquake, and volcanic eruption.

> Then the earth quivered and quaked,
> the foundations of the mountains trembled
> (they quivered because he was angry);
> from his nostrils a smoke ascended,
> and from his mouth a fire that consumed
> (live embers were kindled at it).
>
> He bent the heavens and came down,
> a dark cloud under his feet;
> he mounted a cherub and flew,
> and soared on the wings of the wind.
>
> Darkness he made a veil to surround him,
> his tent a watery darkness, dense cloud;
> before him a flash enkindled
> hail and fiery embers.
>
> Yahweh thundered from heaven,
> the Most High made his voice heard;
> he let his arrows fly and scattered them,
> launched the lightnings and routed them.
>
> The bed of the seas was revealed,
> the foundations of the world were laid bare,
> at your muttered threat, Yahweh
> at the blast of your nostrils' breath. (Psalm 18:7–15)
>
> the earth rocked,
> the heavens deluged at God's coming,
> at the coming of God, the God of Israel.
>
> God, you rained a downpour of blessings,
> when your heritage was faint you gave it strength;
> your family found a home, where you
> in your goodness, God, provided for the needy. (Psalm 68: 8–10)
>
> Eloah is coming from Teman,
> and the Holy One from Mount Paran.
> His majesty veils the heavens,
> the earth is filled with his glory.

His brightness is like the day,
rays flash from his hands,
that is where his power lies hidden.

Plague goes in front of him,
fever follows on his heels.

When he stands up he makes the earth tremble,
with his glance he makes the nations quake.
Then the ancient mountains are dislodged,
the everlasting hills sink down,
his pathway from of old.

I have seen the tents of Cushan terrified,
the pavilions of the land of Midian shuddering.

Yahweh, is your anger blazing against the rivers,
or your fury against the sea,
that you come mounted on your horses,
on your victorious chariots?

You uncover your bow,
you ply its string with arrows.

You trench the soil with torrents;
the mountains shiver when they see you;
great floods sweep on their way,
the abyss roars aloud,
high it lifts its hands.

Sun and moon stay in their houses,
avoiding the flash of your arrows,
the gleam of your glittering spear.

Raging, you stride the earth,
in anger you trample the nations.

You have marched to save your people,
to save your own anointed;
you have beaten down the wicked man's house,
bared its foundations to the rock.

With your shafts you have pierced the leader of his warriors
who stormed out with shouts of joy to scatter us,
as if they meant to devour some poor wretch in their lair.

You have trampled the sea with your horses,
the surge of great waters. (Habakkuk 3:3–15)

"Yahweh, when you set out from Seir,
as you trod the land of Edom,
earth shook, the heavens quaked,
the clouds dissolved into water.
The mountains melted before Yahweh,
before Yahweh, the God of Israel. . . ." (Judges 5:4–5)

But Yahweh is not only powerful, he is also wise. Thus, for example, in Isaiah 28:23–29, Yahweh's wisdom in directing the natural cycles is extolled:

Listen closely to my words,
be attentive and understand what I am saying.
Does the ploughman do nothing but plough
and turn the soil and harrow it?
Will he not, after he has leveled it,
scatter fennel, sow cummin,
put in wheat and barley
and, on the edges, spelt?
He has been taught this discipline
by his God who instructs him.

For fennel must not be crushed,
nor a drag be rolled over cummin;
fennel must be beaten with a stick,
and cummin with a flail.
Does a man crush wheat? No;
he does not thresh it endlessly.
When he has rolled the drag over it
he winnows it without crushing it.
This too comes from Yahweh Sabaoth,
whose advice is always admirable,
whose deeds are very great.

And in Job 5:23, the covenant theology is applied even to Yahweh's relationship with nature:

You shall have a pact with the stones of the field,
and live in amity with wild beasts.

But from the point of view of the Israelites, far more impressive than Yahweh's manifestations of his power and wisdom in the works of nature was his self-revelation in his dealing with his people. For as the second half of verse 2, Chapter 20, of Exodus identifies him, he is Yahweh, who has brought them out of Egypt, the house of bondage. Some of the mightiest hymns of the Old Testament describe the marvels of God's intervention on behalf of his people. We used to recite them mindlessly: Psalms 77, 78, 105, and 106. They were strange, slightly pompous oriental poetry. We did not realize that we were dealing with liturgical hymns that were, if not actually part of the ceremony of covenant renewal, at least a celebration of God's covenant with his people. In Psalm 77, verses 13–20, for example, the Israelites sang of their primordial religious experience of a God who was involved with them.

> God, your ways are holy!
> What god so great as God?
> You are the God who did marvelous things
> and forced nations to acknowledge your power,
> with your own arm redeeming your people,
> the sons of Jacob and Joseph.

> When the waters saw it was you, God,
> when the waters saw it was you, they recoiled,
> shuddering to their depths.
> The clouds poured down water,
> the sky thundered,
> your arrows darted out.

> Your thunder crashed as it rolled,
> your lightning lit up the world,
> the earth shuddered and quaked.
> You strode across the sea,
> you marched across the ocean,
> but your steps could not be seen.
> You guided your people like a flock
> by the hands of Moses and Aaron.

And in Psalm 106:43–48, Israel acknowledged its weakness in responding to the demands of the covenant; but it also celebrated the fact that if Israel forgot the covenant, Yahweh did not.

> Time and again he rescued them,
> but they went on defying him deliberately

and plunging deeper into wickedness;
even so, he took pity on their distress
each time he heard them calling.

For their sake, he remembered his covenant,
he relented in his great love,
making their captors mitigate
the harshness of their treatment.

Yahweh our God and savior,
gather us from among the pagans,
to give thanks to your holy name
and to find our happiness in praising you.

Blessed be Yahweh the God of Israel,
from all eternity and for ever!
Here, all the people are to say, "Amen."

Israel's encounter with God, then, was not merely an experience of "nature mysticism." Yahweh, indeed, worked in the sun and the moon, the stars and the fertility cycles, and the storms and volcanoes and earthquakes. But he was recognized as dominating these events because Israel had encountered him in another context, a context of his being involved in their *history*. Yahweh was not first recognized in the storm-volcano theophany of Sinai; he was first encountered when he brought Israel out of Egypt.

The "Thou" who is Israel's God is a God of power and love *and* action. He is involved not merely in gracious affection in *hesed* for his people. He is also involved in the course of human events, and the eschatological and messianic expectations which Israel would later develop were but a natural and logical conclusion from its conviction that God is directing the course of human events toward a *purpose*. Israel might not have understood Father Teilhard's idea about progression toward an "omega point," but it had the same fundamental insight. Indeed, one perhaps ought to go further and say that if it had not been for the Sinai experience, Teilhard would never have thought of the "omega point." Nor, indeed, would the human race have developed the concern about history and evolutionary viewpoint or the secular, political eschatology which is so typical of liberal progressivism in Europe and the United States. For it is in the notion that Yahweh brought us out of Egypt that we have the root origins of the belief in progress. Human affairs are not an endless cycle, constantly repeating itself in an endless series of representations and reincarnations. Human events do not follow routine paths, as do the cycles of fertility and the progression of the stars across the heavens. Because God directs the course of human affairs, there is a beginning, a middle, and, as Israel came to understand eventually, an end—a "day" of Yahweh in which his work is finally accomplished.

It is one of the paradoxes of the contemporary world that men are no longer ready to believe that God *acts* in history but are willing to believe in historical progress and in the possibility of secular eschatology. The belief in human progress is one of the driving forces of Western culture, even though that belief has recently eroded somewhat under one of those periodic attacks of romantic pessimism. The appeal and attractiveness of Charles A. Reich's *The Greening of America* is to be found precisely in the fact that it is a progressive, eschatological response to pessimism. It is a reassertion of the basic Western assertion that history has point and purpose.

I have always been baffled as to why men can believe in progress and not believe in God (whatever it means "not to believe in God"). For if there is progress in human events, if there is a development toward a goal, it certainly cannot be attributed to Darwinian evolutionary process, for man has evolved biologically relatively little in the last hundreds of thousands of years. If, indeed, we are moving in a direction there is some Force directing us, and if one is willing to concede the existence of that Force, it seems to me that one implicitly concedes that the Force is benign, else why would it be directing us toward improvement and growth? This benign, directive, evolutionary Force, I should think, is not much different from Yahweh on Sinai.

It is now popular and fashionable to decry belief in the progress of the human race and to predict that we are bound for disaster; but even those who announce the new apocalypse do so in a messianic and eschatological vocabulary. They demonstrate their obvious conviction that if we change our ways (if we repent of our sins, in other words), we can be saved; disaster can be averted and progress away from our present condition may then still be possible. Even those who reject the myth of progress are still caught in its categories, its rhetoric, and, on occasion, even in the style of its religious origins.

I am not prepared to try to defend the myth of progress, at least in its more simple secularized forms. But it is difficult to understand why so many people can accept progress as one of their primary intellectual and cultural perspectives and still find it hard to acknowledge some sort of "Principle" of progress. Why are they willing to buy part of the myth and not all of it? (In truth, they seem to believe the more dubious part.)

I do not know how Yahweh acts in human history. I am not sure how God is involved in human events. This is a complicated philosophical and theological question, which I think has never been really satisfactorily answered by philosophers and theologians. Perhaps it does not admit of a satisfactory answer. I often wonder why Catholic theologians seem so little aware of the process philosophy of Alfred North Whitehead and Charles Hartshorne (and the process theology of their disciples, John Cobb and Schubert Ogden). There are a number of problems with this process philosophy and theology; both its assets and liabilities are beyond the scope of this book, but at least Whitehead and his disciples had no trouble at all dealing with the notion of a God who acts. I would think that attempts to come to philosophical and theological grips with the activity of God ought to be very high on the agenda of Christian theologians.

Israel, of course, was a notoriously unspeculative and unmetaphysical people. It would have been at a complete loss to explain how Yahweh was involved in its history. It would not have known what to make of the distinction between the natural and the supernatural. It could not have responded to our question: Do you think that Sinai was an ordinary or an extraordinary intervention of God in human affairs? It only knew that it had experienced in a unique and overwhelming way the presence of Yahweh in the events of its history. Yahweh was *there*. He was, to use a modern colloquialism, "where it's at." Israel couldn't have cared less *how* he was present.

As more rational and sophisticated men, we do care *how* Yahweh works. It is certainly legitimate and appropriate for us to attempt to arrive at some explanation. Ultimately the question is not how Yahweh acts but *whether* he acts. Or, to put the issue on a somewhat more abstract and less anthropomorphic level, is Reality truly gracious? Is it loving, benign, and involved in profound concern with us? There are all kinds of reasons for saying no—and some for saying yes. But whether we decide that the Really Real loves us with a *hesed*, a loving kindness, or not cannot be resolved by philosophical debate. *How* the

Real loves us is far less important than *whether* it does. Our decision about whether it does or not is as much an act of faith for us as it was for Israel at the foot of Sinai.

The other gods are excluded from Israel's cult for the simple and obvious reason that they are not Yahweh. To have anything to do with the other gods is not only unfaithful, it is foolishness. They have neither the power nor the concern nor the love that Yahweh has. The literal translation of verse 3, Chapter 20, of Exodus is "You shall not have other gods before my face." (The Hebrew words are *al panai*.) The face is not merely the front part of a man's head; it is also his presence. God's face among men (even though no one is permitted to see his face) means that God is present among men. That man may not "see" him, that is, look upon him, is not important. God is present among them, and the presence of other lesser powers is excluded. In effect God says, "Why, when you have my presence, should you need the presence of other gods?"

In Exodus 33, there is an interesting juxtaposition of two different traditions among the Israelites about the "face" of Yahweh. In 33:20, Yahweh says, "You cannot see my face, for man cannot see me and live." On the other hand, in 33:11, we are told that "Yahweh used to speak to Moses face-to-face, as a man speaks with his friend." The two traditions are not necessarily inconsistent. Yahweh is thought of as being present as a friend, a friend whose presence one can almost feel physically; and he is present so overwhelmingly and powerfully (in our terminology, so infinitely) that we cannot possibly grasp him with our human powers of perception or description.

It is easy to be affronted by the Sinai myth. I suspect that one of the reasons why we convert the twentieth chapter of the book of Exodus into an ethical code is that an ethical code is not so much an "insult to our intelligence" as is a God who claims to be so powerfully and lovingly involved in human events. We know that the human race needs ethical codes; we are not at all sure that it needs that sort of God; and, more importantly, we are not sure that we can believe in or accept that sort of God. Much of the history of Judaism and Christianity has consisted of attempts to fuzz the issue, to dodge the challenge of Exodus 20:2–3, to try to persuade ourselves that the important thing is to keep certain rules and not to accept entirely the incredible notion of a God who makes covenant with humans. Some moderns will tell us that in a scientific age it is difficult if not impossible to accept such a covenanting God. No one with any powers of observation would deny it, but that it is any more difficult now than in any previous age seems problematic. On the basis of the evidence available to us, most of the men who have lived since the thirteenth century B.C. who were exposed to the Sinai myth and later to the Jesus myth have done their best to avoid making a decision for or against the myths. Legalism, triumphalism, political messianism played a role in ages past functionally equivalent to that of academic, bourgeois agnosticism in the present.

It is certainly not my purpose here to attempt to persuade the reader of the validity of the Sinai myth. I merely wish to describe it, to describe what it really is as well as I can. I am not affronted if the reader rejects the myth as having no value for his religious life. I am affronted if he rejects it without knowing what it really is. Many of those who call themselves believers and many of those who call themselves unbelievers have this important thing in common: what they believe in or what they don't believe in has nothing to do with the critical myth of Sinai (and Jesus, too, for that matter). The believer believes in an essentially legalistic, organized religion; the unbeliever rejects such a religion—and also a God who is some great hangman in the sky. Neither addresses himself to the question of whether the Ultimate, the Real, the Absolute is also profound, passionate Love, a Love that is *involved* with us. That is the issue, and it has been the issue since Israel encountered Yahweh in the desert. For those who have heard of Israel's encounter, there is no other religious question that has any pertinence at all compared to the one that asks, do you believe that Reality corresponds to Israel's powerful, gracious, committed Yahweh?

There is a second question, of course: If you do, why don't you live in such a way that your faith is manifested? Perhaps the second question is more revealing than the first.

Dean M. Kelley, a Protestant administrator and scholar, has recently written about the apparent continued success of the "conservative" denominations in the United States while the more "progressive" denominations seem to have much less vitality, and, indeed, seem to be losing both commitment and membership. Kelley concludes that the conservative churches are more successful because they still provide "meaning," that is to say, they offer an interpretive system which gives their members symbols with which they can respond to the fundamental questions of human life. The progressive churches, on the other hand, are much less certain about meaning, are not at all sure what they believe in, and hence do not provide their congregations with pertinent symbol systems.

In some of Kelley's analysis it would seem that he almost blames the congregations of these churches for the fact that they have nothing in which they clearly believe. Of course, the problem is much more acute for the clergy and the organizational leadership of the churches. Many of the clerics in the more established, progressive denominations have no clear idea of what it is they believe; hence, there is a strong temptation for them to replace religious symbols with social service, political action, or quasi-professional psychotherapy. There are others in society who are specialists in social welfare, political action, and therapy; there is no reason why a congregation should take a clergyman seriously on these matters unless he demonstrates that he is both well informed and well trained. On the contrary, when a cleric indicates that his enthusiasm and moral commitment is a substitute for information and competence, his people are likely to dismiss him as not worth listening to. A persuasive case can be made, I think, for the argument that a religious leader who does have a meaningful religious symbol system to preach to his people will be taken much more seriously when he turns to social and political problems than one for whom social and political symbolism have substituted for religious symbols.

While Kelley's analysis is admirable, I do not think that there is an intrinsic reason why the more conservative churches should have a monopoly on vital religious symbols. The decline of effective religious symbols among the progressive churches is a historical accident—an accident of history which is probably beginning to happen in Roman Catholicism too. The clergy of the upper-middle-class mainline denominations are generally trained in divinity schools that are adjuncts to the secular universities. Hence, they are likely to be permeated with the paralyzing agnosticism which is for all practical purposes the official faith of most secular universities. Furthermore, since the divinity schools are on the margins of the university, the form of agnosticism which develops there is likely to be naïve and simplistic. Caught up as he is in the philosophical and methodological problems of the university environment and in the constant change of liberal academic fads, the divinity student (and usually his teacher, too) permits himself to be persuaded that God is dead, that religion is irrelevant because man has become secularized, that the religious symbols have become "broken," and that what is needed in the world is not faith but social reform. Thus social and political symbols become all-important, and religious symbols, to the extent that they are understood or accepted at all, recede into the background.

A denomination which is staffed by large numbers of such confused and troubled clerics will cease to be a religious organization in any meaningful sense of the word.

I am surely not asserting that all or even a majority of Protestant clergy think that religious symbols are not important anymore (or, to use that ugly, terrible word, "relevant"). Nor am I suggesting that all or even a majority of the younger Catholic clergy have dismissed the relevance of religious symbols. I am saying that there is a strong strain in the divinity school environment toward reducing the importance of religious symbols and replacing them with other symbols. This is a historical accident, a development from the peculiar social and cultural forces of our time and one which over the long run will pass away, I suspect. In the process, however, many of the more "liberal" denominations may find themselves slowly going out of business.

I do not suggest that the social or philosophical issues of our culture ought to be ignored; but philosophical argumentation can neither establish nor disestablish the validity of religious symbols. Philosophy, in other words, can neither command nor prohibit faith. Furthermore, while social and political commitment is essential for those who accept the Sinaitic or Christian symbol systems, they are essential as a consequence, not as a substitute for them. The question a divinity school student (and quite possibly a faculty member, too) ought to ask himself is, "Do I really believe in a gracious, loving Reality?" If he does, fine. He ought to preach it. If not, perhaps he ought to find another occupation.

I address myself to the divinity school syndrome because I think that it represents in an exaggerated way the misplaced religious issue of our time (though past ages have managed to misplace it, too). Many people will say, "I'm not sure what I believe anymore." As a description of an existential situation, this may be a painful though accurate statement. Indeed, no one can be sure of what he believes in the same way one can be sure of a mathematical theorem. Faith generates a certainty but not that kind of certainty. However, as a persistent religious posture, the "I'm not sure what I believe in anymore" stance is infantile; it is an attempt to escape from making a commitment either to or against faith. When his refusal is accompanied by a disinclination to investigate the religious sources or a scapegoating of institutional religion, then one is forced to conclude that such a person is both psychologically and religiously immature. Organized churches make splendid scapegoats, of course; but the validity of religious symbols have nothing to do with the fragile human organizations that proclaim them. Anyone who announces that he is not sure whether he accepts the religious symbols out of his own past heritage without bothering to find out what these symbols really say about the meaning and purpose of human life is behaving childishly.

The pertinent question to ask someone who takes the stance I have described is, "Do you believe in an ultimately loving and gracious Reality or don't you?" At some point he must decide one way or the other. The frequent response from such a person is to bring up the problem of the existence of evil.

It is a problem well worth discussing. No satisfactory solution of it has ever been achieved and is not likely to be. If the problem of evil could be resolved, faith would not be faith but merely the acceptance of something that was logically obvious. The leap of faith cannot depend on the problem of evil being eliminated. One believes despite evil. If one believes that evil will ultimately triumph and that Reality is not gracious and loving, then the appropriate answer to the religious question is that life is arbitrary, capricious, tragic, and absurd. That is at least a stance that does not attempt to avoid the issue by arguing about the nature of manna in the desert or was Yahweh's voice really heard on Sinai or why isn't the church more vigorous in condemning war. I cannot argue with someone who takes such a stance. I believe he is wrong, but he has made his act of faith and I have made mine. I believe in the loving, gracious, pushy Yahweh, who told the Israelites in the desert and everyone after them that he is that God. The man who postulates an absurd and ungracious universe, or even a "random" one, does not believe it. We may respect each other as human beings, but we have very different visions of reality.

But at least he is honest and consistent, and those who refuse to face the challenge of the religious symbols, who half-believe them and half-reject them, who interpret them in such a way that they are interpreted away, are to be counted among the lukewarm of whom

Jesus spoke. They are the sort of persons who stand at the foot of Sinai and ask Moses when he has come down from the mountain, "Moses, old chap, how about going back up there to work out some sort of compromise with Yahweh so that we can believe him up to a point?" Moses was, if the traditions are accurate, a very hot-tempered fellow, and I think it was probably not too safe to propose such a deal to him, and it is most unlikely that he would have ventured back up the mountain. I think if he had, all might have heard the thunder again—not of anger but of Yahweh's laughing in our faces.

Chapter 6
No Idolatry

⁴**Y**ou shall not make for yourself a sculptured image, or any likeness of what is in the heavens above, or on the earth below, or in the waters under the earth. ⁵You shall not bow down to them or serve them. For I the LORD your God am an impassioned God, visiting the guilt of the fathers upon the children, upon the third and upon the fourth generations of those who reject Me, ⁶but showing kindness to the thousandth generation of those who love Me and keep My commandments. (Exodus 20:4–6)

Most exegetes agree that the words contained in verse 4 are more ancient, and that verses 5 and 6 are a reflection from the point of view of covenant theology. It is also generally supposed that the original prohibition was against an image of Yahweh; only later was this prohibition extended to include images of other gods. In the previous verses, Yahweh had disposed of the other gods; Israel was simply not to have them. This verse is seen now as it was seen originally as God's concern with forbidding Israel to make images of him.

It would be a mistake to think that the ancient peoples identified their god with the god's image. The Old Testament railing against pagan images as though the gods themselves is perhaps something of a rhetorical exaggeration. But while the gods were distinct from their images, they were not independent of them. In Martin Noth's words:

> The basis for it [images] rather lies in the idea, widespread in the ancient world, that an image had a firm connection with the being it

246

portrayed, and that with the help of an image a man might gain
power over the being represented in the image. Israel is forbidden
any image so that the people cannot even make the attempt to gain
power over God or that which is of God.[1]

Yahweh had entered a covenant relationship with Israel on his own
initiative. It was a free choice on his part and a free response on the
part of Israel. They were to continue to relate to one another as free
partners. There would be no magic, no attempt to constrain Yahweh to
act in ways his human colleagues deemed appropriate. The only
constraints on Yahweh were his own generosity and love. The power
of Yahweh is such that it cannot be limited by images or even
contained in the whole physical universe. In the fourth chapter of the
book of Deuteronomy, verses 16–19, this precept of the Decalogue is
repeated with more theological explanation:

> not to act wickedly and make for yourself a sculptured image in any
> likeness whatever, having the form of a man or a woman, the form
> of any beast on earth, the form of any winged bird that flies in the
> sky, the form of anything that creeps on the ground, the form of any
> fish that is in the waters below the earth. And when you look up to
> the sky and behold the sun and the moon and the stars, the whole
> heavenly host, you must not be lured into bowing down to them or
> serving them. These the LORD your God allotted to the other
> peoples everywhere under heaven; . . . (Deuteronomy 4:16–19)

Neither in the heavens nor in the sun, the moon, the stars, nor
anywhere in creation is there anything that can contain Yahweh. He is
holy, mysterious, beyond man's control. He operates in human events,
indeed, but on his own initiative. He is close to them, but it is a
closeness of mystery and love. Israel's trust and confidence is based
on the bare word of God as spoken in his covenant commitment. As
von Rad observes:

> Nature was not a mode of Jahweh's being; he stood over against it as
> its Creator. This then means that the commandment forbidding
> images is bound up with the hidden way in which Jahweh's revela-
> tion came about in cult and history. It would be a mistake to think of

[1]Martin Noth, *Exodus. A Commentary*, translated by J. S. Bowden. Philadelphia:
Westminster Press, 1962, pp. 162–63.

the commandment simply as an isolated cultic peculiarity of Israel. The Jahweh whom Israel was so strictly forbidden to worship by means of an image was still the same Jahweh by whose hidden action in history she was continually kept in suspense.[2]

We must understand that in the ancient world, divine power was thought of as lurking just behind the veil of the physical universe. Images and idols were the passageways through the veil to the inner reality of divine power. What Yahweh told Israel, however, was that even though he was involved in human events—indeed, as we shall see, deeply and passionately involved—he was totally separated from the physical world, above not only its external veils but also its internal "powers." It may have been possible, perhaps, to "break through" to other gods by way of their images, but it was impossible to break through that way to Yahweh because Yahweh wasn't there. He revealed himself not so much through the powers of the natural cycles; he directly intervened in the affairs of his people. In the covenant, he "broke through" to them, not they to him.

There may have been physical phenomena like earthquakes, volcanoes erupting, or thunderstorms related to some of Israel's desert experience of Yahweh. But their fundamental religious encounter with him had nothing to do with natural phenomena at all. They became conscious in the desert that he had made them a people; and he had done this not because they had idols of him or not because there was a storm or an earthquake. He did it because he had chosen to involve himself in their events. Yahweh was a God of history because in historical events and not in natural phenomena or in cultic worship, Israel first realized its full power.

This kind of God was completely different from any other god available to the peoples surrounding Israel. It was small wonder, then, that in times of trouble or confusion, Israel was tempted to turn to gods with whom they could deal in the old fashion. At various times, perhaps, there may have been idols even of Yahweh. The prophetic denunciation of idols in later years can only be understood as an insistence of the unique nature of Israel's original experience of Yahweh.

The relentless shattering of cherished concepts of God which occupied the pre-exilic prophets stands in a theological relationship

[2]Von Rad, *Old Testament Theology,* Vol. I, *op. cit.,* p. 218.

which is perhaps hidden, but which is, in actual fact, very close to the commandment forbidding images. Any interpretation which deals in isolation with the impossibility of representing Jahweh by an image, and which does not see the commandment as bound up with the totality of Jahweh's revelation, misses the crucial point. . . . [3]

So, the prohibition of images is not merely a fussy regulation that a touchy God imposes on his people to keep them in line. It is rather an inevitable and logical consequence of the nature of the divinity that Israel encountered at Sinai.

In days gone by we generally skipped over the commandment forbidding graven images with a fairly light heart. If we were Catholics, we had to admit that there were statues in our churches, but we explained blithely that while the pagans at the time of Israel believed their gods resided in the statues, we knew better. Our statues were only representations to remind us of God or the saints to whom we were devoted. I am certainly not an iconoclast of the sort of the notorious Leo the Isaurian, who went about smashing statues in Constantinople back in the eighth century. It is possible to have sacred images and not vest them with sacred power. I suppose that large numbers of Catholics did have the proper understanding of sacred images and did not in fact think that the image gave them some kind of "stranglehold" over the saint with whom they were dealing. I also believe that there is psychological wisdom in the cult of the saints. It is not inevitable that a saint be converted to a surrogate God, who will play a role vis-à-vis us like the one the idols played for the neighbors of Israel.

While idolatry may not have been completely absent from the cult of the veneration of statues or the cult of the saint in pre-conciliar Catholicism (in post-conciliar, too, for that matter), there is a wide range of appropriate behavior in our relationships with God. Our behavior becomes inappropriate only when it becomes magical; that is to say, when we allow ourselves to be persuaded that we have some surefire technique or formula for dealing with God or when we believe that we have found a method for guaranteeing that Yahweh's ways become our ways.

The problem, then, is not so much veneration of images or the cultivation of the cult of saints. The problem is idolatry in a much

[3]*Ibid.*, p. 218.

more fundamental sense of the word. The late Paul Tillich did us all a great service when he pointed out this more basic idolatry and defined it as "making absolute the relative."

The relative becomes absolute when anything religious—a symbol, a cult, an image, a philosophical or theological system, an ideology, an organization, a legal structure, a distribution of decision-making power—becomes more important in the practical order than the God these things are supposed to manifest. When the most important reality in my concrete, everyday religious life becomes a statue or a saint, a parish or a church organization, my own position in the ecclesiastical power structure, or Thomism or opposition to abortion or even a crusade for peace and racial justice, then I have become an idolater. I have taken something that is relative and made it absolute. I have decided that I could "break through" to Yahweh by my virtue or my zeal or my ecclesiastical importance or my commitment to the cause of his Church. Yahweh doesn't require commitment to his Church; he wants us to be committed to *him*. The Church, philosophy, theology, ideology, Catholic education, the preservation of parishes, or whatever else might involve our religious interests are only relatively important. We can fool ourselves if we believe that in these relative things we can confidently and at all times encounter Yahweh. Yahweh, on the contrary, is where he wants to be, not where we want him to be.

Tillich, particularly in his earlier years, vigorously insisted that Roman Catholicism was guilty of idolatry because it identified divine power with ecclesiastical structure. While he may have overdone it, I am inclined to think that Tillich made a very important point. Surely, on the theoretical level few Catholics would have made such an identification, but for all practical purposes many of us believed and many of our leaders claimed implicitly if not explicitly that the organized Roman Church "possessed" God, and that he could only really be found in the Church. Furthermore, we also came very close to claiming that loyalty to the institutional Church was the same thing as religion and was the appropriate worship of God. The triumphalism so dearly beloved by the Roman curia for several centuries has by no means been driven from the field even today. It was idolatry pure and simple. I would also insist that the identification (in deeds if not in words) by many bishops of the cause of God with the preservation of their own ecclesiastical power is also idolatry. The late John Courtney Murray used to say of a prominent archbishop (and who that archbishop was varied from circumstance to circumstance), "He is an absolutely honest man. He would never tell a lie save for the good of the Church." Murray was joking, but not really; and it is commonplace that many American bishops have lied so often to their priests and their people that no one believes them anymore.* They will justify their deception on the grounds that it was necessary "for the good of the Church," though they may not use those words exactly. But, of course, this is to make the "good of the Church" absolute. What is important is the survival of the Church as an ecclesiastical institution and not as a proclamation of the Good News of honesty, integrity, and trust, which, one would have thought, is the purpose of the Church's existence.

It does seem astonishing that these men apparently do not understand that if the Church is worth preserving and if it is to be preserved, then God will preserve it, not the hierarchy. Whenever we come to believe that the accomplishment of a religious goal depends uniquely and solely on us, we have become idolaters. And worse than that, we do not really believe that Yahweh is our God and that he has made a covenant with us, a covenant that he will promote with loving-kindness.

I am not advocating administrative irresponsibility. I am insisting that the exercise of the administrative responsibility is a relative good and not an absolute one. We do the best we can, and if it be God's will that our work succeeds, then we rejoice. If it does not succeed, then we must still be convinced that in the long run Yahweh will triumph. If we don't believe this, we don't believe in Yahweh and we have no business in a position of ecclesiastical responsibility.

It is easy, of course, to criticize bishops. After all, they do so many things worth criticizing. But the temptation to idolatry is by no means limited to the hierarchy. It takes great courage to yield our own convictions, desires, aspirations, expectations to God and substitute trust for magic. Rather, we constantly put Yahweh to the test: "If you do this for me, then I will believe in you. If you do not do it, I will doubt your goodness." Thus, parents, shaken to the roots by the birth of a retarded child, may be strongly tempted to question the goodness of God. Such a temptation is understandable, but if we attempt to impose on Yahweh a reduction of his covenant by crying out for the elimination of a specific personal anguish, then we have become

*Please observe that I said "many "—not most, not a majority, but "many."

idolaters. We have made a certain relative good—admittedly of tremendous importance to us—an absolute good. We are not accepting Yahweh's promise of love; we are rather imposing conditions on him. We are telling him what behavior we insist on as appropriate. We have, in effect, created a graven image for ourselves, for we are postulating a God who can be subject to our demands. Such a God has nothing to do with the Yahweh of Sinai. If the very heavens cannot contain him, if the whole physical universe cannot contain him, how do we expect to contain him with our conditions, requirements, and stipulations?

These are tough words, but I don't see any way to escape them. We either believe in Yahweh or we don't. If we do believe in him, then our lives have to be lives of total trust, no matter what goes wrong—even death. Eventually, as Charles de Gaulle once remarked, we "shall not fail to die." Death itself is a relative evil compared to the absolute strength of God's love.

Jesus repeated this prohibition of idolatry when he pointed out that the Yahweh who provided for the birds of the air and the flowers of the field would certainly provide for us. Jesus did not, obviously, guarantee the elimination of human suffering; all he assured us was that God's love was more powerful than any suffering and would eventually triumph over it.

This is very hard to believe, but then no one ever maintained that it would be easy to believe Yahweh or Jesus. It is much easier to deal with a God on whom we can set some minimal conditions, one who will in return for certain services rendered by us guarantee some stability and reliability in our lives. Such a God would be a comforting, responsible, reasonable God. And when all is said and done, this is the God with whom most of us deal most of the time; but we must face the fact that if that is the God we want, we might just as well forget about the Israelite and the Christian religions, for the God of the Sinai myth and the God of the Jesus myth is not that kind of God at all. In his self-revelation, he is the only absolute; everything else, all human aspirations and enterprises, are relative. That is a terribly arrogant position for him to take, but once we understand who he claims to be, then we are forced to admit that any other posture would be a denial of what he is. A God you can deal with is a nice cozy God, but he is really no God at all.

I am not, be it noted, an anti-institutionalist. I am committed to the

Roman Catholic Church and value deeply its religious traditions. Even though I am appalled at the corruption and incompetence of many of its leaders, I still believe that it will persist all the days, even unto the end. I am also convinced that for all its weaknesses and ineptitudes, it is the only community in which I can encounter the God in Jesus. I am also convinced that it is the best community for encountering Jesus. But once all these things are said, it seems to me that every Roman Catholic who is true to the best of his own tradition must assert that the organized Church structure is a means and not an end; that many of us, especially leaders, but followers too, have turned it into an end; and that is not only idolatry, it is a perversion of the best of the Catholic tradition.

Heaven protect us if the only way Yahweh can work in the world is through the ignorant and incompetent men who are Church leaders—indeed, there is a long record of ignorance and incompetence dating back to the beginning. Any church made up of human beings runs the risk of being presided over by incompetents most of the time. Our faith does not depend on the intelligence of our leadership (for which thank God!). But both those who feel constrained to assert that incompetent leadership is good leadership and those who spend all their religious energies fighting incompetent leadership are in fact idolaters. In both cases, something relative—indeed, quite relative—has been made absolute.

The hierarchy has no monopoly on idolatry. We are told, for example, by some young people that unless the Church takes a vigorous stand on racial justice, they will not think that Christianity is worth believing in. I think the Church should seriously condemn injustice. I also deplore the past failings of the Church in racial matters, and I applaud the zeal of young people to improve racial relations in our country. I am outraged by what has been done to black Americans, and I think it is time to eliminate bigotry, discrimination, and prejudice from our society. But having said all these things, I must insist that the crusade for racial justice, no matter how holy, how admirable, how morally excellent, is not a religious absolute. The only religious absolute is God; and to make one's response to God dependent on the ethical stands of the Church is idolatry.

Similarly, many Catholics are extremely excited about new movements in the Church. For some of them their religious lives have become centered in sensitivity training or pentecostalism or the cursillo movement or, more recently, various attempts to link Christianity with the occult. Each of these movements may have considerable wisdom in them; each may be admirable; each may merit a good deal of our religious attention. But when any becomes the center of our religious life, when any becomes our absolute religious concern, then we have made for ourselves a graven image, and we have reduced our relationship with God to a technique, a method, a formula.

The Church's record in dealing with women is abominable. One of the canons of the present code of canon law equates women with children and idiots. The hundreds and thousands of women religious in the world are governed by a number of antiquated Italian gentlemen in Rome. Although it certainly has nothing to do with the essence of our doctrine, we have for scores of years insisted that woman's place is in the home—and many of us still insist on this despite John XXIII's endorsement of feminism. We use the most absurd reasons to defend the prohibition against women priests. For all these reasons (and more), the feminist movement in the Church is critically important; but it is no substitute for God. Nor is denouncing the Church's stand on birth control a substitute for God. Nor is any movement, activity, commitment, interest, or concern a substitute for God.

I am speaking of the practical order of our everyday lives. In theory, we are all perfectly willing to admit that feminism, racial justice, peace, birth control, pentecostalism, clerical celibacy, sensitivity training are not at the center of our religious commitment. But for all practical purposes, most of the time we so readily live as if those perfectly legitimate but relative interests were indeed absolute. They preempt our emotional concerns, they demand all of our vital energies, they occupy most of our "religious time." Theoretically they may be recognized as relative, practically they have become absolutes.

One good way to test ourselves is to ask how much of our "religious" conversation is devoted to these issues and how much to God's love? And if the truth be told, most of us are at perfect ease in talking about the latest "relativity" in our religious life; we are not in the least bothered by recounting the latest faith healing or tongue-speaking experience in our pentecostal group. We are not at all embarrassed when it comes to talking about the Church's discrimination against women. We are absolutely confident when we talk about the immorality of racial injustice. Then when it comes time to talk about God, we stumble, we are vague, we express doubts and bafflement; and in all likelihood we say nothing at all—mostly we have nothing to say because we have not thought much about the subject. We have been too busy, in other words, dealing with the really important things.

The last of the golden calves was not the one Moses destroyed.

The religious and devotional and social issues with which we are concerned are important. I would argue, however, that they are only appropriate for members of a Yahwistic religion when they are pervaded and transformed by a commitment to and a consciousness of the powerful, loving God who is at the center of our religious life and in whose ultimate goodness and triumph we have complete trust. One can tell whether a man is an idolater not by what he does but by the way he does it.

Some commentators see in the first sentence of verse 5, Chapter 20 of Exodus a statement of liberation. Yahweh is freeing his people from idols. There is no need to bow to or serve lesser deities. Man is now free to enter a covenant with the real God as a partner and not as a slave. No concern, no commitment, no cause is important enough to reduce us to slavery. If we yield ourselves over to a movement in such a way that the movement dominates us, then we are not only idolaters, we have become slaves. Yahweh no more wants us to be slaves than he wants us to be idolaters. Only if we have a conviction of the ultimate graciousness of the universe are we sufficiently confident of ourselves, of our own goodness and the goodness of creation, to be involved in a movement and still sufficiently detached from it so that it does not dominate us. It is absolutely impossible for a Yahwist to become fanatic. A fanatic is a man dominated by his cause. A pretended Yahwist who permits a cause to dominate him has departed from the covenant with Yahweh to sink into idolatry. There have been a lot of fanatics in human history who identified their causes—no matter how noble—with Yahweh; that identification is idolatry and slavery. Those of us who choose to be fanatics had better beware, for Yahweh our God describes himself in the second sentence of verse 5 as an impassioned God. Passionate people tend to be intolerant of idolatry, hypocrisy, and phoniness.

The words used in verses 5 and 6 to describe the quality of Yahweh's relationship with his people are extraordinary. It would only be in much later years that prophets like Hosea and Jeremiah and Ezekiel would make explicit use of sexual imagery to describe the relationship between Yahweh and his people. Those who first set down the Decalogue and those who added the commentary contained in verses 5 and 6 (commentary which, incidentally, is apparently on verse 3 as well as verse 4; hence, on the whole revelation, not merely on the prohibition of graven images) did not choose to develop the covenant symbol into a marriage symbol. It was perhaps because of their fear that such symbolism would easily be confused with the fertility symbolism of Israel's neighbors. It was only in later years, after Yahweh was firmly established as the Lord of fertility, that his relationship with his people could be described in sexual imagery. When Jeremiah and Ezekiel used such imagery, they minced no words:

> The word of Yahweh was addressed to me saying:
>
> If a man divorces his wife
> and she leaves him
> to marry someone else,
> may she still go back to him?
> Has not that piece of land
> been totally polluted?
> And you, who have prostituted yourself with so many lovers,
> you would come back to me?—it is Yahweh who speaks.
> (Jeremiah 3:1)
>
> The Lord Yahweh says this: For having undressed and let yourself be seen naked while whoring with your lovers and with your filthy idols, and for giving them your children's blood—for all this, I am going to band together all the lovers who have pleasured you, both those you liked and those you disliked, I am going to band them together against you from all ground; I will strip you in front of them, and let them see you naked. (Ezekiel 16:35–37)

Verses 5 and 6 of Chapter 20 of Exodus indicate that if the marriage symbol was not implicitly present in the covenant symbol, then at least the vocabulary used to describe the covenant would almost inevitably give rise to a later sexual symbolism. For example, the word *hesed,* which means "an overflowing of kindness and love" describes an extremely intimate human relationship. In Hosea's description of the relationship between himself and his prostitute wife—a symbol of God's relationship with his unfaithful people—he says, "I will betroth you to myself forever,/betroth you with integrity and justice,/with tenderness and love''; (Hosea 2:21). It is the word *hesed* that is here translated as "tenderness."

The word "love" in verse 6 of Exodus 20 is *'ahabah*, which can mean "to desire," "to breathe after," "to love," "to delight in." It is, for example, the word that is used to describe the relationship between the sexually aroused bride and groom in Chapter 2, verses 2–3 of the Song of Songs:

> —As a lily among the thistles,
> so is my love among the maidens.
> —As an apple tree among the trees of the orchard,
> so is my Beloved among the young men.

And the word that our text translates as "reject" is *sane*, which can mean "feel a sexual revulsion." (See 2 Samuel 13–15.) Thus, when the people turn away from Yahweh, they are behaving like a wife who turns away in disgust from her husband's aroused and passionate tenderness and his desire to make love. The "guilt" of verse 5, Exodus 20 is a translation of the word *awon*, which means "twisted" or "bent" or "distorted." A wife who rejects her husband's love is abnormal, frigid, sick, perverted.

Thus, Yahweh offers his people tenderness and demands an aroused response to that tenderness. Those who turn away in revulsion from his tenderness are perverted, and those who respond with openness and trust he will shower with affection. For he is *el kana*, which we usually translate (even in the Jerusalem Bible) as "a jealous God." It is more appropriately translated by the text of the Hebrew Torah we are using in this book as "an impassioned God." Yahweh is involved, passionately involved, with his people. He offers them wildly passionate love, and dismisses as perverted those who turn away in revulsion from such love.

This analysis of the words in verses 5 and 6 indicates that what is being described is not a God who is eager to work judgment on his people but rather the statement of a passionate, aroused lover.

In later years, Israel's religious thinkers began to use explicit sexual imagery to describe the covenant love; but this religious development was relatively minor compared to the original development in which Yahweh was described as entering a personal relationship with a people. Once the relationship was conceived of as an I-Thou interaction in which God became passionately involved with his people, it was a logical step to compare the covenant to a marriage.

The thought of Yahweh lusting after the body of his bride will be offensive to many prudes and puritans. What the imagery attempts to convey, however, is the fact that human sexual arousal is a relatively weak emotion compared to the passion of God's love for his people.

Those who will be offended by the imagery will be inclined not to take the imagery seriously. There is something undignified about a God who permits himself to be described as "lusting for his creatures." In addition, it is also incredible that God should pursue us with a passionate tenderness the way the groom pursues the bride in the Song of Songs. We may even applaud the imagery as being beautiful, but still refuse to live lives in which we really believe that the Ground of Being, the Ultimate, the Absolute, or *ipsum esse,* as we used to call him familiarly in the days of scholastic philosophy, really relates to us as a passionate lover. Beautiful symbol, yes, but scarcely one that can be taken literally.

But what must be said is that to the extent the symbol is inadequate, it is meager rather than excessive. It does not describe Yahweh's love passionately enough. Sexual arousal may be the most powerful and pervasive positive emotion that a man can experience. It is an inadequate description of Yahweh's love; his passion for us is not less powerful but rather infinitely more so.

There is another implication of the sexual imagery of the Old Testament. A relationship between a husband and wife is constantly in a state of evolution and development. It has its ups and downs, its successes and its failures, its excitements and its discouragements. No man or woman with any experience of marriage expects instant perfection in the relationship. Nor does any couple really think that their marriage can reach such a state of perfection that no further growth or development is possible or required. Surely, the relationship between Yahweh and his people corresponds to this phenomenon of marriage as a developing relationship. The words in Ezekiel and Jeremiah that we quoted above show how much trouble and conflict there was in the love between Yahweh and his people.

If we think of our relationship to God as rather like marriage, we then understand both the need for constant development and also the inevitability of discouragement and setback. We are caught in a relationship with a passionate God; he does not demand perfection of us; he does not demand a smooth course in the relationship; he does not demand that we eliminate all failure or even all infidelity from our lives. What he does demand is that we continue to respond to his love. Faith in Yahweh does not generate religious perfection; it merely generates a determination to keep trying. Commitment to Yahweh is not the end of faith, it is only the beginning. The convinced Yahwist is not the perfect man, nor even necessarily the good man; he is, rather, the man who has taken a certain existential posture vis-à-vis the deity and has committed himself to working out his life possessed by his conviction of the validity of the symbolism of a passionately aroused God. The Yahwist believes that he has been "caught up" by such a passionate God, and he tries to live a life which demonstrates response to such passion. But he understands that far more important than the perfection of his response is the fact that he continues to respond no matter how strong the discouragement or how many the failures.

There are, then, two issues. The first is, do you believe in a God that corresponds to the Yahweh symbol? Secondly, how passionate is your life as a response to the God so symbolized?

In individual human beings the answers to these questions are tangled and confused. Our faith is always weak and shabby. Yet, in the midst of lies and indecisions, hesitancy, doubt, and equivocation there is frequently to be found a solid kernel of faith, a faith which many times seems to exist almost despite ourselves. We may have surrounded ourselves with all kinds of idols; we have done everything we can to blur the issue, to beg the question, to avoid the challenge. Yet there is still a part of our being that believes and responds and loves.

What is important for all of us is not to judge the extent of the faith or the response of others but to look honestly at our own faith and response. As I examine my own heart, I know that I accept, indeed, with a powerful intellectual conviction, the idea of a passionately gracious universe; but I must be wary of becoming too confident over that conviction, for I am by training and temperament an intellectual— someone who deals with words and ideas. For me to "accept" an idea and to develop it into "conviction" is not all that difficult an exercise. What I must doubt is whether that intellectual conviction pervades very much of the rest of my being.

I proclaim that the fundamental religious issue is not the Church or birth control or the philosophical and historical problems of interpreting the Old and the New Testament myths. I insist, rather, that the central question is, do the Jesus and Yahweh myths describe a gracious Reality to which I am prepared to commit myself? I also announce, at least implicitly, that I have made such a commitment. And yet, whether my life is pervaded by trust, joy, hopefulness, and a "radiation of graciousness" is a question about whose answer I must remain extremely skeptical. I am one of those who spent his earliest years in the midst of the Great Depression, a time filled with both the general tragedy of those years and the special ones in my own family. When I see movies of the little boy I was before the disaster of the Depression, I am astonished at what a joyous, spontaneous little child he was. I have to go the very depths of my own consciousness to find even a trace of that joy remaining.

Seriousness, diligence, responsibility (why else would someone write so many books?), a sober, at times grim dedication to work— these are the realities that have filled my life as long as I can remember. What else does one do, after all, when one has unconsciously accepted responsibility for the Great Depression?

But it is very difficult for a child who has taken on such an awesome responsibility to live a life of passionate and joyous romance with a gracious God. His intellect may say one thing, but his primal, semi- and unconscious emotions say something quite different. After all, the Depression may come back.

I am not saying these things to justify my own inadequacies as a Christian. However, mine are the only inadequacies that I feel qualified to discuss. One could come to the issue of adult religious commitment with better experiences than mine, but, Lord knows, one could also face the question of the graciousness of being with far worse ones. Each of us, in other words, has a past to transcend. We have inclinations of personality both genetic to the human race and specific to our own experience that make us very hesitant about the leap of faith and commitment required to surrender ourselves to the *hesed* of the *el kana,* the loving tenderness of a passionate God. Our fight against these tendencies does not end when we make an intellectual commitment to that God. On the contrary, the fight has just begun.

But then part of the commitment involves the belief that our fears and our hesitations, our built-in personality weaknesses and neurotic distortions will not, in the final analysis, be overcome by our efforts. They will eventually be swept aside by the 'ahabah, the aroused love, of God.

Chapter 7

The Name of
the Lord

You shall not swear falsely by the
name of the LORD your God; for the LORD will not clear one who
swears falsely by His name. (Exodus 20:7)

Verses 7 and 8 of Exodus 20 in the Torah, are the second and third
commandments in the Catholic tradition (in other traditions, the third
and fourth). They are, in a sense, transitional commandments. Verses
1–6 of the twentieth chapter of Exodus are essentially a description of
the kind of God that Israel encountered in the desert. Verses 12–14
shape the broad context of the moral behavior deemed appropriate for
a Yahwist. Verses 7 and 8 are both religious and moral. They set down
certain proscriptions, but they are of secondary importance compared
to the religious truth which motivates them.

The Catholic who grew up in the years before the Vatican council
cannot help but be surprised when he begins a serious study of the text
of Chapter 20 of the book of Exodus. It turns out that in most cases
things we thought the commandments forbade are either a minor part
of what the text really means or have nothing to do with the intent of
the text. We believed, for example, that the second commandment
regulated the use we made of the names of God and Jesus and also
forbade "dirty" language, which included everything from "damn"
to the scatological and the obscene. The differences between profanity,

scatology, and obscenity were never very clear. They were all lumped together in our consciousness under the category of "bad language" or, alternately, "swearing." I remember one good nun seriously arguing that to say to another, "Shut up," was a violation of the second commandment.

This peculiar hangup was not unique to us. Apparently the proclivity of late Judaism to substitute "Adonai" for "Yahweh" in the text of the scripture also resulted from a misreading of this commandment.

In its original context, the commandment meant something very different. What it prohibited was the misuse of religion, a misuse based on the same assumption that led men to build idols. Just as the idol gave the worshiper some control over the god, so in the ancient world the use of the name of a god gave one control over the deity. Thus, if one used God's name, one had God at one's disposal. Idolatry is forbidden in the first commandment, magic is forbidden in the second; for neither by the use of idols nor by the use of God's name can we control what Yahweh does.

In the ancient world, a man's name represented his reality, his essence (if we may be permitted the use of the scholastic term). When you named something, as did Adam in the garden, then you dominated it, controlled it, because you had grasped its reality. As Martin Noth says, "Anyone who knows a divine name can make use of the divine power present in the name to effect blessings and curses, adjurations and bewitchings and all kinds of magical undertakings."[1] Men were told that God's name was Yahweh in order that they might praise him and call upon him, but not that they might use that name for frivolous purposes, for God's name is his presence, his *sehenah*, his glorious majesty in our midst. Yahweh is the Lord of creation, the mover of history, the passionate lover. To try to use his power and his presence for silly or trivial purposes is an insult, and he who misuses religion for unreligious purposes is a hypocrite. The phrase that the Torah in our translation renders as "will not clear" is the verb *yenakeh,* which can also mean "will not be proclaimed pure or innocent." Another way of putting it, then, is "He who invokes religious power for frivolous or trivial purposes will be deemed a hypocrite." There is no

[1]Martin Noth, *Exodus, op. cit.,* p. 163.

more scathing denunciation of hypocrisy in the Old Testament than that to be found in Amos 5:21–25:

> I hate and despise your feasts,
> I take no pleasure in your solemn festivals.
> When you offer me holocausts,
> . . . . (line missing)
> I reject your oblations,
> and refuse to look at your sacrifices of fattened cattle.
> Let me have no more of the din of your chanting,
> no more of your strumming on harps.
> But let justice flow like water,
> and integrity like an unfailing stream.
> Did you bring me sacrifice and oblation in the wilderness
> for all those forty years, House of Israel?

What Yahweh is seeking from his people is not a vain and foolish approach to religion but a righteous one. Since the word "righteous" is used frequently in the Israelite religious tradition to describe both God and the people, it is appropriate that we determine what the word means. Needless to say, it does not mean righteous in the sense of "self-righteous," as it is usually used today. The righteous person is upright, serious, responsible, sober—not in the sense of being dull, but rather in the sense of reacting with appropriate seriousness to serious events. The Hebrew word for righteous is *zedek*. In its primary sense it means "one who is judicially vindicated," but the judicial vindication presumed that the person was originally innocent and that his claim was just. A righteous judge is one who awards the verdict to an innocent defendant; he is a man who behaves appropriately in the circumstances in which he finds himself. He is an upright person in the sense opposite to the *awon* or person twisted in the sense described in the last chapter.

In our contemporary vernacular, a man of *zedek* is "straight" or "sincere." He is not a phony; he enjoys integrity and credibility. To use *zedek* of Yahweh, then, means that he is the sort of God you can count on, you can trust; he means what he says, he is a responsible, reliable God who possesses both integrity and credibility.

A people who have *zedek* are serious, mature, and responsible in their response to Yahweh. They deal with him as he has dealt with them. They do not use religion for frivolous purposes; neither do they pretend to a religious superiority they do not possess. Professor Williams raises the question of why Yahweh's threat is against those whose religion is trivial or frivolous:

> But why the terrifying threat? Why include here the stern admonition when no such admission follows, for instance, the sixth commandment? Precisely because this commandment is so easily broken. Murder, adultery, theft, and the like are overtly willed acts. Even belief in other gods is usually a conscious deed. Hypocrisy in religion, however, can begin almost without notice. We can use God's name irreverently without even realizing the deed has been done. Therefore it is particularly necessary to remind the believer of the consequences.[2]

And the consequences of frivolous and hypocritical religion are not so much consequences Yahweh wills as the inevitable consequences that vain religion brings upon itself. For if religion is converted from an end to a means—and that is what this commandment is about—then Yahweh disappears. What we have left may be magic; it is certainly no longer religion.

The late social psychologist Gordon Allport in his researches on the various dimensions of religion shed considerable light on vain and frivolous religion. Allport was fascinated by the finding that those who seem to be most religious on a number of measures of religiousness (such as church attendance) were also the most likely to score high on measures of prejudice, discrimination, and bigotry. He began to wonder how it could possibly be that those who professed faith in a gracious and loving God could themselves be so ungracious and unloving in their relationships with others. He proceeded, then, to develop a social-psychological instrument which measured (at least in its initial forms) two "dimensions" of religiousness: the intrinsic and the extrinsic. Those who were extrinsically religious "used" religion. It brought them peace of mind, reassurance, security in dealing with the problems of everyday life. Those who were intrinsically religious viewed religion not so much as a way of acquiring peace and security but rather as a means of opening themselves out to the world and to

---

[2]J. G. Williams, *Ten Words of Freedom, op. cit.,* p. 139.

their fellow men. Not surprisingly, Allport's research demonstrated that it was only the extrinsics who were prejudiced. Those who professed an intrinsic religion were the least likely of all his respondents to be bigots.

I remember a meeting convened by a Jewish agency to discuss research it had commissioned (by two gentile researchers) on religiousness and anti-Semitism. These two worthy scholars had discovered, not surprisingly, a correlation between religiousness and anti-Semitism. They had not, however, taken Allport's theory into consideration nor used his scale to discriminate between intrinsic and extrinsic religion—an omission that most of the social scientists in the group felt was an incredible display of professional incompetence. But some of the Protestant and Catholic social actionists present at the meeting would not accept a distinction between intrinsic and extrinsic religion. As one of them pointed out to us, "You can't define your religion the way you want to. You're stuck with those who are extrinsically religious and you've got to assume responsibility for them."

Of course he was quite wrong. Any religion does have the right to determine what style of religious behavior is expected of its members. In the Yahwistic tradition, extrinsic religiousness is hypocrisy and vanity. Yahweh will not render a judgment of innocence or cleanliness on those who use religion as a means to obtain personal security. If Yahweh will not assume responsibility for the extrinsically religious, there is no reason why Yahwistic religion must assume responsibility for them. Unquestionably, some of the behavior that has gone on in the churches may have reinforced extrinsic religion, though I think most psychologists would agree that the roots of extrinsic religiousness are to be found in childhood relationships with parents and not in one's early or later encounters with a church. If it turns out that those who are intrinsically religious do indeed accept Yahweh on his own terms and are also more inclined to racial prejudice, then Yahwism is in deep trouble. If it is not only those who pursue religion as a means of finding peace and security who are bigoted but also those who open themselves out in response to a gracious universe, then Yahwism is a fraud. But neither Judaism nor Christianity causes prejudice. On the contrary, when they are taken seriously they eliminate it. The problem is not that authentic Yahwism can coexist with prejudice, for it cannot. The problem is that many of us who profess to be followers of Yahweh do, in fact, use his name in vain, convert his worship into other purposes, and, while professing faith in Yahweh, in fact we are narrow, frightened, insecure, bigoted human beings. I suppose the churches can probably be faulted for not doing all they can to facilitate people's development out of this narrow, extrinsic, magical, frivolous approach to religion. But the failure then is of religionists, not of the religion. It is a failure of those who follow Yahweh but who do not take him seriously rather than of Yahweh himself and those who do take him seriously.

The religion of Yahweh is not intended to be a formula, a how-to-do-it technique for solving problems and achieving emotional security. One need only walk through any religious bookstore to see several shelves filled with how-to-do-it religious books. Such volumes purport to provide either the wisdom or technique for achieving salvation. Simply by purchasing and reading these books we can become faith healers, pentecostals, Buddhas or yogis, satanists or Jesus freaks, Christian radicals or masters of extrasensory perception. We can learn about alchemy, reincarnation, enhancement of our sexual lives through Yoga, charms, potions, and spells. We can discover how to obtain the truth from the I Ching or the Tarot cards or the study of macrobiotic diets.

In many of these manuals, there are grains of truth. But one truth most of them seem to miss is that salvation is not a matter of technique or formula, of special skills, or of Gnostic wisdom—at least it isn't in the Jewish and Christian traditions. Yahweh promises us his love and the confidence and peace that go with possessing that love. He doesn't promise us peace of mind and soul, added sexual potency, personal security, and success in business or the elimination of worry and anxiety automatically from our everyday lives. Religion is not a way of achieving self-fulfillment, personal maturity, or satisfying human relationships. The man of faith obviously has powerful motivations to break out of the fears and insecurities and anxieties that stand in the way of maturation and adult relationships, but Yahwism is no substitute for psychotherapy and psychotherapy is no substitute for Yahwism. Yoga may, for all I know, be an interesting and useful technique; it has no more to do in itself with authentic response to Yahweh than did the Nine First Fridays or the Sorrowful Mother Novena or the recitation each day of fifteen decades of the rosary. These devotions could have been authentic. For many people they did in fact represent an opening forth in trust to a gracious God and an ultimately benign universe. For others, they were religious techniques designed to produce personal security and confidence in one's own value and worth. Salvation does come from Yahweh, but it comes as a gift and is accepted in faith. It can be neither earned nor guaranteed by any technique or method hitherto devised. Neither the speaking of tongues nor the going on pilgrimages, neither devotion to Our Lady of Perpetual Help nor extrasensory perception have of themselves anything to do with a serious response to a serious God. Such devotions may for some people be a serious response—so may concern about ESP. There is a place for gimmickry in human life, and there is a place for technique and method in religious development, too; but technique does not guarantee us salvation and cannot pretend to give us peace and confidence. Salvation is a gift of the Lord that has already been given, and peace and trust come only from the acceptance of that gift. Techniques and methods are useful for developing the self-discipline necessary to live lives of gracious and trusting response. They are ways we overcome the residues of fear that still impede us from being joyous followers of Yahweh.

As long as I live, I will need to make constant effort against the morose and melancholy proclivities of my personality. On the other side of the coin, it will require never ending self-discipline for me to be able to live in such a way that the remains of the frolicsome leprechaun that I was in my earliest years can come more and more alive. I am therefore constrained to learn as much as I can about how to combat the neurotic and frightened aspects of my personality. I must adopt forms of self-discipline to focus my energies so that the part of me that responds best to Yahweh can become more and more typical of the person my friends and colleagues encounter.

But such formulae, methods, techniques, and insights are no substitute for faith and no guarantee of the peace that comes with faith. If I attempt to convert my painfully acquired wisdom and self-discipline into the center of my religious behavior, then I have become guilty of the religious frivolity and vanity that this commandment forbids. For what Yahweh wants, unaccountably enough, is not my efforts but me. It does not follow that my efforts are worthless or that Yahweh condemns them. On the contrary, I daresay he expects them, but if I am not confident enough of Yahweh's love to believe that he delights in me even when I am grim and morose, then all my efforts toward greater wisdom and greater self-opening are not at all superior to the sacrifices and burnt offerings so roundly denounced through his spokesman Amos. My righteousness comes not from my own efforts but from Yahweh who made me and loves me. My efforts must continue, but as a consequence of Yahweh's love, not as either a substitute for it or a cause of it.

It is difficult to understand why from Yahweh's point of view our most serious, dedicated, painful efforts are vain, frivolous, and trivial. Rushing blindly through divine office, rigidly making that half-hour meditation before Mass every morning, conscientiously reciting the stations of the cross every day during Lent, weighing that last ounce of lunch so as not to violate the fast, or, more recently, standing on our heads in some contorted yoga posture—all these are difficult and painful, and Yahweh doesn't give a damn about them. If we are Jewish, we may choose to keep all the dietary regulations; if we are Islamic, we may choose to make pilgrimage to Mecca; and if we are Catholic, we may, depending on our particular stance at the moment, say the rosary and go to Mass every day or speak with tongues at a pentecostal meeting. Splendid. These may be acts of great virtue on our part. There is nothing wrong with them. On the contrary, there may well be much that is right with them. But such activities guarantee nothing. Any peace and security we obtain from them has been gained as a result of a vain and frivolous use of religion.

It is very hard to understand that in our relationship with Yahweh the only thing that really counts is our response to his love.

A while back, I was asked by the *New York Times* literary supplement to do a lengthy book review on some fifteen paperback volumes on "the new religions." I could not help but conclude that Yahweh stood in a very poor competitive position compared to the gods of the how-to-do-it manuals. There is something very reassuring about a technique or about a form of wisdom that somehow or other is an "inside secret." Compared to the surefire technique for the hidden wisdom, Yahweh has little to offer. Those whose religious lives absolutely require security and the safety that comes from a technique or a formula had better stay away from Sinai. There isn't any technique to be learned there, nor any wisdom that has been hidden down through the ages. What was offered at the foot of Sinai was not a method but a covenant, not a how-to-do-it manual but a demand for a trusting relationship with a passionate, almost crazy God. Small wonder that the how-to-do-its are selling so well.

Chapter 8
The Sabbath

⁸Remember the sabbath day and keep it holy. ⁹Six days you shall labor and do all your work, ¹⁰but the seventh day is a sabbath of the LORD your God: you shall not do any work—you, your son or daughter, your male or female slave, or your cattle, or the stranger who is within your settlements. ¹¹For in six days the LORD made heaven and earth and sea, and all that is in them, and He rested on the seventh day; therefore the LORD blessed the sabbath day and hallowed it. (Exodus 20:8–11)

Of all the commandments the one demanding the holiness of the sabbath day is the one that most befuddles the scholars.* It is generally agreed that nobody knows for sure what the origins of the sabbath custom are. There can be no doubt that other tribes and peoples in the ancient Middle East kept some sort of seven-day cycle. However, the seventh day was apparently a taboo day, a day when bad spirits were abroad, and it was risky to attempt any work. The sabbath was perhaps in its origins an evil day in which nothing was done for fear that the demons would fight or destroy what man had done. The custom had the obvious social function of providing rest for both slaves and animals, and it may well be that enlightened rulers used the seventh-day superstition as a pretext for easing somewhat the burden of those who had no means of protecting themselves. In the theologi-

*The reader should be reassured that I am not working on this chapter on Sunday. Indeed, I have taken a solemn resolution that I shall never again work on a book on Sunday—well, at least not unless it is absolutely essential.

cal explanation contained in verses 9, 10, and 11, there is a trace of this, for not only are the Israelites to be free from labor, so are their slaves, the strangers among them, and even their cattle. In the version of the Decalogue contained in the book of Deuteronomy, the point about lifting the burden of slaves is emphasized:

> Remember that you were a slave in the land of Egypt and the LORD your God freed you from there with a mighty hand and an outstretched arm; therefore the LORD your God has commanded you to observe the sabbath day. (Deuteronomy 5:15)

If Israel was freed from its slavery by the Lord in the land of Egypt, so it should at least reach forth its arm on one day and free its slaves and servants and strangers in the camp from the burden of work. As Professor Williams puts it with his characteristic elegance:

> Israel is called to celebrate the Sabbath as a reminder of her freedom from slavery, which God wrought through the Exodus. Each Sabbath day should be marked by a return of that feeling of glorious relief experienced as Israel crossed the Sea of Reeds. Israel is called to rejoice, their days of servitude are over, and to consider with compassion the servitude of others.[1]

But obviously the whole context is now changed. The sabbath may be a day of the mysterious and the uncanny. It may also be a day in which burdens are lifted, but the uncanny is now not frightening or threatening and the burdens are lifted not because of fear of taboo, not because the sabbath is an unlucky day, but, on the contrary, because it commemorates the luckiest event in the history of Israel: its encounter with Yahweh. The sabbath is a holy day, a day on which Israel rests from its work so that it may engage in other activity and celebration.

We have no idea from the sources available to us how this transformation came about. The sabbath custom was part of the religious "baggage" that Israel carried with it into the desert. In the transforming experience of the Sinai encounter, the sabbath was transformed too, indeed, almost stood on its head, and fused into the new religious synthesis. Israel now rested not out of fear but because of delight. The sabbath was the day of the week set aside to experience in a special

---

[1] J. G. Williams, *Ten Words of Freedom, op. cit.,* p. 151.

way the ongoing encounter between Yahweh and his people. It was not a time of major covenant renewal, for that took place, at least in the early days, only every seven years; but it was a time when the joys of the covenant were recalled more explicitly than they were during the rest of the week.

The sabbath, then, became part of history. It was a recollection and a celebration of a past event, but also a recreation of that event. While in its origins it may have been part of some natural cycle (though it is difficult to link a seven-day week with a lunar month), in Israel's case the sabbath day was torn from the natural context and given historical importance. It was no longer part of the fixed cycle of the universe; it had become involved in Yahweh's saving intervention in human events. It recreated the past and it directed the way toward the future.

Whatever the origins, then, of the sabbath custom, for Israel it became the Lord's day. As Rabbi Heschel in his beautiful book *The Sabbath* puts it, "Sabbath is one of life's highest rewards, a source of strength and inspiration to endure tribulation, to live nobly. The work on weekdays and rest on the seventh day are correlated. The sabbath is the inspirer, the other days the inspired."[2]

Heschel points out that as a religion of God's intervention in history,

> Judaism is a *religion of time,* aiming at the *sanctification of time.*
> Unlike the space-minded man for whom time is unvaried, iterative,
> homogenous, to whom all hours are alike, qualitiless, empty shells,
> The Bible senses the diversified character of time. There are no two
> hours alike. Every hour is unique and the only one given at the
> moment, exclusive and endlessly precious.[3]

Heschel adds, "The Sabbaths are our great cathedrals"; the Sabbath is a day of *menuha,* a day of happiness, stillness, peace, and harmony. Heschel quotes the ancient catechism as saying, "What was created on the seventh day? Tranquillity, serenity, peace, and repose."[4]

The Sabbath is not a day when one is forced to cease all human activity. Heschel says, "The Sabbath is a reminder of the two worlds— this world and the world to come. It is an example of both worlds:

---

[2]Abraham Heschel, *The Sabbath: Its Meaning for Modern Man.* New York: Farrar, Straus & Young, 1951, p. 22.
[3]*Ibid.,* p. 23.
[4]*Ibid.,* p. 22.

For the Sabbath is joy, holiness, and rest; joy is part of this world, holiness and rest are something of the world to come.''[5]

The Sabbath provides the same *menuha* as does Yahweh the shepherd offer calm in the green pastures, for the ''still waters'' are called *menuhot*. It is beside these peaceful waters that we sit in repose on the Sabbath. The ancient rabbis even called the Sabbath ''the Bride,'' ''the Queen,'' because it was the most glorious and beautiful event of their lives.

Heschel says, ''On the Sabbath it is given us to share in the holiness that is in the heart of time . . . eternity utters a day.''[6] He describes the relationship of the Sabbath to the rest of human life as follows:

> Six days a week the spirit is alone, disregarded, forsaken, forgotten. Working under strain, beset with worries, enmeshed in anxieties, man has no mind for ethereal beauty. But the spirit is waiting for man to join it.
>
> Then comes the sixth day. Anxiety and tension give place to the excitement that precedes a great event. The Sabbath is still away but the thought of its imminent arrival stirs in the heart a passionate eagerness to be ready and worthy to receive it.[7]

Then the Sabbath candle is lighted and ''just as creation began with the word 'Let there be light,' so does the celebration of creation begin with the kindling of lights.''[8]

> And the world becomes a place of rest. An hour arrives like a guide, and raises our minds above accustomed thoughts. People assemble to welcome the wonder of the seventh day, while the Sabbath sends out its presence over the fields, into our homes, into our hearts. It is a moment of resurrection of the dormant spirit in our souls.[9]

There is no doubt about the sublimity of the themes developed by Rabbi Heschel, and while such themes are surely not explicit in Exodus 20, they are legitimate conclusions from it. If the sabbath is a

[5]*Ibid.*, p. 19.
[6]*Ibid.*, p. 65.
[7]*Ibid.*, p. 65.
[8]*Ibid.*, p. 66.
[9]*Ibid.*, p. 66.

holy day, a day blessed and hallowed by the Lord, and if, as Deuteronomy says, it is a day that commemorates the Lord's bringing Israel out of Egypt, then it is a day when people experience the peace, the tranquillity, the joy of special contact with the Lord. It may have taken some time for Israel to come to the understanding that the holiness of the sabbath was the same as the holiness it encountered at Sinai, but once that connection was made, the insights which Heschel summarized were inevitable.

And it surely seemed legitimate for Yahweh to ask for a day for himself. If he had made covenant with his people, then his people surely owed him at least one day of the week when they could explicitly reflect on the covenant and commune with him in loving acceptance of his graciousness. It also made sound psychological sense. It was easy to forget about Yahweh unless one day was devoted to him. Furthermore, a God who didn't demand at least one day out of seven of his people's lives could not, after all, be that much interested in them. Finally, a God who sanctified time by his own intervention in human events could easily seem to disappear from time unless he had a day to himself. The sabbath was the day of Yahweh, signifying both the commemoration of Israel's encounter with him in the Exodus and on Sinai and also, eventually, in anticipation of the Day of Yahweh when his work would be accomplished with the coming of the eschatological age.

Of course, legalism raised its ugly head, and what became important on the sabbath was not so much the joy, tranquillity, serenity, and peace, not so much the contemplation and reflection, but rather the avoidance of work. The laws, the regulations, the details imposed to make sure that no work was done ceased to be a means and became an end in themselves. Jesus was not the only rabbi to denounce vigorously those who became so concerned about the letter of the sabbath that they no longer understood this particular day. The denunciations of Jesus and other rabbis did not eliminate legalism, as the specifications of our theology books of not so long ago made clear. They carefully determined just how much work on Sunday resulted in serious sin and how much omission of Mass was necessary so that it would have to be repeated. The ultimate absurdity (for me, at least) came in a theology class where we were told with a perfectly straight face that crocheting was not sinful on Sunday but knitting was (I think it was that way, but for all I remember now, it may have been the other way around).

The result of such legalism is that the sabbath is ignored by an ever increasing number of people. Many if not most Jews feel that it is impossible in modern life to keep all the requirements of the sabbath observance (though increasingly some of the sabbath ceremonies are returning to Jewish family life). The servile work regulations of the old moral theology were so absurd that they have been thrown out the window by most Catholic clergy and laity. Furthermore, Catholics are beginning to take the same attitudes toward Sunday churchgoing as do their Protestant brothers. It's a nice thing to go to church if you want to, but one is certainly not going to hell for all eternity if one decides to sleep late. Some serious younger Catholics, in fact, insist that they will happily go to Mass one day a week, but not on Sunday, both because Sunday Mass is a drag and, besides, no one has the right to tell them what day they have to go to Mass. Finally, in certain aggressive Catholic circles, the decision to "drop out" of Sunday Mass obser-vance "because I don't get anything out of it" is taken to be a badge of how enlightened and advanced one really is. Sunday Mass, in other words, may be all right for superstitious pre-conciliar Catholics, but it is scarcely required for sophisticated, "modern" Catholics.

Anyone who reads through Rabbi Heschel's profoundly moving pages can readily see how all this is beside the point. Those who drew up the servile work regulations and who insisted that if you came in before the creed you did not have to repeat Mass but that if you came in after you did, not only misunderstood the nature of Yahweh's love for us, they also misunderstood the whole purpose of the sabbath.[10]

Sunday is the day when the Lord our God comes to us. It is a day when our more frantic activities should grind to a halt so that we may have the peace, the tranquillity, the serenity to commune with our God, to reflect on our lives, and to renew our covenant of faith and love with Ultimate Graciousness. One cannot do that by showing up in church for forty-five minutes on Sunday morning (or now, the night before). Staying away from the lawn mower on Sunday afternoon or venturing over to the parish church in the morning has nothing to do with a joyous celebration of the Lord's covenant with us; it has even less to do with a serene, peaceful, contemplative reflection on God's

---

[10]I realize, of course, that the Christian service on Sunday is not quite the same thing as the Jewish observance of the sabbath. In the early Church, Jewish Christians kept both days for different purposes. In the larger sense, however, Sunday is obviously a continuation of the sabbath because it is the day consecrated to the Lord.

love and the purpose and meaning of our lives. We feel that once the "obligation" of Sunday has been honored, we are now free to engage in such undeniably important activities as poring through the Sunday newspaper, watching the pro game on TV, struggling through expressway traffic to visit places we don't want to, and all those other contemplative, reflective activities Americans do to "kill time" on weekends.

Indeed, as one of those many Americans who usually work a seven-day week, I was profoundly embarrassed by Rabbi Heschel's book. A whole day for reflection and tranquillity? What would I do? Surely, he doesn't mean that I should stop reading or writing or listening to football games? He couldn't possibly be insisting that during the summer I should give up wrestling with the wind and the waves in my *Leprechaun.* If I can't do these things or if I can't attend those critically important rituals of American society, the weekend conferences, what is there left for me to do?

Take tomorrow, for example. It is Sunday, the Lord's day, the Christian sabbath. I will certainly have to work on the next chapter of this book. I have to interview some teenagers for an article I may write for *The New York Times Magazine,* and then, in the evening, I must give a lecture at the O'Hare Airport Chapel (never can tell when you're going to need help there), and, finally, I must prepare for what is going to be an extremely hectic week. Reflect? There won't be any time. Be tranquil? Not without the help of a pill. Serenity, peace, joy? What the hell are they?

If there is something obviously wrong with those who thought that sabbath joy and tranquillity could be imposed by precise legalistic regulations (be they Talmudic rabbis or moral theologians), there is something equally wrong with those who profess to be followers of Yahweh and find almost no time in their lives to commune with him. If we believe in a God of history, a God who intervenes in time and makes it holy, then how come we have so little time for him? How come we work so frantically, as though everything depends on how much we can squeeze out of time and nothing depends on how much he can put into time?

It is all the more surprising when one stops to consider that the amount of time most men must work in middle-class American society is much smaller than that required of working men ever before in human history. We manage to fill up our time, of course, and we manage to fill up our expanding leisure with a wide variety of time-killing activity. In the peculiar combination of university and church that constitutes my environment, a seven-day week is an absurdity. It is absurd not merely because no one is requiring it of me (save occasionally) but because after four or five days of productivity, one really has nothing left to produce; tranquillity and reflection are really the only meaningful alternatives—unless, of course, one must run away to another nutty conference. I find things with which to fill up my weekend for the same reason other people do: if there weren't such things, I just wouldn't know what to do with myself. It would be nice if we could take a few minutes or a few hours of our time on a Sunday afternoon to reflect on Yahweh's leading Israel out of Egypt and entering into covenant with them at the foot of Sinai, or even possibly, just possibly, to reflect on the risen Jesus to whom Sunday is supposed to belong. That would be very nice, but there isn't any time for it.

I am not talking of moral obligations, and I certainly do not advocate a return to a puritanical "blue laws" approach to the sabbath. I am saying that those of us who profess to believe in a God intervening in time and directing history ought to be able to devote a little more time—our time and our history—to religious reflection and tranquillity. Obviously, it doesn't have to be done only on Sunday, and obviously there are going to be some Sundays in our lives when it cannot be done. The point is that Sunday is as good a day as any and probably better than most. (Save for parish priests in parishes which, unlike the one I live in, have large Catholic populations. For the typical American diocesan priest, Sunday will never be a day of reflection and tranquillity. One must say Mass, preach, distribute Communions, and, above all, count the money—not much time for serenity in the midst of all that!) Sunday is the day when most of us do not work and it is the day which is traditionally thought of as "the Lord's day." I have no suggestions as to what *must* be done on the Lord's day, and I certainly am in no position to exclude the National Football League from the list of appropriate behavior; but I think the sabbath has to be approached from another viewpoint than from the perspective of "what must I do" or "what must I not do."

The appropriate question to ask ourselves on Sunday evening is, do I approach the beginning of the new week with more serenity, tranquillity, joy, and faith than I was conscious of last Friday evening?

If the answer to that question is not yes, if we have had no experiences throughout the weekend that deepen our faith, that heighten our religious sensitivity, that bring a little bit more of tranquillity and serenity into our lives, then religiously speaking the weekend has been a waste and we must wonder whether we really believe that our God is a God that sanctifies human time. If we believe that Yahweh has made covenant with us, that Yahweh is to be experienced not merely in certain places but also, and more especially, in the development of human events through time, then we must face the fact that certain times belong to him. If he does not have certain segments of our time as specifically his, then our consciousness of him will simply fade away from all other segments of time.

My colleague Martin Marty has suggested that our weekends away at the "second home," which is becoming a part of middle-class life, may spell the deathblow for Sunday observance. He may be right, but I would like to rephrase the problem. The question for the churches is not how to get people to go to Mass when they are away at their summer homes or out in the country camping or engaged in some other frantic effort to get away from it all with large groups of other people who are also trying to get away from it all; I think the question is, do we have enough faith and confidence in the goodness of God really to trust ourselves to relax? We must address ourselves to the human and religious problem of discovering satisfying, rewarding, taxing, tranquilizing, challenging uses of the tremendous amount of new leisure time we have available. Most of the compulsive behavior during leisure time in American society (and I include here my own compulsions) is the result of the fact that we feel guilty when we aren't doing anything. If tranquillity generates guilt, then we certainly have no time to deal with Yahweh. Oh, of course we will go off to pay our respects to him on Sunday morning in church; but that's *doing* something. A time of reflection, contemplation, prayer, spiritual and personal growth? Well, that's not *doing anything*. The stern Protestant ethic, which infects most Americans, warns us that we must do something, even if it's only going over to turn on the TV to watch a Charlie Chan movie that wasn't very good when it was made in the 1930s. Any activity, in other words, is better than having to face ourselves, and, of course, if we cannot face ourselves, there isn't much hope that we can face the Lord our God.

It will be hard for religious leaders to persuade their people that some of the new leisure time must be used simply to slow down and to reflect. Slowing down and reflection are not only absolutely essential prerequisites for prayer, they are also in themselves an act of faith and trust, a manifestation of response to Yahweh's graciousness. We will have a hard time persuading the people of this because obviously we do not believe it ourselves. There are meetings to go to, events to be planned, and, yes, even books to be written.

Religious leadership that is unable to acquire some tranquillity and serenity, that does not bear witness to its faith in the gracious God by finding some time to relax and reflect, and does not permit serenity to permeate at least some of its time is in no position to condemn a compulsive, materialistic society. Nor does it have any legitimate complaint when its parishioners venture forth on the expressways on Friday night looking for serenity and tranquillity some other place besides the parish church.

Let me put the matter as bluntly as possible. If we who are Yahwists, clergy or laity, do not believe strongly enough in a trusting, gracious God who has entered into an intimate and passionate relationship with us, then it is very dubious that we will ever find time for peace, joyfulness, and celebration in our lives. There is certainly a strong question as to whether we really believe in the Yahweh whom we profess to honor. The third commandment is part of the covenant to the extent that those who really honor Yahweh, who have really entered into covenant with him, will not only have no trouble devoting some of their time to him, but will wait eagerly for those moments when the Sinai covenant will be renewed.

Chapter 9
Children and Parents

Honor your father and your mother, that you may long endure on the land which the LORD your God is giving you. (Exodus 20:12)

With the fourth commandment we turn to the more specifically ethical components of the Decalogue. I have argued as the basic theme of this book that the twentieth chapter of the book of Exodus represents not so much a moral code as an account of a religious experience. The covenant symbol describes an encounter between Israel and Yahweh, and the Decalogue is part of the ancient covenant form. The principal stipulations of the covenant between Yahweh and his people are contained in the first two and possibly three of the commandments (or the first three and four of the commandments, given the Jewish way of numbering them). The essential stipulation of the Decalogue is that we should respond with love to Yahweh's passionate love for us. The more explicitly ethical stipulations contained in commandments four to ten (five to ten in the Jewish numbering) ought to be interpreted in the light of the covenant symbol and the religious experience that that symbol manifests to us.

My colleague John Shea has pointed out to me that there is a danger in the approach to symbol interpretation that both he and I use. Christians can view the religious symbol as a "truth to be applied." The symbol will be taken as an intellectual statement from which certain conclusions are to be drawn, and then these conclusions are to be lived out in our lives as evidence that we understand and believe the symbol. Yahweh has made covenant with us; therefore, we will engage in certain specified behavioral activities as evidence that we believe in the covenant and are honoring it in our lives.

I think Father Shea's point is well taken. It would be very easy to regard verses 12–14 of the twentieth chapter of Exodus as a concrete, practical application of verses 2–11. In the first section of the chapter we are told the truths we believe in, and in the second section we are told the practices in which we must engage. This approach to religion has so permeated the Catholic tradition for so long that none of us are really immune from it. It is very difficult to extirpate it from our religious lives.

But this is not what is expected of us at all. A man who gives himself over to a religious symbol, who accepts it as a guiding and illuminating force in his life, does not so much "apply it" to his concrete behavior as he "puts it on," makes it a perspective, a viewpoint, indeed, a set of eyes through which he views the world. A religious symbol is not applied, it is embraced. One does not deduce certain specific modes of action from it. On the contrary, one immerses oneself in it and discovers what the world looks like from within a commitment to the religious symbol.

A proper approach, then, to the second half of the Decalogue is not to see it as application of the first half but rather to ask ourselves how, once we have accepted the idea of Yahweh's gracious covenant with us, that idea will affect our behavior with our fellow men. The issue is not what kind of things we are required to do for our parents and what sort of things we don't have to do. The appropriate approach is to ask how relationships between parents and children look when both parents and children believe in the graciousness of a covenanting God.

The fourth commandment as we presently have it is obviously aimed at adults, so it is describing not the relationship between young children and their parents but rather that between adult children and their aging parents. The instruction given does not so much require obedience as it does "honor." Indeed, the literal translation of the Hebrew word would mean "give weight." That is to say, Yahweh tells his followers that they will treat their aging parents with honor and reverence and respect. And he promises them that if the parents are reverenced and respected they will "long endure on the land which the

Lord your God is giving you." It is generally agreed that the Lord is
not so much promising that as a special added extra reward he will
grant long life to those who honor their aging parents. Rather, he is
asserting that honoring the aged is a necessary prerequisite for a
healthy and successful society. There are two passages in the Old
Testament which develop in more explicit detail the respect owed
aging parents. The first is Leviticus 19:3: "You shall each revere his
mother and his father, and keep My sabbaths: I the LORD am your
God," and the other is Ecclesiasticus 3:1–16:

> Children, listen to me your father,
>> do what I tell you, and so be safe;
> for the Lord honors the father in his children,
>> and upholds the rights of a mother over her sons.
> Whoever respects his father is atoning for his sins,
>> he who honors his mother is like someone amassing a
>> fortune.
> Whoever respects his father will be happy with children of
> his own,
>> he shall be heard on the day when he prays.
> Long life comes to him who honors his father,
>> he who sets his mother at ease is showing obedience to
>> the Lord.
> He serves his parents as he does his Lord.
> Respect your father in deed as well as word,
>> so that blessing may come on you from him;
> since a father's blessing makes the houses of his children firm,
>> while a mother's curse tears up their foundations.
> Do not make a boast of disgrace overtaking your father,
>> your father's disgrace reflects no honor on you;
> for a man's honor derives from the respect shown to his
>> father,
>> and a mother held in dishonor is a reproach to her
>> children.
> My son, support your father in his old age,
>> do not grieve him during his life.
> Even if his mind should fail, show him sympathy,
>> do not despise him in your health and strength;
> for kindness to a father shall not be forgotten
>> but will serve as reparation for your sins.
> In the days of your affliction it will be remembered of you,
>> like frost in sunshine, your sins will melt away.

The man who deserts his father is no better than a blasphemer,
   and whoever angers his mother is accursed of the Lord.
   (Ecclesiasticus 3:1–16, Jerusalem Bible)

In the Leviticus segment there is emphasis on the legal role of the
father and the mother. They have certain "rights" over their children.
But Ben Sira, the author of Ecclesiasticus, makes a rather different
case, and one which may be more in keeping with the spirit of the
Decalogue. We are to help our parents in old age; we are not to
humiliate them; we are to respect them; we are to be kind to them,
because this is the sort of behavior that will guarantee us a good
reputation in society and also a similar response from our children
when we become old.

There is a good deal of psychological insight in Ben Sira's rather
worldly-wise advice. As we deal with our parents, so our children are
likely to deal with us—not because of any extrinsic religious judgment
on us but rather because our children will learn from us how we deal
across generational lines. If the self-indulgent heroes and heroines of
contemporary "youth culture" have such contempt for their parents,
the reason may very well be that they have learned such a model of
appropriate transgenerational behavior from the contempt their parents
had for *their* parents. If old people are shunted aside into nursing
homes, treated with impatience and contempt in the house, and
deprived of the opportunity for any useful or productive contribution
to society, then the children of these aging people should not be
surprised when *their* children treat them with equal contempt, even
though that contempt may be displayed over different issues and
different fashions. Today's youthful radicals, so filled with hatred for
the failures of those "over thirty," could well ponder the fact that
these attitudes and styles of behavior toward their predecessors will
become an ingrained part of their personalities, which will undoubtedly rub off on their own children and guarantee similar hatred from
them. He who does not respect and reverence his parents will not be
respected and reverenced by his children. The habits of one generation
are visited upon another generation, not so much by religious guilt as
by powerful mechanisms of personality development and psychological socialization. No matter what our parents say to us, the way they
treat our grandparents will shape our attitudes toward them, even if
they and we are unaware of it. In a society where there is little respect

or reverence for the elderly, children will certainly have little respect for the middle-aged. Children who are yet unborn will someday do to their parents precisely what is being done to parents today.

Obviously, not all American adults treat their aged parents with contempt. Furthermore, most young people are not of the youth culture and do deal with their parents in a respectful and reverent fashion (a respect and reverence which is not obscured by extreme casualness of style). But there is a strong tendency in American society to disregard the old (and you are old today, I am afraid, after your forty-fifth birthday). That tendency will guarantee an equal tendency for young people to write off all those over thirty as worthless sellouts, from whom nothing important can be learned.

The fourth commandment requires compassion. It declares that in a society without compassion for the aged, there will not be enough trust or respect for the society to persist long. One of the most atrocious vices of our time is that of selective compassion. We worry about those who are dying in Vietnam (and we certainly should) but we worry little about our own aged. We demand sympathy and under-standing for the blacks as they strive for equality in American society (and indeed we should), but we are rather less likely to require sympathy and compassion for ethnic middle Americans or for middle-aged liberals or for the men who fought in the Second World War who still believe that there are things to be said for patriotism. Some points of view are to be considered with every possible allowance made for the context in which they are spoken, and other points of view are to be judged rigidly and harshly without any regard for the context in which they are spoken. For some groups we must make every possible allowance and try to understand their behavior in the context of all the excusing factors that may be at work; others are to be written off as guilty without any such allowances made. Collective guilt is imposed on whole bodies of people, and all their members are to be judged guilty until proven innocent, while in other cases even individuals clearly guilty of obvious crimes are to be excused because of what "society has done to them." Furthermore, it is absolutely imperative that we have scapegoats and that guilt and blame be distributed among them with all the care and precision that is possible.

There is an incredible amount of arrogance, rigidity, and intolerance in this effort to determine who is guilty and who is innocent, who must be excused and who must be blamed. It is not enough that a society discovers where mistakes have been made, lies been told, and even where individual immoral actions were committed; guilt must be distributed up and down across the length and breadth of the society, and everybody must be made to confess guilt and to expiate their sins.

Under such circumstances, of course, there is little room for universal compassion or sympathy. Whole generations are written off as guilty, with the only question being, who is more guilty and who is less guilty? It is necessary that sins be punished and even then they are not to be forgiven.

Well, that is one way to run a society, I suppose, but in any human community where a number of people have appointed themselves inquisitors to hunt out and punish the guilty, trust and compassion vanish. If all whites are racists, then there is no reason for black people to try to enter relationships of sympathy and compassion with whites. Many Americans—probably more white than black—would argue that trust between whites and blacks is impossible, and they would also argue that trust between the old and the young, the rich and the poor, the educated and the uneducated is impossible. If this argument is proclaimed frequently enough, it may become a self-fulfilling prophecy. If compassion and trust disappear from a society, the social environment will become a jungle.

It is decreed, in effect, that everyone must become like us—the "us" being whoever is issuing the decrees. Social peace and harmony will be established not by learning how to live with those who are different from us with some kind of trust and respect; it will come rather from eliminating differences, from everyone's sharing the same values, the same perspectives, the same interests, and the same commitments. There is no room for diversity, we are told, in a modern democratic society.

This is nonsense of course. A peaceful society comes not from the elimination of diversity but from the integration through conflict, compromise, and trust. A mature adult is not someone who demands that all others adjust themselves to his values; he is secure and confident in his own values and is able to deal with respect and integrity with those whose values are different.

It is very difficult to put up with those who are different from us. Most of the conflicts in human history have been fought over rather small differences of language or skin color or nose shape or eating habits. He who is different is not to be trusted. If he is given the opportunity he will do us evil, therefore we do evil to him before he can do it to us. The incredible massacres in Bangladesh were worked by one Muslim group on another, with the only difference between the two groups being that one had somewhat lighter skin than the other. Even a common religion, then, cannot prevent massacres among populations who are slightly different from one another.

It may be extremely difficult to live with diversity, but it does not follow that we can eliminate it or that we should seek to. The fourth commandment tells us, as I understand it, that we must learn how to live with those who are different from us and look upon them with respect, tolerance, honor, and patience. Yahweh demands that we have compassion for those who are not like us.

Following Father Shea's advice and trying to put ourselves within the covenant symbol and look at the human phenomenon of the conflict that comes from diversity, what light does that symbol shed on conflict and diversity?

It is very hard to answer this question. Traditional theology has seen human diversity as the result of original sin and has argued that were we without sin there would be one race, one language, one nation, one religion. It has always seemed to me that this argument is absurd. While much of the evil in the world has come from human diversity, so have almost all the riches of human culture. It would be a sad, dull, monotonous world if everyone was like everyone else. In addition, even if we could eliminate diversities of language, creed, and race, we would still be faced with the fundamental diversities of sex, age, and intelligence.

It seems to me that from the point of view of the covenant symbol a number of things can be said about diversity. First of all, Yahweh loves all men. Even if his initial covenant was with Israel, it was made with them because they were a priestly people, who were to bear witness to Yahweh's love to all other nations and eventually to be a channel for Yahweh's salvation to the nations. If Yahweh loves everyone, then young must love old, white must love black, poor must love rich, hardhat must love hippie, Republican must love Democrat, and Saxon must love Celt.

But I think more than that must be said. If Yahweh loves them, then there must be something good in them, and those things which are different in them exist not as a threat to us but for our education, our enlightenment, and our enjoyment. The diversity of the world's peoples is the result of Yahweh's plans to enrich human life. It is a great splendid joke he had played on us, a joke which, alas, we have been too dull and dense to understand.

The most important point of all is that if we really believe in Yahweh's loving graciousness, then we can afford to be lovingly gracious to others. I take it that this is the fundamental principle of Yahwistic ethics. We are able to love others because we have strength and confidence in God's love for us. We do not have to be suspicious or distrustful or afraid of others because we know that Yahweh will take care of us. We can offer ourselves in open, trusting relationships to those who are different from us because they are no ultimate threat to our existence. There is nothing they can do to take from us the most important thing in our lives, God's love for us.

Obviously, we have a long way to go before such trust and confidence becomes typical of relationships among individuals and nations, and there are no simple shortcuts on the path to a world that is free from suspicion and hatred.

Compassion becomes possible when we no longer have to fear others, and Yahweh's covenant dispenses us from fear. It does not make life easy; it does not eliminate social conflict; but it does assure us that no threat, however powerful, can destroy the core of our being, which is in a permanent and indissoluble covenant with the Lord our God.

It becomes possible, then, in the narrow instruction of this commandment to honor one's aging parents because, even though they may be difficult and demanding, even though they may stand for different values, even though their ways may not be our ways, still they are in no way a threat to us. They are of no danger to us; there is nothing really important that we have that they can take away, at least not permanently. There is conflict between generations, of course, and there always will be, just as in human society there is likely to be conflict among the different racial, religious, and ethnic groups. But conflict need not mean mutual destruction, nor need it exclude sympathy and compassion. All human relationships, even the most intimate and loving, are marked by ambivalence. Faith in Yahweh cannot eliminate ambivalence, but it does make possible the honest recognition of it, which is the only necessary prerequisite for mature love. It also makes possible compassion and sympathy in the midst of conflict.

There is relatively little compassion in the world, not much sympathy, not much ability to tolerate diversity, and relatively little honoring of aging parents. But the reason for these phenomena is not that Yahweh's command has not been heard; it is that we have never yet had enough faith to give us the strength and the courage, the confidence and the trust to honor the commandment.

Chapter 10
Our Fellow Men

You shall not murder.
You shall not commit adultery.
You shall not steal.
You shall not bear false witness against your neighbor.

It is interesting to ponder the fact that but one verse of the twentieth chapter of Exodus in the Torah sums up the four commandments that occupy most of the space in our catechisms and our moral theology books. We spent one whole semester in our seminary years on *de justitia* and another whole semester on the course *de sexto*.[1] Such an expenditure of time seemed reasonable, for obviously it was the sixth and the seventh commandments, and to a lesser extent, the fifth and the eighth, which were the really important ones. Most sins that were committed were against these commandments (and it was no secret, of course, that the sixth commandment was most likely to be violated). It never occurred to us that it was rather peculiar that the really important commandments were all found in one verse. We never asked why Yahweh spent so much time talking about unimportant things like strange gods and so little time talking about adultery or theft. We were, of course, only too willing to make up his mind for him and establish extremely complex rules as to what sort of thievery was "mortal" sin and what sort was "venial" sin. Even more elaborate

[1]Which meant, of course, "concerning the sixth commandment," not sex.

systems were established determining how, when, and where we were to make "restitution" to others for violating the seventh commandment. Among the things we learned, for example, was that if we burned down Peter's house, intending to burn down Peter's house, then we had to pay "every last cent" toward rebuilding that domicile. But if we burned down Peter's house thinking it was Paul's house, we were not bound to restitution to Peter because we didn't intend to harm him. It didn't make much sense then and it makes less sense now.

I am not saying that regulations regarding human property are unimportant, though I am inclined to think that in a society like ours, they might more appropriately be left to lawyers than to theologians. Nor am I prepared to say that there are no moral issues in sexual relationships; clearly there are (though there may be religious and theological issues of greater moment than the quantities of female anatomy which may be displayed without committing more than a "venial" sin).

The fundamental criticism to be leveled against the old moral theology is not that it was frequently absurd in its casuistic conclusions. Its basic flaw, rather, was that it thought it was the business of religion, and particularly of Yahwistic religion, to lay down specific guidelines for human behavior that would have universal application independently of time and space. I do not believe that any serious moral theologian at the present would argue that the details of an ethical code can be deduced from the Christian symbol system. On the contrary, even in the old days most of our moral argumentation fell back upon the so-called "natural law." But our "natural law" was not quite the same as it had been for Cicero or even Thomas Aquinas. It was not what most people in most times and most places thought was appropriate behavior; it was rather what moral theologians and papal advisers thought ought to be moral behavior for all people in all times and all places. "Natural law"—in the sense of traditional human wisdom—is the basis of all ethical systems (even if the frequently hated phrase "natural law" is not used). But if ethics is the result of natural human wisdom, then a revelatory experience of God ought to add nothing in particular to the wisdom that the race already possesses. It may have been appropriate for future priests, deeply involved as they would be in assisting people to make agonizing moral decisions, to be well informed about the various traditions of ethical wisdom, but to treat that wisdom as something that could be deduced from Israel's experience of Sinai in the desert or the early Christian's experience of the risen Jesus was both to falsify the experiences and to trivialize the arduous work of ethical reflection.

There are, as I will argue in a later chapter, very strong ethical implications of the covenant symbol. But these implications neither add to nor subtract from human ethical wisdom. What they do, rather, it seems to me, is prescribe a certain style of behavior, a certain approach to human problems and human decisions which will mark the man whose being is permeated by the religious symbol to which he has given himself. There is not a necessary difference in the concrete programmatic response of a Jew and Christian on the one hand and a pagan on the other to a given problem of social injustice. The covenant symbol does not provide any better insight into the nature of the problem or necessarily any better solution for it. The difference between the Yahwist and the pagan is to be found in the *style* and *manner* with which they approach the problem and the people involved in it.[2]

In the post-Tridentine Catholic Church, it was not perceived that the basic contribution of religion to ethical decision was a style of behavior and not a detailed set of moral answers. The answers grew more and more elaborate and more and more detailed, and yet they

---

[2]Since I accept Schubert Ogden's principle for the verification of religious symbols, I must assume that the validity of the covenant symbol is to be tested by its ability to "re-present" in a most powerful way the fundamental assurance man has from the very structure of his being about the purpose and worth of human existence. The covenant symbol, then, reinforces a primordial and very hesitant instinct that all men have, that Reality may be gracious and even—however inchoately it may be felt—that love is at the core of the universe. Thus, it is altogether possible for a pagan and a Yahwist to have not merely the same programmatic response to a social problem but also the same stylistic and attitudinal approach to it. What the Yahwist brings that the pagan may not have quite so fully is a powerful explicit religious symbol that underwrites, reinforces, strengthens, and confirms the appropriateness of the response style. Or to put the matter more concretely, the Yahwist has a much more powerful symbol that demands of him universal human love. This may not seem to make a very great deal of difference. Why would a man's behavior be especially unique simply because his core religious symbol demands more explicitly and more powerfully the universality of love? One, however, need only inspect the human condition to see how little universal love there is. One may develop the understanding that all men are to be loved as one loves oneself without having the Yahwistic symbol, but the symbol is still of tremendous importance, as becomes obvious when we observe the behavior of that relatively limited group of men who have given themselves over completely to it. Furthermore, anyone who thinks that the nature of a man's explicit central religious symbolism is not important to his behavior simply does not understand the powerful and pervasive influence of symbol systems on human activity.

could not keep up with the appearance of ever more complicated problems and ever more splendid opportunities for sin. The moral theologians tried, heaven knows, and each year the "Moral Guidance Notes" in the Jesuit journal *Theological Studies* revealed the erudition and intelligence of those theologians who strove desperately to keep up with man's skill at inventing new sins.

They kept falling more and more behind, and questions of abortion, artificial insemination, "test-tube babies," the death penalty, war, foreign policy, racial justice, stealing government papers, advertising, political propaganda, the environment, population staggered the most resolute moral theologians. Even in the serenity of the preconciliar Church, they were necessarily falling further and further behind in their codifications of "the Catholic answer."

If the moral theologians are not as sure as they used to be, editorial writers, columnists, political activists, college professors, ecclesiastical bureaucrats, and Jesuit poets are only too willing to provide detailed and specific instructions about what the only possible moral response to a given problem should be.

If anyone can draw back a moment from the controversy that rages about these critical ethical issues of our time, a number of things become apparent: First, there are many inconsistencies in moral positions. For example, militant Catholics who are deeply affronted by abortion seem rather less concerned about napalm and free-fire zones in Vietnam. On the other hand, the good liberals who are horrified at the deaths of already born children in Vietnam are not apparently very much concerned about the deaths of fetuses in the twenty-fourth week of pregnancy. Those who are concerned about abortion being legal murder are not terribly troubled by the death penalty, nor are they much disturbed by the horrors of the American penal system. Some of the American Irish are quite properly outraged by the British treatment of Catholics in Ulster, but they lost no sleep over Bangladesh. The brutality of some police forces is rightly condemned, but there is little concern among many of those who protest the police behavior over the brutality of criminals who prey on innocent people, both black and white. Those right-wing political leaders who campaign on vigorous law and order tickets seem undisturbed by the thought that the most popular techniques for restoring law and order are the abolition of rights by which citizens are protected from oppression.

There is some reason to be suspicious about alleged moral wisdom that is not deeply concerned about its own inconsistencies. There is even more reason to be concerned about moral wisdom that attempts to substitute one form of rigid ethical requirement for another. Thus, those who argue (as did one Catholic psychologist in my hearing recently) that no one should have a child until after three years of marriage are as rigid and authoritarian as those who argue that everyone should try to have a child in the first year of marriage. Those enthusiastic supporters of feminism who, implicitly at least, assert that every woman should have a career are no more to be thought of as permissive than those who insist that every woman belongs in the home. Similarly, those who say that a woman should have absolute control over what happens to her body (an argument in favor of abortion) may not be much different in their simple approach to complex issues than those earlier Catholic theologians who argued that a woman had no control over what happened to her body.

There is a plenitude of simple solutions, of authoritarian regulations, of inconsistent and self-righteous rules of simple idiocy masquerading as moral wisdom.

In addition, there is an almost pathetic eagerness to believe that "things are changing," that, for example, as one article in *Newsweek* put it recently, "There is a burgeoning number of homosexuals." There may or there may not be more homosexuals. It may simply be that homosexuality is somewhat more public than it was in the past. One would think, to hear the celebrants of the sexual revolution, that pornography, adultery, and fornication were relatively recent developments in the history of the human race. It is possible that there were some major changes in sexual practices among college young people in the 1920s. Most of the research evidence suggests that there hasn't been much in the way of change since then, but one need only read some of the accounts of life in colonial America or investigate, even superficially, the sexual practices in those parts of the rural United States supposedly untouched by the influence of the mass media to realize that neither the Roaring Twenties nor the Radical Sixties have really developed anything particularly new in the way of sinfulness.

The real change is the emergence of a group of people—psychologists, counselors, student health advisers, and other "experts"—who attempt to persuade young people that promiscuity makes for personal growth. (They do so usually in the name of a very unsophisticated variety of Freudian psychology.) Such advice is used as an argument against the "rigid" taboos of the past. Rigid the taboos certainly were, and unhealthy too, for that matter, but it does not follow that there was not a kernel of very important wisdom contained within the rigidity of those taboos. William Shannon, writing in *The New York Times Magazine,* makes this point very well:

> Some modern parents are already so defeatist on sexual issues that they are having their 14-year-old daughters fitted with diaphragms or given prescriptions for the pill. But the powerful emotions surrounding the sexual act cannot be screened out as easily as the sperm. It is those emotions which young people have to learn to manage.
>
> Children of both sexes have to be taught what wise mothers have always told their daughters, which is that an intimate and important experience is cheapened and coarsened when it is divorced from love. If persons use one another like disposable plastic cartons, the emotional content of the experience becomes comparably trivial. There are those who argue that sex can be completely pleasurable even if one barely knows one's partner or loathes him or her. I would suggest that most young people are not so tough or neurotic. Whatever they may protest to the contrary, their feelings are engaged in the sexual act and their feelings are bruised when it leads nowhere.
>
> In sexual relations as in other areas of life, Americans have to relearn the satisfactions of self-denial and anticipation. It would do no harm to 16- and 17-year-old boys and girls to know the facts about sex and yet not engage in intercourse. A certain amount of frustration and tension can be endured—and with good effect. Only modern Americans regard frustration as ranking higher than cholera in the scale of human afflictions. An older, wise attitude regarded self-restraint as a necessary part of becoming mature and creative. But if our children are to learn how to wait and how to discipline themselves, they will have to acquire these habits long before adolescence.[3]

I am sure that most therapists of integrity and experience would be in fundamental agreement with what Shannon says.

It is true that no one will go to hell or become unfit for marriage because he or she has engaged in premarital intercourse. It does not follow, though, that premarital intercourse is a healthy, enriching

[3]William V. Shannon, "What Code of Values Can We Teach Our Children Now?" *The New York Times Magazine,* January 16, 1972, p. 52.

experience. Much less does it follow that one can detach sexuality from permanent or quasi-permanent commitment without risking serious harm to selfhood.

I would argue, however, that norms regarding who sleeps with whom are more appropriate for ethics than theology. The Christian symbol system has better and different things to say about marriage than determining when enjoying the bustline of someone who is not one's wife stops being venially sinful and becomes mortally sinful. Ethics cannot be divorced from religion completely, for ultimately man's view of what is Real has a powerful impact on his determination of what is Good; but a viewpoint about what is Good cannot be converted into a detailed ethical system without severe distortion.

I intend in this book vigorously to resist the temptation to engage in arguments about specific moral issues, for that would merely continue the mistake of equating the Sinai covenant with ethics and moral theology. I propose here, rather, a discussion of how those who accept the covenant symbol must make their moral decisions in an environment of incredible complexity, how one facilitates the development of "moral intelligence," and, in the next chapter, how this moral intelligence can be applied by nations. How does a man who has "put on" the covenant symbol respond to the dizzying complexity in which he finds himself?

There are, of course, many people who believe that it is immoral even to concede that there is complexity in ethical decision making. "I think it's a mistake," said a faculty member at an elite American university to me, "to tell young people how complicated social problems are, because complexity is an excuse for not being involved."

There are those who think that while a sophisticated and uninvolved student may be apathetic, an unsophisticated and involved young person may be a fanatic. There are even those who would prefer apathy to fanaticism. But the faculty member's comment neatly summarized two critical issues currently facing American higher education:

1. Is it possible to balance an awareness of the intricate complexity of social issues with moral commitment?

2. And, if it is possible to achieve such a delicate balance, has higher education any role to play in the development of such a balance?

The traditional stance of elite American higher education has been to shy away from questions of morality. One prominent college president has remarked, "There are two kinds of human development, intellectual and moral, and the college is only interested in the former." Furthermore, research scholarship has worked under a commitment to be value-free. Scholarship may indeed teach the virtues that are required for its own ends, but, whatever the scholar's own opinion, his scholarship is supposed to be neutral on other moral issues. Yet the youthful militants (and some not so militant) were incensed at what they took to be the immorality of their institutions and of many of their teachers. They demanded that colleges take moral stands that facilitate development of moral commitments in their students. Nor did the demands seem to be all that new. In a recent study done for the Carnegie Commission on American Higher Education by the National Opinion Research Center, it was discovered that the strongest predictor of satisfaction with their alma maters among alumni in their late twenties and early thirties was whether the college had contributed to the development of values and goals for life. One of the 1961 alumni—a Jewish businessman—summarized his feelings on the subject in very clear terms:

> College is supposed to teach a person how to think and how to live. A person must learn the *meaning of life,* and unless a person learns this he will be unhappy forever, and will probably make others unhappy. My college tried to mold my intellect, which I have since realized is not man's most important faculty. Man's spirit, his soul, is totally neglected by college just as it is neglected by our materialistic world, and as a character in "Karamazov" says: "Without God anything is possible." And now we are witnessing the world crumbling around us simply because man has lost sight of his true essence, his soul.
>
> I am very unhappy about the materialistic, money-grubbing world I live in, but I am optimistic, because the kids of today seem to have an understanding of their essence and morality.

The problem of morality versus complexity is one of the most knotty issues with which man has wrestled. If one chooses in favor of complexity, then it would appear that one must deny the relevance of general moral principles. On the other hand, if one commits oneself firmly to morality, then there is the grave danger that reality will lose its lamentable grayness and appear in tones of black and white.

The liberal anti-Communists of the 1940s and 1950s, at least in part because of their opposition to John Foster Dulles' moralistic approach to foreign policy, emphasized the complexity of political and social positions. Writers such as George Kennan, Walter Lippmann, and Paul Nitze came close to concluding that because of the subtle and intricate nature of foreign policy problems, the nation had little or no choice but to base its positions on what it perceived as its own most enlightened self-interest, since moral principles provided little or no practical conclusions. Similarly, social scientists proclaimed "the end of ideology" and seemed persuaded that most social problems would yield to planning and technical competence rather than ideological visions. Finally, the ethical situationists insisted that moral decisions had to be made in concrete circumstances, illuminated only by the overriding imperative of love.

But enlightened self-interest in foreign policy produced Vietnam; the unquestioned competency of the *Public Interest* school of social scientists did not in two liberal Democratic administrations notably improve the state of American society; and the imperative of love from the situationists did not modify relationships between white and non-white in American society. The people were lied to, some were oppressed, others were killed, students were dehumanized by the multiversity. Even though moral evil had been defined out of existence, it did not seem to go away.

The Movement was a swing away from complexity back toward morality. While situation ethics still reigned supreme on matters sexual, the young and their not-so-young admirers took vigorous moral stands on political and social issues. They did not hesitate to denounce roundly the liberal anti-Communists and those who spoke of the end of ideology as "immoral."

But just as an awareness of complexity uninformed by strong moral values could produce Vietnam, so strong moral values enlightened by an awareness of complexity produced the fanaticism of, let us say, the Weatherman faction of the SDS. Professor Kenneth Kenniston has pointed out in a number of articles how the student protesters have moral values which are much more autonomous and internalized than those of nonprotesters. More recently Kenniston has added the observation that internalized morality by itself does not necessarily produce a balanced human personality. Other personality dimensions must develop at the same time as the moral value systems if the young person is not going to end up a highly motivated zealot.

And of zealotry we have had more than enough.

I am very skeptical of the enthusiastic moralist. The men who murdered John Kennedy, Robert Kennedy, Medgar Evers, and Martin Luther King, Jr., all presumably thought of themselves as very moral men. We can dismiss them as insane bigots, but the step from single-minded moralism to bigotry or insanity is a short step. If I am forced to choose between Machiavelli and Torquemada, I will cheerfully choose the former. The Machiavellis of the world have caused some human suffering and tolerated much more, but they are rank amateurs at creating human misery compared with the Torquemadas.

Nor will it help to argue, as do the disciples of Professor Marcuse, that my morality is better than yours and therefore you must adhere to my morality even if I have to force you to. Such an argument may have some short-range effect if he who poses it happens to enjoy more force than his adversary; but if he possesses less force, then he may find himself oppressed rather than oppressing; and if the force is relatively equal, the result is likely to be the bloodbath of religious warfare. To be moralistic is bad enough, but to be moralistic about one's moralism is a guarantee of violence and tyranny.

But, surely, there has to be some middle course between Torquemada and Machiavelli. I am inclined to think there is, though, beyond doubt, he who tries to assume such a middle position often finds himself poised precariously on the edge of a razor.

Four propositions may be offered to define the limits of that razor's edge:

1. Even in the post-Freudian, post-Marxist age there are such things as good and evil. No matter how complex the issues, technical competence is not enough to arrive at decent and humane solutions. Dialogue between moral principles and technical complexity is difficult and intricate, but attempts must not be abandoned.

2. There are no simple answers to any of the problems facing the American nation. To pretend that there are is to be irresponsible. Thus Professor Wald's response to the question of how the United States could withdraw from Vietnam "by land, sea, and air" was facile and witty but was not in the strict sense of the word a response at all.

3. Men of good will, intelligence, and complexity can agree on moral principles and still disagree on the application of these principles. To claim moral sanction for one's own solution and to repudiate others as immoral brings one dangerously close to fanaticism. Thus, most men by 1968 were agreed that the war in Vietnam should come to a speedy conclusion. Furthermore, some sorts of conclusions—thermonuclear war, for example—were clearly immoral, but, nevertheless, no single plan for disengagement was so obviously *the* right one as to be able to claim unique moral excellence. We may disagree and argue vigorously with those whose disengagement plans seem to us to be inadequate, but we ought to be wary of doing so in the name of the superior morality of our plan. Similarly, men of good will agree on the evils of racial injustice, but it does not automatically follow that, let us say, busing school children has a unique claim to moral excellence as a means of eliminating discrimination. Those who support busing may be able to marshal a telling case against those who oppose it, but the case is not so overwhelmingly clear to enable the advocates of busing to claim a superior *morality* for their position.

4. The intelligent and educated person is able to maintain involvement in social problems without becoming a fanatic. It is not necessary to have zealots in order that we might have reformers. Young people may have deep and permanent commitments to working for social change without needing to create scapegoats on which they can blame social problems.

Underlying these four propositions is the assumption that there is a dimension of the human personality—which we will call moral intelligence—which can be developed in the maturation experience. This moral intelligence is not developed by faculty members who, as John McDermott puts it, see "themselves as embattled missionaries to the culturally philistine." It is rather, I think, the capacity to reexamine and clarify one's own values repeatedly in the light of concrete situations in which one finds oneself. Moral intelligence is the habit of not letting the picture of the complex gray reality which constitutes the political and social world be blotted out. The morally intelligent person is not satisfied with his own coventional wisdom, whether that wisdom inclines him to withdraw from problems that seem too complex or to charge into the problems which seem simple.

A classic example of moral intelligence at work was the behavior of the Kennedys at that point in the deliberations during the Cuban missile crisis when consensus had almost been reached for the bombing of Cuba. Attorney General Kennedy argued vigorously that such surprise attack was completely foreign to the traditions of the American republic. Characteristically, he asserted, "You're not going to make my brother the General Tojo of the 1960s." The issue was a complex political question and the solution to it was necessarily a political solution. One may disagree with that solution, but the point is that a far more dangerous and violent solution was averted, not so much in terms of political pragmatism (though surely there was an element of that) but in terms of a moral vision by which a nation had lived. One regrets that Mr. Kennedy was not present in 1965 to raise the same question when the decision was made to escalate the Vietnamese War.

The decision not to bomb Cuba is an excellent illustration of one of the peculiarities of moral intelligence. It is relatively easy for the morally intelligent man to know what not to do: He does not bomb Cuba, he does not get involved in a land war in Asia, he does not tolerate racial prejudice, he does not dehumanize college students. But it is much more difficult for him to know what to do positively to implement the values that are implicit in decisions about what not to do.

Can higher education make any contribution at all to the development of moral intelligence? I think it will not do so by direct and explicit effort. The thought of a course entitled "Moral Intelligence 101" is absurd and appalling. Equally appalling, but not so absurd, is the thought of faculty members subtly trying to convert students to their moral viewpoints, and, be it noted, these attempts of conversion are by no means limited to denominational colleges. I would suspect, rather, that moral intelligence is learned, if it is learned at all in a college, through interpersonal osmosis. Young people learn to exercise this virtue primarily because they have seen their teachers exercise it.

Faculty and administrators of a college, therefore, would contribute to the development of moral intelligence in their students by the following kinds of behavior:

1. They must demonstrate compassion for *all* people and not merely for those groups for whom it is currently fashionable to have compassion. Compassion for blacks is admirable, but so is compassion for Polish ethnics. When ethnics are discussed solely in terms of being a "barrier to social progress" they are not treated as human beings. J. D. Salinger's "fat lady"—even if she is Polish—is still Jesus Christ.

2. The faculty member or administrator must refuse to indulge in scapegoating as an outlet for his frustration. Blaming of individuals is great therapy for our Oedipal problems but it has nothing to do with either education or morality.

3. The campus adult will beware of reifying labels. Such catch phrases as "the Establishment" or "the military-industrial complex" or "the power structure" may be very useful political slogans but they are not accurate and precise descriptions of the reality of the social order. A faculty member may know that the Establishment is a myth but his youthful disciple may take it as a literal reality (only to be disappointed someday when he discovers that if there were an Establishment it would run things much more smoothly).

4. The faculty member or administrator will resolutely refuse to provide simplistic answers to complex questions. No matter how strongly he may feel about war or technocracy or race—and if he is fully human, he must feel strongly on all three—he will not betray his students by leading them to believe that all that is required to solve these three problems is common sense, moral righteousness, and enthusiasm. Furthermore, he will display proper reserve and skepticism about the latest fads and fashions in the academic world, no matter how strongly endorsed these fads and fashions may be.

5. The adult who is interested in the development of moral intelligence among the young people on campus will not hesitate to warn them that one of the most pernicious phenomena in the human experience is that mixture of guilt and self-righteousness which the late Ronald Knox once described as "enthusiasm."

In other words, if young people are to learn moral intelligence at all they will learn it from association with men and women who have strong moral commitments but who constantly are in the process of clarifying and revising their commitments, men and women who refuse to give up the struggle for a better and more humane world but who also refuse to impose their own contingent applications of moral vision on others as the only kind of authentically moral decency.

It is not easy to stand on the razor's edge between zealotry and apathy, but then it never has been. Perhaps that's why so few have tried.

We may have betrayed a whole generation of enthusiastic and idealistic young people by letting them believe that there were simple answers and that instant response to political activity was possible.

Recently, a veteran (at twenty-six) student leader said to me, "My generation has lost on everything; we lost on the war, we lost on McCarthy, we have been excluded from the black movement, we've lost on educational reform, we've lost in the struggle against poverty. It looks like we will either have to make our peace with the system or turn to communitarian groups and a separate culture. Either way we won't have much impact."

The young man had much less self-pity than most students (though he certainly lacked the stringent honesty about himself that a Bernadette Devlin can display). He was not an extremist. He never had permitted himself too many illusions. Yet he was weary and worn. He seemed unaware that political and social change take time, effort, and patience. He lacked faith that reform is possible, and he lacked the moral intelligence to understand that it is immoral to quit at twenty-six. Someone had failed to communicate to him the nature of the social reality in which man must live.

Again, a girl who had served a sentence in a federal prison on a narcotics charge commented, "The ones I really despise are the faculty. They had all their bright liberal fashions. They said it was all right for us to experiment with drugs, but they didn't have to go to jail and I did."

Finally, a student writing in criticism of the University of Chicago's student newspaper's stand on drugs asserted, "I am a pothead, an experienced tripper, a speed freak, and at one point I was mildly hooked on heroin. . . . I am not Levi [Chicago's president], I am not the fuzz, I am not Student Health; I am just a student, more screwed up than most, who earnestly hopes that somebody out there will profit from my unfortunate experiences. The sum total of my experience is that dope is bad. . . . I hate dope; but if I had my hands on an ounce of pure pharmaceutical cocaine, I would keep injecting it until it was gone or I was dead. . . . I just wish people in responsible positions . . . would think about the other side of the drug controversy."

I am not blaming the problems of these three young people on their college experiences. Presumably, much that went before the college years provided the roots for their difficulties. Nor am I arguing that the college should try to inculcate moral principles; it should not and probably cannot. Finally, I am not trying to defend the war, the administration, drug laws, or even the Establishment.

I am arguing that there are certain habits of mind which are an essential part of the disciplined intellect that enables one to approach moral issues with a sense of nuanced respect for the complexity of reality. If this respect is not to be found among many young people, the reason may be that it is not found among many of their teachers either.

Chapter 11
Morality and Foreign Policy

One of the most discouraging aspects of the moral complexity in which we find ourselves is that with all the good will and sincerity in the world, we still seem to make disastrous mistakes.

When I was growing up during World War II, my older friends who returned from the military repeatedly informed me that if we won the damned thing, the only reason would be that the other side made more mistakes than we did. Reading Liddell Hart's *History of the Second World War* in an accidental but bizarre counterpoint to the Pentagon Papers, I was forced to conclude that that judgment could be made not only of the Second World War but of most of human history, and, in any case, plowing through Liddell Hart and the Pentagon Papers is not an experience calculated to give one much confidence in the present condition of the human race.

Hart views the Second World War as unnecessarily begun and unnecessarily prolonged. Most of the great victories were more the result of the mistakes of the losing side than the genius of the winning side. Some of the most notable Allied triumphs, for example, were caused by previous Allied defeats which enticed Hitler to overextend himself.

Winston Churchill emerges from Liddell Hart as an inept blunderer. His ill-conceived campaign in Greece caused the English to lose the advantage they had gained in the western desert, and the consequent series of incredible disasters there were responsible for the fall of

Singapore, as Churchill poured vast quantities of personnel and resources into each new blunder in the desert.

The casualties and destruction caused by stupidity on both sides were immense, and disasters like Hiroshima and Dresden are ample evidence that even in a war in which one side is engaged in legitimate self-defense, folly can lead to the worst kinds of immorality. A side which produced a "Bomber" Harris is in no real position to be critical of an Adolf Eichmann.

The men who inhabit the Pentagon Papers are remarkably like those who inhabited the Allies' side in Liddell Hart's history. They are guilty of immense folly, folly which it is as easy for us to recognize from hindsight as it was difficult for them to see at the time. Men make a mess out of things, not only evil and malicious men but also good and well-intentioned men, not only men of limited intelligence, like General Westmoreland and "Bomber" Harris, but men with very considerable intelligence, like Dean Rusk and W. W. Rostow. The human race is not very good at arranging its behavior, and when it gets into matters such as foreign policy and war, the historical lesson is that bad things get worse. The blindness, the ignorance, the stupidity, the folly, the arrogance, the narrowness, the rigidity, the inflexibility that led to the Vietnam mess did not come into the world in 1950. These qualities were present in superabundance during the Second World War and certainly in every previous war in which men have engaged.

The appalling thought is that there is no real way to guarantee that it won't happen all over again.

What did we learn from the Pentagon Papers that we did not already know? I do not mean, of course, that there are not *facts* the papers revealed to us which were previously known only to a very few Americans. I mean that the *lessons* of the Vietnam War were all known before and they did not prevent us from getting into it. If we had not learned them by 1960, what reason is there to think that we have learned them by 1970? How can we prevent the same things from happening all over again?

It might be said that the government should have learned not to lie to the people, but there is little reason to think that if all the secret decisions were revealed when they were made there would have been much difference in the public attitude toward the war. Even if Lyndon Johnson had announced before November of 1964 that the war in Vietnam would probably have to be expanded, he would still have beaten Barry Goldwater. Public disillusionment with the war was based on the fact that it went on too long and involved too heavy a price for something that did not seem worth it. It is extremely doubtful that any public in the world would be moved by arguments more sophisticated than that. It is not good to lie to the people. Dishonesty, be it that of Franklin Roosevelt in the 1940s or of more recent administrations in the 1960s, destroys the credibility of a government. The American people believed they were not being told the truth about the war long before Daniel Ellsberg's arrival on the scene. If everything in the Pentagon Papers had been released to the public a month after it had been written, it is extremely unlikely that the slow but implacable pace of public disenchantment with the war would have been much accelerated.

A second lesson might be that the American government should never get into long-term limited wars in faraway places where the casualty rates will be high and the national interest is not obvious. Such a rule is certainly a good one. Harry Truman would undoubtedly endorse it. But scarcely a decade after we ought to have learned this definitively in Korea we seem to have had to learn it all over again. Dean Rusk, in a television interview, lamented the fact that the war did not have the kind of public support necessary to see it through to a successful conclusion; but what in the world made Mr. Rusk think that such a war could sustain public support for very long? We have had to learn the lesson of Korea all over again. Maybe twice in a quarter century is enough to make the lesson stick, but it seems that man's capacity to learn from past mistakes is tragically limited.

Or, it may be urged, more attention should be paid to questions of morality in determining public policy issues; but, as Daniel Patrick Moynihan has observed, defending democracy in Southeast Asia is an exquisitely moral stance. It may not be mine or yours, but it is a moral stance. Few people are explicitly immoral. Harry Truman justified the bomb on Hiroshima in terms of the lives it would save, both American and Japanese, compared to the lives lost if an invasion of the islands of Japan had been necessary. We may not like such a moral justification, but the problem about falling back on moral arguments is that one man's morality is another man's madness. Those who directed the war in Southeast Asia, it will be said, had little concern for human life, but they would surely reply that they had immense concern for human life; they were convinced it was necessary for the United States to take the stand it did so that many millions of human lives would not be blotted out when all the dominoes fell over. One fights a limited war, the argument goes, in order to avoid a total war. I am not saying that I accept this argument or that I agree with its morality. I am saying that while concern for morality and respect for human life are admirable, they do not automatically dictate policy decisions. It is not hard to find moral rationalizations for almost any policy decision, and, beyond that, men of sincerity, integrity, and good will can disagree endlessly on what moral policy is. We have had few more moral secretaries of state than John Foster Dulles, and as the Pentagon Papers make clear, he was of decisive importance in the beginnings of America's post-Geneva involvement in Vietnam.

It is frequently asserted that the United States did not have a clearly thought-out foreign policy; but the Pentagon Papers make it clear that we did have a policy. It was called "containment" when George Kennan first enunciated it back in the forties and then it became known as "collective security," and then, more recently, the "domino" theory. It was a vigorous, consistent, well-thought-out policy, and in many respects it was a successful one. Western Europe was preserved, the expansion of the Soviet empire was prevented, and the slow breakup of Communist unity may very well have been facilitated by the check to Russian ambitions. I do not at this point wish to get into a detailed argument about the successes and failures of post-World War II foreign policy, particularly in Europe. I simply want to assert that the policy was viewed as successful by most sections of the American public and even by most members of the liberal intellectual establishment. One wonders, for example, why the *New York Times* does not reprint some of its own editorials of the late fifties and the early sixties. Would we find in them any more serious questioning of the "collective security" approach than we find in the Pentagon Papers? This is not to criticize the *Times,* but merely to suggest that we did indeed have a policy, a policy that was endorsed by almost everyone. In retrospect, we stuck to the policy too long and applied it in times and circumstances where it was not only not pertinent but devilishly dangerous. But that, of course, is the problem with policies. One never knows when to abandon them, and the record of the human race generally forces us to the conclusion that policies are almost always abandoned when it is too late.

It might be suggested that what we need is more intelligent men in government. Surely no one can read the Pentagon Papers with the perspective that hindsight gives and not conclude that there was a vast amount of stupidity in the American government during the 1950s and the 1960s, and yet the level of academic and administrative intelligence in the American government during the Kennedy and Johnson years was probably higher than it had ever been before in the nation's history. Was there ever a time when there were more Ph.D.s in the federal government or more Harvard men or more men who could claim to be intellectuals? The intellectual community is now eager to repudiate the war quite possibly because it is all too aware that some of its most distinguished members must bear a heavy burden of responsibility for having gotten us into it. If there is any lesson to be learned at all about intellectuals in government from the Pentagon Papers, it is that it is probably a good thing to keep them out.

I don't really believe that, but I wonder whether that astute domestic politician Lyndon Johnson would have proceeded down the path to political disaster if he had not felt intellectually inferior to the brilliant Ph.D.s from Harvard who were advising him on foreign policy. Looking back, what might have been appropriate would have been more political shrewdness and less intellectual brilliance.

But perhaps we will solve the problem if we build into the government a system which guarantees that there are men who will say no. However, the Pentagon Papers make clear that there were "no" men all along the way. General Taylor, for example, did not like the "search and destroy" strategy. George Ball opposed involvement in the war. Roger Hillsman opposed its escalation. Even McNaughton and McNamara came eventually to disagree, but they had sold the President on a policy and the policy was now being carried out by Westmoreland and the President. It was not for lack of hearing the opposite side of the question that the Vietnam tragedy came into being. At one point, it would seem, the President may have stopped listening to everyone but the military, but apparently that period did not last very long. What was lacking, perhaps, was a man of the influence in Johnson's administration that Robert Kennedy had in the prior one. Such a man of political shrewdness and historical perspective combined with a very high position in the decision-making structure is probably an accident, however, and that is a very thin reed on which to build our hopes for the avoidance of more tragedy.

It is now clear to almost everyone that we should not have become involved in the Vietnam War. One must simply say that such clarity was enjoyed by very few people seven years ago. We will not make the Vietnam mistake again. Indeed, we will probably not make a mistake even similar to it again, but given the folly of man, the complexity of the human condition, and the ever more sophisticated power of self-destruction available to us, do we have any reason to believe that we will not make other mistakes equally as bad if not worse? It is my melancholy conclusion that there is little reason to be hopeful about our capacity to avoid other equally serious tragedies in the future.

There are many confident people, however. One hears no more self-doubt from the critics of the men responsible for the documents in the Pentagon Papers than one can find in the documents themselves. There seems to be an abundance of men who are very sure of themselves, absolutely confident that they know what is to be done, and absolutely certain that their wisdom and their morality are superior to the wisdom and the morality of those who governed us in the sixties. I envy such men their confidence and their certainty. I do not, however, understand how they come by it, for in style if not in substance it is the same sort of certainty that marked the positions of "Bomber" Harris and W. W. Rostow. Sometimes I am prompted to think that the wisdom of a policy stands in inverse proportion to the confidence and the certainty of the men who advocate it.

How can those who so eagerly support new American policies in world affairs be so certain that disaster, suffering, and death will not follow from their policies, too? I am not saying we should not have new policies; on the contrary, it is clear that we should. I am simply saying that I am terribly uneasy in the presence of men who are convinced that they know the answers.

And I am troubled and confused by the unintended-consequence phenomenon which Liddell Hart saw so frequently in the Second World War. I wonder whether historians in the future will see a connection between the Vietnamese War and Mr. Nixon's bold steps toward a new policy toward China. Will the historians say that the Vietnamese tragedy was a necessary prelude to a long era of peace and good relations between the United States and China? Such a possibilty suggests that human affairs are appallingly complicated and confused. A lot of straight lines may grow crooked in human affairs, but then occasionally it turns out that a crooked line may go straight.

Professor Brezenski has suggested that if the United States and the Soviet Union did not possess nuclear arsenals there would almost certainly have been a conventional war between the two countries sometime during the last quarter century. I do not know whether such an analysis is correct or not; in the nature of things, one cannot be sure, but it is a possibility, one that those who were so enthusiastic about unilateral disarmament might pause to consider.

One must take a stand, of course, for we cannot be so befuddled by the confusion and complexity of human events as to stand paralyzed before them, but we must be fully aware of the uncertainties, the complexities, the unintended consequences, good and evil, and the possibilities of mistake that are inherent in the policies we advocate. We must also, it seems to me, be fully aware that we might be wrong and that those who disagree with us and criticize us may not only be in good faith but might also possess as much wisdom as we do—if not more.

Most human political policies fail. The only question is, how badly do they fail? What is desperately needed among both policymakers and critics is more self-doubt—not the self-doubt that paralyzes but the kind that makes us a little less than absolutely certain. I find the absence of doubt reprehensible in the men who wrote the Pentagon Papers. I also find it reprehensible in their critics. In the final analysis, the human race divides itself not into left or right, liberal or conservative, but into those who see the world as complicated, confused, uncertain, and ambiguous and those who see it as clear and simple. The latter are those who will destroy us all.

It is not enough to say merely that things are complicated. If we believe in a loving and gracious Reality, then there must be something that that belief contributes to our actions in moral situations, no matter how complex they might be.

Chapter 12
The Style of a Believer

The follower of Yahweh living in the contemporary world must make his decisions in a context of great complexity and with the awareness that no matter how hard he tries, there is a good chance that he will make many mistakes. He also must come to understand that if the arguments presented in the last two chapters are correct, his religion does not provide him with a set of ready-made answers to all human problems. Rather, it gives him a world view, which shapes and colors the style of his behavior without necessarily prescribing the content of that behavior in a given situation.

The Yahwist may not do something that his pagan friends would do, and the reason may have little to do with a different moral code. A young person committed to the Sinai symbol is not likely to join his teenage friends in stealing jeans from a clothing store, not because he knows the theft is wrong and they think it is right. Both they and he know it is wrong. A businessman at a convention may stay away from a house of prostitution to which his colleagues are going, not because he has a special revelation telling him that adultery is wrong. His colleagues know that infidelity is as wrong as he knows it is. The young person and the businessman act morally because their religious convictions provide them with more powerful motivations for moral action.

In other words, if you really believe that you are in a covenant with Yahweh, there are some sorts of things you simply don't do, because they are inappropriate for a member of the covenant community.

While there is much moral complexity in the world, there are also many situations in which the difference between right and wrong is perfectly clear. Theft, murder, lying, adultery are wrong, and while it may not always be obvious what those things are, there are many times when it is obvious. The Yahwist avoids these sins not because he needs his religion to know that they are sinful or even because he expects Yahweh to come down from Sinai in fire and thunder to destroy him for his sins. Rather he is conscious of just the sort of person the covenant makes him. He understands that there are some kinds of behavior that clearly and explicitly violate the terms of the covenant.

What Yahweh said in the specifically moral stipulations of the covenant was, in effect, "You didn't need me to tell you that theft, murder, and adultery were wrong. You knew without me that you shouldn't do those things. I am saying now that if you are one of my people, you will follow your own sound moral instincts and cease those sorts of activities, for they are beneath the dignity of those who have entered into covenant with me."

But we are dealing with prohibitions. It is frequently quite clear what a follower of Yahweh will not do. When faced with certain options he will have no doubt that there are some he ought not to choose. It is much more difficult, however, for him to discover what positively he should be doing. As I remarked in the previous chapter, moral principles may be useful for deciding what kind of foreign policy not to engage in, but they are much less useful in indicating what sort of positive foreign policy one should develop. Similarly, on the level of the individual person, the thirteenth verse of Chapter 20 of Exodus describes outer limits beyond which no Yahwist will go. However, what positive actions he will take within those limits is mostly up to him. Some of his positive decisions will be the same as those of his pagan friends and neighbors and yet different from some fellow Yahwists of sincerity, intelligence, and good will.

It would be quite possible, for example, that for reasons exactly the same as those arrived at by nonbelievers, a young Yahwist would refuse to serve in the war in Vietnam. At the same time, it would be possible for an equally committed, equally sincere believer to decide that, however many evils may have been associated with the war, it is his duty to serve there. We ought not to be surprised that those who are of the household of faith may differ on specific applications of moral issues. Indeed, we had better become accustomed to such differences, because they are likely to increase rather than decrease in our increasingly complex moral situations.

I am not suggesting that both decisions are of equal moral value or that both young men have with equal accuracy evaluated the situation about which they are deciding. In the objective order, one man has made a correct judgment about the war and another man an incorrect one. My own inclinations are to think that the first young man was accurate in his evaluation, but it is the nature of the complexity and ambiguity of decisions which must be made on such issues that it is very difficult for anyone to be certain at the present time which decision was correct. In order to make my point as vigorously as possible, let me say that I can envisage a situation in which the man who refuses to serve in the war is less moral than the one who serves eagerly and enthusiastically. If he who refuses to serve is arrogant and righteous about his own goodness, if he has contempt for those who decide differently, if he makes sweeping judgments about whole classes of people from the heights of his own superior moral rectitude, if he converts his own agonized and difficult moral choice into a "formula religion" which guarantees him "peace of soul," if he thinks that he is now excused from any further efforts at religious and moral growth and that he is dispensed from further generosity, openness, and trust with his fellow human beings, then for all the correctness of his moral judgment, he is not part of Yahweh's covenant. He has responded to a gracious God not with graciousness in his own personal life but with narrowness, rigidity, and pride.[1]

On the other hand, he who decides that it is his duty to serve in Vietnam may do so with the full consciousness that his decision could be wrong, with great humility and openness, with the willingness to change his mind and to learn and grow, and with a powerful commitment to respect and generosity in dealing with everyone, even those who are his enemies. We may have under such circumstances an incorrect reading of the context of a moral situation yet a style of behavior which is appropriate for a religiously committed person.[2]

---

[1] Let it be clear that I am not suggesting that such attitudes are characteristic of those who have decided not to serve in Vietnam. I am merely asserting that in such cases where these attitudes may be found, we may indeed have moral excellence but we do not have a follower of Yahweh.

[2] Of course it is possible for someone who decides to serve in the war to give way to

To put the matter even more bluntly, the one who serves in Vietnam may return humble and uncertain. He may say, "I am no longer sure about the rectitude of my decision. I did the best I could under the circumstances. I may have been right, but I may also have been mistaken. I will have to live with the uncertainty." The man who refused to serve may go through the rest of his life with the absolutely unshaken conviction that there is no doubt about his rectitude and the immorality of those who decided differently. I would have no hesitation in saying that the former young man is the more religiously admirable of the two.

I have deliberately chosen an example where at the present time the sympathy of most readers will be with the one who refuses to serve in the war to illustrate as powerfully as I can my point that in areas of great moral ambiguity and complexity what distinguishes the religious is not so much the substance of a decision as its style. It is more religiously admirable to make a mistake with a style of graciousness, openness, and love than to be right with a style of arrogance, rigidity, and contempt. Obviously, of course, the most desirable result of all is a decision which is both more morally appropriate than the other and also carried out with a style of graciousness and love.

But it is easier to spot the covenant moral style—if we may call it that—in action than to describe it theoretically. How ought one to behave if one views the world from within the context of the Sinai myth? All that can be done in this book is to present a sketchy outline of some of the characteristics of the covenant style.

1. *The person who is committed to the covenant is "secure" in his moral behavior.* He is not at all confident that he is immune from making mistakes. On the contrary, he is probably more willing than others to admit that he may be making mistakes, but his sense of worth and dignity as a human person is not rooted in his perfection. He can more readily come to terms with his fallibility because he realizes that his worth and value are not negated by it. Yahweh has made covenant with obviously fallible people; he apparently does not consider that to be an obstacle to *hesed*. If Yahweh can live with our weakness and proneness to mistakes, then, presumably, we can live with them too.

---

self-pity, to be cruel and exploitive in his relationships with the people of the country, and to deteriorate morally, religiously, and humanly while in the combat area. My point is that neither objective decision necessarily guarantees religious or human growth.

We do not enjoy making mistakes; we are not complacent about the incorrect moral decisions we make, but neither are we obsessed by them. Furthermore, since we are capable of admitting our errors of moral judgment—to say nothing, of course, of our sinfulness—we are also capable of learning from our mistakes and of evaluating decisions that were made with sincerity but with improper readings of all the circumstances. The Yahwist is less concerned about proving his own blamelessness than he is about understanding what happened, learning from it, and growing in personal wisdom so that a similar mistake will not be committed. He is sorry for his mistakes and sorry for the sinfulness, such as it may have been, which resulted from them. But he is not paralyzed by guilt. If the gracious God who loves him is willing to forgive—and there is nothing clearer in both the old and the new covenants than that God is only too willing to forgive—then the follower of Yahweh is willing to accept forgiveness and begin his life again, sadder but wiser. Because he is secure in his covenant with Yahweh, he does not fall apart under the strain of mistakes and sinfulness.

Let us take an extreme example to make the point. A man and woman, each in reasonably happy relationship with their respective spouses, are brought together in the context of their work. They enjoy each other's company and become good friends. The attraction grows more powerful and they find that, while they continue to give their marriages prime importance, this new relationship is also deeply meaningful to them emotionally. One evening a crisis in their company forces them to work overtime, and when they finally leave the office they pause for one and then several drinks. Almost before they know what is happening they are in a hotel room together committing what must certainly be called adultery, though at the moment of action they are suffused with enormous pleasure and joy. The next day the two are utterly overwhelmed with shame. Neither has ever been unfaithful before. Both are convinced that they have desecrated what were fundamentally happy marriages. They are paralyzed by guilt over what they have done and they wonder how they can possibly expiate the ugliness of their sin.

I would argue that it is precisely at this point that religious issues become paramount. Shame is an appropriate emotion; what they have done is shameful. But guilt and emotional paralysis are not appropriate at all and may be counterproductive, because guilt is likely to weaken a marriage now suddenly perceived as threatened and to force the two people closer to one another in a continuation of the adulterous relationship, a continuation which might not occur if they were able to move beyond guilt and self-reproach to understanding and self-forgiveness.

If these two people are firmly convinced of Yahweh's love for them, they should be capable of leaving the exact measurement of their blame to God. It may very well be, to use the old pre-Vatican category, that what they did was no more than venially sinful. They were caught in a concatenation of circumstances and events which, temporarily at least, deprived them of their full freedom and they were swept along by impulses and passions of which they were only dimly aware and over which they had very little control. On the other hand, it may be that for a long time the two of them had been kidding themselves and each other about the nature of their relationship; even a little bit of objectivity would have warned them that they were skidding toward unfaithfulness. But the point is that in the shame of the morning after they are in no position to decide. They may never be in a position to decide. What they did was certainly not done, to use the old terms, "with full and free deliberation," but neither were they absolute slaves to forces beyond their control. They have no rational choice, then, but to live with the realization that their culpability is indeterminate. They are not the greatest sinners that ever lived. On the contrary, they may be only relatively minor sinners, but neither are they completely free from sinfulness.

Since they can do no more about determining their precise guilt, the appropriate question to ask is, what did the incident reveal about themselves, their personalities, and their relationships with their spouses and with each other? They must also ask themselves and each other what sort of mistakes they might panic into because of the neurotic guilt that becomes terribly intermingled with the authentic shame that they both feel. In other words, it is much more constructive to ask, What mistakes did we make? Why did we make them? What can we learn from them? than it is to ask, How guilty are we? Expiation consists more of intelligent analysis and growth in understanding than in self-torment. Obviously, mistakes were made that brought them to the hotel room and obviously, there was sinfulness involved; but the mistakes do not have to be repeated, nor does their shame have to lead to other mistakes. Their sin, paradoxically enough, provides them with the opportunity for religious and personal growth, for becoming better human beings, better marriage partners, and, quite possibly, even better friends. They expiate their sin not by yielding to overpowering guilt, not by imposing the burden of knowledge on their spouses, but by honestly and realistically facing themselves, asking what mistakes were made, and determining how the mistakes arose.

Obviously, it is not easy to respond to such a difficult, traumatic, and complicated moral crisis with confidence and the self-possession that I described in the past paragraphs. One has to be willing to admit that one is a sinner and that one is still lovable. One has objectively violated a precise stipulation of the covenant, but if one really believes in the covenant, one knows that he is not excluded from the covenant because of this violation, that on the contrary it is incredibly easy to remain part of the covenant despite one's sinfulness. If Yahweh is ready to remit sinfulness, then the sinner must also be ready to remit it. This does not mean that he did not sin; it does mean that his sin neither destroys him nor deprives him of the amazing lovability that Yahweh sees in him. The Yahwist's faith symbol enables him to accept himself as a sinner, transcend the sinfulness, and, in an echo of the Easter liturgy *O felix culpa,* profit from his sin.

The old moral theology would have insisted that the two sinners "separate" immediately. One or the other would have to seek employment elsewhere. But such a quick answer, while in some circumstances appropriate, may in other circumstances not be. It may turn out that the two people are sufficiently able to evaluate and to understand what happened so that they know that they can continue the relationship without a repetition of the incident and without endangering their other and more important commitments. All they can do in the circumstances is to try with as much sincerity and intelligence as they can to make a tentative decision. They must face the fact that their relationship has been changed; their friendship has manifested itself once in a physical union that they could not help but enjoy. This intimacy, even though they are ashamed of it, is a fact of their relationship that they will be unable to change and which will have an influence of its own on the continuation of the relationship. They will have to integrate into their friendship the factuality, the pleasurability, and the shamefulness of the hotel room experience. To be able to do this will require not only a great deal of personal emotional maturity but also a great deal of faith. The covenant symbol should facilitate such an integration, but it will certainly not make it easy.

Can they be sure that the incident will not be repeated? Obviously they cannot; nobody can be sure of anything. Even if it should be repeated, the repetition would not make them unable to receive Yahweh's saving and forgiving love. It would mean sin, shame, and the need for a far more rigorous evaluation of the chain of events that led to the repetition. It would certainly indicate that now there is at least a reasonable presumption that the relationship is too risky to continue. Even a repetition of the sin—to whatever extent it was a sin—could still be turned into an opportunity for religious and personal growth if the two people had deep enough faith in God's love for them.

I deliberately describe in detail this imaginary (though hardly infrequent) event to emphasize that the covenant symbol does provide powerful personal resources for responding to the experience of one's own sinfulness and one's own inadequacies in evaluating the circumstances of moral decision making. The Yahwist can live with his mistakes; he can even learn from them.

2. *The man who is committed to the covenant symbol strives to respect the personhood of all of those in the moral context in which he acts.* He may offend some, he may have to defend himself against others, but he does so without either denying their humanity or turning them into objects which he can use for his own pleasure or as pretexts for his own selfishness. Furthermore, he is aware that the tendency to objectify and to blame others is present in all of us and affects our moral behavior and decision making. It is not so much a question of eliminating exploitation and scapegoating from our personalities as recognizing them, allowing for them, and limiting their influence.

Presumably, the couple described above will have to face the fact that to some extent they were exploiting one another. They were not merely enjoying free and open friendship, they were seeking something from the relationship that they were not finding in their marriages. Perhaps this "something" was lacking in their marriages precisely because they were not "free and open" enough in that relationship. They may have been "using" one another because they had been "using" their respective spouses. On the "morning after," they may be powerfully tempted to continue the exploitation either by heartlessly dropping the other now that one had achieved the aim of exploitation or, more probably, continuing the relationship without facing its exploitive component and at the same time actively and more directly pursuing more exploitation.

There may be at the same time a strong tendency for them to project their own guilt onto others. The transference of blame from oneself to someone else is pervasive in human relationships, particularly in intense and intimate ones. Blaming the other is a form of exploitation and objectification—which in its turn justifies more exploitation and objectification. It is dishonest, cheap, and snide, but anyone who thinks he is immune from it is only kidding himself.

The Sinai covenant makes it clear that Yahweh is only too ready to forgive sin, but it also makes it clear that, passionate God that he is, he will not tolerate hypocrisy. Exploitation and scapegoating are forms of hypocrisy. Rarely do we exploit others explicitly (though sometimes the rationalizations and justifications for exploitation are so transparent that we know the exploiter isn't even fooling himself), but all of us are tempted to "use" our parents, our children, our friends, our lovers, our spouses, our colleagues, our superiors, and our subordinates. It is terribly difficult to deal with another subject—a person with hopes, aspirations, fears, and anxieties like our own. We turn others into objects because they are so much less frightening when we can depersonalize them. Prostitution is a classic example of objectification. Physical pleasure can be enjoyed without the messiness of trying to relate to another subject. Prostitution is only a caricature of the objectification and exploitation that pervades our lives. Yahweh may love us all as persons, but we find it terribly difficult to cope with the responsibility of being part of a covenant community in which we must covenant with others as Yahweh has covenanted with us. The strain of dealing with our role opposites as subjects—while at the same time not giving ourselves over to maudlin bathos—is extremely wearing. We can probably only tolerate the strain if others support us both by treating us like subjects and challenging and encouraging us to deal with them and with everyone as subjects. It is for this purpose that we have a covenant community, and in the new covenant it is for this purpose that we have a Church. The Church is nothing else but a group of human beings trying to support one another in the difficult challenge of responding to Yahweh's gracious love by being graciously loving to everyone with whom Yahweh has peopled our environment.[3]

[3]For a discussion of this concept of the Church as a community supporting us in our efforts to deal with others as subjects rather than objects, as persons rather than things, see my book, *What a Modern Catholic Believes About the Church*, Chicago: Thomas More Press, 1972.

3. *He who has committed himself to the covenant symbolism is able to be humble in his moral behavior.* He is quite conscious that he does not have all the answers. He is aware of his own mistakes and is able to accept them and try to learn from them. He acknowledges that he has no necessary monopoly either on knowledge or on moral insight and that others may be both more accurate in their evaluation of situations and more courageous in their personal decisions—even though he does not confuse accepting extreme positions with moral wisdom.

He who believes in the Sinai myth has strong and unassailable notions about the graciousness of God's love, but because the strength of his religious commitments is so powerful, he is able to listen to and learn from others. His humility is obviously related to the personal security we discussed previously. He finds that his value and his worth does not depend on the invariable correctness of his moral judgments but on Yahweh's love. Furthermore, his humility is also grounded in his respect for others as persons. Since the others are subjects, not objects, they are capable of knowledge and insight and wisdom, and they must be listened to instead of being dismissed out of hand. The follower of Yahweh has enough personal and religious strength from his own commitment that he is able to listen to others.

Unlike certain varieties of the species *Liberalis academicus,* the member of the covenant community feels under no constraint to accept the moral perspectives and decisions of others and make them his own—especially when the moralities of the others are stated with deep and powerful passion. The Yahwist, unlike the liberal faddist, has convictions of his own, but precisely because he is secure he is able to listen to others, perhaps to learn from them, and certainly understand them in the context of their own backgrounds and ultimate symbol systems. Similarly, he has no need to try to impose his morality or his symbols upon others. He will explain them with all the vigor at his command, and he will argue about his own moral convictions and decisions with as much integrity and persuasiveness as he possesses, but neither his faith nor his morality depend on the acceptance of others and therefore he has no need to constrain others to agree with him. He knows where the ground is on which he stands and is confident of the value of that ground even if there are others who refuse to stand on it. He does not arrive either at his religious symbols or at his moral decisions by counting noses. If others wish to move their noses and their brains to another religious and moral position, the Yahwist does not feel the need, much less the compulsion, to abandon his position. His strength comes not from the consent of others nor from his ability to impose his will on others nor from the ease with which he can turn others off when they disagree with him; it comes from the covenant that he knows Yahweh has entered with him.

4. *The man who believes in the covenant symbol has no need to become a Grand Inquisitor. He does not succumb to the temptation to "do good."* He does not go around attempting to protect others from their ignorance or sinfulness. He does not view his mission in life as saving others from the misuse of their freedom. Yahweh gave freedom to all men and to each man; it is between Yahweh and the other person what sort of relationship the two of them develop. A man committed to the Sinai myth knows damn well that he can't force Yahweh into anything. He also understands that Yahweh is not going to accept any attempt to force another of his servants into anything. The covenant is a free commitment on both sides, and those who attempt to force others into it do so at the risk of discovering that they are not really part of the covenant themselves. The missionaries who converted the Chinese with the promise of rice, the kings who brought their whole people into the Church, the pastors who "train" everyone in the grammar school to go to confession on the Thursday before First Friday, the parents who force their children to attend Sunday Mass, all have one thing in common: unlike Yahweh, they are not prepared to permit people to be free. One must conclude that the Sinai myth did not have a very powerful hold on their religious and moral lives.

5. *The convinced Yahwist claims freedom not only for himself and his kind but for all men.* The sabbath commandment proclaims rest not only for the children of Israel but for their slaves and for the strangers who are living in their camp. Some commentators think that the word used in the commandment "Thou shalt not steal" means "Thou shalt not steal thy neighbor's freedom," that is to say, "Thou shalt not turn your neighbor into a slave." Furthermore, the denunciation of false witnesses seems to be aimed at dishonesty in legal and quasi-legal proceedings. Thirteen centuries after Sinai, Jesus would rail against injustice, oppression, and hypocrisy; and the Israelite and Christian religious traditions at their best are in constant protest against oppression and injustice. Unfortunately, some members of both traditions, particularly (sad to say) the Christian tradition, have permitted themselves to become so identified with the status quo in its various times and places that they have become not merely part of oppressive social structures but vigorous defenders of such oppression.

One need not go as far as the so-called "political theologians," who argue that the Church must criticize everything and that the essential role of the Church is social criticism. One cannot escape the conclusion, however, that those who believe that Yahweh has entered into covenant with his people must be horrified at the thought that the people of Yahweh—now understood to be the whole human race—are anywhere in the world victims of tyranny, injustice, and oppression. Outrage at oppression is not the same thing as advocacy of simplistic solutions to social problems; and passion to expand human freedom is not the same thing as self-righteous denunciation of those who, despite serious efforts, have not been able to eliminate injustice. The fight against tyranny and oppression is a long one, and as we have suggested, a complicated one. It is not likely to become completely successful in our day or perhaps ever until the Day of Yahweh comes. But if those who believe in the Sinai myth realize that social reform requires competence, patience, skill, persistence, and perseverance, they must also understand that given the covenant symbol which has enveloped them they have no choice but to be angry and appalled at the things man is still doing to his fellow men. If it is necessary—and I am convinced that it is—to insist that much that passes as Christian social criticism is naïve and romantic, it is also necessary to insist that sophisticated social criticism and long-range commitment to social reform are not adequate for the follower of Yahweh unless they are combined with passion and anger at the fact that men still stand in the way of Yahweh's graciousness.

It is difficult, of course, to combine passion with sophistication; the young are more likely to be passionate, the old more likely to be sophisticated, and those of us who stand in between are, alas, unlikely to possess enough of either quality. Yet because it is difficult to combine anger and an awareness of complexity, it does not follow that those who are committed to the Sinai covenant are excused from their obligation to try to combine both qualities. Those whose lives have been grasped by the covenant symbol are men and women who are permanently committed both to enthusiasm and excellence, the former because they understand the secret of Yahweh's love, and the latter because nothing less is an appropriate response to his loving graciousness.

6. *The Yahwist takes risks.* Because he is confident of the fundamental graciousness of the universe, he knows that it is not necessary
to play everything safe, and while he is not an incorrigible gambler
who must risk everything, he still understands that human, personal,
and religious growth occurs only when one is willing to take intelligently
reasoned chances. Since he knows that in the long run nothing can
separate him from Yahweh's love, he knows that even when he seems
to lose, he really doesn't.

One of the besetting problems of upper-middle-class American
youth—particularly those whose parents spent their formative years in
the Great Depression—is their inability to risk themselves. Fear of
making decisions about career, marriage, and children and their
reluctance to expose their total selfhood in complete and enthusiastic
dedication to what they are doing are widespread among American
young people. They constitute the most serious problem that the
counselors and therapists who deal with college and graduate school
students must face. Many young people find it much easier to be
content with unimaginative mediocrity, within which one can argue
that one has never really failed, than to take the big risks, which,
indeed, give one the opportunity for success but also force upon one
the risks of failure. I have known doctors, lawyers, poets, journalists,
and sociologists who are content with "just getting by," because
anything more than that is entirely too risky. I have also known young
people who make great progress in understanding and insight in
therapy, but resolutely refuse to act on their understanding and insight
because if they give up their neurotic defenses they will have to take
the risk of straining toward excellence, and in that risk is the
possibility of failure.

Such young people obviously did not acquire much self-confidence
in their families, and neither did they acquire much faith in Yahweh. It
is intolerable that anyone who has put on the Sinai covenant should be
content with mediocrity. If Yahweh is gracious, if the universe is
good, then it is necessary that man live his life to the fullest. A
narrow, timid, small, unsatisfying existence is anathema.

There was once in moral theology a theory called tutiorism. According to this theory, it was required that a person always follow the
"safer" moral course. Most theoretical moralists reject tutiorism as a
practical basis for moral actions, but an implicit version of it was an

important part of our educations. "No one will ever go to hell," we were told, "for doing the safe thing." Quite apart from the question of going to hell, the dictum was wrong because erring on the side of safety is no guarantee that we will adequately respond to that passionate, headlong God of ours.

There is one example of tutiorism, in practice if not in theory, that I mention, if somewhat hesitantly. There is in the modern world an increasing awareness of the variability of human friendship. Intense friendships are possible between people who are not married to one another without other fundamental commitments they may have being violated. These friendships are widespread, but they are, I think, an especially severe dilemma among celibate religious, who are wondering whether close friendships with obvious and at times powerfully sexual overtones are compatible with their celibate commitment.

I hesitate to comment on this question because it is still an obscure and difficult one, and I do not feel qualified to discuss it with any confidence. I am convinced that my friend Eugene Kennedy is correct when he says that these relationships are only for the mature and the self-possessed and are not to be sought as an end in themselves. I am also convinced that it is extremely easy to engage in self-deception in this area. Finally, I think such friendships are only possible without serious danger when the people who engage in them have no question or doubt about the permanency of their fundamental commitment.

But with all these qualifications it still seems to me that it is necessary to make the point that although these relationships may have a certain amount of risk in them, it does not follow that they are evil and should be abandoned. Because I have alluded in passing to such friendships in some of my other writings, I receive some mail from people in such relationships who are plainly troubled. It is very difficult, indeed, impossible, to make any intelligent comments on a particular relationship when one does not know the people involved. But insofar as one can make a judgment from a letter, I often find myself convinced that the relationships described to me were not only quite harmless but also making an important positive contribution to the personal and religious growth of the people involved and to the exercise of their apostolic vocations. I could understand their troubles, for their feelings sometimes were quite strong and led to displays of affection of which they were, I think, deeply ashamed. Furthermore, almost in the nature of those relationships, there were few if any friends they could turn to for support in working out the problems involved.

However, occasionally it seemed that the people involved had every reason to be confident that they would neither end up in bed with one another or leave the ministry. What tormented them and prevented them from enjoying the blessings of their friendships was the fear that they were doing something risky or unsafe. They felt it would be *safer* to terminate the relationship altogether.

Unquestionably, it would be safer, but as is evident in this chapter, safety of itself is not an appropriate criterion to determine human moral behavior. Whether the calculated risk in the relationship is worth sustaining because of the obvious benefits of that relationship to the people involved is a decision which must be made in each case by the two people. No universal principle can save them from the agony of working out a decision for themselves. However, once they have made their decision, it seems that it would be appropriate for them to put aside their worries and to continue with their work and their affection for one another. What if something goes wrong? they may ask. To which one is forced to reply that something may go wrong in any human relationship or, indeed, in any human endeavor; and if "things go wrong" despite reasoned, mature caution to prevent such an occurrence, then one must simply evaluate the situation again. Worrying about the possibility of things going wrong can easily be a self-fulfilling prophecy and in any case it violates the trust and confidence which should be characteristic of the moral behavior of those who are committed to the Sinai myth.

I suspect that there are some readers who will go over these paragraphs word for word, looking for a "solution" to a "problem" they are facing. But no matter how often they reread this section they will find no solution for their problems. I do not believe that these relationships should be defined as problems. They are challenges, and how people respond to the challenge is up to them, not to me. All I am saying is that in this set of circumstances, as in every other, neither general principles nor a practical version of tutiorism excuses us from the agonizing and ambiguous responsibility of forming our own consciences and making our own decisions.

7. *Those who embrace the covenant symbol realize that they are never excused from effort.* If you believe in a gracious God and a

universe that is "out to do you good," you are simply never allowed to quit. There are some situations and some relationships that may well be beyond redemption. One should be most reluctant to abandon a marriage commitment, for example, but it is a sad and inescapable fact that some marriages simply cannot be salvaged. Some pastors will never learn how to be friends with their junior colleagues; some superiors will never be able to be secure in the presence of their subordinates. Some employers will never be able to deal honestly with their employees. Some delinquents are incorrigible. Some sick people will not be helped by either surgery or therapy. No matter how much time, energy, and work we put in, there are still many times in our lives when we lose. The intelligent man knows when he has lost and goes away to try again somewhere else.

Nevertheless, to abandon hope for reconciliation or its functional equivalent must only very reluctantly be done and certainly not because one has been beaten once or has lost once or has taken a chance once and been rejected. The committed Yahwist does not think he is excused from trying again. If the universe is gracious, if Yahweh loves us, then we are committed to improvement—to improving ourselves, to improving our relationships, to improving the world. We must be under no illusions that it will be easy; it will require work, energy, discipline, sacrifice. And those efforts cannot be ends in themselves; they are means to other and more noble ends; they are transfused and transformed by a commitment to goodness by way of a full acceptance of a universe that is gracious and loving. The Yahwist does not run away. Just as Yahweh did not quit when Israel whored with false gods, so his follower does not resign from the fray when the going gets tough.

8. *Perhaps the most obvious manifestations of the Yahwist's moral style are a refusal to hate and a commitment to joy.* Those who believe in Sinai can grow very angry, not merely at ideas or at principles but at people. They may even find that they have no choice but violence, though they are most reluctant to do so. No matter what happens, they simply cannot hate for very long. It may well be true that others have done them great evil, but the evil is transient and Yahweh's loving graciousness is permanent. If Yahweh does not hate us because of our evil, then we are surely in no position to hate others because of their evil. This is a hard saying. Hatred is one of the most beloved of human possessions and we are reluctant to give it up. Most of us, I suspect, keep lists of our enemies and wait eagerly for the appropriate day when we can "settle" with them.[4] Perhaps the measure of our lack of faith in the Sinai covenant is the amount of hatred still lingering in our personalities—limiting, constricting, deadening. It is precisely because hatred persists—and its principal ally, fear—that we are unable to be joyful. For joy is the ultimate mark of the follower of Yahweh. We can go forth to do battle with the Amorites (these now lurking inside ourselves instead of out on the desert) with a song on our lips only if we are confident that we have been possessed by a dazzling, gracious God. If there is no joy in our hearts, if we are frightened, narrow, angry, anxious men and women, then we have not put on the Sinai symbol; we have not really committed ourselves to the covenant myth, and we don't really believe, at least not with nearly enough strength, that our God does in fact love us.

My list of the characteristics of Yahwist moral behavior is obviously only a very tentative beginning. But the list shows that the covenant myth, even though it is not explicitly concerned with ethical systems and even though it does not provide precise answers to the many specific moral problems we face, nonetheless has extraordinarily important implications for human moral behavior. The security, reverence for persons, humility, moral outrage, courage, durability, trustfulness, and joy of the committed Yahwist ought to make him someone who clearly stands out among his fellow men.

If not many committed Yahwists stand out among their fellow men now, I suppose the reason is that not very many of us are all that committed to the God who revealed himself on the fruitful mountain.

---

[4]I will admit that I have such a mental list. (Some people I know actually have the list written out.) Alas for my Gaelic ire, whenever I encounter such an enemy in person, it vanishes. How foolish of me to be angry at them in the first place.

Chapter 13
Covetousness

You shall not covet your neighbor's house: you shall not covet your neighbor's wife, or his male or female slave, or his ox or his ass, or anything that is your neighbor's. (Exodus 20:14)

The last two commandments, in the Catholic numbering (the last one in the usual Jewish and Protestant numbering), forbid covetousness. One is not supposed to covet either one's neighbors or one's neighbors' goods. The Hebrew word *hmd*, which is used here, does not usually mean "admire" or "wish to have" but rather "to lay plans to take." If one's neighbor has a surplus of goods or a beautiful wife, it is not sinful to admire his possessions, nor is it necessarily sinful to wish that one had equally desirable possessions. Yahweh's stipulation rather is that we do not permit ourselves to be so attracted by a neighbor's wife or goods that we lay plans to snatch them from him.

The Israelite religious mind had a horror of covetousness quite possibly because in any closely knit community one man's success is another man's failure. In the book of Micah, Chapter 2, verses 1–2, the prophet powerfully elaborates on the prohibition of covetousness by putting the following words in Yahweh's mouth:

Woe to those who plot evil,
who lie in bed planning mischief!
No sooner is it dawn than do it
—their hands have the strength for it.

> Seizing the fields that they covet,
> they take over houses as well,
> owner and house they confiscate together,
> taking both man and inheritance.

In the pre-conciliar catechism, the ninth and tenth commandments were taken to be addenda to the sixth and seventh. Coveting our neighbor's wife meant "having dirty thoughts." Coveting our neighbor's goods meant envying his possessions. There never was very much concern about the tenth commandment in the old Church. We agonized at great length over the actual theft and had little time to worry over plans to steal. However, the detailing of the variety of offenses that could be committed through "impure thoughts" was extensive. While it was conceded that sexual fantasies (though the words were never used) were only sinful if one "consented to them," the impact on most religion classes about "impure thoughts" was such that most Catholics seemed to think that sexual fantasies had to be confessed in the sacrament of penance. How human beings could live in a world peopled by bodies approximately half of which were of the opposite sex and escape sexual fantasies was never made clear. In the moral theology books and the catechism, the ideal solution appeared to be to withdraw into a monastery where the half of the world's bodies of the opposite sex would never appear. A happy solution, and not quite so drastic, for many Catholics was to admit in the confessional that they had "dirty thoughts" but to affirm that "I didn't take any pleasure in them." Most of us who were confessors were willing to accept descriptions of mitigating circumstances without bothering to wonder how sexual fantasies could fail to be pleasurable, much less if there was much point in engaging in them if they weren't.

For all the *foolishness* to be found in this exaggerated moral rigorism, there was an important point, although those that made it rarely understood its full implications. The final stipulation of Yahweh deals not only with external human behavior but one's internal dispositions. But it is not the sixth and ninth commandments only that are underwritten by Yahweh's last stipulation; it is the whole Decalogue. It is applied not only to man's outward activity but also to his interior orientation. One of the Talmudic commentaries observed, quite appropriately, "He who violates the last commandment, violates all of

them." If all of man's heart and mind are not given over to the
covenant, then his external behavior is meaningless. Covetousness is a
symptom that a man has not really put his trust in Yahweh; he still puts
his trust in himself. He covets that which is his neighbor's even to the
extent of planning to take it from his neighbor because he is not
confident that Yahweh will honor the terms of the covenant and
therefore believes that he must provide for himself. He is restless and
dissatisfied with what he has and wants what someone else has
because he believes that he can find security in his possessions. The
one who has truly given his heart over to the covenant knows that
security can come only from Yahweh.

The final stipulation of the covenant says the same thing as Father
Shea, whom I quoted in another context earlier in this book, that it is
not nearly enough to profess external faith in Yahweh's goodness.
Man must rather take to himself the covenant commitment and permit
it to permeate and pervade his whole being, so that his trust in Yahweh
is not merely a matter of external assent but becomes a profound
personal commitment that transforms everything he does. Until a
symbol is internalized in that fashion, it has not really become a
meaningful religious symbol at all. The final stipulation of the Decalogue demands that we internalize the covenant relationship by forbidding covetousness. No one who believes that Yahweh is his God is
permitted to put his security in himself. The Yahwist does not covet
because he does not need his neighbor's wife or goods for his own
well-being and happiness. Certain as he is of Yahweh's love, there is
no reason for him to scheme to take things from his neighbor.

This theme will recur in the New Testament. Commentators on the
story of "the rich young man" tell us that the point made by that story
is that the young man's problem was not so much the refusal to give
up his possessions as it was the refusal to give up the personal security
that the possessions provided. Indeed, Jesus' warnings against the
perils of riches were not so much against material abundance in itself
as rather the illusion of security that material abundance can give to
the rich man (and by the standards of the New Testament, all but a
tiny minority of contemporary Americans would be considered rich).
There was no necessary merit in poverty in the teaching of Jesus, but
the poor man could not delude himself into thinking that he was the
master of his own fate. To this extent he was free from one of the

self-deceptions possible to the rich—and possible to virtually everyone in a society where food, clothing, shelter, and medical care are relatively accessible to most of the population.

What Jesus criticized in the rich was what various prophets criticized in Israel's disastrous foreign policy. The Israelite kings thought that they could be secure and confident in their power if they made appropriate military alliances. The prophets warned them that the strength of the Israelites came not from military alliances but from Yahweh. When treaties became a substitute for the covenant of Yahweh Israel was doomed.

Neither in the Sinai covenant nor in the teaching of Jesus was there any mandate for personal or national irresponsibility. One is not to cease work in the fields under the assumption that Yahweh will provide manna. The point, rather, is not to delude oneself into thinking that even the most abundant harvest guarantees one's life or happiness. If one puts one's heart in the treasure of the harvest and if one's heart belongs to the harvest and not to Yahweh, he is not part of Yahweh's covenant.

The Yahwist works hard in the fields (or its functional equivalent in the modern world), and he hopes that the fields bear fruit because eating is better than starving, but he is not obsessively concerned about the harvest, for he knows that even if it fails, he will not be separated from Yahweh's love. Worry about the harvest is foolish because it will have no impact on the harvest and, more serious, it calls into question the sincerity and power of Yahweh's love.

If covetousness is defined as the conviction that we must rely on our own efforts, not merely to eat and to stay alive but also to justify the worth, dignity, and value of ourselves as human beings, there can be no doubt that covetousness is indeed a besetting problem for mankind, particularly in the modern, industrial societies, where one's worth is measured by wealth and success. Contemporary man must devote his thought to what he shall eat and what he shall drink and what he shall put on, because if his food and drink and clothing are not up to the expectations of his status, he can be written off as a failure. We covet not merely because we are not sure of Yahweh's gracious love, we also covet because our value and reputations as human beings depend upon the effect of our covetous behavior.

Much of the accumulation of wealth, pageantry, and pleasures which may be observed in the world around us is rooted in psychological and human insecurity. We surround ourselves with goods and services to reassure ourselves of our worth and to protect ourselves from attacks by those who hate us. The accumulation of money we can never spend, goods we will never use, and pleasures we never really enjoy are all means of self-defense. They do not eliminate the reckoning of death or even postpone it. They give us the illusion that we are in control of our lives, that Yahweh does not hold us in the palm of his hand.

Partly by choice but mostly by chance, I live on the margins of a number of large institutions, neither a part of nor fully accepted by the Church or the academy. I used to flatter myself into thinking that the combination of decisions that moved me out on the margins was proof that I was a man of faith and could take the kind of risks that are expected from a servant of Yahweh. I am now more inclined to believe that there is also a strain of the compulsive gambler in me, and that the disaster of the Great Depression was so powerful an influence on my youth that my propensity for risk taking is evidence of my seeking an abundance of security that the world is incapable of providing. Deep down in my personality somewhere I want the absolute guarantee that the Great Depression won't occur again.

This line of thought occurred to me one day when a colleague remarked, "Greeley, you're the kind of man who enjoys doing things that bring people to the margins of society, but you don't like having to live there." The insight of this observation struck me very forcefully. As I look back over my life, I can see how the decisions I made inevitably pushed me to the margins. While there are obvious strategic advantages in freedom and flexibility and the independence that comes from marginality, I must confess that I find it difficult to live with the realization that I don't really belong anywhere. It seems to me that most people on the margins are not so bothered as I am by being excluded from full acceptance in both the Church and the university. The issue is complicated, and like everyone else, I am a jumble of confusing and contradictory emotions and motivations. I am not suggesting that all my life decisions have primarily been motivated by emotional insecurity and lack of faith. There is a strong and vigorous part of me that really enjoys the ambiguous role I play. I would certainly not give it up without a fight, but I would be kidding myself if I thought my "life project" was totally free from neurosis and infidelity.

I have lapsed into autobiography again because I cannot presume to judge any other man's motivations. I suspect that my experience is common enough. Most of our "life projects" are a combination of strength and weakness, of health and neurosis, fidelity and infidelity. If we had it to do all over again, we might very well make exactly the same decisions, but they would be purified from fear, insecurity, and the hoarding of treasures to protect us from the fragility and vulnerability of human existence. Rather than wishing that we could do it all over again, however, what we ought to do is face the infidelity in our lives and begin to reduce it. If my faith in Yahweh were strong enough, if I had given myself over to the covenant symbol more completely, I would not especially mind a life on the margins, because I would understand that all human beings live on the margin that stretches between birth and death, yet no man with whom Yahweh has bothered to covenant could possibly be marginal. Whenever I covet something to belong to, a "place of my own," I should remember that I do belong to something—a covenant. There is also a place of my own—at the foot of Sinai.

The final stipulation of the Decalogue, then, means that Yahweh wants more than just external professions of confidence and trust; he also wants a confident and trusting heart, one that is so fundamentally secure in the graciousness of Being that it need not waste its time with foolish, trivial worries about wealth and pleasure. The Yahwist does not have the time and energy for such shallow concerns. The covenant has liberated him. He does not covet because he does not *need* to covet. He is free to devote himself to other, better things.

Chapter 14

The End—
The Beginning?

Thre are those who wish to reconstruct the past and those who wish to destroy it. On the one hand, many Christians yearn for the "good old days" when the Ten Commandments were "taken seriously." On the other hand, there are Christians who wish to strike down the Ten Commandments as irrelevant.

The thesis of this book is that both positions are misguided. One can make no decisions about the Ten Commandments until one understands what they are. To reject them as an irrelevant moral code or to attempt to reconstitute them as a relevant one is fatuous activity if it turns out that they were never intended to be a moral code at all. The nineteenth and twentieth chapters of Exodus are not the beginning of an elaborate legal system; they are rather a record of a theophany, a manifestation by and an experience of the deity. The myths and the symbols which record the Sinai experience do not have whatever value they still possess because of their capacity to direct specific moral responses to specific moral issues. We investigate the Sinai symbols to see whether there is in them wisdom about the nature of the Real; whether, as Schubert Ogden has phrased it, they re-present to us our basic assurance of the purpose and worth of human life. In his book *What a Modern Catholic Believes About Heaven and Hell*, Father John Shea describes the Catholic attitude toward religious symbols out of the past:

There is a strong conserving strain in the Catholic tradition. The Christian is an incurable saver. He drags his whole past with him into the future. He would move quicker if he scrapped many of the things he carried, but he cannot bear to lose an alternative perspective or a possible truth. An ancient religious practice or a dusty doctrine may capture and communicate an undying aspect of the human situation. At the present moment its meaning may be obscure but that does not mean its truth is dead. The Christian hoards wisdom; he is reluctant to part with anything.[1]

The question that must be asked is whether the dry, old, dusty Decalogue may possibly contain a truth about the human religious situation that is timeless. Many of us may decide that the passionately aroused Yahweh of Sinai really has nothing to say about the nature of human existence, but if a decision is made to reject Yahweh, let him be rejected for that reason. It is foolish to turn Yahweh off because we don't like his commandments. If we are to turn him off, let us do so because we do not believe that Reality is that gracious and that loving.

But what happened to the Decalogue? How did it get converted into a stuffy, rigid legal code, when in fact it was initially a theophany? Paul Ricoeur has suggested that there is an almost incurable human tendency to make religious symbols the object of faith rather than the means of faith. We believe not in the reality that is revealed by the symbols but in the symbols themselves. The symbols cease to be means of communication between man and God and become idols. From Ricoeur's point of view, we are presently engaged in an exercise of iconoclasm; we are smashing the idols so that we may recapture the symbols. But it is not enough to dispose of the idols. One must also examine the symbols almost, as it were, from the beginning.

The situation in which language today finds itself comprises this double possibility, this double solicitation and urgency: on the one hand, purify discourse of its excrescences, liquidate the idols, go from drunkenness to sobriety, realize our state of poverty once and for all; on the other hand, use the most "nihilistic," destructive, iconoclastic movement so as to *let speak* what once, what each time, was *said,* when meaning appeared anew, when meaning was at its fullest. Hermeneutics seems to me to be animated by this double

[1]John Shea, *What a Modern Catholic Believes About Heaven and Hell.* Chicago: Thomas More Press, 1972.

motivation: willingness to suspect, willingness to listen; vow of rigor, vow of obedience. In our time we have not finished doing away with *idols* and we have barely begun to listen to *symbols*. It may be that this situation, in its apparent distress, is instructive: it may be that extreme iconoclasm belongs to the restoration of meaning.[2]

The most critical issue vis-à-vis the Sinai symbols is revealed when we ask what they say to us about the nature of God, and of man, and of human life. When we pose the question this way, the answer may very well be that Sinai is absurd, but no one who has faced the challenge of the Sinai symbols can assert that they are irrelevant.

For the Yahweh whom we encounter at Sinai is not merely a God to be explained and understood. He is also a God demanding a response. All religious symbols, of course, demand some sort of response, but there is nowhere in the whole repertoire of human religious symbols one more insistent on a response than the Yahweh symbol. Paul Tillich puts the matter with his accustomed clarity and vigor:

> Man is always put before a decision. He must decide for or against Yahweh, for or against the Christ, for or against the Kingdom of God. Biblical ethics is not a system of virtues and vices, of laws and counsels, of rewards and punishments. All this is not lacking, but it appears within a framework of concrete, personal decisions. Every decision is urgent; it has to be made now. When it has been made, it has far-reaching consequences. It is always an ultimate decision—a decision of infinite weight. It decides man's destiny. It decides the destiny of nations, the selected one as much as the others. Every generation in every nation has to decide for or against righteousness, for or against him who is the God of righteousness. And in every nation, including the selected one, the decision against righteousness means self-destruction.[3]

We have two tasks: to listen to what Sinai says about Yahweh and, having heard the Sinai myth, to decide how we are going to respond to it.

It is difficult to listen to a symbol and avoid the extremes of

---

[2]Paul Ricoeur, *Freud and Philosophy: An Essay on Interpretation*, translated by Denis Savage. New Haven: Yale University Press, 1969, p. 27.

[3]Paul Tillich, *Biblical Religion and the Search for Ultimate Reality*. Chicago: The University of Chicago Press, Phoenix Books, 1964, p. 45.

recreating idols or destroying the symbol. Our temptation is to strike out and destroy, particularly when we are angry at the tyranny that idols have exercised over our lives. We are suspicious of the Catholic tendency to hoard wisdom, and in our ignorance and suspicion we feel inclined to say, "To hell with it all! Let us start over and let the dead symbols of the past bury their dead."

But if it is difficult to pass beyond iconoclasm to understanding, it is even more difficult to pass from understanding to faith. We may conclude our listening to the Sinai symbols with the willingness to concede that Yahweh is a fairly impressive God, but such a confession is not faith, and when we have the choice of taking the great leap of faith or going back to smashing idols, pushing the idols around seems a much less demanding enterprise. I am in no position to force anyone to make an act of faith, but as a follower of Yahweh, however inadequate my discipleship may be, I insist that he deserves a hearing at least. It is a monstrous distortion of who and what he is to think that the self-revelation which took place on Sinai was nothing more than the proclamation of a legalistic code. You don't have to like my God—and I admit that there are times when he is a terribly difficult sort of deity—but you should at least dislike him for the right reasons.

This volume is a sequel to my book *The Jesus Myth,* and I think that for Christians the order is appropriate. We first encounter Jesus and then through him come to explore the Old Testament and encounter his father, Yahweh, on Sinai. Once we have explored the Sinai myth, we are then faced with the difficult question of whether the cross and resurrection symbols add anything to the Sinai covenant symbol. The idea of personal resurrection, of a relationship between God and the individual person in addition to his relationship with the people, the emphasis on the universality of Yahweh's revelation, and even the insistence on unselfish love all antedated the coming of Jesus. Late Old Testament Judaism had concluded to a belief in resurrection and a personal relationship between God and individuals. It had also become universalistic in its higher theory, if not in practice. So the uniqueness of the Jesus event cannot be found in any of these phenomena.

But the question of what the resurrection adds to Sinai is an absurd one. How can you add to a revelation that says that God is passionately in love with his people, that the universe is not only benign and gracious but madly in love? Jesus did not say anything fundamentally new. He rather renewed the old theophany of Sinai.

But of course, to a Christian the symbol of the Jesus who died and now lives again adds richness, intensity, and detail to the Sinai symbols. The parables of Jesus describe even more elaborately than Sinai did the madness of our loving God. The cross and the resurrection are much more specific promises of the ultimate impact of Yahweh's love for us than the Sinai covenant contained. It is not a new Yahweh that we encounter in Jesus but rather a more highly developed, more explicitly stated, and more richly symbolized Yahweh. Jesus may not add anything to the fundamental message of God's love for us—for to that nothing can be added—but Jesus does represent the length and the breadth, the height and the depth of God's love. The marvelous thing about the Great Secret is that it is one we all knew from the beginning. Every human being perceives it dimly. Israel learned it more clearly in the desert around Sinai, and Jesus came into the world to tell us all that the Secret was really true, that it was all right to be surprised because the great surprise was yet to come.

And like his father Yahweh, he stands expectantly and says to us, "What are you going to do about that?"

PART THREE

The Mary Myth

At morning's first misty light
They came out of the primal bogs
And worshiped in the holy woods.
They tended the sacred fire
And sang of the land of promise
   beyond the seas in the fabled west.

They told tales of heroines and gods
Sad Deirdre, mighty Finn
Noble Dermot, frenzied Maeve.
Then Podraig—
And soft as summer rain
A new and loving god
   came gently to their dreams.

Ah, great men they were—and women too
But it's all over, 'tis the end.
We shall not see their like again.

Bards and monks, scholars and saints
Bishops and kings, hermits and pilgrims
They printed the books and taught the schools
   and claimed they prayed the whole night long.
By the smoking peat the learned scholar
With weary eye and bobbing head read his sacred text;
And zealous Pangar Ban pursued the local mice
While Holy Brigid kept a great pool of ale
   for the welcoming of the King of Kings.

Doubtless brave and a little mad
They lit the lamps of Europe
Conquered the conquering Dane
   and then lit the lamps again
While Holy Brendan sailed to the land of promise in the west.

Insula sanctorum? Not always.
Still, great men they were—and women too
But it's all over, 'tis the end.
We shall not see their like again.

Through rocky fields they walked, down the muddy lanes
Past the empty cottage and by the youthful corpse

On to the leaky ships, across the mountain sea.
Sick, hungry, poor, afraid.
Into the slum, the tavern, the gutter
The mill, slaughterhouse, the early tomb.
Like Holy Brendan they sailed to the land of promise in the west
and found hatred, misery, and sudden death.

Oh, yes, great men they were—and women too
But it's all over, 'tis the end.
We shall not see their like again.

Out of their neighborhoods they climbed
Onto "the cars," into "the force"
Teacher and priest, mayor and doctor
Lawyer and crook, nun and nurse
They sang, they danced, they talked the whole night long.
They cried at births, they laughed at wakes.
They drank, they talked, they fought
and then they talked again.
And on dark gray autumn afternoons
they prayed for the triumph of Notre Dame.

Indeed great men they were—and women too
But it's all over, 'tis the end.
We shall not see their like again.

So it is all over now.
And tears flow at the country club
For all the glories that were
And all the greatness that might have been.
We made it at last in the land of promise
And damn proud we are.
We showed them. We won; we got in.

It is the end of our tale
But what does it matter?
We glow briefly in the sun's lingering flame
As, martini glass in hand, for the final time
we pray for the triumph of Notre Dame.

Ah, great men we are—and women too
But it's all over, 'tis the end.
They shall not see our like again.

So lean thinker and towering poet
What are you two doing here?
Have you not heard my sad refrain?
The tale is told, 'Tis over, finished, done.
Join the others at the wake
  and sing and drink to the end of it all.
Poet and wise man, druid and monk
Migrant and rebel, monsignor and cop
All dead and buried in the ground.

Today in the land of promise, can it be? Is it true?
Are there still some of us around?
Are there stories yet to be told?
A few mysteries still to be probed?
Songs to be sung, work to be done
  in the melting pot that didn't melt?
Not yet curtains for the crazy celt?

So, generous teachers and loyal friends,
The sun still rises over the misty bogs,
Not all that far from Scarsdale to Mayo
  or from Kerry to Oak Park.
Let it then be writ on the morning sky:

God help them all.
But it is not the end.
They shall indeed see our like again.

ANDREW M. GREELEY
June 21, 1976

A Note About the Illustrations

The illustrations in this book are not merely decorations but are an integral part of the arguments:

——The five Christian images of Mary are more important indicators of Mary's role in the Christian tradition than any theological writing. All are women—even the ethereal Spanish girl painted by El Greco. All are sexual creatures, all represent sharply defined "feminine functions," all represent profound and powerful experiences of sexual differentiations as revelatory of the sacred. It is a pity that women were not encouraged to create their own marian art since then we would have, from both men and women, images of the Christian experience of femininity as revelatory of the sacred.

——The black and white pagan art is designed to show the structural and functional similarity between the experience of sexual differentiation as sacred in Christian and non-Christian religions. Thus both the Tibetan Tara and the Medieval ivory figure present the image of the "young girl as divine." The Michelangelo barrelhead madonna and the prehistoric Sardinian madonna both reflect the experience of woman as mother. The Egyptian Horus with her dead son parallels the Michelangelo pietà. And the modern pagan representation of the attractive goddess of love, Eriu, is roughly analogous to the virgin daughter of Zion whom Yahweh desired in the Botticelli *Annunciation*.

The contemporary Irish drawing is interesting because it represents a legendary Irish goddess in a mixture of modern advertising-poster art and ancient celtic decorative themes—but not completely free from some (perhaps unconscious) marian influence. The ancient Irish drawing from the burial passage at New Grange may depict the three different roles of women in prehistoric and preceltic art—mother at the beginning of life, spouse during the course of life, and death (pietà) at the end of life.

It has been wise, perhaps, to keep secret the fact that Ireland gets its name from an ancient celtic goddess of sexual love!

Ivory Madonna (anonymous)
—COURTESY OF MUSÉES NATIONAUX, PARIS

Pietà (Michelangelo)
—St. Peter's, Rome

Tondo Doni (Michelangelo)—UFFIZI, FLORENCE

Sardinian goddess
with young god

Tibetan Tara

Isis with Horus

Three-spiral pattern
—NEW GRANGE,
IRELAND

Annunciation (Botticelli) — UFFIZI, FLORENCE

Assumption of the Virgin (El Greco)
—Courtesy of The Art Institute of Chicago

Ériu — Jim Fitzpatrick © 1976

Prologue

Our Lady's Day in Harvest Time

The blue mantle hangs useless from the peg
Dust and darkness dim the window
Stale air presses heavy on the land
Summertime—and yet we are cold.

No passion in the empty house
No laughter in the shabby garden
No rapture in the frigid heart.

Long gone she who used to wear the sky—
Bright Brigid, sweet Astarte, gentle Net;
Long gone, too, bewitching teenage peasant
Who bore the world anew

Who tamed the Norman fury
Who warmed the Saxon soul
Who kept alive the Polish hope
And calmed the crackling Celt.

Worthless the mantle and brown her garden
For whom the whole world once sang
"Dei Mater Alma."

The generous belly, the breast soft and warm,
The merry eye, the tender hand—all long, long gone.

Now the icy ideologue, the ivory ikon,
The sickly cult, the papal text,
The dry debate, the dismal "no."

Where gone, Madonna, and how long?
Alive? Well, in what galaxy?
And we orphans, chilled and alone,
Among the rotting roses.

The wind shifts,
The mantle lifts,
White fingers on blue cloth,
Flashing brown eyes in the sudden sunlight,
A smile explodes against the gloom.
Laetare, Alleluia!

A.M.G.

Chapter 1

A Return to Mary?*

This is not a book about Mary; it is about the God who is revealed to us through Mary. This is not a book about women; it is about human nature as it is revealed to men and women through the "masculine" and "feminine" dimensions of women.

It is, therefore a book about hope. The God who is revealed to us in Mary is a God who inspires hope; and in the reproductive powers of the human race, in the fertility of the womb, humankind has experienced from the beginning the biological ground of hopefulness: we may die but the species continues.

We go to Mary, then, to learn about God. We go to women, then, to learn about ourselves. I intend this volume to be an exercise in neither

*There are critics who will argue that only a woman should write about the femininity of God. Such an argument is ideological romanticism. Only the young should write about the young, only the nonwhite should write about the nonwhite, only Jews should write about Jews, only married people about marriage, etc., etc.? Such an ideology is also anti-intellectual, reactionary, and oppressive; I will not dignify it with serious discussion. The question about any book ought not to be what are the ascribed characteristics of the one who writes it but how good it is. Men have at least as much interest in God being female as do women—though perhaps their interest is from a different perspective. This book is written from the male viewpoint because the writer is male. Presumably in some of the man-hating, quasi-lesbian circles of "the movement," this will be enough to make the book an exercise in chauvinism. Too bad for them. A woman might have different insights into the femininity of God than a man; so much the better. Fortunately humankind is blessed with the special insights and experiences of both sexes.

traditional Mariology nor the contemporary feminism—though I do not deny the value of either. I assume all the titles and doctrines of the traditional Mariology, and I assume all the critiques of contemporary feminism; but I write neither about new titles of Mary nor the old oppression of woman by man (or its converse). I write about the God revealed in Mary and the human nature revealed by woman, a God of hope and a people of hopefulness despite themselves.

Hope is currently in bad repute—mostly, I suspect, because it has been confused with naïve evolutionary optimism, an optimism which died in Europe on the bloody battlefields of 1917 and was buried in the Hiroshima explosion of 1945. In this country full realization of its death struck home in the assassination-riot-Vietnam-Watergate nightmare of the 1960s and early 1970s. Unable to distinguish between optimism and hope, many thoughtful Americans, disabused of their optimism, are giving up hope too.

Robert Heilbroner begins his immensely successful book, *An Inquiry into the Human Prospect,*[1] with a question he admits he would hesitate to ask aloud if he did not believe it existed unvoiced in the minds of many, "Is there hope for man?"

Will there be a future that has anything else but a continuation of darkness, cruelty, and disorder? Heilbroner says no. Does worse impend? Heilbroner responds yes. Part of the problem, he insists, is that we have discovered once again that man does not live by bread alone. "Affluence does not buy morale, a sense of community, even a quiescent conformity. Instead, it may only permit larger numbers of people to express their existential unhappiness because they are no longer crushed by the burdens of the economic struggle."[2]

He concludes his melancholy but clear and painfully honest prognosis for the future of the liberal, secular, rational, democratic society (of which he is both product and interpreter) with a quest for a myth, a symbol around which we can rally our will to survive. The Promethean spirit has brought us trouble; perhaps from another figure in Greek mythology we can find peace.

With some sense of pride Heilbroner offers us the symbol of Atlas, "bearing with endless perseverance the weight of the heavens in his hands." We must resolutely bear our burdens, we must preserve the very will to live, we must rescue the future from the angry condemnation of the present: "It is the example of Atlas, resolutely bearing his burden, that provides the strength we seek. If, within us, the spirit of

Atlas falters, there perishes the determination to preserve humanity at all costs and any costs, forever.''[3]

An Inquiry into the Human Prospect is a profoundly melancholy and depressing book, although I cannot help but admire Heilbroner's clear-eyed courage. Atlas, I suspect, is but a projection of the steely determination of Heilbroner's own spirit. Equally pessimistic books, though lacking Heilbroner's stoicism and self-discipline, have been written by Loren Eiseley (who suggested that the evolutionary process made a mistake when it produced humankind), Richard Goodwin, and Peter Schrag.[4] There is also the infamous *Meadows Report,** which turns out not to be much as either economics or computer science but is pretty effective apocalypse.

I wonder whether the wave of doom and gloom is merely the latest fashion among our intellectual and cultural elites. Is *An Inquiry into the Human Prospect* only a successor to *The Greening of America?* Charles Reich was a Pelagian who believed in the endless perfectability of humankind (carried out by a messianic younger generation—made up mostly, it would seem, of Yale students). Heilbroner is a neo-Manichee struggling bravely in the face of doom. Will the late '70s see the pendulum swing back to the Pelagianism of Reich?

However, both Heilbroner and Reich share a common theme which I think represents a major shift in the thinking of intellectual leaders in the North Atlantic community. Both are engaged in apocalypse; both see the end of the world as we now know it; both have abandoned faith in the Enlightenment worldview; both see the failure of the liberal,

---

*Dennis L. Meadows, et al., *The Limits to Growth.* New York: Universe Books, 1972. For a devastating critique of this book see H. S. D. Cole, ed., *Models of Doom: A Critique of The Limits to Growth.* New York: Universe Books, 1973. See in particular the response of the Meadows team on pages 239 and 240 of the book. The Sussex University critics have utterly destroyed the economic basis of the Meadows prophecy of doom. The MIT researchers take refuge in a response that is prophecy and apocalypse, indeed one might even characterize it as religion instead of economics.

This book is not an exercise in economic analysis; however I would note in passing that the enthusiasm of many religious leaders and spokesmen for zero economic growth has not persuaded me that it is either necessary or desirable. On the contrary, all the evidence I am aware of suggests that zero economic growth would be an unmitigated disaster for humankind. The notion that resources are limited is at best a half-truth and at worst a dangerous falsehood. Competent geologists, agriculturists, and biologists have repeatedly argued that while there may be problems with individual resources, there is no foreseeable shortage of any basic raw material in the world. Unfortunately, these sane and sober men do not seem to capture the imaginations of religious leaders.

rational, democratic ethic. Heilbroner also sees a failure of socialism as well as capitalism. Reich confidently expects rebirth, Heilbroner pessimistically expects doom; but both see the modern world as having come to an end. Reich rejoices, Heilbroner laments; but neither sees in the future a place for the easy rationalistic confidence of the Enlightenment.

And here we might mention a third contemporary prophet who mixes Heilbroner's pessimism with Reich's romanticism. The modern world, the world of the Enlightenment, has indeed come to an end for Theodore Roszak, and somewhere out beyond the wastelands the counterculture, equipped with *The Whole Earth Catalog* and other such resources, is beginning to build a new "gnostic" civilization. Roszak is less pessimistic than Heilbroner but not nearly so easily optimistic as Reich. For him, the square society is likely to limp on for a long time. Reich seeks salvation in Consciousness III; Roszak seeks it in the poetry of Blake, Wordsworth, and Goethe. The Meadows team wants to return to some kind of pre-Judeo-Christian state of nature (in which there would be no electricity for the computers). Heilbroner grimly takes the weight of the world on his shoulders and offers us the myth of Atlas as we bravely and patiently await our doom.

Well, maybe.

But as my colleague William McCready remarked to me, "Atlas is the name of a tire. Whoever built a cathedral to honor a tire or wrote a love poem in praise of one?"

At the turn of the century, a remarkable prescient American intellectual addressed himself to the same questions that torment our present intellectuals. Anticipating air flight, nuclear energy, and the computer before any of these wonders were invented, he asked what room there was for humankind in a world dominated by the dynamo:

> What are we then? The lords of space?
> The mastermind whose task You do?
> Jockey who rides You into space?
> Or are we atoms whirled apace
> shaped and controlled by You?
>
> We are beggars! What care we
> For hopes or terrors, love or hate?

What for the universe? We see
   only our certain destiny
In the last word of fate

> HENRY ADAMS,
> "The Virgin and the Dynamo"
> from *Prayer to the Virgin of Chartres*.

It was not, however, to an obscure, unimportant Greek mythological figure that Henry Adams turned as a focus for his emotions in a response to the dynamo. He turned to another symbol of the Western culture:

Simple as when I asked her aid before;
Humble as when I prayed for grace in vain
Seven hundred years ago; weak, weary, sore
In heart and hope, I asked your help again.

You who remember all, remember me;
An English scholar of a Norman name,
I was a thousand who then crossed sea
To wrangle in the Paris schools for fame.

When your Byzantine portal was still young
I prayed there with my master Abelard;
When Ave Maris Stella was first sung
I helped to sing it here with St. Bernard.

When Blanche set up your gorgeous Rose of France
I stood among the servants of the queen;
And when St. Louis made his penitence,
I followed barefoot where the King had been.

For centuries I brought you all my cares,
And vexed you with the murmurs of a child;
You heard the tedious burden of my prayers;
you could not grant them, but at least you smiled.

> HENRY ADAMS,
> *Prayer to the Virgin of Chartres*.

There is no way that the American intelligentsia as represented by such writers as Schrag, Goodwin, Meadows, and Heilbroner will turn to the smiling Virgin of Chartres. Even though they may have lost hope in their Enlightenment rationalism, they are still so much products of the Enlightenment that they could only smile in amusement at the thought that the smiling Virgin might have something pertinent to say to the modern world.

Still I wonder. The Marian symbol is surely one of the most powerful symbols in the Western tradition. Virtually every major painter from the fifth to the sixteenth century painted at least one Madonna. Great cathedrals sprang up all over Europe and still stand. Poets sing her praises, including such improbable characters as Petrarch, Boccaccio, Francois Villon, Shelley, Byron, Rilke. Football teams enter battle in her name. It will be a long time before a football team named after Atlas is number one. On the basis of history, if nothing else, in any competition between Heilbroner's Atlas and Henry Adams's Virgin of Chartres, there isn't much doubt who would win.

If Enlightenment rationalism is truly moribund—and the signs that it is are overwhelming—then we have entered into an era of the open marketplace for religious symbols. Heilbroner's push for a sustaining symbol in Atlas is merely the beginning of a search which is likely to occupy the North Atlantic world for a considerable time to come. Under such circumstances, the Mary symbol ought at least to be reconsidered on the possibility that a symbol which has had as much power for most of the history of the Western world as it did may still have some power of illumination in our time. It may be that our predecessors—not all of whom were howling savages—saw something in the Mary symbol that we have missed. What they saw might well be something we can ill afford to neglect.

There are signs that the reevaluation of the Mary myth has already begun. From his perspective out beyond the wastelands, Theodore Roszak remembered at least one thing from his Catholic background:

> The early and medieval Church remained pliable enough to accomodate to some degree the widespread need for myth. The major manifestation of this was the cult of the virgin, which elevated the inconsequential figure of Mary to a stupendous symbolic stature. Here was the mother goddess Christianity lacked, worked up out of the meagerest historical material by the mythic imagination—a triumph of collective visionary power at times so sweeping that the virgin nearly crowded out the official trinity. Of course, the theology of the church deftly delimited mariology; but that had little meaning at the level of popular worship or artistic creation, where the virgin rapidly

occupied the psychic ground that had always been held by Isis, Cybele, Magna Mater, and their ageless sisterhood. After all, how poor and unbalanced a religion it is that does not find place for the Divine Mother.[5]

Lynn White, in his book *Machina Ex Deo*, comments: "The virgin mother, undefiled yet productive, bearing Christ into the world by the action of the Spirit of God, is so perfect an analogue of the most intimate experience of the soul that that powerful myth has sustained dubious history; for to the believer, myth and history have been one."[6]

Harvey Cox notes in his *Seduction of the Spirit*:

Our overly spiritualized sentiments about immortality reveal yet another way in which our curious blend of technology and Victorianism has removed us from our own bodies. If pressed to a choice between symbols, I vastly prefer the Assumption to Ethical Culture. If God is dead, Mary is alive and well and she deserves our attention.[7]

He adds later, "I don't think we should overlook the fact that in some of her manifestations Mary is not just a woman but a powerful, maybe even a liberated woman."[8]

A Protestant writer is also prepared to contend that Protestantism has made a serious mistake in its opposition to the virgin:

Ignoring the place of the Blessed Virgin in the Incarnation and the whole process of salvation has given Protestantism a harsh thoroughly masculine emphasis. . . . The absence [of tenderness and affection] in Protestantism has led to an overemphasis on a harsh prophetic picture of God with its attending preoccupation with judgment. . . . The development of a mature Mariology in Protestant thinking could do much to temper the harsh portrayal of the God of judgment and provide it with a healthy (and I might add, scriptural) concept of a God of mercy.[9]

The research and thought out of which this book has grown began with two observations: the Mary symbol had overwhelming power for almost all of our predecessors, and a number of perceptive observers outside the Roman Catholic Church see value in the symbolism precisely at a time when Marian devotion seems virtually nonexistent among progressive Catholics. It seems that we had another example of what I modestly term "Greeley's Law": non-Catholics start something the day after Catholics abandon it. I am not advocating a return to the Marian devotion of our Catholic childhoods; I am rather recommending a reevaluation of what the Mary symbolism really stands for on the grounds that Mary might be extremely relevant (to use a good if frequently abused word) for the problems of our time—at least as relevant as Atlas if not substantially more so. I began this investigation with no other predispositions. I am surely not trying to defend Mary, nor am I trying to rehabilitate her. (On the basis of the historical evidence, she needs neither defense nor rehabilitation.) I am certainly not trying to "apologize" in either sense of that word for traditional Catholic teaching. My Marian piety was nonexistent when this project began. The most I started with was a fascination with the history of the Mary myth and a hunch that there was more to be said about it than Cardinal Carberry's lugging the Fatima virgin around St. Louis.*

I therefore propose in this book a reevaluation of Mary from the point of view of the social sciences, or at least from the point of view of a social scientist. I will contend that Mary is a symbol of the feminine component of the deity. She represents the human insight that the Ultimate is passionately tender, seductively attractive, irresistibly inspiring, and graciously healing. I will argue that the Mary symbol arises out of the human "limit-experience" of sexual differentiation and as such she can legitimately be called a "sex goddess." Mary is, in other words, part of a great tradition of female deities, all of whom reflect the human conviction that God has feminine as well as masculine characteristics, a conviction arising spontaneously and inevitably from the profound, disturbing, and shattering experience of sex differentiation.

Among the many excellent recent treatments of the subject of the role of myth in religion, one of the clearest is Ian Barbour's *Myths,*

---

*The word "myth is used in the title of this volume and throughout to mean a story which is a "mysterion," a "sacramentum," a revelation of a "Great Secret." Religious myths may or may not have a historical "referent." In the Jewish and Christian traditions, if myths are not grounded in historical events, they lose all value. To say, therefore, that the Mary story is a myth is not to say that it is a legend. It is a story rooted in historical events, which is a revelation of a Great Secret.

Some Christians are still uneasy when they hear this technical use of the word "myth." It is a good word with a precise and proper meaning, and one that lends itself to scholarly analysis. Christians should not be nervous about its use.

Models, and Paradigms. According to Barbour, myths offer ways of ordering experience, inform man about himself, express a saving power in human life, provide patterns for human actions, and are enacted in rituals (pages 21–22). Barbour observes (page 23), "In the Western religions myth is indeed tied primarily to historical events rather than to phenomena in nature. This difference is crucial for conceptions of history, time and ethics, but it need not lead us to deny the presence of myth in the Bible. Divine action is in itself no more directly observable in history than in primordial time or in nature."

Obviously such an approach to the Mary myth is different from most previous ones. I do not reject either the contribution or the validity of those approaches; I am adding a new one.

I hope at all costs to avoid the battle of the Reformation over Mary (one of the most unseemly and foolish conflicts in the entire history of Christendom). The antipathy of some of the reformers and their followers to Mary was a disastrous mistake, as were the Catholic superstitions which in part caused the antipathy and the triumphalism which followed. In the view I propose to develop in this book, it will be seen that the reformers were quite correct in insisting that Mary had taken on a quasi-divine role in the Catholic tradition. They were wrong, however, in thinking that such a role detracted from the worship of God; for we shall see that Mary, like all feminine deities, reflects a central component of the deity and does not detract from its fullness. On the other hand, I think Catholic apologists have made a serious mistake by denying the obvious connection between Mary and the goddesses of pagan antiquity. In their overanxious fear that Mary would lose her uniqueness, they lost a powerful weapon in the controversy with the reformers and also an insight which might have enabled them to make Mary a much more pertinent symbol to fill the religious need to see the deity as both masculine and feminine. In excluding the feminine component of the deity, the reformers, as Dickson remarked in the passage quoted above, missed a very important and indeed a well-nigh universal component of human religious experience. It may be that the perspective offered in this book will provide a context in which the last of the Reformation battles over Mary can be resolved. But I do not wish to pause overlong on what surely must be in our age an obsolete conflict.

Nor will I put much emphasis here on the specific Marian doctrines proclaimed or discussed by the Catholic Church. I surely do not deny such doctrines, and I think the paradigm that I will develop will be able to subsume them. However, my interest is not in specific doctrine but in religious symbolism, and I would contend that the doctrines may be best understood as theologically directed attempts to explicate the symbols (some attempts being more successful than others, no doubt).

I will not repeat in this book the work of contemporary Scripture scholars on the Marian passages in the New Testament. Such works are readily available and can be consulted by anyone who is interested.[10]

The four primary scriptural images of Mary—the New Eve, the Church, the daughter of Zion, and the Virgin—will fit into my paradigm. But much of the present controversy, in particular over the nativity narratives (important in its own right), is not pertinent to my basic purpose.

I have consulted the works on Mary by the great theologians of our time: the Rahners (Karl and Hugo), Schillebeeckx, Laurentin, Congar, Semelroth, and Thurian.[11] I fear that none of these books has been particularly helpful to my purpose; mostly, I suspect, because the theological method at work in them permitted the authors to take no serious consideration of the contribution to the study of the theology of Mary that might be made by the history of religions. Juniper Carol's three-volume *Mariology* series, Frank Sheed's *The Mary Book,* and Hilda Graef's Marian history have been useful for source material, but I fear the three authors would find my use of that source material surprising, to say the least.[12]

Since my approach emphasizes so heavily religious symbolism, I have leaned much more on poetry and art than has traditional theology. The best available collection of Marian verse is still Sister Therese's *I Sing of a Maiden*; two collections of art by Henri Gheon and one by Jean Guiton have been helpful to me.[13]

Just as I have no desire to contend with Protestants about Reformation controversies over Mary, I am resolved not to argue with the traditional Mariologists within Catholicism. I have cited some of the literature of that tradition to make it clear to critics who will arise from these quarters that I am not unaware of their work. I must say in all honesty that the high Mariology of the theologians is simply not very trenchant. And the popular Mariology seems bent on multiplying titles and miracles (where it survives at all) and is likely to turn off both Catholics and non-Catholics.*

I will confess to being most impatient with popular Mariology even in its present moribund state. It is creepy, and does a great disservice to Our Lady, who has been a prisoner of creeps far too long. I see little purpose in this book in spending time and energy arguing with those to whom no one listens.

My approach to the Mary myth combines elements of sociology, the history of religion, and some of the most recent developments in what might broadly be called "language" theology. My definition of religion and my notion of the role of religious symbols is based on the work of Clifford Geertz and Thomas Luckmann; I have developed this component of my research in my book, *Unsecular Man*.[14] For the material from the history of religions, I am indebted to Mircea Eliade and (with some reservations) to the Jungian, Erich Neumann.[15] The theological input comes chiefly from the work of Langdon Gilkey, Paul Ricoeur, Peter Berger, Nathan Scott, Thomas Fawcett, Ian Ramsey, and especially David Tracy.[16] The last-named writer has brilliantly synthesized much of the best in current theological thought. I am deeply in his debt.

In the following chapters I will attempt to show how I have combined these three different areas of religious thought into my own approach (I hesitate to use that overworked word "method") to religion. I am very carefully stating in the first two chapters both what I am doing and what I am not doing. I do this in order for the reader to have no doubt about my context, my perspective, and my purpose. The approach I have elected to use to better understand the Mary myth is new, perhaps startlingly so. Like everything new it runs the risk of being misunderstood. I take it for granted that many of the things I say will eagerly be snatched out of context and distorted by hostile reviewers. By carefully describing my sources and my approach and excluding questions which are not explicitly pertinent to that approach,

---

*Perhaps the weakness of most of the current Catholic theology about Mary is that the authors are unwilling to take the step that the history of religions enables them to take and see Mary as a reflection of the femininity of God. Still, one theologian saw such a step over a half century ago. Pierre Teilhard de Chardin spoke of the "biopsychological necessity of the 'Marian' to counterbalance the masculinity of Yahweh." He argued that the cult of Mary corrects a "dreadfully masculinized conception of the godhead." [Quoted in Henri De Lubac, *The Eternal Feminine* (London: Collins, 1970) p. 125–6].

I hope to minimize misunderstanding and distortion. There are many aspects of Marian devotion and Marian theory which I do not discuss in this book; it is not, therefore, to be concluded that I do not believe in these Marian doctrines or that I think they are unimportant. My concern in this book is not to repeat old approaches but to explore a new one. My approach should be judged not by whether it is true or false; it is an approach and not a statement. I would rather be judged on whether my approach is useful or not. Those who find it so are welcome to use it; the others are welcome to forget it.

Some readers of an earlier draft of this volume have questioned whether I am an "orthodox" Roman Catholic because I do not assert my belief that Mary is the "Mother of God." I must confess to mild annoyance about this propensity to hunt heresy (which I had thought went out with Vatican Council II). Just because someone does not *assert* his acceptance of a particular doctrine does not mean that he does not *accept* it. I cannot understand why it is necessary to go through a ritual of repeating all the doctrines one accepts so that one may be judged "orthodox" as preliminary to proceeding to the work at hand.

Of course I accept the *theotoxos* (*"mater dei"*) title. It has an honorable history of 1500 years, and no Catholic Christian could possibly reject it. I feel that I deal with it at great length in the Madonna chapter of the book. If I do not spend time on the explicit "Godbearer" title, the reason is that many modern readers can cope with it only if they understand the "communication of idioms" thesis of Christology. Without such understanding, the assertion that Mary is the Mother of God will not only be paradoxical (which, like all good limit-language, it ought to be) but incomprehensible. But to develop an explanation of the "communication of idioms" would take us into Christological problems beyond the scope of this book, as well as the competency of its author.

However, to say that Mary is "the mysterion," the *imago dei,* is not to give her a lesser title than *theotoxos* but a greater one. To put the matter differently, Mary is the *imago dei* because of her maternity. As Jesus himself said in response to praise of his mother, "Rather blessed are those who hear the word of God and keep it." In other words, blessed are those who reveal and reflect the goodness and love of God.

The thesis of this book, then, is that Mary reveals the tender, gentle, comforting, reassuring, "feminine" dimension of God. Surely such a thesis is so traditional as to be pedestrian.

Some commentators on earlier versions have also complained that I do not acknowledge that Mary is an object of faith in herself, and that I do not confess my faith in all the things we must believe about Mary. To make Mary the object of faith, I think, would be to fall guilty to what the Protestants have accused Catholics of doing for centuries. There is only one object of faith—God. All the "doctrines" we believe are about God. They all manifest God to us, reveal something of his nature, give us some hint of his love. This book is not about Mary. It is about God revealed to us through Mary. Those who are horrified by such a strange idea should read what St. Thomas has to say on the subject (II-II, 1, 1). One quotation should suffice for our present concerns: *"Objectum fidei is unun; non solum in actu quo credimus sed id quod credimus."* * The "quod," of course, is God.

The core of my approach to Mary is a paradigm, a four-celled "model" that represents four aspects of the Mary myth—Madonna, Sponsa, Virgo, and Pietà—which correspond to four elements of the human "limit-experience" of sexual differentiation. It is important to understand what a model is to a social scientist: it is a tool for examining reality, not a description of what reality is. Whatever elegance and symmetry there may be in an intellectual model is gained at the price of eliminating much of the complexity, diversity, the ambiguity and "messiness" of the world the way it really is. If one wishes to engage in generalization and abstract thought about the real world, one must schematize, divide, order, and organize the phenomena of experience. One must insert discontinuities where there is continuity, division where there is unity, clear definitions where there is in fact a steady flow of complex phenomena. A model, even the most elegant one—I might even say especially the most elegant one—is necessarily a distortion of reality because it is a simplification of reality.

There is no harm in any of this as long as one keeps in mind that the model is *not* reality. A real problem arises when any model-builder (or his disciples) begins to confuse the model with reality, and indeed

---

*Translation: "The object of faith is one, not only the act by which we believe, but that which we believe."

identifies the model with reality so that the model becomes more real than the phenomena which it tries to subsume and organize. But we who are model-builders are much like the little boy with his airplane; we are terribly proud of our creations. We are tempted to act as though the real world is an affront when it doesn't fit neatly into our elegant systems.

Thus the Freudian paradigm of id, ego, and superego is an extremely useful tool until we permit ourselves to think that there is actually out there somewhere a reality of the human personality, a segment or a force or a division which corresponds precisely to the notion of Freud's model. When we think about it, of course, it becomes clear that the human personality is much more complicated than the neat, tri-layered picture the Freudian theory presents, or the "collective unconscious" of the Jungians, or the binary models of Claude Levi-Strauss. They are all so attractive and elegant that it is easy to begin to think of them as precise descriptions. It is not evident that Freud, Jung, or Levi-Strauss failed on occasion to succumb to the temptation to view them as such; certainly many of their followers have done so.

I want to make clear from the very beginning that my model for the Mary myth is nothing more than a way of organizing data, a perspective from which one can view phenomena, a tool for a very good, sometimes at best, suggestive, and sometimes relatively weak, analysis. But it is an abstraction, a schematization, a simplification of a reality that is in every instance far more complex, elaborate, subtle, and indeterminate than my model. Those religiously inclined people who are used to apodictic certainties in their approach to religion will be appalled at the notion of a religious model as a perspective instead of an absolutely unchallengeable description. So be it. Reality, even religious reality, is far too tangled and fluid to be captured by apodictic certainties.

All models, then, are to some extent metaphors. Freud's three-layered self, Jung's collective unconscious, Levi-Strauss' binary world are all approximations; all say in effect, "The world is *like* . . ." Every model is in some sense a form of "limit-language"; it is designed to startle us into a perception that we did not have previously, to give us an insight that we hitherto lacked. Religious models, as we shall see, are limit-language par excellence. They differ from other models, it seems to me, in degree and not in kind. My four images of Mary are nothing more than an attempt to shatter our old perceptions of the

Virgin symbolism and help us to see it in a new light.* If we then see Mary in a new light, she in turn becomes a model that shatters our perceptions of ultimate reality and helps us to see it in a new light. She guides us to see ultimate reality not only as creating, organizing, ordering, directing, planning, bringing to completion but also tenderly caring, seductively attracting, passionately inspiring, and gently healing. The purpose of this book is not to teach new doctrines or to deny old ones; it is merely to offer new perceptions, new insights, a new structuring of experience. If new language is used, the reason is that new language can produce, or perhaps renew, experiences. I invite the reader to judge this book on this criterion: Does it provide him with new or renewed experience of the illumination shed on the human condition by the smile of the Virgin in the way Henry Adams was renewed in the shadow of Chartres?

Two final comments: First of all, I am not merely asserting that the Mary myth is a useful way to propound the femininity of God in an era when feminism is strong. I am arguing that the structure and function of the Mary myth are designed to reveal the femininity of God. The theologians may have missed the point or have been afraid to touch it; but the poets and the painters have not—nor have the Christian faithful. My attempt, then is not to offer a new interpretation of the Mary myth but to make articulate and explicit the function of the myth from the beginning.

I am not a theologian. Yet I cannot pass this book off as sociology. It is an exercise in the margins between the two disciplines. Perhaps it is even theology done from a sociological perspective. In the past I have inveighed mightily against theologians who cross the boundaries

*For purposes of clarification I perhaps should add that my fourfold paradigm is a "model about a model." For within the Mary myth itself there is a model (the "structure" of the myth, to use Barbour's phrase) which purports to tell us about God.

In the text I may go too far in the direction of what Barbour calls "instrumentalism," denying to a model any reality beyond its utility as a tool. Anyone interested in this not unimportant methodological distinction should consult Barbour (*op. cit.*) The model, he tells us, should be taken "seriously" but not "literally." Deductions from the theory to which the model leads must be carefully tested against the data. The model is a mental construct, not a reality; but the critical realist "tries to acknowledge both the creativity of man's mind and the existence of patterns in events not created by man's mind." We must grant the model some "provisional ontologic status,"which means we believe that there are "entities in the world something like those described by the model . . . there is some isomorphism between the model and the real structures of the world" (p. 42). Still, the critical realist "makes only a tentative commitment to the existence of the entities something like those portrayed in the model" (p. 47).

of sociology without respect for sociological method; I am therefore conscious of the risk of making the same mistake in reverse. Hence I have turned to two theologians, David Tracy and John Shea, as an apprentice striving to learn and to respect the methods of their discipline (in this case, a method they both use). As I understand them, they tell me that I have not too egregiously violated the rules of theological methodology. I am grateful for the education in theology I have received from them, but like all other teachers, they should be dispensed from responsibility for their students' errors.

I experienced renewal in the writing of this book. My devotion to Mary was almost nonexistent. There is now a statue of Mary in my garden. The next thing I need is flowers. In the meantime, I turn to the substance of the book with the prayers of that incorrigible sinner, François Villon.

> Lady of Heaven and earth, and therewithal
>   Crowned Empress of the nether clefts of Hell,—
> I, thy poor Christian, on thy name do call
>   Commending me to thee, with thee to dwell,
>   Albeit in nought I be commendable.
> But all mine undeserving may not mar
> Such mercies as thy sovereign mercies are;
>   Without the which (as true words testify)
> No soul can reach thy Heaven so fair and far.
> Even in this faith I choose to live and die.
>
> O excellent Virgin Princess! Thou didst bear
>   King Jesus, the most excellent comforter,
> Who even of this our weakness craved a share
>   And for our sake stooped to us from on high,
> Offering to death His young life sweet and fair.
> Such as He is, Our Lord, I Him declare,
>   And in this faith I choose to live and die.
>
>   FRANÇOIS VILLON (1431–1485),
>   *His Mother's Service to Our Lady,*
>   translated by Dante Gabriel Rossetti from the French.

Chapter 2
Religion, Experience, Symbols, Language

$$W$$e moderns think of religion as creed, code, and cult. It is a series of propositions to be believed in, a set of moral practices to be followed, a body of ritual to be observed. A man's religiousness is measured by his denominational attendance, his church affiliation, his acceptance of certain doctrinal propositions, his adherence to certain moral norms, and his performance of certain approved rituals. It is all very neat, orderly, and rational. If the sociology of religion has generally not progressed beyond the measurement of such phenomena, the reason is that most sociologists of religion, like most of the rest of us, are very much products of the Enlightenment, and see religion as essentially propositional.[1]

In fact, however, such a rationalistic view of religion describes neither what religion has meant to people in the past nor what it means to most people today. Religion is humankind's way of wrestling with the ultimate; it is the set of answers, usuallly in nonpropositional form, to the most fundamental and basic questions a human has about the purpose of life and of the world in which he finds himself. Indeed, religion is an explanation of what things are all about. Creed, code, cult, church are all derivatives; they flow from the basic worldview, the fundamental interpretive scheme. They are important, indeed, but decidedly secondary to the intuition of the real, which is the primal and revelatory religious phenomenon. Clifford Geertz provides a useful definition of religion from this perspective. Religion is:

(1) a system of symbols which acts to
(2) establish powerful, pervasive, and long-lasting moods and
    motivations in men by
(3) formulating conceptions of a general order of existence and
(4) clothing these conceptions with such an aura of factuality that
(5) the moods and motivations seem uniquely realistic.[2]

Religion, then, is a symbolic interpretation of ultimate reality that
provides templates, guideposts, road maps according to which people
can chart their way through the obscurities of life, particularly as these
obscurities are manifested in the most ultimate questions of purpose
and meaning that a human can ask himself.

But why does religion appear in symbols before it appears in closed
propositions of catechisms and theology books? At one level the
answer is simply that when one deals with the most primal or the most
ultimate, prose is not enough. The proposition appeals mostly to the
intellect; the symbol appeals to the total personality—will and emotions, as well as intellect. But more must be said. Religion appears
first of all in symbols, in dense, complex, multilayered, polyvalent
pictures, stories, rituals, because religion takes its origin from experience, and religious communication is primarily designed to lead to the
replication of experience.

The Enlightenment witticism of Voltaire that man creates God in his
own image and likeness, has been repeated often. God, the Ultimate
(or whatever we choose to call it), was a product of man's dreams, his
self-deception, his wish fulfillment; but it could more accurately be
said that man creates himself in the image and likeness of the God he
experiences. Religion takes its origin in experience, and humankind
shapes its life in the context of the view of ultimate reality it derives
from its experience. Religious symbols are not merely a way of
passing on the basic truths that one individual or a group learn from a
religious experience which gave rise to their religious faith; symbols
are in fact designed to recreate the experience itself, to produce in the
one who views the symbol a religious experience like that which led to
the creation of the symbol.

But what kind of experiences produce religious symbols? They need
not be the ecstatic variety described by such different authors as
William James and Abraham Maslow. Such experiences are far more
common even in our modern "secular" world than many people had

thought. (Approximately two-fifths of the American public has had such extremely intense ecstatic experiences.[3]) Ecstasy is not required for a religious experience. Basic issues arise implicitly or explicitly, consciously or unconsciously, whenever we brush up against the stone wall that creates the boundary lines of our existence. When we push up against our own finite limits we find ourselves wondering what human life means, and in that experience of finitude we obtain a hint of an explanation, a fleeting glimpse of an answer.

The scientist wonders whither come the imperatives that move him to work and discipline his efforts. The ethicians wonder why we have an overriding sense of moral obligation. Lovers locked in passionate embrace, the mother wiping away the tears of her child, a tired and weary pilgrim refreshed by a clear spring morning, light breaking through the clouds, a parent or a spouse dies, a friendship ends in bitter quarreling, one fails, one realizes that one is old, one knows suddenly that one will die—all these are or can be, in Father David Tracy's words, "limit-experiences." The scientist knows that his science cannot measure the imperatives that set him to work; they are beyond the limits of his knowledge. The ethician knows that his ethics can never reveal their source. The lovers understand that however strong the passion that unites them, they are still two separate persons, and both are doomed to die; the mother perceives that these tears she can wipe away but that there will be others to fall later in life that no one will be able to wipe away. We cannot always help those we love and there will come a time when they will not be able to help us. Life is finite, and within the boundaries of life our own particular existence is hemmed in on all sides by physiological, biological, psychological, and sociological limitations. We may be pilgrims of the absolute, we may hunger for the infinite; but the being that we experience in our daily lives is all too fragile, all too finite.

And yet . . . and yet . . . In such experiences of limitation we also may experience something more. The limit can become a horizon that not only defines where we are but also suggests that there is something beyond where we are. In the limit-experience we bump up against the wall that imposes a boundary on our finite existence; but then, perhaps only for a fraction of a second, we find ourselves wondering why the wall is there, how we exist in relation to the wall. Is there something or perhaps even some*one* else on the other side? And every once in a while, in such horizon- or boundary-experiences, we have the impression that perhaps the wall moved a bit, or maybe we heard someone whispering on the other side of it.

I am not suggesting that limit-experiences are a "proof," as the old logical, rational arguments were. We do not argue that the limit may be a horizon, the boundary a disclosure; we rather sense it intuitively as a briefly glimpsed possibility.

The power of the limit-experience to "disclose" reality to us is in its power to stir up wonder. For we sense not merely the limitations on our existence but the gratuity, the giftedness of that existence. And if existence is gratuitous and gifted, then it may also be gracious. And if there is graciousness, from whence does it come? The limit-experience, then, is a "religious experience" precisely in its capacity to stir up wonder in us about grace. The scientists and the ethicians wonder about the imperatives that preside over their disciplines, the mother wonders about the marvel that is her child, the two lovers wonder how such great joy as is theirs can possibly be. Faced with the limitations on human affection and friendship, we wonder how friendship can be possible at all; and finally, pressed up against the wall of death, we are still baffled by the phenomenon of life and by the refusal of life to give up hope even when we can see no farther than the wall of death.

The horizon-experience, then, is a revelation. It does not provide an "answer" to the agonized problems that our limitations impose upon us; it is a revelation in the sense that it is a "hint of an explanation"; it offers us a fleeting glimpse of the possibility of grace; it gives us a hint, sometimes subtle, almost imperceptible, and at other times powerful, that there is "something else" going on in our lives, and if there is, there may also be "something else" beyond the horizon. Religion, necessarily and inevitably, is about that "something else."

Such experiences are "rumors of angels," "signals of the transcendent," or, in David Tracy's more metaphysical words, "disclosive of a final, a fundamental, meaningfulness [which] bears a religious character."

These "disclosive" experiences reveal to us a world of meaning beyond the everyday, and this world is that through which religious symbols come. One might even say that it is a world out of which religious symbols explode. As Tracy notes: "Such a 'world,' by its strange ability to put us in touch with what we believe to be a final, a 'trustworthy,' meaning to our lives may also disclose to us, however hesitantly, the character of that ultimate horizon of meaning which religious persons call 'gracious,' 'eventful,' 'faith-full,' 'revelatory.' "[4]

Limit-situations and limit-questions pose the fundamental religious issues, and, on occasion at least, they also suggest what the answers might be. Our thrust for self-transcendence—in scientific search, in moral and philosophical reflection, in celebration, in service, in love—runs up against Something Else (or Someone Else) which is perceived as having set boundaries to self-transcendence; and more than that, this Something Else is also perceived as responsible for both the self and the thrust for transcendence; or, alternately, it is the object of our longing for transcendence. It is perceived as having set a limit which is not permanent, as having created a stone wall which may eventually tumble down, as having drawn a boundary line, but a temporary one—or, to anticipate the theme of this book, it is perceived as a seductive lover, teasing us to go only so far but seeming also to promise that she (he) may be willing to give even more.

In the limit-experience one experiences oneself as thrust into being, and one wonders about Being: Which is the ground, the origin, the goal of such a thrust? To be thrust into being is gratuitous. We did not ask for it; it was simply given. We wonder, therefore, about the nature of Being. Whence comes this gift? (It is possible, incidentally, to be technically a philosophical atheist and still state the question in this fashion. Martin Heidegger,* who taught us to ask the question in this way, denies that Being is the same as God. He describes himself philosophically as an atheist.)

It follows, therefore, that anything that shares in Being, any being, can be the occasion of a limit-experience. Any being can be revelatory of Being. There was a time when our simple ancestors saw the whole world animated by spirits—a tree, a rock, a wind, a star were all revelations of the sacred reality because each of them was animated, inhabited by some sort of spirit. Nathan Scott observed that in the animistic frame of reference, everything was sacramental, at least potentially, because everything was capable of revealing the sacred world, the real world at work behind the ordinary events and phenom-

---

*There is a charming and true story about Heidegger, a sometime Jesuit seminarian, in his old age arranging flowers in a country church for the celebration of the anniversary of a Jesuit relative. The old philosopher genuflected each time he passed the tabernacle. A curial official present for the festivities turned to a distinguished theologian who had studied under Heidegger and asked, "But why does Heidegger genuflect? Isn't he an atheist?" To which came the ironic reply, "A rationalist like you wouldn't understand."

ena of daily life. Some things could be sacraments because everything was sacramental; some realities could be especially holy, especially revelatory, because all reality was fundamentally holy and revelatory. Scott also argues, rightly I believe, that even if one abandons—as modern humans must—the animistic worldview, one can still see the whole of reality as sacramental. If one accepts the idea that all beings are revelatory in Being because all beings participate in Being, grace—in the sense of the revelation of the given-ness of our existence—comes from some sacraments, because everything is potentially sacramental. Grace is everywhere, or, as Karl Rahner says, "everything is grace."

There are, of course, certain human experiences with a special capacity for revelation, but they have this special capacity because everything has potential for revelation. Some things are especially sacred because everything is primordially sacred. As the poet Richard Wilbur puts it:

> . . . Oh maculate, cracked, askew,
> Gay-pocked and potsherd world
> I voyage, where in every tangible tree
> I see afloat among the leaves, all calm and curled,
> The Cheshire smile which sets me fearfully free.

RICHARD WILBUR
"Objects"[5]

I will argue in this book that sexual differentiation is sacramental in the sense that it has an extraordinarily powerful potentiality for creating in us a boundary or limit-experience, an experience in which the harsh wall of our own finitude is almost brutally encountered but which is also an experience of the revelation of the possibility of graciousness beyond the wall.

Two things must be noted about sexual differentiation as sacrament: Like all other sacraments, it need not be sacramental. While it has the capacity of inducing limit-experience, sexual differentiation need not do so, and most of our experiences of sexual differences are not very clearly or very explicitly limit-experiences. Secondly, sexual differentiation is sacramental because the whole material world is sacramental. Sexual differentiation can reveal to us both the limits of our own quest for transcendence and the hint of a possibility of breaking beyond those limits precisely because it participates in the mystery of a universe that in both its totality and its individual parts imposes limits to and poses questions about the possibility of transcending the universe itself.

What does it take for a thing to be a sacrament, for an object or a person to become a revelation, for an experience of a thing to become a disclosure? As Thomas Fawcett remarks, "A disclosure of any kind is only possible when something within a man's experience confronts him in such a way that a response is evoked within him."[6] When a thing becomes a disclosure, it also becomes a symbol. Trees, flowers, tiny animals are simply things; but when they are carried in a spring procession, they become a sign that spring has come. Even this really isn't a disclosure until the signs "produce specific reactions in us, [until] they operate at the personal level of emotion and imagination [and] something new appears to be given in the experience they create."[7] The flowers, the tree branches, the animals are not merely a sign that spring is back, they have become a disclosure sign precisely because they create in us an experience of bumping up against the limits of the cosmos. The signs which announce spring speak of both death and life; the world is not dead, it constantly overcomes death. I see that sign; it forces me to consider my own death and discloses to me in one way or another that death is not ultimate. The thing has become a sign, and the sign in its turn, because it has evoked tough questioning and a tentative answer in me, has become a symbol.

Note well what has happened. The thing which has forced a limit-experience on me now becomes the symbol by which I interpret my experience and communicate it to others. This transformation of a thing into a limit-experience and a revelatory experience occurs, according to Fawcett in three moments:

(i) The presence of an existential need.
(ii) The moment of disclosure or perception itself.
(iii) The embodiment of the experience in symbolic form.[8]

The existential need has to be there to begin with. There has to be some predisposition toward a limit-experience before the thing can produce such an experience. I can see the dune grass turn green every year and just remark to myself, "Well, it's spring again." Unless there is some need in a particular spring in the depths of my personality to wonder about the mysteries of life and death in the universe, the second and third steps of the limit-experience may not occur. I can encounter a beautiful woman on the street and experience nothing else than a slightly increased level of sexual fantasy unless there is some kind of powerful existential puzzling going on inside of me about the diversity of humankind and the baffling differentiation of that kind into male and female, a differentiation combined with an urge toward unity between male and female. Without the predisposition to wonder, all things, even the most exciting things become commonplace. But when the predisposition to wonder is there, then everything is potentially sacramental, and some things are overwhelmingly so.

Fawcett sees two phases in the process of a thing becoming a sacrament (my phrase, not his):

The Descent
   i. The presence of an existential need;
   ii. The moment of disclosure or perception of need;
   iii. The symbolization of ontological anxiety.

The Ascent
   i. The descent becomes the basis for further disclosure;
   ii. Creative disclosure or perception;
   iii. Symbolizations of integration and wholeness.[9]

So I sit on the side of my dune with a need in the depths of my spirit (mostly unrecognized) to find some answer to the apparent chaos and absurdity of a human life that will surely be snuffed out in death. I then perceive that the dune grass is becoming green again; the grass is being reborn after a winter's death. "My God," I say (more in exclamation than in prayer). "The grass is reborn." It grows older without weakening, without becoming infirm. I too am growing older, but unlike the grass I move inevitably toward death. I have now symbolized my own ontological anxiety about death.

But I continue to stare at the grass. It seemed to be dead last November, but now it is alive again. Can it be that I am less important than the flowers of the field or the grass of the dune? I perceive that somehow, some way, life is stronger than death, that my life is stronger than my death. And so I celebrate the rebirth of the grass, the coming of spring, with a new sense of peace and serenity and wholeness. Life conquers death, and my life will ultimately conquer my death. Thus the symbol is transformed into limit-experience.

Or I encounter an extraordinarily beautiful woman. She is human like me but separate from me, distinct from me, not identifiable with me. I have been lonely, cut off, alienated, but have scarcely noted any existential need for union. In the experience of this beautiful woman, I perceive my alienation, my loneliness. It matters not whether I sleep with her. (The first person pronoun is used here in the general sense, *not* in any autobiographic sense.) Even if we do make love, the moment of union with her is fleeting, and I perceive in it that I really am not "at one" with her, that I am distinct, lonely, cut off. My ontological anxiety has now been symbolized in my relationship with that woman, and in its explicitness I am forced to probe more deeply into the dilemma of loneliness. But I also perceive that in the differentiation that comes from our separateness and distinctiveness, there is also goodness, for she is tender and seductive and inspiring and gentle. She draws me out of myself both physiologically and psychologically. She discloses to me, and I perceive, that differentiation is a prelude to loving integration, and that which is separated can also be joined. If I feel cut off from myself, my friends, my world, from the ultimate forces that are at work in the universe, this woman becomes a sacrament to me that such divisions and separations and isolations can be transcended, and that differentiation is a prelude to wholeness.

Note that this experience of sexual differentiation can arise out of any encounter with a member of the opposite sex as long as there is a predisposing (perhaps unrecognized) existential need. The encounter can be the permanent relationship of a marriage or a chance passing on the street in which not a word is said. Note also that the experience of sexual differentiation, which is as commonplace as breathing, need not be sacramental. Sexual differentiation need not become a symbol; that it frequently has done so is beyond all doubt; that most of the time it does not become so in our lives is also beyond all doubt. Sex is not automatically a sacrament, but a lesson of human history is that it can easily become so.

What has happened in these two sacramental experiences? I have dealt with reality through an habitual structure of perceptions.* In my structured perceptions, dune grass and lovely women are parts of the environment, attractive and appealing in their own ways, doubtless, but quite ordinary and commonplace. But in a particular encounter in which these things** become sacramental, a peculiar dialectic is set up between my existential needs and the revelatory power of the thing. Thus, between my yearnings for self-transcendence and the thing's unique and special capacity to reveal Being, the dialectic is established that reveals the pain of the limit-experience, consciously and explicitly hints that something beyond the experience may be perceived, and transforms the thing itself into symbol which embodies both my perception of the problem and my grasp of the hint of an answer.

Because of the dialectic that is set up, the ordinary structures of my perception have been shattered. The grass is no longer a green flora on my duneside; it rises in revolt, as it were, against such casual, structured perception and demands to be seen for what it is, a wondrous, marvelous splash of green which some playful spirit has tossed on my dune, perhaps as compensation for last year's erosion. "Look at me!" the grass screams. "See what I am! Learn from me about the Being which I reveal." The grass, then, shatters the structures of my perception and becomes a symbol which is a focus, a prism through which my perceptions are restructured. The grass serves three roles; it shatters my old perceptions, but only once I have agreed implicitly to the establishment of the dialectic; it reorganizes my perceptions into a new configuration; and it accompanies me as a symbol which will recall for me the experience I had on the dunes and enable me—if I am a poet—to share that experience with others.

Similarly, the woman also virtually screams at me (when my existential needs force me to be open to dialogue with her): "I am not merely part of the environment. I'm not part of the scenery. I am a person like you, but different. I am cut off and lonely like you, and in the difference between us lies the possibility of unity. In that unity we

*The French philosopher Merleau-Ponty notes that humans organize and structure their experience simply because it is impossible to deal with an unstructured flow of consciousness. Such a structuring is a biological trait we have in common with the higher animals, though there is in humans, of course, in addition to the unconscious, biological structuring of experience, a conscious, reflective structuring. However, this latter builds on the former, which underpins and supports it.

**To call a beautiful woman a "thing" is not male chauvinism, merely an assertion that she shares the physical universe with me.

have together is the union of all things in whatever is ultimate." The woman, then, forces me to recognize my own "cut-offness"; she becomes a revelation of the potential unity of all things, and in that moment becomes a symbol—a symbol that does not cease to be a human person, of course. She remains a symbol around which I can organize my newly restructured perceptions of unity and diversity, of alienation and love. As a symbol, my relationship is not fleeting; she recalls to me my limit-experience of isolation and a hint of an explanation about unity which responded to that limit-experience. She not only has restructured my perceptions, she is a permanent reminder of that restructuring, and hence a guarantee that I will not slip back. Finally, should I be a poet or a novelist or a musician, she is a symbol through which I can communicate to others my limit-experience and the dazzling insight that comes from the shattering of old perceptions and the creations of new structures.*

A limit-experience is essentially an experience of old perceptions being shattered and new ones being structured. It requires a dialogue between my existential need and the revelatory power of something else that shares the cosmos with me. At the core of the experience is the symbolization of that with which I am in dialogue. When, therefore, I speak to others of my experience, I necessarily fall back on the symbol because in one very real sense, the symbol *is* the experience.

Note that the symbolization of the thing, which is at the core of a limit-experience, is action-producing. I do not sit and look at the grass passively after it has intruded itself sacramentally into my life. I set out to work with a song on my lips (Well, I would if I could sing!) and joy in my heart. Restructured perceptions lead to restructured living. One lives in response to the world one perceives; if one perceives the world differently, one lives differently. When I fall in love with a woman who reveals to me the existence of passionate tenderness in the cosmos, my behavior undergoes a transformation. I yearn to be with her, I sing about her, I praise her to all I know. If she is already mine and I am already hers, I desperately wish to make love with her precisely because of my experience of her as a valid and

---

*All of this, of course, is highly schematic. It leaves out that when our sacramental encounters are with other people there is a necessary dialogue of respect for the other person's limit-experiences which may be going on simultaneously.

authentic "other," I experience a powerful yearning for unity. She has restructured my perceptions, and in the process she has inevitably changed my behavior.

We act, therefore, as a result of limit-experiences. The apostles experienced the risen Jesus, and then went forth and preached him. The nature lover sings, the lover makes love. The apostles preached for years before they wrote about it, and only then did they begin to turn to theology. One reflects on the symbol and its meaning only after one has lived—perhaps passionately—the renewed life the symbols have made possible. Reflection is derivative; action is primary. Reflection focuses on both the symbol and the subsequent action, and tries to explain to others—especially those to whom the symbol is not an effective means of communication—what the experience incarnated in the symbol and embodied in one's life really means.

There is a unity in human religious experience simply because the number of things which are almost inevitably sacramental is finite. The sky, sun, moon, waters, stones, trees, the rebirth of nature in spring, special places and times, sexual differentiation, fertility, the life cycle—these are sacraments in virtually every culture the world has ever known. Eliade, in his *Patterns of Comparative Religion,* suggests a universality of sacraments is simply the result of general structures of human existence. Each of those sacramental things are important for all humans by the very fact that they are humans. Thus one does not need to have to postulate anything quite so elaborate as the primal archetypes of the collective unconscious of the Jungians.

If there is a fundamental similarity of religious experience, there is also a great plasticity and diversity of the way in which the various "supersacraments" might be encountered and interpreted. The rebirth of spring (my dune grass) can be greeted by gentle, restrained processions or by wild orgies; one can respond to sexual differentiation as limit-experience in ways as different as the smiling Virgin of Chartres is from temple prostitution. There are primal symbols in the sense that certain things in the world have almost universally overwhelming sacramental power, but these primal symbols can take very different forms as they become the carriers of different specific religious limit-experiences, and as specific religious insights have grown out of these experiences. Everyone experiences the rebirth of spring a little differently. The great religious leaders and founders have their immense influence precisely because their experience of the sacramental things which are available to all of us are profoundly new and original, and because the power with which they elaborate the symbol of their limit-experience calls forth similar new or renewed experiences and insights in their followers

Mary is part of the universal human experience of sexual differentiation as a sacrament of alienation and dealienation, of diversity and unity, of the combination of opposites in the one. Mary reveals, as do all goddesses, the feminine aspect of the deity. We do not see the same kind of deity in Mary that we do in Astarte or Kali, for example. The basic experience of shattering and restructuring of perception is the same in any experience of sexual differentiation, but the way the structures are shattered and the new organization that is imposed upon them by our encounter with the particular symbol (whether we are the first to encounter it or whether we encounter it through others) can be very different. The Mary symbol reorganizes, restructures our perceptions in a very different way than does the Kali symbol. Both reveal to us the combination of masculinity and femininity in the deity, but that which is revealed about the deity and that which is integrated into our personalities by the symbol is very, very different in the Mary experience than that which is revealed and integrated in the Kali experience.

Furthermore, even a specified limit-experience symbol like my encounter with the woman on the street, or the early Christians' encounter with Mary, is not a neat, orderly, unambiguous, simple reality. The thing which reveals itself to us reveals itself in its fullness; it is dense, multilayered, polyvalent. It says many things to us simultaneously, some of them surely paradoxical, some of them even contradictory. One who has fallen in love knows full well that no set of logical propositions is adequate to describe the complexity, the paradox of the beloved. One tries to say everything at once and ends up babbling. All things are complicated, and those things which are most likely to be sacramental are especially so. The best we can do when we leave off simply repeating the symbol and attempting to take just one aspect of the symbol to describe it, is to risk distorting the symbol substantially by neglecting its other aspects. I describe the seriousness and intelligence of my "mythical" loved one, but having done that, I may make her sound terribly dull because I have not had an opportunity to simultaneously describe her humor and playfulness.

So it is with limit-experiences and the language we use to describe them. It is not merely that such language is "odd," as Ian Ramsey says. If one is speaking of limit-experience, one must use special language simply because limit-experiences are different from the ordinary experiences for which ordinary language is appropriate. You don't describe an event in which a thing becomes a symbol in ordinary prose; you must fall back on metaphor, parable, paradox; you must introduce a "qualifier," as Ramsey says, which indicates to the listener or the reader that you are now using words in their limit-sense and not in their ordinary sense.

Of its nature limit-language involves tension. The two terms of the metaphor which is latent in limit-language must be in some tension if they are to produce the startling and perception-shattering experience in the listener which religious language is designed to produce. Such statements as "The first shall be last, the last shall be first," "He is dead but has risen," "She is a mother but a virgin," represent limit-language use of words—words used to convey limit-experiences. Paul Ricoeur says that the language we use to describe the limit-experience, which a symbol both created and attempts to repeat, goes to the limits of language. The language of religion does not so much deny the ordinary as it intensifies it. In Father Tracy's words, it is "an intensification of the everyday." The unexpected happens; a strange world of meaning is projected which challenges, jars, disorients our everyday vision precisely by both showing us the limits to the everyday and projecting the limit character of the whole."[10]

Limit-language, then, is designed to convey a limit-experience, to convert a thing into a symbol. It is language designed to make the symbol "explode with a linguistic power that discloses possibilities for human existence which seem and are beyond the limit of what our ordinary language and experience might imagine."[11]

Such writers as Dominick Crossen and David Tracy have shown that the very language of the Gospel parables has been designed to establish tension, to cut through existing structures of perception with the sharp knife of paradox. There is tension built into, for example, . . . the juxtaposition of the words "good" and "Samaritan," or "first" and "last," which, even before we hear the stories, catch us by surprise and set us to wondering. Both in their substance and in their language the parables are paradoxical, shattering, exploding, and disclosing narratives. Every child, and the child in every one of us, is ready to plead, "Tell me a story." For the role of stories is to explain life, and the good stories, in their very substance and in the structure of their language become revelation. In the shattering, disturbing, confusing, and challenging parables of the Gospel we are confronted with "one possible mode of being in the world: to live with explicit faith, with complete trust, with unqualified love." The story asks us to consider the possibility that we can live a life of fundamental trust, confidence, and total commitment to the goodness which has exploded out of the story and is seeking to take possession of us.

Thus, attempts to persuade us to perceive a thing as a symbol results in necessarily odd, unusual, and apparently bizarre language. The explanation of symbols cannot be made to fit the dimensions of ordinary discourse precisely because it is concerned with shattering forms and structures of everyday perceptions and the discourse that may flow from it. But symbols and the language that attempts to describe them are ambiguous in a second sense also.

When a thing becomes a symbol, it speaks to us all at once, and much of what it has to say we hear very dimly indeed. When we describe our experience to someone else, when we attempt to produce in him the same shattering and restructuring of perceptions that occurred in our experience, when we try to turn the thing into a symbol for him, it is altogether possible that the experience which is produced in him will enable him to see something in the symbol that we did not see. Suppose I write a poem about my dune grass. I have not heard clearly everything the grass has to say, but if my poem produces a similar experience in someone who reads it, he may not hear everything I have heard but he may well hear something clearly but dimly perceived by me; and he may also hear something that was really there when the grass spoke to me, but which I missed completely. In reading my poem, he searches not so much, or at least not entirely, for the meaning behind my words, which I have designed to convey the kind of experience the grass produced in me. He also, and perhaps more importantly, is trying to find the meaning "in front" of the words; that is, what does the grass say to him when it has produced in him through the mediation of my words an experience similar to mine of a thing becoming a symbol. For example, I may not have noticed at all that thin, apparently weak roots of the dune grass indeed hold my great and mighty dune together, and if it were not for the grass, wind and rain and snow would wreak havoc with my dune (assuming the lake waves should leave it alone). Like me, the reader of my imaginary poem experiences the limit-situation of the death and rebirth of nature, but he also experiences an aspect of that rebirth which is truly there but which I may only dimly have perceived or missed completely—the powerful binding force of a reborn nature which holds the potentially disintegrating inanimate reality together. (And, of course, he thereby perceives all kinds of ecological implications of my experience, which I either missed or only vaguely sensed.)

Mind you, he is not distorting my experience; he is not reading into it something that is not there; he is having the same experience I did (or one very similar) through the mediation of my words. But he is perceiving something deep and latent in the ontological reality of the experience that I missed.

Similarly, I may know a woman for years and suddenly discover an aspect of her personality that hitherto had been shrouded in mystery. Indeed, if I am not constantly discovering new things about her, our life together has become dull and routine. It is not that I am reading something into our experience together that was not there; nor is it that she suddenly becomes someone she was not before. This aspect of her selfhood was always there and was always speaking to me, but our dialogue has only today developed to such a stage that I perceive her speaking to me about this aspect of her personality. I am not "getting behind" the meaning of our original experience of each other; rather, I am now "in front of" that experience and seeing in it something I never saw before.

It is a phenomenon something like this that Paul Ricoeur has in mind when he speaks of the "prospective" sense of a text. When one searches for the "prospective" meaning of a symbol, one does not merely or even principally ask what he who first articulated that symbol within a specific religious tradition perceived consciously or explicitly; one asks, rather, what illumination are we able to receive from experiencing the thing-turned-symbol or the problem of being-in-the-world as we experience them given our situation, our information, and our insights today? If we permit the thing-turned-symbol to shatter our perspectives as it shattered the perspectives of its author, and then go on to reorganize our perspectives, what new structures of perception emerge for us? Can the limit-experience that he produces in us through the language by which he describes his experience give us illumination from the thing-turned-symbol that he missed, dimly perceived, or, in fact, couldn't perceive within the context of the time and place of his experience?

Metaphors, symbols, myths are open-ended. No limits can be set, notes Ian Barbour, to how far the comparison in such a figure of speech can be extended, because it has an unspecifiable number of potentialities for articulation left for the hearer or the reader to explore. "It is not an illustration of an idea already explicitly spelled out, but a suggestive invitation to the discovery of further similarities" (p.14). It is precisely because a symbol (like a parable) is open-ended that it can be extended to new situations. The symbol presents a comparison to be explored, insights to be discovered, a many-faceted flow of images to be enjoyed. It illumines one's situation so that one sees aspects of reality which one might otherwise have missed; and at the same time the contact with a newly illumined reality can reflect back on the symbol itself and enable one to discover a potential extension of the basic comparison that was hitherto unperceived.

If a symbol were merely a logical proposition, the possibility of our finding new illumination in it would be nil; but the symbol is an experience and a record of an experience; and experience, as we have said before, is complex, dense, multilayered, and polyvalent. Another man's symbol may produce in us experiential insights that it did not produce in him without doing violence either to his experience or to the symbol which enabled him to share it with us. Obviously we must be careful that the experience is indeed the same or fundamentally similar to his. A symbol is not an inkblot into which we read our own preconceptions and needs independently of its own objective integrity. He who claims to have experienced, in an encounter with a symbol, revelations that are exactly the opposite of the insights of the author and of the insights of a long tradition of those in a community which shared the experience with the author, ought to seriously question whether it is the same symbol and the same tradition of which he claims to be a part. He who encounters the risen Jesus, for example, and announces bravely that in his encounter he has learned that death conquers life, has not had an experience which shares any historical, psychological, or existential continuity with that of any Christians from the apostles to the present. It may be an interesting experience but it is not a Christian one; and it is not the same experience or even a fundamentally similar one to that of the apostles on Easter.

Still, with the caveat that the symbol is not an inkblot and that we must respect the validity and the authenticity of the author's personal experience and of those who are part of the tradition the author began, it is still possible for us to receive illuminations from the thing-turned-symbol that were but dimly perceived or not perceived at all by those who first experienced it.

It is possible, I should think, that as theological discussion of Ricoeur's "prospective sense" develops, a way will be found out of many of the knotty problems that cling to the development of doctrine which has plagued Christianity for centuries. However, such solutions will only be possible for those who carefully put themselves into the context of the theological approach being described in this chapter, and who refrain from quick judgments about the meaning of symbols.

Symbols do not "compete" within a religious tradition. They do not so much describe different limit-experiences as they describe different aspects of the same primal Great Experience. There may be a "core" symbol or a "privileged" symbol, but the others are reflections of it, not its competitors.

The "privileged" center of a symbol system is not diminished by the existence of other symbols organized around it. The central symbol of Christianity is conveyed in the paradox "Jesus who was crucified is risen." Exactly the same passionately loving, passionately renewing God is revealed by the symbol embodied in the paradox of the "virgin Daughter of Zion who gave birth to the new Adam." There is obviously no competition between the two, and while the former is "privileged," it is necessarily contained in the latter—as it is in every other symbol of the Christian system.

From the point of view of the logic of religious language, the Reformation argument about honor to Mary detracting from honor to Jesus is absurd (which is not to say that all the reformers' objections to some forms of Marian devotions were absurd). There is no need at all to limit God's exuberant graciousness by insisting on only one religious symbol as being fully legitimate for a tradition. This book happens to be about the great experience of Christianity as it is reflected in the Mary myth. As I have indicated in an earlier book, *The Jesus Myth*, Jesus died and risen is the "privileged" symbol. God, not being a Calvinist, permits us, indeed encourages us (if the history of religions is any proof) to have other symbols which reflect the core symbol.

Both limit-experiences and those things which are most disposed to become the symbols that trigger and incarnate such experiences are in themselves radically neutral. One can encounter a grace, a sense of given-ness, or one can encounter absurdity. The existential need may be resolved by a reordering of perceptions into a new and more gracious constellation, or the need may be frozen into the old structures of perception which become bravely and stoically accepted in the face of an impulse, an urge toward a new structure. John Shea in his *Challenge of Jesus* (Thomas More Press, 1975) shows ingeniously how a tree—one of the universal things-that-may-become-symbol—was a sign of graciousness for Avery Dulles and a sign of despair for Jean Paul Sartre. What one does with a thing-becoming-symbol is shaped to a considerable extent by one's culture, one's personality, one's biography. I would maintain that there is a strain toward graciousness in a limit-experience, but it is one that can be resisted.

Schubert Ogden is surely correct when he suggests that there is built into the structure of our personalities an assurance of the fundamental purposiveness of our existence. The limit-experience can produce a symbol that "re-presents" that assurance, but one is free to reject an assurance of purposiveness as wish fulfillment and self-deception. Such rejection means a denial of a powerful thrust of our personality, but it can be and has been done—often.

In this book I intend to ask what illumination we can receive for the problems of our time by permitting ourselves the limit-experience of the thing-called-sexual-differentiation becoming the revelatory symbol that is incarnated in the Mary tradition. More simply, what we can learn for our own time by encountering Mary; what we can learn by permitting ourselves the same experience (or a fundamentally similar one) of the Madonna, the Virgo, the Sponsa, and the Pietà which other Christians have been experiencing for nineteen centuries. One must be faithful to their experience, but one must also be faithful to oneself and the situation in which one finds oneself in the world. Tracy describes theology as ". . . reflection upon the meanings present in our common human experience and the meanings present in the Christian tradition . . ."[12] It is precisely because the shape of our common human experiences changes through time—though always maintaining a continuity with the past, of course—that we can find richer and fuller and more illuminating meaning in our reflection upon the Christian tradition.

I have repeatedly referred to a symbol producing in us the same or a fundamentally similar experience which the author of the thing-turned-symbol had when in the dialectic of encounter his perceptions were shattered and restructured into new and better configurations. There is a problem here. No man can have the exact experience of another. Peter's experience of the risen Jesus was not John's; and neither of their experiences was exactly the same as the one that knocked Paul from his horse on the route to Damascus. My experience is not yours, neither of ours is Henry Adams's; and we three twentieth-century Americans do not have exactly the same experience as did St. Bernard.

But what does it take for the experience of the risen Jesus or of Mary to be "fundamentally similar" through time and space? To my knowledge no one has addressed himself to this problem, although there is an obvious common-sense answer to it. There were clearly differences in personality and "existential need" in Peter, John and Paul, you, me, Henry Adams and St. Bernard. It was obviously the same Jesus, for example, that both apostles encountered; and who would question that there was any fundamental difference between Bernard's Virgin of Chartres and the one Henry Adams encountered? The real problem arises when one gets to borderline cases.

I would submit that the question comes down finally to the new configurations of perception that emerge from a limit-experience. When the thing-turned-symbol shatters the old routines and habits with which I view the world, and reorganizes the raw materials of my perceptions into a new pattern, is there a "fit"? It need only be rough and approximate, of course, but the fit between my constellation of perceptions and those to be found among those who have had similar encounters from the beginning must be apparent. My personality is indeed different from St. Bernard's; the world in which I live is different. It would be unthinkable for there not to be very considerable differences between my experience of Mary and his. He emphasized aspects which I think are unimportant; I will emphasize elements which he but dimly perceived and others of which he could not possibly have thought. But allowing for these differences of personality and environment, is my response like Bernard's? Is it a response of enthusiasm and joy to an Ultimate which is perceived as passionately tender? I think that it is, and that I can, therefore, claim continuity with Bernard. There is a "fit" between my reordered structures of perception and his. We may sing different songs to the Virgin, but it is the same Virgin who tells us both of God's loving graciousness.

One more point must be made about the symbol that both creates a transforming limit-experience and incarnates the memory of that experience so we can share it with others. The symbol almost always appears in the form of a story, which we made oblique reference to earlier with a quotation from Tracy's book discussing the Gospel parables. The age-old cry of the child, "Tell me a story," is in fact a primal cry of the human race. We find ourselves caught in the middle of a story—like a movie that we began to watch in the middle. We don't know how or why the story of humankind began, and we don't know how it will end for either the species or for us as individuals. The transforming symbol purports to tell us about the beginning and the ending, and by so doing it shatters our old perceptual structures and orders new ones into new configurations. But the thing-becoming-symbol can enter the dialectic between our existential needs and our perceptions, not as a sort of disembodied figure floating around timeless like a Platonic Idea or a Weberian Ideal Type. The thing becomes a symbol precisely insofar as it manages to embody itself in story, an image rooted in our perception of our reality. The parables of Jesus have the impact they do precisely because in them the language of symbol, limit-language, appears in story form. They begin as all good stories must with the words, "Once upon a time . . ."

Like "Once upon a time a decree went forth from Caesar Augustus . . ."

At the heart of the limit-experience is a sensation of "given-ness," of "gifted-ness," or, to use the old word, "grace." The scientist discovers that the intelligibility of the universe is a given; it is *there,* and whence it came his science knows not. It is a gift, utterly astonishing and gratuitous. The philosopher finds a common human moral faith (infinitely varied in its applications, no doubt, but still common in its basic norms). Such a faith—the underlying premise of all moral discussion—is as gratuitous as is the intelligibility of the universe. Thus, in the limit-experience one not only bumps up against the hard outer boundaries, the horizon of one's own understanding and experience, one also encounters (or can encounter) something that appears to be a grace or a gift lurking on the boundary which suggests something else—a giver, perhaps—beyond the boundary.

It is when a thing is perceived as a gift, as a grace, that it can shatter our perceptual structures and begin to build new ones. When I beheld in my astonishment the marvelous gratuity in the being of my dune grass, then I found myself facing the apparent graciousness of a Being which (or who) thrust the grass into its being. Similarly, the attractiveness of someone who is sexually differentiated from me becomes a symbol—a thing-turned-sacrament—precisely when I begin to wonder about the utter gratuity of that differentiation. She becomes grace when it dawns on me that there is no particular reason why such a marvel had to exist; the fact of her existence—particularly of her existence for me—is a sheer gift, pure grace. She is *there*, no longer now as merely a lovely part of the scenery, but a mysterious gift *to me*, a gift to which I had no right and which didn't have to be. She remains herself, of course, but now she is a sign of mystery, a rumor of angels, a grace-bestowing sacrament.

When grace floods into my personality through such an experience, the old structures of perception are not only shattered, they are swept away. Since I now see the thing differently, as *given*, I now see everything differently. Such a limit-experience need not happen, of course. The grass can remain a sign of the return of spring and not invade my consciousness as a sign of grace and a symbol of resurrection. Similarly, the woman may remain a mere thing; she may even become a thing-that-is, a self like my self, yet still not a thing-turned-sacrament, a self perceived as sheer gift. In most cases, the grass and the woman will *not* become signs of grace, and the giftedness of things will not be noticed. But the point is that they *can* become signs of grace and hence can be transformed into symbols.

Obviously I am using the words "grace" and "sacrament" in somewhat different senses than they were used in the old catechism and theology manuals. "Grace" here means the capacity of a reality to possess our perception with the utter gratuity, the sheer given-ness of its existence. "Sacrament" is a thing-becoming-symbol which reveals to us its graciousness and the graciousness of Being in which it is rooted and from which it has been thrust into a being of its own. I would contend, by the way, that this use of the words is primary, and the old catechetical and apologetic use of them was derivative.[13]

In summary, then, religion is a set of symbols growing out of limit-experiences in which we bump up against the boundaries of our horizon but also perceive that there may be something beyond those boundaries. In a limit-experience—at least in one in which we receive a "hint of an explanation"—a thing becomes a sacrament, a revelatory symbol which dialogues with our own existential need, shatters the old structures of our perception, and gives us new insights by reordering and renewing our perceptions into new structures. The thing-turned-symbol constructs the new configurations of perceptions which move us to action, provides us with a memory of the past experience to sustain us in action, and also becomes a means of communication by which we can share our experience with others. Religious preaching and teaching is essentially the art of trying to induce in others the same limit-experiences that we have had and that the founders of our religious tradition have had.

All things are potentially sacramental. All have the capability of converting themselves from things to symbols. There are certain things, including sexual differentiation, which have special sacramental power. Their overwhelming importance in the human condition has made them sacraments in almost every major human religious tradition. These universal symbols, however, take on many different specific forms, depending on the experience of the specific religious tradition. Even within a context of a given tradition, different humans at different times and places will experience different illumination from the fundamentally similar religious experience generated by the symbol.

The language with which we describe our limit-experience and the symbols which cause and preserve them is necessarily odd or special language, language which startles, jolts, reveals, stirs up expectations and hopes. Language which conveys a symbol is like the symbol itself: it intensifies the ordinary and everyday, and opens up new possibilities for our life in the world.

In the "method" or the "approach" that I have laid out in this chapter, there is immense possibility for preaching and religious education. It is not a possibility that I think will be seized in the near future; it will require hard work, constant rethinking, and the abandonment of many old emphases and techniques. I am convinced, however, that the "method" is an excellent one for dealing not only with secularist unbelievers but also with faithful parishioners. In my own experience, it is much less offensive to traditional Catholics than some of the bizarre techniques of religious education currently being practiced in American Catholicism.

In any event, I now propose to apply this method to the limit-experience of sexual differentiation and to Mary, the most dazzling symbol of the transforming power of that experience. Even the moody early Romantic William Wordsworth could not escape the dazzling power of Mary's charm:

> Mother! whose virgin bosom was uncrost
> With the least shade of thought to sin allied;
> Woman! above all women glorified,
> Our tainted nature's solitary boast;
> Purer than foam on central ocean tost;
> Brighter than eastern skies at daybreak strewn
> With fancied roses, than the unblemished moon
> Before her wane begins on heaven's blue coast;
> Thy Image falls to earth. Yet some, I ween,
> Not unforgiven the suppliant knee might bend,
> As to a visible Power, in which did blend
> All that was mixed and reconciled in Thee
> Of mother's love with maiden purity
> Of high with low, celestial with terrene!

WILLIAM WORDSWORTH (1770–1850)
"Sonnet to the Virgin"

Chapter 3

The Androgyny of God

There is a story about a white male chauvinist racist who presented himself at the gates of heaven and demanded admission. A suspiciously dusky looking angel told him that there was just no way he could get in. The new immigrant wanted to know why, and he was informed that God didn't like him. Since he had been a pious Presbyterian all his life, the man was astonished. "Why doesn't God like me?" he asked.

" 'Cause God, she's black!"

The story is intended to be ironic, of course. We all know that God is an elderly white male with a long beard.

But in fact God is both masculine and feminine, and may well have been thought of as a woman long before she/he was ever thought of as male.

Primitive humans were convinced that all attributes existed as one in the divinity, and that therefore there was every reason to think that both sexes should be more or less clearly expressed together.[1] Eliade comments:

> Divine androgyny is simply a primitive formula for the divine biunity; mythological or religious thought, before expressing this concept of the divine two-in-oneness in metaphysical terms or the theological terms (the revealed and the unrevealed) expressed it first in the biological terms of bisexuality.[2]

The fertility deities are generally either hermaphrodites or female one year and male the next. The vegetation deities (Adis, Adonis, Dionysius) are bisexual. In Australia, with its very primitive aboriginal religion, the primal god is androgynous, just as he is in the most highly developed religions such as may be found in India. Siva-Kali are sometimes represented in the Indian religion as a unity. The Tantric Indian mysticisn is designed to identify the initiate with the "divine pair" by making him androgynous.[3]

As ultimate reality and absolute power, God simply cannot be limited by any attribute whatsoever. Egyptian, Greek, Scandinavian, Iranian, and even Chinese gods were either expressly androgynous or carried residues of their more ancient androgynous condition. The emergence of divine couples (Saturn and Juno, for example) are in most cases later fabrications or reformulations of primeval androgyny. There are, as Eliade comments, innumerable cases of divinity being addressed as "Father and Mother."[4]

Alan Watts traces the theme of the primordial pair in his book *The Two Hands of God* by way of the Yin and Yang themes in Chinese philosophy.[5] He quotes one Chinese text that gives the explicitly sexual connotation of the Yang-Yin unity: "One Yang and one Yin, that is the fundamental principle. The passionate unity of Yin and Yang in the copulation of husband and wife is the eternal rule of the universe. If heaven and earth did not mingle, whence would all things receive life?"[6]

In a more recent work, *The Two and the One,* Mircea Eliade adds that in several of the Midrashic writings, Adam was androgynous: "Adam and Eve were made back to back out of a joint at the shoulder; then God divided them with an ax-stroke, cutting them in two."[7] Another Midrashic writer argued that the "first man was a man on the left side, a woman on the right." This slipped into Christianity through two variants of the Gnostic sect. For Simon Magnus, the promordial spirit was male-female, and the Essenes thought of the "celestial man," Adamas, as a male-female; and therefore Adam, a celestial "reflection" of Adamas, also had to be androgynous.

Plato viewed the archetypical man as bisexual and spherical in form, and his neoplatonic disciples (some of them Christian) imagined human perfection as an unbroken unity. Such philosophical specula- tions were rooted in earlier mythological convictions. The goddess Hera, the goddess of marriage, was originally androgynous; there are statues of a bearded Zeus with six breasts; in some cults Hercules was dressed as a woman. In Cyprus, Aphrodite had a beard, and in Italy, Venus was bald. Dionysius was addressed as a man-woman; he started out as a stout bearded fellow, though later he became much more effeminate. The sober Romans, never ones to take a chance, hedged when they addressed the deity: "Whether you are a man or whether you are a woman..." or "Whether you are a god or a goddess..."

Enough evidence has been produced to make the point. Eliade even sees some traces of this androgynous theme in the writings of early Christianity. In the Gospel of Thomas, for example, Jesus is quoted as saying, "When you make male and female into a single one, so that the male shall not be male and the female shall not be female, then you shall enter the kingdom."[8] Elsewhere in the same apocryphal Gospel, Jesus is pictured as saying, "When you make the two become one, you will become the son of man, and if you say 'Mountain, remove yourself,' it will remove itself."[9] In the Gospel of Philip the division of the sexes—Eve being made from the body of Adam—is the principle of death: "Christ came to reestablish what was thus divided in the beginning and to reunite the two. Those who died because they were in separation, He will restore to life by reuniting them!"[10] In the somewhat more reliable Second Epistle of Clement, Jesus is asked at what moment the kingdom will come, and he replies, "When the two shall be one, the outside like the inside, the male with the female neither male nor female."[11] Clement of Alexandria records the response of Jesus to Salome (in the Gospel according to the Egyptians) when that exotic dancer wondered about the fulfillment of the prophecy. He answered in terms she would doubtless understand, "When you have trampled on the garment of shame, and when the two become one, and the male with the female is neither male nor female."[12]

These apocryphal Gospels are either quasi-Gnostic or have strong Gnostic influences, but Eliade sees some influence of the same perspective in the famous quote in the third chapter of the Epistle to the Galatians, "There is neither Jew nor Greek, there is neither slave nor free, there is neither male nor female; for we are all one in Christ Jesus." Against the background of the other texts, it seems by no means impossible that Paul's choice of words and phrases, if nothing else, was influenced by the androgynous speculation that was rife in his time.

The theme continued to be played in a minor key in Catholic

theology through Maximus the Confessor, John Scotus Origina, and Nicholas of Cusa. Origina thought of God as a primal unity; the division of substances began with God and continued progressively up to and including human nature, which was divided into male and female. This division was the result of sin, but it will come to an end with the forgiveness of sin. Male and female will be reunited, and the circle will then begin to turn back to the primal unity of God. The reintegration is anticipated in Christ. Maximus the Confessor even suggests that though Jesus was born and died a man, in his risen state he was neither man nor woman.[13]

Nicholas of Cusa operated on a much higher level of abstraction. God was the *coincidenta oppositorum,* the combination of opposites—a notion Cusa probably picked up from the pseudo-Dionysius. Indeed, according to Nicholas, *coincidenta oppositorum* is the least imperfect definition of God.

Eliade sees this theme of the combination of opposites running through theology, metaphysical speculation, mythical cosmologies, orgiastic rituals in which behavior is reversed and values confused (the Saturnalia, the Mardi Gras, the Carnivale), mystical techniques for the union of contraries, and in rites of androgynization:

> One can say that all these myths, rites, and beliefs have the aim of reminding men that the ultimate reality, the sacred, the divine, defies all possibilities of rational comprehension; that the *grund* can only be grasped as a mystery or paradox . . . The best way of apprehending God or the ultimate reality is to cease, if only for a few seconds, considering and imagining divinity in terms of immediate experience; such an experience could only perceive fragments and tensions.[14]

The ultimate reality, then, is a primal unity. Creation represents a fragmentation of unity; reintegration involves putting the fragments back together again. The Pauline notion of "restoring all things in Christ" surely shows the influence of this primal religious theme.

To many who have not made a detailed study of ancient or primitive religious myths much of the material I have cited above may seem bizarre. The statues on Hindu temples which show male and female copulations in an incredible variety of different positions strike us as being nothing more than pornography in stone. Obscene they may be, deliberately erotic they surely are; but they also reflect the almost universal human notion that in God the masculine and feminine are blended in unbroken unity. However startling and odd the androgynous themes may be, we must admit that the scholastic philosophy in which we were raised taught us that all human perfection exists in an infinitely superior way in the deity. If masculinity and femininity are perfections, then they must exist in God—so the scholastic could argue (in infinitely superior fashion, no doubt). Therefore, no matter how strange we find the androgyny myths, we must admit that even though we never heard of it in school, the notion of an androgynous deity is certainly not incompatible with the religious perspectives in which we were raised.*

*Merlin Stone, in When God Was a Woman (Dial Press, 1976), argues that God was feminine before becoming masculine, and that in the primordial food-gathering societies, matriarchy antedated patriarchy. Only later did the masculine god enter as a secondary and lesser consort of the Queen of Heaven. Still later did he expel the goddess from the divine court and set up a patriarchal and eventually chauvinist society. Obviously the most chauvinistic of the male gods was Yahweh, who got rid of his consort and imposed terrible oppression on women.

Stone's book is a useful review of the literature on the female deities, but the data will not support her model. Indeed, most sweeping evolutionary models of human change go far beyond the existing evidence. The more we know about primitive peoples (modern or ancient) the more difficult it becomes to fit specific tribes into an evolutionary paradigm. Surely there is no real evidence to support the old notion (first advanced more than 100 years ago by Bachofen in his Mudderech) that humankind has evolved from matriarchy to patriarchy. The reality seems to be that matrilineal (inheritance through women), matrilocal (living with mother's family), and matriarchal (women in governing roles) customs coexist at the same time and in varying patterns with one another and with patrilineal, patrilocal, and patriarchal customs; and that there is no great correlation between these customs and religious convictions. Thus the Celts and the Romans both had mother goddesses but women had far more freedom (virtual parity in many respects) in Celtic society than in Roman. Similarly Hebrew society had no (official) female deity but in practice Hebrew women seem to have had more power and more rights than did Roman women.

The research challenge is not to describe general models (many of which smack of female chauvinist ideology) but to ask under what circumstances one can find specifically a link between religion and social customs. Yahweh had no consorts (officially, at any rate—popular devotion to the Queen of Heaven obviously continued in Hebrew folk religion), but Yahweh also had many feminine characteristics—tenderness, warmth, and attractiveness.

Stone says not a word about the reappearance of the Queen of Heaven in the guise of Mary—which makes one wonder about how ideology can blind a writer. We do not have enough historical monographic work to detail the relationship between the slow improvement of the lot of women under Christianity (in comparison with the Hellenistic world) and the Mary cult, though there seems to be little reason to doubt the connection. However, correlations can run in either direction. It may well be that the more elevated role of women in Christianity ("neither Jew nor Gentile, male nor female, but all one in Christ Jesus") made possible the rise of the Mary cult.

Men are in a position to dominate women because they tend to be physically stronger

When we are forced to think of it, we must admit that God is neither male nor female. To put the matter differently, in God that which is most attractive in maleness and that which is most attractive in femaleness are combined in a higher unity. It is certainly proper, then, to think of God as he/she or she/he. The cautious Romans with their *"Sive Deus, sive Dea"* were theologically precise. For convenience' sake, we have chosen for the most part to address God as male; however, there is no reason either philosophically or religiously why one could not, for convenience' sake, make exactly the opposite decision and, following the example of Juliana of Norwich, address God as "our loving Mother." My argument is not that one must or should address God as female; simply that one may.[15]

The feminine goddesses of antiquity, then, represent the fact that the "feminine principle" is present in the deity. They are developments from more primitive androgynous deities, in all likelihood, and of course they reflect the human experience of sexuality as sacred. Fertility is a good, indeed an indispensable thing, and fertility involves sexuality; then surely sexuality must be found in the ultimate and the absolute. But it is difficult to deal with an ultimate that is masculine and feminine at the same time. Therefore, we have gods and goddesses, and underlying the vast systems of ritual and cult we build to those deities there is still the notion that in whatever is *really* ultimate, the two are combined.

Indeed, if anything, the female deities, or the female divine forces, seem to have emerged before the male ones. There is one major difficulty, of course, in trying to get at the religious behavior and beliefs of prehistoric peoples; and that is that they were prehistoric. The data from which archeologists, physical anthropologists, and prehistorians work is at best very uneven and ambiguous. I am astonished at the elaborate and complex theories these scholars can build up with the kind of data which, if it were available to a

---

and (apparently) more aggressive. Also women are at a special disadvantage during the childbearing and nursing years. The extent to which this domination of the weaker by the stronger is a direct correlate of religious belief is a matter for research and not for theoretical or ideological assumption. But the presence of a female deity does not necessarily impede such domination—as the Graeco-Roman world makes clear.

Still, in one sense the thesis of Stone is undeniable. When God is completely lacking in feminine traits, as is the God of some Calvinists, there will be hard times for all weaker creatures—women, children, black slaves, American Indians, and Irish natives, among others.

sociologist, might well lead him to throw it in the wastebasket. I intend no criticism of these hardworking, creative, and sometimes extremely ingenious men and women; they have no choice; they must do the best with what they have. Still, they and we must be very cautious about accepting their theories.

It is undoubtedly the case that a substantial number of female figurines have been found in caves all over Europe, the Middle East, and Asia. It is very *likely* the case that these figurines have religious and cultic significance, but we do not know for sure since none of us was around to see what our cave-dwelling ancestors did with their figurines. The argument that the grossly shaped bodies of the statues indicate an abstraction which could only reflect some sort of religious purpose is persuasive, although I wonder if archeologists tens of thousands of years from now might not argue from an uncovered cache of *Playboy* centerfolds that these were clearly religious artifacts.

Similarly, there were certainly strong matriarchal themes and social structures to be found in many archaic societies. In such societies it is also true that the mother goddess was more important than the father god: but it does not necessarily follow that matriarchy represented a peaceful and loving stage in human cultural evolution that was replaced by an aggressive, warlike patriarchal culture and social structure. Johann Jacob Bachofen's famous work, *Das Mutterrecht*,[16] is an extraordinarily ingenious organization of the data which cannot be ignored by anyone interested in the study of the history of religions. It is not, however, a description of what actually happened historically in the sense that a Woodward and Bernstein article in the *Washington Post* is. The occasional writer (frequently feminist) who assumes that an evolution from matriarchy to patriarchy is a certainly established historical phenomenon (one that ought to be reversed) shows no awareness of the complexity and the ambiguity of the data of prehistory. In fact, patriarchy and matriarchy are entwined, combined, and follow one another in bewildering patterns. They are "ideal types" and not simple stages of the evolutionary ladder.

I make these qualifications because I think it important for the reader to understand that a good deal of the data available to us about ancient religion is still very complex and obscure.

With all these qualifications it is still true that in the Paleolithic Age there seems to have been an intense devotion to the Great Mother goddess: "With the Stone Age sculptures of the Great Mother as a goddess, the Archetypical Feminine suddenly bursts upon the world of men in overwhelming wholeness and perfection. Aside from the cave paintings, these figures of the Great Goddess are the earliest cult works and the works of art known to us.''[17]

One may wonder about the ''archetype'' to which Neumann's Jungian ideology commits him. One may also wonder after looking at those rather grotesque figures like the Venus of Willendorf, the Venus of Menton, the Venus of Lespugue, and the Venus of Laussel (see Plates 1 and 2 of the Neumann book) if they are all that ''whole'' or ''perfect.'' The modern observer may consider them to be rather ugly, though on second thought he may reflect that they are, after all, not that different from a Picasso drawing. Indeed, with some modification, the Venus of Lespugue could easily take her place in Richard Daley's Civic Center next to the Picasso ''thing'' (or, as we call it in Chicago, ''da ting'').

The figurines are between twelve and twenty thousand years old, and more recently, some have been found in Russia that may be as much as fifty thousand years old. They have ranged from the Pyrenees to Siberia and throughout the Near East and the Orient. Neumann points out that of the sixty Stone Age sculptures available to us at the time of his writing, there were fifty-five female figures and only five male figures. Furthermore, the male figures were poorly executed and did not seem to have any cultic significance. The female figures clearly run to a type and were executed with not inconsiderable skill. While it is not certain that these figures had cultic significance, I think it is apparent that they represent the importance to our cave-dwelling ancestors of those powers in the universe which are perceived to be feminine. For the purposes of this book, such a conclusion seems sufficient.

The figurines do not look very human. The heads are usually shrunken and misshapen, the buttocks and the primary and secondary genital areas are greatly exaggerated. Since we know from skeletal remains that that is not the way Stone Age women looked, and since the artists seemed to be reasonably skillful at making figurines appear as they intended, one has to conclude that the statues are symbolic and hence quite possibly religious. One need not go into elaborate theories of the collective unconscious nor speculate about the bizarre sexual tastes of our predecessors (not much different from ours; perhaps they might well have found the *Playboy* centerfolds a bit bizarre). To conclude, these indeed are figures of a female deity, a Great Mother, the pregnant goddess of fertility, a symbol of the reproducing, protecting, and nourishing dimensions of reality. Neumann puts it nicely:

> One means by which early man could represent the numinous magnificence and archetypal uniqueness of the Feminine consisted in an expressive "exaggeration" of form, an accentuation of the elementary character. Here the body feeling plays a decisive role. The individual who created and the group which worshiped these works were unquestionably fascinated and attracted by the corporeity, the exuberant fullness and massive warmth, that emanate from such a figure. (This is the justification for applying the term "sensuous" to such works.) The attraction is identical with an unconscious accentuation of the infantile, and for this accent the goddess is an adequate image of the elementary character of containment.[18]

I see no need to fall back on "unconscious accentuation of the infantile" any more than the "collective unconscious" to explain the existence of the Venus figures, though I would not completely exclude the analytic models in either. The women kept the fires going in the caves, they brought children into the world to keep the tribe alive, they held the group together while the men went out on the hunt, they probably bound up the wounds of the injured hunters and took care of sick children. It is not too much of a romantic exaggeration, I think, to suspect that they consoled, caressed, and reassured the exhausted and weary food-searchers, as well as offering them sexual satisfaction if not affection (and who are we to say that affection was absent in the caves?). Small wonder that divine powers were thought to operate through women.

Fertility was the great mystery, and no sophisticated modern looking at a newborn child in his mother's arms can escape completely a sense of fascination and mystery at the awesome phenomenon of reproduction and continuation. Fertility was to the primitives, as well as to many sophisticated people since them, not only sacred but *the* sacred thing, *the* sacrament, *the* revelation; for it sustained the human race in its existence, whatever happened to its individual members. As civilization developed it was also responsible for the continuation of the fields and the flocks on which the emerging villages, towns, and cities depended for their food, clothing, and continuing sustenance. If ever there was a manifestation of the divine power, it was in the phenomenon of fertility.

A woman, then, as a locus of fertility was an especially sacred thing. As such, she was the object of both reverence and fear. She was both fascinating and terrifying, something to be worshiped, but also something to be the object of taboos. Divine powers were indeed potentially benign, but they could also be terrifying and destructive. One was wise to be wary when dealing with the sacred.

The hunter, the warrior, the vigilant guardian of the flocks was aware as well of the fact that a woman could "unman" him. In a state of sexual arousal he was no longer capable of hunting food, protecting the flocks from marauding predators, or fighting off enemies. He may also have discovered, though this is problematic and speculative, that once sexually aroused, a woman was capable of far more pleasure than he, as well as almost insatiable sexual demands. When the passions of the women of the tribe were fully unleashed (perhaps during the annual orgy) they were quite capable of thoroughly disrupting the fragile social structure of the tribe.[19]

It seems reasonable to assume that there was both fear of female sexuality as well as awe and reverence for it among primitive and archaic peoples. It was a sacred force, and sacred forces were to be both reverenced and feared. To what extent this fear is responsible for the repression of women in many cultures up to and including the modern is problematic. Many of the customs and social structures which have emerged could as easily be explained by the fact that when infant mortality rates were high (as they have been at all times in human history until very recently), the time and energies of women were consumed by childbearing and childrearing. Under such circumstances, the secondary role of women in the tribe or in the village or city may have been a custom based more on pragmatic than on protoideological reasons. Still, fear for something sacred may also have played a role. Surely no one even today would say that fear of the opposite sex has completely vanished from the human condition.

Whatever may have been the case in the caves and in the very primitive food-gathering and hunting societies that developed after the Ice Age, it is surely true that by the time we get to the pastoral and agricultural societies at the dawn of history, fertility had become the central theme of religious activity. It was not merely that fertility cults were part of religion; religion had become a fertility cult, for fertility was now the dominant force in human life. The flocks must produce, the fields must spring into life or large numbers of people would starve. When dealing with a force that crucial and that powerful, one simply had to treat it as sacred.

As time passed the goddesses became more human in their appearance and more attractive. By five thousand years ago, Egyptian and Cretan goddesses were quite lovely, and had they appeared on a street in a modern city would doubtless attract more than cursory attention. In addition, certain definite themes were beginning to appear. There is a "madonna" figure from Cyprus which may date from the twentieth century B.C. (Plate 32), and other "madonna" figures discovered in Hittite and Egyptian cultures; indeed Neumann pictures (Plate 38) an Isis with Horus figure from 1700–2000 years B.C. that might almost have come out of the Renaissance. The pietà aspect of goddesses may be found in some pre-Roman Sardinian statues (Plates 46, 47), and extremely nude goddesses from Babylon, Greece, and Crete (Plates 54–56) demonstrate the sexual potency of the female goddess images. (Some of these erotic goddesses, incidentally, are equipped with snakes, suggesting, perhaps, the risk a man runs when he permits himself to be seduced into the body of a woman.)

There are also goddesses of death. Among them is the lovely Egyptian, Nut (a lady one would not mind encountering in life or death (Plates 90, 91); and among those far more fearsome goddesses of death, whom one would avoid under all circumstances if possible, is the Indian goddess, Kali, the Devourer (Plates 65–67). The ambivalence about the death dimension of the female deity is clear from the art. Kali, for example, is in some of her manifestations truly a fearsome devourer; at other times she is far more gentle and attractive, tender and consoling (Plate 182). In the latter form she seems to be mother or elder sister to the liveliest of all the Eastern goddesses, Tara (Plates 183–185). Similarly Lilith, the Sumerian goddess of death, has strange webbed, clawed feet, but the rest of her is quite nicely feminine (Plate 126).

As prehistory turned into recorded history, the feminine sacred principle began to undergo differentiation. The divine female power was seen as life-giving and life-taking-away. It is from Mother Earth we are born and to Mother Earth we will return in death; it is a woman who brings us into the world and, quite probably, it is a woman who holds in her arms the head of the wounded hunter or warrior or sick child. The Earth Mother who receives us at death could be thought of as either gentle consoler or fierce devourer. Woman further provided sexual mystery and sexual reward. She brought life, pleasure, excitement, death; and the various woman goddesses reflected the implicit conviction that life, pleasure, excitement, and death themselves reflected components of the perfect unity of the ultimate and the absolute.[20]

Joseph Campbell writes about the *Shakti* of Hindu religion and summarizes the symbolism of the female deity (describing the statue of the Javanese Queen Dedes, Shakti of Adi Buddha):

> The important sanskrit term *shakti,* meaning power, capacity, energy, faculty or capability has here been used in a technical sense basic to all Oriental religious thinking, namely to denote the energy or active power of a male divinity as embodied in his spouse. Carried further (by analogy), every wife is her husband's shakti and every beloved woman her lover's. Beatrice was Dante's. Carried further still: the word connotes female spiritual power in general as a manifest; for instance, in the radiance of beauty or on the elemental level in the sheer power of the female sex to work effects on the male. It is operative in the power of the womb to transform seed into fruit, to enclose, protect, and give birth. Analogously on the psychological plane, it is the power of a woman to bring a man to his senses, to let him see himself in a mirror, to lure him to his realization—or destruction.[21]

I would quickly add that the feminine spiritual power is part of the human condition and exists in both men and women. It is called "feminine" because of the obvious analogy between this psychological power (which is present and admirable in both men and women) and the biological functions of the woman. Doubtless this analogy has been widely abused in oppressive distortions of the ' eternal feminine" as applied only to women, but such abuse does not invalidate the universal symbolic use of the analogy in virtually all the religions of humankind. Extreme feminist ideologists may not want to use it—and that is their privilege—but they are dissenting from the universal practice of humankind, and in all likelihood from the propensities of the human preconscious (bracketing, as irrelevant to our purposes here, the Jungian paradigm of the collective unconscious).

It is interesting to note—and Campbell does not do it—that some students of ancient Semitic religion think that the "Shekenah" (the "power" or "glory" of Yahweh) was once a female consort of that fierce old desert warrior god long before the Sinai experience of the wandering Hebrews.

To some extent this differentiation of the goddesses into separate categories is artificial. An individual goddess took on many shapes and forms in the different cults that were offered to her. Still, by the time of classical antiquity, there was a rough division of labor established among the goddesses: Venus was not into the same thing that Diana was into, and Athena and Juno tended to have different spheres of action. The experience of sexual differentiation obtained in the encounter with the feminine is, of course, a single experience, but there are many components to it; and those components, from early history to classical antiquity, are more and more sharply discriminated. The giver of life, the sexual lover, the source of inspiration, the receiver in death (either compassionate or destructive)—these are the various ways men encountered women and women came to know themselves in their encounter with men. It was naturally assumed (though implicitly and mythologically rather than metaphysically) that these same characteristics could also be encountered in the absolute and the ultimate. The goddesses acted as intermediaries between the experience of the feminine in ordinary life and the assumed existence of the feminine as a component of the ultimate.

We wonder about the mentality of the artist of these female images. Was he working from mythological insight? To what extent was he simply bemused by the woman who was his model (in his imagination if not in physical presence)? The more ancient the figure the more abstract and mythological seems to have been the artist's perspective. The cave figurines could scarcely have been fascinating as women to the person who carved them; but certainly the more recent (5,000 years ago) Middle Eastern figurines begin to take on enough human characteristics that one suspects the artist was depicting a real woman as well as a divine force. Isis and Nut are goddesses, but they are indeed attractive women, and by the time we get to the Grecian Venuses, one simply has statues of beautiful women to whom the name of a goddess has been attached.

We must remember, however, that the Greeks had no trouble at all seeing their statues as religious. We see them more as beautiful women, because the distinction between the religious and the secular was not nearly as sharp for them as it is for us. If there is a feminine component of the deity, one might argue, there is no reason why that component is any better revealed to us in a Venus of Lespugue than it is in the Venus de Milo. All things are potentially sacraments, and if sexual differentiation is a limit-experience par excellence, there is no reason in the world why the Venus de Milo cannot be a symbol as well as a thing.

And she sure is pretty.

Neumann develops an elaborate paradigm based on Jungian theory to organize humankind's experience of the feminine and the goddesses which symbolize this experience.[22] He sees the experience of the feminine as being ordered along two dimensions, the elementary and the transformation. The elementary, or "central symbolism of the Feminine," is expressed in a generalized equation which purports to schematize the basic experience of the Feminine: Woman = Body = Vessel = World. The central symbolism of the feminine, then, is not the sun so much as the moon. Woman as world or as earth gives life and then takes it back; Woman as moon, as transformer, gives renewal, rebirth. Hence, the two dimensions of the experience of the feminine are the dimension of birth and the dimension of rebirth. Combining these two dimensions, Neumann produces his elaborate paradigm. (See Neumann, p. 82.)

The axis "M," running from upper left to lower right of the circles represents the maternal dimension of the feminine, the woman as the source of the earth and of life, woman as earth from which life springs and as earth to which life returns. The "A" dimension, running from lower left to upper right, represents woman as the source of rebirth as transformation, as the moon which seduces and inspires. Both dimensions have a positive and negative pole: a good mother which gives life and a bad mother which destroys it; a positive transformation which exalts the spiritual side of man and a negative transformation which drags him down into ecstasy and pleasure. One has four different kinds of goddesses then: Demeter and Isis, goddesses of fertility; Kali and Gorgon, goddesses of death; the platonic Sophia, the Greek Muse, the Christian Mary (in Neumann's model) as a source of positive spriritual ecstasy, and Astarte (and I might add Venus) as the symbols of physical ecstasy.[23]

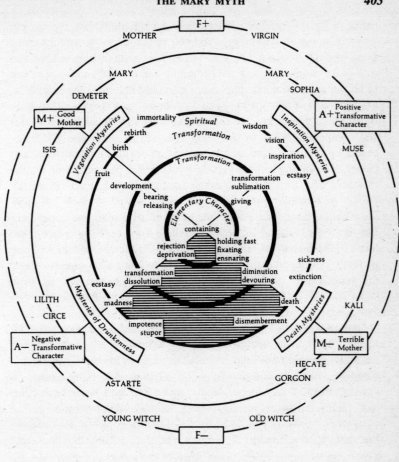

Figure I

So in Neumann's ordering of the data of the history of religions, I observe four different aspects of woman as perceived by both men and women: (1) woman as source of life, (2) woman as inspiration, (3) woman as source of sexual satisfaction, and (4) woman as absorbing in ego-destroying death.

Now of course life, death, inspiration, and pleasure are what human existence is all about; and somehow or other it can be found in every major religious symbol. Religious language does not try to say different things in its various symbols; rather it tries to say the same thing in a different way. Any good religious symbol tries to reveal to us that the ultimate is both the beginning and the end and the occasion of all our inspiration and pleasure. One could rearrange the manifestations of almost any major symbolic theme in a paradigm such as Neumann's. However, because human sexuality is such a powerful and compelling force in our daily life, sexual gods and goddesses reveal to us their "hints of an explanation" with immense force and clarity. They tell us about certain fundamental parameters of human existence and certain fundamental dimensions and structures of the human personality. Some variations on the sexual symbols are more illuminating than others, and none of them, of course, are completely free from the cultural limitations of their own time and place. One turns to the history of religions for symbolic themes, not to seek for perfectly developed symbols but to strive to learn what one can about the propensities of humankind to interpret the varieties of their experience so that, having ordered that experience, they can respond to it.

Neumann's chart is a model, a paradigm, and not a photograph of reality. We human beings do not go around with our brains and memories divided into compartments like those on his chart. Neumann's paradigm, like all good paradigms, is a tentative working model, an ordering of the data which indeed is thought to have some connection with reality but by no means to be a definitive description of it.

In other words, if you find another model more useful for ordering the data of the history of religion and for linking the gods and goddesses with psychological and social experiences of human life, by all means use it. But I think it not unreasonable to suggest that in the experience of the opposite sex (and the traits of the opposite sex one perceives in one's own sexuality) the Other is perceived as linked to the rediscovery of self, the loss of self, pleasure, and inspiration. Neumann's model is a useful way of depicting those experiences.

One can certainly agree that Neumann's schema is a useful way of ordering the data without having to buy the philosophical and psychoanalytic theory that underlies it. Woman as symbol can reveal the universe as giving life or taking it away (either destructively or compassionately); she can also, as symbol, restructure our perceptions to view the universe as inspiring us to nobility of thought and effort, or as seducing us to ecstatic frenzy. This may be a useful way of describing the experience of sexual differentiation as a limit-experience, as one that shatters our old structures of perception and reorders them into new and potentially transforming configurations. Other ways of ordering both the data of our experience and the data from the histories of religion are surely possible. Neumann's seems useful, and I propose to use it with some modifications throughout this book.

What I am about is by now probably clear to the reader. In the next chapter I shall explore the origins of the Mary myth. I will show that even in its beginnings the myth contained, however inchoately, the four themes schematized by Neumann: woman as mother and as death, and woman as source of spiritual inspiration and physical ecstasy. I shall then in subsequent chapters analyze the four experiences of sexual differentiation and Mary's role as a symbol that illumines the ambiguities of these experiences and reveals the feminine aspect of the deity, or, if one wishes to be Heideggerian, reveals the feminine aspect of Being at work in these experiences. If it be true that Mary as Madonna, Virgo, Sponsa, and Pietà can illumine the experiences of sexual differentiation, even in our own time, and by so doing provide us with the new direction that comes from shattering old structures of perceptions in response to our existential needs, then Mary is alive and well and smiling at us just as she did at Henry Adams at Chartres.

As David Tracy has pointed out to me, there are two aspects of sexual differentiation as limit-experience—or perhaps two different though related experiences. In the first, one experiences the gifted-ness, the wonder of sexual differentiation: there is another who is like me yet different, one who is a complement to me, a challenge to me, a fulfillment of me both biologically and psychologically. I will find (or can find or could find) fullness and completion through union with the other, and that union will not only be serviceable for the species (if I think of that at all) but joyous and "wonder-full" for me.

In the second experience, flowing sometimes but not always from the first, I discover simultaneously the androgyny of the other and the androgyny of myself. There is a rhythm in all intimacies and in heterosexual intimacy particularly. Indeed, the most exciting joy and pleasure frequently come precisely from the rhythmic alternation of roles and functions. One gives then gets; one takes then yields; one conquers then surrenders; one pursues then is pursued; one hides then reveals; one attacks then retreats; one is passive then dominant. In such a rhythm one discovers in the spouse the twin poles of androgyny. The most dainty and shy woman becomes the passionate and aggressive attacker. The most direct and forceful man becomes a weak and passive plaything. There is joy in both the changing roles of the other and of the self. Not only is the spouse capable of playing both masculine and feminine roles, the self is capable of being both masculine and feminine, of releasing with pure delight those aspects of the personality which normally the cultural environment compels him or her to hide.

Sexual intimacy between two humans does not always follow such rhythm. It is easier to settle into one or the other role and not run the risk of departing from it. But if there are fewer risks, there is also less excitement, less challenge, and less pleasure. A monophonic relationship is not nearly so much fun as a stereophonic one (if I may be excused the metaphor); nor is it so nearly likely to produce either the limit-experience of sexual differentiation or the even more intense limit-experience of discovering the grace and the gracefulness of one's own androgynous personality. In this latter experience one receives a hint—a "rumor" from one of Professor Peter Berger's angels—that the self is most like the ultimate precisely when it is caught up in the rhythm of alternating "masculinity" and "femininity." Surely at the height of passion the rigid role constraints that the culture imposes tend to slip away (although we can resist the tendency), and we experience not merely pleasure but a liberation, a freedom, an abandonment which enables us to be something more than we usually are. As the various components of our personality blend together in an ever more rapid alternation of the masculine and the feminine, of the pursuer and the pursued, we get a hint of what it must be like to be God—the One in whom the pursuer and the pursued (the first and the final cause) are perfectly blended.

There are two errors which must be avoided if one is to understand the symbol as an occasion of a limit-experience and the medium by which that experience is shared with others. First of all, the modernists, who lacked our sophistication in understanding the nature of symbols, as well as the detailed research of such scholars as Eliade, were wrong when they saw the symbol as a kind of free-floating inkblot which could be interpreted by a new age in response to its own problems without any particular respect for the form and structure of the symbol itself. The symbol has its own morphology that cannot be violated by the interpreter precisely because there is built into the thing-which-becomes-symbol a structure and being of its own. The annual rebirth of nature at springtime is a rebirth. One may make many different things of it, but one violates the morphology of the symbol when one claims to see in it, for example, a call for political revolution. Revolution may be appropriate under some circumstances, but it is not the reality revealed by the spring symbol. Spring is not a sacrament of revolution; it is a sacrament of rebirth.

However, while the morphology of the thing-become-symbol gives a certain direction and strain to the limit-experience, which the thing occasions as it becomes symbol, it does not predetermine the nature of the experience, the substance of that which is revealed in the experience, or the content of the limit-language which is later used to describe the experience. The tree indeed calls to mind the fact that heaven and earth are linked, for example, but in Jean Paul Sartre's experience of it, the link was absurd and irrational, while in Avery Dulles's experience the link was gracious and benign. Thus, as wrong as the modernists are those proponents of a "perennial religion" who see all the symbols of the great world religions revealing the same fundamental truths. Rebirth has a very different substantive meaning for those who experienced the first Christian Easter and for those who reexperience it today than it had for their pre-Canaanite ancestors when they celebrated the spring fertility rituals. Easter also went beyond what the first Christians had experienced in their pre-Easter/Passover celebrations.

There was and is morphological similarity (which makes the history of religions possible as an academic discipline) among early nature fertility rites, the Jewish Passover, and the Christian Easter. But there were differences in the content of the experiences and differences in the substance of what is reported through the symbols which re-present those experiences to the faithful. Quite simply, the message of personal survival (of Jesus and eventually of ourselves) that is at the depth of the Easter experience was not present in the nature fertility rituals, and at best only ambiguously present in the Second Temple Jewish Passover. There were hints of such possibilities, but they were not taken seriously or fully. In the Christian Easter, the hint of personal survival becomes the core of the experience and hence the experience itself (both in its original and its re-presented form). It is categorically different from (though not completely unrelated to) its predecessors.

So, too, with the experience of sexual differentiation and the androgyny of God. There are morphological similarities between Mary and the mother goddesses of antiquity; she is not completely unrelated to them. She and they are rooted in the experience of sexual differentiation, as a sacrament of the androgyny, the *coincidentia oppositorum* of the ultimate. But it is rather different feminine aspects of the ultimate which are revealed by Mary than those which are revealed by Kali or even by Tara. The Christian experience of sexual differentiation as sacrament is different from the Indian or Tibetan related experience. The combination of morphological similarity but substantive differences in limit-experience is possible because humans come to such experiences with different existential needs and different antecedent worldviews, and because the symbols are dense, multilayered, polyvalent in their own reality. They are not formless inkblots, but neither are they propositions which admit only of very narrow and restricted interpretation.

It might well be argued that the fertility rites prepared the way for Easter, that Nut (the tender Egyptian goddess of the underworld) prepared the way for Mary. Humankind had to know the paschal lamb of the pre-Sinai Semitic tribes and the Passover of Pharasaic Judaism before it could know the risen Jesus of Easter. It had to know the tender Nut and the life-giving Demeter before it could know Mary the virgin mother.

At one level of argumentation this need hardly be questioned. Human religious consciousness does indeed evolve. But at a deeper level I do not think that we have yet thought through clearly the theological and psychological explanations of the mechanisms by which this progress occurs. Such questions are beyond the scope of the present book.[24] I will be content to assert here that Christian religious experience and Christian religious faith, which is both revealed and re-presented in such experience, is not totally unrelated to humankind's other religious experiences, but it is categorically different from them. I say this not merely because I am a Christian but because the most elementary analysis of what the symbols portray as the core of the Christian experience demonstrates that the Christian experience is drastically different from its antecedents and rivals. Mary may be "like" Tara or Nut or even Kali. It may help us to understand Mary better if we compare her with Tara, Nut, and Kali. We see how she, like they, resulted from the limit-experience of sexual differentiation and reveals an androgynous deity. But unless we are totally blind, we cannot avoid the immediate recognition that Mary is a very different woman than they and reveals a very different kind of deity. It is not merely that Mary is a historical person and that they are not (although that difference is critical); Mary is the only feminine religious symbol who reveals a God passionately in love with his people. You can fear, respect, and even worship Kali and Tara and Nut; but for Mary you write a poem or a love song.

And that is a difference of absolutely decisive importance for the whole of humankind and for the rest of human history.

Some Christians have been uneasy on occasion with the comparison of Mary with her predecessors, sisters, and rivals. They are men and women of faint heart. In any such contest Mary is a sure winner.

Mary, indeed, is part of the tradition of feminine deities, for like her predecessors she reveals the feminine dimension of an androgynous God.[25] But if she is part of this tradition, Mary is clearly superior to it. One need only compare the art inspired by Mary with that inspired by her predecessors to see both the similarities and the striking differences between them. I wonder how students of comparative religion, and those early Catholic apologists who frantically tried to respond to them, could have thought that the similarities eliminated the important differences. I also wonder why the theologians who wrote about Mary in the 1950s and 1960s failed to realize that the history of religion was on their side. One need only compare the images of Kali or of Diana of the Ephesians with, let us say, the young woman in an Annunciation painting by Fra Angelico or Bonfigli to see that one is in very different worlds. It is not of Kali that we sing.

> I sing of a maiden that
>   Matchless is,
> King of all Kings is her son
>   I wis.
>
> He came all so still
>   Where his mother was
> As dew in April
>   That falleth on grass.
>
> He came all so still
>   To his mother's bower
> As dew in April
>   That falleth on shower.

He came all so still
  Where his mother lay
As dew in April
  That falleth on spray.

Mother and maiden
  Was ne'er none but she
Well may such a lady
  God's mother be.

"I Sing of a Maiden"
—Anonymous

Chapter 4
The Emergence of Mary

There is much that is noble in the pagan goddesses. Fertility, ecstasy, inspiration, reunion with the cosmos in death—all these qualities could stir up artistic and religious genius. They could also, unfortunately, easily be perverted. Orgies, human sacrifice, ritual prostitution were the dark side of the fertility cults, a dark side which all too often became dominant.

It would be wrong, however, to think that there was no anticipation in the pagan worship of the Queen of Heaven to the Christianization of that cult in the honoring of Mary. On the contrary, despite the sexual excesses and the persistence of human sacrifices beyond boundaries of the empire, there were strains in the pagan cult of the Queen of Heaven which almost seemed to demand transformation. One can almost go so far as to say that if Mary had not come along, the pagans might have had to invent her. The Roman writer Apuleius (in a translation by Robert Graves) describes his experience of the Queen of Heaven in the Isis cult:

> The apparition of a woman began to rise from the middle of the sea with so lovely a face that the gods themselves would have fallen down in adoration of it. First the head, then the whole shining body gradually emerged and stood before me poised on the surface of the waves. . . .
>
> Her long hair fell in tapering ringlets on her lovely neck, and was crowned with an intricate chaplet in which was woven every kind of flower. Just above her brow shone a round disc, like a mirror, or like

411

the bright face of the moon, which told me who she was. Vipers rising from the left-hand and right-hand partings of her hair supported this disc, with ears of corn bristling beside them. Her many-colored robe was of finest linen; part was glistening white, part crocus-yellow, part glowing red, and along the entire hem a woven bordure of flowers and fruit clung swaying in the breeze. But what caught and held my eye more than anything else was the deep black luster of her mantle. She wore it slung across her body from the right hip to the left shoulder, where it was caught in a knot resembling the boss of a shield; but part of it hung in innumerable folds, the tasseled fringe quivering. It was embroidered with glittering stars on the hem and everywhere else, and in the middle beamed a full and fiery moon. . . .

All the perfumes of Arabia floated into my nostrils as the Goddess deigned to address me: "You see me here, Lucius, in answer to your prayer. I am Nature, the universal Mother, mistress of all the elements, primordial child of time, sovereign of all things spiritual, queen of the dead, queen also of the immortals, the single manifestation of all gods and goddesses that are. . . . Though I am worshiped in many aspects, known by countless names, and propitiated with all manner of different rites, yet the whole round earth venerates me.

[From Apuleius, *The Golden Ass,* Robert Graves' translation, p. 268–71. Robert Graves, *The Greek Myths,* Penguin, 1960.]

Still, there is no point in attempting to gloss over the excesses of the fertility cults, particularly those which were practiced in the land of Canaan by the neighbors of the Hebrews. The things that went on in the high places may not have been as bad as the prophets thought but they clearly were considerably less than attractive. The consoling and homey aspects of the worship of the Queen of Heaven existed side by side with much more savage practices that to the prophets of official Yahwism were thoroughly unacceptable. We probably need more research to know how depraved the Canaanite fertility cults got. But the opposition of the prophets was only in part practical. They could not accept the identification of the deity with the life forces of the cosmos on theoretical grounds even if there were no practical abuses in such cults. The prophetic objection to the fertility cults was finally theological.

Therefore, when Yahweh, that pushy old desert Semitic storm god, elbowed his way into human history in the Sinai experience, he quite pointedly warned his followers against the fertility cult. There was only one god, and his name was Yahweh. Whatever other deities might have existed were inferior to him and not to be taken seriously. The cosmos was his show. As he ironically informed Job, humans were not around when he made it. He was not about to abide any competition from the bizarre deities who had set themselves up in the deity business—either male or female.

Fertility was not excluded from the new Israelite cult, for they, like all other people, needed to insure that the crops would produce food for the coming year. But one did not now guarantee fertility of the fields by worshiping the fertility forces of the universe or by engaging in ritualized sex. One guaranteed fertility by worshiping Yahweh. It was not so much, as Walter Harrelson points out in his brilliant book, *From Fertility Cult to Worship*,[1] that conflict between Yahweh and Baal was one between a god of fertility and a god of history, for Yahweh dominated both history and fertility.

So the old pagan fertility festivals of unleavened bread and the paschal lamb were combined into a new feast which honored not fertility powers but the Lord who dominated fertility and everything else:

> God was the giver of fertility, but Israel could not coerce fertility or even participate in the process through cultic acts. The task of man was radically secularized. Man was to till the soil, remove the rocks, and clear additional acreage. He was to fight the recalcitrant forces of nature in a world twisted by his own sin, wrestling food from the earth. This was his part. The rain came at God's behest; the earth produced because God had arranged in its creation that it should do so. All fruits of the soil, all fruit of the womb, were gifts of God—for Israel as much as for her neighbors.
>
> What was eliminated was the necessity or even the possibility for Israel—faithful Israel—to strike some bargain with God, to induce the earth to produce or even to participate culticly in the earth's renewal.[2]

In fairness to the pagans, who were the neighbors of the Israelites, it must be said that there probably was some kind of vague distinction in their minds between the powers of fertility and the god and goddess who animated these powers. But in popular practice, belief, and cult, this distinction was pretty well erased. One worshiped the process itself, one integrated one's life through cultic behavior into the process. One became part of the divine power of fertility. The symbol, for all practical purposes, had become more than a sacrament and almost the reality which it revealed. By uniting oneself ritualistically with the symbol, one obtained a certain power over the reality which worked in and through the symbol. More simply, if one committed ritual prostitution with a priestess of the fertility goddess, one obtained some kind of power over that goddess (in addition to whatever personal pleasure one might have experienced) and constrained the goddess to see that the fertility process would indeed produce the abundance that the tribe or village needed.

No one constrained Yahweh to do anything. He did what he did out of his generosity, his goodness, his love. He was not caught up in these processes of nature; he could not be dealt with by those who integrated themselves into the process culticly. He was Yahweh; he did things his way, and nobody forced his hand with ritual.

The feminine deities, therefore, vanished from the scene. Neumann's suggestion that the "Shekinah," the so-called "glory of God in exile," is a feminine component of Yahwistic religion is not very persuasive. There may have been a Shekinah goddess at some stage of the game, but by the time we come to the Yahwism of the prophets, she had long since vanished from the scene.

The purified and secularized fertility cult of the Passover, and the worship of Yahweh as the Lord of history and the Lord of fertility (and Lord of everything else, for that matter) did not, of course, exorcise the fertility goddesses from the popular religion of ordinary people. The prophets railed against Baal and his consorts; they warned the Israelites of false worship in "the high places" and against the adoration of idols, most of which were probably fertility gods and goddesses. Yahweh continually warns through his prophetic spokesmen that his people were not to go off "whoring" with false gods. Such a choice of verb leaves little doubt that it was a regression to fertility cultism that they had in mind.

The struggle between Yahwism and the more ancient pagan fertility rituals was a long and fierce one, and while Yahweh had pretty well swept the field clear by the time of the Second Temple, the periodic construction of pagan temples and the willingness of some Jews to worship in them despite the denunciations of both the Pharisees and the temple priesthood indicates that the goddesses may have retreated and gone underground, but they were not completely destroyed.

However, sexual differentiation had by no means been eliminated from the Yahwistic religion. It reappeared in a new and extremely important manifestation. Yahweh was the spouse, Israel was the people, his bride. Yahweh's intervention on Sinai was the beginning of a divine love affair with a fickle, unreliable but still very attractive spouse. Otherwise, why would Yahweh be interested in the first place? This image of the people as the bride of Yahweh caught up in intimate union with a passionate God (the word "passionate" is unfortunately translated as "jealous" in most versions of Exodus 20) is implied even in the very ancient Sinai stories. It becomes obvious and explicit in the sexual imagery of such prophets as Osee, Ezekiel, and Jeremiah. The Christian notion of the church as the spouse of Jesus is obviously indebted to the Jewish symbolism of Yahweh's romance with his people. In the later prophets this romance was frequently symbolized in the figure of the Daughter of Zion. In the rhetoric of Jewish religious writing, there is a technique called "the corporate personality." A single person, real or imaginary, is equated with the whole people. The Daughter of Zion is spoken of frequently as though she were an individual, but in fact she represents the corporate body of Israel. It is the romance between Yahweh and the Daughter of Zion which leads to the conception and birth of the messianic age. Passages with this theme abound in the later prophets:

> This Yahweh proclaims to the ends of the earth:
> Say to the daughter of Zion, "Look, your savior comes,
> the prize of his victory with him, his trophies before him."
>
> (Is 62:11)

> Shout for joy, daughter of Zion,
> Israel, shout aloud!
> Rejoice, exult with all your heart,
>   daughter of Jerusalem!
> Yahweh has repealed your sentence;
> he has driven your enemies away.
> Yahweh, the king of Israel, is in your midst;
> you have no more evil to fear.

> When that day comes, word will come to Jerusalem:
> Zion, have no fear,
> do not let your hands fall limp.

Yahweh your God is in your midst,
a victorious warrior.
He will exult with joy over you,
he will renew you by his love;
he will dance with shouts of joy for you
as on a day of festival.

(Zp 3:14–18)

Sing, rejoice,
daughter of Zion;
for I am coming
to dwell in the middle of you
—it is Yahweh who speaks.

(Zc 2:10³)

One can also find liturgical texts which echo the theme:

In his winepress the Lord has trampled
the virgin daughter of Judah.   (Lm 1:15)

How can I describe you, to what compare you,
daughter of Jersalem?
Who can rescue and comfort you,
virgin daughter of Zion?   (Lm 2:13)

She has done a deed of horror,
the Virgin of Israel.   (Jr 18:13)

Yes, I hear screams like those of a woman in labor,
anguish like that of a woman giving birth to her first child;
they are screams of the daughter of Zion, gasping,
hands outstretched.   (Jr 4:31)

Writhe, cry out, daughter of Zion,
like a woman in labor,
for now you have to leave the city
and live in the open country.   (Mi 4:10)

According to such writers as Wilfred Knox and Geoffrey Ashe, the figure of "Wisdom" in the Old Testament is feminine. Knox, in his *St. Paul and the Church of the Gentiles* (Cambridge 1939), says bluntly that there can be little doubt that personified wisdom is both feminine and "on the divine side of the gulf which separates man from God." She is, he argues, a Hebraeicized version of the Syrian goddess

Astarte. In his book *The Virgin* (London: Routledge and Kegan Paul, 1976), Ashe notes that the Jewish community in Elephantiné in Egypt reverenced the Virgin Anath (a Canaanite goddess) as in "some sense attached to Yahweh" (p. 31). Anath had many of the wisdom characteristics of Greek Athene. Ashe concludes that "the background presence of a female deity in Judaism toward the beginning of the Christian era is rather more than conjectural. While one set of texts evoked the Virgin Daughter of Zion, another evoked the Virgin Wisdom dwelling in Zion, trailing phantasms of a pagan past behind her" (p 31).

There were, then, still traces of the female deity even in the most refined manifestation of Yahwism—and much stronger traces, it would appear, in Hebrew folk religion. It is precisely to those traces that we must look if we are to begin to understand the emergence of Mary.

Robert Graves, in his translation of the *Song of Songs* (London: Collins, 1973), suggests that it was in fact a bridal sword dance performed in honor of Anath, who at that era of her development was a goddess of war and battle (a devourer as well as a virgin?). One need not accept all of Graves' speculations, some of which seem pretty thin, to realize that there was far more myth in the Hebrew religion than one would perceive merely from reading the prophets. Indeed the apocalyptic revival of the post-exilic years probably was a return to the imagery (always modified by the Hebrew sense of history) of Near Eastern creation myths. Yahwism, in other words, was a mulitfaceted and polyvalent religion with room for many different components, including many survivals from paganism which it had absorbed. The female deity was still around, now either absorbed in the tenderness of Yahweh or continuing as the Daughter of Zion or the Wisdom of Zion or as the shadowy patron of human love and marriage.

Sexual differentiation as limit-experience, then, is by no means foreign to the Jewish religion. On the contrary, in the later prophets it became one of the dominant themes. But the sexuality of later Yahwism is quite different from that of the fertility cults. Yahweh dominates fertility completely; sexuality is his gift to humankind, but it is a gift that reflects and symbolizes his love for his people.

The daughter of Zion theme was taken over by the Church, which saw itself as a new Zion. Given the religious atmosphere of the time when Christianity developed out of Pharisaic Judaism, such a development is not at all surprising. In retrospect, what is astonishing is that all the old goddesses came creeping out of their caves, went through an extraordinary rehabilitation, and emerged in the person of Mary, the mother of Jesus.

The early Christians were no better disposed than their rabbinic Jewish brothers and cousins to pagan deities. They abhorred the grotesque, depraved, and corrupt rites associated with the residual remnants of fertility worship. The reformulation of the old cults in the Gnostic wisdom religions was even less acceptable to the early Christians. Under such circumstances one would have expected the Christians, like their rabbinic Jewish relatives, to resist with all the power at their command even the slightest concession to the tradition of the female deities; for these deities, in the circumstances in which the Christians encountered them, were frequently quite depraved and always enemy to the Good News. It wasn't merely Diana of the Ephesians who was the natural enemy of St. Paul; in a few short centuries she, Athene, and Aphrodite were gone. But they were replaced from within the Christian religion itself by a new symbol of the feminine component of God, and it was to emerge as the most powerful of all the feminine sacred personalities. It must have been a surprise for everyone.

As one pours over the history books of the early Church, it is not really clear how Mary emerged as the new symbol of the feminine component of God. However, it is clear that by the early second century, Christian writers were speaking of her as the new Eve; by the late second or early third century, drawings of her appeared in the catacombs, and by the middle third or early fourth century, direct and explicit devotion to her was well under way.

There seem to have been two factors at work in the emergence of Mary as an object of devotion. First, the early Christians were caught up in a fantastic exuberance that we can barely imagine today (and which, alas, we all too rarely try to imitate). The excitement of the renewing event of the death and resurrection of Jesus had created an extraordinarily powerful liberating experience for many of those who had become followers of Jesus. They were free from old laws, old fears, old constraints, old customs. The world was new; it had been born again, and therefore the early Christian apologists could proclaim that whatever was good, whatever was true, whatever was beautiful, whatever was admirable in the human condition was not only not opposed to Christians but actually already Christian. Art, music, literature, poetry—there was no opposition between these things and the Christian experience. On the contrary, they were already part of such an experience. The dying Roman Empire might be a political threat but nothing could be a cultural threat to these exuberant and self-confident Christians. Whatever was good was Christian. If the good was somehow mixed with the bad, that was no problem; the bad could be swept away and the Christian remain whole and clean. So the various local deities were transformed into saints, and the feminine goddesses were integrated, rehabilitated, and transformed into Mary. Whatever was good in the worship of the goddesses was already Christian and ought to be saved; and whatever was bad could be excised and dismissed as not constituting a very serious threat. Did there seem to be some similarity between Mary and Diana or Juno or Athene or Aphrodite? The early Christian shrugged his shoulders. So what? Mary was also strikingly different from her predecessors, and no one could seriously believe that her preeminence could be threatened by those pagans. Thus, I suspect, is the way it went. The early Christians were much more casual about the similarities between Mary and the pagan goddesses than were the later reformers or the counterreformers or the early students of comparative religion and the Catholic apologists who tried to argue against them. The early Christians, unlike their successors, knew what Diana was like; they were much more interested in the differences, not similarities, between her and Mary.

In any event, this exuberance for all things good and for all things human probably created a context in which Mary could emerge as a Christian symbol between the end of the first century and the beginning of the fourth. But the mere existence of such a context does not explain why Mary did in fact emerge.

For this explanation we will turn to the theological method that many of the early Christian writers chose to follow; the "argument from type," or "typology." John McKenzie in his *Dictionary of the Bible* defines it as "an exposition which presents the persons, institutions, or events of the Old Testament as 'types' of persons, events, or institutions in the New Testament."[4] Thus figures and events in one section of Scripture are seen as anticipations (though, at least in the more intelligent typology, *not* as literal predictions) of figures and events in another section of Scripture. The early Christians did not invent this technique; it was already in use in the Old Testament. In Isaiah, for example, the restoration of Israel after the exile is described in the terms of Exodus; hence the restoration is in a sense a reenactment of the Exodus. While it is surely the case that some of the typological arguments of the early Christian writers were exaggerated and almost bizarre in their passionate and convoluted development of allegorical similarities, it is still true that typological argument is not all that different from that used by the historians of religion, or even that used by the Jungian psychologists—that there is a certain unity in human religious experiences. Or, as one might put it from the viewpoint of a believer, there are similar themes in the dialogue between God and man, and an early manifestation of theme may anticipate a later manifestation of it, which in its turn may reflect back to an earlier explication of the theme. In the terms of this book, both the "type" and the "antetype" are the same thing-turned-symbol, the same fundamental insight into the nature of the universe that produced similar structures of perceptions and the ordering of similar new configurations.

God creates, God liberates; Adam symbolizes the former, Moses the latter. The creation and liberation of God are manifested once again in Jesus, who in this symbolic and hence very real sense is both the new Adam and the new Moses. He is a symbol that continues the same limit-experience (or a similar limit-experience) which was integrated earlier in the symbols of Adam and Moses.

The early Christians vigorously used the typological argument that Jesus was the new Adam, and especially in their dialogue with their Jewish confreres. St. Paul himself, very early in the game, had begun to reason in this fashion. But if Jesus is the new Adam, the beginning of a new creation, the first partisan of a new humanity, the father of a renewed humankind, who was the new Eve? If there was a new Adam, there had to be a new Eve. Who was the new mother of us all? The jump could not have seemed very great to the one who first made it. Jesus was the new Adam, the father of us all; Mary, his mother, was the new Eve, the mother of Jesus and the mother of all of us. With that jump, Mary emerged as the Christian symbol of the feminine aspect of the deity. The Christian myth was rooted in the limit-experience of sexual differentiation, the Christian transformation of all the goddesses who had gone before—and perhaps the most powerful religious symbol in the Western heritage was born.

But when did it happen? In attempting to answer this question I encountered a paradox, which, as far as I can find, no one else has noticed. The "new" Scripture studies take away from us virtually all historical information about the mother of Jesus. This is a severe blow to the theologians who have blithely assumed that Scripture provided at least some kind of historical information about Mary upon which they could rely for their theological reflections. But if contemporary exegesis has lost the historical Mary, it has enabled us to find the theological Mary much earlier than the theologians might have expected. From the point of view of the theologian of only moderate sophistication in exegesis, "theologizing" didn't really begin until the second century. One could not therefore expect a Marian theology before that time. There was, of course, some kind of theology in the New Testament, but it was not basically theological as much as it was historical (though the modern theologian would quickly add that it was certainly not history the way we mean history). But for the exegete, the New Testament, while containing important historical elements, is made up essentially of theological reflections by the earliest Christians of their experience of the risen Jesus. Hence the exegete has no problem at all in finding the typological theological reflection going on even in the books of the New Testament. The theologian sees Marian doctrine emerging perhaps in the middle of the second century, while careful, responsible, professional exegetes like Raymond Brown, John McHugh, and Lucien Deiss have no difficulty at all in finding Marian theology in the New Testament itself. And an increasing number of Protestant writers, such as Max Thurian, are also prepared to concede (some gracefully, others not) that there is, particularly in St. John and St. Luke, an unquestionable Marian theology. This discovery, of course, knocks into a cocked hat most of the Reformation-Counter-reformation arguments over Mary. One may still legitimately dispute the form and shape of the Marian cult; one can no longer deny the presence of explicitly Marian doctrinal themes in the Gospels.

Note the price that has to be paid for this revolution: if one contends—and I believe now that one must—that what the New Testament has to say about Mary is theological, typological, and symbolic reflection for the most part, one has placed Marian themes back almost to the beginning of Christian reflection. But the cost is the loss of virtually all historically reliable information about Mary herself. In terms of unity among Christians and understanding of Mary as a symbol articulating the limit-experience of sexual differentiation as a revelation of the feminine component of God, the cost may not seem too great; but for those whose devotion to Mary has always depended on the possession of solid historical fact, it may be a devastating blow indeed. We have placed a theological or a symbolic Mary back to almost the beginning of things, but what has happened to the real woman who was the mother at Bethlehem and the mother at the foot of the cross? Do we have the symbolic Madonna and Pietà at the cost of having lost the real one?

We surely have lost precise, detailed information about the historical Madonna and Pietà. We know nothing of what she looked like, what she thought, how she responded to critical situations—at least we know nothing with any kind of historical confidence. The absence of such precise, actual historical knowledge may not be too great a price to pay as long as we do not lose Mary as an actual, historical person. If the Mary symbol becomes detached completely from the actual Mary, then however admirable the symbol may be, it cannot really claim to be Christian. Christianity, like Judaism, is a historical religion. (Though, as my colleague and friend Roland Murphy points out to me repeatedly, it is not merely a historical religion. Salvation history is a basic and fundamental theme of Yahwism; it is not the only theme.)

If Mary is a symbol divorced from a historical personage, then she certainly is an admirable substitute for some of her depraved predecessors, but she is not then a sacrament, a revelatory thing of the God of history who presides over history.

However, I do not think this is a serious problem. We do know that Jesus had a mother. We know that there was a woman who brought him into the world, and we know much about him—his enthusiasm, his passionate sense of urgency, his joyfulness, his sense of intimate union with the Father, his flaming proclamation of the victory of good over evil and of life over death, his promise of resurrection for all of us. We know his courage, his wisdom, his insight, his incredible command of poetic language. We know the startling, shattering, disturbing, paradoxical nature of the language he used in his proverbs, his proclamation, his parables. In knowing him, we surely know much about his mother in the sense that anyone who knows a remarkable man must postulate a remarkable mother. This is not, I would submit, a sentimental romanticism. It is a solid psychological truth. The mother of Jesus had to be an extraordinarily intelligent, courageous, devout, and charming woman. She could hardly have been anything else. It would seem to me that this solid psychological truth provides us with all the historical information we really need—as pleasant as it would be to have more. I think it more than justifies virtually all the devout reflection that believing Christians have traditionally made on the New Testament data. While these data can no longer be considered historically valid, they still may be viewed theologically and are perfectly compatible with the kind of person that Mary must have been. No one can take the mother of God away from us; only a fool would try.

David Tracy, commenting on an earlier version of this manuscript, has noted that it would be a mistake to concede that this mode of knowing Mary through Jesus is a second-class form of knowledge. On the contrary, we know more about the kind of person Mary must have been from the study of her son than we would from the stories in the Scriptures themselves, even if those stories were as historically precise as an account in the morning's *New York Times*. Suppose that you knew a handful of incidents in the life of a woman. Then you met her son and had an opportunity to be with him for a substantial period of time, to listen to his teaching and to observe his actions. Would you think that the few facts about his mother were more important than the certain judgments you would make about her from knowing him? Jesus as the source of our knowledge about his mother is a much better "sacrament" (revelation of truth) than are the New Testament stories about her—whatever historical value these stories may have. Do you know more about Mary from her obedience to the angel or from the knowledge of Jesus her son?

There is profound psychological truth in this concept of the son as sacrament of the mother. But there is also truth in the opposite direction. If we know Mary through Jesus, then having reflected on what his mother must have been like, we come back to Jesus and know him better. The mother is also the sacrament of the son. When we know Mary through Jesus we are able to translate the qualities of Jesus into "feminine" form; and by seeing the feminine sources of the personality of Jesus, we are able to return to that personality and see more easily and readily the feminine aspects of the personality itself. By knowing Mary through Jesus, in other words, we are able to come to terms more fully with the androgyny of the personality of Jesus, and thus we know Jesus through Mary.

And through the two of them there is revealed to us the fullness of the unity of opposites in God. It is by knowing Mary through Jesus and Jesus through Mary that we encounter the androgynous. I hesitate to speak of psychological inevitabilities or necessities in such matters as this, but it is still difficult to see how this perennial human insight of the *coincidentia oppositorum* could have been integrated into the Christian religious tradition—and transformed by it—unless there was some relationship like that between Jesus and Mary. A woman whom Jesus reveals and in whom he is revealed seems to be psychologically indispensable for the Christian religious vision. Indispensable or not, such a woman certainly emerged historically.

I must insist that the comments of the past three paragraphs may be stated in the terminology of contemporary psychology, but they are not merely speculative. They are a description of what in historical fact has been the role of Marian devotion in Catholic Christianity. Catholic devotion to Mary is not based merely or even primarily on the handful of incidents—as beautiful as they may be—related in Scripture. It is based principally on the knowledge of her son. With that knowledge we return to the scriptural incidents and interpret them in light of what we know she must have been because of who her son was. I am not proposing, therefore, any new form of knowledge about Mary but merely pointing out what our knowledge of her has always been and the sound psychological foundations on which that knowledge is based.

I find myself wondering if perhaps we might not be able to say something more—though here I am out on a very long limb. The traditions which the authors of John and Luke have reworked as the basis of their theological reflection are clearly much older than the two Gospels. Apparently they go back to Palestinian sources which may be as old as the middle of the first century. (Indeed it is possible that they may go back to a single common source. There seems to be a relation between the Johannine and Lucan Marian sources, and there is certainly a relationship between their theological reflections.) Whence came these stories? We do not know at present, and it would be a return to the gratuitous confusion of the piety and history which marked an earlier generation of Catholic writing to say that traditions could be traced to Mary herself. But one need not, I think, go that far. If they are not necessarily traditions from Mary, might they not be traditions about Mary as an actual person? It is safe to assume that there were people in the early Church who knew her and who were fascinated by her as the mother of Jesus. If her personality was as strong and vigorous as it almost must have been to have been the mother of such a son, it seems reasonable to imagine that she must have had an extraordinary impact on those who knew her. Could it be that the ease with which the Church began to theologize about Mary so early, probably even before Luke's Gospel was written, could be explained by the contact that some of the early Christians had with the person herself?

At best, Mary casts but a fleeting shadow across the pages of the New Testament; but it was a very long one indeed, stretching down through the whole history of Christianity.

The principal sources of New Testament theological reflection on Mary as the new Eve are contained in the Lucan infancy stories and in the Johannine Cana-cross narratives. The best available treatment of Luke is contained in John McHugh's *The Mother of Jesus in the New Testament*[5] and the best commentary on the Johannine passages is to be found in Raymond Brown's Anchor commentary.[6]

I shall not endeavor to repeat in detail the brilliant exegetical arguments of these authors. Each should be read in its entirety. However, after reading two commentaries, there can be little reason to question that the typological theme of Mary as Daughter of Zion, the New Eve, the Church, and the Virgin were already strongly at work in the Church by the year A.D. 70.

How explicit the Daughter of Zion theme was in the mind of the author of Luke is a matter of minor scholarly debate. Lucien Deiss has no doubt at all that it was in the author's mind explicitly. Max Thurian parallels passages from Luke and from Zephaniah which certainly seem to support the notion that the author was deliberately imitating Zephaniah:

Zeph. 3	*Luke 1*
14. Sing aloud, O daughter of Zion!	
Shout with delight, O Israel!	
Rejoice thou,	28. Rejoice thou,
and exult with all your heart,	
O daughter of Jerusalem!	full of grace!

15. The Lord has taken away the judgments against you,
    he has cast out your enemies.
    The King of Israel, the Lord is in your midst;

    You shall fear evil no more.

16. On that day it shall be said to Jerusalem:
    Do not fear, O Zion;
    let not your hands grow weak.

17. The Lord your God is in your midst,

a victorious Savior.
    He will rejoice over you with gladness;
    he will renew you in his love.
    He will exult over you with loud singing
    as on a day of festival.

(30. for you have found favor with God.)

the Lord is with thee.

(33. He will reign over the house of Jacob forever...)

30. Do not be afraid, Mary;

    for you have found favor with God.

31. Behold, you will conceive in your womb and bear a son and you will call his name JESUS (Yahweh Savior).

The original Hebrew of the Lucan account would make quite obvious these literary similarities between the messianic proclamation of Zephaniah to the daughter of Zion and the angelic Annunciation to Mary, but even the Greek text makes it clear.[7]

McHugh implies somewhat more cautiously that the influence of Zephaniah on Luke may have been preconscious or unconscious: "If anyone had asked him outright, 'Do you mean that Mary is the Daughter of Zion foretold by the prophets?' he would have replied that this title summed up perfectly all that he meant to say."[8]

So Mary, then, either implicitly or explicitly becomes a corporate personality in the infancy stories. She is the spouse of Yahweh representing the whole people to whom Yahweh is committed in passionate love. Jesus is born of the love between Israel, as represented by Mary, and Yahweh. Note well that this is not the pious reflection of a later age. This is the response of the very early church to a powerful limit-experience. It is proto-Christian theology, arising out of the awesome shattering of old structures of perception that was caused by the Christ event.

The Eve-Church typology in which Mary is seen simultaneously as the New Eve and as the Church, the mother of the new creation, the loving mother of us all, becomes quite explicit in John's Gospel. Raymond Brown has no problem in seeing the "woman" in the apocalypse relating to Mary as "woman" in the Cana narratives, and Mary as "woman" at the foot of the cross.

Two paragraphs in Father Brown's commentary summarize his careful analysis:

> Having seen the relationship of the three scenes in the Johannine corpus in which the woman (Mary, the mother of the Messiah, as a symbol of the Church) appears, we may now interpret the conversation at Cana. On a theological level it can be seen that Mary's request, whether by her intention or not, would lead to Jesus' performing a sign. Before he does perform this sign, Jesus must make clear his refusal of Mary's intervention; she cannot have any role in his ministry; his signs must reflect his Father's sovereignty, and not any human, or family agency. But if Mary is to have no role during the ministry, she is to receive a role when *the hour* of his glorification comes, the hour of passion, death, resurrection, and ascension. John thinks of Mary against the background of Gen iii: she is the mother of the Messiah; her role is in the struggle against the satanic serpent, and that struggle comes to its climax in Jesus' hour. Then she will appear at the foot of the cross to be entrusted with offspring whom she must protect in the continuing struggle between Satan and the followers of the Messiah. Mary is the New Eve, the symbol of the Church, the Church has no role during the ministry of Jesus but only after the hour of his resurrection and ascension.[9]

Several years later, in his commentary on John's crucifixion account, Brown repeats, completes, and qualifies ever so slightly the same analysis:

> Jesus' mother is the New Eve who, in imitation of her prototype, the "woman" of Gen ii–iv, can say: "With the help of the Lord I have begotten a man" (cf. Gen iv 1—Feuillet, "Les adieux," pp. 474–77). Perhaps we may also relate Mary the New Eve to Gen iii 15, a passage that describes a struggle between the offspring of Eve

and the offspring of the serpent, for "the hour" of Jesus is the hour of the fall of the Prince of this world (John xii 23, 31). The symbolism of the Fourth Gospel has a certain resemblance to that of Rev xii 5, 17 where a woman gives birth to the Messiah in the presence of the Satanic dragon or ancient serpent of Genesis, and yet also has other offspring who are the targets of Satan's wrath after the Messiah has been taken to heaven. It is interesting that the offspring of the woman in Revelation are described as "those who keep the commandments of God"; for in John xiv 21–23 we are told that those who keep the commandments are loved by Father and Son, so that a beloved disciple is one who keeps the commandments.

By way of summary, then, we may say that the Johannine picture of Jesus' mother becoming the mother of the Beloved Disciple seems to evoke the OT themes of Lady Zion's giving birth to a new people in the messianic age, and of Eve and her offspring. This imagery flows over into the imagery of the Church who brings forth children modeled after Jesus, and the relationship of loving care that must bind the children to their mother. We do not wish to press the details of this symbolism or to pretend that it is without obscurity. But there are enough confirmations to give reasonable assurance that we are on the right track. Such a symbolism makes intelligible John's evaluation (xix 28) that this episode at the foot of the cross is the completion of the work that the Father has given Jesus to do, in the context of the fulfillment of Scripture. Certainly the symbolism we have proposed is scriptural (and thus this episode of the crucifixion falls into line with the other episodes that emphasize Scripture so strongly). And since the symbolism is centered on Jesus' provision for the future of those who believe in him, in many ways it does complete his work. He shows to the very end his love for his own (xiii 1), for symbolically he now provides a communal context of mutual love in which they shall live after he is gone. The revelatory formula "here is . . ." on which we have commented, is truly appropriate in this scene, since Jesus' mother and the Beloved Disciple are being established in a new relationship representative of that which will bind the Church and the Christian.[10]

So, in the two Johannine passages of Cana and crucifixion we see the three symbols combined: the New Eve, the Church, and the fruitful Daughter of Zion. Brown carefully notes that these theological themes in John must be kept distinct from a later Mariology "which will attach importance to the person of Mary herself; . . . the Johannine stress is on Mary as symbol of the church. Both in Luke and in John,

Mariology is incipient and is expressed in terms of collective personality."[11] A Marian theology, then, is present in incipient form in both Gospels, although it is a theology of type, of collective personality and not a theology of devotion to an individual person. One may choose to see in it three symbols or one; either Eve, Church, and Daughter of Zion, or simply Mother. It is the limit-experience of maternity that produces the thing-turned-symbol that Mary the mother of Jesus has become in these two Gospels. In subsequent chapters of this book, I choose to use the three symbols to fit my four-cell paradigm, because there are different emphases in each of the three symbols. The Daughter of Zion is the beloved spouse, the Sponsa of Yahweh; Eve, the mother of us all, is the Madonna; and the Church (with perhaps some stretching) is the loving mother who gives us life, and then as Pietà receives us back into death.

There remains the virgin symbolism in Luke's nativity story. It is generally agreed by exegetes that Luke did intend to teach the virginal conception of Jesus. The debate current among exegetes is whether the theological discussion of the virginal conception of Jesus in Matthew and Luke is in fact a theologoumenon, that is, a story created to make a theological point, or whether it is a reflection on historical fact. The two principal Catholic writers who have addressed themselves to this question, Brown and McHugh, differ somewhat. McHugh is far more confident than Brown that the account of the virginal conception is not a theologoumenon. Brown insists that "Scripturally I judge that it is harder to explain the virginal conception by positing theological creation than by positing fact."[12]

I am not qualified to comment on the discussion, although I agree with Brown's point that "it should be clarified for Catholics that the doctrines of the sanctity of Mary and of the incarnation of God's Son are not logically dependent on the virginal conception."[13]

In other words, the power of the Mary symbol remains unshaken no matter how the exegetical discussion is finally resolved. As Brown notes, the fact that all generations have called Mary blessed depends much more on the fact that she was the mother of Jesus than on biological phenomenon or exegetical debate.

I would add that as important as the discussion is and as intelligent and courageous as is the work of such gifted scholars as Father Brown, it would be a mistake for all Catholic attention to be fixed on what is fundamentally a technical issue within the subject of Mary. I have noticed that as I discuss the themes in this book with Catholics, such immature (at least it seems so to me) fixation prevents many Catholics from paying attention to Mary's central role as a symbol growing out of the limit-experience of sexual differentiation and revealing the feminine component of God—of being a sacrament of the ultimate as being passionately tender.

But how do we relate the Virgin Mother symbol to the other three New Testament symbols of Mary (as a corporate personality if not as an individual)? Brown says that "Matthew and Luke are interested in virginal conception as a sign of divine choice and grace, and as the idiom of a Christological insight that Jesus was God's Son or the Davidic Messiah from birth..."[14] I think more can be said. Virgin Mother is limit-language par excellence. It is disconcerting, shattering, disturbing, and paradoxical, as all good limit-language should be. I would suggest that the purpose of this limit-language is to reveal to us (is to be a sacrament for us) that with the coming of Jesus a new creation began. Just as Adam had no father but God, so Jesus had no father but God. With the coming of Jesus humankind is renewed, decisively and dramatically. The virgin part of the Virgin Mother paradox (a classic example, incidentally, of the tension-intensification dynamism at work in limit-language) emphasizes the total renewal of the human condition that took place in the coming of Jesus, which is precisely what Neumann's Jungian model says is the function of the "positive transformative" character of the feminine archetype. Mary the Virgin, it will be remembered, represents transformation, sublimation, renewal, a new beginning on Neumann's schema.

So all four of the New Testament Marian symbols, Daughter of Zion (Sponsa), Eve (Madonna), Church (Pietà), and Virgin Mother (Virgo), are related to the central theme that with the coming of Jesus humankind began again. Jesus was the new Adam, marking the beginning of a New Creation and the dawn of a new day for humanity. His mother was a new Eve, the bride of Yahweh, the Church who tenderly cares for us after the departure of Jesus. And the virgin-mother represents in her virginity the total renewal of creation.

There were, then, elements of both the Jewish and Christian scriptures that could provide justification for the transformation of the pagan Queen of Heaven—the pagan manifestation of the femininity of God—into a Christian Queen of Heaven. We know very little, however, of the precise history of this transformation. It was certainly linked with the decision of the early Church to absorb all that was good, useful, and beautiful in paganism—a decision of great courage and even greater hope. (And we do not know precisely how this decision was made either.) However, once it was determined that, unlike official Jewish Yahwism, official Christian Yahwism had nothing to fear from baptizing pagan customs and cults, the popularity of the Queen of Heaven was such that she surely was going to emerge in Christian dress.

Geoffrey Ashe* has the best available summary of the historical information available to us presently. His thesis of a popular Mariology that preceded the official cult (and about which the official Church had some doubts at first) is persuasive, although his speculation about a formal underground Marian church that actually worshiped Mary is based on extremely slender grounds, I think.

It also seems reasonable to agree with Ashe—at least until later research proves him wrong—that the turning point was the triumph of popular devotion over official hesitation at the Council of Ephesus. Ashe thinks that the emergence of Mary as *Mother* in the fifth century (in the fourth century she was predominantly *Virgo*) was a response of Christianity to the horrors of pagan invasion by seeking protection and security in the arms of a mother. Ashe's comparison of the religious functions of Mary with those of her predecessors is enlightening, even though it must be considered speculative because we have no other evidence of what was on the minds of our fifth-century predecessors.**

> The citadel had fallen. Proclus, who had launched the attack, became Patriarch of Constantinople. Rome itself took the lead in a proliferation of Marian churches, new or rededicated. Its own Santa Maria Maggiore quickly acquired a vast mosaic on a triumphal arch,

---

*Geoffrey Ashe, *The Virgin* (London: Routledge & Kegan Paul, 1976).

**Another useful work with a good deal of information on the scriptural as well as Apocryphal origins of the Mary cult—and some helpful psychological and anthropological speculation—is *Alone of All Her Sex, the Myth and Cult of the Virgin Mary* by Marina Warner (Knopf, 1976). Unfortunately Ms. Warner's work is not free from an ideologically rigid anti-Catholicism. Her concluding prediction ("The virgin will recede into legend . . . emptied of moral significance and [of] . . . its . . . real powers to heal and harm.") is what one would expect from a young woman who believes her own age is the hinge of human history. Ms. Warner's predictions may of course be right, but one may be pardoned for withholding final judgment till more data are in. Mary has been around a long time and is not likely to vanish just because Ms. Warner thinks she has become obsolete.

depicting the Virgin enthroned and glorified. Almost every large city throughout the Empire followed suit in architectural homage. Predictably perhaps, several of Mary's churches stood on ground once sacred to female divinity. Santa Maria Maggiore replaced Cybele's temple on the Esquiline hill. In due course Santa Maria in Arocoeli, on the Capitoline, succeeded to a temple of the Phoenician goddess Tanit. Another Roman church adjoined Isis's sanctuary near the Pantheon, another was on a site which had long been consecrated to Minerva, the Roman form of Athene. This last goddess, virgin daughter of Zeus, handed over to the new Virgin in a number of places, notably the Greek city of Syracuse, and Athens itself.

The lingering popular cults made the same transition. Rustic shrines of Aphrodite in Cyprus turned painlessly into shrines of Mary, where she is hailed to this day as *Panaghia Aphroditessa*. Goddesses surrendered their functions to her. Like Cybele she guarded Rome. Like Athene she protected various other cities. Like Isis she watched over seafarers, becoming, and remaining, the "Star of the Sea." Like Juno she cared for pregnant women. Christian art reflected her new attributes. She wore a crown recalling Cybele's. Enthroned with her Child she resembled Isis with Horus. She even had touches of Neith about her. The title and office of Queen of Heaven passed to her naturally from Isis, Anath and Astarte, and preserved her own Collyridian character.

(Ashe, pp. 192–193)

The historical questions of the precise process of the rise of the cult of the Virgin remain to be answered. However, for the purposes of this book, it is enough to say that there seems to be a thrust in human religions to search out symbols that reflect the femininity of God. Such symbols were available—though perhaps vaguely—in the official Yahwism of the Second Temple era and in the surrounding matrix of Graeco-Roman culture. They found their way into the New Testament. After some hesitation, Christians decided that it was safe for them to let these symbols develop into a Christianized cult of the Queen of Heaven. Such a process was practically inevitable once Christianity decided to take the risk of absorbing all that was good and beautiful in paganism.

Prophetic Yahwism—as part of the great "axial era" of human history—discovered a God who ruled supreme over the forces of nature but was independent of them. The prophets objected theologically to the Queen of Heaven cult because they could not reconcile the cult with the transcendent God to which they were committed. Later on, Christian Yahwism would restore the Queen of Heaven to her throne because in the explosion of hope that was the Easter experience, Christians were able to be far more confident of their ability to honor a God who was love without falling into either the excesses of the fertility cults or the theological error of transcendentalized God. This confidence does not seem to have been misplaced. The fear of the prophets was not the fear of reformers. Whatever might be said about the mistakes and excesses that have sometimes marred the Mary cult, the new Queen of Heaven presided over no orgies and affected not in the slightest faith in divine transcendence.

The reformers, incidentally, are not to be blamed for misunderstanding the concern of the prophets; they did not have available the conceptual tools or the research evidence we have.

The question must remain, however, as to whether the paradigm of the female deity as mother, virgin, spouse, and death is a construct of contemporary scholars useful for ordering the data yet fundamentally artificial or whether it reflects a conscious model used by the ancients. Did they see four distinct but overlapping functions of the female deity?

There is evidence to believe that the ancient Celts were quite explicit about the paradigm, and that the pre-Celtic peoples of Ireland may also have consciously distinguished between the (connected) roles of the woman-god. Thus Irish mythology deals with various triads of goddesses responsible for birth, mating (combining the virgo and sponsa roles), and death. The triadic goddesses are variously known as Morrigan, Machu, and Badh; or Danu, Anu, and Brid(get); or Banba, Eriu (whence the name Erin—Ireland), and Aodhla. Their roles overlap and sometimes they change roles, with who does what depending on who is telling the story. Often the high king of Ireland is having ritual intercourse with several of them (busy man, he).

Without going into the complexities of Irish mythology in elaborate detail,* it is clear that the functional distinction of roles was a self-conscious model among the Celts. Furthermore, according to some speculations, the famous triple spiral in the Newgrange Passage

---

*See, for example, John Sharkey, *Celtic Mysteries* (London: Thames and Huston, 1975).

tomb (County Meath) also represents the three aspects of the role of the feminine divinity in the continuous pilgrimage of man through life—birth, reproduction, and death. Explicit and self-conscious modeling of the different functions of the earth mother, then, goes back a long, long time—perhaps as much as 5,000 years.*

These are not, I must insist, themes of a later piety, of a medieval personal Mariology or a pious sentiment. These themes are more or less explicit in the New Testament, antedate the writings of the New Testament books, and go back very close to the beginnings of Christianity itself. They are also themes which correspond to the various symbols of the feminine as sacrament, as revelatory of the female component of the godhead, and are also to be found among the goddesses whom Mary replaced.** The question remains whether these themes might continue to be adequate expressions of the limit-experience of sexual differentiation as we encounter that experience today. Do the themes of Madonna, Sponsa, Virgo, and Pietà still shatter our old structures of perception and reorganize them into new configurations in which we can find light, illumination, and direction for our lives?

> The Christ-child lay on Mary's lap,
>   His hair was like a light.
> (O weary, weary were the world,
>   But here is all aright.)
>
> The Christ-child lay on Mary's breast.
>   His hair was like a star.
> (O stern and cunning are the kings,
>   But here the true hearts are.)
>
> The Christ-child lay on Mary's heart,
>   His hair was like a fire.
> (O weary, weary is the world,
>   But here the world's desire.)

---

*For an imaginative modern presentation in the ancient Celtic styles of the various Irish goddesses, see Jim Fitzpatrick, *Celtia* (Dublin: De Danann Press, 1975).

**I am grateful to my friend Herman Schmid, S.J., for pointing out to me that the first Christian Feast of Mary is the feast of "Conceptio Christi"; it was celebrated on a special Sunday of the year probably in the first century—the same Sunday on which the creation of the world and the resurrection were also celebrated. The first Christian feast, really only a special Sunday since all Sundays were resurrection days, then linked creation, conception, and resurrection.

The Christ-child stood at Mary's knee,
    His hair was like a crown,
And all the flowers looked up at Him,
    And all the stars looked down.

G. K. CHESTERTON,
"A Christmas Carol"

Madonna

Celtic Madonna

What do you see, freckle-faced mother
Out there at the horizon's line?
Your steel-blue eyes miss not a move
And your viselike mind retains it all.
Friend or foe? You're not yet sure
Probably a friend, so that's okay
But whoever, be fairly warned.
"Touch this kid of mine
And you'll get a bloody nose."

Strong arms, clenched fist, tough jaw
Red-haired Irish beauty indeed
And ready to smile and laugh
And set the whole world dancing
    with her own lilting spirit song
But "mess with this son of mine
    and you'll end on the flat of your back."

"O, it's only you, creation's Lord
Sure, come right on in
Yes, he's a very nice boy
We'll keep him, thank you much,
I'll take care of him for you
Because he's only mine for a while
But as long as I'm in charge
You won't have to work overtime."

Not a warlike race
Given to peace and love
Never started a fight
But never about to run.

"A fierce woman?
Oh, no, not me
I just take care of my own
Your mother would understand."

The physical foe will be put to rout
And the newer psychic demon exorcised
He'll be free to grow
And accept himself
And chase his dazzling dreams
And never doubt the ground of love
On which we stand and from which he came.
And anyone who messes with him
Will get a bloody nose.

Mystic boy, tow-haired son
    of neighborhood jumprope champ
The world is in your eyes
Your mother has offered it to you
Warm and sensitive you will always be
Life is more painful when intense
But also much better fun
Laugh the way she laughs
Fight the way she fights
Live the way she lives
You may get a few more bloody noses
But also a lot more passionate love.

                                        A.M.G.

Chapter 5

Madonna
Dei Mater Alma

Before I turn to my paradigm I want to insist that the exercise in which I am engaged is one of reflection and explication and not of persuasion. When one deals with religious symbols, one does not argue about them. One merely lays out the symbol for people to look at. If they are attracted to it or transformed by it, fine. If not, no amount of argument will persuade them. I am not engaged in any enterprise of trying to sell Marian symbols to anyone. I think the impact of the Enlightenment is so powerful on America's intellectual elite that no symbol, however transforming its character, can possibly speak to them. Things are things, and that's that. If one assumes on *a priori* grounds that there is no graciousness, then surely one will not encounter grace in anything. Heilbroner's hope that Atlas may be a transforming myth is, I think, doomed to be frustrated.

Nor do I wish to persuade my Protestant brothers and sisters that they have been missing something as a result of their fierce exclusion of Mary from their theological and devotional lives. Some Protestants see that already, many do not. I have no ambition to force insight on those who will not receive it.

Finally I am not trying to sell anything to Catholics. The traditional Mariologists—few as these may be—will be far too scandalized by what I have attempted even to listen to me. The more modern, sophisticated Catholics will dismiss my efforts as a frivolous attempt to resuscitate religious symbols which are long-since dead. I have no doubt that some brittle, bitchy, feminist reviewer will tell me that modern liberated woman simply cannot find anything meaningful in Marian symbolism. So be it.

I do not wish to argue with modern Catholics, traditional Catholics, Protestants, atheists, Jews, agnostics, women. I am not arguing with anyone. I am describing a symbol system and hinting at some of the implications and illuminations that might exist there for our world. It may be possible that Mary can still ignite grace-revealing limit-experiences for some humans. It is for those who are willing to admit this possibility and for them only that I am writing. Those who want to argue should find someone else to argue with.

I propose to take each one of the four major Marian themes—Madonna, Virgo, Sponsa, Pietà—and run it through a paradigm of fourteen cells. Figure 1 (p. 403) both illustrates the paradigm and applies it to the theme of the present chapter.

First we describe the aspect of sexual differentiation which in the given context has the capacity to produce limit-experience (Experience of Sexual Differentiation). Then we look at the biological roots of this capacity (Biological Origin), and the broad archetypal symbol which expresses this biological reality (Cognate Symbols). We will then consider the pagan goddesses who incarnate the experience (Ancient Goddesses). Next we will see the New Testament origins of the typology which applies this limit-experience to Mary (Type), and then we describe how Christians have described Mary as the thing-turned-symbol (Mary Symbol).

We then examine the existential need which predisposes us for the limit-experience in question (Existential Need); and then we explore the perception-shattering aspect of the limit-experience itself (Limit-Experience). Then we will see what kind of grace is revealed to us in the shattering experience (Grace that is Given), what illumination is obtained and organized into the new configuration of perception (Illumination). Next we turn to the results of the limit-experience which was initiated by the Marian symbol (Action). What are its implications for action in our contemporary world? What does it reveal for a man's self-understanding and a woman for hers (Man-Woman Implication)? Finally, we give an example of the symbol in poetry (Poem) and art (Plastic Art).

There is a dialectic involved between the overarching symbol and our own symbolic experience which must be kept in mind. We experience maternity as it is disclosed in the world around us; we then encounter Mary as Madonna, perhaps in a leap of imagination from a specific maternity experience of ours. Human-as-mother calls to mind Mary-as-mother, and Mary illumines human-as-mother. The overarching symbol, then, has the power to intervene in a particular limit-experience of ours to bestow sacramental power on the thing we have experienced. There are then really two symbols at work though they may be linked into one symbolism. It is the presence in our life or our cultural background of Mary as Madonna which enables us, or perhaps merely disposes us, to see the grace of the Madonna in an encounter with that aspect of sexual differentiation which we call maternity. The Madonna, in other words, illumines the world in which we live so that the various things we encounter acquire a much stronger potentiality for breaking through the barriers of the hardened structures of our perceptions and engaging in revelatory dialogue with our existential needs.

The most elemental dimension of the experience of sexual differentiation is maternity. Biologically, psychologically, and theologically the image of the mother is primal, and indeed all the other images of woman are derived from it and flow back into it. (Hence the verses of the *Ave Maris Stella* must be rearranged somewhat so that we consider first of all the Madonna theme.)

There are three different ways in which we can experience maternity, each one of which has a powerful potentiality for inducing a limit-experience. Each of us had a mother. It was the primal biological relationship of our lives, and one of the two most important psychological relationships in the development of our personality. We have, of course, internalized our mother; and whether she is alive or dead, her image is permanently implanted in our personality, and we carry it with us for the rest of our lives.

Secondly, many of us have been and are mothers, or are married to women who are mothers. We know not merely what it is like to be brought into the world, nurtured, protected, cared for, played with, admired, loved by a mother; but we also know, either immediately or through observation, what it is like for a woman to bring her own child into the world and to nurture it, protect it, play with it, admire it, love it (and occasionally also to shout at it, discipline it, and wish for the moment that it were in Afghanistan).[1]

Finally, we have the experience of encountering maternity as a part of everyday life. A woman carries a child onto the bus or the airplane (and you mutter a devout prayer that the child will not be in the seat next to you and scream the whole trip); a baby flirts with you behind his mother's back in a supermarket; we see a mother attempting to protect her child from the horrors of war revealed in an ugly, painful scene on the evening TV news; a woman walks down the street pushing a baby buggy; we walk through an art gallery filled with Renaissance madonnas.

There are almost overwhelming emotional currents released by such encounters with maternity. We remember in the depths of our souls (unconsciously, perhaps) what it was like to be mothered, to be cared for, to be protected, to be loved. Indeed, much of the activities of our lives are driven by latent personality dynamisms which seek to recapture the security, the affection, the total care and concern which we experienced in infancy. We want someone to take care of us the way mother did—and not a few men marry the women they expect to be surrogate mothers, who will be their loving, devoted slaves for the rest of their lives.

Mothering is part of any intimate human relationship in the sense that we expect those who love us to be at least on occasion passionately tender toward us, to assume the responsibility of "taking care" of us. In marriage, then, a spouse does indeed mother the other, although for the emotional maturity and happiness of both, there ought to be other dimensions to their relationship too. There is no contradiction in saying that a husband must "mother" his wife on occasion. He is gentle and tender with her, "taking care" of her. One of the problems, of course, is that a man may not feel free to develop a sufficiently androgynous personality, and the feminine aspects of his selfhood atrophy; he is quite incapable of having any maternal dimension in his relationship with his wife. She may mother him—for her that comes relatively easily—but he may refuse to "mother" back, since for him, such behavior is quite difficult. The lack of symmetry in their marriage can be discouraging, frustrating, divisive.[2]

Mother love gets perverted in many cases. Women hate their children, use them, project their own frustrations and fantasies into them. Such are the tragic effects of human sinfulness. Still, anyone who has seen a new mother proudly carrying her child into church to be baptized knows that the biological-psychological thrust toward pride, tenderness, admiration, protection, reverence, and delight between a mother and a child is one of the most fundamental powers in the universe. There are some environmentalists and some feminists who have come to despise motherhood as a combination of oppression and pollution. I surely have no intention of arguing with people who hold such a viewpoint, although I must admit to being skeptical of the argument that holds that a woman's desire to have a child of her own to hold in her arms is culturally caused. I will cheerfully concede cultural conditioning; I will also concede that there are some women who do not want or are afraid to have a child. Still, I do not anticipate the time when even a majority of women will not feel proud of and passionately tender toward that strange, delightful, disturbing, and at times maddening combination of angel and devil they have brought into the world.

The primary element of sexual differentiation, then, is that women bear children and men do not. Women become mothers, men do not. (Men can act maternally, of course, and my assumption is that some maternal component in a man's personality enriches it rather than weakens it.) The experience of maternity, either in oneself or in someone else, is the core limit-experience of sexual differentiation. The mother gives life; she brings life into the world. The phenomenon of childbirth is commonplace; thousands of children are born every day. Birth need not be a limit-experience at all. (Although in research on mystical ecstasy done by William McCready and myself, the birth experience often triggers a mystical interlude—in fathers almost as often as mothers.)

That childbirth is an experience intimately related to religion is testified to by almost all the cultures humankind has ever known. For religion, of course, is concerned with the great mysteries of life and death, and in maternity one has the quintessence of the mystery of life. In the great religious image systems, the fertile womb of the mother is linked with both the container, the vessel, and with life-giving waters. It is not merely in the Book of Genesis that life springs from water. In almost all of the religions the world knows that out of water comes life, out of mother comes life.

Psychoanalysts are persuaded that in most dream symbolism water stands for the maternal womb. Indeed, the brilliant founder of the Chicago Institute of Psychoanalysis, the late Franz Alexander, wrote three volumes arguing just this point. In the world religions and in the human unconscious, then, water, mother, vessel, earth all converge to represent one life-containing, life-bestowing symbolism.[3]

The Great Mother is the primal goddess both psychologically and historically. The feminine aspect of the ultimate is the life-bestowing dimension of God as opposed to the life-ordering or masculine dimension. In most religions, creation represents an ordering of primal chaos rather than, as in the later Jewish and Christian view of things, the production of something out of nothing. In the pagan worldviews, life antedated creation, and it was the male deity or demiurge who slew the female dragon Chaos. Out of the parts of the slain primal chaos the male deity put together the ordered universe. If the female deity did indeed precede the male one in human cultic behavior, and the evidence from the caves suggests this, the reason was that our archaic predecessors thought of life as the raw, primal force that antedated any attempt to order and contain it, and that always threatened to erupt and break out of the ordinary compartments into which creation had placed it. The mother goddess, then, was the source of life, but the life force she gave was potentially destructive; it was raw, undisciplined, hard to contain. Humans had to tame that force by orderly cultivation of the fields and by domestication of the flocks. In some sense the human condition was a struggle to impose restraints and limitations on the raw power and vitality of the feminine life-giving force.

The Kagaba Indians describe it as well as anyone:

> The Mother of Songs, the mother of our whole seed, bore us in the beginning. She is the mother of all races of men and the mother of all tribes. She is the mother of the thunder, the mother of trees and of all kinds of things. She is the mother of songs and dances. She is the mother of the older brother stones. She is the mother of the grain and the mother of all things. She is the mother of the younger brother Frenchmen and of the strangers. She is the mother of the dance paraphernalia and of all temples, and the only mother we have. She is the mother of the animals, the only one, and the mother of the Milky Way. It was the mother herself who began to baptize. She gave us the limestone coca dish. She is the mother of the rain, the only one we have. She alone is the mother of things, she alone. And the mother has left a memory in all the temples. With her sons, the saviors, she left songs and dances as a reminder. Thus the priests, the fathers, and the older brothers have reported.

Song of the Kagaba Indians, Colombia[4]

Isis in Egypt, Demeter in Greece, Juno in Rome, Ishtar in Phoenicia, Artemis in Archaic Ionia, Artargatis in Syria, Rati in Indonesia, Kali (in her more positive manifestations) in India, and such ambivalent Aztec earth goddesses as Tlazolteotl and Coatlicue in Mexico (both of whom, like Kali, were also death goddesses) have cousins all over the world.

One does not have to accept Neumann's Jungian psychology to agree with his summary of the role of the mother goddess in human religion:

> Thus the Feminine, the giver of nourishment, becomes everywhere a revered principle of nature, on which man is dependent in pleasure and pain. It is from this eternal experience of man, who is as helpless in his dependence on nature as the infant in his dependence on his mother, that the mother-child figure is inspired forever anew.
>
> This mother-child figure, then, does not betoken a regression to infantilism, in which an "adult" becomes a child, or is moved with nostalgia by the mother's love for her child; rather, man in his genuine identification with the child experiences the Great Mother as a symbol of the life on which he himself, the "grown-up," depends.[5]

When we move from pagan religions to Yahwism, the context changes dramatically. Eve is indeed the mother of us all, but she is not a goddess, she is an all-too-human earthbound person. The Eve of the Old Testament is probably a transformation and a humanization of a pre-Sinai Semitic mother goddess. The aim of the author of Genesis is obvious. Eve may represent the origin of human life; she may be the mother of us all; but she is not a goddess or a life force with specific power unto herself. She is rather a creature of Yahweh who gives life. Mary, too, is a human and a historical personage, a person who lived and died at a specific time in human history. She is not identified with the power of fertility, she is not the goddess who directs the raw, primal vitality inherent in reproduction of all life; she is the servant of the Lord, the agent of Yahweh. But it is still through her that Yahweh chooses to bring life to the world. She represents the rich, abundant, variegated creativity with which Yahweh has blessed the earth. Therefore she reveals to us the life-giving, the feminine dimension of Yahweh. She quite properly emerges as the Madonna, because she is a sacrament of Yahweh our loving Mother.

Christian poetry about Mary as Madonna, as Great Mother, is almost endless. Much of it is pretty bad, but from the fourth to the nineteenth centuries, Mary the Mother has inspired some of the finest poetry ever set on paper. Aurelius Clemens Prudentius tells us that she is the mother of a new age of golden life:

Sentisne, virgo nobilis,	Know thou, O Virgin, noble-blest,
Matura per fastidia	That through the timeless tunneled
Pudoris intactum decus	glooms
Honore partus crescere?	The blinding beauty of thy soul
	With childbirth splendor flames and
O quanta rerum gaudia	blooms?
Alvus pudica continet,	
Ex qua novellum saeculum	What joys are fountained for the
Procedit et lux aurea!	world
	Within thy womb's well, deep and
(*Aurelius Clemens Prudentius*	white,
(348–413) Hymn XI of the	Whence streams a new-created age
Cathemerinon, *verses 53–60*)	And golden light, and Golden Light!

(Translated from the Latin by RAYMOND F. ROSELIEP)

A thousand years later two anonymous bards sing the same song of praise:

Mater, ora Filium
ut post hoc exilium
nobis donet gaudium
beatorum omnium!

Fair maiden, who is this Bairn,
That thou bearest on thine arm?
Sir, it is a King's Son,
That in heaven above doth wone.

Man to father hath he none,
but himself is God alone;
of a maid he would be born
To save mankind that was forlorn.

The kings brought him presents,
Gold and myrrh and frankincense,
To my Son, full of might,
King of kings and Lord of right.

Fair maiden, pray for us
Unto thy Son, sweet Jesus
That he will grant us of his grace
In heaven high to have a place!

"Fair Maiden, Who Is This Bairn?"
—ANONYMOUS

Mary is a lady bright,
She hath a son of mickle might,
Over all this world she is light,
    Bona natalicia.

Mary is so fair of face,
And her son so full of grace,
In Heaven (may) He make us a place,
    Cum sua potencia.

Mary is so fair and bright,
And her son so full of might,
Over all this world He is light,
    Bona voluntaria.

Mary is both good and kind,
Ever on us she hath mind,
That the fiend shall us not bind.
    Cum sua malicia.

Mary is queen of everything,
And her son a lovely king;
God grant us all (a) good ending,
    Regnat Dei gracia.

"Nunc Gaudet Maria"
—ANONYMOUS

Mary the Mother is called upon to help and protect us, to care for us as she cared for her son. The son was innocent and deserved her care; we have little reason to claim in right Mary's protection. We still plead for it. In the anguish of Geoffrey Chaucer, who was all too well aware of his own sinfulness:

And thou that art the flower of virgins all,
Of whom Bernard has such a love to write,
To thee now in beginning first I call!

Comfort of wretched us, help me recite
Thy maiden's death, who, through her merit bright,
Won life eternal, vanquishing with glory
The fiend, as men can read here in her story.

Thou daughter of thy son, mother and maid,
Thou well of mercy, sinful souls' physician,
In whom for goodness God to dwell essayed,
Thou humble, yet enthroned in high position,
So didst thou lift our nature with thy mission
That He that made all nature thus was won
To clothe in flesh and blood His only Son.

Within the blissful cloister of thy side
To man's shape grew the eternal Love and Peace,
Lord of the threefold universe, and Guide,
Whom earth and heaven and ocean never cease
To praise, Thou, spotless virgin, for a space,
Bore in thee, maiden still in every feature,
He that Creator was of every creature.

In thee are mercy and magnificence,
Goodness and pity in such unity
That thou, that art the sun of excellence,
Not only helpest those that pray to thee,
But often times, in thy benignity,
Freely, before men any help petition,
Thou dost appear, and art their lives' physician.

Help me, thou lovely, meek, and blesséd maid,
Who banished now in bitterness must dwell;
Think on the wife of Canaan, she who said
That dogs would feed upon the crumbs that fell
Down from their master's table. I know well
that I am sinful, wretched son of Eve,
And yet accept my faith, for I believe.

And since all faith, when lacking works, is dead,
So give me now for work both wit and space.
That I from darkness be deliveréd!
O thou that art so fair and full of grace,
Be advocate for me in that high place
Where there is endless singing of "Hosannah!"
Mother of Christ, dear daughter of St. Anna!

And from thy light my soul in prison light,
Where it is troubled by contamination
Of this body, and the heavy weight
Of earthly lust, and all false inclination;
O heaven of refuge for us, O salvation
Of all souls whom distress and sorrow neighbor,
Help me, for I will now attempt my labor!

Invocatio Ad Mariam (From the Prologue to the Second Nun's Tale)
by Geoffrey Chaucer (Translated into Modern English by
Frank Ernest Hill)

And that enigmatic son of the Renaissance, Desiderius Erasmus, turned to the Greek language that he helped restore to Europe to pray that the mother who brought life back to the world would free him from his sinfulness:

Hail, Jesus' Virgin-Mother ever blest,
Alone of women Mother eke and Maid,
Others to thee their several offerings make;
This one brings gold, that silver, while a third
Bears to thy shrine his gift of costly gems.
For these, each craves his boon—one strength of limb—
One wealth—one, through his spouse's fruitfulness,
The hope a father's pleasing name to bear—
One Nestor's eld would equal. I, poor bard,
Rich in goodwill, but poor in all beside,
Bring thee my verse—nought have I else to bring—
And beg, in quital of this worthless gift,
That greatest meed—a heart that feareth God,
And free for aye from sin's foul tyranny.
Erasmus, his vow.

"Votive Ode" (At Our Lady's Shrine in Walsingham)
(Translated from the Greek by J. T. Walford)

About the same time a much more simple poem was written in Spanish describing the marvelous events at Bethlehem:

White and crimson, cheek and breast,
O Virgin blest!
The pledge of love in Bethlehem

A flower was on the rose-tree's stem,
O Virgin blest!
In Bethlehem in sign of love
The rosebranch raised a rose above,
O Virgin blest!
In the rose came forth a flower—
Jesus, our high Lord of Power—
O Virgin blest!
The Rose of all the rose-tree's span,
God in nature and a Man—
O Virgin blest!

> "Cantiga" by GIL VINCENTE (1470–1540)
> (Translated from the Galician-Castilian by THOMAS WALSH)

Even the strange, half-mad Lord Byron could pause amidst his self-advertisements to wonder about the Madonna who brought life to the world:

Ave Maria! blessed be the hour!
 The time, the clime, the spot, where I so oft
Have felt that moment in its fullest power
 Sink o'er the earth so beautiful and soft,
While swung the deep bell in the distant tower,
 Or the faint dying day-hymn stole aloft,
And not a breath crept through the rosy air,
And yet the forest leaves seem'd stirr'd with prayer.

Ave Maria! 'tis the hour of prayer!
 Ave Maria! 'tis the hour of love!
Ave Maria! may our spirits dare
 Look up to thine and to thy Son's above!
Ave Maria! oh that face so fair!
 Those downcast eyes beneath the Almighty Dove—
What though 'tis but a pictured image—strike?—
That painting is no idol, 'tis too like.

> "Ave Maria" (From *Don Juan*, Canto III, cii, ciii
> by GEORGE GORDON, LORD BYRON (1788–1824)

But of all the Madonna poems, my own favorite is that of the good nineteenth-century Jesuit, Gerard Manley Hopkins, who combined the

simplicity of the medieval bards with the complex rhythms that
astonish the most modern of poets.

> May is Mary's month, and I
> Muse at that and wonder why:
>   Her feasts follow reason,
>   Dated due to season—
>
> Candlemas, Lady Day;
> But the Lady Month, May,
>   Why fasten that upon her,
>   With a feasting in her honor?
>
> Is it only its being brighter
> Than the most are must delight her?
>   Is it opportunest
>   And flowers finds soonest?
>
> Ask of her, the mighty mother:
> Her reply puts this other
>   Question: What is Spring?—
>   Growth in every thing—
>
> Flesh and fleece, fur and feather,
> Grass and greenworld all together;
>   Star-eyed strawberry-breasted
>   Throstle above her nested
>
> Cluster of bugle blue eggs thin
> Forms and warms the life within;
>   And bird and blossom swell
>   In sod or sheath or shell.
>
> All things rising, all things sizing
> Mary sees, sympathizing
>   With that world of good,
>   Nature's motherhood.
>
> Their magnifying of each its kind
> With delight calls to mind
>   How she did in her stored
>   Magnify the Lord.
>
> Well but there was more than this:
> Spring's universal bliss
>   Much, how much to say
>   To offering Mary May.

When drops-of-blood-and-foam-dapple
Bloom lights the orchard-apple
    And thicket and thorp are merry
    With silver-surfèd cherry

And azuring-over greybell makes
Wood banks and brakes wash wet like lakes
    And magic cockoo call
    Caps, clear, and clinches all—

This ecstasy all through mothering earth
Tells Mary her mirth till Christ's birth
    To remember and exultation
    In God who was her salvation.

"The May Magnificat"
GERARD MANLEY HOPKINS (1844–1889)

It seems to me that the essence of Mary as mother goddess, Mary as a sign of fertility, Mary as symbol of the raw, life-giving power of Yahweh is caught up in those lines, "What is Spring?—/ Growth in every thing—" It's all there—the raw, primal power of fertility, the awesome mystery of life, the elementary, biological fact of maternity, of nature's motherhood. In the poem it is embodied as "Flesh and fleece, fur and feather,/ Grass and greenworld all together," and all combine to proclaim the endless generation. Nature's motherhood, "All things rising, all things sizing/ Mary sees, sympathizing" is part of Hopkins' Christian song, but he sings of an experience that goes back to the grotesque (to us) Venuses of our cave-dwelling predecessors. It is an experience that probably goes back to the dawn of mankind, to the time when a man was overwhelmed with astonishment at the sight of an infant in his woman's arms.

I would submit that the images of Hopkins, Byron, Chaucer, Erasmus, the nameless medieval bards, and the elegant Prudentius tell us far more about the power and the meaning of the Madonna than theology books could possibly portray. Poetry is much better at conveying limit-experience than scholarly theology.[6]

As for the Madonna in plastic art, one could argue until Judgment Day about which paintings were the best. I would walk through the whole Uffizi Gallery in Florence just to look at Michelangelo's *Holy Family on the Barrelhead*. Hans Memling's *Adoration of the Angels* in the Prado in Madrid, the fourteenth-century sculpture in the Notre

Dame church in Riom, France; Donatello's relief in Turin, Leonardo da Vinci's *The Virgin and Saint Anne* in the Louvre, Van der Weyden's Flemish madonnas—all represent dimensions of motherhood. Some of them are very spiritual, some are very earthy; but all reflect the mystery of birth and of the passionate protective tenderness, the fierce dedication and devotion of a mother toward her child. While it is unfashionable now to be very enthusiastic about Raphael and Botticelli, the melancholy, reflective *Virgin with the Pomegranate* of Botticelli and the gentle serenity of Raphael's *Virgin with the Blue Veil* come mighty close to producing limit-experience in me every time I look at them, as does da Vinci's *Madonna of the Rocks*.

But when all is said and done, I still find myself back in the Uffizi looking at Michelangelo's *Holy Family*. The tender concern in the eyes, the playful pride in the slightly parted lips, the vigor of the body of the Virgin ever ready to hold and to protect the child. Oh, it's all larger than life, of course, and the Virgin may have an arm muscle to frighten Muhammad Ali; but she is a mother you wouldn't mess with. No one is ever going to hurt that child while she's around.

The strength of the Michelangelo madonna, the ever-so-slight satisfaction on the Virgin's face as she looks at the child against her breast in the Van der Weyden painting, the thoughtful, almost melancholy reflection on mystery in the Botticelli paintings, the fascination in Raphael's blue-veiled mother with her sleeping child, the mystic rapture of da Vinci's mother of the rocks, the life-giving mother of Prudentius, the sin-forgiving mother of Erasmus and Chaucer, the warm but distant mother of Lord Byron, and Hopkins's Mary—the sympathetic onlooker of the rebirth of nature in May—are just a handful of the images and pictures of Mary the madonna that emerge from Christian art and poetry.[7] Irrelevant for our time? Well, maybe, but then so much the worse for our time.

What is the human existential need with which maternity as illumined by Mary seeks to dialogue? Just as maternity represents the most fundamental and primal and vital of life-giving forces, so existential anxiety, the fear of sickness unto death, is the most primal and elementary of human fears. Maternity means life; anxiety and fear mean death. Maternity is a response to despair. Indeed, in the poems of Byron, Chaucer, and Erasmus cited above, the wrestling with despair becomes quite explicit. Even in Hopkins, the celebration of

May can only come from one who has already lived through the darkness of December.

In the Madonna we encounter the dilemma, the ambiguity, and the conflict between life and death. We know the Madonna's child will die, as will the child of every mother, even our own. We move dangerously close to despair. What point is there in life if it is all to be snuffed out in death? Is there no purpose? No love? No grace? Is this surging creativity to be blotted out in oblivion? Are the life-producing forces to be routed ultimately by the life-destroying forces? Can we respond to life only with a brave, stoic despair?

Our perceptions have been caught in the hardened, rigid structure of the common defeats in life—discouragement, frustration, sickness, old age, death. And then we encounter maternity as illumined by the Madonna. We can glance over the lines of the poetry that extols her and walk quickly by the paintings that portray her and nothing will happen. But once the existential need for meaning has become powerful (and that may never happen), we may stop to read, we may stop to look, and we may pause to reflect on our own experience of woman as mother. We become aware of the overwhelming power of life; we think of the surge of fertility each year in the spring, of "flesh and fleece, fur and feather,/ Grass and greenworld all together." Doubtless there is death and destruction all through the world, doubtless we shall die; but here is maternity, fertility, birth, life, rebirth. We are now up against the limits of our own existence, the horizon of our own being; but we also perceive life, and we perceive it as a gift, a given, as something wildly, madly, exuberantly gratuitous. "All things rising, all things sizing."

What is one to make of this "ecstasy all through mothering earth"? It is grace; it claims to reveal; it claims to be a sacrament of something else. It is a gift. Might there possibly be a Giver, a Giver of whom fertility, maternity, even the lovely-eyed Madonna are but a pale reflection? Can it be so? Might it be so? Is it so? Is there passionate, life-giving tenderness out there beyond the horizon of our life?

If we have been sufficiently captured by maternity-turned-symbol, by the grace that the Madonna as sacrament has revealed to us, then we can begin to hope once again. The shattered structures of our perceptions are organized around a symbol which has captured our experience of rebirth. "Life and Death are inseparable on earth for they are 'twain yet one and death is birth.''[8] The symbol takes possession of us; our perceptions are restructured, and we begin to move.

Where do we move? Well, we move to the earth that is the source of the gift of life. We commit ourselves to bringing joy and happiness and peace and love to the earth. If we are followers of the Madonna, there is no room for despair, no room for hopelessness, no room to give up or quit. Servants of Mary who have committed themselves to political and social reform do not withdraw from the contest when the going gets tough and when they suffer repeated setbacks. They do not despair because the Enlightenment-socialist dreams have turned into nightmares, they do not seek stoic gods like Atlas to wait bravely for the end, they refuse to listen to the prophets of doom; they set out to build and rebuild with no fear for the ultimate outcome. Their hope is not based on economic projections, political assessments, computer models, or ideological convictions. It is based on their faith that the earth is graceful, that the world is gracious, that it is a given, a gift, a reflection of a Giver who is as tender and gentle, as passionate and as generous as the Madonna.

The followers of Mary do not, heaven save us, abandon economics, politics, planning, projections, or even computer models, but they find in them neither the source of their faith nor the depth of their commitment. Their faith is not rooted in social science or social ideology but in a vision of a world animated by the passionate, life-giving tenderness of which the Madonna is a sacrament.

Is that the way things really are? Is the ultimate really the kind of life-giving love that is reflected in the Madonna? A cautious world says probably not; the followers of Mary have made the opposite choice.

It is but a step from saying that the life-giving power of earth symbolized as life-giving love in Mary reflects the life-giving love of the ultimate to assert further that the earth is Mary's garden. Such a symbolic and poetic statement merely means that the earth is a sacrament; it is sacred and must be treated with reverence and respect and awe and a sense of mystery. If the earth is Mary's garden, you don't rip it up or rip it off. Respect for the physical environment is not just a new notion dug up to give relevance to an outmoded symbol that one is trying to rehabilitate for the modern world. Respect for the environment, on the contrary, is at the very core of the Mary myth—though the phrase "respect for environment" is new. If "all things rising" reflect through Mary the life-giving love of God, then all the rising things on earth are mystery. To pollute, abuse, corrupt, destroy these things is a sacrilege.

You cannot have a successful environmental movement unless you restore a sense of reverence and awe to the human community. If the cosmos is a machine or a set of mathematical formulae or an empty collection of random atoms, then why should we respect it or reverence it? Why should we not exploit it to the fullest? Why should we worry about what or who comes after us? Everything will be wiped out in nothingness eventually, so why not take what we can get now? This is not a very noble way of thinking, but it is a very human way. Most of the ecological enthusiasts, captives of the Enlightenment still, seem to think you can respect the environment without reverencing it, that you can have concern about the environment without seeing any mystery in it. Guilt and fear are their two primary weapons, because that is all they have to motivate people. The cosmos has been drained of mystery and of the sacred. For some, environmental concern can become an ideological movement that serves as a substitute for religion. Fine for them, but most of humankind will respect the earth again only when they see it once more as a park, a paradise given to them by God but still belonging to him. The earth will be Mary's garden or a trash heap.

The Mary myth is not the only one that can provide a restructuring of perceptions and illumination and direction to respond to the critical issues of our day. There may well be other symbols that work just as well or perhaps even better. Still, if we are going to save the earth, it damn well better become someone's garden.

As we try to sort out the meaning of masculinity and femininity in an era that is rethinking sex roles, Mary may well be the best available argument for the androgynous personality, the personality that combines the essence of each sex. For if God is androgynous—and that's what the mother goddesses reveal to us—then it is all right for humankind to be androgynous. In principle, almost any one of the female deities could underwrite the upgrading of women. There is no particular reason why it has to be Mary. But she is the only mother goddess currently available. Astarte, Lilith, Demeter, Isis, Ishtar, Nut, Kali, Coatlicue, Rati, Ceres, Tlazoltoatl—that crowd—are not around much these days. You might not like Mary particularly, but if you want someone to convey the idea that God is androgynous, she is about all you have (unless you want to return to the mother goddesses of witchcraft, which not a few people seem to be doing).

G. K. Chesterton finds in Mary the appeal of hearth and home and the traditional wisdom of the fields:

> The dark Diana of the groves
>   Whose name is Hecate in hell
> Heaves up her awful horns to heaven
>   White with the light I know too well.
>
> The moon that broods upon her brows
>   Mirrors the monstrous hollow lands
> In leprous silver; at the term
>   Of triple twisted roads she stands.
>
> Dreams are no sin, or only sin
>   For them that waking dream they dream;
> But I have learned what wiser knights
>   Follow the Grail and not the Gleam
>
> I found One hidden in every home,
>   A voice that sings about the house,
> A nurse that scares the nightmares off,
>   A mother nearer than a spouse,
>
> Whose picture once I saw; and there
>   Wild as of old and weird and sweet,
> In sevenfold splendor blazed the moon
>   Not on her brow; beneath her feet.

"The White Witch" G. K. CHESTERTON,
The Queen of Seven Swords

For women, Mary symbolizes the awesome power of femininity. To be a woman does not mean to be quiet, retiring, weak, diffident, inferior; it means to be strong, powerful, creative, dynamic. One can afford to be tender, gentle, loving, caring because one knows that these are not signs of weakness, that they can coexist with aggressive, strong, outgoing, directive behavior. If Mary reflects an androgynous God, femininity is as good as masculinity.

And if there is nothing weak or effeminate about life-giving love, about maternal love that is both passionately tender and fiercely protective, there is no reason why a man must retreat behind the shield of hypermasculinity; he can afford to be tender, sympathetic, caring because Mary reveals to him that these qualities are signs not of weakness but of strength. If God can be tender and passionate, if God is reflected by Mary as a source of maternal life-giving love, then the tender, gentle man is not weak but strong. In the God who is revealed to us in Mary, masculine and feminine are blended. Among the followers of Mary, sharp, exclusive, and oppressive distinctions between men and women are not appropriate. As Professor Robert Higham has pointed out, the sharp demarcation line between men and women, against which the feminist movement is quite properly revolting, is a relatively modern development, a product of the Enlightenment passion for clear and sharp distinctions. Women did not lead armies into battle in the Crimean War. (They certainly couldn't have done any worse than the male generals did.) Nor can one imagine cathedrals being built to women in the France and England of the nineteenth century.

I am not suggesting that traditional Marian theory or piety anticipated the feminist movement. Nor am I denying that corrupt Mariology has been used by some people in the Roman Church to underwrite the most benighted and oppressive attitudes toward the role of woman. The *Kirche und Kinder* view of women was far more appropriate for a pre-Christian peasant society than it is for Christianity. That so many Christians mouthed it and distorted Marian imagery to support it is a sign of how strong and persistent has been the worldview of peasant paganism (which bubbled to the surface with terrifying horror in the Nazi movement in Germany).

But the feminist movement today is hardly derived from older Marian theory, at least not in any explicit sense (though a case could be made that Christianity developed a culture through the Mary symbol in which feminism could eventually emerge). I am content with a much more modest statement: the high tradition of Mariology is compatible with a theory of the role of women which emphasizes the freedom, independence, strength, passion, and responsibility of maternity. It is less compatible with one that emphasizes the quiet, docile, retiring, passive, fragile role of woman that was so dear to both the Victorians and the Nazis, as well as to some of the fertility cultists of the Catholic Church of not so long ago who seemed to believe that the number of children one had was a measure of how well one had discharged maternal functions and responsibilities.

The argument needs only to be minimal. There is reinforcement in the Mary myth for both environmental concern and feminism, and there is no consolation at all in the myth for those who do not care about the environment or who want to keep women in dependent positions. Indeed, the thought of a follower of Mary being dependent would be funny were it not that so many people badly misunderstand the Mary myth and think of her as weak and passive. They know nothing of the origins of the maternal symbol in religion and understand little of it in their own religion. In fact, the symbol stands for massive, awesome, life-giving strength, a strength that is combined with fierce protectiveness and passionate tenderness which reflect a God strong enough to be tender and passionate enough to overwhelm us with his/her life-giving love.

What is the world all about? What is the nature of everything? Is it an idiot's tale, random chance, a plot? If it is a plot, what is the plotter like? It cannot be a romance or a tender love story—or can it? The person who wrote one of the earliest extant poems to Mary in the English language thought it was, and a mother was at the heart of the story.

> Be glad in heart,   grow great before the Lord
> for thy comfort,   and build up glory;
> hold thy hoard locked,   bind fast thy thought
> in thine own mind.   Many a thing is unknown.
> True comrades sometimes fall away, tired,
> word-promises grow faint;   so fares this world,
> going swiftly in showers,   shaping its destiny.
> There is one faith,   one living Lord,
> one Baptism,   one Father everlasting,
> one Lord of peoples   who made the world,
> its good things and joys.   Its glory grew
> through this passing earth,   stood for a long time
> hidden in gloom,   under a dark helm,
> well screened by trees,   overshadowed by darkness,
> till a brave-hearted maid   grew up among mankind.
> There it pleased Him   who shaped all life,
> the Holy Ghost,   to dwell in her treasure-house—
> bright on her breast   shone the radiant Child
> who was the beginning   of all light.

> "A Brave-Hearted Maid"
> from the Old English by MARGARET WILLIAMS

Madonna

Experience of Sexual Differentiation	Maternity
Biological Origin	Birth, nursing, taking care
Cognate Symbols	Earth, water (womb), home, hearth
Ancient Goddesses	Isis, Demeter, Juno
Type	Eve, the source of life
Mary Symbol	Madonna
Existential Need	Discouragement, despair
Limit-Experience	Vitality of cosmos, life-giving love
Grace That Is Given	Inexhaustible and passionate tenderness of life-giving love
Illumination—Restructuring of Perceptions	Hope
Action	Protection and improvement of the earth (Mary's garden)
Man-Woman Implication	Acceptance of androgyny
Poem	"May Magnificat" (Hopkins)
Plastic Art	*Holy Family* of Michelangelo

Virgo

Hymn to My Favorite Three-Year-Old

Surely, leprechaun child, a mistaken name
What 'tween you and the frenzied queen of old.
Giant blue eyes, curly red hair, winsome smile
A perfect little lady in every way
Sweet, lovely, innocent
Charming all who cross the stage
The pride of the nineteenth ward
The inestimable Nora Maeve.

Who can resist your grin
Who imagine the slightest temper
Who deny your smallest whim
But let them try
And they'll have their lunch
They'll see the fiery, the frenzied
The inextinguishable Nora Maeve.

No need to fight,
Conflict quite beside the point
We'll do it my way, of course
Pleasant, reasonable, cooperative
Who can possibly disagree
    with sensible Nora Maeve

Shape up world, get your act in line
Ready or not, here she comes
And take it from us
She'll accept none of your guff
'Tis time to prepare the way
Here comes the imperial and imperious Nora Maeve

Enough of your nonsense, disordered cosmos
No more loafing on the job, guardian spirits
Let's get this show on the road
Fagablough, look out, here she is!
Hell on wheels, pretty Nora Maeve.

Mommy and daddy, Liam and Andy, Sebi too
And all the rest of you
To receive your orders get in line
All hail her High Mightiness
The grand duchess Nora Maeve.

And God up in heaven
'Twas your idea, after all
You who renew the human race
    through girl children such as she
Maybe you're ready for her
If so, 'twill be a better world
And in years to come they'll chant her praise
And we'll say, oh yes, we knew her when
The famous, the saintly Nora Maeve.

A. M. G.

Chapter 6

Virgo
Atque Semper Virgo

The symbol of Mary as Virgin is the hardest of all to explore in the modern world. Part of the problem comes from misunderstanding the symbol. It is, as we said in Chapter 4, part of a limit-language paradox, Virgin Mother. It is *not* a symbol of sexual "purity" or repression. At least in its origins and in its high tradition, the Virgin symbol represents renewal, transformation, the beginning of a new creation. Unfortunately for all too many Catholics raised in the last fifty years, Mary's virginity speaks not of the transformation of humankind but of measurements of hemlines and necklines, of singing "Mother Beloved" at the beginning of a high school prom, and of a whole range of detailed sexual prohibitions and restrictions. Mary's virginity was equated with frigidity for all practical purposes, particularly in the more recent northern European Catholic tradition and especially (God forgive us for it) among the Irish Catholics.[1]

The symbol of woman as positive transforming force, which is deeply rooted in most religious traditions and, if we are to believe the Jungians, also firmly embedded in the human unconscious, is not easily understood in a modern world which worships orgasm as the only meaningful sexual interchange. Curiously enough, the gonadal determinism involved in orgasm worship is justified in terms of the sexual liberation allegedly made possible by Freudian psychoanalysis. Freud, of course, had a much more differentiated and nuanced view of human sexuality, but the distance between the real Freud and the pop

Freudianism which sees orgasm as the only self-fulfilling expression of sex is a very great distance indeed.

Nevertheless, most relationships between men and women do not culminate in genital sexuality. A mother, a daughter, a professional colleague, a friend can all be strong feminine influences in the life of a man without there being any genital sexuality involved. Furthermore, even two people who have intercourse together are not—save in the fantasy world of *Playboy* and *Penthouse*—making love all the time. There are nongenital interludes and episodes in their lives which occupy far more time than those periods they spend in bed with one another. While the influence a woman has on her man in facilitating the growth and transformation and renewal of his personality is linked with lovemaking, it is also distinct from it and persists even when intercourse becomes impossible for one reason or another (physical separation, for example).

Such observations are so obvious that they almost do not need to be made except for the fact that the current fixation on orgasmic satisfaction (understandable, perhaps, after a long era of puritanism) seems to make it impossible for many people to consider any other dimension of human sexuality.

A serious literary exception is Gabriel Fielding's little noticed but brilliant novel, *Gentlemen in Their Season*.[2] Bernard Persage, the hero, has a wife, a mistress, and a friend. The first presides over the cozy, reassuring domesticity of his home and family, the second leads him off to Calais on a great love affair which doesn't quite work out, and the third—a lutanist, composer, and an intellectual—is the only one of the three to whom he can talk. Most of the reviewers of the book could not understand the relationship between Persage and the friend, Emily Link; but surely such a refusal to understand was caused by ideological blinders. If Bernard had gone to bed with Emily, it would fit the conventional wisdom of pop Freudianism. For her to remain a transforming influence in his life—as common as such friendships may be in the real world—is still an affront to orgasm worship.

Yet the transforming influence of the opposite sex is an obvious datum of ordinary life. A woman comes into a room where there are a group of men. The language changes, the conversation becomes more impressive, and the competitive behavior among the males to make an impression noticeably increases. The ideologues of the woman's movement will argue, of course, that the change in language and conversational subject is sexist, and that if women were permitted into the same life-situations as men, conversations full of vulgarity and obscenity would continue undiminished with the appearance of a woman. Surely in some occupational and social situations where such liberated women are present, such transformations of language and conversation will not happen. Indeed, when a woman is present the men may compete not so much to elevate the language as to make it even coarser. Familiarity may breed contempt, and so much the better the movement would argue.

In fact, all the feminist ideology in the world will not change the propensity of members of one sex to try to impress members of the other. No man likes to lose a tennis match while women are watching. He is humiliated. The presence of women—perhaps a special woman—in the audience motivates him to try much harder to win (unless, of course, he is a tennis pro whose motivation for victory is quite independent of the sexual composition of the audience). Nor will all the feminist ideology in the world ever bring about a situation in which it makes no difference to the average golfer whether he tees off in front of a mixed audience or not. If there are women present, there is no way he will not try harder. (And alas, the game of golf being the diabolic enterprise it is, he is thereby much more likely to make a fool of himself and slice the ball three fairways away.)

This desire to impress a member of the opposite sex is quite unrelated to whether one is sleeping with him/her or not. A man wants to impress his wife every bit as much as he wants to impress a strange woman or a woman he is courting. It is a normal human response to try to impress a person. We want the other to like us, to approve of us, to admire us. If the stranger happens to be a member of the opposite sex, we simply try harder. Obviously such an urge to impress is rooted ultimately in the radical possibility of having intercourse with the other person, but normally intercourse will not occur, and is not even a remote possibility in the minds of the people involved. The presence of a member of the opposite sex heightens our consciousness and transforms our behavior quite independently of how honorable our intentions may be.

The consolation of a tender nurse when one is sick, the efficiency of a coolly competent assistant or associate when one is in the midst of confusion, the reassurance of a mother or a sister or a daughter when one is lonely or confused, the laughter of a friend at a party when one is distressed or depressed are all examples of the transforming and renewing impact of sexual differentiation. In a happy marriage, the wife plays all these roles—nurse, organizer, mother, mistress, daughter, provider of comic relief.[3] Lovemaking between husband and wife integrates all these other and transforming dimensions of their relationship. Yet, over the long haul in their marriage, it is precisely their ability to use sexual differentiation as an occasion for a mutual transforming and renewing experience that will condition the payoff each receives from genital sexuality.

The experience of the transforming power of sexual differentiation is universal. (Or as the dean of students remarked in the seminary—as close to an all-male world in the 1940s as one could imagine—"after a while, you begin to imagine that you hear the click of heels on the sidewalk.") This transforming power is biologically rooted. A member of the opposite sex "arouses" us. In many circumstances the physical arousal is slight or virtually nonexistent, but the psychological arousal remains and persists. In that arousal, our consciousness is heightened and our behavior is transformed either dramatically or very little, but enough so that we are aware of the potential for transformation and renewal.

However difficult it may be to sell the notion of woman as a source of transformation, inspiration, and renewal to the modern world, this aspect of sexual differentiation was obvious to our archaic ancestors. The gate, the tomb, the central pillar of the house, the enclosure, the cattle pen, the village, the city, and ultimately the nation were conceived of as female in nature. As Neumann says:

> The woman is the natural nourishing principle and hence mistress of everything that implies nourishment. The finding, composition, and preparation of food, as well as the fruit and nut gathering of the early cultures, are the concern of the female group. Only the killing of large animals falls to the males, but the life and fertility of the animals were subordinated to the Feminine, since hunting magic, the magical guarantee of success in the hunt, lay in her province, although it was later taken over by the male hunting group. This rule over food was largely based on the fact that the female group formed the center of the dwelling, i.e., the actual home to which the nomadic males again and again returned.[4]

The woman, then, is primordially the natural, nourishing principle, the mistress of all that implies nourishment—house, table, hearth, and bed. She is responsible, of course, for physical transformation, for the cooking, the maintenance of the house, those primal activities of transforming the world. In the Roman mythology, there was even an oven goddess, Fornacalia, on whose feast day the national bread was baked. An old Roman proverb announced, "The oven is the mother."

Moreover, the woman had charge of the medicines, and so the feminine deity who was already responsible for the crops, the herds, and the fruit became the numinous agent in charge of curatives, intoxicants, and poisons. The woman, according to Neumann, learned the mysterious powers of fermentation and intoxication as the gatherer and storer of plants and herbs. From this wisdom it was but a step for the woman, and the goddess experience through her, to become the shaman, the sibyl, the priestess, and the wise woman. Woman became the "manna" figure, the Ceres, the lady of the wisdom bringing waters from the depths of the murmuring aspects of the fountain. Then, in one more step, the female goddesses of transformation emerged as the nymphs, the wood spirits, and finally, the graces and the muses.

Indeed, Neumann argues that the notion of a virgin-mother goddess is by no means unique or original to Christianity. It is the son of the virgin mother who renews the earth:

> The childbearing virgin, the Great Mother as a unity of mother and virgin, appears in a very early period as the virgin with the ear of grain, the heavenly gold of the stars, which corresponds to the earthly gold of the wheat. This golden ear is a symbol of the luminous son who on the lower plane is born as grain in the earth and in the crib, and on the higher plane appears in the heavens as the immortal luminous son of night. Thus the virgin with the spica, the ear of grain, and the torchbearer, Phosphora, are identical to the virgin and the child.[5]

It would be a mistake to push Neumann's insight too far, for there is obviously substantial difference between the transforming and renewing virgin mother of the fertility cults and the transforming virgin mother of Christianity, but the idea is not completely foreign to the human religious tradition (which does *not* necessarily mean that the Christian theme of the virgin mother is a symbol without any grounding in actual historical event).

The mother goddess as a source of manna, the source of spiritual transformation, reaches her height of development in the figure of Sophia, or Wisdom, in late antiquity. She is not abstract, disinterested knowledge but rather the wisdom that comes from loving participation. As Neumann puts it: "Just as the unconscious reacts and responds, just as the body reacts to healthful food or poison, so Sophia is living and present and near, a godhead that can always be summoned and is always ready to intervene, and not a deity living inaccessible to man in numinous remoteness and alienated seclusion."[6] Neumann notes that the Christian figure of the Madonna sheltering humanity under her mantle corresponds rather neatly with this late pagan notion of Sophia. And of course Beatrice is Sophia transformed and personalized in Dante's *Divine Comedy*.[7]

The spiritual mother or the virgin mother, the Sophia of the pagans, is indeed the mother goddess of earlier antiquity; but, as well as being the agent of transforming others, she has been transformed herself. She communicates now not so much a life of earthbound materiality as a life of the spirit. She is interested not merely in reproduction and caring for the child but also in the whole man through the whole process of his spiritual development. In Buddhism, Kwan-yin is the transforming mother; in India, Shakti and even Kali, in her benign manifestation, becomes a spiritual mother; and in Yoga, Tara—the One Who Leads Happily Across—is the spiritual mother (complete with the lotus and the lily which symbolize spiritual transformation).

Old paganism, then, saw the goddess as the source of transformation, mostly that transformation that came from drugs and intoxicants. Later paganism reconceptualized the transforming mother as a spiritual force, calling forth the highest and the most noble in the creative powers of human beings—though that did not necessarily exclude the use of drugs and intoxicants. The sibyl or the seer frequently uttered her wisdom under the influence of narcotics.

The moon, the gentle, numinous orb in the sky at night, became the natural symbol of the transforming goddess, as did the lotus and the lily and sometimes the tree. The goddess of transformation was perhaps a fertility goddess in her origin, but she became one of spiritual transformation, of wisdom, of human renewal as the years went on.

Mary, the Virgin "full of grace," is not discontinuous from the transforming mother, the wisdom-giving virgin of the world religions. She is the spiritual mother, the mother who consoles, protects, watches over her children not merely in physical infancy and childhood but throughout the course of their spiritual development. For her to be full of grace does not primarily describe the state of her own spirituality; it means that she is full of graciousness *for us*. As the virgin mother, the renewing and transforming woman pours over us the renewing waters of graciousness. The virgin mother is the mother who *cares*.

The human existential need, which opens us up to the limit-experience of woman as inspiration, transformation, and renewal, is the limit-experience of weariness. It is related to the experience of death anxiety described in the previous chapter but distinct from it. When we are weary "in the middle course of life" (as Dante has put it), or indeed at any other course of life, it is impossible to surmount the ennui of routine, monotony, mediocrity, ordinariness, the mundaneness of our life. The sheer boredom of our everyday life drags us down into a rut from which it seems impossible to get out. "Oh, weary, weary is the world." Our vitality is spent, our exuberance is gone, our creative energies are exhausted; the muse (literally, in this case) no longer speaks to us. There seems no point in trying because everything we do is doomed to failure. It is at this stage of the game that we are open to renewing experiences in the sense that we desperately need such experiences. We may fall in love—wisely or not—or fall back into love again as we rediscover (perhaps for the first time) our old love. We may be caught in a numinous experience, perhaps one of ecstasy, which draws us up out of ourselves, renewed, reinvigorated, transformed. Mary, the virgin mother, is the Christian symbol that illuminates our weariness, our discouragement, our frustration, and draws us in tenderly and compassionately to an experience which inspires and transforms us, gives us new life. She is the virgin mother presiding over our rebirth, just as in the birth of Jesus she presided over the rebirth of humanity.

What is it about Being that is revealed to us in these limit-experiences of transformation, which run the full range from falling in love to mystical ecstasy? When the thing becomes a symbol and in that becoming renews us, what is the grace that is given? What is the

insight that is provided? The virgin mother as renewing sacrament—
what aspect of the androgynous deity does she reflect upon us?

The renewal experience is essentially an experience of fidelity.
Ecstatic, mystical experiences are brief, numinous instants in which
we see the whole purpose of the universe converging, and we see our
place in it. It all *does* make sense; there *is* a purpose; there *are*
promises which are being kept. That which in a limit-experience is
revealed as life-giving love through the madonna aspect of the Mary
symbol is now revealed as faithful love, love with plan and purpose,
love which does not repent of the promises it has made, love which
draws us up out of ourselves and integrates us into its dazzling unity,
love which bathes us with joy, serenity, peace, confidence, and
sometimes even literally heat and light. After such an experience,
weariness and discouragement are no longer possible; we have been
transformed precisely because the old structures of perception trapped
us in the mud and mire of weariness and randomness, and they have
been reintegrated into a new structure of confidence. Before the
experience, everything seemed random, loose, unintegrated. There
was no animating spirit at work—no wisdom, no sense in the casual,
disordered phenomena of our life. Now, after the experience, we have
a whole new constellation of perceptions in which we see purpose
animated by gentle and powerful love, and we see ourselves integrated
into that purpose. To love life is not purposeless, aimless, useless; not
unintelligent, not blind; it is rather directed, purposeful, concerned,
involved with us.

One need not undergo such an ecstatic experience of the numinous
to be renewed, inspired, transformed. Nor need the limit-experience
be a shattering once-and-for-all event, for there is transformation and
renewal in everyday life. It need not necessarily be associated with
sexual differentiation, though that is indeed a powerful and important
occasion for transformation and renewal. A gentle breeze at the end of
a hot day, a rain shower at the end of a dry summer, the first warm
breath of spring after months of cold, the smile on a child's face when
we come home after a hard day's work, a kind word from someone we
have helped are all revelatory of the existence of a reality that is "full
of grace." The Mary symbol deepens, enriches, reinforces, and
illuminates these episodes of transformation and rebirth that are
available to us in our everyday life, if only we are willing to pause to

consider them. It is not all vain and purposeless. Our efforts are not wasted; we are reborn, we can start again.

The illumination that invades our personality in the restructuring of our perception in the limit-experience of spiritual transformation is the illumination of trust. One can trust the cosmos because the cosmos and the purpose behind it are reflected to us in the transforming experience of the protective, revitalizing virgin mother. If one can trust the ultimate, if one can trust the universe, if one can trust life, then one can trust one's fellow humans—not naïvely, not innocently, not without caution and sophistication certainly, but it is not necessary any longer to cut oneself off in alienation, isolation, fearful cynicism and suspicion. You can risk yourself in relationships with others because even if you get hurt, the tender virgin mother, reflecting the tender, renewing God, will drape her great blue mantle around you in protection. Your heart may break if you risk yourself in trust; Mary will put the pieces back together again.

This is not merely sentiment. Mary protecting us under her mantle is an image that reflects the protective power of life-giving, life-renewing love. To believe in the virgin mother's protective mantle is to believe in love. To dismiss that protective mantle as a meaningless, sentimental image is to reject the notion that there is life-renewing love at work in the cosmos. One may not like the imagery of the virgin's mantle, of course, but one must recognize that such imagery is rooted in the sacred Scriptures, persistent throughout the whole Christian religion, virtually universal in the more developed forms of paganism, and, if we are to believe the Jungians, rooted in the depths of the human unconscious—or, if we prefer Eliade, rooted in the structure of common human experience. Dispense with Mary's blue mantle, if you wish, but understand that it is a powerful image of the protective power of the transforming goddess.

If it is possible to trust, then it is possible to make commitments which are permanent and which will not be withdrawn when one grows weary, frustrated, and discouraged. These commitments can be made to other human beings, particularly to a spouse, parents, children. They can be made to friends, organizations, careers, vocations. One does not abandon a career or a vocation merely because one is tired of it—at least not if one is open to the limit-experience of spiritual transformation.[8]

One can also make commitments to causes not out of immaturity but out of maturity, not out of weakness but out of strength, not out of fear but out of confidence, not out of suspicion and hatred but out of trust and love. When the cause for which one stands receives frustration, setback, failure—as do all causes—then one has the resourcefulness, the resilience, the strength to bounce back and start over. He who has been through a decisive limit-experience of transformation and renewal knows that quitting is a luxury he cannot afford and an escape he does not want. Mary, the inspiring, transforming, renewing virgin mother, from whom came the Christian worldview—the most decisive of renewal experiences, the rebirth of humankind—incarnates and symbolizes the human capacity to be transformed and renewed and the divine love at work in the world striving to transform and renew our troubled, battered, weary souls when we are caught in the frustrations and discouragements of "the middle course of life," whenever that middle course might be.

One can reject the possibility of renewal; one can deny that there is any transforming, inspiring force at work in the universe. Then the virgin mother full of grace will seem a deceptive and foolish symbol. But if you do reject the virgin mother, reject her on the grounds that you do not believe in the possibility of renewal and transformation, that you do not believe in a life-restoring, life-transforming love at work in the universe. Reject Mary because you believe that weariness is the revelation of things the way they really are, that suspicion and cynicism are more appropriate responses to the human condition than trust and commitment. These are very plausible grounds for dismissing Mary full of grace as a relevant, outmoded, and deceptive symbol. But do not dismiss her because of what some nun told you in grammar school about patent leather shoes or low necklines, or what some priest preached to you at retreat about "impure thoughts." Do not dismiss her as a frigid, negative sex goddess; do not dismiss her as a fertility idol demanding from you as many children as possible. Do not dismiss her in the name of a pop Freudianism which believes that orgasmic satisfaction is the only thing in sex that really matters. None of these false images of Mary or oversimplified bits of conventional wisdom have anything to do with what the virgin mother full of grace really stands for. Men and women who are striving to work out their relationships at a time when sex roles are being reexamined can see the virgin mother as a by no means irrelevant religious symbol, for she stands as a rock-hard sign that transformation, rebirth, renewal is possible in a human life and in a human relationship.

Under normal circumstances, a renewal experience of sufficient power to shatter our weariness and restore our confidence in the fidelity of Being will come out of our marriage relationship. If a man cannot inspire and renew his wife and if a wife cannot renew and inspire her husband, then renewal and inspiration will not be likely for either of them. Some relationships have deteriorated so badly that there is simply nothing left. In others, there was nothing to begin with, and in still others the psychological incapacities of one or both partners are such that the relationship cannot become one of renewal or rebirth without major and lengthy psychotherapy at least. Still, we cannot sit around waiting for the numinous to invade our personalities in a full-blown ecstatic experience; nor can we expect that the casual love affair, for all its exciting and invigorating promise, will really do anything more than divert us from the weariness and discouragement of our lives. In ordinary circumstances, renewal is not to be found elsewhere—in another lover, another job, a trip to the Orient, or an interlude in a monastery (Buddhist or Christian). It is normally to be found by seeking the transforming and renewing the elements in one's present environment. One of the most lamentable aspects of the human condition is that we carry our psychic environments with us. Everywhere we go becomes eventually just like the place before. Whatever love we have becomes eventually very like the last one.

Husbands and wives in the "middle course of life" remain skeptical about the possibility of change, renewal, transformation. Cynicism, suspicion, sophistication (usually of the pseudo variety) all lead them to ridicule the notion that anything can change in their relationship. It is absurd and foolish to think that there is even the faintest trace of potential for rebirth and renewal. Things are what they are and they are what they are going to be; nothing can change them. The woman has long since abandoned any notion of inspiring her husband. She is content to coexist, to accept, and to nag intermittently (or perhaps interminably). The husband expects no inspiration from his relationship with his wife. All the mystery, allure, and fascination has gone out of her. He takes her for granted. She is commonplace, ordinary, part of the environment. There may be no conflict of magnitude, no tensions which threaten to destroy the relationship, but nothing much exciting is left in it either, and both have become indignant and perhaps even angry at the suggestion that there was any possibility of transformation, inspiration, romance, mystery, discovery, adventure in their relationship. To inspire one's spouse, to renew and to restore, to give oneself over to the revitalizing and renewing mystery that is one's spouse require imagination, confidence, and openness of the sort that is all too rare at any time in life.

Mary, the renewing virgin mother full of grace, stands as an implacable symbol that renewal is possible, that one can begin again just as humankind did when Jesus came into the world. One can trust, one can take risks, one can begin to explore the mysterious, the numinous, which lurks just beneath the surface of the most ordinary and the most everyday, the most routine and the most matter of fact, the most commonplace. Man and woman may not want to take the image of the virgin mother of Bethlehem as a symbol to illuminate the possibility of renewal and to underpin and reinforce the efforts at renewal. They may not believe that the cosmic renewal experience at Bethlehem makes possible the transforming limit-experiences in their own relationship. If they do not wish to believe that, it is their privilege, of course. If they feel that the image of virgin mother is absurd as a symbol by which they can renew their love, then one cannot argue with them and would not try to persuade them.

They may well assert that a symbol which has stood for sexual oppression in their childhood can hardly be expected now to serve as a symbol of sexual playfulness.[9] In fact, whatever they may say, it is still the case that the virgin mother is a symbol for renewal, of beginning again, of starting all over again; it is a symbol of possibility. Mary as the protector of sexual playfulness in an ever-renewing relationship between husband and wife may be offensive to puritans and ridiculous to those who think all possibility of renewal has gone out of their relationship. Mary as the protector and proponent of renewal through sexual playfulness is consistent with the very deepest meanings of the Mary myth. Mary supports renewal, rebirth, starting all over, beginning again wherever such frightening, fascinating, wonderful experiences are to be found. Falling in love again, we are told by those who have done it, is much more fun than the first time around. Similarly, being born again was a much greater adventure for the human race than being born for the first time.

Venantius sings of the glory of the virgin mother who renews the cosmos:

> Where troops of virgins follow the Lamb
> Through the streets of the golden city,
> Who is she walks in the lily throng
> Clothed with the sun,
> Her mantle flowing like an azure wave
> To the jewel pavement?
> High in her arms for all to adore
> She holds a Man-Child.
> She leads the mystic song that swells and soars
> Like the noise of many waters,
> With the voice of her own *Magnificat*.
> The glory of virgins is she, a maiden mother.
> O Mary, where your Jesus leads, you follow,
> The first of pearl-pure human souls.
> The prize that reckless Eve has tossed away,
> You stretch a generous hand to give again,
> And draw the earth's sad exiles
> To their promised land of joy.
> O doorway of the mighty King!
> O radiant threshold of His light!
> Life-giving Virgin!
> Nations redeemed praise you with jubilation.
> Jesus, Son of Mary,
> Father and loving Spirit,
> Glory to You forever and ever. Amen.

"O Glory of Virgins" (*O gloriosa virginum*)
by Venantius Fortunatus (530–609)
(Translated from the Latin by Sister Maura)

A medieval German bard sees Mary passing through the forest with blossoms of renewal springing up in her wake:

> Mary went through the thorn-wood wild;
> Mary went through the thorn-wood wild
> That had borne no blossom for seven years.
>
> What did she carry beneath her heart?
> Without a pang—a little child
> She carried gently beneath her heart.

And on the thorn-boughs roses stood
As she carried the sweet child through the wood;
Upon the thorn-boughs roses stood.

> "Mary Passes"
> (*Maria durch den Dornewald ging*)

The strange, complex, half-mad genius Savonarola sees Mary renewing the city of Florence after the plague has passed:

O Star of Galilee,
Shining over earth's dark sea,
Shed thy glorious light on me.

Queen of clemency and love,
Be my advocate above,
And through Christ all sin remove.

When the angel called thee blest,
And with transports filled thy breast,
Thy high Lord became thy guest.

Earth's purest creature thou,
In the heavens exulting now,
With a halo round thy brow.

Beauty beams in every trace
Of the Virgin-Mother's face,
Full of glory and of grace—

A Beacon to the just,
To the sinner hope and trust,
Joy of the angel-host.

Ever-glorified, thy throne
Is where thy blessed Son
Doth reign: through Him alone,

All pestilence shall cease,
And sin and strife decrease,
And the kingdom come of peace.

"O Star of Galilee" by GIROLAMO SAVONAROLA (1452–1498)
(Translated from the Latin by R. R. Madden)

Shelley, in the midst of his incorrigible love affair with nature, sees Mary lurking behind transforming dynamisms of the world and pleads with her to eliminate the imperfections of his work:

> Seraph of Heaven! too gentle to be human,
> Veiling beneath that radiant form of Woman
> All that is insupportable in thee
> Of light, and love, and immortality!
> Sweet Benediction in the eternal Curse!
> Veiled Glory of this lampless Universe!
> Thou Moon beyond the clouds! Thou living Form
> Among the Dead! Thou Star above the Storm!
> Thou Wonder, and thou Beauty, and thou Terror!
> Thou Harmony of Nature's art! Thou Mirror
> In whom, as in the splendor of the Sun,
> All shapes look glorious which thou gazest on!
> Ay, even the dim words which obscure thee now
> Flash, lightninglike, with unaccustomed glow;
> I pray thee that thou blot from this sad song
> All of its much mortality and wrong,
> With those clear drops, which start like sacred dew
> From the twin lights thy sweet soul darkens through,
> Weeping, till sorrow becomes ecstasy:
> Then smile on it, so that it may not die.

> > "Seraph of Heaven" (From *Epipsychidion,* lines 21–40)
> > by PERCY BYSSHE SHELLEY (1792–1822)

Henry Adams, having looked at the smile on the Virgin of Chartres and having prayed ironically to the Dynamo, comes back to the Virgin to pray "Before your majesty of grace and love,/ The purity, the beauty and the faith;/ The depth of tenderness beneath; above,/ The glory of the life and of the death." He prays to her now as he imagines he prayed once before with Saint Bernard and Saint Louis:

> Help me to see! not with my mimic sight—
>   With yours! which carried radiance, like the sun,
> Giving the rays you saw with—light in light—
>   Tying all suns and stars and worlds in one.

> Help me to know! not with my mocking art—
>   With you, who knew yourself unbound by laws;
> Gave God your strength, your life, your sight, your heart,
>   And took from him the Thought that Is—the Cause.

Help me to feel! not with my insect sense,—
  With yours that felt all life alive in you;
Infinite heart beating at your expense;
  Infinite passion breathing the breath you drew!

Help me to bear! not my own baby load,
  But yours; who bore the failure of the light,
The strength, the knowledge and the thought of God,—
  The futile folly of the Infinite!

"Prayer to the Virgin of Chartres"
by HENRY ADAMS (1838–1918)

It may be Chicago chauvinism on my part, but my favorite image of the mystical transforming virgin is the El Greco *Assumption* in the Chicago Art Institute. The lovely Spanish girl with her broadly flowing red and blue robes is lifted up to renewing heaven, and at the same time she bathes in new light the whole world beneath her. And one can go back to the fifth-century praying Virgin at the archbishop's palace at Ravenna to see the outstretched arms of the virgin mother looking very much like Sophia or a Greek muse or a Cretan goddess of renewal from two millennia before. Clearly, her arms are outstretched in a plea for protection for all of us who are desperately trying to survive and renew ourselves. Roger van der Weyden's Virgin as intercessor is praying for us that we might be renewed, that we might be able to start over again. The beautiful woman being crowned by Jesus and the Father in Velasquez's *Coronation of the Virgin* represents the renewed, revivified humankind if anyone ever has. And in both El Greco's and Michelangelo's *Last Judgments* we see Mary, the tender, renewing, protecting mother, interceding for us against the stern punishments of divine justice.[10]

The virgin mother stands for a second chance. In pagan antiquity, in the depths of the human psyche, in the structures of human experience, in the renewed humankind depicted by the paintings of El Greco and Velasquez, in the passionate plea for protection from such diverse characters as Shelley and Savonarola, and in the vision of the possibility of renewal in the medieval German singer, and the tired, weary New England aristocrat, Henry Adams.

It is possible to start over again, to begin anew, to be reborn.

If only we were not so tired.

Fair is the hue of your mantle, Mary—
  (Take me to shelter, take me to hide!)
From the deep skies of Heaven it drank all its color,
  In the deep pools of Heaven my mantle was dyed.

Fine is the cloth of your mantle, Mary—
  (Take me to shelter, take me to hide!)
Ah, careful was the carding and careful the spinning,
  And piteous the shearing of my dear Lamb's side.

Warm is the web of your mantle, Mary—
  (Take me to shelter, take me to hide!)
It is woven of rare wool, woven of fair wool—
  The soft white fleece of my Lamb Who died.

Draped like a queen's is your mantle, Mary—
  (Take me to shelter, take me to hide!)
Yea, God hath exalted His handmaid, Who made me
  Mother of His Word and His Spirit's bride.

Full are the folds of your mantle, Mary—
  (Take me to shelter, take me to hide!)
That all generations be shielded and succored,
  The cloak of their Mother is a deep cloak and wide.

Ah, wrap me around with your mantle, Mary—
  (Take me to shelter, take me to hide!)
Child of my sword-pierced soul, I shall guard you,
  Little blood-brother of the Crucified.

> "The Mantle of Mary"
> —PATRICK O' CONNOR (1899–   )*

Virgo

Experience of Sexual Differentiation	Transforming, inspiring, renewing
Biological Origin	Arousal, heightened consciousness (face-eyes)

*Appeared in *I Sing of a Maiden: The Mary Book of Verse* by Sister M. Therese (New York: Macmillan, 1947), p. 320.

Cognate Symbols	Moon, lotus, lily
Ancient Goddesses	Shakti, Kwan-yin, Muse, Sophia, Tara
Type	Eve, the beginning
Mary Symbol	Virgin full of grace, the new beginning
Existential Need	Weariness
Limit-Experience	Renewal, transformation
Grace That Is Given	Implacable fidelity of life-giving love, which is also life-renewing
Illumination—Restructuring of Perceptions	Trust
Action	Commitment
Man-Woman Implication	Both man and woman can inspire and renew, and can surrender to inspiration and renewal
Poem	Percy Bysshe Shelley, "Seraph of Heaven"
Plastic Art	El Greco, *The Assumption*

Sponsa

Gardener in a Bikini
(For Norman and Lou and the boys down at the harbor)

Not a full-blown classic nude
Nor an overdressed, fluffy Victorian
But Earth Mother on the American Plan
Brown, tall, supple
Womanly splendors taut and trim
Lithe nakedness made even more appealing
   by a few ounces of pale blue cloth
And tenuous bits of string.

Girlish allurements to be enjoyed
But not in passive repose
Neither statue nor bathing beauty
But Cybele in movement, most seductive
With youthful body hard at work
In the vigorous ordering of your garden.

Ethnic Venus with a swinging hoe
Each disciplined movement of arm and handle
Hip and thigh, a creamy tasty delight
Even to the angels who pause in work
   to marvel at the Creator's designing wit
And enjoy the noontime show.

Middle western nymph, cool, poised, confident
Heedlessly unaware and yet proudly aware
   of your own unclothed loveliness
Slender waist, long tan legs,
Flat belly, soft and shapely shoulders,
Curving back, caressed by a single lucky strap
A public indecency in most ages past

Now a familiar scenic attraction
On any summer day.

Engineered, machined, mass produced? Well, maybe
But the boys in the slow moving cars don't mind
As they envy the roses their start of delight
    when you swiftly bend over them
To dispatch an offending weed
And your rich full breasts
Push against thin blue restraint
Eager to spill out among the flowers
And dim the luster of their blossoms
While your rounded derriere stretches tight
The snug bikini bottom
And invites a friendly swat
From every passing male.

Elegant and delectable innocent
Sexy, bouncy and a good gardener too
Free as few women have ever been
To sport unclad in the summer sunlight
To be yourself, to reach for life
To be mistress of your own fullness
Come a long way, but expecting much more
Inviting affection, promising pleasure, demanding happiness
A big demand and requiring more from you
    than piebald breasts and saucy tail
(Though in truth they will surely help)
And much from the rest of us too.

Yet you know little of life and love
And nothing of suffering and old age
The bittersweet pleasures and the numbing pains
    that too quickly dim the youthful glow
Nor will you escape the greedy death
Which already has turned the leaves you rake
A dry and dusty brown.

But at this garden noon, I do not doubt
That the beauty from which you came
Captivated by his(her) own creation

Seduced by his(her) own seduction
Will fall victim to your active charms
And be caught in his(her) own trip of love.
Your grace will never end.

A. M. G.

Chapter 7
Sponsa
Ave Maris Stella

The Madonna and Virgo symbols both deal with the giving of life. That which is beneath and beyond and within and outside of everything both gives life and renews it. The mother is the source of physical life, the virgin mother the source of spiritual renewal. The other two images, Sponsa and Pietà, are "death" images. The Pietà receives us in loving tenderness back into the womb of the earth at the end of life; the Sponsa, the seductress, deprives us of the individuality and the rationality of life in the frenzy of orgasmic release. Orgasm is a kind of death in that our other interests and concerns, even the other functions of our bodies, are temporarily suspended as our whole beings concentrate on the release that comes from sexual union. For a brief instant it is almost as though we have stopped living and have completely been absorbed by the elementary biological forces of the universe. With the Pietà we experience permanent death, and whether it is pleasurable or not remains to be seen.

Just as there is considerable difficulty in adjusting our perspective to understand the relevance to the contemporary world of Mary as virgin mother, so there are difficulties and obstacles that must be eliminated before we can understand Mary as a symbol of the limit-experience of sexual differentiation as manifested in sexual passion. It might be argued that Mary didn't have sexual intercourse, so how could she possibly symbolize the intercourse experience, particularly since Catholic Christianity has maintained, and apparently still maintains, that it is better not to have sexual intercourse than to have it? Indeed, the church even once maintained through some of its greatest theologians that sexual intercourse was sinful even between husband and wife if it was done "merely" for pleasure.

Physical desire is the most obvious, the most demanding, the most disturbing, and the most intensely pleasurable aspect of sexual differentiation. Spiritual love, transformation, constant mutual renewal may have more long-run psychological payoff; they may also be essential for the creation of a context of relationship in which physical love may survive and develop. Nonetheless, for sheer intensity of pleasure, orgasm simply can't be beat—a phenomenon that must have been obvious to the human race from the very first time it began to reflect on anything. There is good and bad sex, of course; still, bad sex is better than no sex, and about this bit of folk wisdom there is no disagreement.

The overwhelming power and pleasure of physical union between the sexes was obviously sacred to early humankind. It was terrifying and frightening in its capacity to absorb the total concern of the individual. When its furies were released the fragile social structure of the primitive tribe or the archaic village could be torn apart. A band of hunters or warriors or shepherds returned to the camp with just one thing in mind: they wanted women. If it was their own camp, their own women would do; but if it was the camp of another tribe, their women would do too. Nothing else mattered until this primal need was satisfied. Sexuality might indeed be something sacred, but it was the source of the fertility which kept life going; but it was also sacred because of the terrifying strength of its demands, the intensity of its pleasures and the temporary destruction of the capacity to do anything else when caught in the heat of sexual arousal.[1]

Lust is the passionate desire for union with the body of a member of the opposite sex. It is, of course, fundamentally a matter of hormone levels in our bloodstreams, but since humankind is an interpreting animal, one who of necessity gives meaning to all his experiences, lust and the tension release which satisfies it are far more than biological and physiological phenomena. Because of their intense power and force, they are interpreted and given meaning within a context of sacredness.

The various fertility goddesses could easily be transformed into goddesses of orgy and orgasm. Festivals in honor of Lilith, Astarte,

Aphrodite, and Venus may have begun primarily with a concern about integrating humanity into the fertility process of the universe; but the ritual intercourse frequently involved in such cults was undoubtedly pleasurable. As human religions evolved, in many cases the ritual intercourse became an end in itself. To please the goddess of fertility and to integrate oneself into the life-giving processes was distinctly a matter of secondary and often unremembered importance as the fertility cults developed—or decayed.

Once a ritual or a festival became identified with the breaking down of sexual restraints that were necessary to keep a community together, the breaking down became the important phenomenon and its ritual significance was easily forgotten. We gather on New Year's Eve to celebrate the end of an old year and the beginning of a new one; but after a while, that's hardly the name of the game. We go off to New Orleans at Mardi Gras time to prepare for Lent. Similarly, what remains of the *Carnivale* in Europe, particularly in Germany, may in principle also be a preparation for Lent—but who keeps Lent anymore?

So, too, the rites marking the change of the season—the winter and summer solstices, the vernal and autumnal equinoxes—are theoretical times when one celebrates the death and rebirth of the god of light, while at the same time commemorating the harvest, the vintage, and the eventual promise of the return of nature. As events dealing with light, fertility, and life, these four seasonal changes easily became involved with sexual differentiation, and with an understandable leap, with rituals of sexual release. The pent-up and repressed sexual energies of the society were unleashed first of all to unite oneself and one's society with the primal reproductive powers of the cosmos, but also, secondarily, to provide socially legitimate escape from sexual tensions. By the time of the Saturnalia, as we know it in the Roman Republic and Empire, the primitive and archaic religious overtones were long since lost. The Saturnalia was a feast of lust in which one worshiped (if that is the word) sexual pleasure. As a social function, it doubtless had a utility of a sort, but any connection with the old fertility rites of the mother goddess was vestigial. The immense power and pleasure of sexual release was honored, and the sexual goddesses like Venus and Aphrodite became the most important feminine deities in the pantheon. Lots of people had a rip-roaring good time.

I would not suggest that ritual orgies were without religious experience. On the contrary, the breaking down of barriers and the reversal of roles were a return to primal undifferentiation, a return to the *coincidentia oppositorum* which was supposed to mark the Beginning. There was religious and cosmological symbolism as well as the release of social tensions in a festival in which sexual limitations and restrictions were swept away. Furthermore, there was surely a valid religious insight that lust reflects a divine power in humankind; but as we moderns need little imagination to realize, it was very easy for the religious dimension of orgasmic festivals to get lost. Was Venus a goddess to be worshiped or simply a girl to be lusted after? For most people she was probably both, but in very uneven proportions.

The religious insight about the divine aspects of lust go back almost to the dawn of human religion as we know it, insofar as we know anything about it. In some religions the physical world emerged as the result of intercourse between the male and the female deity. In others, it is the lust of the divine beings for one another that produces the rebirth of spring each year, and in still others it is lust and passion between a particular people and its god—whether that god be male or female—that ensures the survival and perpetuation of the tribe. The continuation of its harvest and its vintages were in fact the result of intercourse (sometimes ritually reenacted with temple priestesses) between the deity and its people. The Israelites were not the first people to imagine that their god had embarked on a love affair with them. What was unusual about the divine romance with Israel was not the romance but the god who had fallen in love so passionately with his people.

Nor is it in principle an unreasonable assumption about the deity that with the exception of hunger and the protection of one's life there are no human passions anywhere near as powerful as the desire for sexual release when aroused. The sweating, writhing, screaming frenzy of a man and woman in the final stages of intercourse is evidence of how fierce and furious is sexual desire. Something that strong, humankind has argued traditionally, must give us some hints about whatever is ultimate, absolute, and final. If lust is powerful and God is powerful, then there may well be some kind of lust in God, or some thing in God which is powerful in him as lust is in us. But what could be the object of divine lust? It might be other deities, or it might be individual human maidens with whom the god becomes enamored, or it might be the whole of his creation, particularly his people. Lust is the desire for unity, the desire to merge one's personality, however transiently, with another's, to lose oneself in the breaking down of the barrier of sexual differentiation, to form a oneness out of two fleshes. If God craved unity the way we crave the body of another, then who was the object of his craving for unity? The answer was a startling, and it must have seemed blasphemous to many, insight: God craved union with us. Once people began to think that way, a decisive revolution had occurred in human religious consciousness. It might be a long time before the kind of God who had fallen in love with his creatures would be the sort of person you would invite to your house for supper. After all, many of those lusty, roustabout, horny gods of antiquity were thoroughly disreputable characters. Yahweh, as in other things, was something else altogether. It was not the bodies of your maidens or your matrons He wanted; it was the whole personality, body and soul, of the people. As time went on, it became clear that he wanted the whole personality, body and soul, of each individual of the people. Yahweh lusted not after our bodies but after us, and then, religiously speaking, it became a whole new game.

So the people became the bride of Yahweh, and Israel, God's people, became personified as the Daughter of Zion for whom Yahweh felt a passionate lust, a lust which would produce eventually a messiah, who in his turn would preside over Yahweh's messianic age. We may have come a long way from orgies at the temple of Venus to Yahweh's passion for the Daughter of Zion. The religious thought has been transformed obviously, refined and elevated; but the imagery and the religious insight are fundamentally the same: in God's relationship to us, there is something like the passionate longing that we feel at the height of our lust for the body of one who is sexually different from us. God may be the passionate aggressive male pursuing us in a frenzy of sexual arousal (and such images are frequent enough in the later prophets of the Old Testament), or he may be a woman tempting us, teasing us, leading us on alternately discouraging and encouraging us, promising, revealing, hiding, disclosing, covering, uncovering, but always enticing us. Whether God is the passionate aggressor or the passionate temptress, the message is the same: God wants us and he is leading us on or pursuing us toward eventual union.

In the Old Testament the image of the Daughter of Zion is the corporate personality, Israel, which is the object of Yahweh's passionate love. In the New Testament and later Mariology it is Mary who is the individual person for whom God felt a passionate attraction. This merely conveys the age-old human insight that God loves us with a power and force and strength that makes human sexual arousal look mild and moderate by comparison. A man pursuing the body of a woman who has utterly enthralled him (captivated, imprisoned, captured—whatever other similar word of enslavement might be appropriate) so that nothing will stand in his way or stop him until he has merged his body with hers is a weak and meek thing compared to the way the absolute feels about us. A woman who uses every guile and wile and attractiveness, every inch of her flesh, every curve of her body to capture a man she passionately wants looks modest when compared with the wanton deity who has created the entire glorious universe to attract and seduce us.

This religious insight may be offensive to some and absurd to others, but it is what Mary, the Daughter of Zion, with whom Yahweh has fallen in love, represents. We may reject as ridiculous the notion that God feels about us the way we do about a man or a woman in the height of sexual arousal. Things *cannot* be that way; it would either be offensive or ludicrous. For some, the image of a sexually aroused God is dirty, for others, it is altogether too good to be true, and we know better than to believe it. However, such an image is still one of the fundamental themes of the Yahwistic religion, and it is captured for Christianity by the symbol of Mary, Daughter of Zion.

The symbols can be played in two directions. We can think of God as a sexual attacker aggressively pursuing us, or we can think of God as the sensual temptress seductively attracting us. Once one concedes the androgyny of God, either approach is valid; or, more properly, both approaches are valid. Indeed such is the case in many human love affairs where the pursuer is pursued. The sexually attacking male, if he has any skills at all, is teasing, arousing, enticing; and the sexually tempting female, if she has any wiles at all, knows when to stop being passive and take the offensive. Our religious insight as Christians leads us to believe that God, too, plays the game both ways.

If there is a God, it is surely the case that he both seduces and attacks us, both tempts us and pursues us. We may be horrified to think of him in such a way either because we think that such a God is inappropriate, or (and more correctly it seems to me) because such a God is too frightening. Of course there is no obligation to think of God that way. One can conceptualize the deity in any way one wants. The point is that if one concedes there is a God involved in the human condition, the image of temptation and pursuit becomes inevitable. If you don't like the image, don't use it, but to deny its validity and inevitability you have got to deny either the existence of passionate love at the core of the universe or assert that there is such a passionate love but that for some inexplicable reason it doesn't care much about us.

So Mary is the spouse of Yahweh, the one after whom Yahweh lusts. But each of us is the spouse of Yahweh, and whether we want to think of God as feminine or masculine, as attacking us or tempting us, is entirely a matter of our own personal religious choice and taste. God as the pursuing male is an image that is open and explicit in the Christian religion; but God as the woman, attractive, charming, fascinating, is also strongly pictured in the Christian heritage through the Mary myth. Mary reveals God to us as alluring, tempting, charming, arousing, attracting.

The existential need as a prelude to the limit-experience of an encounter with a passionately aroused Being is, I think, a combination of alienation, constriction, restraint, loneliness. We are cut off; we are alone; we are isolated; we are alienated; we are hemmed in, restricted, hung up, constrained by our own fears, anxieties, suspicions, skepticism, cynicism. We then encounter a thing which invades our personality, attracts our attention, demands our interest, arouses our wonder and awe, and consumes us with its "being-ness." The thing, whatever it is, becomes a symbol for us, a sacrament, a revelation of gifted-ness precisely insofar as it can momentarily command our whole attention, attract our whole selfhood, and impose upon us the obligation to abandon ourselves to it completely. That thing-turned-symbol under the influence of Mary as Sponsa can be almost anything. Most obviously it will be a member of the opposite sex, but even the grass growing on the dune can invade me, take me over, absorb my attention, and demand that for a few moments at least, I become abandoned to it, totally absorbed by the wonder and marvel of its being, possessed by its attractiveness, entranced by its graciousness, dominated by the goodness for which it is a sacrament.

In the act of abandoning myself through the gift of the thing-turned-symbol, I abandon my old structures of perception. They are shattered. It is no longer necessary to be restrained, constricted, cut off, suspicious. Having given myself over to this being, I can, if I will, give myself over to Being. The new structures of perception which emerge from the limit-experience are looser, more open, more flexible, more sensitive, more in communion with other things. I now approach the world not with fear, suspicion, or inhibition but with joy, liberation, abandonment.

In lovemaking there comes a point when abandonment of some sort takes over. The proprieties, the decencies, the restraints drop away and basic, elemental urges dominate. When that point of abandonment is reached, both partners know that they will couple. There is nothing tentative, preliminary, or preparatory left. The situation is to a considerable extent, though not completely, of course, dominated by the biology and physiology of their bodies. They have "let go"; they have "turned on"; they have yielded themselves more or less willingly, more or less skillfully, more or less gracefully, more or less pleasurably to one another. The surge of liberation, of abandonment, of letting go in intercourse is paradigmatic of the letting go which happens in the limit-experience.[2]

When abandonment of any sort becomes a limit-experience, a sacrament of grace, a revelation, through the impact on us of the being of the thing to which we have given ourself, then there is revealed to us the glorious gift and liberating seductiveness and passion of the ultimate. In the limit-experience of abandoning ourself, we encounter the other, which has both attracted and pursued us into this act of abandonment. We have met only life-giving love, not only life-renewing love but now also pursuing and attracting love, challenging and demanding love, love which wishes to absorb us, love which invites us to lose our self in it, love which demands abandonment and which repays our abandonment with freedom.

Freedom is the illumination offered to us through our restructured perceptions when we permit ourselves to fall under the spell of Mary, Daughter of Zion, the beloved Sponsa of Yahweh. If the world is animated by a passionate lover, the cosmos is directed by a seductive temptress; if our life is dominated and guided by one who is calling us to ever greater love, then there is nothing to be afraid of. Oh, we still have our fears, our existential fear of nothingness, our fear of death, our inhibitions. Our neurotic little fears that we so carefully preserve from childhood are real enough, but they do not cut us off from others, they do not imprison us, they do not bog us down, they do not constrict or restrain us. We have abandoned ourselves to a goodness that we have encountered and experienced, to a grace that has taken possession of us; and we are free to live and love and laugh and rejoice.

So much of our life is constraint. We are afraid of what others will say, afraid of what will happen. We are afraid of losing the few things we have acquired. We fear having our defenses swept away, of being stripped naked psychologically to stand revealed as utterly worthless, a "no thing." If we give ourselves over to joy and freedom, all these precious things we have will be lost, and from being a "no thing" we will slip into nonbeing; we will merely die, we will cease to exist.

Mary, the Daughter of Zion, Mary, the beloved Sponsa of God, Mary the Bride of Yahweh, stands as a symbol that exactly the opposite possibility is available to us. If we merely abandon ourselves to the passionate goodness in the universe, if we say with her, "Be it done unto me according to Thy word," then we become free. (This is, incidentally, a long process, not a single decision. It may require and can coexist with a therapeutic experience.)

If you are imprisoned in the chains of your own fear, then there is nothing to celebrate, but if you are liberated by a love that captivates your heart, then not only can you celebrate, you must celebrate. Mary the Madonna moves us to the action of protecting and enriching the world, Mary the Virgin moves us to the sustained commitment to the people of the world, and Mary the Sponsa moves us to joyous celebration of the glories of the world. It is of the nature of the symbol, as we observed in Chapter 2, that it moves us first to action and then to reflection. Our theologizing about the salvation revealed in the Daughter of Zion is not a precondition to our celebration. On the contrary, our lives of celebration are the phenomenon with which theology begins to reflect. Joy is a *locus theologicus,* an occasion for theologizing and not the result of it. In Luke's infancy narratives, Mary sings a hymn of praise; she does not write a doctoral dissertation or an article for a scholarly journal.

I spoke in an earlier chapter of the exuberance of the early Christians which permitted them to absorb so many of the good things they beheld in paganism and make them their own. The exuberance that resulted from their encounter with God proved hard to sustain. Some Christians still have it, of course, but to all too many Christians, Teresa of Avila's prayer that God "deliver us from sour-faced saints" still applies. Too many of us have lost our energy and our enthusiasm, our faith in the power of rationality, civility, liberal democracy, and scientific technology to humanize the planet. I am in categoric disagreement with the prophets of doom and the mad, self-destructive proponents of zero economic growth. I do not accept an economic or scientific analysis which views either natural resources or energy as vanishing from the planet. On the contrary, I think the evidence suggests just the opposite. There is reason for short-term concern, of course, about the expanding populations of certain countries of the world and the short-run supply of energy, particularly as long as the rulers of the oil-producing countries can casually threaten to demolish the world's economy. I certainly do not see any reason for us to be wasteful of resources either. There are problems of both environment and resources. There will likely be famine in the short run no matter how generous the developed countries are, there may be serious worldwide economic depression within a decade or so, and we could blunder into ecodisasters (though probably not anything like the ecodisaster of the Black Death). But over the long run there seems to be no solid economic reason to abandon faith in science, technology, civility, or the liberal democratic system. Indeed, as I read Robert Heilbroner, his problems are not ultimately political, social, or economic. He has lost his faith in human nature and human society.

My call for joy and celebration is not based on naïvete about the economic, environmental, and population problems of the world. Such problems are far more serious than many American Catholic Christians are willing to admit to themselves; they are not nearly as disastrous as some of the prophets of doom would claim. In the final analysis, however, Christian joy and celebration cannot be rooted in economic analysis. We rejoice in having abandoned ourselves in passionate love of an aggressive and seductive deity regardless of the economic and political outlook. We can chant the Magnificat to the Daughter of Zion even with the Black Death moving through the streets of our city.

If we as American Catholics think it is necessary to be gloomy to gain acceptance in some quarters—to be invited to Martha's Vineyard for a summer weekend among the disenchanted intellectual and cultural elites, for example—then by all means let us be gloomy, but let us also at least admit to ourselves that it's a game we are playing. We don't really mean it. Let us retreat into caves or catacombs at night, gather around the statue of the virgin and laugh and stamp our feet in joy. We fooled the prophets of doom once again. Let us never take the prophets of doom seriously, and heaven save us from taking ourselves seriously. Let us stand in the shadow of Mary, with her gentle, half-amused smile, and abandon ourselves to the exuberance and joy which comes from being Christian.

All this may not be your cup of tea. You may not enjoy abandoning yourself to celebration and exuberance. You may think there are too many things wrong with the world and with the human race to permit any expression less than sour to pass over your face. I shall not attempt to persuade you, but we shall miss you among Mary's company. You have misunderstood altogether what God revealed to us in his love for the Daughter of Zion.

Finally, if there is passion in the universe, indeed unrestrained passion which is both reflected in and the cause of human passion, then the passions we humans feel for one another have certainly been legitimated, reinforced, sanctified. If we are to abandon ourselves in joyous celebration to passionate being, then surely it is not only legitimate but virtuous to abandon ourselves in joyous celebration to one another. Granting that social conventions must necessarily restrain the raw, elemental power of sexual arousal from tearing society apart, and granting, too, that there will be differences of opinion and swings of fashion back and forth between restraint and liberty in the expression of social conventions, there are still no grounds in the Mary myth for prudery, puritanism, inhibition, frigidity in the relationship between husband and wife. On the contrary, the Mary myth incarnates the worldview which advocates joyous abandonment of restraint in the relationship between a man and woman who are committed to one another. Discretion, respect for privacy, good taste, sensitivity are all still required; but experimentation, playfulness, joyous abandonment ought to be characteristic of the sexual relationship of those who believe that God is a passionate lover, a ravisher, a seducer, a temptress all combined.

It is not always the case, and it has not always been the case. One need only read many of the great Christian theologians like St. Augustine to see that Platonic suspicion of human sexuality has pervaded Christian thinking for a long, long time. One need only recall the mission sermons of not so long ago to see that grass roots Christianity was pervaded by the worst kind of prudery and puritanism. There are no grounds for either Platonism or puritanism in the Christian symbol system and no grounds for it in the myth of Mary the Daughter of Zion after whom Yahweh lusted (if, in the New Testament, only as a corporate personality).

That both Platonism and puritanism survived as long as they did is merely evidence of how long it takes a new mythology, a new set of symbols to break the hold of an old worldview. The history of sexual thought in the Christian era has yet to be written. Most scholars who address themselves to it do so with little data and lots of preconceived notions. One of the few who have approached the matter with both an open mind and a respect for data is Herbert Richardson in his book *Nun, Witch and Playmate*.[3] Richardson argues that the emphasis on virginity in the Christian tradition was in fact a reaction against Platonic views of sexuality in the world of Hellenistic antiquity into which Christianity came. The human spirit was viewed as a slave, or at least a prisoner, of the physical body, particularly of its sexuality. Differentiation between the sexes was absolute, and the woman was absolutely inferior because she was more captive of her sex than the man and more likely to imprison him in the demands of her body. "Real" friendship was spiritual and only possible between members of one's own sex. One had a wife, of course, for release of sexual tension and so that the family might be perpetuated, but friendship was another matter. Often, of course, there were sexual overtones to the friendship, though Plato argued through Socrates that ideal friendship was independent of the body.

In Richardson's view of things, the Christian attitude was quite different. Sexual differentiation could be transcended, and men and women could be friends in the power of the Lord Jesus. It might be necessary for them both to be virginal in order to sustain such a friendship, but virginity was then seen, not as a judgment that sexuality was evil but an act of faith that in Jesus friendship was no longer constrained by sexual differentiation. It was out of this perspective, Richardson argues, that the courtly romantic love of the Middle Ages first emerged, with its emphasis on erotic but not genital sexuality; and then, in more recent times, the revolutionary notion that marriages and friendship could be combined. According to Richardson, virginity as a way of life was a step in a historical evolutionary process toward our present day notion of the combination of marriage, romantic sex, and friendship—an ideal toward which most humans are still striving.

There is a certain plausibility in his theory; it seems to fit the data currently available to us. But we should not forget another source of Christian faith and practice, besides the Platonism of the high theological tradition and the puritanism of some of the expressions of practical moral guidance, as Father Godfrey Dieckman has repeatedly insisted. If one looks at the liturgy, particularly the worship service around the celebration of marriage, one finds an entirely different set of themes. Marriage was a sacrament, a revelatory event. It disclosed the love of God for his people, the Church. There was no trace of puritanism, prudery, Platonism there. To the extent that there were any influences outside the Christian symbol system, they were from the relatively joyous paganism of the Teutonic and Celtic tribes, and not of the grim and glum paganism of the neo-Platonic empire. The mixture of old fertility and sexual practices with the new Christian symbols of God's love for his people and of the Church as the bride of Christ may have been uneven and uneasy, but apparently it never bothered the people themselves very much. There is still much research to do on this subject, and as far as I am aware, not many people are doing it. An interesting folk custom of peasant Poland is that the bride and groom recited the Magnificat after their first union. I am dazzled by the rich religious and sexual implications of such a custom. Doubtless, pagan fertility goddesses and goddesses of sexual love lurked around the marriage bed in pre-Christian times, but in this peasant custom, the Slavic versions of Aphrodite and Juno are dispatched by the Daughter of Zion, whose words are spoken by the bridal couple as they rejoice and give thanks to God over the union they have begun. There is no Platonism, no puritanism, and no paganism either in such a custom. In terms of the religious symbolism of the Mary myth, such a custom was profoundly right.

What of celibacy, then? What of those who choose to forgo orgasmic satisfaction and human love in marital intimacy? Richardson sees it as a step in the evolution of Christian thinking. Most Protestant Christians and an increasing number of Catholic Christians (perhaps even a majority) are now convinced that consecrated virginity is outmoded, that happiness, self-fulfillment, good physical and mental health require that one have a spouse. Some would even suggest that those who chose celibacy in the past were probably a bit strange, and those who choose it today, in a post-Freudian age, are crazy. Does my suggestion that Mary, the Daughter of Zion, the beloved of Yahweh, the revelation of God's passionate lust for his creatures, a symbol which can easily preside over joyous and celebratory abandonment in marital intimacy, conflict with the existence of consecrated virginity? Does everyone, in other words, have to have orgasm? Does everyone need the warmth and intimacy of family life for their healthy physical and psychological development?

The answer is an obvious no, I think (though both the "obvious" and the "no" will be unacceptable to many readers, I fear). To write off the great celibate saints of the past as psychic misfits is a narrow, rigid intolerance of the various modalities of being-in-the-world. There is no reason in psychoanalytic theory to deny that sublimation can be psychologically healthy. Nor is there any evidence in the psychological measurement literature to show that those who lead lives of consecrated virginity are any less mature, any less fulfilled, or any less satisfied than married people. There are, God knows, misfits in the religious and priestly life, and there are certainly misfits in the married life. I doubt that their particular states of life have much to do with the dynamics of their difficulties.

Consecrated virginity is one way of responding to Yahweh's love. It is a way of reacting to the grace that is revealed to us in limit-experiences. It is a way of serving and loving other human beings. To deny that many healthy, heterosexual human beings can have rich and rewarding lives in this form of love and service is to deny an obvious fact. Because many who chose a celibate life mistakenly are unhappy in it does not mean that by its very nature such a life need be any less happy than one of marital intimacy. Both have their problems, both have their payoffs. I very much doubt, for example, that Catholicism could have sustained the faith and the organizational commitment of the immigrants in the United States without a celibate clergy and religion. Furthermore, to deny that a life of such service is a mystery, a sign, a revelatory act, a grace which reveals to others the presence of a passionately loving God—or at least the conviction of human being that there is such a passionately loving God—is to deny the obvious.

The charism of a vocation of consecrated virginity is not given to everyone. Part of the problem today may be that not so long ago we imposed such charisms on people who didn't have them. Such a style of life clearly has to be a matter of free choice. But, I will insist, there is no contradiction between such a free choice and the myth of Mary as Sponsa, the reflection of Yahweh's lust for his people. For if Mary, as that symbol, provides legitimation and reinforcement for the abandonment and the joy of orgasmic union which celebrates human life, it by no means imposes an obligation for such union. There are many ways one can abandon oneself; there are many ways to celebrate; there are many forms of service in which one can rejoice. In the Father's kingdom there are many mansions. Those who would herd everyone into just one have no respect for the variety, the diversity, the pluralism the Father encourages in his kingdom on earth.

Those Christians who would exclude consecrated virginity from an honored place in the Christian life are guilty of more than just doing violence to an ancient tradition. For what they are doing in effect is to impose an obligation to marry. It is a rigid and authoritarian dictum that one who does not marry is either a misfit, unfulfilled, or perhaps not altogether heterosexual. Such a cynical, narrow view is all too widespread in contemporary American Catholicism. This may be in part because consecrated virginity was extolled in such a way in times gone past that marriage looked decidedly second rate. Now that we celebrate the joys and glories of marital intimacy and sexual orgasm with religious support, it seems logical enough to downgrade the worth of consecrated virginity. Human beings feel it easier to say "either/or" instead of "both/and." Still, there is no reason why both states should not be glorified. Anyone who has a tolerant, open personality should find it rather easy to do so. The symbol of Mary, the virgin Daughter of Zion, is sufficiently broad to reinforce all deep, passionate, powerful commitments that we humans can make, as well as every joyous, celebratory abandonment in which we give ourselves over to the goodness of being.

Images of Mary as the beloved of a passionate God abound in the poetic literature. Thus St. John of the Cross makes clear in one of his poems the passion involved in God's choice:

Then He summoned an archangel,
Blessed Gabriel by name.
To a lowly girl called Mary
The Divine archangel came.

For with her cooperation
This great mystery could be.
With her flesh the Word was clothed
By the Blessed Trinity.

All three Persons worked that wonder,
Though in One alone 'twas done.
In the womb of Blessed Mary
Took her flesh the Incarnate Son.

He that erst had had but Father
Had a Mother likewise then,
And He was conceived in Mary,
As have been no other men.

Hers His flesh and hers His dwelling
Ere His human life began,
Wherefore He is called together
Son of God and Son of Man.

> "Romance VIII" by SAINT JOHN OF THE CROSS (1542–1591)
> (Translated from the Spanish by E. Allison Peers)

And Robert Southwell, who was scarcely a saint, engaged in a pun to make the same point:

Spell Eva back and Ave shall you find,
    The first began, the last reversed our harms;
An angel's witching words did Eva blind,
    And angels' Ave disenchants the charms;
Death first by woman's weakness entered in,
In woman's virtue life doth now begin.

O virgin breast! The heavens to thee incline,
    In thee their joy and sovereign they agonize;
Too mean their glory is to match with thyne,
    Whose chaste receite God more than heaven did prize.
Hail fairest heaven, that heaven and earth doth bliss,
Where virtue stars, God, Son of justice is!

With haughty mind to Godhead man aspired,
    And was by pride from the place of pleasure chased;
With loving mind our manhood God desired,
    And us by love in greater pleasure placed:
Men laboring to ascend procured our fall,
God yielding to descend cut off our thrall.

> "Our Lady's Salutation"
> by ROBERT SOUTHWELL (1561–1595)

The love affair between God and Mary is celebrated in our own time by W. H. Auden in a conversation between Mary and God with Gabriel as go between:

GABRIEL

Mary, in a dream of love
Playing as all children play,
For unsuspecting children may
Express in comic make-believe
The wish that later they will know
Is tragic and impossible;
Hear, child, what I am sent to tell:
Love wills your dream to happen, so
Love's will on earth may be, through you,
No longer pretend but true.

MARY

What dancing joy would whirl
My ignorance away?
Light blazes out of the stone,
The taciturn water
Burst into music,
And warm wings throb within
The motionless rose:
What sudden rush of Power
Commands me to command?

GABRIEL

When Eve, in love with her own will,
Denied the will of Love and fell,
She turned the flesh Love knew so well
To knowledge of her love until
Both love and knowledge were of sin:
What her negation wounded, may
Your affirmation heal today;
Love's will requires your own, that in
The flesh whose love you do not know,
Love's knowledge into flesh may grow.

MARY

My flesh in terror and fire
Rejoices that the Word
Who utters the world out of nothing,
As a pledge of His word to love her
Against her will, and to turn
Her desperate longing to love,
Should ask to wear me,
From now to their wedding day,
For an engagement ring.

GABRIEL

Since Adam, being free to choose,
Chose to imagine he was free
To choose his own necessity,
Lost in his freedom, Man pursues
The shadow of his images:
Today the Unknown seeks the known;
What I am willed to ask, your own
Will has to answer; child, it lies
Within your power of choosing to
Conceive the Child who chooses you.*

"Dialogue between Mary and Gabriel"
(From *For the Time Being—A Christmas Oratorio*)
by W. H. AUDEN (1907–1974)

The haunted, melancholy Oscar Wilde looked for something else
but found in Mary, the Daughter of Zion, the supreme mystery of love:

Was this His coming! I had hoped to see
A scene of wondrous glory, as was told
Of some great God who in a rain of gold
Broke open bars and fell on Danae:
Or a dread vision as when Semele,
Sickening for love and unappeased desire,
Prayed to see God's clear body, and the fire
Caught her brown limbs and slew her utterly.
With such glad dreams I sought this holy place,

*Copyright 1944 and renewed 1972 by W. H. Auden. Reprinted from *Collected Longer
Poems*, by W. H. Auden, by permission of Random House, Inc. and Faber and Faber Ltd.

And now with wondering eyes and heart I stand
Before this supreme mystery of Love:
Some kneeling girl with passionless pale face,
An angel with a lily in his hand,
And over both the white wings of a Dove.

"Ave Maria, Gratia Plena"
by OSCAR WILDE (1856–1900)

Francesco Petrarch, that worldly wise son of the Renaissance, felt
the same throb of cosmic passion:

Fair Virgin,
  Vestured with the sun!
Bright shining one,
  Star-crowned:
Who such sweet ultimate favor found
  From all eternity
With the great primal Sun
  That from the height
He stooped in thee to hide the light
  Of His Divinity:
Now shall my love upraise
  New measures in thy praise,
Though to begin without thy aid were vain
  And without His,
Who, joined with thee in love, shall ever reign.
  Thee I invoke who never turned deaf ear
When ardent faith called to thee without fear.
  Virgin, if our poor misery,
    Our trafficking with pain,
In thy deep heart stir pity,
    Incline to me again;
Once more on thy sure succor now I lean,
Though of base clay am I
  And thou be Heaven's queen.

"Ode to the Virgin" by FRANCESCO PETRARCH (1304–1374) First stanza.
(Translated from the Italian by Helen Lee Peabody)

In all of these poems, there are two crosscutting themes of passion.
There is first of all the abandonment of God who gives himself over in
love to his people as personified and represented by "some kneeling

girl with a passionless, pale face,'' as Oscar Wilde puts it. There is also the theme of abandonment, of joy, of celebration, of exuberance, of freedom that comes from the poet himself, caught up as he is by the sacrament of grace, by the manifestation of gracefulness that he beholds in the virgin Daughter of Zion. Petrarch, Wilde, Auden, Southwell, John of the Cross are all very different men, but all sing in praise and exultation of what they beheld.

Paintings of the visit of the angel to Mary often portray her with such restraint that many moderns would see her as passionless. My own incorrigibly romantic tastes will be revealed no doubt with my selection of El Greco's and Fra Angelico's Annunciation paintings. The young woman of Fra Angelico seems overwhelmed, reduced to stunned silence which does not hide the passionate determination of her response. El Greco's virgin is astonished—so much so that her lovely lips are open in surprise; but she too is no weak, diffident child. Indeed, I have the impression that the virgin of El Greco's *Annunciation* can hardly wait to begin the journey to Elizabeth. She is filled with good news; she is ecstatic with joy. Her abandonment, her surrender has been an experience of wonder but also one that demands celebration.

Van der Weyden, Memling, Botticelli, and Bonfigli have all created portraits of the Daughter of Zion which are admirable in their expression of modesty, discretion, and surrender. Only Botticelli's *Daughter of Zion* (in the Uffizi), however, seems to be a woman of strength and passion, a woman capable of responding to God's strong love with a powerful love of her own. The Botticelli virgin matches God's passion with passion of her own, God's strength with strength of her own. The mere tilt of her head is proper enough, but I suspect that the propriety conceals an abandonment and joy that is both intense and utterly unshakable.

Bonfigli's adolescent in his annunciation painting has not yet responded to the message of the angel disguised as a dove, but it is quite possible that when she does, she will turn into a hoyden, running out of the house and down the road in breathless excitement. At least that's what I hope she would do.

There is a certain quietness in both the poems and the paintings of the Annunciation. Yahweh consummates his union with the Sponsa, the Daughter of Zion, subtly, gently, almost imperceptibly. It is a strange kind of passion to us humans. The passion we know is rather the opposite, so we are tempted to say that if that is how God's lust works, it must not be very powerful after all; if that is how God's hunger for union with humankind manifests itself, he can't be all that hungry. Yet even in our own experience as creatures, great passion can be communicated with the light touch of hand on hand. Moreover, and more importantly, God's ways need not be our ways. The universe apparently came into existence as the result of a shattering explosion— the proverbial "big bang" of astrophysics. How appropriate, then, for God to begin again, to renew his romance by something rather like a very light tapping on the door, so light that at first we barely hear it.

John Donne sees Yahweh's passion for Mary existing even before time began. His language is gentle, subtle, delicate, and elegant, yet fully expressive of Mary's grace.

> Salvation to all that will is nigh:
>   That All which always is All everywhere;
>   Which cannot sin, and yet, all sins must bear;
> Which cannot die, yet, cannot choose but die—
> Lo, faithful Virgin, yields himself to lie
>   In prison in thy womb; and though he there
>   Can take no sin, nor thou give, yet, he'll wear
> Taken from thence, flesh, which death's force may try.
> Ere, by the spheres time was created, thou
>   Wast in his mind—which is thy Son and Brother,
>   Whom thou conceivest—conceived; year, thou art now
> Thy Maker's Maker, and the Father's Mother:
> Thou hast Light in dark, and shut in little room
> Immensity, cloistered in thy dear womb.

"Annunciation"
by JOHN DONNE (1573–1631)

Sponsa

Experience of Sexual Differentiation	Pleasure, lust
Biological Origin	Orgasm (Vulva)
Cognate Symbols	Moon, planets (Venus)
Ancient Goddesses	Venus, Astarte, Aphrodite

Type	Daughter of Zion
Mary Symbol	Sponsa, desired of Yahweh (corporate personality in the New Testament)
Existential need	Aloneness, isolation, restriction, inhibition
Limit-Experience	Passionate abandon
Grace That Is Given	A love that pursues and attracts, invades and tempts
Illumination—Restructuring of Perceptions	Freedom
Action	Celebration
Man-Woman Implication	Playful pleasure
Poem	W. H. Auden's "Dialogue between Mary and Gabriel"
Plastic Art	Botticelli's *Annunciation*

Pietà

The Black-Eyed Wife

A great man lies dying
Gray, haggard, hollow
But there is worse than death in this room
With its thick rugs and rich drapery
Energies and forces fill the air
Fearsome, primal, ancient
Spirits, good and evil,
And something terrible in between.

I like it not
This roar of heaven's wars
My holy oils irrelevant
My priestly words drowned out
By the din of spirit's battle.

Outside the peaceful lake, the routine traffic
But here a struggle which was old when the galaxy was new.
In the next room friends' quiet conversation
Here the sizzling electricity of good and evil
Love and hate, order and chaos invisible.
Evil has come to conquer a good man's soul
Chaos to reassert its fearsome hold
Hatred to open its dread abyss.

None of this for your local parish priest
Against them my poor prayers weak and vain
I do not deal with demons and seraphim
With psychic principalities and powers
I only minister the Final Rites.

Through the demons which haunt this room
The black-eyed girl moves

With steady confidence
She knows these demons, understands their power
Young in years but as old as they
A psychic lightning rod
More a target perhaps than he.

It is for two souls they fight
Amidst the swirling currents of dark and light.
And, powers of good, as always in retreat
I'm sorry but please don't count on me.

The black-eyed wife straightens the sheet,
Smooths the spread
Gently wipes his brow
Calmly takes his hand
Softly repeats the prayers
Her sensuous warmth routs the haunting chill
The angels begin to hum
And mother church quietly goes to work.

The two mothers, church and wife,
Will not give up their son
Save to the One Who Is to Come
Then tenderly the black-eyed girl
Yields her man to another
Who some day must explain . . .

It is finished, the day is done
The demons cackle but they know they're lost
The powers crackle but their energies are spent
Strange things yet to happen
But no matter for the black-eyed woman
She weeps but she knows that she has won.

Outside the lake still serene in the setting sun
Mine a minor role in this eery drama
And I do not want another.
Irrelevant to the mighty contenders,
Priests with holy oil are common
Indistinguishable, they come and go.
Yet Something tells me as I leave

"This night there was more at stake
Than you will ever know"
And it's nice to think
As you drive off in the night
That the side you were on
Was the side that won.

A. M. G.

Chapter 8
Pietà
Felix Coeli Porta

The Pietà symbol in the Mary myth is the most complicated of the four symbols both because it combines seemingly opposite experiences and because, as Neumann suggests, the "negative elementary character" of the experience of the feminine "originates in inner experience" and cannot be derived from any "actual and evident attributes of woman."[1] Neumann asserts that the "Terrible Female" is a symbol for the unconscious, and hence the "Terrible Mother takes the form of monsters. . . ."[2] He goes on, "In the myths and tales of all peoples, ages, and countries—even in the nightmares of our own nights—witches and vampires, ghouls and specters, assail us, all terrifyingly alike."[3]

> Just as world, life, nature, and soul have been experienced as a generative and nourishing, protecting and warming Femininity, so their opposites are also perceived in the image of the Feminine; death and destruction, danger and distress, hunger and nakedness, appear as helplessness in the presence of Death and Terrible Mother.[4]

It is from the earth that life comes; it is the earth to which life returns. The earth is the great womb; it produces us in life, it devours us in death. It is the place from whence we come, the place to which we go to rot. If woman is like the womb and like the earth, then she is both the giver and the destroyer of life.

One may not have to go to the unconscious, however, to discover human experiences that may explain the relationship between the female goddess and death in most of the world's religions. Sexual intercourse, as we noted previously, is like death in that most of our other interests and faculties are suspended transiently, and temporarily we "lose consciousness" (if we do not become "unconscious") at the height of pleasure. Similarly, given the very high infant mortality rates of primitive and archaic people, the mother must have had many dead children in her arms in the course of her childbearing years. Birth and death were linked not only psychologically, but when home and hearth were being assaulted, women became fully as destructive warriors as their men. Finally, when an injured shepherd or huntsman lay dying by the fireside, it was the woman who cradled his head in her arms—often the same woman who brought him into the world.

The primitive mother goddess, the goddess of earth in which all things decay, the devourer of the dead bodies of mankind, the mistress and the lady of the tombs, is a very ancient divine personage. In the most ancient figurines we have from India, Kali, the goddess of death, is already the major figure in the pantheon. Neumann describes this worthy lady in three of her manifestations:

> The most terrible of the three images of Kali is not the one with the inhuman many arms, hideously squatting amid a halo of flames, devouring the entrails that form a deathly umbilical cord between the corpse's open belly and her own gullet. Nor is it the one that, clad in the nocturnal black of the earth goddesses and adorned with the hacked-off hands and heads of her victims, stands on the corpse of Chiva—a barbaric specter whose exaggeration of horror makes her almost unreal. The third figure seems far more frightful because it is quieter and less barbarous. Here the hands strike us as human. One is extended, the other strokes the heads of the cobras almost as tenderly as Isis caressing the head of her child; and though the phallic animal breasts are repellent, they recall the similar breasts of the African mother goddess. But with its hooded head, the cobra that is twined round her waist like a girdle suggests the womb—here in its deadly aspect. This is the snake that lies coiled in the lap of the Cretan snake goddess, forms the snake robe of the Mexican goddess Coatlicue, and girds the loins of the Greek Gorgons. And the hideous bloody tiger's tongue of the goddess is the same as hangs down flame-spewing between the tusks and bestial striped breasts of the Rangda witch, or darts from between the gnashing fangs of the Gorgons.[5]

Hathor, the Syrian cow goddess, is a first cousin or perhaps even a sister to the hippopotamus goddess of the underworld; and Medusa, the Gorgon, and Hecate are similar forms of the feminine as destructive death. However, if one really wants to encounter the Terrible Mother in all her unbridled fury, one must go to Mexico. Ilamatecuhtli, the Aztec goddess of death, presides over human sacrifices and destroys her son, the male warrior god, after ripping out his heart and castrating him. She must be one of the most degraded religious conceptions humankind has yet produced.

Neumann points out that some of the death goddesses are almost the mother goddesses in slightly different forms. Demeter, Ishtar, and Hathor are normally life-producing goddesses, but they can also be life-destroying goddesses. They are keepers of the gate of life and can make life stand still by closing the womb of living creatures. They may be mistresses of the East Gate, the Gate of Life, and at the same time preside over the West Gate, the Gate of Death and Hell. (The word "hell" is derived from the German goddess of the underworld, "Helle.")

This ambivalence about the source of life is psychologically understandable without postulating a collective unconscious or an archetype. While the life-giving power of the cosmos does indeed bring us into the world, it also brings us into the world to die. Everything which is born, dies; everything which comes alive, eventually corrupts. Whoever is responsible for life is also responsible for death. Whoever gives birth also produces that which is dying already. Humankind experiences joy at the birth of a child, but it also realizes that that child is born to die. Reality, whatever it is, brings us into being only to take that being away. Life and death are one. That same elementary dynamism which creates also destroys. Small wonder, then, that the woman, the bearer of life, is also seen as the bearer of death.

So we humans are ambivalent about life, but we are also ambivalent about death. We do not have to postulate a death instinct, a *Thanatos,* as did Freud in his later writings, to know that there are powerful, self-destructive dynamisms in the human personality. But there are also many times in the course of life when cares, worries, frustrations, pain become too much and death appears as a liberation, an escape, a peaceful sleep. So we are ambivalent about the source of life and the end of life. Both may look terrible on occasion, and both may also on occasion look attractive. The Egyptian goddess, Nut, early became the benign goddess of death who embraces the dead man against her bared breasts and offers him rebirth of a sort. The monster Ammit is replaced by the Mother Isis who holds the body of her dead son in her arms awaiting his rebirth. Even the fierce and fearsome Kali takes on a benign form, appearing as the goddess of rebirth and resurrection with her breasts available to provide nourishment for new life. Tara, the Buddhist transformation of Kali, represents the most gentle and most peaceful of resurrections.

The primal chaos is feminine in the typical ancient cosmology. Creation comes from the slaying of the feminine and the ordering of its parts by the masculine. But the life-giving forces are still feminine. When we die, we return to raw creativity; we are destroyed, but we are also reunited. We rot and corrupt, but in that corruption we are integrated once again with the raw, elementary forces from which we came. There is, if not joy from this reunion, at least a sense of peace. When we are dead we are freed from the burdens of life. Death may be a hideous fate, but it may be also a gentle and peaceful sleep.

So death may be at some times devouring and destructive, at other times gentle and tender; but at all times it is implicit in the life-giving forces of the universe. And may not the raw, primal creativity, which produces us and destroys us, bring us new life once again? Nut and Tara, at least, suggest that such rebirth is possible.

There is nothing of the devourer or the destroyer in the New Testament image of Mary. As a corporate personality she represents both Zion, after whom God lusted, and the Church, the loving mother of us all. The Church surely is not in Christian theory (whatever it may have become in sad actuality) a devouring mother, but it does reintegrate, reunite. Baptism, by which we are initiated into the Church, is a death and rebirth experience in its clear and obvious symbolism. We are buried in the waters of baptism in order that we might rise again purified. We put off the old man in order to put on the new; we die to what we were in order that we might live in Christ Jesus. To come alive in the Church one must pass through a kind of death; one must molder in the tomb with Christ (in the waters of baptism) in order that one come alive again with Christ to a new life here on earth as prelude to permanent life in the kingdom with the Father. Mary is the archetype of the Church. She sees us through this spiritual death and presides over our spiritual rebirth. She held the dead body of Jesus in her arms (against her breasts in Christian plastic art, just as did the ancient death goddesses of old). But she held the dead Jesus only as an interlude in preparation for his resurrection. So she accepts us into the earth (as a type of the Church) through a temporary process of death from which new life will emerge in Christ Jesus. The Church reintegrates humankind by first requiring that individual humans must die in order that they might live again not in suspicion and mistrust, which separates us from our fellows, but in generous love, which unites us to one another. Mary the Pietà becomes a "goddess" of death insofar as she and her type, the Church, preside over the death and rebirth experience of baptism.

The Pietà is the loving mother who presides over the destruction of old life and its renewal in baptism. She is also the loving mother who will preside over the final death and resurrection at the end of our lives, of which baptism is in Christian theory the anticipation and the guarantee. Baptism, St. Paul tells us, is the *arabon*, the down payment, on final resurrection.

There is a striking similarity between Mary the Pietà and Isis or Nut as goddesses of death. All hold a beloved son in their arms in death as a prelude to rebirth; all display the gentle, tender, accepting, reintegrating aspects of death. That which tenderly gave life receives it back again tenderly in death. But there is another side to Mary, the symbol of death, which can certainly be found in popular piety if not in the Scriptures. Mary the mother, like her antetype, the Church, can be a fierce and destructive protector of those who assault her children. So various cults of Mary became identified with persecuted and oppressed peoples who sought religious and political freedom. She became also part of the symbols of national identity as well as at times a militant nationalism. Our Lady of Guadalupe was the religious rallying point of Mexican Christians during persecutions, and she survived the decades of religious oppression undiminished. Icons of Mary watch the masters of the Kremlin as they go to and from their daily tasks. The Black Virgin of Czestochowa represents the quintessence of passionate Polish nationalism and religious fidelity. Campostella and Walsingham were once fierce symbols of national identity for Spain and England. Mary was one of those responsible for sending Joan of Arc into battle, and, according to legend and G. K. Chesterton's poem, she inspired a tired and weary Alfred to take up the sword again to do battle with the Danes at White Horse Vale. Many of the IRA "provos" carry the rosary in their pockets.

The image of Mary, then, with the seven swords of sorrow in her heart, but a single sword of militancy, liberation, revolution in her hand, is certainly part of the Christian tradition. The militant, violent, warlike mother who protects her children fiercely may have no basis in Scripture, but it has considerable basis in history and psychology. The militance, anger, and fury which might be called the "dark side" of the Mary myth is demonstrated, for example, in the anonymous sixteenth-century protest against Cromwell's destruction of the shrine at Walsingham:

In the wrecks of Walsingham
   Whom should I choose,
But the Queen of Walsingham
   To be guide to my muse?
Then, thou Prince of Walsingham,
   Grant me to frame
Bitter plaints to rue thy wrong,
   Bitter woe for thy name.

Bitter was it, on, to see
   The silly sheep
Murdered by the ravening wolves,
   While the shepherds did sleep.
Bitter was it, oh, to view
   The sacred vine,
While the gardeners played all close,
   Rooted up by the swine.
Bitter, bitter, oh, to behold
   The grass to grow
Where the walls of Walsingham
   So stately did show.

Such were the works of Walsingham,
   While she did stand:
Such are the wrecks as now do show
   Of that holy land.
Level, level with the ground
   The towers do lie,
Which, with their golden glittering tops,
   Pierced once the sky.

Where were gates, no gates are now:
   The ways unknown

Where the press of peers did pass,
  While her fame far was blown.
Owls do shriek, where the sweetest hymns
  Lately were sung:
Toads and serpents hold their dens,
  Where the palmers did throng.

Weep, weep, O Walsingham,
  Whose days are nights:
Blessings turned to blasphemies,
  Holy deeds to despites;
Sin is where our Lady sate;
  Heaven turned is to hell:
Satan sits where our Lord did sway—
  Walsingham, oh, farewell.

> "A Lament for our Lady's Shrine at Walsingham"
> —ANONYMOUS.

The shrine is once again established at Walsingham—as it is at Guadalupe and Czestochowa. One may not consider Hilaire Belloc's poetry the acme of expression, but the militant, even belligerent, image of the Church in Mary is fiercely captured in his "Ballade to our Lady of Czestochowa." Mary in the poem is the goddess of death who will receive the battling Hilaire when he dies. She will move him and those who believe as he does "to vengeance in the glories of the bold," in particular against modern politicians who can be bought and sold and who preside over a civilization that is "a crumbling sty."

I

Lady and Queen and Mystery manifold
  And very Regent of the untroubled sky,
Whom in a dream St. Hilda did behold
  And heard a woodland music passing by:
  You shall receive me when the clouds are high
With evening and the sheep attain the fold
This is the faith that I have held and hold,
  And this is that in which I mean to die.

II

Steep are the seas and savaging and cold
  In broken waters terrible to try;

And vast against the winter night the wold,
  And harborless for any sail to lie
  But you shall lead me to the lights, and I
Shall hymn you in a harbor story told.
This is the faith that I have held and hold,
  And this is that in which I mean to die.

III

Help of the half-defeated, House of gold,
  Shrine of the Sword, and Tower of Ivory;
Splendor apart, supreme and aureoled,
  The Battler's vision and the World's reply.
  You shall restore me, O my last Ally,
To vengeance and the glories of the bold.
This is the faith that I have held and hold,
  And this is that in which I mean to die

Envoi

Prince of the degradations bought and sold,
  These verses, written in your crumbling sty,
Proclaim the faith that I have held and hold
  And publish that in which I mean to die.

"Ballade to Our Lady of Czestochowa"
by HILAIRE BELLOC (1870–1953)

Such fiery hymns of the Church Belligerent, not to say the Church Berserk, may seem slightly less than appropriate for our own more irenic age of ecumenism and internationalism. Mary, the "help of Christians," leading John of Austria to victory over the Turks at Leponto seems much more appropriate as a Counterreformation image than a modern one, so in the remainder of this chapter I shall emphasize the Pietà dimension of Mary the Mother of Sorrows, the Mother of Death, as opposed to the image of Mary the Sword-carrier. It would be a mistake, though, to think that the latter theme is not an authentic part of the tradition of the Mary myth or that it does not reveal something of the fierceness of the Church which even in an ecumenical age has a role to play as passionate defender of truth, freedom, and justice. Finally, Mary, the warlike mother, also reflects the deity who for all his love and tenderness can legitimately be thought of as fiercely angry at oppression and injustice, at persecution and suffering and misery. The Yahweh of the Old Testament became furious at the persecution of the innocent; Mary, leading troops into battle, reflects the same aspect of God.

Mary the Reconciler, I think, is a far more pertinent symbol than Mary the Militant Mother who distributes machine guns. Still, there are times when humans must fight, times when reconciliation does not work, times when civil and urbane politics must yield to violence. I would believe that in the present world circumstances reconciliation is a far more appropriate strategy than revolution. Of course, even in the politics of reconciliation and coalition-building, competition, confrontation, and conflict are essential parts of political methodology. Defending human rights, your own and other people's, necessarily involves conflict and confrontation even if it is done within a system which seeks to build an overarching consensus. Mary the fierce, protective mother could surely be thought of as one who presides over struggles for freedom, justice, and dignity. Mary, sword in hand, can appropriately be thought of as a leader of crusades against all evils of oppression, injustice, and bigotry.

Still, by far the stronger aspect of Mary as the goddess of death is the Pietà, the Mother of Sorrows, who receives the dead body of her son into her arms. The human existential need which precedes dialogue with the Pietà symbol is, I think, ambivalence about life. Sometimes our weariness with life is the result of frustration, disappointment, failure. It has become a rut out of which we need to be jarred. But there is a deeper weariness of life which is conveyed in the notion that we are pilgrims wandering through a vale of tears. We are created with a hunger for the ultimate, the absolute; and all imitations become unsatisfactory after a time. We are thrust into being when the reality of our existence is severed from physical integration into the universe. We come into the world crying, in part because we are protesting the indignity of our thrust into being. Neither the time nor the manner of our existence are matters about which we were consulted. So we wander through life hungering, yearning, searching for the absolute, more or less enjoying life, but realizing that the taste of even the greatest pleasures is all too fleeting and only briefly distracts us from our urge to be reunited again with that from which we were sundered by our entering existence as a separate, individuated, person. Our ambivalence about life is essentially the result of our dissatisfaction with the individuation that means separation. We wish that we could be lost again in the great cosmic processes from which we emerged.

The limit-experience which can follow such an existential need is that of dying to the individual self and being absorbed in the cosmic collectivity which can give us a new, more serene and peaceful life. Loss of self is part of any moderately intense religious experience. The mystics tell us that in their moments of ecstasy the "other" (whatever it may be) takes over their personalities and is by far the more real of the two who participate in the encounter. The lonely, anxious, restless, dissatisfied self is almost swept away and absorbed by whatever it is that takes possession. The individuation that began at birth is temporarily suspended. (And it does not follow, as many psychoanalysts argue, that ecstasy is a regression to an infantile state.)

In less dramatic limit-experiences, we also discover the transiency of life and the contingency of the individuated self. The grass will grow up every year on the side of the dune even after I am dead. The trees I plant this autumn will be here long after I am forgotten; beautiful women will still walk down Michigan Avenue; the first vespers of Christmas will still be sung. The cosmic process, the human experience will go on. I am but a grain of sand on the beach, a drop of water in the ocean.

There is something overwhelmingly terrifying about this discovery of the contingency and the temporariness of the individuated self. But there can also be at the same time an experience of great peace and serenity. One takes up life for a brief period and then returns it. It was a loving and benign power which gave us life, it will be a loving and benign power that receives it back. In the experience of something having been given, of oneself as "gifted," there is the impulse to return that which was given generously, freely, serenely; to respond to grace with a gracious gift in exchange. To be separated, to be thrust into being is good, though it is a limited and imperfect good; but to end the separation, to be accepted back into Being is terrifying, yet it also seems to be good. From our realization of contingency there also flows great peace and serenity. We know from research on dying that at least in sudden-death episodes, the final instant is one of peace and serenity bordering on ecstasy. Those who have miraculously survived certain death attest that those moments have a profound effect on the rest of their lives.

Similarly, those who have had mystical experiences of death testify that while there is great terror surrounding their experience there is also great peacefulness, relaxation, serenity. If one is freed from the necessity of clinging fearfully to the shreds of being that is the individuated self, the result apparently can be not defeat and despair but peace and, in fact, a vigorously reconstituted and more relaxed self.

The old structures of perception are shattered by such limit-experiences. Life is something that is not to be clung to; we can care and at the same time not care. There is no need to be panicky, defensive, threatened, insecure. Having "lost" ourselves temporarily to the thing that has invaded us and become a symbol, we emerge with our perceptions restructured, viewing the world and its problems, worries, and troubles with a greater sense of the transiency and contingency of all things. From this improved perspective we are able to give ourselves more effectively to the world, since now we work from peace, not from terror.

In other words, in a limit-experience where we discover our own transiency and contingency, our own reality as being and not Being, we in fact die to the old man and rise to the new. Baptism is intended to be a limit-experience. In the very depths of its symbolism it reminds us of the day we come into Mother Church and that henceforth our life will be brief, and as the waters are poured over our heads, so in the not too distant future, the holy waters will be sprinkled on our caskets. But by the very fact that at baptism we accept the transiency and contingency of our lives, accept the existential limitations of being an *ens ab alio,* we then become free to live with the peace and serenity, the generosity and the openness that have come from resignation. We have learned to care and not to care.

In the limit-experience of obtaining peace and serenity through acceptance of death something else is given. There is another gift, another sacrament, another grace. Having come to terms with ourselves and the finitude of our existence in the arms of the Pietà, and having experienced, astonishingly enough, resurgence of vitality and energy, we encounter the amazing phenomenon of rebirth. Having died, we are reborn; having been baptized, we rise to new life; having died to the old man, we now give life to the new man. The acceptance of death does not mean cessation of effort; it means new, more peaceful, better controlled, and more effective effort. Dying, we are reborn.

So what the hell is going on?

There may just be no other limit-experience quite like that one.

> For birth hath in itself the germ of death,
>   But death hath in itself the germ of birth.
> It is the falling acorn buds the tree,
> The falling rain that bears the greenery,
>   The fern-plants moulder when the ferns arise.
>   For there is nothing lives but something dies,
> And there is nothing dies but something lives.
>   Till skies be fugitives,
> Till Time, the hidden root of change, updries,
> Are Birth and Death inseparable on earth;
> For they are twain yet one, and Death is Birth.

"Ode to the Setting Sun"
by Francis Thompson (1859–1907)

The rhythm between life and death, the periodicity, the alternation is the most baffling of all limit-experiences. One approaches the horizon of one's life, accepts it, and then finds that the horizon has been changed, transformed. Why, once we have accepted death do we then experience rebirth? What kind of game is being played out there beyond the boundary? Who is shifting the limits around?

Such a limit-experience is not new. Nut and Isis were resurrection goddesses before Mary became the Pietà. All three represent the fundamental human insight that the experience of the acceptance of death paradoxically leads to a sense of rebirth. To link Isis, Nut, and Mary is not to say that the revelations of the three goddesses are exactly the same. It is merely to assert that the Christian conviction of ressurection builds on the limit-experience that is universal in the human condition. Jesus' dead body, which was taken gently and lovingly into the arms of his mother, has risen; and in our experience of the dead and risen Jesus, we encounter the best symbol available to re-present our unshakable conviction that human life does make sense, as well as our paradoxical intuition that death is birth and dying is a prelude to rising again.

For Catholics, the Church, the prototype of Mary, is also the Pietà, a loving mother tenderly leading us to a life of repeated deaths and rebirths, an endless progression of putting off the old man and putting on the new in Christ Jesus. As sons and daughters of the Church, we die a thousand deaths throughout our lives in order that we might have a thousand and one rebirths. The Church imposes fierce challenges and demands on us; it demands—at least in its better moments—that we live as though we were already in the eschatological age. It requires us to die to our old fears and anxieties, our defenses, our vindictiveness, our cynicism every time we renew baptism as we bless ourselves with holy water. In each new death the Church, our Mother, requires of us and also (again, in her better moments) makes available to us rebirth to a new life. We must, as St. Paul says, think of ourselves now as dead to sin but alive to Christ Jesus.

What is revealed to us in the limit-experience of accepting death? What is the grace we receive? What is the thing that invades us and becomes the symbol, now also a sacrament? What is going on out there beyond the boundaries? The hint we receive is that the love that brings life, the love that brings renewal, the love that pursues us and seduces us so passionately is also a love which will eventually receive us back into all-embracing unity in which the separateness, the isolation, the alienation of the individuated self is absorbed once again into the totality of Being. But—and here is the core of the paradox of this limit-experience—we also intuit that the love beyond the boundaries, by so absorbing us back into primal unity, will not in fact destroy whatever is most truly us but liberate it and enrich it. The self will not be annihilated but will be transformed. He who loses life shall find it.

One may or may not accept this grace as revealed in the sacrament which is the Pietà. One may accept the paradox of life which bestows death and death which bestows life with great serenity and confidence and never articulate the limit-experience in the limit-language terms of "life after death." But whatever language one uses it is still hard for us cynical, skeptical, cautious, fearful, life-clinging humans to really accept the grace that is given to us in the limit-experience of resignation. It is, of course, only a hint of an explanation, and in that hint very few details are provided. We can refuse to accept the hint because it is too good to be true; it must be wish fulfillment or self-deception. It probably isn't true. But what if it is?

And that is the most basic religious dilemma for humankind.

The illumination that we receive from the Pietà—or from any symbol which plays a similar function in a limit-experience—is one of resignation and peace. It is no longer necessary to be anxious, to be worried. We accept death, and in the peace which comes from that acceptance we are able to live. We are able to care and not to care; and in the serenity born out of the confidence that comes from resignation, we care far more lovingly and far more effectively than we ever did before. We have found the peace that the world cannot give.

So we can turn to the remainder of our lives—fifty years or five minutes—with an attitude of acceptance. We do not abandon our commitments, we do not neglect our obligations, we do not mitigate our celebrations; but we stop worrying. We still change what we can, but we do not become upset about what we cannot change. We love with all the power at our command, but we are not shattered by the discovery of how inadequate and incomplete that love so frequently is. We celebrate with fantasy and festivity, but we are not disheartened when the festivity breaks down and the fantasy ends. We don't especially like it when it rains on our parade, but parades are still good things, rain or shine.

Acceptance and resignation, therefore, do not mean passivity. They are not cop-outs; they do not mean that we turn away from our fellow humans. Rather, we learn from the limit-experience of resignation that all things human are transient and fragile, and that it is foolish to rant and rave about their imperfections. One does what one can while one has time; but one has not failed because the messianic age had not appeared before one's twenty-fifth birthday. Furthermore, one understands that effective action for other human beings does not require high levels of guilt or fear or neurotic anxiety. Indeed, the service of other human beings is far more effective when it is done in a spirit of peace and serenity, when it is done to reflect the graciousness of the universe rather than to do penance for one's own guilt. A man who has been through the limit-experience of losing his indivuation and rests in the loving arms and on the soft breasts of the Pietà simply does not believe in neurotic guilt as an effective and sustained motivation for human behavior. Those who consider it necessary to keep guilt levels high in order to change society are merely revealing how desperately they cling to their own transient, contingent individuated self. They think that guilt is necessary to sustain commitment and that commitment defines being. In fact, however, commitment really only begins when guilt is replaced by that peaceful resignation that generates new life. To be effective in one's social commitment one must first of all die to the old self that seeks self-validation through the commitment and rise to the new self which is capable of giving generously to others without any fixation on the self-as-giver. Only when one has lost one's self can one make the gift of self. He who loses his life shall find it. More than that, he shall be able to give it.

Mary, having lost everything that mattered to her at the foot of the cross, was then able to give herself to the whole of humankind: "Son, behold thy mother."

Such generous, resigned, peaceful giving of oneself is absolutely essential in the intimate relationship between man and woman. He who goes into marriage to validate his masculinity or she who enters it to validate her femininity is bound to be frustrated. For in marriage you do not seek something you don't have; you rather seek to give something you already possess. One priest I know hopes he will be able to marry eventually, because, he says, before he dies he wants to have someone to love him. Wanting to have someone love you is indeed an admirable goal, but it is not a good reason for getting married. On the contrary, the only reason for getting married that makes much sense is that you want to love someone else. One marries not to possess but to be possessed.

Intimacy, to be successful, requires acceptance, resignation, peacefulness, the loss of self which is an absolute prerequisite for the discovery of the self. In a happy marriage both husband and wife must die to their old selves in order to be born again. The new selves they discover in the interchange and the dialectic of their relationship will join in the Pietà at the foot of the cross in surrender of their old stubborn, tenacious, vindictive styles of keeping other humans at bay. They must sweep away the protective shield of their defense mechanisms and become vulnerable to one another. In the limit-experience of accepting death, one radically and profoundly accepts one's own total vulnerability as being; one recognizes not merely that it is possible to get hurt but that one will get hurt and will be ultimately hurt in death. Then one is able to risk being hurt in intimate union with another. More than that, one knows that one will be hurt and, lamentably, one will also hurt; but it does not end there. For if you resign yourself to the inevitability of being hurt, you also acquire peace, serenity, confidence, self-possession, and you can give yourself to another and accept the other in return. One will be hurt, but one will have joy; one will have joy, but one will be reborn. The tears will come, but they will be wiped away in joy. To protect one's vulnerability is to prevent injury, but then one cannot be possessed. If one cannot be possessed, one is quite incapable of possessing.

In the limit-experience of resignation and acceptance, one lays life down gladly and generously. In human intimacy one not only dies to the old, selfish, separated self, one dies for the other person, the other who has lured one into the snare of intimacy and promises a rebirth, a new life, if only one will give oneself to the total vulnerability of death. Intimacy is a limit-experience in the strict sense of the word. In the other who demands that we die that we both might live is the advance agent of that Other who is lurking behind the boundary wall of life itself. I think that second Other claps his hands with joy when we are first beguiled into her/his tender trap and brings us to death and rebirth in the seductive clasp of intimate human relationship.

The theme of sorrow turned into joy has been echoed repeatedly in poetry. John Mauropus, a Greek poet of the eleventh century, sings of the Lady of the Passion:

O Lady of the Passion, dost thou weep?
   What help can we then through our tears survey,
If such as thou a cause for wailing keep?
   What help, what hope, for us, sweet Lady, say?
"Good man, it doth befit thine heart to lay
   More courage next it, having seen me so.
All other hearts find other balm today,—
   The Whole world's Consolation is my woe!"

"Our Lady of the Passion by JOHN MAUROPUS.
Translated from the Greek by ELIZABETH BARRETT BROWNING

Two hundred years later, the Franciscan bard Jacapone da Todi wrote the famous *Stabat Mater,* whose thundering Latin verses have lost much of their power, alas, for those of us who had to hear them sung badly during those seemingly endless Stations of the Cross services in which we were imprisoned through all our years of Catholic schooling on Fridays in Lent. Still they are magnificent and ought to be listened to:

Virgin holiest, Virgin purest,
Of that anguish thou endurest
   Make me bear with thee my part;

Of his passion bear the token
In a spirit bowed and broken,
   Bear his death within my heart.

May his wounds both wound and heal me;
His blood enkindle, cleanse, anneal me;
   Be his cross my hope and stay:
Virgin, when the mountains quiver,
From that flame which burns for ever,
   Shield me on the judgment-day

Christ, when he that shaped me calls me,
When advancing death appalls me,
   Through her prayer and storm make calm:
When to dust my dust returneth
Save a soul to thee that yearneth;
   Grant it thou the crown and palm.

> *Stabat Mater* by Jacapone da Todi (1228–1306)
> Translated from the Latin by A. de Vere

An anonymous sixteenth-century author echoes the theme of the mixture of suffering and joy:

The holly and ivy,
When they are both full grown,
Of all the trees that are in the wood,
The holly bears the crown:
   The rising of the sun
   And the running of the deer,
   The playing of the merry organ,
   Sweet singing in the choir.
The holly bears a blossom,
. As white as the lily flower,
And Mary bore sweet Jesus Christ
To be our Savior

REFRAIN

The holly bears a berry,
As red as any blood,
And Mary bore sweet Jesus Christ
To do poor sinners good:

The holly bears a prickle
As sharp as any thorn,
And Mary bore sweet Jesus Christ
On Christmas day in the morn:

The holly bears a bark,
As bitter as any gall,
And Mary bore sweet Jesus Christ
For to redeem us all:

The holly and the ivy,
When they are both full grown,
Of all the trees that are in the wood,
The holly bears the crown:

The rising of the sun
And the running of the deer,
The playing of the merry organ,
Sweet singing in the choir.

Rudyard Kipling, of all people, pictured the soldier praying to Mary,
Lady of Sorrows, before going into battle:

O Mary, pierced with sorrow
    Remember, reach and save
The soul that goes tomorrow
    Before the God that gave;
As each was born of woman,
    For each, in utter need
True comrade and brave foeman,
Madonna, intercede.

> "O Mary Pierced with Sorrow" by RUDYARD KIPLING
> (1865–1936), from *Song Before Action*

And Giovanni Pecci, who became Pope Leo XIII, wrote an absolutely
fierce war cry to Mary in which the warrior queen is depicted as
protecting her children from death. Transformation is involved in the
poem, but there is little of the Pietà left in it.

When warfare blusters at high Lucifer's command,
And writhing monsters fume a course from Acheron's land,

With speed of wind and wing, O loving Mother haste!
Shield for the plagued of soul, sword for the heart laid waste!
Crush with thy virgin foot these cobras of the night,
Erect thy son a tower on the Mary-height
Where he may watch the serpents leave, as stars in flight.

"War Cry: To Mary" (*Ardet pugna ferox; Lucifer ipse, videns*)
by Leo XIII (1810–1905)
Translated from the Latin by Raymond F. Roseliep

In the plastic arts, there is a superabundance of riches, beginning of course with Michelangelo's defaced but now restored Pietà in St. Peter's. It is perhaps one of the greatest works of sculpture ever produced in the world. The sorrow, resignation, and serenity of Mary are also brilliantly depicted by Giotto, Fra Angelico, Van der Weyden, Rembrandt, Rubens, Grünewald and Gauguin. I must confess that I find many of these *Mater Dolorosas* a bit offensive. Van der Weyden's version is collapsed into the ground, Rubens's has lost all self-control, Grünewald's looks like she is about ready to die herself, Rembrandt's *Mary at the Foot of the Cross* is on the verge of collapse. As far as my own piety and devotion goes, I much prefer the splendid *Our Lady of Sorrows* of Luis Morales, in which one sees a strong, brave, self-possessed woman accepting death, yet already, despite her sorrow, she is experiencing rebirth. Similarly, El Greco's two *Mater Dolorosas* are much more persuasive; the one in Munich is shattered but still strong, and the one in Strasburg is perhaps a little too self-possessed, too determined. Even Gauguin's sickly green virgin combines strength and peace with her sorrow.

With the exception of some of the overwhelmed and collapsing late Renaissance Pietàs, the women depicted at the foot of the cross in most Christian art are deep, deep in sorrow yet able to cope. They have suffered a terrible loss, but they have not lost their faith. They have plunged into the depths, but they are strong enough to rise up. They are resigned; they have accepted. Despite their sorrow, they are in the process of being born again, anticipating, as it were, the resurrection of their son. This is what the limit-experience of acceptance is all about, and what Mary as Pietà—the Church, our loving mother—is supposed to represent to all her followers.

I left a lei, Lady,
   To say goodby
Before we sailed away
   To where men die,
And vowed to bead on my return
   Fresh buds for dry.

Should I return not, Lady,
   When battles cease,
Grant my vow and promise
   Sweet release,
And lay your leis where I lie,
   And peace.

> "Lady of Peace" *Cathedral: Honolulu*
> by FRA ANGELICO CHAVEZ (1910–   )

Pietà

Experience of sexual Differentiation	Woman as source of what lives only to die
Biological Origin	Death in arms of beloved
Cognate Symbols	Gate, lock, raven, vulture
Ancient Goddess	Nut, Kali, Hecate, Isis
Type	Church, the new Zion
Mary Symbol	Pietà
Existential Need	Futility of life, separation
Limit-Experience	Loss of self in resignation to death
Grace That Is Given	A love which draws all together back into unity—death as a prelude to new life
Illumination—Restructuring of Perceptions	Peace, serenity

Action	Acceptance
Man-Woman Implications	Loss of self to another
Poem	Da Todi's *Stabat Mater*
Plastic Art	Michelangelo's *Pietà*

Envoi

Notre Mère de la Plage Grand

I'm sorry, Ma'am, about those clothes
Blue and white and awful rose
And I'm sorry about the color of the snake
Who so fascinates small fry here abouts

"Why does that lady
Stand on the ugly snake?"
They'll not hear a word from me
About what means old Genesis, Chapter Three

But they don't make great statues any more
And if you are to watch over my garden
I had to take what I could get
And worry about the winter cold

"Our Lady of Wicker Park," they say
But that's an ethnic joke
And we don't believe in those
No group to blame for that sickly rose

So you preside over the stormy lake
The Irish kids, the barking dogs
The roaring motors, the golden sails
My dubious flowers and next door
The great show of lights
Which illumine the weekend nights

A long way from Galilee
And a much bigger lake
Chartres this place is not,
I'm sorry, Ma'am, it's all we've got

My friends are baffled
Why *you* of all people
They don't know about the call
From the lofty New York Times

Not much left to the poor Roman Church
But the only female deity still around
God is woman as well as man
The one who creates also calls
The one who orders also touches
The one who plans also entices
The one who judges also consoles

Silly superstition? Only to the rigid
Caught in dogma's bind
Creepy devotion? Only to the dull
Trapped in dismal fear.

She who came long before the dynamo
And, if needs be, will live long beyond
Mother, wife, muse, morning star
A revelation of God's warming charms
To a cold and bitter world

Not yet time, perhaps, Lady dear
For new spires to climb the skies
But still reign over our poor Grand Beach
(which is no longer beach or grand)
And wait the certain day
When the hymns begin again

And while we wait
I'll not forget
That here on sandy dunes
I, weary and spent,
Worn and beat,
Found you once again.

                                        A. M. G.

Chapter 9

Our Light,
Our Sweetness,
Our Hope?

The wide streams go their way,
The pond lapses back into a glassy silence.
The cause of God in me—has it gone?
Do these bones live? Can I live with these bones?
Mother, Mother of us all, tell me where I am!*

Religion is a system of symbols which purports to illuminate and provide direction for humans as they wrestle with the most basic and fundamental ambiguities in life. Symbols take their origin in limit-experiences in which a person brushes against the boundaries, reaches the horizon of his own existence, and encounters a grace, a sense of something gifted or given. The limit-experience occurs when we permit a thing (which can also be a person) to invade our consciousness and become a symbol, a sacrament, which speaks to us of the limits of our existence and offers the grace which seems to lurk somehow or other just beyond the limits. In such an experience the thing-turned-symbol shatters the old structures of our perception and organizes them into new and different constellations in which we see things more clearly, more profoundly, more penetratingly. The thing-turned-symbol incarnates our limit-

*"What Can I Tell My Bones?" copyright © 1957 by Theodore Roethke from *The Collected Poems of Theodore Roethke*. Reprinted by permission of Doubleday & Company, Inc. and Faber and Faber Ltd.

experience so that we can recall it to our own memory and share it with others. The religious symbols of the great traditions represent the limit-experience of their founders, and enable those who come after them to share the same limit-experience, to receive the same grace as the founders did. But the great symbols serve not merely to link the experience of the founders of our own experience, they also serve as channels of communication in the opposite direction. We are able through the great symbols to link our own limit-experiences, which are necessarily as unique and special as each of us is, with the experiences of those who began our heritage and who have transmitted it to us. The great symbol makes the original experience present to us, preconditions us for our own experience, and then links the grace which is given to us with the graces that have gone before us.

The sheer density of the being of any thing makes it multilayered and polyvalent. If there are some primal things which in all cultures seem to become religious, the thing itself is sufficiently ambiguous so that the limit-experience by which the thing becomes symbol can have different and even contrary meanings in given religious traditions. Furthermore, the great symbols of any tradition will be more richly and fully understood as different generations of believers discover fuller and broader implications in them. To put the matter differently, as each generation has its own limit-experiences from within its own context and perspective, it reinterprets the great symbol which overarches the culture itself.

The result of the radical restructuring of our perceptions that is caused by a thing-turned-symbol in a limit-experience moves us to neither thought nor reflection but to action. Seeing things differently than we did before our existential crisis began, we necessarily modify our behavior, our response to reality in the light of our now fundamentally different way of perceiving reality. It is only when we begin to reflect on our new behavior that we try to describe the experience, to explain the symbol, to share the experience with others through the symbol. When we do so, we necessarily fall back on limit-language (even if our reflections take the form of philosophical theology). The language of paradox, tension, and intensification to which the ordinary rules of language and interpretation are no longer pertinent characterizes limit-language which seeks to describe the horizons of existence. The limit-experience is odd, out of the ordinary; it can only be described by odd language, language out of the ordinary. A religious symbol which can be expressed in a proposition that does not have at least an implicit paradox will turn out to be a very inadequate symbol.

The process can be described (though somewhat artificially) in the circle of Figure 1 (page 403). A ''thing'' intrudes itself into our consciousness in response to an existential need. It produces an ''experience'' that restructures our perceptions and turns the ''thing'' into a ''symbol.'' The ''symbol'' in its turn leads to a modification of ''action,'' and that modification is reflected in ''limit-language,'' which purports to state something important about the ultimate nature of human existence, thus providing us with ''meaning'' by which we can interpret the ambiguities of life. Within the frame of reference which that meaning gives us we can turn to the ''thing'' again for a regeneration of the ''experience.''

This cycle is repeated in both the individual person and in the history of religious tradition. Each time a person or a tradition goes through the cycle, new dimensions of the grace revealed by the symbol are experienced. New aspects of the sacrament invade our personality; new meanings ''in front'' of the symbol are perceived; new and richer language is required to express the experience, the symbol, and the grace revealed.

There are a number of advantages to this mode of religious reflection (or, if one wishes, theological method). Put together from language theology, existential and process philosophy, history of religion, and sociology, it enables one to bypass many of the controversies of the past which are no longer pertinent to our present situation. Two of the age-old problems which have plagued Christian theologians are resolved, or at least become resolvable: the questions of development of doctrine and of the striking similarity of some aspects of Christianity with religions that preceded it and surround it.

Human religious experience is seen as having both unity (based on the fundamentally similar structures of all basic human experiences— light, dark, sun, moon, male, female, birth, death) and a wide diversity (based on the dissimilar modalities by which these things become symbols). Furthermore, since even the great symbols of a religious heritage will trigger different limit-experiences in different times and places, there is room for growth in understanding of the riches of the symbol. It is not so much that we experience Jesus or Mary, let us say, in a unique and special way and thereby get back to what the experience meant to the earliest Christians; it is rather that we, through the symbol and the limit-language passed on to us by our predecessors, experience Jesus and Mary again; and in that experience we get at the meaning "in front" of the symbol, coming to understand the grace revealed in Jesus and Mary in ways that our predecessors could not understand because they did not bring to the experience what we do. Of course we must also acknowledge that our predecessors may have brought to the experiences capacities to perceive that we lack.

The development of doctrine should not be thought of as an evolutionary process in which new and more valuable insights are acquired while the old ones are discarded. Neither can a symbol be interpreted to mean anything the interpreter wants it to mean. A symbol has an integrity and a vitality of its own. There must be a fundamental similarity in the limit-experience produced by the symbol today and the experience the same symbol produced in our predecessors. One must, to put the matter scripturally, experience the same Lord Jesus who had died and risen. If our experience denies the fundamental theme of the experience of our predecessors, it may indeed be splendid, but it is not part of the same heritage, and it is not a response to the illumination of a great symbol of that heritage. If the language we use to describe the limit-experience, which we claim was triggered and formed by a symbol out of our heritage, destroys the basic paradox of the original limit-experience, then it is not the same experience or the same symbol. If in the Christian tradition the paradoxes of the crucified-risen God-man, three-one, and virgin-mother are explained away, then one no longer has Christianity. If the new language we attempt to use lacks paradox, it is not limit-language at all and we are not describing limit-experience. Indeed, we are no longer engaged in anything which could properly be called religious.

The greatest disadvantage in this mode of religious reflection is that it is completely different from the mode of religious reflection in which most of us were raised. We have to bracket temporarily the "method" that was assumed in our religious education and which has become the unquestioned and unrecognized context of our religious thought. To let new insights and assumptions develop in an altered context free from that which was instilled in us when we were young is extremely difficult. We try to twist and distort our perceptions and insights to fit the old categories, the old styles of thought. Then we are comforted, for now we can understand the new in terms of the old and as nothing more than a restatement of St. Thomas's "Five Ways" or St. Anselm's ontological argument, for example.

An alternative to this way of encountering something new in the way of religious reflection is to content oneself with identifying it with a heresy out of the past. The new method is nothing more than Schleiermacher or the modernists or Scotus, and so one can write it off.

I think there are distinct advantages to this method of religious reflection. One can apply it rather easily to all the fundamental symbols of the Christian faith. It will take great patience, of course, to analyze the symbols within a multidisciplinary approach. Perhaps more to the point, the method, once grasped, can be used with considerable effectiveness in preaching and teaching. Indeed, those who have tried it in one form or another report that the reaction of the faithful is uniformly positive, particularly because the method breaks down the artificial distinction between "old Church" and "new Church" or "preconciliar Catholicism" and "postconciliar Catholicism." It is relatively easy also to show people what it is they "always believed" in the expression of a religious doctrine and how that is not only not denied but reinforced and better understood by our new ways of expressing it. The method concentrates, in other words, on the organic continuity between the old and the new and not on the radical discontinuity. (Of course, showing continuity is bound to be offensive to those immature preachers and teachers who believe it is their function to assault and shatter the faith of those who did not receive the superior theological training they had. Such people arrogate to themselves the perception-shattering function which belongs to the symbol itself.)

Another advantage of the method is that to pause and reflect on our own religious lives—as opposed to intellectualizing about religion—is the way a religious life really grows and develops. If one thinks about the cycle of religious change and maturation that has gone on within one's own personality, then the schema of Figure 1 acquires a certain rough and intuitive validity. The laity I know who have been introduced to this method seem to "feel" its rightness and are stimulated by it.

There is a final, and from the religious and theological viewpoint perhaps secondary, advantage. This mode of religious reflection is shaped by the social sciences in part and also feeds back into further social science research. My colleague William McCready and I have been studying religion as a meaning system. We have tried to get beyond such peripheral (it seems to us) measures as church attendance, denominational affiliation, and the acceptance of doctrinal propositions to the basic worldview with which each person approaches the primal poignancy, ambiguities, and problems of human life. We have also, coincidentally, been studying religious experiences. We have just recently grasped the relationship between religion as meaning system and symbol as expression of limit-experience. In further research we will have to link the two, and we will also have to explore, not just the ecstatic limit-experiences but much more ordinary and commonplace limit-experiences. It is apparent to us now that a sociology of religion which is not concerned with the "ordinary" limit-experiences of everyday life will not even begin to cope with what religion means to either the individual human person or the collectivity of human society.

This book is an attempt to apply this mode of religious reflection to the great symbol of Catholic Christianity, Mary, the virgin mother of Jesus. Mary is the Catholic Christian religion's symbol which reveals to us that the Ultimate is androgynous, that in God there is both male and female, both pursuit and seduction, both ingenious plan and passionate tenderness. Mary is the Christian symbol which incarnates the experience of sexual differentiation as sacrament, as grace revealing Something or Someone beyond the horizons of our life, beyond the limits of daily existence. Sexual differentiation has been a source of limit-experience and religious meaning since the beginning of anything we might know as human culture. Mary is the life-giving mother, the life-renewing virgin, the attractive and fascinating Daughter of Zion, and the reuniting, peace-giving Pietà. She reveals to the feminine dimensions of the Christian God, and at the same time reinforces our perceptions of all things, including ourselves, as androgynous in some fashion.

This exercise may be summed up in table form. (See page 540.) I would make two comments on the table. First, there is a reciprocating interaction between the experience of sexual differentiation, the limit-experience, and the Mary symbol. Not all experiences of sexual differentiation become limit-experience; most do not. Similarly, by no means is sex the only thing which can turn a limit-experience into a symbol. Second, there are other symbols besides Mary which can trigger limit-experiences, whether they arise out of the perception of sexual differentiation or from the perception of some other thing that is potentially a symbol.

Thus there is no necessary linkage between the three rows in the table labeled Experience of Sexual Differentiation, Mary Symbol, and Limit-Experience. There is a strain toward a close connection, however. The experience of sexual love is surely one of the most powerful of the potential limit-experiences available to humankind. Furthermore, for most people sexual love is likely to be the most intense if not the only limit-experience in their lives. It is also true, of course, that the nature of the limit-experience is such that it readily admits of description in sexual terms—being attracted, invaded, taken over, surrendering, and taking possession of. It is not only the great mystics who have fallen back onto sexual imagery to describe their ecstatic limit-experiences. Anyone who knows what it is like to give oneself over to the contemplation of a thing-becoming-symbol sees the sexual overtones and implications of absorbing that thing unto oneself.

Finally, because sexual differentiation can so easily become limit-experience, and because limit-experience so easily takes on sexual connotation, a religious symbol based on a great tradition's perception of the sacramental and revelatory grace of sexual differentiation readily becomes both a trigger for limit-experience (sexual or otherwise, but especially sexual) and a means of articulating such experience.

Mary—Madonna, Virgo, Sponsa, Pietà—is a natural trigger for a limit-experience of any kind (in the sense that she creates a context and ambience in which in our existential need we can turn to a thing and let it become symbol). She is also a readily available instrument for describing to others what went on in the experience. Other religious symbols can do the same thing, of course, and often have. I only suggest that Mary, the Christian mother goddess, is an obvious and natural symbol to reflect the femininity which is blended with masculinity in the androgynous God. She is the natural trigger for and expression of sexual differentiation which becomes a grace, a sacrament, a revelation. I also argue that it is inherent in the Mary symbol that she be seen as "presiding over" the limit-experience of sexual love as reflecting God's furious and tender passion for his human creatures. This meaning may be "in front of" the symbol, but it is surely not extrinsic to it. Indeed, particularly in marriage liturgies and marriage customs, it has not been unrecognized in the past.

For the purposes of description it has been necessary to separate in analysis that which is always united in reality. In any experience of a member of the opposite sex that is at all rich or full, all the elements of sexual differentiation are experienced as a totality. One does not see a woman as eyes, breasts, vulva, or womb. One sees the whole person. Mary is Madonna, Virgo, Sponsa, Pietà all at once. One does not experience maternity distinct from inspiration, inspiration distinct from arousal, and arousal distinct from tender consolation. They all happen at the same time. If we select one image from among the others, it is only because that particular image is most obvious in the given set of circumstances. So, too, are the existential problems—discouragement, despair, futility, isolation, restriction, separation, weariness—are all experienced together, though usually one or a few may dominate. Also, in any limit-experience worthy of the name we encounter life being given, life being renewed, life demanding abandonment, and life reuniting us to the cosmos all at once. And the God, or the Ultimate, or Whoever, is always experienced simultaneously as passionately tender, implacably faithful, seductively attractive, and tenderly consoling. So, too, we emerge from a limit-experience (unless we resist the "given-ness" and the "gifted-ness" which such an experience attempts to impose upon us) with a combination of hope, trust, freedom, and peace. One grace, one revelation, one emotion may stand out more sharply than the others, but all are present. Mary is Madonna, Virgo, Sponsa, Pietà. Mary is Woman; and that says it all.

What does woman do to man? (Or, alternately, what does man do to woman?) In the language of modern idiom, they "turn each other on." When we are "turned on" by a member of the opposite sex, we are transformed. The whole idea is that God wants to turn us on. He (She, It, They) wants to remake us. If the Mary symbol has any meaning at all, then it tells us that God prays in a fashion not unlike these words from Roethke's poem "Meditation of an Old Woman":

How I wish them awake!
May the high flower of the hay climb into their hearts;
May they lean into light and live;
May they sleep in robes of green, among the ancient ferns;
May their eyes gleam with the first dawn;
May the sun gild them like a worm;

May they be taken by the true burning;
May they flame into being!*

May we flame into being. Well, that's not a bad idea.

But what are the chances for the one about whom I write? Can she tell us where we are, and even more important, where we should be going? Can she possibly survive in a world that has been variously described as heading for ecological apocalypse and destroyed by a "liberated," "permissive" culture? Is the Lady of Bethlehem an anachronism?

Maybe. Still, if it comes to a competition between Heilbroner's Atlas and Adams's smiling Virgin of Chartres, I think I can venture a bet as to which of the two will win.

> Blessed sister, holy mother, spirit of the fountain,
>   spirit of the garden,
> Suffer us not to mock ourselves with falsehood
> Teach us to care and not to care
> Teach us to sit still
> Even among these rocks,
> Our peace in His will
> And even among these rocks
> Sister, mother
> And spirit of the river, spirit of the sea,
> Suffer me not to be separated
>
> And let my cry come unto Thee.**
>
> T. S. ELIOT, "Ash Wednesday"

*"Old Woman's Meditation," copyright © 1955 by Theodore Roethke, from *The Collected Poems of Theodore Roethke*. Reprinted by permission of Doubleday & Company, Inc. and Faber and Faber Ltd.

**From "Ash Wednesday" in *Collected Poems 1909–1962* by T. S. Eliot, copyright 1936, by Harcourt Brace Jovanovich, Inc.; copyright 1963, 1964 by T. S. Eliot. Reprinted by permission of Harcourt Brace Jovanovich, Inc. and Faber and Faber Ltd.

Four Aspects of Mary

	MADONNA	VIRGO	SPONSA	PIETÀ
Experience of Sexual Differentiation	Maternity	Transforming, inspiring, renewing	Pleasure, lust	Woman as source of what lives only to die
Biological Origin	Birth, nursing, taking care	Arousal, heightened consciousness	Orgasm	Death in arms of beloved
Cognate Symbols	Earth, water (womb), home, hearth	Moon, lotus, lily	Moon, planets (Venus)	Gate, lock, raven, vulture
Ancient Goddesses	Isis, Demeter, Juno	Shakti, Kwan-yin, Sophia, Tara	Venus, Astarte, Aphrodite	Nut, Kali, Hecate, Isis
Type	Eve, the source of life	Eve, the beginning	Daughter of Zion	Church, the new Zion
Mary Symbol	Madonna	Virgin full of grace	Sponsa, desired of Yahweh (corporate personality in NT)	Pietà
Existential Need	Discouragement, despair	Weariness	Aloneness, isolation, restriction, inhibition	Futility of life, separation
Limit-Experience	Vitality of cosmos, life-giving love	Renewal, transformation	Passionate abandon	Peace, serenity

Grace That Is Given	Inexhaustible and passionate tenderness of life-giving love	Implacable fidelity of life-giving love, which is also live-renewing	A love that pursues and attracts, invades and tempts	A love which draws all together back into unity—death as a prelude to new life
Illumination—Restructuring perceptions	Hope	Trust	Freedom	Peace, serenity
Action	Protection and improvement of the earth (Mary's garden)	Commitment	Celebration	Acceptance
Man-Woman Implication	Acceptance of androgyny	Both man and woman can inspire, renew, and surrender to inspiration and renewal	Playful pleasure	Loss of self to another
Poem	May Magnificat (Hopkins)	Seraph of Heaven (Shelley)	Dialogue between Mary and Gabriel (Auden)	Stabat Mater (da Todi)
Plastic Art	Michelangelo's Holy Family	El Greco's The Assumption	Botticelli's Annunciation	Michelangelo's Pietà

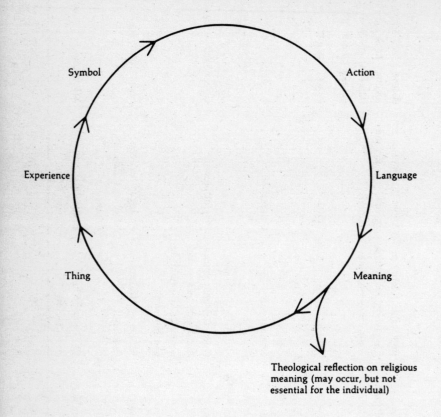

Theological reflection on religious
meaning (may occur, but not
essential for the individual)

Figure II: The Religous Cycle in the Individual and in a Tradition

Notes

Chapter 1

1. Robert Heilbroner, *An Inquiry into the Human Prospect*. New York: W. W. Norton & Company, Inc., 1974, p. 15.

2. *Ibid.*, p. 70.

3. *Ibid.*, p. 144.

4. Loren Eiseley, *The Firmament of Time*. New York: Atheneum, 1960; Richard Goodwin, *The American Condition*. New York: Doubleday & Co., 1973; Peter Schrag, *The End of the American Future*. New York: Simon and Schuster, 1973, and *Man's Eight Deadly Sins*. New York: Harcourt Brace, 1974.

5. Theodore Roszak, *Where the Wasteland Ends: Politics and Transcendence in Post-Industrial Society*. Garden City, New York: Doubleday & Co., 1972.

6. Lynn White, Jr., *Machina Ex Deo: Essays in the Dynamism of Western Culture*. Cambridge: Massachusetts Institute of Technology, 1969.

7. Harvey Cox, *The Seduction of the Spirit*. New York: Simon & Schuster, 1973.

8. *Ibid.*

9. Charles Dickson, "Mariology: A Protestant Reconsideration" in *American Ecclesiastical Review* (May 1974), pp. 306–7.

10. See, for example, John McHugh, *The Mother of Jesus in the New Testament*. London: Barton, Longman & Todd, 1974; Lucien Deiss, *Mary Daughter of Zion*. Collegeville, Minn.: Liturgical Press, 1972; Raymond Brown, *The Virginal Conception & Bodily Resurrection of Jesus*. New York: Paulist Press, 1973; and also the excellent commentary on the Cana incident

and the dialogue at the foot of the cross in Raymond Brown's, *The Gospel According to St. John,* Volumes 29 and 29A. New York: Doubleday & Co., Anchor Bible, 1966 and 1970.

11. Karl Rahner, *Mary, Mother of the Lord.* New York: Herder and Herder, 1963; Hugo Rahner, *Our Lady and the Church.* New York: Pantheon Books, 1961; Yves Congar, *Christ, Our Lady, and the Church.* Westminster, Maryland: The Newman Press, 1957; Rene Laurentin, *The Question of Mary.* New York: Holt, Rinehart and Winston, 1965; Edward Schillebeeckx, *Mary, Mother of the Church.* New York: Sheed & Ward, 1964; Otto Semelroth, *Mary, Archetype of the Church.* New York: Sheed and Ward, 1963; Max Thurian, *Mary, Mother of All Christians.* New York: Herder and Herder, 1964.

12. Juniper P. Carol, *Mariology,* Vols. I, II, III. Milwaukee: Bruce Publishing Company, 1961; F. J. Sheed, *The Mary Book.* New York: Sheed & Ward, 1950; Hilda Graef, *Mary: A History of Doctrine and Devotion,* Vols. I, II. New York: Sheed & Ward, 1965.

13. Sister M. Therese, *I Sing of a Maiden: The Mary Book of Verse.* New York: Macmillan, 1947; Henri Gheon, *The Madonna in Art.* Paris, Tisne, 1947, and *Mary Mother of God.* Chicago: Henry Regnery Company, 1955; Jean Guiton, *Images de la Vierge.* Paris: Editions Sun, 1963.

NOTE: I wish to thank in particular Bishop Thomas Grady and Sister Candida Lund and the library of Rosary College in River Forest, Illinois, for supplying me with these materials.

14. Clifford Geertz, "Religion as a Cultural System," in Donald Cutler (ed.), *The Religious Situation: 1968.* Boston: Beacon Press, 1968, and *Islam Observed.* New Haven: Yale University Press, 1969; Thomas Luckmann, *The Invisible Religion.* New York: Macmillan, 1967; Andrew M. Greeley, *Unsecular Man.* New York: Schocken Books, 1972.

15. Mircea Eliade, *Patterns in Comparative Religion.* New York: Sheed & Ward, 1958; *Myth and Reality.* New York: Harper & Row, 1963; *Myths, Dreams and Mysteries.* New York: Harper & Row, 1960; *The Quest: History and Meaning in Religion.* Chicago: University of Chicago Press, 1969; *The Two and the One.* New York: Harper & Row, 1965; Erich Neumann, *Amor and Psyche: The Psychic Development of the Feminine—A Commentary on the Tale by Apuleius,* translated by Ralph Manheim. Princeton, N.J.: Princeton University Press, Bollingen series 54, 1960; and *The Great Mother: An Analysis of the Archetype,* translated by Ralph Manheim. Princeton, N. J.: Princeton University Press, Bollingen Series 47, 2nd edition, 1963.

16. Langdon Gilkey, *Naming the Whirlwind.* Indianapolis: Bobbs-Merrill, 1969; Paul Ricoeur, *The Symbolism of Evil,* translated by Emerson Buchanan. Boston: Beacon Press, 1967; Peter Berger, *A Rumor of Angels.* Garden City, N.Y.: Doubleday, 1969; Nathan A. Scott, *The Wild Prayer of Longing: Poetry and the Sacred.* New Haven: Yale University Press, 1971; Thomas Fawcett, *The Symbolic Language of Religion.* London: S.C.M. Press, 1970; Ian

Ramsey, *Religious Language*. London: S.C.M. Press, 1957; David Tracy, *Blessed Rage for Order: The New Pluralism in Theology.* New York: Seabury Press, 1975.

Chapter 2

1. For an alternative approach, see William C. McCready, *Report on Ultimate Values*. Beverly Hills: Sage Press, Sage Library of Social Research, 1975.

2. Geertz, *Religion as Cultural System,* p. 643.

3. See my book, *Ecstasy: A Way of Knowing.* Englewood Cliffs, N.J.: Prentice-Hall, Inc., 1974.

4. David Tracy, *Blessed Rage for Order.*

5. From *The Beautiful Changes and Other Poems,* Harcourt, Brace Jovanovich, Inc., 1947.

6. Thomas Fawcett, *Symbolic Language,* p. 174.

7. *Ibid.,* p. 174.

8. *Ibid.,* p. 170.

9. *Ibid.,* p. 172.

10. Tracy, *Blessed Rage for Order,* Chap. 6.

11. *Ibid.*

12. *Ibid.,* Chap. 4.

13. For a discussion of this use of the word "grace," see Joseph Sitler, *Essays on Nature and Grace*. Philadelphia: Fortress Press, 1972.

Chapter 3

1. See Mircea Eliade, *Patterns in Comparative Culture,* pp. 420–424.

2. *Ibid.,* pp. 420–421.

3. *Ibid.,* p. 421.

4. There is at least a trace of this in Christianity. Blessed Juliana of Norwich (not exactly whom one would call a feminist) referred to God as "Our loving Mother."

5. Alan Watts, *The Two Hands of God*. New York: George Braziller, 1963. Watts also suggests that the swastika (in the opposite direction of that used by the Nazis) and the filot, as well as the familiar Chinese circle with two stylized fish, represent the unity of the primordial pair.

6. *Ibid.,* p. 63.

7. Eliade, *The Two and the One*. New York: Harper & Row, 1965, p. 104.

8. *Ibid.,* p. 106.

9. *Ibid.,* p. 106.

10. *Ibid.*, p. 106.

11. *Ibid.*, p. 107.

12. *Ibid.*, p. 107.

13. *Ibid.*, p. 104.

14. *Ibid.*, p. 82.

15. And I hereby repudiate all attempts to shock and scandalize ordinary parishioners by changing the gender of God in religious devotions. Whatever one may do in one's own personal prayer life, one does not reverse two thousand years of custom on a single Sunday morning.

16. Johann Jacob Bachofen, *Das Mutterrecht*. Basle: Gesammelte Werk, Vols. 1–4, 1948–1954.

17. Erich Neumann, *The Great Mother*, p. 94. Plates mentioned here refer to this book.

18. *Ibid.*, p. 104–105.

19. A reason for the annual orgy, perhaps in addition to uniting the tribe with the rebirth of fertility in springtime, was to set aside a time of the year when passions could be given free reign so there would be less reason to throw the tribe into a state of sexual disorganization during the rest of the year, hence "carnival"—*carni-valle*, "farewell to the flesh."

20. Let me quickly assert to the feminist reader that I believe the most fully developed personality is androgynous. Since I am writing here about female gods, I am emphasizing a man's response to the femaleness of woman and a woman's awareness of her own femaleness as it is reflected in the male's response. If I were writing about male deities, I could readily reverse the terms, but then there already is a lot written about male deities.

21. Joseph Campbell, *The Mythic Image*. Princeton, N.J.: Princeton University Press, 1974, p. 217.

22. I am inclined to believe that Catholics are perhaps a little bit too anxious to be swept along by Jungian psychology, feeling that somehow or other Jung's obvious interest in religion makes possible a rapprochement between traditional Christianity and psychoanalysis. In principal, such a rapprochement may well be possible, though the elaborate and frequently obscure Jungian models are terribly difficult to follow, and are, I believe, unnecessary if one wishes to use the history of religion as part of one's theological method. More to the point, Jung is not in particularly good repute with psychoanalysts outside of the relatively small Jungian school; indeed, he is viewed skeptically by most analysts in the Freudian tradition, especially since the publication of the recent Freud-Jung letters. The Jungian models may be interesting and helpful, but the study of Jung is not at present, nor is it likely to be, a means of dialogue between Catholicism and psychoanalysis.

23. Neumann does not discuss Celtic goddesses, but since it is a special interest of mine, I shall. If one strives to get behind the historicized versions of the Christian monks, the Celtic counterparts would appear to be Morrigan

the Virgo, Maeve the Spouse, Brigid the Mother, and Bahd the Destroyer. But the Celtic goddesses tended to switch roles. Morrigan became the wife of the "Dagda the Good God" (rather like the later "God the Father" of the Christians); and Maeve, the "frenzied" mate of each of the kings of Ireland, was frequently destructive. The Irish rivers were also goddesses (such as Sionna and Boann—Shannon and Boyne now) who played at various times different goddess roles. Brigid was the sun goddess. (The Brigid cross of the Christians is an ancient Indo-European sun symbol.) Her feast—Inbolc—was on the first of February, when the westerlies begin to bring Ireland its three months of spring. The goddess's shrine was at Kildare. Interestingly enough, the Christian Brigid also had her feast on February first, she wore the Brigid cross, and presided over a monastery at Kildare. In few countries have the pagan customs been so systematically adopted as in Christian Ireland.

24. It is sufficient here to insist that the method being laid out in this volume is not an attempt to revive modernism or to argue for a kind of universal *"religion perennis."* On the contrary, both positions I reject as errors which violate the assumptions of the present method. Christian religious experience, those different religious experiences occasioned by the same or similar things-become-symbols, ultimately all speak to the same fundamental human questions; and they are occasioned by the same fundamental human dynamisms. But they speak in different voices and give different answers. We may have had to hear some answers before we were prepared to hear others; some answers may be implicitly contained in others; but some may contradict others, and some may complement or fulfill others. They are all hints of explanations, "rumors of angels," to use Peter Berger's phrase. But different angels generate different rumors—and some rumors are much better than others.

My own guess is that God speaks to that which is most open, most generous, most joyous in our own hopes, expectations, and aspirations. When the Spirit speaks to our spirit he touches ever more deeply the resources and the longings of our personalities, and both challenges the resources and confirms the longings. If this is the case for the Christian, Jesus can be seen as God's best Word, which definitively confirms the most passionate and hopeful human longings and definitively challenges the most open and the most noble of human resources. Jesus does not so much tell us something that is completely new as he validates something which we had always (or for a long time) hoped but never dared to believe was possible.

There are many problems with my "guess"—not so much what it says as with what it does not say. Where, for example, does one fit into it the self-revelations of God in the Eastern religions, which seem not only to be different from the Word spoken in Jesus but contrary to that Word? Could the Word have been spoken in another cultural milieu besides that of Second Temple Judaism? What would it have sounded like then? Can it be translated into other and seemingly opposed milieus? How? What about angels whose "rumors" seem to have been monstrously misunderstood—the devouring death goddesses of India and Mexico, to take an example pertinent to the subject of this book? These are tough questions, but I cannot address myself to them here.

25. The pagan probably would have been sophisticated enough in his more serious moments to distinguish between the goddess he was honoring and whatever was ultimate in the universe. The goddesses, then, were no more identified with the One than Mary is identified with the Trinity in Christian thought. In popular devotions, of course, there was much more confusion in both paganism and Christianity. To concentrate on the confusion and to ignore, as it is to be feared many of the reformers did, the sacramental and revelatory nature of a feminine sacred person is to miss the point altogether.

Chapter 4

1. Walter Harrelson, *From Fertility Cult to Worship*. New York: Doubleday & Co., 1969.

2. *Ibid.*, pp. 13–14.

3. *The Jerusalem Bible*. Garden City, N.Y.: Doubleday & Co., 1966.

4. *Dictionary of the Bible,* ed., John McKenzie. New York: Bruce Publishing Co., p. 903.

5. McHugh, *The Mother of Jesus*. Part I, pp. 101–156.

6. Raymond E. Brown, *The Gospel According to John*. New York: Doubleday & Co., Anchor Bible Series, 1966, pp. 101–111, 922–927. One should also consult Brown's extremely careful, cautious, and responsible *The Virginal Conception and Bodily Resurrection of Jesus*.

7. Max Thurian, *Mary Mother of All Christians*, p. 16.

8. McHugh, *Mother of Jesus,* p. 52.

9. Raymond E. Brown, *The Gospel According to John I–XII*, p. 109.

10. *Ibid.*, XIII–XXXI, p. 926.

11. *Ibid.*, I–XII, p. 109.

12. Raymond E. Brown, *The Virginal Conception*, p. 132.

13. *Ibid.*, p. 132.

14. Raymond E. Brown, "The Problem of the Virginal Conception of Jesus," *Theological Studies* 33, 1 (March 1972), p. 7.

Chapter 5

1. I hereby reject all charges of implying that fathers should be absolved from responsibility for taking care of an infant child. On the contrary, I think

the peculiar notion that fathers should be free from such responsibility represents an injustice to both the father and the child. Still, I think few would disagree that psychologically, all other things being equal, the mother's relationship with an infant is more intimate than the father's. The father did not carry the child within his body for nine months and is not biologically designed for infant feeding. (I say "all things being equal," because we know situations in which the mother cares very little for the child and the father assumes the role of both father and mother.)

2. There is also a paternal role in all human relationships in which the strong, vigorous, aggressive aspects of the human personality should emerge and be reciprocated. A man may find it easy to "father" his wife, but she has been forced to let the masculine part of her androgynous personality atrophy and may be quite incapable of "fathering" her husband. Again, the lack of symmetry can disturb the equilibrium of the relationship.

3. The dreams that many of us have of jumping into a large body of water are supposed to represent a desire to return to the secure, comfortable, all protected water environment of the womb. Of course, one should not exclude the possibility that sometimes we dream about jumping into water because we like to swim. As Freud himself remarked, sometimes a cigar is a cigar.

4. Neumann, p.84. Text translated from Preuss, *Die Eingeborenen Amerikas*, p. 39.

5. *Ibid.*, p. 131.

6. David Tracy points out to me that even theological terms are in fact limit-language.

7. I am convinced that if we wish to understand the power of the Mary myth, we must look to poetry and art, and to neither theology nor the desiccated popular devotion of recent times. I would have liked to include more pictures in this book, not as illustrations but as data for religious reflection. Unfortunately, the costs of book publication are such that more plates could not be included. Perhaps there will be a "coffee table" edition of this book. I hope, however, that the reader who is trying to follow my argument will dig out a book of Mary paintings from his local library and reflect upon them, as they illustrate the symbol we are trying to explore.

8. Francis Thompson, "Ode to the Setting Sun."

Chapter 6

1. At least among Irish Catholics after the Famine. Professor Emmet Larkin has noted that pre-Famine Irish Catholicism was something else altogether— less devout, perhaps, but also much less inhibited.

2. Gabriel Fielding, *Gentlemen in Their Season*. New York: William Morrow, 1966.

3. Lest I be inundated by outraged feminist ideologues, let me hasten to add that in a good marriage the husband plays exactly comparable roles for his wife.

4. Neumann, pp. 283–294.

5. *Ibid.*, p. 317.

6. *Ibid.*, p. 331.

7. I think Neumann is on less solid ground when he sees a similarity between representations of St. Anne with the Virgin and Child with the pagan mother-daughter-child paintings of Demeter, Kore, and the divine son, p. 332.

8. I would not suggest that one never revokes a commitment, never leaves a career or a vocation, or never changes one's mind. I merely assert that the limit-experience of spiritual transformation can be a growth-producing, illumination-bestowing event at the time when one is in a crisis of decision.

9. See my book, *Love and Play.* Chicago: Thomas More Association, 1975.

10. I have deliberately chosen to steer away from discussion of the controversial titles and doctrines of Mary because I think such discussion would distract from the purpose I have in mind. Nonetheless, both the doctrines of the Immaculate Conception and the Assumption are theological reflections on the image of the renewing, transforming virgin mother full of grace. They are both ways of saying that when Jesus was born into the world, humankind got a fresh new start; humanity began all over again. The whole earth was renewed, and in that renewal comes potential for renewal for each of us. Like all religious doctrines, these two are exercises in limit-language, and as such they should be interpreted by the rules of language appropriate to this particular style of discourse.

Chapter 7

1. Presumably the women of the returning men had more or less the same reactions. Indeed, it has been argued that given the physiological capacity of women to have multiple orgasms, they may actually have been more sexually insatiable than their men in the archaic communities. One of the reasons for sexual restrictions and taboos and for oppression of women may well have been that the destructive power of insatiable sexual hunger once awakened in women was more threatening to the tribe than male sexual passion. I am somewhat skeptical about this particular speculation, but I have no doubt that in archaic societies, men and women both understood the strength of the sexual urge and hence could not help but see it as sacred.

2. Lovemaking itself can be limit-experience, though obviously it need not

be, and presumably in most instances it is not, save perhaps in a very faint and small way.

3. Herbert Richardson, *Nun, Witch and Playmate*. New York: Harper & Row, Inc.,1971.

Chapter 8

1. Neumann, p. 147.
2. *Ibid.*, p. 148.
3. *Ibid.*, p. 149.
4. *Ibid.*, p. 149.
5. *Ibid.*